The Queen of
INTELLIGENCE
A 9/11 Conspiracy Novel
HARVEY HAVEL

WORKBOOK PRESS LLC
187 E Warm Springs Rd,
Suite B285, Las Vegas, NV 89119, USA

Website: https://workbookpress.com/
Hotline: 1-888-818-4856
Email: admin@workbookpress.com

Ordering Information:
Quantity sales. Special discounts are available on quantity purchases by corporations, associations, and others. For details, contact the publisher at the address above.

Library of Congress Control Number:
ISBN-13:   978-1-960752-55-0 (Paperback Version)
                978-1-960752-56-7 (Digital Version)

REV. DATE: 03/29/2023

The Queen of
INTELLIGENCE

A 9/11 Novel

By

Harvey Havel

© *2023 by Harvey Havel*

Books by Harvey Havel:

Noble McCloud (1999)

The Imam (2000)

Freedom of Association (2006)

From Poets to Protagonists (2009)

Harvey Havel's Blog, Essays (2011)

Stories from the Fall of the Empire (2011)

Two Tickets to Memphis (2012)

Mother, A Memoir (2013)

Charlie Zero's Last-Ditch Attempt (2014)

An Adjunct Down (2014)

The Orphan of Mecca, Book One (2016)

The Orphan of Mecca, Book Two (2016)

The Orphan of Mecca, Book Three (2016)

The Thruway Killers (2017)

Mister Big (2018)

The Wild Gypsy of Arbor Hill (2019)

A Rumination on the Role of Love during A Condition of Extreme Conservativism and Extreme Liberalism, A Political Essay (2019)

The Odd and The Strange:

A Collection of Very Short Fiction (2020)

The Queen of Intelligence: A 9/11 Conspiracy Novel (2023)

For Amanda W.

&

Princess Tatiana, for her help.

"On the broader questions of American foreign policy and intelligence operations during the two decades leading up to September 11, the [9/11] commission's final report is perhaps generous towards the Saudi government and the Pakistan army, but many of these favorable judgements involve conspiracy theories that my book did not address at all, such as whether the Saudi embassy in Washington aided the September 11 hijackers while they were in the United States. Also, the commissioners saw themselves, as they wrote, "looking backward in order to look forward," and they may have managed their published criticisms of Riyadh and Islamabad with future counterterrorism partnerships in mind."

Steve Coll

"As a nation, we believed that history repeats itself. What happened in the 19th century to the invading British would also be the fate of the Soviet invaders. Philosophically, the Soviets believed that history is undirectional, progressive, and does not repeat itself. History did repeat itself, and we did prevail."

General Abdul Rahim Wardak

"What is Caesar's is God's, and to leave it to Caesar is to take it from God."

Sayyid Qutb

"War is not death to young men; war is life. The earth had never more raiment of color as it did that year. The war seemed to unearth pockets of ore that had never been known in the nation: there was a vast unfolding and exposure of wealth and power. And somehow – this imperial wealth, this display of power in men and power, was blended into lyrical music…wealth and love and glory melted into a symphonic noise: the age of myth and miracle had come upon the world again. All things were possible."

Thomas Wolf

"Here beside him stands a man, a soldier from the looks of him, Who came through many fights, but lost at love."

Robert Hunter

An Apology by the Author

Let me begin first by saying plainly that I am neither the narrator of this novel nor do I espouse the same beliefs that this novel herein contains. The narrator is a separate character altogether who is a creation of the imagination. The dear reader may think him unduly crass, misogynistic, and racist, but as the writer of this novel I am not so. While I will admit that I hold certain values that may be outdated, old-fashioned, or out of touch with the mainstream of our generous society of today, it is only because I am too detached from current affairs to have any firm opinions about any of the issues contained herein. No longer do I read the papers, the newsworthy items in glossy magazines, or respond to the commentaries of television pundits. Ever since the end of the Trump Presidency, I have divorced myself from politics and the muck of current affairs, even though their pervasive qualities continue to follow me wherever I go. I try to turn away as best I can when I see a headline of a story or any breaking news on television. I have exhausted my interest in anything newsworthy altogether.

Given that I am not the narrator of this book and that my stances in general are apolitical towards the events that dominate us now, I must also say that this is a work of pure fiction. Even more so, this is a work of historical fiction whose attitudes, opinions, and beliefs no longer apply to our present. The characters in this novel are purely fictitious and in no way are they meant to slight anyone the dear reader my find comparable to real persons. In fact, I commend and applaud the efforts of those who have put their lives in jeopardy to protect and defend our precious country from countless threats, both foreign and domestic.

While this narrative portrays these fictious characters in a negative and perhaps humorous light, it is for entertainment purposes only. This novel is to be enjoyed and not to be a seen as a personal cudgel that bashes any particular political persuasion or criticizes any government servant, department, bureau, or agency. We should see this novel as an artifact forever stuck in the annals of time, a near-forgotten history from the past, more so than any comment or criticism of our government at present or any influential persons that may have had at one time served the public.

The impetus for this novel, however, came after a thorough investigation of a community known as the *Incels*, or those who are involuntarily celibate due to no fault of their own. *The Incels* are members of a community that have grown in number in recent years and has caught the attentions of the press and the interests of concerned psychologists and psychiatrists alike. Careful readers may notice that the narrator may indeed be an *Incel* himself, should the reader find any similarity between the two. While I do sympathize with those who have the terrible misfortune of being a member of this embittered community, it must be known that I am not an *Incel* myself, though I find some of their arguments and theories to be valid. But in no way do I blame any man or woman for contributing to the condition of *Inceldom*. I believe that there are many social, political, and economic factors that have yet to be explored or discussed and play a much greater role in this horrible condition than the reductive argument that there are certain types of men and women who are to blame for such a misfortune.

Nevertheless, in no way do I espouse the same beliefs or attitudes the narrator has, as stated earlier. I will simply say that I find some validity to the *Incels'* ideas through the shards of my own experiences but not the totality of them. Thus, I hope women will not take offense to this work of fiction due to the narrator's attitudes, beliefs, or points of view. In fact, the narrator can be seen as a man who suffers from a heartbreaking obsession with the protagonist and the riddle of his own faulty logic. Neither does this work comment on any societal relationship men and women have today, as it is my belief that the narrator is neither of sound mind nor body. Neither is he mentally stable enough to defend his own beliefs adequately.

As far as the setting is concerned, the cultural norms that defined the months before the tragic event of September 11th were much different than the norms of our present world. It is my sincerest hope that the dear reader will place this work within its own historical context and not confuse this context for any of the events and issues which are at the forefront of our great nation at present. Also, we must remember that, since this is a work of pure fiction, even the events of yesteryear are matters that are more open to interpretation than matters of fact. The tragedy of September 11th, it should be known, affected me greatly, and in no way do I mean to cast aspersions on any figure, public or private, who was involved in it.

As far as its effects on me personally are concerned, on September 11th, 2001, I awoke late in my one-bedroom apartment in Fort Lee, New Jersey that fateful morning. At the time, it was an apartment I could hardly afford. The ceilings leaked. The walls were stained with the black residue of many years of neglect. The wooden parquet floors that cracked beneath my feet every time I traversed each tile had been dulled by many years of decline, mismanagement, and a general effort by the building's owners to save costs over a period of many years since the building's construction. They simply let the building age and wither, ever since these first condominiums were offered to the public, allowing its luxuries and its entire infrastructure to decay without any renovation or refurbishment.

What were once condominiums that typified the glory of

Fort Lee's new prosperity and its sudden resettlement by nearby Manhattanites and those who wanted cheaper ways to commute into work, mostly due to the skyrocketing costs of living and rent increases in the nearby metropolis across the George Washington Bridge, had inevitably fallen into tougher times. Many owners of the units in our building, both past and present, had filed lawsuits in their attempts to force its owners to fix the leaky ceilings, flooded bathrooms, and old, outdated windows and balcony doors. The residents wanted the management to repair the cracks in the broken pool, stock the vacant weight room with updated equipment, and replace the moth-eaten and dusty uniforms worn by the doormen who continued, quite dutifully in their advancing years, to man the front entrance of the lobby. These doormen were mere ghosts who had once functioned well after the first ceremonial shovel had been dug into the pile of dirt inaugurating the building's construction.

But to me, buying the condominium had been a great accomplishment, a milestone, if you will, considering that I had never owned a condominium before, and as it turned out, a condominium that I could no longer afford after only two years of living in it. But I didn't mind. The value of the property had accrued significantly. I cashed out making a tidy profit and left the enormous costs of baseboard electric heating and summer air conditioning far behind.

But after I dressed for work as an assistant to a wealthy writer in nearby Manhattan that morning, I was in a good mood, which was a rarity for me. I never handled the rigors of the two-hour commute into the Lower East Side of Manhattan very well. I had to travel by both bus to the Port Authority directly across the Bridge and by two grueling subway rides into lower Manhattan as well. I always had a damned good reason to be nervous every morning, as I would shake and sweat on the commute, hoping that I wasn't late for work again.

But on September 11th, 2001, I didn't have that problem. By some stroke of divine luck, I had woken up on the early side and even had a little breakfast after a comfortable shower. I rode down the elevator and happily strode into the lobby to begin a leisurely stress-free commute into the city. Even the packed trains wouldn't be so bothersome this time around.

Once I landed in the lobby and headed towards the wide entrance of the building that had an equally wide view of the artery that fed into the entrance of the Bridge, however, I noticed to my horror that the traffic along the avenue – these cars, trucks, buses, and taxis – had all stopped completely. Of course, I panicked, thinking that I would at least be an hour late, maybe more, as a result of the backup that extended all the way down to Edgewater.

"What the hell happened?" I asked the doorman on duty.

He was an elderly Black-American who had manned the doors since the building's founding. He wore a faded captain's cap, an old blue doorman's uniform, and a pair of black orthopedic shoes. This man was usually sleepy and lethargic in the mornings. The years had grown on him and worn him down, such that he always seemed exhausted, tired of life, just waiting for the inevitability of sitting in his living room recliner and watching Yankees baseball until the end of his days. Yet this continuously tired and overworked man was somehow unbelievably excited on a day that would have normally been just another morning of outrage by Fort Lee residents who once again had to confront the city's needless end-of-summer construction on the Bridge.

The doorman usually took the traffic calmly, but on this morning, he had suddenly sprung to life, excited in a way, as though he had finally witnessed something that altered his consciousness and returned him to young adulthood.

"Man!" I sighed up into the air. "I'm going to be late

again."

"The Towers fell," he said excitedly, animated by the rarity of the event.

I had to chuckle at this. The man had finally loosened up and cracked a joke for once in many long years.

"C'mon, man," I smiled in response.

His eyes then lit up immediately when he heard me and said, "I'm serious!"

I again smiled and said, "C'mon, man, how am I supposed to get to work?"

His face metamorphosed into an expression akin to an Army Sargent leading a bewildered platoon into battle.

"Follow me," he commanded.

And I, never thinking in an eye-blink of questioning his orders, hurried behind him trying to catch up. I followed him through a small opening at the rear of the lobby and into a narrow hallway, quickly arriving at a hidden room made just for the doormen of the building. It seemed like a social club especially made for them. On each wall hung their uniforms on wooden pegs. There was a long row of warped, aluminum lockers and an old, rusted fridge, its naked compressor rattling amidst a soft breeze that an oscillating fan could barely push aside. Layered clouds of old cigarette smoke hung motionless in the air. An open soda can on a table, the floor a dull concrete color with a drain in the middle of it, and a small musty couch that must have been purchased at a church charity sale adorned their sanctuary. And at the far corner of the room, in front of the musty couch, an old television set with rabbit ears sticking out from its top blared the local news.

"Have a seat," he ordered.

He then returned to his duties in the lobby as I watched two enormous jet airplanes, one after the other, ram into the Towers at full speed, cutting into their respective floors and setting them aflame in a fireball of orange chaos, and then soon after, a long, fatal pause and then the utter collapse of each Tower, straight down in slow-motion.

I didn't have a reaction just then. Actually, I didn't have a reaction to it for an hour, maybe two. It seemed utterly surreal to me, as though somehow it really hadn't happened. It was occurrence that had been etched somewhere in my subconscious, not really registering until I returned to my apartment upstairs, turned on the news, and watched it for several hours straight. I watched the same footage over and over again the entire day, waiting for explanations that I had already known full well, that Islamic terrorists had finally had their way with us and had finally brought us to our knees after so many years of their bloodshed and our land-robbing, oppression, insults, and hubris. And what did these people who perished in the tragedy do to deserve this? Well, as was usual with an eternal tit-for-tat war of this sort, they had done nothing at all. Nothing.

I was scared. All of New York City was. New Jersey, The Pentagon, and even rural Pennsylvania were also scared. The entire country became frightened and yet terribly excited, like small children we all were, watching our first atomic bomb go off right in front of our eyes. But aside from all of the news that it generated, years of it, in fact, I was scared for totally different reasons. I was dreadfully afraid that, because of my Pakistani and Indian heritage, my skin color, and my position in society as a then-relatively well-off young man, I would be targeted by a gang of unruly thugs and beer-drinkers from the local watering hole if I dared to walk down the street to fetch my groceries.

Suddenly, I became excruciatingly aware that I was

precipitously dropped to the lowest rung of the societal ladder after all of my years at the top of my game. And as the years pressed on, as I had lost my great fortune and traded it in for drunken excess, I remember now how I was completely wrong back then to be afraid of anyone who lived in America.

The American people tend to astound the world with their way of handling intense national tragedies like this. And while I realized that many people who practiced the Islamic faith openly and unabashedly probably didn't have the same experiences I had in the aftermath of September 11th, people actually wanted to know more about my own heritage than ever before. In fact, here in the United States, people wanted to learn about it enthusiastically. People needed to know. People came out of the woodwork who were suddenly interested in me.

Naturally, we had people who immediately switched gears and began to hate Muslims, as they usually hated all sorts of people, but for the most part such hatred, even among Jews, never came to the New York City area as far as I could tell. Maybe elsewhere but definitely not to New York or where I lived in Northern New Jersey. It needs to be said, though, that times for people of my heritage and skin color are much more dangerous as of this writing than ever before, and this is eighteen years after the tragedy of September 11th. It's ironic then that we have completely turned ourselves inside out after the bombing of the Twin Towers.

After it happened, I was embraced by many Americans. There were Indians and Pakistanis who frequented the bar I went to who were also embraced. My best friend at the time was Jewish, and we became regulars at this bar in Hackensack where I had moved shortly after I had slid down the ladder of financial ruin, to the furious consternation of my family who never trusted me with money ever again.

Even though the tragedy had happened only a few miles

away, most of us understood that the roaring good times and prosperous remnants of the Clinton years had suddenly been swept away. But I had little reason to be afraid. While I never wore traditional Islamic clothing out in public, I did imagine that if I had at the time of the tragedy and somehow looked like a traditional Muslim walking down any American street, getting eyeballed all the way, absorbing looks of anger and resentment, then maybe a die-hard American patriot would have spit in my direction. But this never happened, even though many on the street may have known that I was born in an Islamic country.   Months after September 11th, however, I came to know how forgiving America had been to me, how it embraced me, and how it cared for me after many years of my heated complaints about its politics and culture. Naturally, I was completely dumbfounded by the reaction I received from kindly strangers.

Looking back on those times some twenty years ago, I am still dumbfounded. But the greater point is that I should have apologized to the people of our then united country for thinking the worst of them. What's more, America will definitely have to forgive me now for bringing up this terrible, unpalatable catastrophe again in a novel such as this. It "steals [our] sunshine" as a popular tune sang on the Music Television station I watched with abandon back then.

Yet the same question of September 11th still burns in my memory only to have recently resurfaced, because now that we are a completely different country dangerously on the brink of a conflict that may indeed have severe consequences for every one of us, I have to look back, remember, and examine the vicious attack that culminated and ended in horrible tragedy. Because when the Towers were attacked, our world as we once knew it had also completely collapsed. All of the optimism, the prosperity, those worry-free good times of high employment, decadence, good-cheer, libations, revamped ghettoes, all of that had disintegrated with these two Towers.

And then twenty years of war and internal struggle began. Such an imbalance hasn't left us alone since. Our wide political polarity is also a direct result of September 11th. And so, I must return to this event and present at least one theory among millions of theories of how these attacks occurred.

Those who read this novel may not like what they read, and for that I humbly apologize. This novel presents a mere theory of how things may have happened, or better put, it is a fictional account of the causes and effects of the attack that completely ruined us as a nation. This account is unsubstantiated and unsupported by any fact or set of facts whatsoever. It is simply a theory that fits, as all theories tend to do, and in the end, fails to account for what may have really happened in the months preceding the attacks. The concepts and ideas presented in this book represent a theory that in no way should be taken as a factual string of events that I personally believe in.

Yet, I still have two burning questions. First, who benefited from these attacks (*qui bono?*), and second, who is to blame for these attacks (*casus belli?*). These are ages-old questions that loom after every attack ever made in the history of the World from the point of creation and beyond, and I can't shy away from asking these same questions in a novel of this kind. I already have my ideas, but I can't say that I have made up my mind about how the events preceding the attacks came into being.

For worry of giving too much of the novel away in this simple apology, I can at least address the problem of blaming and shaming those who have been openly and publicly assigned the burden of guilt by our government, as governments, in very simplistic and general terms, often have to assign blame when a catastrophe of this magnitude occurs on its own soil. The blame needs to be simplistic in order to be more easily communicated to and more readily digested by the people it serves.

This blame is usually stark, plain, and unwavering. Whether or not we really believe in our government's assignment of blame is totally immaterial, because we all have to follow along with it anyway. The authorities have already decided that there are certain people to blame for the attacks and something must be done about them immediately to protect ourselves from another one.

After a long period of waiting and fierce debate, as recharged Americans we fell into an inevitable war that has continued for twenty consecutive years, and perhaps there is another war, civil or otherwise, just sitting and waiting for us on the horizon. We are presently an empire both at war and at peace at the same time, two paradoxical modes of life operating in the same breath and in the same tongue, almost indivisible and indistinguishable, thereby making our country the most powerful and prosperous on Earth.

But what our country lacks is painfully obvious. We are no longer a happy people. We are no longer so forgiving. We are no longer a people that embraces one another with open arms and tender hearts. We no longer laugh or dance without purpose or planning. We no longer drink too much or let go of the steering wheel for once in our lives. We never make the mistakes we need make in order to open up new and rare opportunities where near perfection now stifles them. In other words, the apple never has a chance of falling on Newton's head anymore. Someone or some algorithm created in our own minds, whether that mind be from our own government or even from the most talented of our computer scientists will instead be waiting there to catch Newton's apple before it hits his head. The forgotten question still looms, however, that no matter how far we have drifted off the mark, who is to blame for the attacks of September 11th, 2001?

We can blame Islamic terrorists for the attacks, and of course, we can easily blame the dangerous political climate at the time on these same attacks, but the origin, the germ of exactly where we are today in its most nascent terms rests with those three-thousand or more innocent people who perished and have since been buried deep in the ground after the Towers collapsed. And there is plenty of blame to go around. Because we have, indeed, become the complete opposite of what we once were as a people. We are no longer Americans, but something else entirely.

But as far as the 'who to blame' question is concerned, let's first discuss the Middle East. Hatred for Israel and all things Jewish by mad terrorists Hell-bent on destruction, for starters, are to blame. The religion of Islam as an abominable cult of hatred and war, a close second, is to blame. Unruly Arab dictators who oppress and torture their own people and mad and savage Muslims who are all fat and filthy rich on their oil, they are to blame as well. The ancient notion of operating Kingdoms instead of what our peaceful and prosperous and far-better Democracy offers our entire world are most certainly to blame. Old Communists in Russia and China and their rejection of capitalism, as always, can also be blamed. And we can always blame Iran, that yearly favorite of ours, whenever it is most convenient for us to blame them for our plight and the contemporary international dangers we now find ourselves in.

But can we, as Americans, be to blame as well? After all, America had once been the happy, prosperous place that had been viciously and innocently attacked, just like Pearl Harbor was, and the 2001 attack basically destroyed what we once had. Because presently, in 2021, we have an entirely new generation raised and bred on war. They have learned that war is inevitable, whether we are the ones attacked or not.

These ideas of how our own government, or those within our own government, secretly but purposely organized, arranged, and executed these attacks, however, have been hovering about our ears ever since those two jet planes first sliced their wings into those tall, magnificent skyscrapers made of steel and glass. It is a question that every citizen has already asked himself or herself, and I guess, for me, it is high time that I at least begin to address those questions here, not only for others, but for myself as well. This novel is the explanation that I've been waiting for, but it is a fictious explanation. It is a theoretical one. In no way is it supposed to be real or true in any way. It is once again a conspiracy theory presented in a novel and has little or no bearing on what actually took place or what others think took place. We all have our own ideas of what caused the September 11th attacks, and they are all equally as valid. We have passed the point of argument and the gathering of evidence. I only have this one weak theory to serve as an example of the many theories that already exist.

Whether or not I believe my own theory doesn't matter at this point, mainly due to the absurdity of even presenting one. And the question still bothers us. Who is to blame? Are we to blame?

We can blame Israel, of course, and how it really is a client state or a colony that uses American tax dollars to buy advanced weaponry and technology in its insatiable quest to extend its own borders and ensure its own survival and prosperity at the expense of its Palestinian and Syrian foes, at least for the present moment, until it boldly reaches outward and touches other areas of the Arab world, like Iran.

We can easily blame imbalanced U.S. foreign policy in the Middle East and how America will forever be bent on its own, obsolete oil industry and its alliance with Israel as the sole arm that defends our economic interests there.

Many may view the depiction our own elected representatives, whether past Presidents or past members of Congress, as valiant, honest, and impartial brokers of peace, when they are downright corruptible and warmongering hawks to the core. Similarly, we can easily blame the Bush Administration who had the most to benefit from September 11th. We can even blame the Clinton Administration for so neglecting conservatives and threatening their way of life to such an extent that the Midwest and the South had to restore much of what they had lost during Clinton's eight years in office. The children of Southern and Midwestern parents had to abandon their family farms and work in automated computer factories in far-off urban centers. No wonder why conservatives hate liberals so much.

We can even go so far as to blame Christians and the religion they practice, because aren't the Israelis and Palestinians really paying for the Christian sins of Hitler and his drive to rule the entire globe for the cause of Christianity and the Aryan race? Imagine that? The Christians are really to blame for the September 11th attacks?

The blame game is infinite, as we can now see, and this is precisely the point that I'm trying to make. We can blame anything and every idea and every religion and everyone on this planet for September 11th, and their ancestors too, such that it becomes an almost absurd proposition to blame anyone at all. I would submit here that there is actually no one to blame for the vicious attacks that occurred on September 11th, 2001. Rather, as this novel will try to demonstrate through the unfolding of a simple fictitious theory, that the September 11th attacks were the result of a vast causal chain of events that led to other events, each single event having an effect which then caused another event to occur, resulting, finally, in these attacks in which three thousand innocent victims were brutally taken from us and removed from their families and friends, these innocents who had lost the only world they had ever known and were robbed of the only real connection to the life they ever thought possible.

Because if we look at the tragedy and how it affected us, we can even address this question in a more philosophical light, as we are lucky enough to have survived all of these years through war and incredible prosperity, no matter how much blood has already been spilled.

In a sense, there is no one to blame for what and who we are now, and as posited earlier, we are all to blame simultaneously. Due to such a dangerous paradox, we can advance the idea, then, that these innocents of September 11th died, not by the hands of others, but instead by some Higher Force, call that Force what you will. In its own way, this Force seemed to ordain their deaths. Because what these innocents really represented were the blood sacrifices this Higher Force had already ordained, the blood sacrifices these innocents all had to make in order save no one else but ourselves. And for this idea and for bringing up this tragedy once again, I truly apologize. Please forgive me, and please forgive this book for what it contains, should it contain anything worthwhile for the dear reader at all.

H.H.

Albany, New York

2021

Chapter One

January 2000 – Washington D.C., USA

A beauty such as hers is not without its cruelty. She had a look that could wreck a man's soul and extinguish whatever hope grows in his heart. But there is no logic to this beauty. It just appears there, and once taken in, it never lets go of its hold. Such was her beauty, and it isn't the type that enlightens or enlivens. Rather, a man wants to capture it for himself so badly, that it changes him into a mad hunter without a strategy, without any tools or weapons, without a voice to coo it near so that he could keep her all for himself with all the greed in his heart. That is the trick – to capture her beauty just for himself, to own her heart, so that she will forever be looking for him, even as she stands right in front of him.

It would be a dream if all she saw was an ugly man. But in this terrible, ridiculous world, such a woman can never be captured by such ugliness, as her world rests in the arms of other men, clones they are, who look alike and talk alike and have the same odors and highbrow palaver. They have the same disposition. She may have held out a sympathetic hand to the ugly and the damned, but she is only meant for the best. And so, the ugly and the damned have to accept her charity, while she gives her body to the type of men we loathe and want dead. And while she feels sorry for these ugly men, she makes love to the clones who have stolen and plundered her heart through every era, decade, and century. There is no disruption to this continuous cycle. To break it would mark the end of Western civilization.

The rare recessive flower opening to a lesser, colorful one in what is an otherwise planned, orderly, and highly cultivated garden will never be salted by anyone except a God whom a man, in the depths of his own madness, has screamed to in moments of his greatest despair. Because the ugly man will never win her heart. He will go so far as to confuse the curse itself – is he himself cursed? Or is the beautiful woman whom he hunts the real curse? But the generational copies of her visage that walk passed him wherever he goes will always remain - each copy different in subtle ways but all equally oblivious to his existence, as women such as she concentrate on those electronic contraptions they thumb in their palms, sorting out other clones who await her arrival at the next dinner party where they all cannibalize each other, if only to protect their collective beauty and sell it to make their millions and declare victory over the Third World, drenching the pitiful parade of the lesser ones with a thunderstorm of their own making.

A woman so fair has to be owned and captured, as that is what heaven and nature had meant by creating her, an agreement between the two, a resolution of sorts to this never-ending conflict that keeps the Earth spinning on its axis, just so the ugly and the damned have her to look up to, for lesser women to dress like her and talk like her, for nations to follow her into endless war zones and broken ghettos just for a glimpse of her figure or a touch of her soft hand. They need her to be placed on pedestals of worship. Otherwise, there would be no point to the grueling procession that begins on the bestial floor and extends to the heavens, no point to the pain it takes for the flower to break through dark soil and emerge as a luminous rose, its petals thin, soft, and delicate, then falling to earth to birth many more of them, killing a world of useless weeds. Because this beauty of hers conquers completely. While smelling of roses, her blonde locks radiate below us like a thousand brilliant haloes, casting a light so blinding that we as her supplicants see that she doesn't belong at eye-level but high above, she a substitute for an ascending sun that warms the planets that circle her crown.

It's curious, then, what the ugly and the damned of this world want with a natural blonde they can't touch, talk to, or kiss. They separate her from the rest, despise the clones who win her hand, or perhaps they need her as a sacrifice, to tie her upon an altar and reveal the truth to her about the humbler men she has been avoiding since the beginning of time. And while giving her body to the clones she has been paired with ever since birth, this woman, not unlike the queen of a nation, obeys the scroll, as she descends from her throne to heal her subjects. Her empathy for them delivers her to the Earth below only to buoyed up again by a society that refuses to let her drift too far down.

Could it be that her natural blonde hair is the reason for this? Or her suntanned buttery skin, perhaps? Do those blue crystal eyes of hers, rammed into the consciousness of every dark-colored boy at an early age, cause a rat race in which a lowly man can never compete no matter how great his own potential? Her body doesn't represent a prize or a trophy to be won, though, as incomprehensible as that may seem. Her descent from the heavens signifies the need to possess her or to cast a spell that only an ugly and damned man could conjure, because there is really no reason for giving her body to those look-alikes, as every man she opens herself to is that way. Her man is always the king on top of the heap, and it is always the same man. It is Hell to witness this process.

It sticks within the minds of those most alone, like a dense fog that constricts blackened lungs that exhale dry, hollow coughs of gross injustice in rapid release. Because the fact that Sherry Aspen lies in bed with the young man she has been paired with is the most intolerable of all injustices. An ugly, damned, and darkish man can only look upon the two snuggled in their bed in their cozy Vermont chalet and be alarmed at the perfection of their bodies together.

She was in the throes of a dream when an irregular breath broke her from a sound sleep. Her soft bronze arms had been wrapped around her lover that night, and she carefully untangled herself from his strong back and neck. She lifted herself up from the king-sized bed and tiptoed into the kitchen to pour herself a glass of cold milk. Outside her window, the first winter snowfall fell upon dry pinecones that were nestled beneath tall evergreens. It forecasted good skiing that morning. As the sun broke over the rolling Green Mountains, she heard a soft wind curling against the windows. Luckily, her muscles weren't at all sore from a full day of skiing the day before. Her boyfriend's muscles, the man she was sure to marry after they both graduated from Georgetown in just a week's time, weren't sore either. They would both be graduating early after winter exam week.

She made sure not to wake him, as the kitchen was close enough to the large room where they slept. After the milk she drank coated her throat, she made a pot of dark roast she bought from the gourmet coffee shop down the access road. It had a chocolate aftertaste to it. She usually liked her coffee light and sweet, but her tastes had changed ever since she met the handsome gentleman who may have one day become her husband. As she sipped her coffee, she heard his breathing, his body rising and falling in the bed that they shared. She would soon wake him by caressing his face, she thought, or maybe running her hand through his thick brown hair. His body was strong and lean, his muscles discernible through the silk sheets under which he slept. She had never beheld such a beautiful body, and as she stared out into the evergreens and up towards the snow-laden mountains, she caught her reflection in the window just then.

She agreed that she was just as beautiful, and together they would complement each other's beauty. They belonged at the dinner parties and the wedding receptions. They were the same, as though they grew up in the same region, or perhaps they looked like cousins from the same stock. They were the ones the commoners saw in the magazines and the television ads, as the rich were just more interesting. They held hands, smiled, and loved life completely, because, believe it or not, such a world did exist. She lived in it exclusive of others who simply lived around it and always wanted to get in it. And those who were scraped off the sides could only cast their stones at the pig-fuck at the center where the two of them stood. The commoners weren't exactly envious of them but upset at the corruption they generated and the unfairness of it all, or at least that's how she saw everyone beyond her circle. If she simply stooped to the outcast, the scapegoat, or the leper, she would have touched their defects with enough of her beauty to last lifetimes, but instead, with her boyfriend and college peers in the way, she stood as an obstacle to the dreams and wishes of the feeble and disfigured ones who fell into the abyss were she had pushed them. So, we cast our stones at them and preach revolution once every century.

There too were the ones who supported and surrounded the couple with ingratiating remarks and sycophantic regards, as they secretly longed to be touched and anointed by their powers and were immediately sucked in just by being mere acquaintances of theirs. And when reality beckons them back to their mediocre lives, these sycophants confirm their secret hatred for the couple. Even if the masses had nothing but iron and lead, they would forge crowns for the couple, kiss their tender hands as rulers of a new civilization that promised beauty and prosperity, as those closest to them quietly weave crowns of thorns for their execution as they slept.

After her coffee, she sat by him on the bed. She ran her delicate hands through his hair. For several moments he did not stir, and so she ran her hands down his back, which soon awakened him.

"What's wrong?" he said, coming out of sleep. "What time is it?"

"It's seven in the morning," she said.

"Sherry, go to sleep. The mountain doesn't open for another couple of hours. We have all day."

"I can't sleep anymore."

He turned over on his back. His chest faced her. She bent down and kissed his lips.

"What's wrong?" he asked.

"Nothing's wrong."

"Then what are you doing up?"

"I was just thinking."

"About what?"

"Our future."

He chuckled at this and said, "what about our future?"

"Can you tell me the story?"

He chuckled again and had her lie down next to him. She curled in close to him, and as he caressed her blonde locks, he began telling the story of their lives together as man and wife one day.

"First, we finish college," he whispered into her ear. "We have to do that. Every couple must do that. I will graduate with a degree in Economics, and soon I'll intern for my Dad's public relations firm downtown. We'll get a nice big house, a place to raise our family, with a wide lawn and a large backyard and a swimming pool. And the house will be close to campus where the both of us are living now. And once I work with my Dad for a few months, I'll fly up to Cambridge, to Harvard Law School, and attend classes there. Once I graduate and pass the Bar, I'll return to DC to work for my father. I'll eventually head the place, you see, but that is not enough. I want to lead. I was born to lead. I'll eventually work with one of my Dad's friends who sits on the Senate, and I'll get to know how things are run in DC as an insider. Then, once I learn the ropes, I'll run for the Senate myself. And do you know what? I'll win."

"For California?"

"Yes, of course. Once I'm a Senator, we can finally live just how we've always wanted to. We'll live on the ocean in Malibu, or how about Santa Barbara? We'll raise our beautiful children there, and everything will be just fine."

"And what about me?"

"Ah, yes. That is the best part of the story. First, you finish school with me with a degree in Biology. And while I intern with Dad, you'll move up to Cambridge and go to Harvard Medical School, as we planned. There, you will train to become a pediatrician who helps troubled kids all over the world, especially those people in those poor places, like Africa and India. Soon, I will follow you up to Cambridge and join you there. After a few years, I will have my law degree, and you will be a licensed medical doctor. We can then get married and have a huge wedding in California."

"What kind of wedding will it be?"

"It will be the most beautiful, lavish, and expensive wedding the state of California has ever seen. All the most important government people will be there, maybe even the President and the First Lady, if their schedule permits. You will be brought into one of the great remaining American families. You, an Aspen of Vermont. Can you imagine it? The joining of two wonderfully open-hearted families? The wedding will be covered by the press and put on all the celebrity TV shows. We'll be American celebrities, because your dress will be the most beautiful wedding dress ever made."

"All of those stars and important people?"

"Yes. They are already friends of the family. They would die to be invited. It will be like Truman Capote's party at the Plaza Hotel in the 1950s, because that's what my Mom and Dad want."

"But my family isn't known at all. Won't people think I'm not good enough?"

"You will be the star who is born right in front of the world's eyes. It doesn't matter whether or not your family is known. You will be a part of *our* family."

"But my family is middle class."

"Not that bad off."

"Compared to yours, mine is poor."

"Well, you don't have to worry about that ever again, okay? Myself and my family will always have your family covered."

"We're a simple farming family," she said.

"I know, dear, but my family will always take care of

your family. I promise. We'll have no problems. Not a worry in the world."

"I will pay you back for medical school. You know that, right?"

"Yes, I do. You will pull your own weight, like you insist on doing. But until that time, I'll be paying for your medical school, and we'll soon be living in Cambridge together until we're both done. And then we'll return to DC and work, traveling to California and back when we need to. This is when I'm a Senator and you're a doctor taking care of all those sick children and infants."

"It sounds so wonderful."

"That's because it is wonderful, Sherry," he said, caressing her cheek. "I just don't know why you're so worried all the time. As long as I'm around, nothing will ever happen to you. You're with me. Sometimes you act like you're a lost little girl in the forest looking for shelter, and you think that every shelter you find is a temporary one. You've got to relax. You're with me. So kiss me, okay?"

She leaned over his hairless chest and kissed his open lips, her mouth taking in his tongue, and together they locked lips, tongues, and bodies. His free hand moved beneath her prairie night gown and traveled along one of her buttermilk thighs. She liked his hand there, and just when he moved it between her legs and up towards the middle, she stopped him.

"What? What's the matter?" he asked.

"I'm not feeling it," she said.

"Not feeling it? We used to make love all the time, and lately you just stop like there's something wrong. Is there something wrong?"

"Nothing's wrong."

"Maybe it's something about me?"

"No, there is nothing wrong about you, or me, or us, or our future, or anything like that."

"Then why can't we make love, Sherry? Something must be wrong."

"There's nothing wrong,"

"Then? Have you been seeing your therapist? What does she say?"

"Why is sex so important to you? Why do we have to have sex all the time? It's like you want it every night."

"We haven't made love in a very long time, Sherry. I just need it. I just do, okay? I need to be inside of you as much as I can, because I have to make sure that you are mine."

"But I am yours. And you're inside my heart. You don't literally have to be inside of me. We have a connection far beyond that."

"Sometimes, Sherry, we need to feel it, our two bodies touching, my skin on yours, my body inside yours. We used to do that all the time. And if we do it now, then we'll be connecting with all of that other stuff you talk about. We will connect emotionally, spiritually, and all of that other stuff."

"It's not 'other stuff.',", she said, climbing off his body. "See, that's the problem. It's just 'stuff' to you. That 'stuff' is all we should need."

"So what are you saying? We shouldn't sleep together ever again?"

"I'm not saying that," as she got up and paced with her arms folded near the foot of the bed. "Let's just take our time, because I want that connection, all three of them burning at once – physical, spiritual, emotional."

"We're going to be married. I love you. Can't you see that?"

"I know. But just stop pushing me all the time. Just get out of bed, get on your Chilly's and pour yourself a cup of coffee. The lifts start spinning in a couple of hours."

"I'm getting sick of this," he said, throwing off the covers. "I don't know how long I can stand this shit."

"Are you saying you won't wait for me?"

"I have no idea what we're waiting for. What are we waiting for? Tell me."

"I want to wait. That's all. I want you that badly."

"You already have me. What's the problem?"

"Not yet," she said. "There's a piece that's missing."

"What?!"

She smiled sympathetically, returned to the kitchen, and resumed staring into the Green Mountains that surrounded the chalet.

"What!" he yelled from the bedroom.

She smiled again and just kept staring out the window. She knew she had him, but she would make him wait until she broke him like a wild stag. A man had to be broken and whipped into shape. Sure, when they first met, she doled it out. That's how she kept him coming back. And for the past year she closed it off, a twist of the spigot of necessary ecstasy until that screw in her mind that had rattled around remained in one place. She needed more of him. His soul, perhaps?

His family had already guaranteed her medical school tuition and the townhouse next to campus. His beautiful noble parents just waited to hear of their engagement. Yet nothing had happened officially. These were just useless rumors and plans in a sea of other useless rumors and plans. He could have repeated the story of their lives a thousand times over, and she still wouldn't have been convinced of such a farfetched fairy tale of love and endless happiness. That one screw that rattled around her head like a mouse running from wall to wall in the attic of her skull plunged her into insecurities that sometimes kept her awake at night. At those times, when the world was dead, she often needed a drink or a sedative prescribed to her by her therapist to help her sleep. It was early in the morning again, and she felt as though she had been up all night. Not sleepy, but exhausted.

Another couple from Georgetown had joined them on their ski trip. They lodged in the chalet next door on her boyfriend's dime. She figured it would be better if she weren't so isolated all the time, if only to avoid awkward silences, fighting off his libido, and getting on one another's nerves. His libido was ferocious at times, and she worried about his getting hot and bothered enough to force her down on the bed and do whatever he willed with her. She knew he wanted her badly enough that morning but not badly enough to force her down on the bed as she had frequently imagined. Good Georgetown gentlemen just didn't do that to the women they would one day wed.

From what her sorority sisters had told her, men commit far greater sins than women. But they also said that men like theirs were simply unlike other men. They had reputations for being true, honorable gents. Sherry and her boyfriend stood out from that flock. They were the King and Queen of the Prom, the star quarterback and the head cheerleader, Ken and Barbie, however her sisters frivolously described them – like Charles and Diana, Jack Kennedy and Jackie Bouvier, Bogie and Bacall, Princess Grace and King Alfred. Such comparisons went on and on, and they thrilled her, even though she never let it show.

She wanted to be a part of something much larger than her own small New England self, ever since her humble rural parents told her that she would one day marry a prince just like the girl in the children's books they read to her before bedtime, these same children's books that never explained anything about the human condition but presented a life that avoided tragic endings. They taught her to expect the fairy tale, not simply dream about them. That expectation had been based solely on her beauty.

Sure, she had brains too, but her beauty always came first. Brains were for the basement, while beauty was for the penthouse. It was that simple. She could have had a thousand brains, but it was more important that she breed more blonde children if only to balance out the population, so that she could be presentable at the places she would one day travel, if only to prove that there was a certain class of people within her great society who would never be bored or lonely, tired or ugly – especially the lonely part, because God didn't make beautiful women lonely for too long. Beautiful women always had someone to go out with or visit at night, friends who flattered them and guys who kept them occupied with possibilities of ultimate happiness, even beyond the grave where she sits next to the heavenly Father and rules over the souls of the damned, if only to gain the good Lord's sympathy for them and rescue her craven flock from the purgatory of never-ending masturbation when no one's looking.

She forgave them of such a sin, because she already knew what they wanted, and what they wanted was she. Men didn't want anything else. But it was far too late. She would wed the Georgetown gent - this young, athletic thoroughbred ready to lead the political classes without even lifting a finger. Sure, they still felt pain, because only their pain was broadcasted over every airwave, newspaper, website, and bubble-gum pop song, and not anyone else's. And together, their pains would be the pains of all, as though everyone shared the same pain – from the starving man in the gutter, the leper who falls in love with the jogger wearing tight yoga pants in the park showing off her ass on a nice sunny day, and finally, to the wealthiest men and women on earth.

Because we all feel pain, and princes and princesses were no exceptions, and because of this, they ought to be excused for not doing too much and succeeding at whatever they did, such that even their simplest mistakes had been rewritten by some fortunate historian who explained them away with the rationale of the great philosophers and sages who haunt the stacks of our most cherished libraries. Sherry and her boyfriend were not meant to fail no matter what they did. Her beauty saved her, and together their happiness, beneficence, and power in a land of bewildered mongrels and feeble minds had been cemented.

By the time they ate a light breakfast and donned their ski clothes, the chairlifts spun, and a few early risers had already dotted the dove-white trails that led from the mountain peaks to the base lodges below. Sherry wore a tight pair of racing pants that clung to her body like a latex condom. She didn't wear anything woolen like the others, but rather let her blonde hair fall behind her and her body stand out. Out of the four of them, she looked like she belonged on a ski magazine cover and not the icy and rocky East Coast slopes where the snow fell heavy and wet.

Her boyfriend dressed more traditionally and so did her friends from Georgetown, her best friend and her best friend's boyfriend. The two guys were fraternity brothers, and the two girls were sorority sisters. Their fraternities and sororities had been paired together ever since their early foundings, and this foursome represented the ideal pairing of traditionally aligned organizations that could only dissolve if another country nuked the university and all of the fair-skinned people who attended it. Only the beautiful women went to the sorority she had rushed. And the favorable, handsome stags went to the fraternity he had pledged, a tribal and ethnic affair that cast its shadow over the undesirables who only wanted a taste of what had been branded into their minds.

Both of their chalets were connected by a slope that led straight to a chairlift at the base of the mountain. Rays of bright sunshine had broken through a partly cloudy sky, and even though it was still very early in the season, there was still enough snow on the ground to have a solid day without the burden of the crowds that would surely populate the area later that season. They even had to take their final exams in a couple of days. Despite this, exam week didn't stop them from the pleasure of their truancy from the august lecture halls and the classrooms of the university. They never had any reason to worry. The classes were easy once they got in, as college was no longer a place to learn but more like an amusement park, the buildings and dorms and events as interesting and anticipated as late-night keg parties and one-night stands. Unless a student wanted to become a professor one day, academics didn't matter. Once the name of the place and the degree that came with it had been embroidered into a student's identity, no one had to worry about academics anymore. A student could read a single book or all the books in all the libraries on campus, and he or she would still graduate with a 'B'. The name of the place counted, but not much else. One could easily get the same education from a public library but without the benefits of getting drunk and laid every weekend. If the tuition could be paid, then a diploma could be issued, as the diploma was that slip of fancy paper that put the student in the running for an entry-level job, if he or she were lucky enough. Otherwise, the kid moves back in with his parents and gets on their nerves.

The group that went skiing right before exam week, however, had nothing to worry about. Their exams would be multiple choice, their scores scanned by machine, their classes a series of gut courses meant to ensure a breezy ride through the time of their lives. It was no big deal. But perhaps they had it tough due to the burdens of privilege. They had the task of navigating the social scene of the university. Since they lived and breathed in the center of all things, they had to play their parts without stuttering their words. They were on display wherever they went. They avoided the parties and courses that compromised their social rank. They also made sure to avoid the people who did not look or act like they did. The beautiful went with the beautiful, the stupid with the stupid, the ugly with the ugly, the damned with the damned.

Sherry had different ideas, though, and this made her even more beautiful in the eyes of the younger students who beheld her on campus. Her beauty was a kind of charity in itself, as though the sight of her visage made the crops grow. She cared about the poor, especially the children, as any future First Lady ought to have cared, but she had little idea how to solve the problem of poverty. Her solution was to become a doctor, but without getting her hands bloody at the same time. She wanted it both ways – to be rich and be poor, she supposed. Blood and guts were not things she was used to. At this time in her life, however, being a pediatrician and the example it would set in a senatorial family fascinated her more than the work it entailed. But because she had to choose Biology to become a medical doctor, she didn't have it as easy as her sorority sisters.

First of all, the sciences had always been tougher than

the humanities, as anything with numbers or organisms turned the in-crowd off, but secondly, a major like Biology required more class time, lab work, and heavier books that she lugged around campus in a Tibetan rucksack that was all the rage in Colorado when they skied there last season.

Her decision to become a doctor had been seen as a sacrifice for those poor children who needed her blessings just to survive. Sherry would soon become the doctor that the children would rather go home with than their own mothers, and consequently, they would long to remain with her than in their own tenement houses on their graffitied city streets at their Cream of Wheat dinners. On that brisk, early Vermont morning, however, their first order of business was breakfast.

An exclusive restaurant abutted the chalet, and the foursome had met there the night before for apres-ski and dinner. A waiter seated them at a large window with a view of the ski mountain. The foursome looked like they had been skiing together since childhood. To the guests, they looked like they belonged in such a place. They ordered eggs, bacon, toast, and coffee, but Sherry made sure to watch her weight too. She left the bacon for her boyfriend, and she ate her egg whites with plain wheat toast, even though she wished it were buttered.

"You're not eating any more than that?" asked her boyfriend.

"I'm not that hungry this morning. Plus, I ate before you woke up."

"God, it's like you don't watch your figure enough already," said her best friend on the other side of her, her auburn hair towel-dry in the sunshine. She had just taken a shower, even though she would soon spend several hours sweating on the slopes.

"Sherry has to watch her figure," said Sherry's best friend's boyfriend. "Otherwise, the gossip around campus would snowball. Isn't that right, Sherry?"

"Honestly, I'm really not that hungry," she said.

"Don't be so dour, honey," said her boyfriend. "You'll have no problem passing that ridiculous Poly-Sci exam. It won't be that hard. It's not like you really need to pass anyway."

"I'm not worried about exam week," said Sherry.

"Then what's bothering you?" asked her best friend. "Are you trying to lose weight?"

Sherry said nothing for a few moments and then said, "Nothing. Nothing's the matter. Sorry. I guess I am just worried about exam week."

Her best friend suddenly summoned the waiter.

"Mamosas all around," she called.

"No, I couldn't," said Sherry.

"Yes!" said her boyfriend. "Great idea."

"This occasion definitely calls for high spirits," said the fraternity brother.

When the flutes of orange juice and champagne arrived at their table, they toasted their ill-timed vacation and downed the Mamosas in one shot. Sherry felt a little better, now that the atmosphere had become cheery and festive.

"That was a fine idea," said her boyfriend. "Feel better?"

"Yes, darling," said Sherry, "I do. I really do. I think I'll finish the rest of my breakfast. I don't want to be tipsy on the mountain."

"That a girl," said her boyfriend, massaging her back

and kissing her on the cheek. "Sometimes she needs a little push."

She smiled a little and ate her breakfast in tiny bites.

"I wonder what they're doing back in Washington?" said her best friend.

"Studying. What else?"

"I mean our people."

"Drinking," smiled her boyfriend.

"Y'know they're partying," said her best friend. "I wonder who hooked up as we slept last night."

"You can bet a lot of them did," said her boyfriend. "We don't let exam week stop us."

"Can we talk about something else, please?" asked Sherry.

They all had a good laugh over this.

"Seriously, it's just sex and partying all the time," said Sherry. "College should be about something more than that, don't you think?"

The three of them looked at each other quietly and then burst out laughing again. Her best friend threw a napkin at her.

"I'm not joking," laughed Sherry.

"God, won't she make a great wife of a Sentor someday?" said her boyfriend.

"Someday?" said Sherry.

They again burst out laughing.

The slopes awaited them, and after she fit her boots on and dipped them into her bindings next to an outside hearth on the restaurant's patio, she followed her boyfriend to the chairlift near the base. The temperature had warmed considerably since early morning. The other couple followed in the chair behind them as they moved forward high above a barren trail of large boulders, thinly covered mud, and blackened snow.

"What kind of wedding will it be again?" she asked him.

He lowered his ski mask and leaned into her.

"It will be the finest wedding the Capital has ever seen. Even the President will be there."

"Ha!"

"You think I'm joking?"

"Yeah, right. I don't expect you to pull that one off."

"My father was a sophomore at Yale when he was senior. You know that? They knew each other well."

"Don't joke."

"I'm not! There's a good chance that the President, or at least a representative of his family, will be there."

"But aren't we on the other side?"

"Honey, it doesn't matter. We're all part of the same team. It doesn't matter if we're liberal or they're conservative. We all manage the government no matter what direction the country turns. All that conflict everyone else sees on television is just meant to confuse people. Everyone gets along. Even though my father is a liberal Democrat, he is still close friends with the Bush's. So, in all likelihood, he will be there at our wedding. You'll see."

"If you ever ask me to marry you."

"If you ever accept."

"What?"

"To marry me."

He kissed her as the chair approached the summit of the mountain. When the four met at the top, they skated along a flat primer of the mountain's many trails until they dove down a black diamond towards the bottom, her skis parallel and her arms poking into the snow with her poles. She looked as elegant as a figure skater. She careened across the face of the trail in splendor, her boyfriend behind her, followed by the two others. As she was a natural Vermonter, her skiing bested the others, even though her friends also knew how to ski well and were no strangers to the sport. Sherry had been taught to ski at kindergarten, and her friends had learned during third or fourth grade. As a bright youngster, she raced on the ski team, winning award after award for the fastest times. She made the greatest contribution to her team. She also trained for the Olympics and wanted to join but chose to immerse herself in academics instead.

She won a much-coveted scholarship to Georgetown, not an athletic one, but a merit scholarship based on her grade point average and high standardized test scores. She was the first member of her family to have attended such a prestigious school, as her parents had attended the University of Vermont, which was not so bad either. She was an only child, and as a result, her parents sunk their hopes and dreams into this one promising product of their love. By the time she entered high school, she was already the most beautiful girl in a state of dairy farms, antiques, ski resorts, rolling hills, mountain bikes, transplants from New York City, white women with soft skin, red lips, long limbs, sky-blue eyes, and long, thin sun-bleached hair.

Her milk-over-teeth beauty went far beyond what most of the New England well-to-do expected of their suburban daughters. And yes, all the boys wanted to date her, and the bad boys wanted to get into her pants, as that was what the whole student body waited for, but she refused all of them until she successfully completed her coursework in exemplary fashion and moved to DC to become a freshman at Georgetown, a school she could have only dreamt of going to. She had the pick of the Ivy League lot, but Georgetown offered her much more than the others, and so her parents leapt at the chance and enrolled her as soon as the dollar amount of her scholarship arrived in the mail.

Her turns on the mountain were tight and sharp. Her muscles flared as she hit a few moguls, her skis turning on a dime and shaving the tops of each mogul, her legs absorbing them effortlessly like pistons in an engine that pumped at lightning speed, her friends in hot pursuit.

Interestingly, Sherry didn't forget about them. They struggled to catch up behind her. She was well aware that they eagerly chased her down the trail. They copied her elegant movements, her knees bent and her body squat. They were more surprised by her amazing talent than envious of it, but they would never admit that to anyone. They tried to beat her down the mountain, but if they ever pursued her too hotly or came too close to her, it would have only resulted in terrible wipeouts.

About halfway down, she stopped and moved to the side of the trail near the trees. Her friends slalomed behind her slowly, and when they regrouped, she said, "is everyone okay?"

But her friends were already out of breath. They had the styles of advanced skiers but were not naturals. Out of the bunch, Sherry was the only natural, and she knew that they knew it. From that midpoint on the trail, she led them to a trail below another chairlift. They skied down the lift-line, as the few skiers from above witnessed their expertise and grace.

They sped down like ballet dancers, their skis tightly parallel, keeping their balance, their edges carving into the snow, the snow spray following the tails of their skis and curling above the evergreens on the trail sides. She knew she looked good, as it was a performance more than recreation that showed her audience on the chairlifts that, even though she came from one of the humbler families in the area, she could ski with the elite and even better than they when it came to an expensive sport that most of the country's population could no longer afford.

Sure, other families tried to teach their children how to ski, but it was too late for them. The wealthy had already purchased all of the mountaintops in the land and doled out its peaks to the highest bidder. For some reason, that's how everyone wanted it, or at least that's what they were told on a routine basis, the mantra of capitalism's greatness pounded into their skulls as though they were premature monkeys tortured in a classified scientific experiment. They said it was actually better for them that way. That is how everyone wanted it – to maintain the exclusivity of the sport, so that it attracted her friends and friends of theirs, the kind that looked like them, and so on, just to maintain a fixed population of beauty in a fixed place, so that it could remain untouched, untarnished, and as pure as the snow they skied on. Anything otherwise would be off-putting. It would cheapen the experience, like a leg too short or a front tooth knocked out of its socket.

After several runs, they gathered at the base lodge for a hot chocolate. The three of her friends wanted to take an extended break after the chocolate had warmed their insides, but Sherry wanted to hop right back onto the mountain and ski several more runs before lunch.

"Don't you want to relax?" asked her boyfriend. "We've already been here for two days. We've skied all the trails already."

"But the more runs we get in, the better," said Sherry in response.

"Sherry's back on the farm again," said the fraternity brother.

"No, she's not," said he best friend, hitting her boyfriend's arm.

"Yes, she is," said Sherry's boyfriend. "She wants to get the most bang for her buck."

"It's a waste is all," she said, embarrassed. "We squeeze out as many runs as possible while there's still time."

"Sherry, my dear, if you want, I could make a few phone calls, have everyone removed from this average mountain, and we could have it all for ourselves. Will that make you happy?"

"That won't be necessary," she said.

Her boyfriend sighed and said, "what I'm trying to say is that we don't have to get the most out of the place by skiing every second of every minute of every hour of every day, okay? You're with us now, not your parents. You have to get used to that. In fact, I say we fly to Telluride tomorrow. How about it?"

"Telluride?!" exclaimed her best friend. "We couldn't. What about exams?"

"They won't miss us."

"You don't have to do that," said Sherry. "Besides, I want to take my Poly-Sci exam. I studied hard for it. I want to graduate the right way."

"I know you do," said her boyfriend, while putting his arm around her.

She smiled bashfully at the gesture.

"My good little Sherry has always been a good student," he said.

"I'm in," said her best friend.

"I'm in too," said the fraternity brother.

"That makes three of us," said her boyfriend. "I can charter the flight from Montpelier right now."

"We are not going to Telluride," said Sherry. "We are going back to campus tonight, and we are taking our exams as planned."

"Sherry, you have to learn how to come out of your shell and live a little bit. You're going to Harvard Med, so you have nothing to worry about."

"But I want to go on my own merits."

"You already are. Just relax."

"I have to take my exams. I'm sorry."

"Honey, when you're with me, you don't have to do anything you don't want to. We don't have to do anything we don't want to. That's the way things are."

"Well, I'm going back to Washington. That's the way I want it."

"I don't want to argue with you, Sherry. I think a few days in Telluride will do us some good. What do you guys say?"

"It's a great idea," said her best friend, as the fraternity brother put his arm around her and smiled in agreement.

"Well," said her boyfriend, "shall we get packing then?"

Even though they had spent only a few hours on the

mountain that morning, they returned to their respective chalets. As soon as Sherry locked the front door behind them, she threw off her boots and ran into the master bathroom. She slammed the door shut. Her boyfriend soon followed.

"Don't get so upset by all of this," called her boyfriend through the door. "Telluride is not at all crowded this time of year."

"Don't play with me," she called from the bathroom. "Once again, you humiliate me to control me."

"What on earth are you talking about?"

"You know what I'm talking about. You know that I want to take my final exams. You just wanted to show everyone who's in control, like you always do. Like you have power over me, which you don't, really."

"Honey, we are flying to Telluride this afternoon. You don't need to take your finals. It's all taken care of."

"You embarrassed me in front of our friends. You always do. You embarrass me in front of my sorority sisters too, every chance you get. Is it because I'm a better student than you are, or a better athlete than you'll ever be?"

"Nonsense. I'm not competing with you."

"It seems that you are. You are always trying to put me in my place, like you have some inferiority complex or something, like you're trying to win a game against me. You always have to win, don't you? All the time. Even when I'm not playing."

She came out of the bathroom and sat on the bed. He sat calmly next to her, placed his warm hand upon her thigh, and stroked her fine blonde hair.

"It's all in your mind, sweetheart," he said. "I'm not trying to outdo you, or overpower you, or show everyone's who's in charge. It's all in your mind. You need to see your therapist when we get back from Telluride, okay? Because I love you. I want us to have a great time. Skiing Telluride will be great this time of year. We are all on board, and we'll leave this afternoon. I want you to be with us. And maybe I can make this all up to you. I didn't mean to hurt you."

His warm hand cupped her outer thigh, as his other hand that had been stroking her hair pulled her neck back and kissed the length of it, his lips moving along its succulent curve towards her exposed shoulder. He moved his hand ever so slowly between her legs. She opened them up for him as he continued kissing her neck and stroking through the tangle of her blonde locks. But as soon as he pressed his hand deeper between her legs and pulled her head down towards the bed, she opened her eyes, saw what he was doing, and stopped him cold.

"What?"

"I don't want this right now," she said. "I'm upset with you. Why would I do anything when I'm angry with you?"

"Are you seriously telling me that you want to go back to DC and take that stupid Poly-Sci exam instead of skiing Telluride? Are you serious?"

"Hey, I studied hard for that exam. I know you don't need to study for anything. None of you do. But I want to take that exam, okay? And I want to do well on it. I can't get away with it like you guys can."

"You could if you chose to."

"So what are you trying to say? That I could choose to miss the exam? How?"

"I'm just saying."

"No. Tell me. Because what you're suggesting is that

I could miss that test under certain conditions, right?"

"You're being unnecessarily difficult, Sherry. All I'm suggesting is that you come with us to Telluride tonight, and everything will be taken care of. That's all I'm saying."

She looked hard into his brown eyes. She tried to read him but couldn't locate his secret agenda. She knew he meant more than what he said. It was something to the effect that, if she were made a part of his prestigious family, she could easily miss that exam if she wanted to. That's the message she found. But he didn't let on that it was. The way he raised his eyebrows told her that he had little idea that she wanted him to propose all of a sudden and to take her petty worries away, as though hers were inchoate afterthoughts of her farming ancestry, the talents she had been born with, and the skills she had learned in her youth. She may have been born another dumb blonde, but everything that came after that she earned. She was sure of it. Luckily, her parents had pushed her, because blondes didn't have it so easy anymore. They needed more than just finishing school to survive. They needed more than the good manners that came with marrying well. They needed to think critically, speak well, and crunch numbers.

She needed to be clever and move beyond the Jane Austen's, the Edith Wharton's, and the *Little Women*. She needed street smarts and common sense, not the knowledge of which side a salad fork belonged or where to place her napkin after a meal was finished. Her sorority sisters had common sense but only applicable to cocktail parties, baby showers, and cotillions. They knew how to trap other men and get half of their money when they divorced them. She had been pulled into that world based solely on her looks. Put her sisters on the street, and the only profession they would most likely succeed at is the world's oldest one.

Sherry faced that danger too, and maybe she would have made a lot of money at it, but she had an example to set for other women – to become the First Lady who saves twig-boned African and Indian children from famine and tribal genocide for all the media to see and laud, while these same images along with her visage transmit through every flat screen television and every mobile phone of every menstruating teenage girl in every shopping mall miles away from the blighted urban ghettos of the inner-cities.

"Are you coming to Telluride or not?" asked her boyfriend.

"I'm going back. This is not the time to be vacationing in Telluride. And even if I did go, I wouldn't feel comfortable going. And either should you."

"You know what you're acting like?"

"What? A responsible college student on a full scholarship?"

"No. A woman who assumes that one day she'll become a Senator's wife."

She felt like hitting him, but she was not that kind of woman. Her hands were too delicate and her soul too gentle.

"I didn't mean that," sighed her boyfriend.

"I'm returning to Washington."

"And I'm going to Telluride," he said defiantly. "I'll schedule a flight for you from Montpelier to DC tonight."

"I'll take the Amtrak from Rutland, thank you."

She then marched into the bathroom again and slammed the door shut. She didn't want to be near him, and she didn't want him to leave the chalet right away either. She wanted him to clean up the mess he created. As she sat on the lid of the toilet and waited for her nerves to calm, she tried to convince herself that she neither needed him nor his family to go to Harvard Med or become a pediatrician. She earned all that she had, not he. She worked hard and pulled herself up by her bootstraps, even as everyone who saw her walk across campus assumed she had been born with it. She valued the education from Georgetown more than any life of privilege, and any medical school in the country would admit her if they took her grades and her recommendations into consideration.

She didn't need his family's reputation. She felt like telling him that, but she knew better, no matter how emotional she was. As she calmed down, she knew her place and even romanced the notion of becoming someone greater than herself, just as they taught her to be in high school – to be somebody in society and not a nothing – because everyone who beheld her at one time or another expected her to stand above the rest and accomplish great things. She wouldn't simply settle down and pump out a couple of kids and marry yet another Wall Street investment banker like so many women of her ilk had done before. She could have been another corporate housewife taking aerobics, yoga, spinning classes, and going shopping for organic foods had her parents not pushed her. She would have pumped out two kids ready for private schools, or at least a public school where all the village families donate to the cause as though it were a private school anyway.

She deserved more, she told herself, and she genuinely deserved to make something of herself, just to avoid being another interior decorator, receptionist at a SOHO art gallery in the morass of Manhattan, a kindergarten teacher at a Montessori school, a corporatized publisher of literary fiction novels, or a good lay for some egomaniacal Hollywood producer, should she run away from home.

She cooled off in the bathroom after thinking these

things over. While she could have gone her own way, she needed him. To be an important woman in a world of meaninglessness and absurdity mattered to her. She could accept nothing less, and she needed to talk with him and make up, but not with sex. She would make sure of that.

Just a year ago, she gave him sex on a regular basis, whenever he asked for it. She played the sex slave, but she shut off that valve after he wanted an endless supply of it. Her boyfriend could have had any pick of the sisters in her sorority. Instead, he made a beeline straight for her. But now she promised to deny him access until she was sure he loved her. She gave him the test drive but not the keys to the car, in other words. It was now his turn to buy it. Such refusals on her part often turned his face crimson red with madness, as she spurned his every attempt to seduce her, because it should never be about the sex. Any kind of marriage based upon how good a couple was in bed never lasted, she believed. She rubbed up against an ideal that she couldn't understand yet, even though everyone who surrounded them thought they were becoming much too adult and mature for their time. She would have rather lain on the bathroom floor and masturbated than have given it up to him that morning.

Under a residue of anger, she finally exited the bathroom and found him packing his clothes for the trip.

"At least let me fly you back to DC," he said. "You don't have to take a train."

She walked up to him and kissed his mouth.

"What was that for?" he asked.

"I'm sorry," she said.

"Me too. I didn't mean it. I just get angry sometimes, because I want to be with you all the time. Because I love you, Sherry. I'll always love you. You mustn't forget that."

"Then you understand why I'm going back?"

"Yes, I do. I'm good at being irresponsible, but that doesn't mean you have to be."

She kissed him deeply and stopped as soon as he cupped his hand around her breast.

"I guess we better get going then," she said, pulling away.

Shortly after they packed, their two friends came in, and they all shared a bottle of red wine.

"I hear Telluride's a difficult mountain," said her best friend. "You're really missing out, Sherry."

"Leave Sherry alone," said her boyfriend, caressing her thigh again. "She's been through enough."

"I wonder what's happening back at the house," said Sherry. "I wonder who broke up with whom, who hooked up, who had an affair."

"Plenty of that happened," said her best friend. "Our sisters really put out before exam week. It's a stressful time."

"Not for my Sherry," said her boyfriend.

She could have taken this for a slight. But there was enough wine in her to laugh at what he said. Her boyfriend laughed with her.

"What's so funny?" asked the fraternity brother.

"I think I know what's going on," said her best friend.

"Then someone, please, let me in on it."

Her best friend pressed her mouth to her boyfriend's ear and whispered. He then smiled, as though he were the cat that swallowed the canary.

"Apparently, she has you wrapped around your little

finger," said her best friend.

"No, I don't," said Sherry, pouring herself another glass of wine. "It's just that he's always so hot-to-trot, and I have to take him aside and talk some sense to him."

"Sherry?" said her boyfriend. "C'mon. Some things ought to be kept private. Please."

"Oh, it's no secret" said her best friend.

"What do you mean?" she asked.

"Everyone knows you've been playing him. You see, Sherry here wants to make sure he loves her enough. Isn't that right, Sherry, dear?"

"Some things ought to be kept private," laughed Sherry. "Please."

By the time they had finished the bottle, they were reasonably buzzed enough to begin their trip to the airfield at Montpelier where her three friends then boarded a chartered flight to Telluride. After they departed, Sherry waited for an hour before her plane left for Washington.

On the flight, she ate a light lunch and drank some more red wine, just because she felt like it, now that she didn't need to be so social anymore. The jet lazily drifted over the earth below. She leaned back and watched the weakening sun acquiesce to a darkening sky. She even took off her shoes, because she was thankful to be alone and away from her friends for the first time in several days. She had preferred being alone than with the others lately. As a result of studying so hard and achieving so much in her younger years, she lived in her head a lot, not because she had an empty head, but because there was too much analysis in there and also too much reflection. But when accompanied by her boyfriend at dinner parties, however, she concerned herself with how she looked and talked and dressed, as though she saw her own reflection in her own mind while mingling with the crowd, wondering how she looked and how she sounded while on his arm. She busied herself with this hard task, as though it were a job that only a few women could handle.

She let him do all the talking at these parties, because at the most important of them, she didn't know anyone. Her boyfriend simply introduced her to other older couples who were established in what they did. And she didn't consider these older couples dead in any way, as some ancient Irish author in a book she read had suggested. Rather, she felt comforted by these older folks. They were kind to her - just as long as she stayed silent and friendly and uninvolved, just as long as she enjoyed herself and got along. She still needed to look good and speak well, because her position demanded it. Those were the demands of the job, as many of the people she met were often friends of her boyfriend's father, some of them professional lobbyists, committee members, and high-profile Congressional leaders.

When they went to these functions, she usually put on the clothes her boyfriend selected for her. She reviewed her table etiquette before each occasion, but she would again keep quiet, as these were luncheons meant to discuss her boyfriend's future. The older folks saved dinner for more social purposes, but luncheons were small affairs with herself, her boyfriend, and maybe someone else in the government. Every once in a while, the government guy would bring his wife or a friend, but it was mostly business talk about the future. These government officials took all the wanna-be kids out to lunch, and in return, they bragged about how great their jobs were or what promotions were in the works for them. But these officials bought them lunches to see how their young investments were coming along.

Her boyfriend dispatched whatever gossip he had gathered from the other parties they had attended on campus, as the kids on the other side of the aisle were from several fraternities and sororities from that other party with which he had been taught to shake hands. By dint of being with him, Sherry mingled with the other side as well. They avoided becoming too entrenched in their own parties. Apart from partisan differences, his father's friends liked to know about the kids of their enemies – who sexually assaulted the girl on campus and got away with it, who had been sent to rehab, which one had been thrown in jail and who had been bailed out, who had failed their midterms and would graduate a year late. Amidst clinking silverware, heavy cloth linens, polite smiles, and endless samples of house wines, the luncheons were informational exchanges. There was no such thing as unimportant information. It all mattered. The official they dined with never knew where or when he would need it, use it, or in which file he would have to encrypt it.

To her boyfriend, these luncheons were more important than anything remotely academic. But with winks and smiles, the officials insisted that he study regardless. It was the right thing to do. But her boyfriend never did and instead specialized in campus parties and wining and dining with the higher-ups. Even these officials sometimes partied on campus and in the city with those students they would have to rely on in the future. These were places where drunken Senators and Representatives took beach-bunny co-eds home with them, provided they secure well-paying jobs for them after they graduate. Sherry found it amusing how all of the Congressmen's assistants were attractive, and the bureaucrats who drank their way through the midnight watering holes of the university also had young, all-female staffers who were amazingly good-looking. But Sherry would never be one of them. She promised herself that she would never stoop so low, because her boyfriend loved her. He wouldn't let anything like that happen to her. No one would dare make a play for her with such a good and important man in the picture. She was off-limits, and everyone in the Greek system knew it. If another kid hit on her, they were dealt with accordingly, and the punishment was severe. Sherry could only imagine it. They hired thugs from off-campus, or how about private detectives who accessed the student's academic records through connections with the Registrar's office and made a few major changes to it.

While her perceptions of these things were a bit farfetched, she believed them anyway, because she knew herself to be the most beautiful girl in the most elite sorority on campus, and other men knew to stay away from her, as bodyguards hired by her boyfriend's family would soon be guarding her in few year's time. She did have friends who were men, though, but these were usually the geek contingent in the fraternity who made it through rush period to write papers for the good-looking brothers or to take care of the star athletes who paid in dollars and in pussy for whatever help they gave them. Not that they needed the money, but they figured they could at least get close to women who looked half-way decent and nail them by being invited to the best parties.

Sherry employed a similar strategy, as she motivated her boyfriend that way, but not for advancement or more power over him. She believed in love and wanted to fall in love. Again, it was all perception, just like how many students on campus believed that she had been born with it when just the opposite was true.

She had been taught that there was nothing like a sperm lottery. She had also been told that important people mated with discretion. Nice and friendly guys wound up single and alone for most of their lives, so she should allow any future husband of hers to have his secrets and keep them to himself. Nice guys had no secrets. They were wet noodles that most women said they wanted but never considered. The more criminal and abusive the man, the more beautiful the woman he gets. Just a fact of life, she was told.

She shouldn't want someone who was honest, sweet, or too kind. There had to be something irreversibly corrupt about him. The nice ones were the mishappen ones. They had something constitutionally wrong with them, as though they just had to be unattractive and would never very perform well in bed. They would never land high-paying jobs, and if they did, they would soon become the same assholes who were there before them. They walked the streets under cloaks of invisibility, so desperate and lonely they were, that women as beautiful as she could easily tell that such sweet and lame men were really going nowhere and would be better suited to live with their mothers for the rest of their lives.

For some reason, women shouldn't want responsible men. Social Darwinism and natural selection had infiltrated romance and everlasting love. Funny, because these nice guys usually found this out later in life when these once-beautiful women are all spent and used up. The nice guy finds out just before kicking the chair out from underneath his feet, wondering why he couldn't have been a brutal bastard like the rest of the men women like Sherry dated much earlier in life. Yet Sherry thanked the powers that be for finding someone like her boyfriend, because the flight did feel comfortable, and she didn't really want to travel by Amtrak all the way down to Penn Station and then the Express down to Washington.

She used to ride the train down from Vermont before her boyfriend approached her at her very first sorority mixer.

From that point on, she either accompanied him wherever he went, or he chartered jets for her wherever she wanted to go. But being alone on a long train ride never suited her well. Faceless strangers often gazed at her for prolonged periods of time, and even the handsome ones kept making pleasant conversation when she didn't want to be bothered or hit on. She expected this on the trains, and although she could have shooed them away, she politely listened to their pickup lines as though she were a toy doll that could easily be plucked by the next good-looking guy sitting next to her.

But the worst was when the freaks and the geeks on the trains sat next to her and only stared from across the aisle. These were usually the bookish fellows with thick, goofy glasses, diabetes, and morbid obesity, reading science fiction novels from the 1940s and breathing heavily from asthmatic conditions. Sherry knew them to be shy souls, but they annoyed her to no end. She felt their eyes walking all over her body. She looked up, and immediately their eyes darted away, as though they feigned their fascination and had never been entranced by her beauty in the first place. The fact remained, though, that they were much too fat to take seriously.

And there was even the minority crowd that thought they had a remote chance with a blonde built for aristocracy. Maybe she wanted a joint or even some coke or a little dope for the long trip. Maybe she was a bad girl they were used to banging in the city – one of those high-class Park Avenue sluts who were intrigued by horny prep school gangsters who dropped ecstasy at the more exclusive late-night clubs. This type passed by her and made strange sounds – sucking lips, snapping fingers, odd gestures, unusual sounds.

A woman like her just didn't belong with such men. They weren't aesthetically pleasing enough to look at. At times on the same route down to DC, she had to get up and move to another train car. She tried to humble herself by telling her boyfriend that he really didn't need to charter those expensive jets. But after a short time, she preferred it. She could eat, drink wine, listen to music, call her parents and friends, and even study for tests. Usually, when her boyfriend accompanied her during the first few weeks of their relationship, when she saw that he was anxious and stressed out over some complicated matter, she would lead him to the back partition of the plane where a bed had been set up, pull down his pants, and pleasure him until he was relieved of his worries. She did that often, and her boyfriend liked that quality about her. She was good at it. The evidence was both pearl-white, wet, and sticky. But after a few weeks of doling it out, she suspected that her boyfriend may have had problems with sex. She protested in the back partition of the plane.

"You don't open up to me anymore. You don't say anything anymore. You just expect me to have sex with you, and then you say nothing, like there's nothing else to talk about. I'm not your whore."

"Did I ever say that?" he shot back.

"Not in so many words. But I can tell when you're not communicating."

"Sherry, sex is a form of communication. I am being honest and open with you when I give myself to you. It's more intimate than any conversation or any hobby we can do, any party we can attend, any vacation we can enjoy."

"I get the point," she said angrily. "Things are going to change."

She then marched back to the front of the plane and remained silent for the rest of the flight.

That was nearly a year ago, and that was the last time she had been intimate with anyone. On many occasions he was close to seducing her, but he had never gotten close enough to seal the deal.

Together, they decided to build a more traditional relationship, since they anticipated leaping into the void of marriage someday. Fate had stitched them together, but in their DC townhouse near his fraternity, they slept in separate beds and kissed each other only when the moment felt extraordinarily right, and more importantly, when she felt romantically and intimately connected. Sure, he could hear him jerk off in the middle of the night when he thought she was sleeping or when he locked himself in the bathroom for long periods of time. They naturally hungered for it at times. She could even sense when he was aroused, not visually, but by having some strange feminine empathy for the plight of man, as though he radiated a torturous vibe, a vibe that suggested his slow self-destruction. But she didn't indulge him. Sometimes, she thought the way in which he tried to break their unspoken celibate contract was quite amusing. Once her sorority sisters found out about their celebacy, it soon became a source of humor for the whole lot of brothers and sisters alike – loaves of bread thrown into a bloodthirsty crowd of the Colloseum.

She grew tired of it, though. Beauty was the first impression she made, and that subtracted from whatever impression people had of her intelligence and intellect. She figured her boyfriend only wanted her for her beauty and not much else. She was a trophy, in other words, for a man who was undoubtedly wealthy and had a future as a public figure and statesman. But she wanted more than that. Working with poor and damaged children was important, but her boyfriend never intended her to be a Jane Goodall, a Hillary Clinton, or a Margaret Thatcher. He wanted her hemmed in, compliant, and looking good on his arm in an evening dress, letting all of those gray Congressmen kiss her hand and pinch her ass once in a while after they drained their glasses.

She understood that she had role to play, and perhaps being a DC, Harvard-trained pediatrician filled that maternal image of a nurturing, caring stereotype that men of power so desired, but she didn't want to remain quiet when she disagreed with a policy, law, or opinion in the op-ed pages of the *Washington Times*. She didn't want to be a bird in a cage like the past prototypes. Her path, however, was not a choice but an obligation. A duty, almost. She was meant to be a Senator's wife. She had been prepared and groomed for it.

By the way he had been playing his power games, she didn't know what he thought. She figured he still had a ways to go before she would let him sleep with her again. She knew he would wait. The thought of breaking up with her was much too threatening to him and his well-known family. They were on the cusp of graduating a semester ahead of schedule, and they were right on schedule to tie the knot, just as the whole of society prescribed in the playbook of every upstanding American family.

The traditional path was the best path – none of this career-first garbage and wearing long pants shit. The most successful people came from strong families that had repeated the same cycle of American procreation. First, get into a prestigious college. Once there, marry a wealthy and good-looking man. Third, repeat for several generations for the desired result. It was a sure formula for American success, no matter where one began. Water finds its own level, and the more a man strived for a body like Michelangelo's *David*, the more likely their success became. The woman looked like Aphrodite.

Over several generations of trying to look like *David* and believing in the same religion from which it came, any guy could land a woman like Sherry. Guaranteed. That was the promise that America offered, and the whole world fell in line with it, not necessarily a dream or an abundance of opportunity, but a systematic and genetic evolution methodically resulting in a more beautiful man, beautiful enough to win the hand of a blonde woman who would rather have nothing to do with any blemish, vulnerability, or aberration in a partner, as though it was her birthright. So be it if they couldn't get along. It mattered little. Their future mattered more. Regardless, the looks of a woman's partner had been the second item on her checklist. The first, of course, was wealth.

Sherry didn't know, though, when he would pop the question. It was a mystery to her and all of their family and friends. She assumed he would ask before graduation, maybe even after exam week when the younger sorority sisters threw their yearly Christmas bash. And no, there were no Jews or Muslims in her sorority. Basically, it was a drunk fest mixer where everyone dressed fashionably but the atmosphere remained cool and calm until things got out of hand later in the evening. This notorious party culminated in a holy Yule-time orgy among the sorority girls and the fraternity boys in a sorority's mansion that had been built a couple of centuries earlier when black slaves lived in basement rooms and kept the wardrobes of their young owners preserved and looking like new.

She snoozed briefly before the middle-aged pilot woke her gently by calling her name. She could feel his breath on her ear lobe. For him it was a cheap thrill.

"We're about there," he said.

By the time the black Lincoln Town Car picked up her, her luggage, and the ski equipment from the private airfield near Reagan International, she headed to their brownstone near the campus ready to confront her fellow sisters the next morning. They would want to know where her best friend and the two fraternity boys went.

Many of the sisters barraged into the dining room where she ate and crowded around the table the next morning. They demanded to know the intimate details of their trip and what had happened to the others.

"They flew to Telluride," she told them over a buttered bagel and a fruit cup.

To say that her sorority sisters could have one day been A-listers in soft porn films was an understatement, and yet they maintained an aura of gentility and purity wherever they went, their secrets sealed in their campus mansion never to escape beyond its Plantation-styled pillars.

"Well? Tell us," said one sorority sister in a pair of tight jeans and a tank top, her black hair falling to her back, and her green eyes imploring Sherry with unbridled curiosity.

"Just tell us," called another sister. "We've been waiting all week. Did he propose?"

"Just answer the question," called another.

"Okay," she said, "I'll let you know that much, but no more. I have to study for my Poly-Sci exam."

"So? Tell us."

"No, he did not propose. Nothing has changed. We are still a couple. Just as before."

They booed, followed by a round of laughter and chatter.

"At least tell us if you slept with him," said another good-looking sister, leaning over the table with her elbows on it, eager to know.

"I'll leave that to your overactive imaginations, sisters," she said.

"C'mon! You can't walk away from that!"

"And with that," said Sherry, "I have some studying to do. I'll probably see you later for dinner."

"Oh, you're such a prude," said another sister.

"Like you're actually joining us for dinner this time," called another.

"I'm not a homebody," said Sherry, finishing her meal. "I miss you guys. You know that."

"But you'll be here for the Holiday Party, right?" asked another sister.

"We will both be here. Don't worry about that. I plan to get plenty tipsy this year."

The sisters wanted to know more about their trip, but she didn't reveal anything that would make them feel less of themselves or envious. She was responsible that way, especially to the freshmen sisters. She never bragged about the lavish gifts her boyfriend bestowed upon her for every silly occasion – the flowers, the quick Caribbean getaways, anything to please her. She hid these things from them, as her boyfriend pampered her beyond anything these girls would ever recognize. Such gifting never spoiled her, though. Rather, she often gave a lot of the jewelry and many of the spa treatment sessions to her best friend, the same sister who flew to Telluride. In fact, Sherry made sure her best friend and her numerous boyfriends went to many of the places her boyfriend took her. While her boyfriend wanted them to travel alone, Sherry insisted that her best friend tag along. It often frustrated him, but he yielded to her wishes.

Sherry and her best friend were in the same pledge class

together. They discovered that they had much in common – beauty, brains, and the same taste in men. They both liked them good-looking, as attraction at that stage of their lives trumped everything else. Their men had to look the part. They were eye-candy to be sucked on at their open sorority parties and private mixers. When they first joined, they preferred their men dumb, compliant, pliable, and reckless. Men were lumps of clay, Rodin's blocks of cement, to be molded by a woman's creative processes. This usually involved training them to treat them well, as all women ought to have been treated, to make them more perfect gentlemen who crawled out of the salty ocean from which they developed and emerged as a species that at least headed in the right direction, towards a degree and not alcoholism, towards fidelity and not adultery, towards hard work and not sloth and the false freedom of doing absolutely nothing and lying on a couch, watching football, and drinking beer.

Her best friend had made many more mistakes with men than Sherry could have ever conceived. But Sherry had the upper hand in beauty. Her blonde hair made men come out of the shadows and try their luck at a losing game. But then her prince came and fit her dainty feet into the glass slipper and danced with her the rest of the night revealed that she was a student on full scholarship and would never be able to afford the tuition at a place as expensive as Harvard. Naturally, he returned to the sorority the very next day. Their coupling had been predestined, even though there were many fraternity brothers she thought incredibly chiseled and highly attractive as well. She simply went along with what the world expected of her and had been paired with the boy who had the looks and the highest potential to succeed.

She sometimes carried her best friend's promiscuity and bachelorette approach to college with her, but over time, the mature approach of having a decent relationship and learning how to love her man proved more palatable an idea or at least a goal to be desired. Yet that endpoint hadn't arrived yet in their relationship. She kept fishing for it, casting a line, as though she tried to snare another achievement, until the same cycle repeated itself through her children when they one day landed spouses of their own. That's how most people did it, she figured. There was no such thing as luck, good timing, or acts of God. The only role her intelligence played was to keep her kind on the treadmill, walking the same path in perpetuity. This would ensure the best possible outcome.

It made sense to her. But she and her boyfriend didn't share much in common apart from the roles they would play in their adult lives. She was independent enough not to need a mutually dependent relationship. They would be a team, a partnership, two economic and political operators on an axis point heading towards the most optimal position on the graph. She didn't need his emotional support, and either did he need hers. The adults saw separate bathrooms in their future. Similarly, she didn't want him to worry or care for her too much, even though he paid for anything she wanted. She was perfectly able to stand on her own two feet, just as long as he paid for medical school, as they agreed. That's all she asked for. It was a mere pittance compared to the resources at his disposal.

If she were with any other man, she would be the one bringing home the bacon, especially to the lonely ones who declared it good enough that Georgetown had its share of hot women who could do anything they damn well pleased after graduation and would always get away with it. After all, God designed only men to be lonely. All loners lived vapid and mediocre lives without her. After graduation, these students pushed paper, masturbated to videos on the Internet, abstained from drugs and alcohol to avoid jail, and kept silent as every conceivable injustice they learned of passed for American exceptionalism. While their bills might have been paid, and maybe a few would be fortunate enough to avoid creditors, lawsuits, and evictions, a loner's precious dreams were whittled down to early glimpses of heaven just to keep him out of the straightjacket of a padded room.

After leaving the sorority house, she returned to her townhouse a few blocks away. The brownstone building stood on a silent street beyond anything noisy or polluted. It had an elevator that moved among three spacious floors. Out front and up the hard and heavy steps, a pewter plaque commemorated the property as a historical landmark that her boyfriend's generosity had saved from demolition. It had been completely and utterly renovated and refortified with the latest of everything – new appliances, windows, stairs, ceilings, rooftops, doorknobs, and bathtubs. After this renovation, eager real estate speculators purchased the derelict properties surrounding it on the sure bet that the abominable DC neighborhood, where the crack dens, the indigent hoboes, and the heroin addicts had been stationed, would be contained by the Georgetown police and co-opted by the university.

Once these properties were resold and had fetched even higher prices from other speculators with bigger wallets, the dregs of the city would then be sent packing to the next ghetto several blocks away. If they hung around the newer, nicer neighborhood, the cops forced them out. And soon, a once-poor neighborhood had reinvented itself.

First, the artists came. Then, the young people who liked to drink and smoke and visit the fashionable bars and restaurants arrived. Then the bourgeoisie moved in. Finally, the wealthy moved in and were praised for single-handedly reviving the neighborhood and giving the once-abandoned area so much of its life and culture back. Yes, the awards, the ribbon cuttings, and the massive tax breaks for more of the sprawl and the biggest return on their investment dollars were hurled at them by a grateful City Hall.

The wealth trickled down to the churches on the outskirts, who, in turn, ran the soup kitchens and the food banks that now fed the same people who had been pushed out. And once a few experienced social do-gooders came in to compete with the churches for grant money to help the battered women, orphaned children, the homeless, and the mentally deranged, the powers that be then cut taxes even more while doling out grants to those cheapest non-profits that held out their hands and claimed they could change these people, train them for the workforce, have them lift heavy boxes, mop the floors, handle the cash registers at dollar stores, and cook bacon and eggs over scalding hot grills at local greasy spoons for less than minimum wage.

The ones who didn't want such jobs were called lazy sonofabitches for sucking on the government tit. Others felt sorry for them and agreed they should be minimally subsidized. And then there were those in the ghetto who saw a way out through the lucrative drug trade. These jokers usually ended up spending their lives in jail. There was really no incentive for them to reform anyway. At least mopping floors, helping poor, disabled people navigate the streets in their wheelchairs, and selling stolen clothing from the Arab convenience stores were things to shoot for. Work would set them free, said the many who looked on in disgust at what they had chosen to make of themselves.

As Sherry walked home from the sorority house, she was oblivious to how the neighborhood had changed over a past decade of failed attempts by the city and the university to eradicate the abandoned homes, the makeshift convenience stores, and the drug dealers loitering in front of them. She lived in a new neighborhood of high value without knowing how it became that way. Blacks, Browns, and Asians just had different family dynamics, and so they lived apart. Living apart was just natural, like the plants and the birds and the many fish found in the sea. It had nothing to do with redistricting, gerrymandering, electoral politics, the rush for jobs, or ancient racial ideologies. It was a natural consequence of a free and open society. Birds of a feather flocked in similar places, even though these were human beings who were far from being animals.

Miscegenation, after all, was such an ugly term. It produced abandoned and displaced people unanchored to any particular culture or nationality. Pure breeds were the only way to go, as Sherry recognized the futility of interracial relationships. The ones that she did see on the outskirts of town when she sometimes traveled in her Black Lincoln Town Car consisted of heavyset women dressed in pajamas and slippers, pushing strollers down ghetto sidewalks, while their black, jobless boyfriends drank tallboys out of paper bags on apartment stoops and project entrances. She would have never felt safe in such neighborhoods, even though she had nothing against the poor blacks and white trash who populated them. If only they tried a little harder or did something with their lives, then maybe they would get somewhere, she thought.

Her boyfriend did promise that, one day, other neighborhoods would also be rehabilitated, but such redevelopment took time. The time span seemed endless, as though it would continue for many generations. It pointed to the population's inferiority, but Sherry battled back thoughts of this, because she knew full well that such thinking was wrong. There was no such thing as racial superiority among people. But she could see that the lighter the color, the more likely the success. A color line, perhaps.

She had heard two blacks talking before one of her Biology classes. They said that white people had remained in their caves, while black and brown people emerged earlier and gathered in the wilderness beyond their dwellings before whites did. This phenomenon accounted for the ferocity, the natural reserve, and the defensiveness of white people towards others. They just didn't get along with other human beings very well, even their own kind. They preferred the private rather than the public, and they fiercely protected their property and their women.

Not much had changed since the thaw of the Ice Age. It made sense, but a lot of it seemed to be based on little evidence. She could only see it on the streets whenever her driver took her shopping, or when she went to the airfield with her boyfriend. There were, in fact, two Washington DCs, and she made sure to stay away from the black parts of it. She may have been mugged or raped in those parts. And rape had always been a deep-seeded fear of hers – to be raped and then killed off, only to have her photograph featured on the six o'clock news.

There were places she shouldn't go, and men she just didn't find attractive either. It wasn't her fault. Blacks and Southeast Asians were just ugly to her. So were Far East Asians with their slanted eyes and yellow, translucent skin. She didn't know what it meant, only that she should stick with her own kind. Interestingly enough, many blacks had already accepted the fact that she found them ugly. They wanted nothing to do with her, as she came from a separate world unavailable to them, if not completely alien. If she were to hit on black men, that might have been a different story, but it was a lie that she could somehow see passed the color of their skin.

She didn't feel guilty about it either, because even though she did see them as colored, she still thought herself special enough to rise above it, should a good black man come along and ask her out. She piled on the bullshit high enough to feel even more secure about her own character. Everyone in the sorority already knew that black men never got the blonde, blue-eyed babe. Her sisters would have said that she could have done much better than settle. It just wasn't done. There must be something wrong with her, they would have said. She would have been disowned or beaten to death by the village mob with their pitchforks, rakes, and shovels. She too would have wound up fat, pregnant, and poor in pajama bottoms and slippers pushing two ugly, biracial kids to the welfare office to pick up her weekly checks. The scenario scared her, and so she stayed away, even if she were remotely curious about a particular black man she saw on campus or even in the city streets. Same went with the other races and nationalities that came near her personal space. She neither looked at them nor talked to them.

For the next couple of days, she received the material for the Poly-Sci exam and ate at the sorority house as often as she could. After taking the exam, she felt she did well on it. It was the last exam of the year, and she had suddenly become a graduate of Georgetown University. Her professors issued grades the very next day, and the Registrar's Office would mail her the diploma in a few weeks. Her boyfriend soon returned from Telluride. The only event that precluded an official end to her undergraduate career and entrance into medical school entailed a visit from a recruiter, an esteemed physician from Harvard Medical School. He was also a top surgeon at Massachusetts General Hospital in Boston. He flew down to have Sherry sign a few papers and conduct a final interview before they admitted her.

It was supposed to be a mere formality, but Sherry knew full well that she had the power to pull the plug on the whole plan, should there be anything that interfered with her ideal view of what kind of pediatrician she wanted to be. She didn't want to let on that she would jump at the chance to go to Harvard. Rather, she wanted to play it cool and equalize the relationship. Harvard should have wanted her just as much as she wanted Harvard. It was a mutual exchange of talent, she reasoned, and she should not show any kind of undue gratitude or overabundance of joy just because they had admitted her. After all, Harvard should be grateful that she wanted to go there. It was a two-way street.

For this meeting, she dressed professionally in a black, pleated skirt that fell to her ankles, a white blouse with a bow, and a black jacket that covered her firm breasts in a diagonal v-shape over her upper chest. It was conservative wear meant to show that the occasion was serious and her entrance guaranteed. As usual, she wanted to make a good impression. She would be the first Aspen ever to go into medicine, and it was vitally important that she make it through the experience and succeed at redirecting her rural ancestry away from the farms to the hospitals where so many accomplished and respected persons had established themselves. She even brandished an antique tea set that her boyfriend had purchased for her up in Vermont, and when the recruiter arrived, she immediately sat him down, served him herbal tea in keeping with good health, along with a couple lumps of sugar as the Brits always did, and a few butter cookies to make the entire presentation classically perfect.

She sat stiffly upright, as though she were an ambassador at a US Embassy. Again, she loved making a good impression. The man was much older, probably in his late sixties. He had all of his hair, mostly white and parted to the side. He was imperially slim and wore a blue blazer and red Harvard bowtie. Out of a slim leather valise, he took out some paperwork and laid it on his lap.

"How was your trip, Doctor?" asked Sherry pleasantly.

"Fine, Miss Aspen, just fine. Your fiance's family had me fly down from Logan. It was pleasant traveling by private plane and not a commercial flight on Harvard's dime, even though I do fly first class everywhere they send me. I appreciate how your family saved the school some good money."

"It's no problem, Doctor. We'd do it again for Harvard. And I'm glad you could make it on your tight schedule. You must be missing a few appointments for this, yes?"

"As an alumnus, I try to make a little time for my Alma Mater to ensure that we admit only the best to our medical school."

"I hope I fall into that category, Doctor," she smiled.

"Consider yourself a part of our family at Harvard – just as you consider us a part of yours."

"That sounds just fine, Doctor."

"Provided everything goes well, you will be admitted. Now I just have a few papers for you to sign," he said, sorting through the stack in his lap.

"Everything already did go well, right? I'm finished with undergrad, right?"

"Yes, but we hope your other things go well too, Miss Aspen," he said with a smile.

"There were no problems with my application, right? Are there any?"

"Just take it easy, Miss Aspen. No, there are no problems with your application. We just want to make sure that you follow through on your plans."

"Doctor, I hate to belabor the point, but I am already accepted, aren't I?"

"Well, not technically, no," he said carefully with a slight look of concern, crossing his legs to the other side.

"I don't understand. Can you tell me a bit more?"

"Miss Aspen, you see, at Harvard, we consider the entire applicant's portfolio and profile, not only the required grade-point averages, test scores, recommendations, and all of those other factors."

"I see. But I did very well on my MCATs. My grades are excellent. My application essay is strong. My recommendations from my science professors are exemplary, right?"

"Of course, Miss Aspen," said the good doctor a bit uncomfortably. "But you see, you are part of the Harvard Family now. And because you will soon become an important public figure in Washington after you graduate, we factor that in as well. Your future standing is very important to us, Miss Aspen. Not only are you smart enough to come to our medical school, but you are also important enough to make the cut, you see, whereas our other applicants simply fall by the wayside. What I'm getting at is that so many young adults from the most prestigious pre-med programs around the world want to attend Harvard Med. The Chinese, the Indians, people from all over the world. But we have a responsibility to make sure our student population is adequately represented, and we pick the ones we think will fare the best and achieve the most after they leave us. You see, Miss Aspen, you are one of those people. Not serving in Washington would only negatively affect your application.

"So please. All I need is your signature on these documents, and I also have to take your body measurements for our files. But don't worry. No one will ever have access to them. We keep these for our records only."

"Okay," said Sherry, she said.

Disappointed with the good doctor's explanation, she stood from the living room sofa and allowed him to record her body measurements for his files. He measured her waist and chest size just to make sure her proportions fit the profile of what Harvard expected of her. Needless to say, the other applicants did not have to do this to get in. Despite all of her bold ideas and talk about getting in on her own merits, she signed all the documents anyway without any objection. After all, she would one day be a Senator's wife, and life was just different for special people like her – those who were not only smart and beautiful, but also women who were to be important figures in the public eye. She thought that this was the time-tested process that all public figures and celebrities had to go through before they could be introduced to the public. She just never realized it before. And despite being groomed for the prestigious medical school, at bottom it also excited her that she was now privileged enough to be on the fast track. Maybe her boyfriend was right. She could have easily gone to Telluride instead of taking that Poly-Sci exam. Either way, it wouldn't have mattered. She still would have graduated and gone on to Harvard.

After the good doctor left, however, her hands began to shake. The world had not worked like the teachings she had grown up with. They didn't apply anymore. She was now in a different world. Her preconceived notions had been smashed over time. She opened her medicine cabinet in the bathroom and swallowed a couple of sedatives to relieve her anxiety. Her thoughts raced to the point of confusion. She took the elevator down to their first-floor dining room, and poured herself a glass of scotch, which she hoped would further calm her down.

After a half-hour and her good spirits restored, she remembered her therapist at the university saying that dark and foreboding thoughts about the future wouldn't last for very long. They had to end at some point. The sedatives and the scotch helped that, and soon, she looked forward to her boyfriend's return and the Holiday Bash at the sorority house the next evening. Bouncing back, she grew excited about being the star of the show as she had always been. And besides, as soon as she had signed those papers, she was suddenly studying medicine at Harvard. There was nothing at all wrong about that anymore. No reason to be remorseful or nervous. The world had fallen back into place. Her life would roll on as destiny had already determined it would. And soon her boyfriend would return to tell her the story of their lives together all over again, what an amazing pediatrician she would soon become, and what a wonderful wedding they would have in Malibu. She saw this unfolding before her lovely blue eyes, as though these phantasms replaced by real people, and of course, her beauty the centerpiece of it all – the Earth circling that one singular quality that she effortlessly sacrificed for others.

That very night, her boyfriend returned, and on the next night, they found themselves in their bedroom looking at themselves in the mirror. She had on a short black evening dress that hugged her body, and he had put on an expensive designer coat and a high-end pair of dress slacks. They stared at themselves for several minutes at various angles, making sure they were the best-looking couple there that night. With their smiles frozen as though they were in front of a camera, they checked their facial features and the folds of the fabric they had draped over their bodies. They looked so good together that it became awkward to forfeit their statuesque positions in front of the mirror. They were getting late, though, and without saying a word to each other, they left the townhouse with butterflies in their stomachs and went by limousine to the sorority house just a few blocks away.

The limousine would have seemed unnecessary, but it wasn't by a long shot. About a couple of blocks away from the party, a line of limos had formed. Their limousine inched forward until a black uniformed concierge opened the doors for them at the pillars of the mansion. Professional photographers and those from the press flashed away at this mesmerizing couple that had just arrived at the most infamous holiday party on campus. Even the students not involved with the sorority looked on behind the photographers as though the front of the mansion were a movie premier. The scene sickened and delighted these students, each one of them bewildered that a single campus party had generated so much attention.

Her boyfriend took Sherry's arm through his, and together they walked through a threshold lined with crimson poinsettias. They had arrived fashionably late, just as they had planned. Once inside, another black man in red uniform took their coats. A cover band played the classics on a stage at the far end of the sorority ballroom. Most, if not all, of the fraternity brothers were there, and together with their sisters, they fed on lobster tails, filet minion, and grilled salmon between drinking massive quantities of beer, wine, and liquor and dancing foolishly drunk and stoned as the night progressed.

All of the sorority girls lived in the mansion, and as the clock circled the dial, people mysteriously vanished from the dancefloor. Many of them adjourned to the rooms upstairs to continue the late-night partying on their own. Sherry, however, had been caught by one of the geeks near the carpeted stairs that led to the second floor. He was a short fellow with horned-rimmed glasses. He would soon go on to be an accountant or some kind of Wall Street analyst after college. He purchased his suit off the rack, she could tell, and their conversation bored her to no end. She just wasn't interested in anything about him, and she let him know this by craning her neck to see if she could spot her boyfriend somewhere, which she could not. She assumed he went upstairs somewhere to have a drink with his fraternity brothers. She hardly paid attention to what this short character said. She only pretended to listen to him talk about how an important accounting firm in New York had just recruited him. He would start his new job that summer and would also be paid a handsome salary fit for someone who had worked there over many years. It took connections, he said, and especially the numerical talent he had been born with.

She nodded her head, desperately wanting to flee upstairs to where the real party was and where her boyfriend could be found, but the accountant just wouldn't stop talking. She had to be polite about it, in keeping with her good manners, and she didn't know if her boyfriend would ever need a good accountant someday, but she excused herself as soon as he took her glass and offered to fill it up with some of the spiked punch. She then raced upstairs to join the popular guys and girls who had been partying on the second floor for at least an hour already, probably drunk and dancing to familiar pop tunes they had sung at other parties earlier that year, she guessed.

When she reached the second floor, she heard loud music blaring through the hallway. Suddenly, out of one of the rooms ran a sorority sister in nothing but her panties, giggling hysterically. One of the fraternity brothers chased her in his boxer shorts. They shot passed her and hid in another room, laughing playfully, until he shut the door and muted the loud interruption.

Sherry figured her sisters hooked up in the many rooms of the mansion, as the later hours of the Holiday Bash had always been reserved for their final chances at getting laid before the semester came to a close. She heard her sisters moaning and gasping with pleasure through the thin walls, and she just wanted to go home with her boyfriend and do the same with him.

Yes, now that they had graduated together, she would let him have his way with her for the rest of the night. He deserved it for being so good to her, so loyal, so kind for putting up with her neurotic need to finish her exams while denying his relentless advances just to make sure he truly loved her. Just as he wanted to be inside of her for all those months he had gone without, so she wanted to take him inside until she came multiple times and finally released a full year of stress, pressure, and fierce argument from her body. She wanted him to come, not just a little, but a lot – a huge gush of it straight into her womb – until they both fell into their bed together too exhausted to move.

She searched the second floor by quickly and quietly cracking open the doors to each room and peeking inside. Most of her sorority sisters were busy fucking the men they had always wanted to fuck during the school year but never had the chance. One fraternity brother had taken two girls to bed, and others simply fooled around beneath the sheets before plunging into each other. Sherry wanted it right away – not later, but immediately, the tingle between her legs like a radar that picked up the signals of his desperate longing somewhere within the sorority house.

Sherry climbed another set of stairs which were narrower than the first. She arrived at the much coveted third floor where her senior sisters resided. She again heard the ubiquitous moaning, gasping, and giggling, the walls breathing with ecstasy and pleasure. When she peeked into the room where her best friend resided, however, there she saw her boyfriend in the nude standing next to her best friend's bed. Her best friend had planted her naked body on all fours and had taken him into her mouth, licking it up and down, his head thrown back and his eyes closed as though receiving signals of bliss from same God who gifted his world with the high privilege he enjoyed.

She stood motionless, observing the two in horror, and when her best friend paused to lick her lips, Sherry ran downstairs, only to be found by the accounting geek all alone on one of the sofas holding her drink in his hand. She marched up to him nearly out of breath and said,

"You, come on. Let's go back to your place."

"You mean, the fraternity?"

"Yes. What did you think I meant?"

"Are you okay?" he asked, getting up from his seat.

"C'mon. Let's go to your place."

"Do you think that's a good idea?"

"What are you talking about?"

"With your boyfriend and all? I don't want any trouble."

"Don't be such a wimp," she said. "I don't want my boyfriend tonight. I want you. So let's leave while we have the chance."

"I don't think it's a good idea," he said.

She walked up close to him and planted a firm kiss on his lips.

"Follow me," she ordered.

She grabbed his hand and pulled him out the door of the sorority mansion. She led him to the fraternity house across the quad. Most of the brothers were still at the sorority house that night, but a few of them loitered the downstairs area of the fraternity as well. They rubbed their eyes and looked twice as she led the soon-to-be accountant upstairs to his room.

His room was small but well-organized. She could tell that he was not a very important or notable member of the brotherhood, but she pushed him into his room anyway, shut the door tightly, and made sure it was locked. The young geek resisted her as much as he could, because he knew what waited for him should the other brothers discover him with the star beauty queen in his room late at night. In fact, she wanted to devour him, attack him almost, just to bring him in line with the rest of the bastards in the fraternal animal world, not to humiliate him, but to teach him how to suffer for her, or even how to kill for her like the rest of the brothers had to do in order to sleep with someone as fine as she. And in many ways, she saw him as an innocent victim who had to grow up. As unusual as it seemed, he had to become a man. They were mismatched – the insufferable pencil-neck geek, sneaking ahead of the line in front of the rest of the idiots who had a hard-on for her, and now the prom queen, ruining her reputation for this half-man, half-child. She would turn this geek into an animal fit for battle, and as a result he would win his future.

And yet she witnessed how nervously he shook as she stood before him, wondering what the consequences would be if she suddenly disrobed in front of him, exposed her trim blonde body, pushed him onto his bed, and smothered his face between her full breasts. She knew she had to do it.

"Listen," he said nervously, "I can't do what you want me to do. I don't want any trouble. Please."

She moved in and kissed him again. But he pulled away.

"You need help," he said. "We can't be doing this now. It's not a good idea, especially with your boyfriend and all."

"I'm done with my boyfriend," said Sherry. "We're over. I'm a free woman, and now I want you."

"Listen," he said nervously, "you're not rational."

"I am perfectly rational. I'm a graduate of one of the best universities in the United States, and I'm about to go on to Harvard Med. How am I not rational?"

"Please, I don't want to have sex with you tonight."

"Why not?! Is there something wrong with me? Do you not find me attractive?"

"You're already taken, I'm afraid."

"Well, fuck you then, you fucking wimp! You four-eyed loser! Sleep with me, or else I'm leaving!"

"I'm sorry," he said. "Let me at least take you back to the sorority house."

"I'm going home," she said angrily.

She grabbed her coat and ran down the stairs of the fraternity house with tears in her eyes. The limousine waited across the quad at the sorority mansion. She covered up her black dress as though she had been betrayed by destiny. She couldn't get the image of her boyfriend and her best friend out of her head, how his eyes rolled back as she sucked him off, up and down, the phallus that was meant for her lips alone.

She stood outside of the townhouse they had made

together and saw that the light on the third floor was on. Apparently, her boyfriend waited for her, and yet she didn't want to discuss it. Not only was she too angry and upset but also too exhausted to deal with his excuses and lies, and perhaps his apologies. Once on the third floor where their bedroom was, he saw him lying on the bed in his bathrobe after having taken a shower.

"Where have you been?" he asked, getting up.

"Looking for you," she said bitterly.

"Your mascara. It's running. Have you been crying?"

"That's none of your concern."

"Honey, what's the matter?" he said, climbing out of bed and approaching her. "Did something happen? Why are you so upset?"

She stepped up close to him. She could smell the alcohol seeping through his skin. She then smacked him hard in the face. He fell back onto the bed and soothed the sting by holding his hand to his cheek, his eyes watering.

"What the hell was that for?!"

"Why don't you tell me?!"

"I have no idea what you're talking about? Have you been taking your meds?"

"Oh? No idea what I'm talking about? Why don't I ask the bitch that sucked your cock tonight?"

He sighed deeply, and his head fell back into the pillows behind him.

"You didn't think I'd find out?" she asked.

"Sherry, you have only yourself to blame for that."

"Excuse me?"

"You weren't putting out. You were starving me for no reason. And all I ever did was love you more than anyone else could."

"How long has it been going on?"

"What?"

"Don't 'what' me. I'm not a fool. How long have you two been seeing each other?"

"It's been going on for a while now, Sherry. You have no one but yourself to blame for it. You just wouldn't make love to me. How's that supposed to make me feel? Do you have any idea what that does to a man at the prime of his life?"

"I don't care. It's obvious you don't love me anymore. Or maybe you never did. Maybe you were just using me."

"That's not true. You were using me. It's the other way around, sweetheart. I gave you everything – money, clothes, a place to stay, your whole fucking future, and then you get all pissy, because someone else gives me a blowjob, because you refused to do it in the first place. What the hell is wrong with you anyway? It's just a blowjob. Don't worry about it. It's not a big deal. I'll tell her to stop doing it."

"You know what? I think you two deserve each other. That's what I think."

"I'm glad you think that, Sherry, because let's be totally frank here, okay? You're replaceable. With just the snap of my fingers."

"Is that what you think? Three years I gave you, and this is what it comes down to?"

"Sherry, you gave all that time up a while ago. It's been a year of suffering for me. Maybe not for you, but for me. You've been selfish, and this time it's going to cost you."

"It's over. You can go to Hell!"

"Get your stuff, and get the hell out of here," he said. "And don't ever come back. I'm having the locks changed."

"That's just fine. Give my best to your wonderful family. And I'm taking my three years back. I never needed you at all. Not once."

She grabbed her purse from off the dresser and fled downstairs to where the limousine had parked for the night. She summoned the driver who then brought her to the nearest luxury hotel where she holed up for the night.

When she got under cool covers, she cried herself to sleep, knowing full well that what she had felt for him was simply a chimera, a fairy tale, an idea of the perfect life that had slipped through her fingers. The dream of being a pediatrician, an important woman one day, a Senator's wife, the jewel of her family line, all of the horseshit with which she had been fed since childhood, all faded to darkness. She choked on her tears so much, that she swallowed a couple more sedatives that she brought with her from the house. She fell fast asleep with her black dress still on.

She didn't sleep well, though. She awoke early the next morning. It was a Sunday, and with haste, she donned her coat and her sunglasses and ran to the nearest bank. She took cash advances out on all of her credit cards that her boyfriend had put in her name. She maxed all of them out. She came out with roughly fifteen thousand in cash. She returned to the hotel and slept for a few more hours. She fell asleep while clutching the thick envelope that contained the flurry of one-hundred-dollar bills. It was all that she had.

Chapter Two

December 2000 – Washington D.C., USA

'What is it about growing old?' he asked himself while gazing at his young granddaughter. She combed the hair of her Barbie doll as he lazily sipped his bourbon and sucked on a melted ice cube to steady its sour flavor. He sometimes drank before he went to work – only a couple of them to get into the mood. He had been doing so for years and had no intention of ever ending the ritual, even though his wife didn't like it. She labeled it a bad habit, especially around their granddaughter who visited every few days to play with her collection of dolls, miniature houses, and cosmetics that she smeared on her face.

The old man remembered his own daughter, and his own daughter was a mirror image of his own wife. It was just how it should have been. His granddaughter had been blessed with dirty-blonde hair, which he considered to come close enough to every elite family's hair in Washington. Even though his own parents, or her daughter's grandparents, had fled the Soviet Union in his youth, he had transcended the barriers that other immigrant families in America dreamed, because in a single generation, he produced an American blonde beauty whom he would marry well into an important family, just as he had planned.

The young child had nothing to worry about. Life

would never be difficult for her. She would have the best of Washington society at her fingertips and would dine and dance with the best of men, so that she would advance her family line and the old man's line along with her. She carried him in her cells, and he would continue to live through her DNA long after he left the Earth. While the old man's wife was a trophy, his granddaughter was the blank check that came with it. It had nothing to do with fate. It was good planning and sound decision-making that forged their pathway to the top. Yes, he knew he would meet his maker soon, but first he had to square things away, tie up loose ends, and repay the people who had helped him along the way.

His son-in-law was a handsome and dashing young fellow of whom he enthusiastically approved. There were many men who wanted his youngest daughter, but he found the right man before she made any stupid mistakes. His daughter liked the artsy types. They would have driven his family straight into the mud, he figured. Better to have her cry over them at any early age. She would look back and realize how right her father had been to wed her to the guy he chose. Talent, creativity, and high intelligence were no match for experience and the laws of good breeding, the buzz of the bourbon ethereal, the room lightening its load. He picked up what remained of his fat cigar, chewed and frayed at the tip, and lit it aflame from a solid pearl lighter a friend stationed in Qatar had given to him several years ago.

There was nothing like the rush of bourbon, the face of his beautiful granddaughter playing near him quietly, and a nice fat cigar in his mouth, his teeth clamping down on the Cuban tobacco leaves, the tangy sweet juices running along his tongue. They ushered in memories of a decadent past. It was a time when men drank their bourbon at will and smoked cigars whenever they felt like it. There were no wives to remind them of bad health. The men exchanged tasteless jokes and made plans for the future, while dragging along their wives to cook and clean and take care of the kids like they were meant to do. 'What happened to it all?' he wondered. The world had turned upside down since then. He couldn't help but feel lost in his own den, his wife coming in from the kitchen with a tray of eggs and dry wheat toast for breakfast.

"Put that thing out," she said. "Not while Millicent is in the room for God's sakes. Now eat your breakfast before it gets cold. And you know you're not supposed to be drinking before work anymore. Look at that belly of yours. Why don't you take a walk in the morning instead of sitting there and staring into space?"

He studied the roundness of his belly, patted it, took another swig of his bourbon, and burped.

"Did you know, sweetie," he said, "man came first, and women came second? From the rib, honey, from the rib! So do me a favor – be a good rib and get me another drink before I shower up, okay, hun? Be a good girl for me."

"Pretty soon you won't be able to get out of that chair, especially with all of those doughnuts you've been eating. I saw you this morning. I'll have to hide them from you from now on."

"I'm in perfect health," he said, patting his belly again.

She giggled at this, and the way the corners of her mouth curved into the dimples of her cheeks reaffirmed that after so many years of marriage, she was still very much in love with him – bourbon, noxious cigar, his blubber, the whole package.

"You're going to be late," she laughed. "It's time to stop playing Barbie with your granddaughter and get moving."

"What if I don't want to go?" he said suddenly. "What if I want to go trout fishing instead?"

"What would the world come to if you went trout fishing? Think about how many people need you at work right now. Think about your fans."

"My fans?"

"Yes. Your devoted fans and the disciples who work for you. Where would they be if you went trout fishing today?"

"You know, sweetie pie, for once in your life, you're starting to make sense. Because as I see it, the world needs people like me. I put in my hours as a sacrifice to this country, to straighten the gate, to level the playing the field, to charge the scroll, to help the helpless. Because the world as we know it cannot go on unless I walk right into that office, do what I have to do, and come home to your flushed face at night and plant a kiss right on your sweet lips."

And then to his granddaughter, "isn't that right, sweet pea?"

"Yes, Papa," said the small child at his feet, now putting a new set of clothes onto the Barbie doll.

"See," said his wife. "Even your flesh and blood agrees, so hit the showers, and no doughnuts before you get upstairs, okay?"

A little tipsy, he struggled out of the recliner, kissed his granddaughter on the crown of her head, and stumbled up the stairs to the top floor. Once in the bathroom, he checked his old body in the full-length mirror his mother had brought over from the Soviet Union seventy years ago. Most of him was made of fat now. His oval stomach obscured what remained below it, and if a man was what he ate, he figured he looked like a giant jelly doughnut. His hair had thinned. His fingernails were nicotine-yellow, and his teeth needed to be aligned and bleached to remove the tobacco stains that had been pressed into its pores. Still overweight after so many years, he stepped under pelting warm water and washed himself.

When he got out, he went to his king-sized bed as naked as the day he was born and checked over the blue pin-striped suit his wife picked out for him. It had a traditional cut and feel, like when he had just started out as an attorney in New York many moons ago. The suit was a new one, made of worsted wool, and it was cool to the touch. It came with a pair of button-down suspenders and a starched white Oxford shirt, making his office uniform unpretentious and cooperative.

"Those Wall Street guys got nothing on me," he smiled.

The suit, as usual, fit perfectly, and with an ankle-length shoehorn, he slipped into a pair of mahogany-colored loafers. Even though he was just a kid from Queens, he still made sure to assert his elite status wherever went, just to remind everyone who was in charge and whom he could scare with just one side glance. That's all it took. His dark brown eyes held his secrets within, as though their colors were merely a front that kept his manic soul from bursting out from within his head.

When the buzz of the bourbon had worn off, he found his wife in the kitchen with his necktie, and she tied it for him, as usual. She had gotten good at it over the years, although it escaped him how she had gotten so good. He mainly admired the colors and patterns of the ties she chose and not the knot, per se. On this late morning, his tie was solid navy blue with a random pattern of anchors on it. After his wife brushed some of his gray hair away from his eyes and patted his rosy cheeks, he looked like the CEO of JPMorgan.

"Okay," she said. "You can have one Boston Crème doughnut."

"Thank God. My Lord, you are one tough bird, lady."

A box of them sat on top of the fridge. He reached up, opened the lid, and dove into it. The eggs and dry wheat toast were his wife's valiant attempt to get him to eat healthily for a change. He ate one Boston Crème doughnut and then a glazed one, and finally a jelly one while sitting on the couch in the large living room watching the news. And then his personality completely changed once the day's information came rattling through the television. The powdered sugar around his lips was the last remnant of domestic life for the rest of his day. As of that moment he was on the job.

His wife and granddaughter knew better than to disturb him as the headlines ran amok. He watched the basketball scores, thoroughly entranced by the many useless teams that won and lost, the same teams, day in and day out, always on schedule, the sportscaster exuding the same level of enthusiasm for a sport the old man had loved since childhood. First, the jelly doughnut. Then, the sports scores. Finally, the headlines. It was this first order of business that placed him in the impervious bubble that no man on earth could enter – the direct link between his darting eyes and a news story that President Bush intended to take a heavier hand with the terrorists who had attacked the USS Cole in October.

Terrorism had now been internationalized, yes. He knew already how effective it was, how dangerous it was, and how it had to be stopped before something happened closer to home, that one thorn in the lion's paw, the rock that sinks into Goliath's skull, the spear that blinds the enormous eye at the center of the Cyclops. That's what terrorism represented – the fear of flesh getting blown to bits and served on a plate for the masses to view. It could ruin an administration if not dealt with properly. Clinton never handled it well. He merely poked at it, jabbed at it, and maybe they spilled a little blood, but the kind of splillage that provoked laughter. It encouraged a more direct engagement with these towel-headed freaks who claimed to be brothers under God's kingdom.

It sounded weird – that a people who took innocent American lives would declare that they knew God. The old man knew about the work President Clinton had done over the years and that maybe they were right, that what the US had done in the name of democracy far exceeded the damage these terrorists had done. But no amount of money would stop them. Even though these towel-headed bastards had no money or military at all, they could neither be bargained with nor appeased. Yet they crippled a US Navy vessel and killed seventeen sailors, this among the zillions of other acts that pecked away at the resolve of the United States.

They were not only religious freaks. They were smart religious freaks at that. They could hijack a plane and spur headlines around the world while summoning even more support from their own countries against the aggressor and occupier of their entire universe: The United States of America, an evil empire hell-bent on confiscating their holy lands, extracting their natural resources, destroying their shrines, and killing their God, just as she had done to the Native Americans and the slaves, and the spics, and the chinks, and everyone who was non-white and non-European.

The old man knew those young punks in the ghettos wanted the Muslims to defeat the white man. Then they could finally get their community centers and gymnasiums and government programs that rich and powerful men who earned their wealth had to pay for. Why some hoary German political scientist from the 1800s wanted to tax the talented, he never understood it.

As these thoughts ran through his aging mind, he realized that the President would now chart a different course with these people. They threatened everything America stood for. What the Muslims failed to understand was that we were only individuals in an irrational and chaotic world. We were in a universe of unknowns. Not a brotherhood of man that bowed to a force that had been conceived through superstition or vague and uncertain synchronous patterns and signs operating in the deliberate winds that constantly changed directions. Such was the danger of the new Islamic wave, the fastest growing religion in America, far surpassing converts to Christianity and Judaism which were two resilient and equally useless fixtures in American life. Religion did nothing compared to good, self-interested, and profitable domestic policy.

But when the television showed Bush up at the podium, he could hardly believe how incredibly dumb he looked, not because he merely looked dumb, but because he just may have been the dumbest President ever elected. That evil prick Cheney was the mind of the operation. The guy never smiled, even during meetings with him. He just stood by his side. The Alfred E. Neuman at the podium smiled, his accent a Northeast derivation of a Texan, as Cheney threatened the press corps with those piercing laser beam eyes of his, because to fuck with Bush was to fuck with Cheney, and no one wanted to be on the bad side of Dick Cheney. Colin Powel on the other side of the President could stage a coup with the snap of his fingers, and yet the soft-spoken soldier had been trained since birth to be way too grateful and ignorant to notice how much power he had over the other two clowns. If only Powell wanted that power, thought the old man. But Powell was a loyal cog. He would never bite the hand of his white masters. Black and ineffectual was how the Republican Party wanted him.

But the old man had a job to do that morning, now that a new administration had taken over. It changed the game for all the other countries around the world. Clinton had a hell of a run, but his time was up. The days of Slick Willy had ended and in came an entire army of Midwesterners, southerners, rednecks, Neo-Nazis, hillbillies, Confederate flag-waving beer-bellied, beard-wearing, and Aryan Nation separatists with the bloody, decapitated heads of socialists spiked on spears. These rubes rode into stylish and sophisticated Manhattan to declare victory. It was their time, and the world knew it - time to invest in oil and defense, and time to make the lazy poor useful again. Charity, less government, low taxes, deregulation, the same predictable garbage. It was wonderful to be alive. Whether or not the dot com crash put an entire younger generation out of work didn't matter. Who did they think these youth were anyway? Did they think that these new stupid super-computers could take over the old economy? These idiot kids didn't even put on a jacket and tie in the mornings anymore. They strolled into their la-dee-fucking-da office spaces, pranced around pretending to be big shit, and thought they could rule the world? Son, he felt like telling people like that, it just don't work that way in America.

The young always shoveled the shit on their father's farm, and that's the way it worked. Amen. And when the pretty young nurses changed the shit-stained diapers of old men at end of their lives, they just better be happy they had a job and weren't sent back to Mexico where they belonged, he thought, as the television faded into a commercial.

"Honey, shouldn't you get going?" his wife called from the kitchen. "The car is waiting."

His granddaughter approached and sat next to him on the couch as the television rattled on.

"It's time for work, Grandpa," said his young granddaughter.

"Shhh."

"Grandpa?"

"Okay, okay. Just hold on!"

"But Granpa!"

"Alright, then!"

"And Grandpa? Can you get me another Barbie?"

He couldn't answer her. There was still too much on his mind to discuss Barbie and Ken and how two human beings mated and all of that bullshit. He wanted more news. He wanted to know more, more of that raw information, what happened inside America as well as outside of it, the reports that came over the wires, those menacing little journalists who knew what he didn't know. He needed to know who moved against whom, which dictator seized power, how the US capitalized on the latest genocide or atrocity, who had to be removed to get the US economy moving again. Because it was no longer a question of voluntary fair trade. Either trade with the US, or US forces opened the market with its muscle. It was as simple as that. Cooperate or get ousted. Simple.

But even though America was indeed the world's only superpower, now that the Soviet Union had disappeared, something always had to fuck it up. Terrorism, yes, but those Middle Eastern locusts had been unleashed by more powerful interests that wanted America to suffer. And then he remembered the classified report on his desk that he read the other day. Vladmir Putin won the Presidency of the Russian Federation.

The report back in his office contained a full description of the man and the role he played prior to the Soviet Union's demise. Putin was Yeltsin's successor. Russia had become a country with but a few powerful and incredibly wealthy oligarchs and the clueless masses who were suddenly slaves to them. Yes, Vladmir Putin - born in St. Petersburg in 1952, sixteen years as a KGB foreign intelligence officer serving in East Germany, producing disinformation for those on the other side of the Wall to ponder over, winner of the Soviet Badge of Honor in 1994, appointed Director of the Federal Security Service under Yeltsin in 1996, and then appointed Prime Minister in 1999. He was the next one. And the more the old man and his stomach full of doughnuts thought about Putin, the clearer it became that this man posed a virulent threat to the United States, no matter how much power the Russians had lost. Putin alone would be the obstacle and the counterbalance to US supremacy in the world and at home.

From what he remembered of the classified report from the Directorate of Intelligence, Putin could easily manipulate American democracy, because he knew its weaknesses only too well. If there were any direct challenge to the US, it was not terrorism, as the classified report noted. Putin and his cadre of oligarchs were the challenge. The emergence of Vladmir Putin as the next Russian President, succeeding that red-nosed, Vodka-drinking clown before him, commanded the old man's attention. Osama Bin Laden was merely a blip on the radar. Putin represented the fiercest threat to American hegemony.

"Look. Barbie is naked!" laughed his granddaughter.

"That's nice, sweet pea," he said, waving her away from the television.

There was something about those electric lights that fed right into his cerebellum, its own kind of hypnosis that did a much better job than the papers or the books. Those poor *Washington Post* fuckers. They really missed the boat to the Information Age. He then picked himself up and kissed his wife farewell.

"I'll wait up," she said.

"Why bother?" said the old man. "Nothing's worked down there for years."

"We can still cuddle, though."

He rolled his eyes, donned his overcoat, and stepped out into the gray winter's chill.

The driver of the jet-black Cadillac limousine held the door open for him, and soon he climbed into the back seat, poured himself another glass of bourbon, reclined on the leather seat, hoisted his stubby legs on the leg rest, and listened to the classical music the driver played up front. He couldn't move. He felt sophisticated, like some of his underlings at the Company, those young Ivy League twirps who kissed his ass all day and begged him for promotions. They bored him. But the one person he could always rely on was his Deputy, a young man as good and loyal as his own shadow, probably the only man in the government he trusted. And when it came to clandestine government work and running a Company that the entire free world relied on, trust was no superficial concept. He never threw around the word 'trust' lightly. The Deputy had served him for ten years. The old man regarded him as a son after his own fell to heroin and cocaine abuse while living the good life in Hollywood. His Deputy was handsome, incredibly bright, and willing to sacrifice his own life for him, even though the old man was much closer to death than his Deputy would ever be.

While the old man ate doughnuts and stuffed oiled grape leaves into his mouth all day, his Deputy survived on boiled cauliflower, vegetable juice, and that wheat grass and orange-carrot shit. While the old man sat in his recliner in his den and drank bourbon, the Deputy jogged and lifted weights at the crack of dawn and made breakfast for his Wellesley wife. An upstanding man he was – the perfect person to withstand the sheer force and power and danger of all that administrative work that no one else could handle.

The Deputy had thrown the javelin as a track and field star in college. He hated the towel-heads as much as he did. He still despised communism even though its day had passed. He hated everything un-American and pledged his life and soul to the country. In many ways, the old man wanted to be like his Deputy, if only he had the time, but he would never be able to measure up to such a handsome, gallant man. Had they been peers or friends in college, or had they shared the same entry-level desk job, his Deputy would have outpaced him.

Interestingly enough, the old man never envied his Deputy. Rather, he saw their relationship as a marriage, a deeply fond relationship between two consenting adults who admired and respected one another. And no, it wasn't like J. Edgar Hoover and Clyde Towlson. Only the FBI would stoop so low as to fuck each other, but never in the Company – except for the effeminate Ivy Leaguers and their Nazi ancestors from time to time – but other than that, the Company had been stocked with decent, clean, heterosexual men and the few women who went both ways, which was an added bonus.

While dense clouds obscured the white orb in the sky like so many winter mornings, the Cadillac sailed down below the Potomac. Sheets of ice blanketed the black water along Route 123 in McClean. The old man sipped at the bourbon and asked the driver to turn up the classical music. The loud music celebrated his arrival at Dolly Madison Boulevard, like rolling out the red carpet. He heard the concerto rise to a crescendo as the violins vibrated in unison, the horns blared, and the cymbals crashed. They approached a checkpoint that sat between a long chain-linked fence above which sharp razor wire had been coiled. It was flanked by concrete barriers to prevent any vehicles from ramming through it or a grenade from obliterating the guards stationed behind them. The driver knew the security people well, and while his windows remained clear and transparent, the old man's windows in the back had been tinted black and made opaque. It could deflect any machine gun fire. The entire limousine was bulletproof. It could block a missile if it had to. It was manufactured from the heaviest steel in the world, straight from the Midwest, he guessed, or even from the Rust Belt where emptied and chained factories stood like carcasses that had once thrived before its unemployed moved to cities that soon became the new cancers of capitalism.

He understood that there was no changing the world. There was no changing America. The world spun on action and not thought. That's how it had always been. The sword was much mightier than any idea that no one read or needed. Novel ideas had been stifled by the mighty American marketplace, and if the marketplace didn't stifle them, the government did. He thought about these things as the limousine entered the Campus' roundabout.

Its buildings within the fences were ugly and nondescript with long antennae and cupped satellite dishes staring into the sky. They may have been tracking alien spaceships that had taken over the nation and the President. Those tools of modern technology were useless, he figured. All he needed was an AK-47 and plenty of ammo. One could do quite well in the world with just those. Communications didn't matter as much as the capacity to kill. The conscience merely followed the ability and skill required to kill, as killing had been ingrained into the very processes of life. Killing was neither a sickness nor an evil. It would never be removed from the face of the Earth, as the civilizations that survived were the most savage and had applied their full intelligence, knowledge, and imagination to killing. His granddaughter would learn this someday, he figured. One needed to gut any sort of emotion or human feeling from life's basic equation in order to move the country forward and prosper where other undeveloped worlds fell to poverty, sickness, and early death. America was, indeed, a fortress. Its boundaries were giant walls from sea to shining sea. They locked out those who sought to sink her. She repelled whatever was thrown at her. No one could get in, and after a short stay, no one could get out either. He chuckled at this paradox. Once the US seeped into the blood, there was no escape. It festered in the brain like a parasite that wouldn't unhook its teeth from its tender, tubular flesh.

The same philosophy loomed large at the Campus that morning. He noticed the unpretentious buildings and the green colors that covered their sides. The fences, the razor wire, the checkpoints, the watchtowers, and its essential impregnability kept everyone secure, servile, and trapped. One could find himself in Paris, Kinshasa, or Tel Aviv and still be stuck inside its perimeter. An eerie phenomenon, yes, but one that at least offered a life that held firm and immutable, like the ugly concrete buildings themselves. And therein lay its charm. There was no fluidity, just a campus stuck in time that carried the weight of its monstrous history and reputation in the flesh and blood of its employees. No one ever escaped.

Once in the company, the Campus became the cemetery plot for a lifetime of anonymous service for a cause that stretched beyond anyone's imagination. The simple need to know sufficed. It motivated its best men. It wasn't curiosity necessarily. It didn't require an interest in any one subject or any one people. Leave that to the State Department. When he first arrived there long ago, the old man had started out searching for answers.

At first, his questions had been so wide that they dwarfed the waters of the Potomac. Over the years, though, these questions had narrowed, and the answers he sought were reduced to bits of information, clues that formed a more genuine philosophy of how the world worked. While the imagination dealt with myths and fantasies, knowledge, by contrast, was the language of action. Knowledge provoked action and presented choices whether or not to act. The imagination, then, didn't really matter much to the old man and was hardly important. How fast a bullet pierced a Kevlar vest painted a more complete picture of the world and the motivations of man than something as ludicrous as time travel or a Black Hole. It took knowledge to build a nuclear missile, translators to interpret the formulas, men with bent backs to extract the uranium from the Earth, and idiots in radiation suits to load the warheads into the tips of those missiles. The imagination birthed spoiled and snot-nosed kids, while knowledge and information produced disciplined men who whacked their children with belts when they talked back, as his own father had done.

He checked himself in the mirror in the back of the limousine. He took his last swig of bourbon. A gust of cold wind blew through his suit when the driver opened the door for him. The last thing he needed was a cold. His wife would have told him to wear his overcoat after getting out, but as usual, he took it off in the back seat. The limo was a boy's club that needed a few Playboy bunnies, a pool table, and a nice, big, fat, chewed-up cigar to make it entertaining. But first came the uncomfortable task of leaving it.

He walked quickly through the blustery air. Two

uniformed guards with loaded automatic rifles slung on their shoulders stood at the entrance. Their unflinching eyes stared straight ahead. They had faces of steel, their jaws tight, their chins wide and square, their gazes fiercely obedient as they stood to attention. No one knew what hid behind their cold masks. They were as emotionless as statues, no matter how frigid the nation's capital had been that morning. They must have stood there nonstop for the last couple of weeks.

The old man wobbled passed them, ambled across the great seal on the lobby floor, and squeezed into a small, old-fashioned elevator at the back of the lobby. He didn't care about the plaques on the wall honoring the dead for service to the country. At this point, death was just a part of life, although he hoped his number wouldn't be called just yet. There were still plenty of cigars to smoke, bourbons to drink, and grape leaves to eat, not to mention the doughnuts and the Yankees on television and the basketball games on the sports channels in the dead of night.

The elevator brought him to the seventh floor. Once the door slid open, he faced a tight foyer with a small table upon which an old Chinese lamp cast a dull light on an eye scanner at the center of a heavy metal vault. He hated this part, as a bright green laser traversed his corneas when he pressed his eyes to it. He didn't know why some idiot in Science and Technology didn't invent something better. Fucking nerds. When the latch opened, he pushed the vault open and faced a large, cavernous office with a heavy desk, a conference table, a bathroom with its own shower, and a few flat screen televisions on the wall in front of a row of couches.

There was nothing remotely palatial about his office, though. After all, he worked for the government and not the court of some gay French king whose ornamented costumes were like the late Liberace's. God, he thought. What a character that fruitcake was, limp-wristed and all. But his wife liked him, so he let it pass. The lack of any royal pretentions crowding the otherwise plain office reinforced the idea that America was a democracy, that America usurped tyranny and replaced it with a representational government that hardly worked, even though he made sure the masses thought it worked and benefited from it, when, in reality, it hardly functioned and benefited only the very few. The masses just wanted their money and their guns, so let them have it. But he had power and a license to end their lives with impunity if he wanted to. He had the moral authority to take lives with no questions asked, because that alone was the true aim of power – to do what God intended – and he shared in some of that power. But he was no king. He had worked long and hard to earn his stripes as well as the chair that cradled his husky bottom.

He swiveled the chair around to the bar behind him, uncapped the last bottle of bourbon that his secretary left, and poured himself another drink. The windows of his office faced a sparse forest defoliated by the winter winds. Out of a humidor he selected a fat cigar. Once again, he made it to the boy's club, only this time he would be there for the rest of the day and possibly late into the night. He turned on the 24/7 news channel that showed the newly elected President of the Russian Federation delivering a speech to Parliament. He promised what the Soviets had once promised, the same promise all new governments promised its people. The Russian Federation would compete on the world stage with the United States with the best poultry and food products available. A chicken in every pot.

The Reds had done it again, and suddenly an idea flared in his mind like a shock that jars dark and depressing thoughts into frenzied arousal. It happened as he stared into the bald, hairless, electronic face of Vladmir Putin.

Putin wanted the Presidency. This he knew, no question. But he also knew that he wanted more than that. Now that the old man had the knowledge that he would rebuild Russia, the Company had to respond. And if he indeed had to look in the rearview mirror to see the future, this new Russian President would draw the same design for Russia that the Soviets did. He realized that Putin would again inch closer to the world's oil supply, and that meant reaching into Afghanistan covertly at first, but then a second all-out invasion to reclaim the blood they had spilled there. Their blood had been drained through the rivers that led right back to Putin's cherished Moscow and his hometown of St. Petersburg. Once again, the threat of another Stalin cast its shadow over the free world, and once again, the old man rubbed up against what his predecessors had faced – the elusive and enigmatic Russian capacity to worm its way into the free world if only to destroy it from within, enslave its people, and absorb it into its own authoritarian regime. Putin's aim was to replace an American system that was truly liberal and free and good and wholesome and extraordinarily Christian and European to the core, the Jews notwithstanding. He wanted what the Soviets had lost. The old man saw it in his face and read it in his eyes.

Bush's Daddy should have conquered Russia when he had the chance. The old man bit into the tip of his cigar, tore off the tip, and lit it on fire with the pearl lighter. In front of him sat a platter of cold grape leaves, the rice tangy and soft, like his mother used to hand-craft in her Queens kitchen. He had them shipped in every week from New York City, the old Greek diner off St. Mark's Place. If he could, he would smoke the cigar and eat the grape-leaves at the same time, but his wife discouraged it. He could not watch the news and think without something in his mouth. It allowed the wrinkles in his brain to breathe. The rice absorbed the oil, and the right touch of vinegar nurtured his ability to think. Combine that with a fat cigar and a half glass of bourbon at ten in the morning on a Sunday, and the perfect workday presented itself.

He finally attained the level of bliss needed to withstand another day of living. He upended an otherwise bleak isolation with the pleasures of life in his office along with the pretty anchorwoman prattling on about the tragedies and sickness of the world. His job as he knew it, his life's work, was to defend the country from anyone who would want to do it harm. He would do it for free if the President asked him to. The houses, the limousines, the tuxedoes, the butlers, and the gifts from foreign dignitaries weren't worth shit to him. Money meant nothing. His job had become his identity, as though his very family name and his entire Mediterranean ancestry had been erased and supplanted by this experiment known as the United States. Yet there was still the swarthy, hirsute Greek in him and the history of his expelled Soviet ancestors. He thereby felt the raw ethnic urge to sack Putin like a radiating cell that attacks a virulent tumor.

As an undergrad, the old man studied the Soviets and how their government operated. He saw pictures of its leaders, the castles of Red Square looking like ice cream cones covered in trippy colors, a symbol of Russia's bizarre tastes and inherent superstitions that made these people completely ignorant of God's grace. They were the collective, the indivisible Eskimo snow tribe. Every man had to stand shoulder-to-shoulder with his fellow revolutionary. If one grew taller than the rest, he was thrown into the Siberian gulag.

He read Solzhenitsyn in one of his literature classes. The professor said that after the great author had defected to the US, he holed up and languished in a Vermont cabin for the rest of his days, suffocating from a lack of decent cold air. From that point forward, the Soviet Empire had always intrigued the old man, especially their studies of the paranormal and the supernatural. He felt that the Soviets were at the cutting edge of a reality that America ignorantly dismissed. They shared the world with the US, yes, but they were also smart motherfuckers who craved recognition and heroism and honor rather than the innate corruption that the greenback brought. Russia's common people cared not for material goods but only for medals and praise from their elders and their statesmen. Of course, they smuggled in Western goods, but the tables gradually turned on them after the defeat in Afghanistan and their cover-up in Chernobyl. Gorbachev finally wanted what the West had. America had individuals. The masses were asses. There was no such thing as a collective mind. The power of the collective had been replaced by the power of the individual. Gorby wanted to be an individual.

But the old man liked plans, certainties, and patterns too. He had been immersed in the Red Menace for far too long during his college days. While in college, he always had a chip on his shoulder, though, because he couldn't make it to the Ivy Leagues. As a young man in law school, however, he had something to prove. He graduated *summa cum laude* in International Affairs, hacked off his Greek roots in Queens, and moved to a bustling DC Metro area that promised American authenticity. There, he climbed the ranks until one of the partners at his law firm brought him into a company of men whose job it was to save America from disaster at every turn. At the time, the Soviets were that disaster, as everything about communism shunned God and liberty. And America had thwarted Russian dreams ever since the Conference at Yalta on the coast of the Black Sea. Stalin walked away in a fit of anger as Churchill and Roosevelt got the better end of the deal. When the Soviet Union crumbled decades later,

America replaced it with the possibility of a democracy.

The old man believed he knew the new Russian leader without ever really knowing him. He knew how his mind worked, his motivations, what he wanted. Putin liked being in command and the feel of power. But he also loved to outsmart his opponents. He thought he could outsmart anyone. He remained perfectly steady and calm, perhaps even kind, gracious, generous, but he could equally destroy anyone who crossed him with a look of those cold Soviet eyes of his. He promised mercy to his enemies like any inexplicably beneficent force before he plunged the samovar straight into their guts. That was Putin – a smart Soviet Red looking like he cared, but a psychopath beneath that jaundiced, bald forehead.

The old man remembered the day the Berlin Wall fell, and he considered that the US should have conquered and enslaved the Russians at that point. But we had to do the right thing, didn't we? We had to give the Russians a break. We made sure we transformed their government into what resembled a working democracy. We were the ones who gave Putin the reigns of power. And the old man had always lamented this terrible mistake. We were too nice to them. We had to do the right thing. Instead of taking the Russian machinery apart, we repaired it, stabilized it, rebuilt it, and resuscitated it. Putin would now roll back the clock.

He stared into the television broadcast of Putin's speech, knowing right away that this one man was the next enemy to defeat. He would try to reclaim what had been lost to the only mega-power the world had ever known. He would rearrange each government apparatus into a whole package, just like things used to be. The US had misjudged the Russian Federation, but the old man would never make the mistake of misjudging Putin. Because in his old age, the old man had far better Soviet instincts than American ones. No country took their challenges as they came. The Russians played chess, and they were good at it. But when the Soviets stepped into a game without any rules in Kabul, they had no idea that mathematics, science, formulas, strategies, and their desperate attempt to implement Mao's war practices to control the random warlords and the undeveloped population would be no match for a bunch of skinny brown rebels with missing teeth, ragged clothes, and old British muskets for their defense. What little hair remained on the old man's arms suddenly stood to attention. He knew right away that he would have to stop the Russian advance. That would also involve Iran.

Russia's relationship with Iran had blossomed over the years, since the end of Iran and Iraq's bloody war. Ever since the US attacked Saddam the first time, the lines had been drawn. The US surrounded Iraq and policed the oil tankers in the Persian Gulf, and Russia kept Iran as a strategic ally perched right next to them. The Russians would move into Afghanistan as a prelude to recapturing the old Soviet satellite states that sat independently and defenselessly along its central and eastern borders.

But Mother Russia still had to have Afghanistan. It already had the topography down, the dismal record of its own defeat, the remembrance of its mistakes and misjudgments, the methods of the Afghani rebels, and their old Communist allies in Kabul who waited in the wings for the likes of Putin to return and usurp the Taliban and the other fundamentalists who had overrun their land. The Russians knew the warlords that needed profits and arms and food. They knew which warlords hated which. In other words, even though Afghanistan was a buffet of chaos and anarchy, Putin would still try to make sense of it like any loyal and dutiful KGB officer too smart for his own good.

After the Soviets pulled out of Afghanistan and had divested from its war of blood, body parts, and frozen corpses, different factions there fought for power. An even bloodier period of civil war unfolded. After Massoud and his Northeast Alliance died, so did Western hopes for democracy in the country. That's when the Taliban took over and cast its net over a normally secular citizenry who cared only that they fed their families and defended their lands. Yes, figured the old man, it was much more complicated than that. While he didn't know the details of the report on his desk, as he had only read the summary, he didn't really need the details. He was already convinced. All he needed was a map. That's how he had learned. And while the devil hid in the details of how the US would deal with the Russians and these other idiot shit-smelling countries, those details would be handled by his Deputy.

The old man waited for him in his office that morning, the dull sun breaking through the clouds for a spell and then hiding behind them again. The forest, blanketed by snow, was forever a fixture beyond his windows. A murder of crows flew between branches. For him, the crows were the perfect metaphor for Arabian wars – one group raiding another without a center, or at least that's how the Bush administration saw foreign policy, now that it wanted to put a dent in international terrorism.

He stood from his comfortable couch, stamped out his cigar in the ash tray, and stuffed a cold grape leaf in his mouth. He paced wildly about the office, his shrunken mind flaring with renewed energy. His mind burned, and just when he saw how events in the world would soon unfold, the chime of the doorbell startled him. He went to his desk and pressed a button. In sauntered his Deputy with a notebook and a

Mont Blanc fountain pen. As usual, his Deputy had dressed impeccably. He wore a black suit, college tie, and had his black shoes shined. He had combed his hair straight back with slick salon gel, and his lean fingers ended at wholesome cuticles and manicured nails.

"Good morning, sir," he said.

The old man turned the television down from his desk and returned to his chair. He invited the Deputy to sit in front of him. He offered him a bourbon, but the handsome middle-aged father of two declined. First business. Then pleasure.

The old man grinned because he knew his protégé well. The old man could instinctively sniff out who was faithful and who would betray him, and this handsome Ivy League attorney would always tell him the truth. He would always do his bidding. The kid was more loyal to the old man than his own father. The Deputy was more than a son, though. He was a protector and a guardian, the child who saved an old man who had crossed pinnacles of madness. Just having his Deputy sitting across from him calmed him.

The old man offered him a grape leaf, which he accepted. He also offered him a doughnut – a Boston Crème. The kid would one day be just like him. He would never deviate from the ideologies and philosophies the old man had ingrained in him ever since he first commandeered Administration. The old man nabbed him as a rising star at Defense, plucked him from the sky, so to speak, as that was his privilege. He sat him down before his throne. The Deputy reminded him that he wasn't dead yet.

He slid the classified file on Afghanistan from the Directorate of Intelligence over the top of the desk. He poured himself another bourbon from the bar and waited until the Deputy finished reviewing the file.

"Well?" said the old man. "Whaddaya think?"

"A thorough report," said his Deputy nervously.

"And?"

"Clearly, the psychopath wants to be on top of the heap again. Isn't that the game? To be on top?"

"Right you are!" exclaimed the old man, delighted by his response.

The Deputy, relieved, eased back in his chair.

"He wants it all back," said the Deputy, crossing his legs, his hands folded on his knees. "He wants what Stalin had. He wants what the Western World took from Uncle Joe at the Crimea. He's coming at us to get even. The report, I feel, sir, is spot on. He wants another crack at Afghanistan. All the intelligence we have points to that. He wants to reclaim it and get rid of those towel-headed cave-dwellers at the same time. Those sand niggers are the thorn in his side. He wants to control them. He doesn't want them crossing into Central Asia. And he'll fight for his beloved Afghanistan, the ancient land that the Soviets were supposed to have. All he needs is to rally his supporters. It slipped through his fingers the first time. A failure of Russian intelligence. An embarrassment for the whole world to see. They finally had to accept that they were inferior to our way of life."

"Yes," said the old man, lighting up the cigar he had previously stamped out. "That's what he's thinking too. He knows that we know that we are thinking about him. He wants to play the game all over again. That shithead. The question now is, do we take the bait?

"You see, son, he wants us to take it, that rat, because we both know that the KGB won the Cold War, not us. We have to remember that. We did everything but the human intelligence work necessary to defeat the KGB. Sure, we staged coups, ran guns, rigged elections, all of the shit we usually do. But while we're playing cowboy, the KGB's turning all of our assets. These are not the Wild Bill Donovan days anymore. We're not cowboys. We need human intelligence."

"HUMINT, sir."

"Whatever it's called. How fucking embarrassing it all was. I don't know if you were around, but the Ames and the Nicholson cases? And then one of our guys gets caught buying intelligence from that Frog official. Remember that one? Assets leaving our classified files on their personal computers? We're now the mockery of the world! People think we're idiots! It's like we're paying our own people to fuck up and leak our own information. Our assets can't go around telling niggers in Congress that we're dumping crack cocaine in their neighborhoods. That's just irresponsible. We look like sick thugs. I mean, someone has to keep the population in line. What with all of those poor illiterate children they keep pumping out and dumping out on the curb? And of course, we have to do the street cleaning for them. We're the ones whom they call demons when we're just doing exactly what they want us to do. We fucked up by bombing the Chinese Embassy in Belgrade. We were sleeping at the wheel when the dot-heads ran their nuclear tests. The Clintons reduced us to ashes. Finally, now that Bush has come in, we can reinstate our damaged reputation as the finest company in the world."

"I totally agree, sir. We just have to move beyond the mistakes of the past. We have new fish to fry. The Muslims."

"Our country is scared shitless of those people. We couldn't have found a more perfect enemy. The perfect enemy is always the same enemy, the fucking towel-heads."

"We use them as a cover for the Russians, in other

words?" asked the Deputy.

"Damn straight. Putin's the real enemy here. Those third-world idiots are just flies on the big lump of shit in Putin's toilet – let's not forget that. The game has changed. We'll start by hiring more Arabic-speaking assets, and no, they don't have to be citizens or residents here. Put 'em on the payroll. Bush will give us anything we need. Bush wants to win, and so do we. Let's win this time and not make asses of ourselves."

"Yessir. We also have all the technology at our disposal – Predator drones, Future Imagery Architecture, In-Q-Tel."

"Whatever," said the old man. "But I want HUMINT. Real human intelligence. The information. That's what gave this Company its life, and that's what Putin feeds on. He already has the upper hand when it comes to that. He's always wanted to destroy the United States. The only way we can destroy him is by converting the public to our militant brand of Christianity and fighting militant Islam. I want a full campaign right away. We'll loosen the bureaucratic red tape for our assets to do the jobs they need to do – to make unlimited contacts and get rid of our enemies without all the paperwork. I want all the paperwork cut in half."

"Yessir."

"And I want all of the foreign spies in the company rooted out. We're going to take risks again, and to get Putin we'll have to skirt the laws. No more gray areas."

"Definitely."

"I want Putin. He's the man we want."

"True," said his Deputy nervously, "but Russia is not the Soviet Union anymore, sir. There are only a few wealthy men he answers to. We'll need to account for that. But in a few years, I could easily see Putin as the lifetime ruler of Russia."

"Me too. We need something here. But what?"

The old man led him to the couch again and turned up the television. He carried the carafe of bourbon with him.

"Son, if I didn't love my wife so much, I'd really like to fuck her," said the old man of the anchorwoman on the set.

"Sir, we can arrange…"

" - Nah. I don't want that anymore. Those days are long-gone. I tried to do it the legit and gentlemanly way when I just got out of law school, but those pretty preppy girls just ignored me. They insulted me. They wanted the Executive branch and those young Senators and up-and-coming Congressmen. They didn't want a nobody."

"It's a mystery, sir."

"Yeah. I thought I was ugly back then. Y'know, just too fat. I had no money. No nice car. I was never as good as those other All-American jocks. I was always too old-school. I liked tradition, hard work, guts, and honor. I liked throwing my coat over a puddle so a girl could walk over it. That was how my mother raised me. That's how I grew up. And soon enough, I was the fat friend who sat in the darkness and loved the beauty queen while the quarterback nailed her. I guess that's why I went behind my wife's back. I repaid all of those young beauty queens by putting them on their knees and sucking my cock. But after so many years of doing that, I fell in love with my wife all over again. How about you? How's your family doing?"

"Well, I'm seeing a few girls here and there, but the best one is a recruit. She'll do anything to get promoted, and I mean *anything*. The girls have always been like that in

Administration."

"We still make sure they look good, right?"

"Yessir."

"So goddamned important. They don't work here if they're ugly, you got that? Soon, this whole damn country will be filled with ugly women. Then, we'll be in real trouble," he laughed.

"Yessir. I would never deviate from that policy."

"Good. Keep it that way. We have no room in this Company for ugly broads, even if they are qualified. You show them the out-door, you got that?"

"Yessir."

"So how are the kids?"

"About to graduate from Andover."

"Where do they want to go?"

"One wants Princeton. The other Georgetown."

"Princeton? C'mon!"

"I know, but she has her heart set on it, sir."

"Bunch of geeks up there. Too many niggers too. Send her to Georgetown, will you, please?"

"The youngest is the stubborn one. She's not the kind that listens to her parents."

"Trust me, I know the type. How're the finances? You got 'em together?"

"Yessir. We suffered a setback when the bubble burst, but so did everyone. We're now plugged into oil and defense. We've moved some into China. I expect a brief lull and then a boom again. That's the way it usually works."

"If you need any cash, you just see me, and I'll get

you some more. That's never been a problem. And if you're looking for the big money-makers, just go down to DI, and they'll give you some good picks. But oil and defense should be good enough. Those young geeks worked so damned hard on their fucking microchips. Now they'll come to us begging on their hands and knees, as usual."

After a few moments the old man said, "I think Putin will try to take Afghanistan again."

"Me too, even though Ukraine sounds more reasonable."

"Nah. Putin's a pompous ass. He wants to make a show of it, just like we did. But the Reds hate the towel-heads just as much as we do. So, he'll divide them. He's thinking, why not kill two birds with one stone? If he takes Afghanistan with the help of his old friends and avoids the bigger prize of Ukraine, which we now support as an independent nation, and if he aligns himself with some of those exhausted and fucked up Hajis in the Middle East, then he moves closer to the prize, the center of where all of our fucking oil is. Two birds with one stone."

"That's what he wants, sir. I can see your point."

"Well, what the hell are you gonna do about it?" the old man said angrily, his jovial mood turning.

"I'll get on it right away. I'll talk to DI right away. I'll go down there right now."

"Good. But before you go, let's drink to another era. A repeat of the first era. Only better. This is the last plan we'll ever have to write. Right now, we keep this small. We get the money going once we find a way in and the lay of the land. I'll let Congress know bit by bit, and soon, our new initiative to contain Putin will be a showcase for the world. Action counts. Nothing else. Unleash the hounds!"

The old man poured him a full glass and, with a smile, watched his Deputy gulp it down in one harsh swallow.

"That'll bring the blood to your cheeks, eh? Now get the fuck out of here, so I can concentrate. And get my secretary in here, so she can take some notes. I need to prepare for my meeting this afternoon."

"Yessir."

Chapter Three

December 2000 – Washington D.C., USA

'A poor Jew never does well in this world,' he thought, while checking his pockets for spare change. He barely had enough in his wallet for lunch. His kid had grown up too fast, and government work had never paid well enough. To be stuck in the basement of the Directorate of Intelligence in a generic building on the McClean campus had become a dull routine after a time. He simply wrote paper after paper about hot zones all over the world.

He remembered how much dough he dished out for his own doctorate, and after thirty years at the Company, he still couldn't pay back his student loans. But the Jewish analyst was definitely good at what he did, or so his superior had mentioned that to him on a number of occasions.

When his superior didn't pat him on the back every now and then, however, the analyst then imagined a life far beyond the gates of the company. And just when a tropical destination far away from Washington became too grandiose and too fantastic to pull him back in, his superior popped in his office again and gave him another pat on the back for a job well done. Such a gesture returned him to the real world and forced him to keep his focus, because he, like the handful of analysts stuck in the basement of the building, needed kindness above all else. When he didn't get praise, something was wrong with the universe.

He never knew that his years of study would lead to a cramped office in a basement. Many times, he thought himself a chump for putting in all the grunt work generating papers that DI probably destroyed after someone upstairs read them and declared them useless. The Directorate of Intelligence ran like any other corporate office on a tight-fisted budget. He had a beige metal desk, used or possibly resold to the company from some other agency, his desktop computer slow and obsolete, and those ugly aluminum shelves for his books and his papers to rest on. It was basically a professor's office but in a dungeon, and in keeping with the location, they kept him at the same pay grade since hiring him in the mid-1970s.

Intelligence made sure it created a competitive environment in which a handful of analysts slaved over their work. As a result, each analyst guarded his research and hardly ever talked to each other. The Jewish analyst could only imagine a day when they would give him a space above ground, so that he could at least take in the sunlight and maybe a squirrel or two gathering acorns under an oak tree every now and then. Instead, he sat under a flickering fluorescent light that usually drove him crazy by day's end. He sneezed every few minutes within the miasma of dust that circulated in the air. He had allergies, and the dust tickled his upper sinuses. He had used up too many handkerchiefs cleaning the fingerprints from the thick plastic lenses that still blurred his eyesight. He never remembered having purposely touched the lenses with his fingers, and so his glasses had to be cleaned every few hours for reasons unknown to him.

Through the steady routine of blowing his nose and cleaning his lenses, he developed the reputation of being a middle-aged man who was very smart, yes, but could never handle any physical work whatsoever. He was too gaunt to boot, and he wore half-blended collared shirts that he bought on sale, all of them either white or slate blue, and this wasn't just because Einstein never wanted to work his mind into the ground by pondering what to wear every day. His shirts felt like cardboard on his skin, and they identified him in the Company as a service worker. It designated him as the guy who always wore those awful, cheap shirts, because he wasn't able to support his family well at his pay grade. If anyone upstairs needed him, they would simply order 'the guy who wore those terrible shirts' to pick up the house phone. But rarely did they summon him from the depths of the basement floor. His uniform, however, made it easier on their absent-minded memories, he supposed, since they could hardly remember his own name. DI had kept the analysts far apart, as though the floors above them tried hard to prevent a basement revolution from reaching the higher floors.

The analyst sometimes imagined such a rebellion too, considering the many revolutions, coups, and military takeovers he had written about. He needed his job, though, and he wasn't so foolish as to take his family and flee DC just as his young son began his first year at the University of Ohio. Considering that he hadn't repaid his own student debts yet either, he thought it self-defeating to project how much money he would loan his son once he actually finished college. If he left the Company, he wouldn't have a job anymore to continue his son's monthly allowance.

In a system such as ours, he guessed, the only way to win his family's love was by earning a paycheck that steadily rose over time. In his case, however, his pay remained intolerably flat. He believed that most fathers won their families over by amassing wealth, and the wealthier the father became, the closer and more loyal his family grew and the more respect he earned. Children all felt it when he had a bad day, or when he favored a child above all the others, for instance. If a father couldn't support his own family, he'd probably take to drugs and alcohol, or perhaps his wife would leave him, and the family would break apart. The analyst wasn't exactly a pessimist, but much of his work always dealt with avoiding catastrophes, and he planned out his personal life no differently, as he desperately wanted his family to stick with him and stay together. He had an ingrained fear that his wife and child would one day disappear, because he was too kind and gentle of a man to make good money.

Every day in that basement, he felt like he walked on a wire, as though a calm breeze would blow through him and easily push him off. It made him a good analyst, though, because much of his research had been devoted to digging deeply into files both on and off the computer to find solutions that may have saved thousands of lives. It was labor, though, and nothing beyond that after nearly thirty years of doing it. In theory, he saved many lives. His mind worked like a chess board, and he labored by positioning the many pieces all over the map until a peaceful solution presented itself. In fact, what he wrote imitated a game which he played against himself. He imagined the different players on the board and executed the unilateral, bilateral, and multilateral actions that boiled everything down to a set of options on what the US ought to do in every possible situation.

Of course, there were never any right or wrong answers – just probabilities of success. No one ever told him that he was off-base or wrong in his research or assessments of the many conflicts in the thornier regions of the world. He simply filed his work on a cloud, and his superior took the file from there and sent it to someone else upstairs. That's all he knew. And the superior would stop by to give him a thumbs up. There was nothing else, though – no opinions, questions, comments, or feedback – only as steady stream of work, as he himself became a computer by filing reports, much like the news wires that pumped out random stories from locations around the world. It was a form of gathering, yes, but the analyst never thought of it that way. He believed his mind and his research meant much more to the Company than that, and he hated thinking of his role as being a mere microchip in a Borg-like apparatus living a life of eating their own shit to stay relevant and to justify their yearly budget increases to Congress.

Yes, morale had been low since the first Iraq War, and the analysts in the office didn't feel very useful as of late. The analysts had to take into account that they were the lowest on the totem pole when it came to their places in the Company. Intellectual work didn't pay very well unless it produced a more powerful weapon that thwarted all the others. But words that spelled out ideas translated into the price of toner ink, copy paper, old, degenerate printers that jammed often, and a clunky telephone in case he needed help from his superior or had to call his wife or son. No one paid attention to a man's intellectual labor that he had learned to honor and cherish as a young undergrad at the University of Ohio.

Ever since the Berlin Wall fell, there was no need for his reports, no need to match minds with that other great superpower that blew the global balance of power completely out of whack when it collapsed. When the Wall fell, it primed America and The United Kingdom to take over the world. And while it was a time of great joy that the Cold War had ended, it spelled doom for the Company. The public no longer needed it. Everyone also assumed that the Company had been corrupt and dirty. It arranged assassinations and fed propaganda to the masses of ignorant Americans, which was true, but it had also grown abhorrent under the weight of easy money, decadence, and the revival of 1960s counter-culture that excoriated the Company's methods.

Ironically, the Jewish analyst believed in the same counter-cultural values that stamped out the Company's relevance. He cherished the idea of peace, and his papers prevented dangerous wars before they ever began. He was exceptional at cutting off an arm or a leg to save the rest of the body. Essentially, that was the Company's overall function as he saw it – to save the many by killing off the few who were sacrificed for the greater good. But the fewer who had to die, the better. His reports were accurate and righteous in the sense that he prioritized the sparing of lives rather than the taking of them. And because he knew it vitally important to resolve conflict as well as protect the lives of the Company's assets, both in operations and in the paramilitary units, he was somehow seen as relic of the past, now that a new President had been elected. Actually, he had become a relic as soon as Bush II was inaugurated into office.

The Carter Administration had been his Golden Age. His reports leaned heavily towards Carter's aims of establishing balance and peace in the Middle East until a disastrous hostage crisis, an oil embargo, and high inflation kicked him and his ideas in the teeth. Then Gorbachev introduced reforms for his people after Reagan abruptly took Carter's place. He never expected the hostage crisis, and ever since then, the company held him hostage in the basement.

The walls began to stink of mildew, the atmosphere nearly choked him to death, and the bastards upstairs wouldn't allow him to see the light of day beyond his windowless room. They wouldn't even let him have a decent cup of coffee, as the cheap contraption they had in the hallway breastfed them a thick, lukewarm sludge that they forced down their throats every hour, on the hour. He had to give up smoking tobacco and cannabis on his off-hours to stay competitive. As new allergies emerged, he grew thinner, reedier, an older man in a jail cell reserved for himself. Older age had left him nervous and depressed, and even though he still had his mind, he could never squeeze together a thin dime from the noggin he had been blessed with. He could only scrounge up a salary that bored his wife and sent his son into K-Mart for his clothes.

It used to be so easy when he grew up in the middle-class DC suburbs from where he came – the Jewish kids and their parents on Hebrew Hill, as the gentiles had called it. The Jews stayed with the Jews, the Protestants with the Protestants, and the Catholics with the Catholics - the same old tired story - before a complete change of consciousness nullified whatever structures the ancient mindset had heaped upon them. Ethnic pockets of the inner-cities and the suburbs could no longer stay cohesive, because after a while, similar people had to fight their own kind and soon branched out into other, crossbred states of nature that mutated and created entirely new organisms. It was a wonder, then, how the religious and racial purity of his neighborhood splintered when he left DC and headed for Akron.

In high school, he had incredibly intelligent and highly motivated Jewish friends who would go on to do what their fathers had done. If one were a son of a doctor, then one became a doctor. The son of an accountant, became an accountant. The son of a dentist, a dentist, and so on, until the species sharpened itself the *nth* degree to become an entire community of super-doctors, accountants, and dentists, and within the community of these super-people, a man had to govern and rule. He or she must reign from the top of the pyramid like the shining eye on the one-dollar bill. That one eye took its seat on the top. It knew all and saw all. But his fellow classmates understood that in a democracy no one could really be ordered by any one eye, and at times, that eye on the dollar bill had to blink. When it did, the midpoint of the pyramid crumbled due to the refusal of this midpoint to buttress the upper layers and nourish the lower ones at the same time.

As the analyst remembered his college days at the University of Ohio, the pyramid had just crumbled, and he lived in the aftermath of its destruction. He stopped attending temple, wore a red bandana and a jeans jacket, and hung out with Blacks, Protestants, Catholics, whomever he chose, just because he felt like it. There were no class or social boundaries. As they sat out on the fields of the college grounds, groups with painted faces and flowers in their hair played bongo drums, smoked cannabis, ate mushrooms, dropped a full range of psychedelics, especially that special one that leaked from a European laboratory and altered consciousness so much that it forced the eye to blink. The analyst had then been pulled into this scene, not as a radical rabble-rouser or hard lefty, but as a free thinker – an agnostic willing to consider other philosophies than those that filled his blood. His search for God began all over again, as if he were reborn.

He did not have to be a Jew if he did not want to be a Jew, in other words. That, or maybe his search for God would lead him back to being Jewish, he still wasn't sure. He could be black if he chose, or a Christian, or a Hindu, or even a Muslim. In fact, one famous Jewish poet he read back then brought Buddhism to the nation and converted many of his followers. The gay poet left a legacy new generations today would think unimaginable. These were the pioneers. A Jew didn't have to remain a Jew, and a Muslim did not have to remain Muslim. The eye had to blink and shut its lid. It neither saw nor contemplated how its entire design and structure collapsed, rendering the world totally blind. And once it was blind, the people were set free.

In his first year in college, the analyst had arrived in Akron a couple of hours earlier than he was supposed to. He carried his suitcase up to his room and discovered that his two new roommates had already arrived. They sat on their respective twin beds and chatted about how excited they were to be a part of the college experience. The analyst had only brought a single suitcase, since he didn't own a car and had to take a Greyhound bus from the Washington transit center. His two roommates were clean-cut boys, just like him. One was from Oregon, and the other was an international student from Egypt. He had a slight accent but spoke fluent English. All three college freshmen were new to the area, and each was equipped with a student handbook that outlined the schedule for new student orientation. They had some time before they had to be at The Science Building for their first meeting. They used that time to introduce themselves. The orientation would be followed by a dinner for new students in one of the many dining halls on their enormous campus.

They had been grouped together by an unknown lottery system that matched similar personality traits and likes and dislikes, but no one really knew the specifics of how the freshmen roommates were matched. The boys assumed they had been randomly assigned and didn't know that they had been put there deliberately. But the analyst already found the Oregonian and the Egyptian very friendly, prepared to study hard, and ready to take part in the life of the university. While they kept their hair shaggy in keeping with the style of the day, they dressed plainly in pedestrian clothing. An onlooker may have assumed that their mothers had bought their clothes for them at their local department stores, which was definitely true in the analyst's case. The boys came from non-deviant, non-criminal, wholesome backgrounds, so whatever items they came with were mundanely mainstream and never veered beyond the stylistic parameters of what their families saw in the ads in the newspapers and on television.

"Hi," said the analyst, sticking out his hand first.

They all shook hands and returned to their spots on their beds.

"I guess we have orientation first?" he asked.

"Yeah," said the Oregonian. "At four pm. It's not too far from here. Where are you guys from?"

"I'm from Egypt."

"I'm from DC," said the analyst. "Just got here by bus. A very long trip, but I finally made it. I do want to see some of the campus, though. Hopefully before orientation."

"I don't think there's enough time," said the Egyptian. "We shouldn't be late for orientation. It's the first important thing we have to do before classes begin next week."

"Yeah," said the Oregonian. "Maybe we should just hang out here, get unpacked, and then go. We should have plenty of time to see the campus before classes start. What are you guys majoring in anyway?"

"Government," said the analyst.

"Business Administration," said the Egyptian.

"Economics," said the Oregonian.

"Wow," said the analyst. "I guess you guys have a lot of money coming to you in the future."

"Why government?" asked the Egyptian. "Maybe you'll be President one day?"

"That's not what most people become in Washington, I'm afraid. My father and my grandfather worked for the federal government. I guess I'd follow in their footsteps.

Why not?"

"My father was in the Egyptian army, and then we immigrated here after the Six Day War. He now runs a convenience store in downtown Los Angeles, but I decided to pursue something different than going into the Army. More than anything else, our family needs money."

"Don't we all," smiled the Oregonian. "My dad runs an auto parts store in Portland. I'm going to work for him after I finish here."

"That all sounds really neat," said the analyst. "I hope we can make the grade here."

"Yeah," said the Oregonian, "but it's such a large university. You never know where you'll end up."

"True," said the Egyptian. "Only the future will tell."

"*Que sera, sera*," sang the analyst. "*Whatever will be, will be.*"

"Right," said the Oregonian. "I guess we should unpack. We'll get to the bookstore later. It's all explained in the handbook."

"There are also clubs and tons of extracurricular activities," said the Egyptian. "So many of them."

"I wouldn't mind joining the chess club," said the Oregonian. "I'm not bad at it."

"Have you guys ever heard of the board game *Diplomacy* at all?" asked the analyst. "They must have a group that plays here."

"Hey, I've heard of that game," said the Oregonian. "They played it in my high school back in Portland. I think it was in history class."

The freshmen boys were excited about beginning the

semester, and the analyst already liked his roommates. They seemed to be good students and would one day become good, law-abiding citizens, which were the type of people his family wanted him to be around. They hadn't met anyone on the floor until, all of a sudden, someone in the hallway blasted a stereo recording of *The Rolling Stones*. The analyst had heard the familiar song on the radio back in DC. The noise flooded the entire dormitory, even though the speakers had been turned out of the windows to face the large expanse of the green lawn in front of the dormitory.

"My God!" yelled the Oregonian. "That's really loud!"

"Won't we get in trouble?" yelled the analyst covering his ears. "It's way too loud. The campus police will come, won't they?"

Suddenly, the door to their room swung wide open, and an extraordinarily large muscular man stood at the opening with his arms gripping the doorframe above him. He had long curly hair, and he wore a University of Ohio varsity football jersey. The dormitory was too small for a man of such a build. The giant needed much bigger ceilings and much wider walls. His body couldn't enter the room without squeezing through it, so he stood in the hallway where the music blared.

"Wake up time, girls!" said the large man, wearing a wide, toothy smile.

"Hi," said the Egyptian above the music. "Who are you?"

"I'm your Resident Assistant," said the large man. "Wondering if you have any questions before the semester begins. We only have this one weekend."

"I have one," said the Oregonian, raising his hand nervously and yelling through the music. "Where is new student orientation? It says that it's in the Science Building, but this map is too hard to figure out."

"Hang on," he said. "I'll be right back with the answer to that."

By the time the giant returned, another *Rolling Stones* tune blasted from the hallway stereo. The giant effortlessly talked over the music with his loud, penetrating voice.

"The orientation location has changed," he said. "You guys have to be at the Fox Theater on the student strip at seven. The doors will open at seven, and you will give these three tickets to the bouncer at the entrance. Got it?"

He picked up a case of cold beer behind him and dropped it by the door. He also threw in a large bag of what the analyst thought was oregano or some kind of food seasoning.

"You," he pointed to the Oregonian, "come here."

Without fail, the freshman boy jumped over to him. The Resident Assistant handed him the three tickets.

"You guys are to finish all this beer and smoke all this green. You then proceed to the show to see the band at eight. But you guys will be there at seven. My boys are at the door and are expecting you. And if you're not there, I'll hear about it. And if that happens, you guys owe me for all of this shit, you got that?"

"But what about the Science Building?" asked the analyst, freaked out by the new development.

"Orientation has been cancelled, dingbat! Now do as I say, or I'll find out about it. I'm glad we understand each other. And if I don't see you there, I'm going to hang the three of you on a goalpost."

"Yessir," said the boys.

"Good," he smiled, shutting the door and thereby

dampening the sound of the music.

"What was that all about?" asked the analyst, shocked by the overture.

"I have no idea," said the Egyptian. "What about orientation? We have to be there, don't we? We'll get in trouble if we're not there, won't we?"

"I don't know," said the analyst, "but we better do as he says. Would you rather have an administrator mad at us or that guy?"

"I agree," said the Oregonian. "You guys drink much beer at home?"

"Never," said the Egyptian. "It's not permitted in my family."

"I've had beer before," said the analyst, "but I never liked the taste of it. Way too bitter."

"I guess I better start, then," said the Oregonian. "We drink a lot of beer back in Portland."

"But what about the green stuff?" asked the analyst, pointing to the cellophane bag on the floor.

"That's marijuana," said the Oregonian. "My older brother smokes it all the time. He taught me how to roll it into cigarettes, but he never let me smoke it. He said I'm too young. He gave me a nickel for every cigarette I rolled. He sold it to the university guys when he traveled back and forth from Eugene."

"It's illegal," said the analyst. "I don't think we should take it."

"I don't think so either," said the Egyptian. "It's not a good idea."

"Okay," said the Oregonian, "but we'll have to carry it

in case he finds us at the theater. The stuff is pretty valuable. We'll just take it with us."

"They won't search us at the theater, will they?" asked the analyst.

"Nah," replied the Oregonian. "I think we'll be alright. Lots of people will be smoking the stuff there, I'm pretty sure. From what I hear, a lot people smoke it these days."

"Well, I'm not," said the analyst. "I don't want to go to jail."

"We won't go to jail," said the Egyptian. "It will be all over the place."

"Okay, I guess," said the analyst. "But you never know with the Feds. They post their people all over the country. They're just waiting to bust people."

"Not in college," said the Oregonian. "I think we'll be alright. We just have to be cool and calm. We should pretend like we're like any other group."

All of three of them eyed the large bag of cannabis on the floor. They didn't know how they would smoke such a large amount of it, especially since they had never smoked it before. It was valuable, so they couldn't dispose of it. They were stuck with the bag, it seemed. They waited to decide what to do about it, because they had plenty of cold beer to drink, which was the other part of the order they were reluctant to carry out.

Each of them drank eight cans. They had started slowly but after one or two, they were off to the races. They talked more about where they were from and what it was like there. The beer inebriated them, and gradually, they grew happier the more they drank. The analyst liked the effect, even though he didn't like the taste. He had been used to cherry cola and maybe a candy bar once in a while, or perhaps some ice cream after his mom cooked dinner. But he never drank something as adult as beer before.

After they finished off the beer, though, their mood lifted like a weight that had been removed from their backs. The analyst was no longer so nervous. He was amiable and garrulous. His roommates reacted in the same manner. The beers had been more than enough. The suds so filled his stomach, that he couldn't drink anymore after a time, even though he wanted to get even more inebriated. He eyed the marijuana which wasn't too threatening anymore. The Oregonian would carry it in during the performance anyway.

It was late in the summer, and a resplendent sun baked the many students traveling on the green. Its light gradually moved across a blue sky with its cotton-candy clouds floating towards some mysterious destination, like lost sailboats on an azure sea. The wide lawn had the greenest grass he had ever seen before. He didn't have sunglasses, though. He only had his plastic glasses for his myopia. He made sure to clean them before leaving the dorm. With his new friends, he walked through the college to where the excitement was supposed to be. But when they arrived at the theater, they found that it had just opened, and they were one of the first few there.

"You guys are a little early," said the big bouncer at the door.

"You mean, no one's here yet?" asked the Egyptian.

"Nope. Probably another hour or so. But you can go in there. You can get close to the stage. It's general admission."

"Wow!" remarked the analyst. "We have front row seats!"

"Not exactly," said the bouncer. "You have to stand. There are no seats in there. But trust me. You should get as close to the stage as possible. It'll be dynamite. You'll get to see the band right in front of you. You guys ever been to a rock concert before?"

The analyst was too woozy to reply, but the Oregonian admitted that they had never been to such an event.

"Well, you kids are in luck," said the bouncer. "Tonight's some band out of Colorado. Real jammin' shit, I hear. I'm going tomorrow night."

"What kind of music do they play?" asked the Egyptian.

"All the good stuff. Lots of people will be here tonight, so you guys should consider yourself lucky. Go on in and go right up to the stage and wait there until the theater fills up. Trust me. You'll have a good time. The sound is great too. 'The Wall of Sound,' they call it. Real primo."

They surrendered their tickets to the friendly bouncer and walked into a nice-sized theater with a pit in which to stand. The theater had an upstairs balcony area that had a couple of bars. A wall of large speakers had been planted on either side of the stage, and the band's equipment had been laid out upon it like a colorful buffet. Drums, a large organ, standing microphones for all the singers, a bass on a stand, and a set of bongo drums with a couple of tambourines thrown in would be played by the band.

"Wow!" said the Oregonian. "I've never seen anything like it."

"Me neither," said the Egyptian. "This is much bigger than anything I've ever seen in Cairo. Nothing like it at all."

"I hope we don't lose our hearing over this," said the analyst. "Those speakers look like they'll blow our eardrums right out."

"I wouldn't worry about it," said the Oregonian. "We're not right in front of the speakers. We can stay here, right in the center. But it sure is weird that no one's here yet. We definitely left too early. I guess we'll just sit on the floor until the show starts."

Within twenty minutes or so a steady flow of older students flowed into the theater and camped out next to them. They were boisterous and smoked joints. They brought back large cups of beer from the bars upstairs. Some of them didn't seem to be drunk on alcohol, though, because they talked strangely and shared how they saw bright rainbow colors swirl together and melt right before their very eyes. A few of them waved their fingers in front of them as though they tried to create shadow puppets at the base of the stage. The analyst had never seen such colorful clothes, their ripped jeans, and the headbands that kept their long hair in place. Some of them held hands and danced in circles while singing strange songs that sounded much like nursery rhymes.

The analyst had never seen such dancing, even in his own temple back in DC. The Oregonian noticed that his older brother had worn similar clothing and had kept his hair just as long, but he seemed perfectly rational at home. But the Egyptian had seen nothing like it and had only read about such dances in the Sufi tradition. As these concertgoers gathered, danced, and smoked joints all around them, the three roommates could only look at themselves in the self-consciousness that comes with those who want to belong. They were the only clean-cut oddballs there. Apparently, their Resident Assistant had played a prank on them. But as the general admissions area filled out, the three of them were pushed even closer to the stage until they were surrounded by dancing, long-haired tribal white people smoking large amounts of cannabis and cheering loudly when the house lights went down.

The analyst was still inebriated, and as a result, he welcomed the new experience. He witnessed shadows moving upon the stage in the darkness. The crowd surrounding him roared with rarefied delight. And then, a guitar chord, a thump of the bass guitar, a few taps of the snare drums, and a riddle of organ keys soon formed into an intelligible melody that rocked the crowd with a sound so crisp and powerful, that he couldn't help but become absorbed by the strange stew of music and bodies that swayed in the darkness. He looked at his roommates, and they were equally amazed. They observed these musicians play and sing lyrics that were supposed to make sense but in no way did, as though the boys had been left out of a hidden secret that everyone else knew about already. But on the left side of the stage apart from the lead players, the analyst beheld the loveliest figure he had ever seen before.

A black woman tapped on a tambourine and added vocals to the melee of song. Her figure was near perfect, her brown African-American skin flawless, and her hair relaxed and long. She sang with full lips and a wide smile. She had the voice of an angel, he was sure of it, and even though the lead players had commanded most of the audience's attention, the analyst couldn't take his eyes off of her for the several songs they played. Within their space, his body soon shuffled to the rhythm. He then began to dance. The woman's clear, sonorous voice and the band's music freed him from the imprisonment of whatever world he had been hammered into. He felt as light as air, becoming a part of a completely new universe within which this one woman was at the center in a tight sequined dress, her tambourine alternately banging on her hips and then her smooth palm. In all of this splendor, the analyst was sure she stared right at him from the stage.

When the bass and the guitar grew louder and, together, the band came to the end of the set, the crowd could only jump and dance with unregulated joy, cheering at the spectacle on the stage and celebrating the bliss shared by their collective mind. The feeling traveled through each individual in the theater at the same time. The analyst had never heard anything like it, and either had his roommates. They looked at each other, as though they had been carted away to a future filled with people of this sort who danced into a frenzy of boundless energy so blissful, that they emerged out of themselves in the unexpected ecstasy only great poets dreamt about. The roommates looked at each other and understood that they were no longer so different from the people surrounding them.

The show continued after a brief intermission. The analyst had never expected such an incredible dazzle of lighting and sound. The black woman in the dress mesmerized him even more as the show pushed the envelope from one jam to another, and when it ended he did not want to leave. He wanted to stand there, hoping the band would do a second encore. But it didn't, and his heart duly sank. But as the three boys moved along the side of the stage towards the exits, they ran into a small crowd of young people waiting in front of a rope. After asking a stoned student, they learned that the small crowd was waiting for backstage access.

"How about it?" asked the analyst of his roommates.

"We're never going to get in," said the Oregonian. "We're freshmen. Look at all the beautiful women. They're all upper classmen. They're the cool crowd. We're not."

"We should at least try," said the analyst.

"Okay," said the Oregonian, "but don't be disappointed when they turn us away."

Every few minutes they let in three or four people. The

bouncer unhooked the rope, and the fans rushed in beyond the black curtain on the side of the stage. They cheered when they were let in, and within a few minutes, the freshmen boys had their turn.

"No way," said the bouncer. "Go home."

"Why not?" demanded the analyst.

"Because you guys are fucking geeks. You think I'm letting you back there?"

"But we love their music," insisted the Egyptian. "We're really big fans. They once sang in Cairo, all in English. And about us, the Qu'ran is translated into many languages, and just because their lyrics aren't in Arabic, doesn't mean that it can't be the Qu'ran."

"What the fuck is that supposed to mean?" asked the bouncer.

"I think what my friend is trying to say," said the analyst, "is that you should never judge a book by its cover. Just because we look like geeks, doesn't mean that we can't fit in back there."

The bouncer thought about it a moment and said, "you know, you kids are absolutely right. Now get the fuck out of here, before I throw you out of here."

The three roommates did an about face, but before walking away, the analyst had an idea.

"Hey," he said to the bouncer, "we have some green."

"Green?" replied the bouncer. "You can't buy your way in here. Get going!"

"I don't think you understand," said the Oregonian.

From his back pocket, he unfurled the large bag of marijuana their Resident Assistant had given them.

The bouncer inspected the bag, unhooked the rope, and let them in without asking any questions. Finally, they were in, and they slapped each other on their backs as they walked through a narrow corridor behind the stage. It opened to a large room with a table full of food and oversized pillows thrown about the floor. Many revelers sat on them, smoked pot, and drank beer. Music played from a small sound system, and it appeared that everyone was having a good time discussing how the show went. Apparently, the revelers seemed to know each other already from previous concerts, as they were fast friends of the band and were privileged enough to follow them around the country. The female groupies had dressed scantily for the occasion. They were camera-ready, their bodies hour glasses wrapped in tight jeans and crop-tops that accentuated the shape of their perfectly rounded breasts.

"I think we're in heaven," said the Egyptian. "Allah be praised. Finally! After lifetimes of struggle."

"I know what you mean," said the analyst.

"We have the bag," said the Oregonian. "We have to be practical, because it was our ticket in. We'll have to share it with them in order to stay here. Or else the bouncer will come back. We stick out like sore thumbs."

"Agreed," said the analyst.

And then he found her – the woman he prayed he would see again. This time, though, she would not get away so easily. Towards the back of the room, the black backup singer sat amongst a group of friends drinking a beer. They passed around a joint and laughed at some joke one of her white friends had made. Determined to break the boundary that separated him from her, he tugged his friends along with him after convincing them to penetrate their circle. They reluctantly agreed, having no knowledge of why the analyst wanted go in, but they followed him because they had no other plan.

When they moved in, they saw that the group had sprawled themselves out on large pillows that had tapestry designs stitched on them. It added more color to the trippy backstage experience. But when they tried to join in the fun, the young adults in the circle turned cold and silent, as though the three freshmen had interrupted an intensely private conversation.

"May we join you?" asked the analyst.

"Guys," said one of the hippies, "why don't you go someplace else. You're really bumming us out with all of that student shit you have on."

"Student shit?" asked the Egyptian. "You mean our clothes?"

"It's your whole vibe, man," said another hippie, toking on a joint. "You're just bumming us out. Move on and bother someone else. You remind me of my kid brother, for fuck's sake. The last thing I want to think about is my parents, man. This is not *Leave It to Beaver.*"

The analyst looked to the singer pleadingly at the far end of the circle. In all truthfulness, he felt like crying, because he felt humiliated in front of her, and he didn't want to be turned away after finding the woman so beautiful. But the singer looked at him searchingly, wondering how to tell him that he just didn't belong in a crowd such as theirs and that he would one day find his own niche but just without her. He would soon forget he ever laid eyes on her and move on to the next fish in the vast sea of ocean animals that would want his attention. But the analyst didn't budge from his spot and lost track of the protestations that the two hippies now threw at his two roommates. He could only stand there paralyzed while looking into her, and she looked into him, hoping he would stop staring and roll his wagging tongue back into his mouth. It was obvious how he felt, but the analyst didn't notice how flagrantly his affection had been showing. The singer could only smile back at him sympathetically, as though she understood his fascination as well as his newfound pain.

When she smiled at him, the analyst knew right then and there that the backup singer must have had many men who loved her, but they all failed to win her heart. What would make his attempt so different, he asked himself, as his fascination with her broke party-going etiquette. But he hardly cared. He wanted to sit next to her. And just when he prepared to speak to her directly, the Oregonian brilliantly brandished the large cellophane bag filled with marijuana to the delight of the abusive hippies. They quickly changed their tune when they spotted these green buds smothered in wet, sticky resin.

"There's a first for everything," said one of the hippies.

"Yeah," said another. "A friend with weed is a friend indeed. Might as well join us. Have a beer too."

The Oregonian surrendered the bag, and one of them dumped out its contents onto a bronze platter in the center of the circle. Some marijuana had already been piled onto the platter, and their weed only added to the massive gross. Another hippie rolled a joint, lit it, and passed it around. Now that the three boys had nestled their bodies amongst them, they drank from their never-ending stockpile of cold beer. It gave the analyst a chance to sit next to the singer. But he was cock-blocked by one of the hippies who wouldn't let him squeeze in. Yet the analyst stubbornly planted his body between them. It was obvious to them all what he wanted. He looked at the wonderfully attractive black singer who smiled weakly at him.

After a few tokes of the joint and a couple of beers, however, a strange feeling came over him. At first, he felt a strange chill on his skin, as though a window or a side door had been opened. He felt a little cold, even though he understood it to be a warm summer's night. He heard the footsteps of other friends and friends of friends saying hello to their group. The music grew louder on the stereo system, and the backstage din hit its peak. And then he was sure what had been bothering him, as a long joint passed several times around him. What they were doing was highly illegal. He could have easily gone to jail. The hippies could have too for smoking pot and drinking too many beers. They could expel him from school. He would have to go back home to DC to face his brokenhearted mother who had saved so much to send him to school.

The idea of confronting his mother while stoned and drunk backstage scared him. He imagined being escorted home in handcuffs by the FBI when they tell his mother that he would be spending twenty years in a federal penitentiary. He didn't have the nerve to talk to the backup singer yet, but he knew he had to, because amidst the sounds of the footsteps all around him, he sensed that the Feds would soon break into the theater and arrest the whole lot of them. The analyst bravely leaned in to her and whispered into her ear, "the Feds may be on the way. We have to watch out."

"What?" asked the singer.

"The Feds. What if they're watching us?"

"Are you the fuzz, man?" she asked. "Are you here to bust somebody?"

"No. I'm just saying we can get into a lot of trouble if we get caught. The Feds are all around this place. You never know when they'll be coming for us."

"What are you talking about?" she asked.

She then leaned over his body and told her tripping friend about what the analyst had said.

"Oh, fuck," said the hippie. "This guy's such a bummer, man."

And then he said to the analyst, "listen, man, why don't you stop bumming her out? Why don't you go somewhere until you've stopped 'noiding? You're hurting the buzz, man. Get your shit together, dude."

The analyst, clearly paranoid over the Feds, turned to the backup singer with eyes that plead for sanctuary. He became a lost puppy dog in a cold winter's rain. She sighed deeply in response, and said, "okay, sweetie. Follow me."

Like a sheltering mother, she got up from the circle, grabbed his hand, and led him out of the exit doors. Behind the theater in the cool summer's breeze stood a fleet of white trailers and a couple of custom tour buses. The analyst had never seen anything like it and had no idea that such a mobile village had been stationed there. Many people reveled in each trailer. He heard a familiar riff of the band's guitarist float into the air. The shapely singer led him by the hand to an empty trailer.

Its interior had also been stocked with large pillows thrown against the walls. He lay down and rested his head on one of them. The singer dimmed the overhead lights and lit a series of earthy-scented candles that smelled of outlandish herbs, strange spices, as well as the scent of a woman's musky body, as that was how he remembered it. She sat down next to him and stroked his hair into place. Her soft fingers felt so good, that he almost drifted off into sleep, until he heard her instructive voice giving him sound advice like one of his attractive schoolteachers once did.

"This scene is not for everyone, sweetie," he heard her saying. "You had a little too much grass tonight, sweetheart."

She continued stroking his forehead and then his face.

"You're so young," she said. "You're not used to this. You see, I've been on the road for six months, so I'm used to it. I graduated from Ohio last year and right after that, we went on tour. It's a business. It's show business, and that's why we end up partying all the time. It's just part of the rock n' roll glamor scene. But that doesn't mean you have to follow it too. Are you still feeling scared, sweetie?"

"I'm fine," said the analyst. "This feels so good. I could stay like this forever."

"You're kind of cute too," she said. "But after tonight, we're heading down to Tucson, and then Austin, and then Phoenix, and on and on. It never ends."

"I'll follow you," said the analyst. "I don't need school. I'll defer a year."

She smiled at this and said, "just think about me when I'm gone. Remember me is all you have to do. You don't have to be with me wherever I go."

"It's not better than the real thing."

"You really have some kind of crush on me, huh?"

"The first time I saw you on the stage, singing."

"You know why they call it a 'crush,' don't you?"

"No. Tell me."

"Because in the end, the person gets 'crushed.'"

"That can't happen," said the analyst. "I'd follow you anywhere."

She smiled again, massaged his forehead, and ran her fingers through his hair.

"I want you to have something to remember me by. It's something we can share, if you're up for it."

"Anything," he said.

She stood up and went to the small kitchen area near the back of the trailer. She returned with a small vial filled with clear liquid.

"Want to take a ride with me?" she asked.

"What does 'Sandoz' mean?" asked the analyst.

"Don't worry about the label. It doesn't mean anything. I'll give you just a little bit, because you've never tried this stuff before."

The singer stuck her pinky in the vial and placed a tiny drop of it on his tongue. She did the same for herself. She then lay down next to him on the nest of pillows. As the flames at the tips of the candles began to trail, the shadows on the walls transformed into outlandish shapes. The sound of the music grew as momentous as the most gifted philharmonic orchestra. The analyst curled up into her soft body. She held him closely to her breast. After twenty minutes, he felt himself leaving this earth and heading towards the planets of nirvana.

The analyst still stared into a spot on the dingy basement wall of his cramped office. He remembered her then as though it were yesterday. And now there was no way back, no matter how hard he wished and prayed for it. It was as though his fate had been purposely built to prevent such a return. He had to move along, like a mule who is whacked by a switch along a barren road, forever moving forward with his load of memories and futile plans. No wonder mules are so stubborn, he thought for a moment as his eyes returned to his computer monitor into which a few electronic characters had been permanently burned. He remembered, though, how young and fresh she looked, her soft skin glowing as they cuddled in outer-space where no one would ever hear or bother them. He recalled the music she played on that trailer stereo, the music growing more profound, and his insecurity and paranoia easing as she held him.

That was almost fifty years ago. He wanted out of the Company. He wanted to retire. He no longer cared about the government or what it did. He found his professional career wanting. The reports he filed no longer came with any reward. He wanted to go home to his wife, but just when he signed off on his computer, two men from Administration blocked his attempted escape from the building's basement. He almost wished they saved the time and buried him alive down there.

"Follow us, please," said one of them.

"What's this all about?" he asked nervously.

"It's classified. You're wanted in the Deputy's office right away. C'mon, let's go."

"The Deputy of the entire Company? Or just the Directorate of Intelligence?"

"The Company," said his supervisor, squeezing in to join the other two. "Just go. I don't know what any of this is all about, but you better go if the Deputy wants to see you."

"I've never met him," said the analyst.

"Either have I," said the supervisor. "He's high up there, so I wish you luck."

He followed the two suited men through several passageways and corridors before arriving at an elevator door without any labels or instructions. The two bookends made sure to stand on either side of him as the elevator took them several floors up to the Deputy's office. He noticed they were armed.

They men accompanied him inside the dark office. They remained inside the elevator when the doors shut, leaving him in the office alone with the Deputy. The large room, he noticed, was completely empty, save for the Deputy's desk and chair. But there was a lone empty chair for anyone who had the misfortune of being ordered to meet him.

The analyst tried to sit down, but before he could, the Deputy raised his hand and instructed him to remain standing. When the Deputy swiveled around in his seat, the analyst noticed not only his fine suit and tie, his slicked-back hair, and his lean build, but also how young he looked. He must have exercised regularly, he suspected.

"I never asked you to sit down, did I?" asked the Deputy, grinning.

He held a thick manila folder in his hands, which he then started flipping through. It was marked classified. Little did the analyst know that the file contained his own employment record with the Company. The Deputy was young enough to be his son, he figured. He looked demonic in the shadows as he perused the file.

"Tell me," asked the Deputy, "how does a liberal, self-hating Jew get to work at my company for so long?"

The analyst was so shocked by the question that he couldn't respond.

"I mean, you are a Jew, right?" asked the Deputy.

"I'm a human being," said the analyst.

"And it says you joined the company in 1976. Is that right?"

"Yes."

"Hmmm," said the Deputy holding his index finger to his chin. "So then why would a liberal, self-hating Jew want to work here knowing full well what we do? I mean, did you know what we did before you joined us in 1976?"

"I worked for the Directorate of Intelligence, because I wanted to serve my country by researching different aspects of our nation's foreign policy and its impact upon other nations."

"Sir," said the Deputy.

"Sir, what?" said the analyst.

"You are to call me 'sir,' or did you not remember to whom you are speaking?"

"I'm sorry."

"Sir."

"Sir, yes," said the analyst, grinding his teeth and standing up straighter.

"From what it says here, you used to write excellent reports, but your personal history is kind of fucked up, wouldn't you say?"

"I don't understand, sir."

"You got your PhD. from Ohio University, which has a damn fine football program. Why not Harvard or Yale? Couldn't make the cut, eh?"

"My grandfather went to the University of Ohio, sir."

"And speaking of your grandfather, it says here that he was the one who got you the job here. That makes sense, because you never were qualified to work for us in the first place. But your grandfather served in the OSS and was quite good at what he did. He then served in Defense, and he's the one who got you in here."

He looked up from the folder in his hands and said,

"funny, because my grandfather fought on the German side during the war, and look where I wound up. I guess some things never change, eh? I have to admit, though, George Weisz was a damn good spy. The work ruined him, I hear. Tell me, has the work ruined you yet?"

"Not yet, sir."

"And you are on the verge of retiring, so your time here is almost up. But according to your financial statements, you don't have a pot to piss in. And that isn't surprising at all, because your wife is a nigger jazz singer, am I right? I mean, come on, man! A fucking jazz singer? What a waste of time. Who does she think she is? Billie fucking Holiday? Were you too poor, ugly, or too much of a good Heeb to marry a white girl?"

"Please, sir, with all due respect, if you could stop – "

"Don't tell me what to do in my Company! You've got some balls coming in here and telling me what to do! Just shut the hell up and answer my questions!"

"Yes, sir."

"But tell me the truth," he smiled again, "is it true what they say?"

"About what, sir?"

"Black chicks. Y'know? 'The blacker the berry, the sweeter the juice?'"

The analyst felt like ripping his throat out, but his only recourse was to stand there and take it. He felt like a dartboard taking his pointed throws. The Deputy was getting closer and closer to the Bull's Eye.

"'Once you go black, you never go back.' Am I right? Oh, it's all true in your case, because you also have a mongrel son who is off in Ohio too. How fucking sweet. Like father, like son. But, I mean, don't you guys have a hard time settling down somewhere?"

"Sir?"

"Well, you're family is not white and not black, and your child must be all fucked up. So where are you people supposed to live? In the ghetto, or in a white neighborhood? Wherever you go, you're not accepted, so how does your family cope with that? Do you hang out with white people or niggers?"

"Sir, we live in a nice, quiet suburban neighborhood not far from here. We have a diverse array of very close friends."

"Did they ever bully your son in school?"

The analyst remained silent.

"Well? Is he a nigger, or is he a white?"

The Deputy questioned him in this vein for some time. He reviewed every detail of his file, his thirty years of work with the company, and by the time he got to the point of why he wanted to see him, the analyst was on the verge of breaking nervously and fainting in fatigue. He wanted to murder the Deputy, but at the same time, he didn't have the courage to jump over the desk, considering what the consequences of striking him in the face would have been. There were men posted downstairs, and he may not have gotten out of the office alive. He had never been treated in such a way by anyone in the Company before. He thought fleetingly that maybe they would commend him for thirty years of service. Instead, the young, snot-nosed Deputy ripped him apart, flayed him, whittled him down to the bone with every question, each of them like a lash flogging his back.

"Let's just say, from the looks of things, you really haven't done too much for your country, and it's sad that someone who has been here for so many years is going to leave on such a terrible note. You'll be getting a negative review from me, this I can tell you, if you ever want a contract job or need a job somewhere else, because it looks like you will definitely need the money, that's for sure. Unless, the jazz singer can rake in something for your kid."

"Sir," said the analyst, "I'm ready to retire."

"I brought you in here, you see, because, believe it or not, this is your lucky day. Your country and I are giving you a chance to redeem yourself, to make some good money, to make your family respectable in the eyes of our wonderful and caring Washington establishment."

"Sir?"

The young Deputy stood from his desk and walked over to the windows.

"I'm going to make you an offer," he said.

"I don't understand, sir."

"You heard me. I'm going to give you a second chance, not only to straighten out your terrible track record, but if you do decide to take this offer, I'll even promote your old, geezer ass."

"Promote me to what, sir?"

"I'll make you Supervisor."

"Excuse me, sir?"

"You heard me. Listen, you've led a really fucked up life, that's for sure, and you married a nigger, sure, but your reports are spot on, or so says the current Supervisor down there in the hellhole where you work. You really are good at what you do, despite your pathetic life. So, I'm going to give you a second chance. If you do this, you will be running things in your division. Quite a boost in pay, wouldn't you say?"

"Yes, sir. I can't believe it."

"Believe it. But what I'm going to ask you to do goes against all of your beliefs, you fucking hippie scumbag."

"Sir, I don't understand."

"We have learned that the new President of the Russian Federation will invade Afghanistan a second time."

The silence in the dark room hung in the air as though a bomb were about to go off.

"Are you sure, sir? That doesn't seem right, considering that Russia will never be as powerful as it once was."

"We've heard differently. As a result, we must prepare to invade Afghanistan before the Russians get there."

"Shouldn't we wait for them to invade first, sir? That would be standard protocol, sir."

"Sometimes, offense is the best defense. We will strike first, and I want you to devise a plan to have us attack Afghanistan, covertly at first, but also gain overwhelming national and international support for what we will be doing."

"Sir," said the analyst, "I appreciate the opportunity, but such a plan is not in my area of expertise. My entire philosophy, actually, is quite different. I'm more of a – "

"A peace-lover. That's what you are."

"Sir, I wouldn't exactly say that."

"Then do this last job, and you'll be appointed Supervisor. You have more experience with the Russians than any analyst in the company right now. You've researched them over and over for the past thirty years, and soon Putin will rebuild Russia into what it used to be. So, take the assignment, not only for the Company, but for the security of our nation as well."

"And if I don't?"

He sighed and turned around to view the snowfall.

"Y'know, he said, "intelligence work is a funny thing, because now that you know about this, you are a threat to our national security, aren't you? I mean, what would happen if you leaked this?"

"I won't, sir. I can promise you that."

"Listen. If you don't do this, we'll just have to deal with you accordingly. You know too much already. Don't you see?"

"I don't understand, sir. If I refuse, you'll do something to me?"

"I'll have your throat slit, you Commie bastard. And if this ever leaks to the press or to anyone else at State or the Bush Administration, I'll not only have your throat slit, but also have your wife's and your son's. She would have a hard time singing her jazz standards without a throat, wouldn't you say?"

"I just don't think I'm the right person for the job, sir."

The Deputy turned to face him and moved in closer.

"You are not only the *right* one, you're the *only* one. This is a black box operation. The only people who know about this are the Director of the Company, myself, and now you. Three people. That's it. You'll do it, or accept the consequences. The choice is yours. We can't have a liberal Jew analyst running around town with this kind of information, now can we?"

"I don't know what to say, sir."

"Say yes to your new role as Supervisor after you plan this out for us. It's either that or, well, I think you already know."

"I'll have to get right on it, then, sir. How long do I have?"

"I want a full report in three days. Once I become the next Director of Central Intelligence after the old man retires, you will come to work directly under me in the Intelligence Division. No questions asked. Do we have an understanding?"

The Deputy held out his hand, and the analyst reluctantly shook it.

The Deputy grinned and said, "you better get a good night's rest. Over the next three days, you probably won't be getting much sleep. You have so little time."

On his way home that evening, the analyst could do no more than wonder how he would ever be able to unravel decades of hardwired political philosophy in three short days. He thought the idea of the United States infiltrating Afghanistan so preposterous that he couldn't even wrap his mind around any strategy that would ever accomplish such a highly absurd and ridiculous mission. As he drove into DC Metro from McClean, he hardly paid attention to the freeways and routes beyond his windshield. He could only contemplate this one atrocious idea and how many lives would have to be sacrificed for it, all because he happened to be at the wrong place at the wrong time.

And then he thought that the only idea that may have worked would be to turn the car around and head down to south of the border, to Cabo St. Lucas or Ixtapa or the Yucatan, or one of those many Mexican exotic locations where he had always wanted to take his wife, just turn his fucking piece of shit Japanese clunker around and drive like hell. But if the Russians found Trotsky, the Company would surely find him anywhere in the world, and he wouldn't be so foolish as to leave his wife and son languishing at the home where those bookends on the elevator would hold them captive until he created the most asinine plan the Company had ever devised. He should have gotten out many years ago, but his wife wanted to continue singing, and his kid needed a degree. He would have sacrificed his life for them. But suddenly, the reality of beginning yet another war with the Russians seemed like a cross much too onerous to bear. The Deputy was right after all. The analyst was a peace-lover. He wanted nothing else for the world. He hated war and what it had done to his generation, not only the sorry souls returning from Vietnam but also those innocents who finally stood up to the natural abuses of government power only to destroy their own families and their own minds, if only to stop a demonic war machine from mincing them whole.

He never picked a side, as a globe doesn't have any sides, he used to think. And yet madness had sprung up all around him, minds soaked in LSD, rage and psychosis wherever he turned, resulting in a country divided just as it was then as he headed home. And to think that he would be the one to initiate the sick cycle all over again just as the ashes of the Cold War were being swept away. He wanted to take his wife and son and leave for some barren island in an altogether different hemisphere. Yet in a 'New York Minute,' the eye in the sky shined upon him and chose him for no other reason than to perpetuate its own cruelty over humankind. Pain without reason, he considered, because now he would have to kill and not save. Perhaps that was the price of being an employee of the Company, no matter in what division or capacity he served. It was lunacy in the first place that one could never leave the company without destroying other people.

The role reversal sickened him. The Deputy had good reason to pick him. No one knew this shit better than he did. Because of his philosophy, the analyst was able to understand all sides and all options over many years of careful study. He understood how every piece on the chessboard moved. He supposed that this came with being a dove and not a hawk. Doves had been granted what hawks could never have – the breadth of their own minds over the dim-witted instincts of using sharp teeth and claws to eat their prey alive. Perhaps it had always been that way, and for some reason, the world just had to have both. The two birds just couldn't live in their separate worlds. Instead, they were fixtures in the tragedy of the natural fuck-up that he now found himself wading knee-deep in. He had three days to figure something out, and then who knew what the Deputy would do? No wonder he wound up slaving away in a basement, while this Deputy ended up running and managing the entire company from up high. Maybe that's what it took to run and manage something.

He didn't stop for gas as he should have. He rolled into his driveway with his tank empty. He had a box full of books and papers that he would use for the project. He knew he had to get started right away. The clock was ticking, but he didn't feel like moving. He only stared at the small three-bedroom home in front of the car. He noticed how old it had become. The pea-green vinyl siding was out of fashion. No one in the neighborhood had a house of such an ugly color. The roof needed retiling. Even the driveway needed repaving. Out of all the homes on the block, his looked the most depressing, as though nothing within it had lived for many years – just two seniors rotting away like corpses buried alive, while their only child flew the coop just to get away from them.

They had plans for their retirement, damnit. Now how

was he supposed to explain this to his wife? She thought he worked for some Congressional advisory committee on Foreign Policy. What bullshit he had been feeding her for thirty straight years. He would have told her if he could have, but if the Company found out, he would have been booted out or even arrested. She never really knew exactly what he did. He made sure to avoid any conversation about his job.

When he walked in from the cold to a nice heated living room, his wife was watching the local news. She looked as radiant and as fresh as when he first laid eyes on her on that stage in Akron many moons ago. She was decked out in a lovely black evening dress and wore a pearl necklace that she had inherited from her mother after she had passed.

"Good!" she said, "you're back. I was worried. We're getting late."

"For what?"

"You forgot? My concert tonight? I'm on in an hour."

"Damn," he said, pounding his head with fake affectation. "I knew I forgot something."

"Well, get dressed. Get your suit on."

He stepped into the living room cautiously and took a seat next to her. He put his arm around her and gave her a peck on the cheek.

"Something's come up," he said.

"Excuse me?"

"Honey, I can't go tonight. The supervisor stuck me with an important assignment. It has to be done in three days."

"You better call him and tell him to give it to someone else. The whole gang will be there. I haven't headlined a concert in a long time. You know that."

He took off his glasses for the hundredth time that day and wiped them clean with his handkerchief.

"I'll be promoted if I do this one last project," he said calmly. "That means a real step-up in pay. We need it, especially with all the bills that have been piling up."

"But you're retiring at the end of the year. What's all this about a promotion?"

"We need a few more years, honey. Just a few, so that we can be totally secure."

"Fuck that!"

She got up from the sofa and stood over him, her breath fuming into his face like a dragon's.

"What the hell did you do?" she cried. "We're done with this. We're selling this house. Work is over for us. It's time to start enjoying our lives instead of working ourselves to death, pinching every goddamned penny, repairing the leaks in the goddamn roof. All of it. What the hell did you do to mess things up? How could you commit to such a thing?"

"We'll have plenty of time to retire, sweetheart, but let's just put one foot in front of the other, okay? I have to start on this project right away. You go to your concert and have a ball. I'm sure you'll be great."

"Yeah, and you won't be there for it. How embarrassing. How am I supposed to explain this to all our friends? Why would I want to perform when you won't even be there? We planned for this months ago. Are you feeling alright?"

"I'm okay, yeah," he said weakly.

She felt his forehead and said, "something's not right with you, because you are definitely not the same person I went to bed with last night."

"I am the same person. I'm just a little preoccupied

with this project right now. It will take a few days, and once it's done, we'll take a nice long vacation to celebrate. How does that sound?"

"Don't try to sweet-talk your way out of this one, baby, because it won't work. It's getting late. There are leftovers in the fridge if you get hungry."

"Please, don't go away angry. You know how I hate that. It isn't my fault."

"Then who's fault is it? Oh, so you just decided all of a sudden to cancel our Golden Years, take a promotion, and then to put the icing on the cake, you can't even make the concert tonight? And you managed to do all this in eight hours!"

"I know I should have talked to you – "

"Damn straight you should have talked to me. What the hell has gotten into you? I'm your wife. We make the big decisions together, like we always do."

"I had to decide right then and there."

"No one ever has to decide right then and there on such things," she said. "You don't have to lie to me. That makes me even madder."

"I'm sorry about all of this, but one day you'll understand. When I leave that stupid department, you'll understand why it had to be this way for a few more years."

"That makes no sense," she said on her way out the door. "You might as well stay in the den if you have to work for the next three days, because I'm too angry to even speak to you. Fuck you and the horse you rode in on."

"I want to be there," he called from the living room. "You know that, honey. I wanted to see you on stage again. You have to believe me. I'll make it up to you. All of it!"

By that time, she had left. The analyst sighed deeply and cleaned his lenses again. He leaned back in the sofa and stared up at the ceiling, exhausted. He wondered how he would ever be able to explain to anyone what he had to do in the short time ahead of him, or why he had to lock himself up for the next three days in his den to get the project done, a project he never even had the nerve to imagine working. He had been stuck with such a horribly inhuman challenge, and if he told anyone about it, neither he nor his family would make it out of Washington alive.

It would be the analyst's last project before he climbed from his sorry state as a slave in a basement. Finally, a man of importance. There was no pretending what his new position would mean to him and his family. It was right in front of him, like fresh bait, and maybe he should accept the fact that people needed to be killed, that war and famine and bloodshed needed to happen, as though it were part of God's divine plan. It sickened him. The whole world sickened him. It was difficult to keep ideals when death and destruction surfaced all around him. And yet a strange new power, the ability and the will to snuff out other lives, took root within his mind.

He had been following the wrong path, perhaps. He had been mislead by an overreach of his own reasoning and emotion to think he could actually prevent the taking of life and the tortuous path to war. Who was he to believe he could do anything about the human condition? He thought he could make a difference when just the opposite was true – that he too had to eat and protect his family and tear bloody meat from the teeth of his jaws, incisors that bit on thick flesh. How exactly would he have survived otherwise?

He locked himself in his den. He grew feverish sitting in front of a large, sprawling map of the world that he had tacked up to his wall. He stared at it for some time, looking at

Afghanistan and the other countries surrounding it. But this time, he didn't have to be so clever as he had been in previous reports. He could now take lives indiscriminately in order to defeat the Russian foe, as he had been given due license to kill and destroy, even sacrifice American lives to win this battle that would one day move the precious country one step closer to the containment of a soon-to-be dictator whose greed would bring the Western world to the brink of destruction, as though the Russian prick actually enjoyed playing czar for the latest generation of Russia's oppressed. Naturally, we had to move in first to prevent him from accessing the Middle East more than he already had. The more influence he had there, the tighter his grip around the nation's throat. But then where did the Deputy get this information about Putin's plans for Afghanistan?

He held back for a moment, taking his eyes off the map. He went into his walnut desk and took out a large bottle of vodka. He poured himself a half glass and sipped the warm liquid. It helped the blood in his mind circulate. He had felt so useless. Unappreciated. Ignored. Getting old without any kind of reward for living a life of restraint and desperation. The hair on his head had grown gray and white, his muscles slack, his clothes old. It had all gone wrong somewhere. The rest of his life had been spent waiting to die, not wanting to live as a man who dreamt of a greater station in life, and now such a station was possible, just as long as he destroyed people, killed off their lives, recreated the same putrid world that he had so valiantly fought against. Even his wife had grown tired of him. His son didn't have much of a future either. He had discipline problems in high school, and his grades had suffered. He spent his afternoons skateboarding instead of doing his homework. He had long curly hair that sprouted from his head in all directions. He hated his clothes so much that he tore them to shreds to fit in with his crowd of anti-social outsiders who had permanent attitude problems. Every family was indeed miserable, but never before had the analyst considered that his own son neither had the drive nor the wherewithal to sustain his own life, should he even want it.

He realized that every man had to kill. Peace was but an illusion created by the weak to dump the dirty work upon the shoulders of the strong. Someone had to kill those who wanted to invade the country, and if we didn't control world affairs, then some other country would. Either we did it or someone else would, and that was the bottom line. Better us than them. Better the fly-ridden boy eating a handful of rice in a parched desert who suffered in hunger than his own son. Better that a few of our paramilitary units infiltrated Afghanistan and killed off a few hundred civilians in the dead of night rather than their killing of our own soldiers several years down the road. Because it doesn't end, he considered.

And if he wanted to change his stars, he had to kill and not merely be appointed Supervisor, but take it, as it was his for the taking. And if he didn't take it, some other bureaucratic fuck-head would take it. Might as well take it, then. He refused to be rendered impotent and useless in his own life. He refused to be sent to an early grave and succumb to the fatigue and exhaustion of an utopian ideal that died many years ago. He had to fight fire with fire and ditch the feeble mind whose tape reel had played John Lennon's *Imagine* over and over and over.

He drank some more of the vodka, now that he was motivated to man-up instead of being such a sissy. If only he had the balls of the Hindu God Kali earlier in his life, maybe he would have been Director of the entire Company by now. Yet he was born at the wrong time, even though he vividly remembered when a rosy return to Eden was possible, when the tree-huggers were winning, sending the war pigs into ignominy and shame. No longer, he thought, as he examined Europe on the large map in front of him.

First, he would have to make the invasion worthwhile for the Bush Administration as well as for the hawks on the continent across the pond. Bush wanted to build up the military. The analyst first proposed that the Defense Department install new long-range missile systems in Europe aimed directly at Russia. This would serve as backup for our conventional troops when they're introduced into Afghanistan for the first time. The defense contractors would make some money off the deal, and the hawks in Defense would also take a cut. Nice, he thought.

Such a proposal took him late into the evening, and still he drank at the bottle of warm vodka, inspired by his amazing reversal of fortune to continue pleasing the Bush Administration for the benefit of the Company and for the sake of his family. But after several hours of work, he collapsed on his chair, drunk. His wife must have returned from the concert, but she wasn't interested in seeing him to bed. This indeed was his finest hour. It was time to rise above the ashes like the phoenix he was meant to be. And with that, he passed out until morning.

Morning came soon enough, though, because his wife banged on the door, asking if he was feeling alright all locked up in his den for so long.

"I'm okay in here, honey," he answered weakly.

"Don't you want some breakfast," she asked.

"I'm fine. I already ate. I'm really busy in here. I can't be disturbed."

"At least have something to eat," she said.

"No can do, honey. Too busy to eat. I have some snacks in here. Don't worry. I'm working hard. I'll be out soon."

"Can't you at least open the door and let me in?"

"It will interrupt my concentration. I really need to concentrate."

"But I'm worried. You've locked yourself in there."

"I know. Just a little while longer, okay?"

"How long?"

"A couple days."

"Well, then come out and call me if you need anything, you hear?"

"Will do. Just pretend I'm not here. Pretend that I'm at the office."

"Fine," she said before going away.

He fell back into his chair. His head throbbed, and his empty stomach felt dry and nauseated. He poured himself another glass of warm vodka. Within a few minutes, he loosened up and was prepared to put in a full day's work. He again thought about the Bush Administration.

The President would want to renew his relationship with the Saudis and manufacture more demand for oil, thereby raising the market price per barrel for crude. That relationship would net international oil producers a lot of money and bring jobs to Texas, the Midwest, and the states along the Gulf of Mexico that were big supporters of the Bush dynasty, considering its interests in oil. Therefore, the best policy would be that which targeted Saudi Arabia and made them a firm partner in another war. The analyst wanted to repair the damage caused by Clinton's Internet economy and anti-oil environmental policies. Just as Reagan did with King Fahd, so Bush II would have to renew his ties with Crown

Prince Abdullah. Both would have to work hard to fight Islamic terrorism and those who desired a pure Islamic state free of Christians and Jews. The Royal family were against the terrorists and their renegade Saudi, Osama Bin Laden, even during the Soviet Invasion of Afghanistan. The Saudi princes were the more moderate forces in the region compared to their powerful Islamic clergy who wanted to keep the Middle East in the Stone Age. The clerics and the terrorists must be stopped.

And as the vodka took greater effect, and as he felt stronger about his capacity to wield the saber of war over the Middle East in order to contain Russia, a barrage of ideas soon swept through him. As the hours progressed, inch by inch, the level of warm, clear vodka in the large plastic bottle dipped until late into the night. As a result of his good feeling and newfound inspiration every few hours, he furiously scribbled down every idea that came to mind, and they came to him in fits, almost like spasms or convulsions of thought that shot down from the heavens and were pounded directly into his skull, shaken and stirred, until they produced something of value.

Second, the company would advise the President to take a very tough and unmerciful hand with these terrorists. The public would support this, because it was always paranoid of the Muslim threat, and there were hardly any Muslims in the country for them to make much of a stink about it. Because Islam was the fastest growing religion in the country, the pro-Christian Bush Administration would like nothing more than to slow this growing trend, especially amongst the Black-American population whose power during the Clinton Administration increased exponentially, and to Bush, most dangerously.

The ideas kept coming all day long in this manner. He

paced the room, studied his maps, poured through books and statistics to hash out the details, drank more of the vodka, collapsed in his chair, and nearly wept with the misery and torture of a man who made answers to riddles deceptively simple.

Third, at the outset, the President had to be convinced to trust the intelligence coming in from the Director of Central Intelligence or the Deputy of Central Intelligence only. Under no circumstances should the Administration trust unreliable sources that did not pass through those two offices. That meant, never trust the FBI when it came to foreign intelligence matters and have the State Department and the FBI report directly to the Director and the Deputy of Intelligence instead. In this way, to prepare the country from what the analyst had just invented, relevant departments in the intelligence services would have to be 'decompartmentalized.' This would have to happen, because the US would then bomb poor Iraq for the second time and remove the irrelevant dictator Saddam Hussein from power in Baghdad.

Why? Well, first, the Administration needed justification, thought the analyst. The President must invade Iraq and democratize it to protect Israel as well as Saudi Arabia from Saddam's supposed expansionist tendencies, even though such tendencies didn't exist anymore. This would force Putin to aid Saddam against the US in Iraq. But see, another war in Iraq would only be a distraction from the company's slow, quiet infiltration of Afghanistan.

The second justification for invading Iraq that the public would readily buy would be the pronouncement that weapons of mass destruction (WMDs) that threatened both Israel and Saudi Arabia had been found in Iraq. Both Israel and the moderate Saudi royal family, then, would form an alliance, thereby throwing the Palestinians under the bus. The company would give the Bush Administration doctored satellite images and phony intercepted phone calls to show how Saddam hid these WMDs. These images would also show Osama Bin Laden's training camps – yes, the same Osama Bin Laden who bombed the US Embassies in Kenya and Tanzania. These images would show PLO training camps and their terrorist fighters poised to attack Israel, because Bin Laden funded the PLO as well. The distraction from infiltrating Afghanistan would not only be Saddam but Bin Laden as well.

The doctored satellite images would be leaked to the press and prove to the American public that Iraq had been playing games again. As a result, the Armed Forces and the Company would get massive funding directly from Congress with overwhelming bipartisan support. Now that the new Middle East proxy war would soon come into play in Iraq, Putin was sure to approach the Iranian regime as the Soviets did at the end of the horrible Iran/Iraq War. Confronting the Iranian regime would win Bush points with the American Zionists and win him even bigger points with the growing American right wing. Iran would always be the people's favorite punching bag, he thought. But here's the catch. The US would have to pretend to confront the Iranian regime, because it would simultaneously have to open clandestine negotiations with Teheran to halt Russian influence from growing there.

The analyst, in a brainstorm, recalled that Soviet/Iranian relations had soured when Khomeni suppressed the Communist Tudeh Party after the Iranian Revolution in 1979. After Khomeni's death, Iran allied with the Soviets to counterbalance US presence in the Persian Gulf. But since the US would now be invading Iraq, the US would now renew its ties with Teheran and enlist it in a fight against 'global terrorism', just as the US had enlisted them to help against the

Sandanistas in the Iran/Contra Affair. This subtle alignment between two well-known enemies, the US and Iran, would stop the Russians from getting too strong a foothold in Iran. So, to sum up, an easy win in Iraq, another proxy war with the Russians in Iran, and finally, the US preparation for an even greater war in Afghanistan, which was where the US really wanted to be. Phew!

But the Company would not mention the Putin threat to the Bush Administration just yet. Actually, Putin wouldn't be mentioned as a threat at all, smiled the analyst, pouring himself another glass. Once Congress awarded the Company and the Defense Department all the money it desired, morale among servicemen and women and employees of the Company would dramatically soar. The end of the Clinton Administration would signal the burial of the Iran/Contra Affair and other embarrassing scandals that rocked the once-solid reputation of the Company. Like his father, Bush II would remake the company into the glorious organization it once was when it had replaced the OSS at the end of World War II.

He knew, however, that the public needed a figurehead to blame for yet another crisis in the Middle East. The public would actually think that the Bush family and their rich Texas cronies were on their usual quest for oil profits. And so, he created "A Muslim Scare" to take root in the public's consciousness. This would take the blame off of the Bush Administration and put it unabashedly on those crazy Muslims who had always hated America and what it stood for.

He hated this idea most of all, as he again wiped down his glasses with his handkerchief. Believe it or not, scapegoating always worked, as it did in Nazi Germany. The plans that he made so far had been so cruel, that he started laughing hysterically until tears rolled down his face. His plans were both preposterous and real all in the same breath, just like he had seen in so many of those dumb Cold War propaganda movies when the nuclear warhead is about to be launched towards Russia. The Company had produced these for the corporate media and the Christian Evangelicals here in the US. But a new Muslim Scare was to be only a very light slap on the wrist compared to Nazi Germany. It would coerce the Muslims to get on board with the fight against 'global terrorism' and the new war against Saddam. It would force the most ardent of Muslims to assimilate into the Western society. Yes, he must do that, because the majority always had to point the finger at the new minority on the block. The Muslims were next on the neverending American hit list.

This scapegoating effect would commence as the first bombs dropped over Baghdad. The Company must inform the President of the situation on the ground at all times. But the Company must also persuade his Administration to occupy Iraq long-term, because the Company will inform the President that Saddam Hussein will also be making an expensive arms deal with Putin to counter American aggression in Iraq. This information will be the final straw. It will justify the occupation of Iraq.

An arms deal would scare the hell out of the Bush Administration. And because of this, the President must then make a public spectacle of this second Iraq War, while knowing full well that he must stop this Russian/Iraqi arms deal from going down. As the spotlight shines on Iraq with all of the new technology the Pentagon will deploy there, the Company will secretly enter Afghanistan without anyone noticing and prepare for a much wider, longer, and colder war to contain Putin.

In anticipation of this incursion into Afghanistan, the Company will put radical Mullahs on the payroll to gain their support and flip their followers to the more moderate side.

The Company, then, would make them more accepting of the West. The President, however, will say little, if anything, to the press. The Administration will keep its cards close to its vest, so to speak. Let the media showcase the War in Iraq on its own terms and have the Department of Defense grant the important interviews to those reporters who sympathize with the cause. The press will make heroes of the armed servicemen who fight overseas and sacrifice their lives for the good of the country. The only information that the President will supply to the public is the constant, repetitive reminder of how terrorism has threatened America and its allies for years. Enough is enough. This meant emphasizing Saddam's WMDs and the new threat posed by another single man, this one terrorist figurehead, this zealot cartoon figure for all of these school kids to hate – Osama Bin Laden. Clinton had been too clumsy and weak to deal with him. It was finally payback time for the US.

The analyst killed two birds with one stone. Get the terrorists and stop Putin cold. What a fucking master plan, he thought, as he collapsed completely and utterly drunk by the end of the second evening.

When he awoke the next morning splayed out on the floor of his den, he immediately felt a viral pain in his stomach. He quietly and calmly retrieved the wastepaper basket filled with his crumpled notes and ideas, and vomited up whatever was left of the warm vodka in his stomach. Apparently, he had passed out, and with a few day's stubble on his face and a ghost-white complexion, he heaved a second time, tears pushing out of his eyes, until his immediate sickness had been expelled. He was terribly sick. He knew that. He was also very hungry. He hungered for his wife's scrambled eggs most of all, the typical breakfast for a hangover, but his skull throbbed so viciously that he could only sit in his chair and stare at the mess he created in his den over the last two and a half days.

And then he remembered what he had planned for the Company. It filled him with enough shame that he just had to look to what his grandfather had given him before he passed away in the 1970s. He opened the side drawer of his desk and pulled out a solid brass pill box. It felt heavy in his hand, denoting it as the guardian of something significant. He slid the top open. Inside was a small white pill of potassium cyanide bequeathed to him by his grandfather before his death.

His grandfather had carried it in Nazi Germany as an OSS officer. He carried it in case German troops captured him in battle and forced him to compromise any intelligence. It was also used to avoid the harsh tortures of the SS. His grandfather told him that it was the most valuable gift any man could give another man, whether he turned out to be a pauper or a prince, and that he should keep it until he absolutely needed to use it. Considering that the Jewish analyst had betrayed every value and principle he had ever known during these three days of delirium, he thought it may have been the right time. But then the Company would have come after his son and lovely wife. They may have bankrupted them, thrown them in jail, or even killed them. He must submit the report, he decided, and no, he didn't want to go to Hell, because his entire life had been spent traveling through it already. He did not want to do it all over again, and he didn't want his wife and child to follow in his footsteps either.

Yet the small white pill promised an easy end to his worries and concerns, an easy end to all of those aptitudes, all of that knowledge, all of that raw creativity that was now being used to destroy thousands upon thousands of lives. He had joined the Company with the goal of doing directly the opposite. But the bottle of vodka at his feet was now empty and uncapped on the carpeted floor.

He didn't have any fluid with which to swallow the pill, and rather than being discovered roaming the house looking for a glass of water, he still had to have something to wash it down with. Swallowing the pill was another obstruction, he thought, before breaking into the light of freedom, like so many other obstacles, until he found yet another way out, another plan that would set things rightly, like so many other times before, once again bailing out the world from holocausts, plagues, and apocalyptic doomsdays, all parceled into a flimsy report like the well-trained monkey that he was, filing report after report like the emotionless automaton he had become. He had to fight the will to kill before he became what he always hated. He had to fight it before he became just like them – another liability to humanity, another destructive force within a world of destructive people, just another drooling wolf chasing the lone lamb who fled for its life.

Out of the drawer where he had stored the pill box, he took out an old flip phone and dialed a number he had often used in his Golden Years. When it connected to another man on the other end, he agreed to meet him in the 'hood at a sit-down fast-foot joint that served typical black ghetto fare – pizza, wings, gyros, hamburgers and cheeseburgers, and of course, fried chicken – all under one roof. They agreed to meet in an hour.

He took his Japanese clunker down to the Black section of the city. The analyst never could understand why neighborhoods had to remain so segregated, but such was the reality of the DC Metro area. Such was the reality of every city in America. DC was no different. He mused that the white majority as a collective had trouble integrating with the black population, but not vice-versa. He was not sure at all, however, if this wide generalization had one shred of truth to it. His wife loved him so much, that it seemed that Black folk just found it easier to integrate, and in some cases, found it easier to blend with whites, as that was the nation's social prerogative in the 1970s. He remembered working on it himself. 'The Great American Melting Pot', he recalled. And the corollary to that came when his beloved Carter lost the election to Ronald Reagan. 'The Great American Salad Bowl'. Perhaps it depended on the swing of the mighty pendulum, or perhaps that wheel in the sky that reset all of the clocks to zero and put everyone on an entirely different path, until that path became as familiar as the lines on the palm of one's hand.

Before he advanced yet another theory of why whites and blacks didn't mix, he easily found parking in front of the fast-food joint. The immediate area smelled of cooked fat, a vapor that blew out of the vents above the front door. The nippy wind clutched him once he exited his vehicle. He kept the envelope containing his classified report within his coat.

These people never cared about what they ate, he thought, when entering the restaurant. It amazed him how some of these black folk ate such garbage and never gained a lick of weight. But it was no accident that they had adapted to this kind of poison. Fresh fruits and vegetables were kept away from them and saved for those the government deemed worth saving. He entered the place angry by the thought but was soon eased by the sight of the man he was supposed to meet. He sat in the far corner of the room, patiently waiting for him.

The analyst ordered a soda first and then sat down in front him. He was near certain that no one from the Company had tailed him, because the Company used intermediaries and contractors, and not assets, to manipulate conditions in the ghettos.

"We meet again, comrade," said the black man checking him over. "You look like shit. You've been drinking that cheap imitation vodka. Not the real stuff. You smell like shit too. What has happened to you, comrade? Why have you come back to us? What is wrong?"

The analyst slid over the thick envelope that he had been carrying in his coat.

"You have no need to call me 'comrade' anymore," said the analyst.

"Ah, but there are many just like you who still believe," he said. "People may die all the time, but nothing can ever destroy an idea. What does this contain?"

"Just read it," said the analyst. "You have to know. You must do something. You must stop this madness – the madness that is my very own creation."

"Like your Frankenstein, eh?" said the black man.

"I was forced to do it, you understand."

"Aren't we all? A common tale. But what do you get out of sharing this with me?"

"Nothing except the promise that you, comrade, will do everything in your power to stop this from actualizing. I cannot do it myself. So, I am asking you."

"Okay, then. I will take it to my people. I guess a 'thank you' is in order."

"Especially when I'm trying to stop a war before it begins," said the analyst solemnly.

"War? What kind of war?"

"Just read what's in there."

"I will. I guess I really should be thanking you."

"Don't," said the analyst. "Just pray for me."

The black man laughed and said, "but you know better than that, comrade. We don't pray."

"Trust me. Just start praying. I never believed in God either, but today I'm going to try."

"You look unwell, my friend. Are you feeling alright? How is your mental health?"

"Just read it. And now I'm going home."

He left his soda half-empty on the table and then ran into the bitter wind. He got into his car and headed home, but before reaching, he stopped by the local liquor store and picked up another bottle of cheap vodka. He hoped the cashier wouldn't already smell it on his breath. He had obviously been poisoned by it the night before. He didn't care what the cashier thought, though. He grabbed the heavy brown bag from the counter and headed home. Once there, he locked himself in his den all over again with the unusually large plastic bottle that would dull the pain of his torn conscience. He wouldn't be noticed by his wife, since she wasn't home. Yet something still remained undone.

He reviewed the plans once again. Once sent to the Deputy, he would make endless and passionate love to his wife, images that turned him on as he sat amidst all of his books, papers, pamphlets, and his map of the cruel world. He would fall into their bed, and she would cover him with her love. He envisioned himself falling soundly asleep while still deep inside of her, spent and relieved, like a boy who remains in his own mother's womb. He pictured her on top of him, but such a chimera was interrupted by that simple tick that he still left something undone with the plan he made. Indeed, he must have, because otherwise, he would have never been so doubtful about it.

He unscrewed the bottle and drank directly from it.

Within moments, he was drunk again, reviewing his papers, trying to find out what he had missed. Yes. He needed the Saudis and the Israelis to ally, but even more so, the US and Israel would permit the Saudis to crush a growing anti-Saudi rebellion in neighboring Yemen. It followed then that the Saudis would turn a blind eye to whatever tactics the Israelis used to get rid of the Palestinian irritant once and for all. Good. But there had to be something else, right?

His mind searched and then turned, and the more it turned, the more it burned, and the more it burned, the more he drank, until he spun out of control, but only for a short moment as he had been granted access to the mind of a God he had turned his back on all of his life. From God, he stole a single idea that would win America the war in the Middle East and would also stop the Russians from invading Afghanistan a second time.

See, the American public had to be completely convinced that yet another war in the Middle East was absolutely necessary to protect them. And when he thought about what had to be done to convince them, he gulped down as much vodka as he possibly could before again vomiting it up in the wastepaper basket. Tears of misery leaked from his eyes, as he remembered why the Company had hired him in the first place – to cut off the arm to save the entire body. The greatest good for the greatest number. It was America's way of culling the population, as it had been done in every great civilization preceding the founding fathers. Sacrifice the few to save the many. His tears flowed, because all of his innocence had been lost so close to his retirement. Not an ounce of it remained. There was never a way of getting around it, was there? There was no way of ever walking away with clean hands, as Pilate had wanted to do so long ago.

He clumsily inserted the final solution into his final

report, ran out of the house, down the driveway to the end of the block, and shoved the thick envelope addressed to the Deputy of Central Intelligence into the mailbox. Just as quickly, he returned to his den and locked the door. If his wife were to return, he didn't want her to see him so defeated by his own beautiful mind.

He sat in his noiseless den. He used to love it in there. It had once been his sanctuary. A man, he thought, was never meant to bear the burdens of the world this way. But that afternoon, his den turned into a dungeon for his sins, a room of whips and chains that stripped the skin off of his back. He couldn't withstand the agony of it. He opened the drawer beside him, took out the small tablet of potassium cyanide, and swallowed it whole.

Chapter Four

April 1980 - Afghanistan

The analyst's black comrade in the fast-food restaurant held the envelope in his hands and was tempted to open it right there but refrained. He would hand it in to his superior at the Russian Embassy and be done with it. Luckily, the cold winter in Washington had coated the streets with ice and snow, because he couldn't stand the summer months in the US capitol anymore. He cherished daylight but not when it brought the discomfort of heat. Sitting in the restaurant while bearing the warmth from a greenhouse effect that cast its hazy light through the windows made him perspire and itch. He also hated the food. He missed borscht with the obligatory dollop of sour cream in the middle of it. They made it especially for him at the best restaurant in Moscow, the place where Kremlin officials discussed their work, new promotions in the party's ranks, and of course, the Americans, always the Americans, all in the language of typical Soviet cynicism that refreshingly told the true tale of the capitalist foe, the condition of humanity, and how only a Marxist revolution could free the enslaved from the chains of aristocratic hegemony in the West. The pizza tasted like poison, and the Coca-Cola he sipped through his straw was watered down in typical capitalist fashion. As expected, the owners of the place had filled half the cup with ice just to save a buck. Typical, he thought.

He remembered his father suddenly and all that he had

said about his life in America before he defected in 1974. His father died just a little while ago, but he remembered his lectures well. His father wanted him to fight the Americans in Afghanistan when the Soviets prepared to invade. He was barely twenty years old back then. The news all over Moscow declared that the Americans, after paying off the Afghani people with their dirty money and inferior technology, had toppled Taraki's Communist government in Kabul. The rebels were now on the march and moved closer into Soviet territory in Central Asia. To stop them, the Red Army would have to support its own communist government by invading.

He remembered what his father had told him when they lived together in Moscow off of Red Square, the tomb of Lenin just a few blocks away and the spires of the magnificent Kremlin poking above the grey cement apartment complexes surrounding it. The Americans had to be stopped by any means necessary, he said.

His father sat in the living room on an easy chair in their compact three- bedroom apartment, while he sat at the kitchen table eating potato dumplings with sour cream and relish. His father stared into his distant memories. His mother had died a year earlier, but his father insisted on keeping her belongings preserved in the spare room. His father couldn't stand the idea of letting her things go. He loved her deeply, and his son saw how tough her death had been on him. It was difficult to live without her. As an older man, the skin on his cheeks and hands had grown smooth, delicate, and paper-thin. From his head fell heavy flakes of dandruff for which he used a strong medicated shampoo prescribed by the chemists down the block. His father was skin and bones in his older age.

Over the years, his son had grown strong, muscular, and fit from lifting weights and running hard on the gymnasium tracks to maintain the near-perfect shape of his black body.

As a student with high marks at the Soviet Union's most elite university, his life from the very start had been meant to serve the Party, as that was how his parents had raised him. After a certain time, he would be sitting on the Politburo and take his place among the most honorable servants of the Republic. But as he ate at the kitchen table, news had already spread throughout the city that the Red Army had been mobilized and was poised to fight. The obvious next step in his career involved joining that fight in Afghanistan. But he didn't want to go, just as his father never wanted to go to Vietnam on the American side when they drafted him nearly two decades earlier.

While he understood that he needed to fight to advance his political career and to please his father, who strongly insisted that he go, there was something so very wrong about fighting there, especially now that the USSR had already outdone the Americans in every facet of society since the Cold War began.

He loved living in Moscow, and as Lenin had envisioned, living in the Soviet Union was indeed heaven on earth. He had heard so many horror stories from his father about living in America that he was thankful and grateful he had been protected and looked after by the State, as everything had been taken care of. Food and shelter had always been provided, and all of the shapely white Russian women and all of the rare Russian vodka he could ever want had always been available. He had been waiting to hear where he'd be assigned for work in the government, but now that an invasion was underway, he may have had to go to war. He had been on the verge of living a carefree life filled with every pleasure he could think of until the news of Afghanistan appeared on posters, state newspapers, and in party radio broadcasts. It had to be done, they said, because those cowboys were marching closer. The fight against capitalism had always been the noble fight, as his parents had taught him since childhood.

But his son wanted the dessert without the labor it took to bake it. The last thing he wanted to do was to join the Red Army. Now that he had just finished his studies, he wanted a break. That his generation had been caught by the toe and dragged into a war that no one his age knew anything about wrecked his plans. It wasn't that he didn't want to serve or flee from serving. It was just that he wasn't the least bit enthusiastic now that his life in Moscow was going so well. He would have rather been closed off in an office or taught as a professor at the same university from where he came. He didn't want to don a uniform and fly to a place that no empire had ever conquered since Alexander the Great. Plus, he had never heard anything positive about Afghanistan to being with.

His father, however, seemed to know his son's thoughts. After washing his plate in this sink, the son was about to run out the door to hang out with his comrades until his father stopped him and called him over. Apparently, he had something important he wanted to discuss with him. With a sigh, he backed away from the door.

"What's your rush, son?" asked his father.

"Nothing, father. It's just that I have plans for the afternoon."

"Why don't we talk for a while. We never get to talk anymore. There are some things I want to show you."

"But father," he said, "I am already late."

"Oh, you can go out with your comrades anytime. I want to show you a few things. Just wait here."

His father went into the spare room where he stored his

wife's things and came back with a heavy gold jewelry box with a red star engraved on its cover. He stood in front of his son and opened it. Within its red velvet interior shined the Soviet Union's highest honor – the Silver Star – given only to those greatest of heroes who had served and contributed to the State and the values and ideals of the Revolution with the highest distinction. It glimmered and gleamed in the soft light filtering through the apartment windows. While the son knew his father had won the medal a few years after he had arrived in the Soviet Union, he had never actually seen the Silver Star before. He was astonished to behold it. It befuddled him as well, because he didn't understand why his father had waited until that very moment to show the medal to him.

"Go ahead, son. You can touch it."

He carefully dipped his fingers into the box and stroked the fine silver of the star. His father had kept it from him his entire life.

"I've always wanted to show it to you, but I wanted to wait for the right moment."

"Why is this the right moment, father?"

He closed the box and returned it to the spare room. When he came back, his father led him to the cushioned chairs in the living room where a small coffee table stood. Before sitting, however, his father led him around the room. His son dutifully followed.

"You see those pictures on the wall? That's your mother and I when we were married in Moscow shortly after she arrived here."

"Yes, she told me, father."

"She was a proud and powerful black woman who served the Party in Angola before being summoned here to serve. We were married soon after. And the next picture is me in a Red Army uniform after I left Vietnam. And next to that, Prime minister Nikita Khruschev awarding me the Soviet Union's highest honor, the Silver Star…"

"Yes, father, I already know all of this. Mother explained it to me a thousand times over. Father, what's on your mind? There's obviously something troubling you."

"Why don't you make us some tea, son," he said.

He moved over to the kitchen area, filled a kettle with water, and set it on the stove to boil.

"Come," said his father, waving to him. "Sit with me."

When the two were comfortably seated on the chairs, his father said, "I'm sure you heard the news about Afghanistan."

"How could I not have? They've been writing about it in *Pravda* for a week straight now. It's all over the radio and the television. I can't imagine what we want with Afghanistan."

"It's the Armed Resistance, my son. Taraki's forces in Kabul have been overrun by rebels backed by the Americans. We can't afford to lose any ground there. We must restore the Party's rule in Kabul. We must stop the capitalists and retake Afghanistan. They are too close to our own borders."

"Something about it doesn't sound right, though. Maybe the Afghanis just want everyone out, both us and the Americans."

"Don't be such a fool. Anyone who goes against our nation and the ideals of the Revolution is always linked to the United States. There's deceit in their ways, son. That's how capitalists have always been. Only they could have funded these rebels who toppled Taraki. The rebels would never be able to do it on their own."

"The Red Army is drafting people for the war," said his son.

"Are you surprised? The resistance against the Americans requires that kind of commitment. Believe me, I know."

"You never said much about your younger days in the US. Why not?"

"I never want you involved with such a place, that's why. When I left that place, I left it for good. I promised never to return."

"But shouldn't we be working towards peace with them? How long can we keep up this struggle against them?"

"Forever, if I had my way. It's a dirty system they have over there. It's corporate capitalism fully backed by their police and military."

"What do you mean, father? I know all about the horrors of capitalism, how the government lies to its people, and how terribly it treats them. But I've never heard anything about it from you."

"How old are you now? You should have already learned all of this."

"Not from you, father. You've never talked about it. You send me to all of these schools where I learn everything about nothing. I don't even know what my own father experienced in the West. You never talk about anything at all."

"It's in the past, that's why," he said bitterly.

"The past is in me, father. It's a part of me. It's within my flesh and blood. It's within my mind, my intellect."

"You don't need to hear about it."

"And you think I'm going to Afghanistan based on

what I've read in books, or the equations I've solved, or for the future that's been magically planned for me?"

"There is nothing magic about it," snapped his father. "You are at the start of a long line of leaders that will serve the Party with honor and distinction. The past means nothing. It never comes back. We progress. We evolve. We move on."

"Without the past, we don't know the present, and we certainly can't know the future."

"Where'd you get that garbage? Don't be smart with me!"

"I'm not trying to be!"

"And watch your tone when you're talking to me!"

His son sighed heavily and said, "I'm sorry to upset you, father, but just tell me some of what you experienced in America."

"You will know soon enough. The Party will publish my biography after I'm gone. You can read all about it then."

"I don't want to hear it from the Party! I don't want to read about it in some history book of dead heroes! I want to hear it from you, my own father. At least some of it. At least a part of it that is meant for me, not the Party, but for me, without reference to the Revolution or Lenin's genius. But from you. Because to tell you the truth, I don't want to fight in Afghanistan. It's a useless war. Just another tragedy. I can sense it, and so can everybody else."

"Shut your mouth!" he shouted. "You will fight! I am ordering you to fight! And if you don't, you will no longer be my son!"

"Then tell me, father. Convince me why I should fight those bastards, and why I should instill the history of the Revolution and the teachings of Lenin and Marx after we have defeated them, so that I can better do the People's will after you are gone. Because right now, father, I can no longer learn from those old history books, newspaper articles, and calculus equations. After a while, they make no sense. Nothing makes sense. It's a resistance for no reason unless I hear it from you, because I admire you. I want to learn from you. I want you to be my father for once."

The kettle on the stove screamed. The water had come to a full boil. He went to the kitchen and carefully poured some black tea into two porcelain cups. He brought them over to where his father sat. Both of them sipped their tea in the aftermath of their heated argument, the taste of the tea ushering in a serenity that hadn't been present prior to that.

"I've only kept it from you, because I wanted to erase it," said his father. "I want to delete it from the history of our family. But I guess the past is never too far behind. Oh, well. I am now forced to tell you some of what I experienced back there, even though it sickens me to do so."

"Then tell me. Just let it out. I'm listening."

"As a young high school student in Boston, Massachusetts," he began, "I believe it was 1968, America's greatest leader, The Reverend Martin Luther King, Jr., was assassinated on April 4th of that year."

His father's voice fell to almost a whisper. His son leaned in closer to him. The old man sipped his hot tea and stared blankly into space, witnessing his past all over again right before his very eyes.

"The whole country erupted," he continued. "The cities burned. The anger hurt us all, and it ran deep. This one man who preached peace, integration, non-violence, and universal brotherhood had been shot down in cold blood. The supposed will of God had also died that day, you see. There was black rioting in the streets – looting, arson, killings. It didn't stop for days.

"When the unrest exhausted itself, when all the smoke had cleared, a new America had been promised to the black man. I must have been eighteen years old at the time. I lived with my parents and my older brother in a neighborhood called Roxbury. It was an all-black ghetto, basically. It was another concentration camp, so to speak, where blacks had been caged, based not only on the color of their skin and African roots as colonial slaves, but also as a people who tried to compete in a ruthless white capitalist system that wouldn't allow Blacks to compete. And I'll explain it to you this way –

"When I was in high school in Boston, my parents made sure my brother and me looked our best and put our best foot forward. Due to the Civil Rights Movement, the black man reinvented himself. My education was of the utmost importance. That was the climate during Dr. King's time, you see. We dressed well. We studied hard. We worked within our churches and communities to provide for others who had little or nothing at all during those hard times. We were on the right track. When I wasn't studying, I was working after school. During the hot summers, I worked as a water boy and an assistant for an all-black work detail and construction company. Integration hadn't settled in yet, you see.

"These strong black workers in the hot summer heat laid warm brick and chipped away at hard concrete with pickaxes, their black bodies slick and sweating in the sun, laboring together like one black muscular machine. Every day I'd go to the construction site and notice how aesthetically beautiful they were. They'd drink from the buckets of water I'd fill, the water from an aluminum ladle running down their hot, overworked bodies like a waterfall, its coldness falling from their mouths and cooling them.

"But after working just a single summer there, I easily saw how exploited we all were. We'd work on structures of glory for a dollar, while the white man, who did nothing, made triple that on our labor without lifting a finger. And then we'd retreat to the ghetto busted, broken, and exhausted, sore and sleepy, not even having enough time to spend with our own families, too tired to move.

"I went back to high school after that summer, and I made sure to put the money I had earned to good use, you see. I bought a jacket and a tie, shoe polish, a hairbrush, and some talc to smell good. I looked smart, son. Really, I did. I wanted to do well in America, especially since the American black man was finally on the move. We were rising. We were promised a better future within our society. I was proud. We all were. But we were also foolish to think that our pride would last very long, because when I went back to school all dressed up, all those white students pointed their fingers at me, called me a nigger, laughed at me, some of them even beat me up. They said go back to Africa where I belonged. They did these things in front of all those pretty white girls in those fuzzy college sweaters and short skirts who laughed along with them. And if you looked at these women with any kind of attraction in your eyes, they'd call over their horde of boyfriends and make sure you got a good beating. Get into any kind of argument with a white girl, and they'd cry rape. The man would come, beat your black ass, and cart you off to jail where your poor parents would have to spend a week's pay to bail you out. That's just how it was.

"So, we black folk always had to keep our guard up, even though they let us into those white schools. Yes, we were laughed at and humiliated, bruised and beaten by males and females alike, make no mistake about it. They were both in on it. But like dutiful scholars, we sought a good future for ourselves. Even though we endured the abuse, we went back day after day and did the best we could.

"While my friends had been defeated by all of this, though, I, however, had different ideas. I saw how those white boys had it. They had the beautiful white women. Nice cars. Nice clothes. Nice houses. All built on the backs of Boston's working class, white and black. You see, even the white folk had to compete for construction contracts. We got ours as a form of charity from City Hall, but we knew we were never meant to succeed at what we did. And son, you must never forget your DuBois and what he said about charity – "almsgiving separates the classes." Never, ever take anyone's charity, son, especially from the white man, because next thing you know he and his army will Christianize you.

"But to continue, being the young, foolish man that I was back in high school, I still had the idea that I could do well in America, that I could still compete my way into a better life in a white man's world. That was what they taught us in the integrated schools. Anyone could do well in America. A black man just had to work hard, be honest, and of course, go to church every Sunday and pray to God. A black man could no longer be lazy or steal anymore for his daily bread. It was capitalism - to generate a profit from what one owned, and in order to own, one had to work hard enough to own. And I wanted the same things the white kids had, because, supposedly, they had to do all those things too in order to do well. So instead of saving up for college, I saved up for a down payment on a brand-new automobile.

"I remember looking at it every day in one of those glossy magazines in the school's library. It was a big, beautiful Ford automobile that even outdid some of those white kids' cars. Every day I worked hard after school at the construction site, saving up my money for that car to prove to myself that

I belonged in America, because I wanted to belong. I wanted to be a part of that American dream they always taught us about. Because the more one owned in America, the more one belonged. The more one owned, the more one mattered in America, you see.

"After another long summer of labor with the workers, I had enough cash for the down payment on that Ford. I donned my usual suit and tie and strolled into the bank like a prince. I was called to the loan officer's desk, and I sat right down in front of him. I told him I needed an auto loan. I told him I already had the car I wanted to buy in mind and also a sizable down payment.

"He was a good, sympathetic old man. He smiled. He was impressed, and damnit, he wanted me to own that car. A good white man that loan officer was, because really, son, and you must realize this – a few bad apples will never ruin the bunch – no matter how badly you are treated in the Western world. Over there, the people are individuals but only as a white collective. Individually, they behave. As a group, they're deplorable. But this white-haired gentleman wanted me to own that car. I filled out all the forms. I just had to wait a week for the bank to check my credit. I had no outstanding debts, because I had never taken out a loan before. I was paid off the books, so I never had a record of my income. I was just a man with a lot of cash who needed a loan for a car.

"A week had passed, and I returned to the bank all ready to get final approval for the loan. The white loan officer looked at me sadly. The bank had denied my loan, he said. He said my credit score was too low. I didn't have a credit history. I didn't have a record of my income. Actually, there was no record that I even had a job. I insisted that I had more than enough money for a down payment. I even showed him the crisp one-hundred-dollar bills that I took right out of my pocket. I just slapped those greenbacks right on his desk and sat in front of him until he admitted that, yes, I qualified for the load if he had his way. I could have easily afforded that Ford. But he just shook his head sadly. He said I needed a legitimate, well-paying job, like a job in an office, or in a factory, or some kind of union job with an income that the IRS could collect taxes on. And I had none of those.

"I collected the cash off his desk and left the bank to the mocking laughter of the white customers waiting on-line for the tellers. I ran out of there with tears in my eyes. I lost faith in capitalism right then and there. I would never be able to get one of those white jobs with the white folks. Such a system was never meant for the poor. Only for the rich. Because even though I struggled to finish up high school, before I knew it, they drafted me to fight in Vietnam against a people who would have treated me much better than any white capitalist ever would, this I can tell you.

"We were an integrated platoon in Vietnam, but we were all from poor backgrounds. Most of the men who had to do the killing and the dying in the war were the poor folk. Funny how wealthy capitalists never fight their own wars, eh? Even the best of them have had to kill others somewhere in their family's history in order to rise to the top of the heap. They had to kill others they didn't even know to make their blood money. They grew up that way – all of those games, like 'steal the bacon,' 'king of the hill,' and 'capture the flag' – all of that bullshit and all of those lies. And after their forefathers did it, they made the poor man kill for them once they got theirs, so their white debutant daughters could go to those fancy schools and marry those professional white boys from the country clubs.

"In Vietnam, I must have killed hundreds of Khmer Rhouge with my machine gun. Each kill did a tap dance on my head, son. I killed children in villages, their mothers, some of them pregnant. I gunned down fathers and grandfathers who had nothing to do with the war. I raped a few Vietnamese women. I torched whole villages and sent families wandering into the fields half-naked and starved with nowhere to go, only then to be taken prisoner by Pol Pot's men and thrown into torture and slavery. That's the kind of man I became.

"After a while, I killed without even knowing it, without even batting an eyelash, all for God and country. Killing became ingrained, you see. It was a part of me, a part of my common sense in the bush. When three-quarters of my platoon was killed off in Khe Sahn, I didn't even shed a tear for them. Neither did I want revenge, because by that time I had become such a stone-cold killer that I was unable to feel and unable to think. I had lost my humanity, son. I hardly remembered Boston or the family I had been ripped from. I just kept humping and killing, humping and killing, as I was ordered to do, just like the capitalists had trained me to do. You see, son, the wealthy had taken my humanity away to feed their own kind. Once again, they exploited the poor to protect themselves – their land, their cars, their own freedoms and liberties – while enslaving us and forcing us to kill for their own sons and daughters. Because that's what the capitalist system does, white or black. It exploits everyone and everything within range, so that one man must destroy another for a shot at the crumbs left under the rich man's table. The ghettos in America that I remember so well are merely deep pools of former slaves drowning. These black folk are selected to do the white capitalist's bidding, whether it's shining their shoes or killing innocent children in foreign lands.

"But when I went to Vietnam, I realized that the poor white man had it no easier than I did. They also were concentrated in their pools, in their own disenfranchised labor camps, always sent to work generation after generation. The problem with America, son, has never been racial in my view. The problem with America is systemic. A system in which the exploitation of the poor, the sick, and the weak is an indelible part of the fabric of everyday life over there. And that exploitation is a result of capitalism. Necessity can never be the mother of anything when it is necessary that a mother starves to death. Her children that just happen to survive capitalism's cut must rely on the basest qualities of humanity in order to feed themselves while they watch their own parents starve. They must kill and steal and cheat to advance just one more rung. Those who do it best become the leaders of the capitalist society, until everyone tries to get ahead. America is an entire nation of ruthless capitalist murderers without a shred of humanity to them. And I, being a handmaiden of the capitalist state in Khe Sahn, returned to Saigon having lost three-quarters of my platoon.

"When the US pulled out of Vietnam in 1974, instead of returning to Boston, I remained in Saigon. Over a period of a month, over a period of heavy drinking it hit me what I had done in those rice fields and villages. All I could do for a week straight was weep for the dead, weep for what I had done, not only for the lives of those who had fought with me, but for my own bloodied conscience. I wept for all of humanity, wept for how foolish we all were for ever fighting in Vietnam in the first place. I stayed in Saigon, which then became Ho Chi Minh City after the Americans evacuated. I surrendered to the Khmer Rouge Intelligence Services there. I asked them to take me to the Soviet Union. I wanted them to kill me, but instead they obliged and sent me on a transport to Moscow.

"I earned the Silver Star, because out of the ashes of

capitalism, I told everyone in the Soviet Union I had found a much better life in a communist society. I learned a better way to live from some of the most gifted minds in the Soviet Union. Sure, I struggled hard to adapt, but when I became confident, I joined the Red Army in a supervisory role and aided the KGB in keeping the Kremlin safe from anything that smelled remotely of American capitalist vermin. I could easily sniff them out – those white CIA pigs. They were so easy to spot. I was good at it, because I already knew their total lack of honor, their reptilian minds, their white arrogance, and their hubristic pedigree as idiot sons and daughters of the landholding wealthy elite in the West. For this, they awarded me the Silver Star, just like they awarded it to the famous intellectual W.E.B. DuBois who had the courage and singularity of purpose to escape capitalism's concentration camps and emerge victorious into service of the Revolution and what is stands for. Like him, I earned the Silver Star, and for that, the State that I still serve provides me with a new life, a lovely wife from Angola, and a son ready to fight against a country that only intends to put you back in chains, as they will do again if they ever win in Afghanistan.

"If we don't resist, you too will be forced to give up your humanity and kill for them, just as I had to. That's why you must go to Afghanistan. Here in Moscow we get to sleep in the apartments we build – all of us as equals. What we build belongs to us all, as a collective. No one exploits us here. We are members of the Party, equal in the eyes of the state we serve. If the Americans gain one inch of territory, they will take another yard of it. That is what their system demands. They will lie, cheat, steal, and kill to get that one inch, and do it again to an even greater degree to take that yard. That is what they are about, and that is why we must stop them by any means necessary."

'By any means necessary' had been the refrain rotating in the son's mind as he lead a platoon of five other young soldiers on a mission to the small town of Ruhki on the western side of Afghanistan just a year later. Together, this platoon flew at low altitude in a Soviet SU-25 aircraft, the hull vacant save for his troops seated on opposite sides of each other. They carried heavy parachutes on their backs, and an open cargo bay door made the inner hull unbearably loud. He couldn't even hear himself think. The aircraft shook and jostled their bones. Up front, he saw the two pilots clutch their ancient controls and communicate coordinates back and forth to base camp. They wore beige, plastic headsets.

As he scanned his troops, he could tell that the long conflict against a variety of groups vying for control of Afghanistan had made them all gravely depressed, as this was another mission out of way too many. Somehow they had made it out alive from the worst fighting any platoon the Red Army had seen. They had no idea if they'd ever make it back to Russia, and if they did, it would have been useless to return anyway. Each of them had been irrevocably altered by the conflict to live the same way again. That being known, however, the black captain had been convinced by his own father that he must fight the Americans 'by any means necessary.' He knew his mission perfectly. He made sure his strung-out platoon knew the mission perfectly as well. Any deviation could have easily resulted in, not only their own deaths, but the deaths of other Soviet troops in nearby battles.

The platoon had been sent to repair a broken pipeline that the Afghan rebels had blown up and lighted on fire using Pakistani-made explosives near the town they now flew towards. They were to parachute into Ruhki, eliminate anyone living there, repair the breach that had been gushing the precious Soviet oil all over the surrounding countryside, and get out by helicopter alive if they were so lucky.

While the mission seemed fairly straightforward to the captain, in no way would it be easy. The *mujahideen* had their wily ways, as they had perfected the art of the surprise ambush. And while the captain knew that his side was losing the war, he still had to keep his troops in line and motivate them just enough to complete the mission without getting themselves blown to bits.

He also felt the same unrelenting depression they felt –the war-weariness that came with the inability to remember their former lives in Moscow. It had been a running joke in his platoon that the whole of the Red Army might as well have stayed in Afghanistan for the rest of their lives. They were dying by a thousand cuts. The Soviet Union was now a foreign land with a foreign people who knew nothing of what they had been doing or how they had gradually morphed into crazed, sick, and drug-addicted former versions of themselves who would scarcely be able to find their way out of their own minds let alone Afghanistan itself. Grand memories of home had been replaced by the need to smoke hashish, mainline heroin, and maintain the delusion that they may indeed make it back safely to Kabul without getting their legs blown off by the countless landmines scattered all over the roads and within the maze of trails that cut through the craggy mountains. As they prepared for yet another landing below, they each knew how useless it was to find any kind of pride in the disaster of Afghanistan. They simply laughed at their own jokes, smoked blocks of black Afghan hash, injected whatever heroin they could, and forced down as many dirty glasses of the common man's vodka to gain any semblance of relief. The only thing they looked forward to came at the end of each day, after they had crossed the flat rice fields, hiked the red roads strewn with rubble and large rocks that twisted and sprained their ankles, and endured the plumes of orange dust that blinded their eyes in the haze of hot sun that beat upon their backs. At the end of each march, the night promised a couple hours of restless sleep with one eye open, nervously waiting for the next rebel ambush.

As the landscape below rolled along like a diseased picture show, the platoon had been content to sit in their seats lazily as the aircraft descended upon a red dirt road in the middle of nowhere. The village of Ruhki, according to his estimation, was a couple hours west of where they would parachute in. When they jumped, each of them had been poised and ready to kill off an entire village, which included its mothers and children, just like they had done countless times before. They then hoped to return to Kabul as a reward for a job well done.

That evening, they only looked forward to nighttime in Ruhki, where they would decamp, sleep for a little while, and dream vaguely of the pleasures of their former lives. Sharp boulders would serve as their pillows. Red dust would cover them. Occasional scorpions would bite their naked flesh beneath their Soviet-issue uniforms, and rattlesnakes would surreptitiously slide into their sleeping bags after they drifted off to sleep.

But they already looked too far ahead of themselves for their own good. Just then, the green light flashed, and an annoying, buzzer jarred them out of their daydreaming. They filed along the hull of the aircraft towards the open cargo door, the hot breeze slapping their burnt cheeks and chapped lips. One by one they leapt from the plane into the vacuum of a fiery sky with their parachutes tucked into their backpacks. They plummeted towards the scorched earth like they had done hundreds of times before. Halfway between heaven and earth, they released their parachutes, the air sucking up their bodies. They drifted to the rubble below like teardrops falling from the eyes of the sun.

Once all of them were down, they gathered their parachutes and collected the equipment that floated down with them. They then gathered together on the barren plain to unpack and distribute their equipment. Each soldier carried a Kalishnikov rifle and an AGS-17 grenade launcher. They filled their backpacks to the hilt with food rations, clothes, Yaras, which were cartons of Soviet-brand cigarettes, and other items they needed on their long march into Ruhki. They had little idea what waited for them there. They could only imagine it.

They couldn't begin the march without their sapper in the lead. The sapper carried a metal detector that scanned the ferocious terrain for hidden landmines. These metal explosives were as commonplace as ammunition. They were scattered everywhere beneath the earth. The sapper led the pack into the blank foray of what may have very well been their last mission before the landmines ravaged their lower bodies off. The sapper, a short but muscular red-faced Russian from Ukraine, checked his equipment to make sure it functioned properly. A Yara cigarette hung from his lips, its smoke billowing into their air without obstructing his vision or stinging his eyes. He tested the monitor and the headset on the detector. Ironically, the sapper was treated as though he were a lowly janitor when the opposite was actually true. His perspicuity and conscientiousness were arguably the most important virtues the platoon had going for it.

"I hate this piece of shit," said the sapper, sweeping the immediate area in front of him. "This thing's gonna blow our dicks off. No one's used its since Stalin."

The black captain put his helmet on, a shadow of a beard growing on his face, and approached the sapper from behind.

"Does it work?" he asked.

"Yes, captain," said the sapper. "It just takes a little time to warm up, this piece of shit. It'll be ready in a few minutes. I'll have to test it a few times."

"There's no rush," said the captain while scanning the snow-capped mountains beyond the flat plains. "We have plenty of time."

"What else is there in this shithole but plenty of time," he laughed. "They gave us an outdated sweeper, captain."

"Keep working on it."

The other soldiers all sucked on their Yaras several feet behind them. Their eyes were fixed to the snow-capped mountains, its rocks as sharp as razors. One trip or fall upon the edge of one of the rocks could give a soldier a wound so wide that it would take at least a couple of hours for a medic to stitch it up. Even the rocks strewn about their feet posed a threat. They couldn't exactly walk on them or step on them. They meandered through them, making sure not to land directly on any of them. Without a helicopter there was no way back to Kabul. Only if the mission ended successfully would they be found by base camp and flown back from Ruhki.

They stood alone under a sun that soon weakened above them. Each of them remained forever vigilant for a rebel ambush or that one landmine that would send a soldier back to Moscow or St. Petersburg in a body bag. The black captain ordered them to check their equipment, load their grenade launchers, and ready their rifles. With helmets on and their bodies already drenched in sweat, they moved out along a plain that soon led to a flat dirt road over which the ever-present film of red dust strangled the brightness from the sky.

For a while, these young soldiers remained silent, acclimating to yet another dangerous mission. All of them, except the captain at the front of the platoon, chain-smoked. Cigarettes were a fixture of the war they could not do without. They became extensions of their hands, a necessity, like their tattered boots, their toothbrushes and water purification tablets.

"Don't all talk at once," said Soldier #1. "This place isn't as awe-inspiring as it looks."

"Especially if we're going to be buried here," said Soldier #2.

"We'll use these rocks for gravestones," said Soldier #3.

"While the ghosts piss on them and laugh their toothless asses off at how stupid we Russians are for ever coming into Afghanistan," said Soldier #4.

"Yep, exactly," said Soldier #5. "But first they'll cut our heads off and make us convert to Islam."

"I can't wait to get out of this hellhole," said Soldier #2.

"There's no such thing as Hell in the Soviet Union, remember?" said Soldier #4. "Unless you've been to Afghanistan, of course. There's no leaving this gulag once you've been sentenced here."

"You've got that right," said Soldier #5.

"Is that all you do? Agree with everybody all the time?" asked Soldier #1.

"No," replied Soldier #5. "I love it here. That's why I always agree with all of you. I aim to please."

They all laughed, until the black captain whispered hotly, "keep it down," as he continued scanning the mountains. "Your voices are carrying all over the place."

"Sorry, captain," said Soldier #1. "There's no use talking anyway, since we're already dead."

The captain could not deny the veracity of this statement.

"Just shut up," ordered the black captain.

But the soldier was right. They were already dead. They died a long time ago. They had become like the rebels themselves – ghosts traveling along a barren road with a deafening silence all around them, together yet totally alone, a fierce wind swooping into their eyes, nostrils, and mouths, the heads of their cigarettes decapitating every few minutes and the curses under their collective breaths muted while fishing out lighters from their shirt pockets and smoking yet another one.

The captain understood that they both existed and didn't exist. They had to follow base command blindly without knowing the effect it had on the war. He was told what to do, and he carried out his orders without even questioning them. He had been instructed to handle the entire war that way. All he could do now was speculate, and given what little information had had been given about the sheer number of Soviet deaths and casualties and also from the antagonistic landscape he had never quite gotten used to, he knew the Red Army had already been defeated. And yet he still marched, because that's what they ordered him to do. That was his function. He knew nothing more and had been told nothing less. He carried only old images of Moscow – those vodka-infused nights with Soviet women on each arm kissing and tonguing his lips and dancing at the local discotheques way into the early morning. Then, suddenly, as he walked upon jagged rocks, the poem he had once read while at the university came to mind. *A Dream Deferred.*

And if the captain's dream was to return to Moscow and visit his old comrades from the university, all of them having returned from the war alive, friends whom he remembered well, all of them once sitting at a large roundtable in a candle-lit restaurant overlooking Red Square, a place with heavy dining utensils made of pure silver and thick cotton tablecloths and napkins, a sophisticated waitstaff catering to their every need, where everyone wore their finest suits and dresses and munched on stone-wheat crackers and Beluga caviar on gold-rimmed plates, sipping French champaign as they had done during the ages of the Russian Czars, but only this time with the understanding that the essential value of their labor for and allegiance to the Revolution amounted to these luxuries that only the Soviet state could bestow upon its most important heroes, and if suddenly this dream had been deferred, only to be replaced by thin, narrow canyons and rocky sides of coal-black mountains, deep red ravines and steep, tiring slopes, snow-laden uphill trails with subzero winds whipping against their bodies, keeping them confined, incarcerated almost, while picking up bloody body parts from the frozen roads, carting off their fallen comrades riddled with bullets into helicopters, pushing those who were lucky enough to live in locked-down wards in Kabul as they wandered around in circles and laughed to themselves without anyone hearing them, then what happens to that person once his dreams had been deferred?

For the captain, the reality that unveiled itself had been the only reality he had ever known, his men covered with festering sores, their bodies dirty, wrinkled and desiccating in the hot sunlight, sagging under the weight of their heavy and bloated backpacks, the odors of their bodies as pungent and raw as rotting meat, as they marched along yet another empty road that had already maimed their souls. They had moved beyond death and into another dimension that demanded brute survival and the brutal killing of anyone in their path. Because that was all they had become. They weren't human beings any longer but the single-minded function of the death and destruction of others, and ultimately, the killing of their own selves, only that they had become oblivious to this danger, as they began their trudging through the canyons and rice fields like zombies, poisoning farmland, livestock, and water wells, while imagining the Afghan kids hungrily feeding on their poisons before bedtime, their mothers telling them ancient stories of their forefathers before Allah returned them to their heroic ancestors up in heaven.

The poisoning of the water wells was the easy part. The difficulty came when they came upon the rice fields. With the water wells, they simply had to pour pouches of cyanide into them and wait for the powder to dissolve and spread into the fresh, cool waters that melted off the virgin peaks. This killed many more people than gun battle alone, or so the Red Army thought, as the Soviet strategy had been modeled on Mao Tse Tung's strategy to "kill the fish by draining off the water." It was similar to salting soil, rendering the rebel fields useless and thereby starving an entire population. Better to destroy the water supply, the food, the cattle, and any and all vegetation, but when it came down to burning the rice fields, they always had to be careful. As night slowly descended upon them, they knew that any size fire could attract the ghosts who were watching their every move just waiting to ambush them. No matter how much the platoon was a muddy and tattered guerilla force, they looked like they had been tied to the back of a Jeep and dragged through the rubble on the plain.

The condition of their bodies also matched their minds. After one soldier lit the blow torch and commenced burning one of the large rice fields beside the road they were on, he pulled out a brass pipe and pressed a thick chunk of black hash into its bowl. He lit it up and inhaled deeply.

"It's beautiful, isn't it?" he said to the black captain who ordered him to burn the field and then stood beside him to watch.

"Keep focused on the job, comrade," he said quietly.

"Yessir, but you have to admit, it is beautiful. It's like a painting I once saw by an artist in Stalingrad. The flares are like wildflowers coming out of the ground."

"Just keep torching the field until everything is burnt, comrade."

"Yessir."

The captain then found the other troops smoking the *kaif* and cigarettes. At every field they burned it was also an opportunity for them to take a break. And even though the sky had darkened and the clouds had blackened above them, they still could not resist the opportunity to soothe their short-circuited nerves.

One of the soldiers from behind pulled out a picture from his pocket. He shared it with the others.

"My girl from Crimea," he said with a toothy smile.

The soldiers fought for the picture, as though they desperately needed to see this woman, as though she were the only living feminine creature left on the planet.

Soldier #4 lunged for it first, but the soldier with the picture pulled it away.

"I need it for tonight," said Soldier #4.

"We have to share it," said Soldier #1.

"She's what we're all fighting for anyway, right?"

"Right," said Soldier #5, who always agreed.

"Shut the hell up," said Soldier #1, and then to the picture-holder, "give it to me. My world for a blonde, blue-eyed slut from the Crimea."

"Here," said Soldier #3. "You need something to calm you down," passing over his pipe of hashish, which Soldier #4 lighted and took a long, deep, and slow inhalation. He coughed up warm smoke from the pit of his burnt lungs.

Soldier #4 soon stopped laughing and stood in his boots, frozen, staring into the burning rice field, entranced by its array of flame, as though he returned to the comforts of home just then.

The rest of the soldiers looked at him and laughed. But this laughter was short-lived, as they saw the black captain, as dull and as sober as the road they trodded on, march towards them angrily.

"If you idiots don't shut the fuck up," he barked, "I'll hang every one of you, you got that?!"

"Sorry, captain," they all seemed to say at once.

"You guys want to fuck around, you can do it at Lubyanka back home."

"But captain," said Soldier #4, "I'm sorry for bringing it up, but it's beautiful, is it not? Can't you see it, captain?"

The captain understood that the *kaif* talked through them. In a sense, the poisoning of the wells and the burning of the rice fields were indeed beautiful, but only to them. To him, it represented all that he hated, as though hatred, purported to be such a dirty word and that actually meant hatred of the self and the killing of others, had now been manifested in everything he saw, and he hated what his platoon now found beautiful. But still, he cared for his men, and he had a job to do. And so, like a good man, as a man of respect, a man of duty and honor and courage, he had to fulfill his mission, because that was his job, and he was a man defined by what he did and never by what he thought. Therefore, in order to be the man he wanted to be, he had to act and not think. Whether or not he hated the beauty of the burning rice field did not matter. It was, in a sense, irrelevant. And whether or not his men found the now-burning rice field beautiful or not did not matter either. The mission mattered. The job mattered. The end-all of being the man to whom he ultimately aspired became his only and penultimate goal.

"Yes," said the black captain quietly. "You are right. It is beautiful, comrades."

"Captain! You're finally coming around. You agree with us for once. Really?"

"Yes, comrades, I do," he said. "And do you know what else I find beautiful? When our sapper discovers a landmine. There is beauty in that. I agree wholeheartedly. When we poison the wells with the drive of our labors, there is beauty in that too. Comrades, it's beautiful the way you hold your rifles, the way your hard fingers pull the trigger, your stances when you fire them and kill these ghosts. There is beauty and music in our mission, like our own Shostakovich. Like being at a Bolshoi performance in Moscow. Yes, there is beauty in hearing their cries and their pains and then witnessing their blood flow from the holes in their skulls, while their bloody madness spills into the hot dust and nourishes their soil. Because what we are doing here is giving life. We are giving these people life, not death. We are liberating them from the capitalist pigs they are being killed by. We are liberating them from who they are at this point in time."

"Yes, captain," said Soldier #4. "I see it now. I see exactly what you mean."

The troops surrounding him hung on to his every word. They all huddled together and watched the rice field burn, the fire entrancing them all. And when the captain ordered them to move out, they all hurrahed under a heavy sky above them and were finally motivated and excited to find beauty in all things and their own past actions, the actions that began to release the hatred within the captain's own self until he hated himself completely enough to kill more rebels again.

They finally finished their *kaif* and *Yaras* and moved along the road, feeling calm now and ready to focus on the mission. They saw up ahead a round woman riding a tired Missouri mule. This mule had a bundle of cloth on its back, and this woman, no matter what she looked like, was as beautiful as the place they were in. She wore a cotton shawl that had been dyed soft red. She was plump but young. She tried to turn around, but the troops advanced upon her immediately. They surrounded her and the mule and looked her over with smiles on their faces.

Soldier #5 was the first to say something to her, but she just nodded her head and didn't understand what he said. The black captain had busied himself scanning the horizon after having passed ahead of the woman on the mule. She headed in the opposite direction, probably towards a *kishlak* near Kandahar. Perhaps she had her family there and transported goods from one province to another.

"Search her," said the captain, still scanning the horizon, as though he had eyes in the back of his head.

"Yes, captain," said Soldier #5. And then to the woman, "get off of there."

"I'm just passing through, comrades," she said. I'm

headed southwest."

"Well, you're a long way from home for a woman so alone out here. Get down off that mule, before I pull you off."

The woman did what Soldier #5 commanded. After she stood beside her mule on the road, Soldier #5 pulled off the cloth bundle from the mule's back and searched it.

"These clothes are pathetic," he said.

He searched underneath the mule's belly to find another cloth bundle, but it did not contain clothes. It contained something much different.

"Get away from that mule," commanded Soldier #5 of the woman.

His fellow soldiers gathered around the mule and carefully watched as Soldier #5 untied the bundle from the mule's belly. He untied the twine after throwing the bag onto the road for all of the men to see. In the bag he found two bolt-action British Enfield rifles. The other soldiers smiled. Soldier #3 shared the news with the captain who kept watch up ahead.

"Look at what we found, captain!"

The black captain, now jarred from concentration, returned to his platoon who again seemed to smile all at once.

"Strip her down," ordered the captain.

"With pleasure, sir," said Soldier #3.

Soldier #1 held her, and Soldier #2 covered her mouth so she couldn't scream. They threw her to the ground, ripped off her shawl, pulled off her shoes, and then ripped her dress off down the middle. She lay on the ground squirming under the weight of Soldier #4. Soldier #2 tightened his grip over her mouth. Soldier #3 ripped off her dress fully and searched it.

"Captain, she has nothing on her."

"Good," said the captain. "You know what to do."

"Yes, captain."

The soldiers, delighted by her naked, tan flesh, smiled and chuckled quietly as they held her down, her mouth covered, their hands feeling up her tender and soft breasts, her round, warm belly, and her hairy legs. It was then that Soldier #2 spread her legs wide apart, pulled down his pants, and entered her as she squirmed beneath his weight and tried to scream. But even though she tried, these screams only existed in her own head, as each soldier took their turn. Once they were finished and relieved, Soldier #1 took out his pistol from his holster.

"But what about the child," protested Soldier #5, referring to a possible future pregnancy.

"Shut up!" said Soldier #4. "The kid will be an outcast in his own land. We're saving the kid, you idiot!"

Soldier #1 aimed his pistol at her head and pulled the trigger.

"Now dump her," said the captain, returning to his point up ahead, the mountains a mysterious sight to behold, as he wondered when the next ghostly ambush would come.

In their relief and with newfound willingness, the troops put on their clothes again and swung her naked corpse to the side of the red dusty road. They collected their heavy backpacks and resumed their march towards Ruhki. They had captured the two Enfield rifles just as they had been ordered to do on previous missions. The spoils of the kill were now Soviet state property.

They had dreamed of women, and so suddenly they were relieved of the burden of that dream. Even though her body cooled on the side of the road, they still wanted more of her. They still had enough strength and relief to keep going for a few more hours before nightfall. They lit up *Yaras* again while trudging up a slope into the mountains. They were exhausted but also at such peace that they didn't feel fatigued. Once they approached a crooked pass that cut through the peaks, they were on guard again, afraid again, able again to accomplish their mission. Only the mission mattered, remembered the black captain, and not anything else.

The crooked pass dipped until they were in a canyon surrounded by mountainsides. A hard, heavy rain began pelting them. They donned their grey ponchos. The captain understood that he did his duty, as he had resurrected and rebirthed his men as he had always done.

The same red dust typical of the plains was also typical of the crooked path they marched on. The trick involved maneuvering around the sharp rocks and boulders on the trail while scanning the mountainsides at the same time. They could have easily been the target of gunfire from rebel enclaves above them. These enclaves were carved into the mountain's rugged walls. A spray of bullets from American-made 76mm mountain guns, AK-47's, and AK-74 rifles could have easily torn through their state-issued bullet-proof vests. They also had to be deadly quiet.

They spoke in whispers, as their voices within the canyon could have carried from one side of its narrowness to the other, thereby alerting the rebels to their whereabouts. As the rain continued to soak their bodies, they waded in ankle-deep red mud while being careful not to trip or twist their ankles on rocks that jabbed into the soles of their feet like serrated knives. Without looking where he walked, however, Soldier #2 stepped on one of these rocks at a wrong angle. He let out a loud yelp. He twisted his ankle, fell to the ground, and banged his knee on another rock on his way down into the wet mud.

Soldier #3 immediately rushed to him and muffled his mouth as he writhed in pain. He clutched his ankle with one hand and his cut-up knee with the other.

"Shut the fuck up," whispered Soldier #3 hotly into his ear. "There are ghosts everywhere."

Soldier #2 could only grunt into his wet palm. The rest of the platoon waited on them as a matter of course. Soldier #5 took out some medical supplies – bandages and surgical tape – and wrapped and bound his ankle and patched up his bleeding knee. Soldier #2, his body stuck in red mud, remained there until the immediate pain subsided. The wet of the rain bled through his uniform, and soon he grew cold and deadly afraid of catching fever, should his immune system buckle at just the wrong time.

The captain stood at the front of the pack, aiming his rifle at the recessed enclaves that could have easily been filled with silent ghosts waiting to ambush them. He figured the other men would tend to the injured Soldier #2, who finally lifted himself out of the red muck and hobbled his way in line with the others. Because he yelped every few feet, the platoon thought it best to seal off his mouth with surgical tape, lest he alert the ghosts. It may have seemed cruel to tape Soldier #2's mouth shut like that, considering how much he suffered, but each of them knew full well that human kindness in war, in and of itself, was an inherent evil that must be overcome for the greater good of their very survival. This survival depended on luck as well, they figured, as they each carried their Russian superstitions with them. They even had to be careful to quiet the sound of their boots as they sucked up mud like suction cups. Soldier #2, twisted ankle and all, collapsed on the muddy ground a few times just to relieve himself of the intense pain that came with marching.

After a time, the other soldiers left him behind, wanting to escape the misery of the canyon as soon as they could, lest the rebels fire upon them from above. But just as they thought they had acclimated to the heavy rains and thick mud, a fierce cold wind blew through the canyon. The winds brought an equally fierce cold. The canyon soon sounded like a pipe organ, its noise bouncing against the mountain walls and filling their ears with melodies of futility, as though they would never get through the canyon without more injury.

To their relief, however, they saw a slight opening a mile ahead of them. Soldier #2 struggled to keep up, but not even the black captain cared very much about the straggler. Better to leave him behind as an offering for the ghosts than risk the lives of the others in the platoon. Better not to risk the mission than to drag along this one careless soldier along.

The captain based his own ability to survive on luck also, as though he had been born from the loins of ethnic Russians who had believed in the paranormal and held superstitious tendencies all of their lives, even though his parents were foreign born. Because when the platoon exited on the other side of the canyon and trudged in the muck of yet another crooked pass that ascended into flat, browning plains, he saw a flush of Eucalyptus trees in the shadowy distance as well as a break in the sky above, a future space under which they would all soon drop their gear and rest their weary bones. The pipe organ that blew through the canyon softened its melody and volume. The wind died down and the torrential rains, its water sharp, returned to its natural calm.

Nevertheless, with their boots and calves caked in wet mud and their uniforms soaking wet despite the protection of their flimsy ponchos, Soldier #2 wandered out of the canyon and finally marched to where the ground was more level and the mud much thinner. The others even had the unimaginable wherewithal to wait for the injured straggler, not due to any feeling or soldierly comradery, but simply because they were so tired that they all had to stop. The captain felt for his troops even though he knew he shouldn't, as though any feeling for them were akin to a terrible curse that would ultimately lead the Soviet army to lose the war. But they waited for Soldier #2, who approached them with blood leaking through his bandages and a loosened boot that let his swollen ankle breathe.

He came to them out of breath and limping. The captain had the brilliantly strategic thought of killing him right then and there to lighten the load. The last thing they needed was excess baggage. As he looked around at the faces of the exhausted men, the captain knew his troops thought the same, and they would have easily shot Solider #2, had he ordered them to.

"Next time, be more careful," he said to Soldier #2. "And that goes for the rest of you," he barked. "Watch where the hell you're walking. Anyone who gets injured from here on in, we're leaving you behind for the snakes and the scorpions to eat, you got that?"

"Yessir," they all said weakly.

The captain didn't allow them to rest for too long, though, even though all of them wanted to have another go at their hash pipes. Instead, he ordered them to collect their muddy gear and march away from the canyon, the sapper returning to his lead position canvassing the ground that eventually led to a level road several miles ahead of them. Gradually, the rains stopped, and once they arrived on a level plain, the air turned as dry as before, and the plains on either side of the road were still as infertile as a virgin twisting in the hot, nomadic breeze.

The skies had darkened considerably, the clouds had parted and opened a universe filled with bright, twinkling stars. The captain ordered them to keep marching, but they were grateful enough to dry off in the hot air, the mud on their lower bodies stiffening their clothes. Like clay breaking off of them, chunks of mud fell from their uniforms. They were happy to be alive, but they knew full well not to show it. The captain wanted to make it to Ruhki soon. He kept them moving, and fortunately for them, they didn't have any duties to perform, like burning more rice fields, poisoning more water wells, or killing off more livestock.

They approached the outskirts of Ruhki and marched alongside several wild Arabian horses that danced along the plains like children released for recess. If they could, the soldiers would ride these horses bareback and desert their beloved army through Eurasia and blend in with the Muslims there who were were rumored to shield Soviet deserters. But the troops craved heroin more than riding these wild horses out of the war. The black captain made sure to keep them moving, always moving, chasing the Dragon, so to speak, rather than contemplating desertion. The horses, however, were a good sign. It meant they were close to Ruhki. But it also meant more *dushmen* lurked about. They still had to keep quiet. They only heard their collective breathing and panting, sweat dripping from their brows, until, suddenly, the temperature nosedived. Dusk faded into night along the road.

As the hot breeze turned cold, as was typical with the climate, they marched even faster just to keep from shivering, their hot breath filling the immediate area with puffs of warm vapor from their blackened lungs. They were relieved when they came upon a small cluster of hovels spread out in all directions. These hovels had been dug from the ground up. They were primitive but sturdy.

The captain ordered the troops to search each dwelling carefully. They turned out to be empty but contained abandoned cushions, blankets, and dented cooking utensils. When they walked further into the village, the soldiers encountered many more of these abandoned dwellings, but the entire *kishlak* was deadly quiet. It had been deserted, or a local warlord had relocated the people living there. The only living things that roamed the area were several abandoned dogs and a few ugly jackals that Soldier #4 chased away with the butt end of his rifle.

"Very well," said the captain. "The pipeline is about a mile up the road, beyond the *kishlak*. We'll camp here for the night, but remember to keep your voices low and your guard up. We'll rest here and move out again at dawn."

"Finally," clapped Soldier #1, dropping his rifle and heaving his heavy backpack to the ground. "We made it through all that shit."

"What a shitty country," agreed Soldier #3. "How can anyone ever live here?"

"This place is not even fit for a corpse," said Soldier #1, pulling out a fresh pack of Yaras and lighting up. And then to Soldier #2 who limped up to the group, he yelled "and you, you idiot, go build the fire. You could have killed us back there."

"But I didn't, now did I?" said Soldier #2 wisely.

Soldier #1 moved in on him, but the other soldiers restrained him.

"Let it go," said Soldier #3. "We're all tired and hungry. We have until dawn, so let's use it."

The platoon set up camp hastily. They did not care about how the camp looked or whether it met the codes outlined by the Red Army. The captain had his own tent apart from the rest. Soldier #3 built the captain's fire for him and boiled water for his tea. The rest of the platoon gathered around the fire Soldier #2 had painstakingly worked on. They arranged their tents around the fire accordingly. Within the abandoned village, they made their own smaller version of a free Soviet state among the dwellings of those who had been fighting them with 19th Century muskets and American-made AK-47s.

"This country of fuckhead terrorists can take over the whole of the Soviet Union if they wanted to," said Soldier #1.

"The Afghans couldn't give a shit about the Soviet Union," said Soldier #3. "All they care about bread and fucking, just like any normal person on earth. No wonder we're getting our heads handed to us."

"Hey, we taught these fuckers how to fight," said Soldier #5.

They spread large tarps on the ground to guard against the cold wet mud. While the plains were as dry as bone, the *kishlak* told another story. Luckily, they had enough of a water supply to fill their helmets and wash their gnarled hands, blistered feet, and scarred faces. Once this was done, they broke out state-issued tins of lamb's meat and rice, the staple food of Afghanistan and the only food the Red Army issued. And even though they ate from these tins whenever they were on missions such as these, they never grew tired of them. The *dushmen* relied on *biryani*, and so did the platoon, as though they had connected with the very same people who wanted to be rid of them.

"Gangur would have been proud," said Soldier #1, lapping at his food.

The longer the Red Army remained in Afghanistan, the harder it became to differentiate between who was Russian and who was an Afghan fighter. Their uniforms were different, but their mindsets had melded to the fierce landscape. The Soviet-made lamb's meat would never measure up to or be as succulent as the Afghan's native *biryani*. But to the troops, the meal was the best they had ever tasted, even though they had yet to encounter any fighting so far on this mission. They didn't have time for breakfast or lunch that day, and so they lapped at several miniature meals until their bellies were full. The black captain in his separate area of the utopian camp ate in silence, studying the map of the road that would lead them to the broken pipeline. Repairing the pipeline would be infinitely harder than getting there. The journey there, he decided, was the easy part.

He soon walked over to the others who had by now finished their meals. He ordered Soldier #3 and Soldier #4 on point. They would have to remain awake through the night in case any rebels showed up to the party. In other words, the troops could celebrate their arrival at Ruhki, just not so enthusiastically. They could sleep until dawn and get in a few hours except the ones on point. They would all leave together in the late morning.

The injured Soldier #2, the bastard of the bunch, tended to the camp. He would clean the camp in the morning and make sure they left without a trace. It was a job well-suited for a compromised soldier, as his untouchable status, apparently, was well-deserved.

The captain also kept watch but in his own particular way. While he understood the need for his platoon to rest, he certainly didn't trust the two soldiers on point to sit and stare into the blank darkness without taking a break themselves. The captain had to be especially careful, as the two soldiers were ordered to keep their wandering eyes peeled on any traces of *dushmen* ghosts. The captain had the double duty of keeping watch for *dushmen* as well as those on point.

The members of the camp soon broke open their bottles of cheap vodka, soupy caviar, and, of course, their hash pipes. The captain permitted them to behave like human beings, because at this point, they weren't human beings anymore. Far from it, in fact. Their revelry would keep them going, keep them smiling, keep them joking just long enough to seal the pipeline and kill whoever stood in their path. And as the fire raged and the smokeclouds of premium *kaif* billowed up around them, the captain sipped his hot tea and poked at the lamb's meat in its tin tray, courtesy of the state apparatus.

It wasn't long until the remaining soldiers danced around the raging fire, drunk on state-issued vodka and stoned on native Afghan hashish.

"We're heroes," laughed one of them, dancing.

"Only the bureaucrats are heroes," laughed another. "Only the idiots get the medals."

And then one of them confiscated the picture of the Crimean blonde. Even the captain could feel her penetrating blue eyes from where he sat, as he observed the derelictions of his soldiers. They rolled in the cold, wet mud, fighting over the photograph and laughing like disturbed children.

"Hey, the KGB is making money on her. Give her back to me!"

"The KGB is making a lot of money on this war," said another. "It's what they do in war."

The captain permitted it. They had to seal the pipeline.

The soldiers agreed that they should take turns with the picture. But Soldier #5 muscled his way into the lead. He was strong, tall, and well-built for the machinery of war. He wrestled the photo away from the others and retreated with it behind one of the abandoned dwellings several yards away. The others understood the importance of making love to this woman, the only love a place like Afghanistan afforded. The others smoked more of their *kaif* and drank more of the cheap vodka while waiting for their turn.

Behind the dwelling in the soft darkness, Solider #5 looked into her blue eyes, caressed her soft, buttery skin, pulled off her bikini top, and thumbed the tips of her firm breasts while gazing into the soul of her eyes, discovering the vulnerable child within her always running into the arms of other men while avoiding him just because she could, because he was the only real love she could be with. They were worlds apart now, she and Soldier #5, and maybe once in a while he was granted the momentary release of seeing her in such a photograph, and maybe she would want him in the same way, even though the chances of his ever finding her alone like this were slim to none. The world powers had forbidden such a romance.

But on that night, he wasn't such a lost cause, and she wasn't so distant. He spoke to her without words, without language, as she walked through his life with her soul visible through her blue eyes, her guard finally down, his hands moving along her smooth back, dancing with her in some ridiculous club at the edge of oblivion, the two of them moving together in uncanny harmony suggesting the eternal absence of other men – just the two of them alone in the darkness, this mismatched couple – one a gruesome and fierce product of pain and the other a sophisticated deity of disturbing beauty who could never be caged and could never speak to him, wouldn't say anything, just hang on to him, only to vanish in the next instant and flutter away as a free bird into the arms of another soldier and then another and then another.

After relieving himself with a flash of heavenly bliss and delight, she fluttered away again, ready to capture the next man and never allowing her heart to be possessed in return. The war had made it so. The State had made it so. Old men in suits had made it so. Lubyanka had made it so. Afghanistan had made it so. She was a curse to all men who ever had the privilege of beholding her, even within the folds of a dog-eared photograph that had been so manhandled and overused that it had become hard to discern the woman from the moist and flimsy wad of photography paper crushed in his palm.

When he returned to the camp, he held back tears, because he missed her already. He couldn't stanch the blood from the wound in his heart. He handed the photograph over to her next insignificant client. He collapsed into the mud and filled the hole she had left in him with the swift gulps from a vodka bottle they had been passing around the fire. He pulled out a small cellophane bag, pinched the brown pasty powder between his thumb and forefinger, and snorted it up his nostrils.

Within moments it transported him far away, so far, in fact, that his muscled, ever-ready body slumped deeper into the mud. The pain that had built up over several years of dangerous missions had soon drained from his exhausted body, his nerves numbed, his limbs enclosed within a protective cocoon of love and bliss, as though there really was a heaven and that heaven was Afghanistan. Such a concept was not to be believed by any soldier whose job it was to kill, poison, torture, and maim. But on this night, he found such a place, a bliss so profound that it put him into the most restful sleep he had since his last mission.

Each soldier had the same stab at this same oblivion. The captain could only look upon this scene from his tent several yards away, sip more of his tea, and plan to kick them to life the very next morning, even if he had to shoot them to wake them.

Fairly soon, the other four soldiers around the fire were laid out in the same manner as Soldier #5. As an early dawn casually shifted into its usual place and blotted out the night's prior revelry, only the captain had stayed awake the whole night through. He kept watch on his platoon and the entire camp. The fire had died down to hot embers. His only source of energy, cup after cup of piping hot tea that he had been drinking every half-hour, kept him alert. His training didn't allow him to sleep. Staying awake all night had never presented a problem for him. The Red Army tortured him well enough during his days at the military that they made sure he never rested peacefully again.

For the black captain, the pinkish sun emerging over the black mountains was a welcoming sign. The new day meant the surety of routine. The machinery of war had its own comforts for those who willingly complied. But as he filled his tin cup with yet another round of black Russian tea, he heard something twitch behind the dwellings they had passed earlier that evening. His hands froze, and his ears perked to investigate the anomaly. He was a startled rabbit who knew intuitively that an early morning ambush had come knocking on the sanctity of their camp's door at a time when they were least prepared for it. He would have cursed and berated himself had he the time, but again, a man of thought and reflection had little place in an irrational universe. He relied on pure instinct, as though all those years at the university were ridiculous nonsense, just scribblings of madmen on rotted chalkboards. The classy women of Moscow with their hijacked Western garb were merely illusions that belonged in the far recesses of space. He knew it was over right then and there. He instinctively, however, had to kill as many ghosts as he could to clear the way for the next package of Soviet meat that would come to repair the same pipeline he had failed to repair.

He carefully reached for his Kalishnikov and also his helmet. He trodded on the frozen mud to where his soldiers had blacked out on alcohol and dope. He came upon Soldier #3, whose snoring could have alerted the *dushmen* to their whereabouts. The captain made a hard fist and whacked him squarely on the chin. Immediately following this, the captain muffled his cries with the palm of his hand.

Soldier #3 may have indeed believed that the captain had wanted to murder him, simply because he was a substandard soldier for sleeping on the job. But once his bulging eyes saw the captain pressing his forefinger to his lips, the soldier knew exactly what he meant by this show of early-morning affection. It allowed the captain to wake up Soldier #4 in the same rude manner. And when the two recalcitrant point men were fully conscious and had been successfully brought back into the war, they reached for their helmets and their rifles and woke up the other soldiers in the same rude way, their bodies covered by a thin layer of frost. But they were much too late, because they were outmanned by seven, maybe eight ghosts who had the advantage of having observed their every move from behind the abandoned dwellings.

The ghosts came at them from all sides and angles, and they riddled the three soldiers lying around the ashes of the fire with bullets from their AK-47s and Enfield rifles. These three were killed immediately without pain. They wouldn't have known it anyway. They wouldn't have felt it. They were too doped up from the night before to notice it. They were easy sacrifices. But the two remaining soldiers and the captain fired their Kalishnikovs indiscriminately at the *dushmen* who slowly closed in on them. It forced the black captain and the two others to fire in retreat, running backwards against the outskirts of the abandoned village.

Soldier #3, now in full retreat, tumbled into the mud near another abandoned dwelling and fired at the *dushmen* from the ground. But it was useless. A *dushman* came in silently from the side of him and killed him by pumping a series of rifle shots into his torso. The soldier could only clutch his body in pain until the toothless *dushman* walked up to him and pumped a rifle shot into his skull. It at least gave the black captain and Soldier #4 time to take up safe positions and fire like mad at the series of *dushmen* that closed in on them. But the captain had excellent marksmanship and killed off half of them with an efficiency and skill that was commensurate with his impeccable training and rank. Soldier #4 on the other side of him several yards away took down two of them, maybe three. There were two more ghosts left. They hid behind a series of desert bushes back towards the village where the platoon had camped.

The black captain again pressed his forefinger to his chapped lips, signaling Soldier #4 to keep quiet. He then pointed to the bushes where he suspected the remaining *dushmen* hid. Now on offense, the captain and his only soldier left crawled in the mud. Soldier #4 followed his lead. They both elbowed their way to the extreme sides of the bushes. They wanted to attack them by pinching them in the middle. The quick-thinking captain picked up a rock in the mud next to him, and once close enough, threw it in front of the bushes. Immediately, the two *dushmen* unthinkingly fired at the diversion. It was then that the captain and Soldier #4 hopped to their feet and attacked them from opposite sides, piercing their brown, turban-headed bodies with bullets until they were dead, their souls returning to their brand of heaven.

The captain checked the area to make sure there were no

remaining *dushmen.* And then he dropped his weapon to the ground, looked up into the glowing red sky and sighed heavily. Soldier #4 simply fell to his knees and wept uncontrollably. The captain walked over to him after he was certain that everyone else in the immediate area had been killed and there were no remaining survivors.

"We're not done yet, comrade," said the captain. "We still have to get out of here alive. Or did you forget that?"

"I can't handle it anymore, captain," cried Soldier #4. "I just can't take this place anymore. We're locked in here. Like prisoners we are, captain."

"On your feet, soldier! Right now!"

"Yessir," he said, rising to his feet and wiping away his tears.

"You stay here," ordered the captain. "I'm going back to get the supplies and the signal flares. We're all clear now. Just wait here and don't move. Keep your eyes open."

"Yes, captain."

But after he returned with all of the supplies he could carry, he found Soldier #4 sucking on his hash pipe, calming his shattered nerves. The soldier then pulled out a pack of Yaras and sucked one of them down as though it were his last cigarette on earth.

"It's okay," said the captain. "If it shuts you up, it's fine. We'll just settle here for a little while until we can make sense of things, okay? Then we have to get the hell out of here."

"But what about the bodies, captain?" asked Soldier #4, his body shaking.

"Let's not worry about that now. Just be ready to move out in a half-hour, once you've calmed down."

"Yes, captain."

They both slumped in the mud, and it was clear that the *kaif* had calmed him. The captain, however, had no need for such sedatives. His nerves were strong. But ever since his last mission, his attitude towards the war had changed direction. There was no optimism left in Afghanistan. It seemed ridiculous that he should keep fighting a losing war. But as far as the general attitude of the Red Army was concerned, his was more positive than the lot of them. The cynicism of the army had been so bitter, that they could only joke about the horror show of Afghanistan. They had to laugh at it in order to avoid shooting themselves over it. There was little alternative. It was akin to being tickled in the armpits by the fires of Hell. The captain knew it but preferred not to let the sore of Afghanistan fester in his mind. He had to keep moving until, through some stroke of luck, the war ended. He had to keep hard rather than forfeit his duties to the soothing properties of the *kaif*. It didn't appeal to him. He thought himself above it, and in many ways, he had to be above it to survive the monstrosity of the place.

By the time Soldier #4 had settled down, it was time to move. The captain got to his feet and nudged his only remaining soldier with his boot. Without a word, the stoned soldier stood and donned his gear. They then headed into the desert away from Ruhki. The objective was to get into the wide-open spaces of the desert and fire their series of signal flares, so that a helicopter, hopefully, would rescue them. But when they launched the first round of flares into the bright sky after they distanced themselves far from the *kishlak*, they attracted not a helicopter, but even more *dushmen* from behind. The captain had taken that risk, and once again, he ended up on the losing side of the bet. There was no helicopter in sight, just shadowy apparitions chasing them into the open desert.

They ran from them as fast as they could, sweat bleeding through their uniforms. Soldier #4 could hardly breathe. Too many cigarettes and too much *kaif* had gotten the better of him. But he ran for his life, huffing and puffing the whole way. From behind, the captain pushed him forward and ordered him to keep running. But once Soldier #4 was out of breath, he had no choice but to collapse to the ground. The captain immediately took a knee and fired into the distant haze behind him as the *dushmen* fired forward. At this point, Soldier #4 got to his feet and ran wildly again into the open desert.

The captain had taken out most of them with his expert marksmanship, yes, but there was one left, and this *dushman's* skills were better than the others. The captain had to run in retreat again, chasing and then catching up to Soldier #4 whom he again pushed forward. But then there came the problem of the landmine that Soldier #4 landed on. As soon as the Pakistani-made device exploded below him, half of Soldier #4's leg blew off and flew into the air. It landed behind his bloodied body, right in front of the captain, who then tripped over the leg. The captain went tumbling head-first into a sharp rock that gashed the side of his head. But the explosion, no matter how unfortunate, also brought with it another diversion. War was instinct, and he had little time. With blood spilling into his eyes, the captain sat up and fired his rifle into the cloud of red dust and dirt that billowed up all around the explosion. He squeezed the trigger so hard and for so long, that he wasted his entire clip on this one *dushman* that had chased them down. Once the gunfire stopped, he heard the shrill shriek of a dying ghost. It was over. The captain had killed yet another enemy attacker.

He would have rested and sighed heavily into the hot air again had he not have to tend to Soldier #4's leg. The soldier's Soviet-born blood flowed from his thigh onto the desert floor, his every heartbeat pumping an ocean of blood from him. He wailed and shook and soon fell into shock. Once he determined that the final *dushman* was dead, the captain doffed his heavy backpack, ripped off his shirt, and made a tourniquet out of it. But the soldier was losing blood quickly. The captain couldn't delay any longer. With blood in his eyes, he reached for the signal flares again and fired off the last two high into the air. The only option left now was to wait with the wounded soldier who had passed out from the sight of his own missing leg and the blood that pooled under his body. It was a sanguinary mess. And they waited, the hot sun beating down on them. And they waited some more, hoping for someone to respond. The captain could do nothing so long as Soldier #4 still lived and breathed. He could only think about their woeful situation.

He wanted to kill the unconscious Soldier #4 and then travel to the next *kishlak* on his own. Either that or wait and hope they both made it out alive before more *dushmen* came. But he wanted to kill him, and this suddenly became his instinct – to preserve himself and make it out of the war alive. But the more he actually thought about it, the more he realized that he should wait and save both of their lives rather than merely saving his own. It was a puzzling dilemma. He resented this inadequate soldier as well as his dope-sniffing, hash-smoking, and vodka drinking ways. He was a curse on the Red Army, and he now appeared as a curse to him, the mirage of an escape to the next village tempting him.

He resented his father for ever sending him into this ridiculous war. They might as well have been stranded there, because even if they made it out of Afghanistan alive, nothing would have ever been the same for them anywhere else in the world. It was better to live out the rest of his life miserable in Afghanistan than to live in misery anywhere else. The State would never tell its people what happened in this foul desert, how thousands of soldiers had been killed off, how those who made it out alive were now addicts and mental cripples, about how within months of their arrival the ferocity of the landscape itself defeated the Red Army before it even had a chance to launch their full-scale invasion. At least the Afghanis had something to fight for – their natural need to eat, fuck, and shit. But what did he fight for, he wondered. Stalin? Kruschev? Mao? Breshnev? Really?

The fight against American imperialism had hardly been worth a drop of Russian blood, considering how the Red Army couldn't even protect itself against a horde of shit-brown *kafirs* using ancient technology to drive out a nuclear-charged superpower. And they did die that day. Did die.

The captain spat on the ground and cursed his entire existence as a lone helicopter chopped its way through the desert air and calmly settled on the ground in front of them. Two pilots ran out from underneath the rotating blades. They tended to Soldier #4 first. The captain could only spit into the red, hot dust several times more, cursing himself, because he knew full well that he would have killed Soldier #4 had the helicopter not found them. It had been the last lapse he had made while in Afghanistan.

This black captain, now an expert GRU asset at a hole-in-the-wall chicken place in the DC ghetto, felt along the side of his head for the indelible scar that carried the memory of these awful lapses he had made some fifteen years ago. And for supposedly saving Soldier #4's life, for protecting him, and for killing off all those *dushmen* back in Ruhki, he was awarded the Silver Star, just like his father many years before.

Chapter Five

January 2001 – Washington D.C., USA

In his elegant suit and tie, the Deputy gazed into the dense, snowy forest surrounding Langley and resolved not to throw himself out of his fifth-story window. He had been meaning to for a long time but never had the nerve to withstand the terror and pain of the fall. The idea stuck with him while in and out of bed with his beautiful wife and also in meetings with the Old Man who said he had forgotten about such feelings years ago. It was something The Deputy had to get through, like a milestone in his career or a mid-life crisis. But the Deputy had never been to war before. He had never been battle-tested. He was too young to enlist during the Reagan years when there had been a split between an old anti-war guard and a new Cold War reorganization of the armed forces. He had been caught in between. If he recalled correctly, he never registered for the Selective Service either.

Instead, he applied to the Company, went through all of the necessary training, and because of his high pedigree, his prep school and Ivy League ancestry and legacy, and his genuine good looks, he became a high-functioning bureaucrat with a mind that could cut glass. But it wasn't all of the paperwork or the pressures of the job that bothered him. It was the knowledge of how many lives of the Company's American loyalists and those countless Third World troops who had to die in order to fill the coffers of the Treasury Department, both foreign and domestic, that he had to sacrifice in order to win small, stupid battles. Most of all, he hated how corrupted his mind had become while planning and executing these jobs properly. All they had taught him at those silly little prep schools back then was how to be virtuous, honest, and true to oneself. What a departure he had made from those ideals.

He remembered his Classics teacher. He was a mild-mannered fellow with round, horn-rimmed spectacles. He always wore heavy, tweed suits and bowties. He was old back then, his head bald, and his skin ashen-white. And when his teacher invited him to dinner at his residence just outside of campus one night, he told him that he really didn't care how high he went on the totem pole of success, how many riches in the world he would one day amass, or how contented he would one day be later in life. His teacher wanted his star pupil and good young friend to be virtuous. Always virtuous. The two broke bread, drank wine, and talked about his future within the framework of what it meant to be virtuous, as though it were that quality alone that sustained a man in Western Civilization, just as it sustained the Ancient Greeks and Romans.

The Deputy remembered cheating on his teacher's final exam a couple of weeks later. He wrote notes in blank blue books and snuck them into the exam room. Once the exam proctors weren't looking, he took them out and used them to write his essays. No one noticed a thing, not even his Classics teacher who gave him the highest grade in the class. After all, he needed good grades to get into a good college.

But as the Deputy stood in his office at Langley and looked into the forest outside, he realized how low he had gone and what a liar, cheat, and bastard he had become after all of his years in government service. It wasn't something he could easily explain away. The things he had done since his old Classics teacher saw him last were inimical to any concept of virtue. He couldn't remember all of the women he fucked and how many men he had fucked over. There were, in fact, plenty of people who hated him and wanted him dead, but the list was so long, he preferred not to know whom. That wasn't the point. The greater point was that he did this all in the name of his country and the job at hand. Yet he couldn't move forward without looking back at all the garbage he had collected over the few years. He still wanted to throw himself out the window.

He should have been fine by now, but he considered that, if he got what he really deserved, he should have been washing cars in the DC ghetto. His forfeiture of virtue kept pecking at his soul. His sins could never be washed. His life was an unsolvable riddle in this sense. He had forever been charged with doing the Company's dirty work, which further pushed him into even greater sin without the chance to reverse its treacherous course. Perhaps suicide would be his way own way absolution. But he had to return to the job at hand, always the job at hand, as though there were no separation between his own self and the Company that gave him an identity, because he sacrificed himself for the good of his country. There was at least a part of him that still remained pure. Preserving such a purity about him may have been stupid and idiotic of him, but it was the purity of sacrificing himself for the welfare of the Company that kept him working. It had always fallen back to that. But he couldn't ignore that his soul was dead. He gave it up for a view of the forest behind Langley and his predictable movement up the chain of command towards oblivion.

He was no stranger to the information he had to hide. A cheat, a liar, and a fiend was what he had become. He had ordered the deaths of many with his signature. He manipulated stock prices to keep the Russians and the Chinese from infiltrating American markets, no matter how many innocents had lost their life's savings on legitimate trades. He understood that the only elements holding his beloved country together were the lies and the consistent and continuous propagation of those lies. The weak were destroyed. The strong abused the weak until the weak were too distraught to fight for themselves. The most beautiful and most desirable women always loved and worshiped the most sadistic of men. This was what survival demanded. Yet he still tried to preserve that sliver of purity that merely whispered into his ears that he should throw himself out the window while he still had the chance. It would have been a just punishment for defending his country, for murdering the innocent to protect the guilty.

There was no innocence in America anyway. Perhaps there never was. No purity either. The lack of these killed him slowly. The assets in the Company were irreversible scumbags high on their own power, as though they actually knew something the average observant bum on the street didn't know. The name of the Company itself became a misleading moniker that had little association with the truth. The Company's truth amounted to the same garbage he waded through, day in and day out. In other words, for the Deputy starved of virtue, there could never be contentment or rest. It was not knowledge that created power, but knowledge that created the corruption that, in turn, coerced him to do what the clandestine information gleaned from his operatives forced him to do.

When it came to defending the country, though, he had no other choice. National defense became that fundamental excuse that permitted the violence and death that had been the foundation of his everyday life. But he didn't know how long he could go on sacrificing himself to protect the good of the masses. If the public knew of the things he did, they too would see him as a heathen. His sacrifices were a form of leprosy. There was a supreme human value in avoiding the likes of him. He was no more and no less than a leper unworthy of a cure. He figured that his only positive quality was his ability to discern this leprosy about himself, even though he was way too far gone now to turn back. That ability to identify his disease was what remained pure about him. He believed that once the President and the Old Man appointed him Director, he wouldn't be able to see himself as a leper at all.

He eyed his desk at the far end of the room – a television posted to one of the walls, a long leather sofa, and a bar full of liquor from which he never drank. His office was not as nice as the Old Man's, but it was damn good for a man so young. In the quiet and stillness of his office the Deputy returned to work. He didn't have to worry about being second best to the Old Man anymore either. Once the Old Man kicked the bucket, he would have his office upstairs.

He ambled over to his desk where a picture of his wife sat between his computer and his telephone. He needed his wife then, just to feel someone wholesome, alive, and healthy, the direct opposite of what he was. After sitting there for a few moments, he picked up his phone and called in his assistant who was stationed just beyond his door. He needed his wife, and his assistant was the only substitute available. His assistant had been hired for that sole purpose – to be the woman available to him whenever he needed her.

The Company had its minions for certain purposes, and his lovely young assistant, only a few years out of college and wearing a short skirt and dark leggings, walked in with her usual computer tablet. She looked like a woman who would never suffer very much in life, even if it turned unexpectedly tragic. She was naturally happy, as though her parents designed her that way. She was intelligent enough to do well at any corporation that may have hired her. He figured she had a boyfriend in the city somewhere whom she would one day marry, but even if the guy were as well-kept as she, she would still do anything for her Deputy. And yes, the way she looked that late morning turned him on.

Judging by the smile on her face, she must have known she had this particular effect on him. It wasn't that she wanted anything greater than his mentorship. It wasn't that she had any secret ambition other than being who and what she was. One day, she would be married, just like all the other assistants they hired. Like the others, she submitted willingly and completely to his power as Deputy. She knew her place and her role. So, when he pushed himself away from his desk, his young assistant, on cue, put down her tablet computer, knowing what he needed.

She walked behind the desk, smiling the entire way there. She knelt before him and undid his pants. The Deputy stroked her soft, brown hair, while she smiled cleverly as she took him in her hands. She slowly licked him up and down until taking him completely in her warm mouth. It didn't take long before the Deputy sighed and relieved himself in her. After swallowing all he had, she wiped her lips with both of her fingers, zipped up his pants, and walked out of his office, returning to the othe world on the other side of the door. The Deputy soon felt energized and new.

With the assitant's help, he was finally ready for a lunch appointment she had made for him nearly a month ago. It was that difficult for anyone outside the Company to meet with him. It seemed sometimes like the only link to the outside world rested with his beautiful, young assistant, who did anything for her boss.

The car and driver picked him up out front of the Langley complex. He didn't really care whom he had to meet with that day. As usual, he hadn't been prepped at all. His assistant managed all of the important details of his work, while he focused on the bigger issues. He had little interest in making connections with those on the outside. As an administrator, he focused on internal matters that dealt directly with national security. When he had to leave, it usually meant he had to tolerate the nonsense of Company diplomacy that was more of a trait of the wet-noodles at State.

He had to take the Jewish analyst's plan to the old man later that afternoon, for instance, to make the old man comfortable and secure. He considered himself a good right-hand man and had gained the old man's trust over several years of governing all three branches of the Company.

There was always an international crisis that the President wanted dealt with. Yet the Company was much more than a simple function of the Executive branch. It was an organization unto itself—independent and without the same checks and balances that plagued other, lesser agencies. It never really had to answer to Congress. It simply supplied it with how much it needed and gave brief, convoluted summaries of what it needed the money for. It supplied intelligence briefs to the President. The outgoing President, however, had lacked confidence in the Company's abilities. He deflated its power and demoralized its staff. Luckily, a Presidency that had very little trust in the Company had ended after eight brutal years. Perhaps this was the only development that the Deputy had to be thankful for. The Company had a new lease on life with the new President.

His driver dropped him off at *Joe's Seafood*, a popular restaurant for Washington's higher-ups. He wasn't at all hungry, but a functionary from the Ukrainian Embassy had been waiting for several months to meet him. He told the Matre'D who he was, and the effete, smallish man, who dressed meticulously in a black suit and tie, directed him to a back room with a large bar and an arrangement of tables covered in white linen. There, alone at a table in this silent, empty section of the restaurant sat this no-name functionary. Another cog in the machinery.

He was much older than he. He was bald and overweight. He had already started in on a plate of broiled scallops. When the Ukrainian stood to welcome him, he offered him a plump hand wet with lemon juice and melted butter. Reluctantly, the Deputy shook it but not without wiping his hand clean with the napkin on his lap. He disliked him already.

"What can I do for you?" asked the Deputy.

"Oh, come now," laughed the Ukrainian with a wide smile and jagged teeth. He also had a thick accent. "Stay a while. Have something, no? Courtesy of Ukraine."

"I'm not hungry."

"Ah, you really are no fun, are you? That's what I heard about you."

"Please, let's keep this brief. I have a busy day."

"Such is your reputation, Mr. Deputy. All work and no play, eh? Yes, I have heard about you. Never any time for the finer things in life, like enjoying the fruits of the countries that help you."

"I think it's the other way around. We don't need help from anyone, especially from Ukraine."

"Oh? So, you wouldn't be interested in what we've found out about the loyalists in the Kremlin?"

"You're not going to tell us something we don't know already."

The Ukrainian chuckled as he bit into a scallop. He chewed with his mouth open, and the Deputy avoided looking at the mashed bits of scallop on his tongue. He barely missed the spittle that flew from the Ukrainian's lips.

"We want your Company and our government to work together," he said. "We would like to invite some of you to the Ukraine to help monitor our expansionist neighbors next door. You would be working directly with us. We will share what we have discovered already."

"How many are we talking about?"

"Give us ten."

"Operatives? Analysts? Scientists? What?"

"Operatives, of course."

"To do what, may I ask?"

"We have our people in posts inside the Kremlin. They are real good. But we need your help transferring them out of there and back into Ukraine."

"Protection?"

"Precisely, Mr. Deputy."

"And what do we get in return?"

"Assuming that they are returned safely, we can offer you all they have collected about our mutual friend. We can initiate a cooperative sharing arrangement."

"So, my people will remain in Ukraine after that?"

"For a few years at least, yes."

"But we don't need you for information on Putin. We already have assets in the Kremlin."

"Oh, you'd be surprised about what we've learned about our mutual friend, Mr. Deputy. You'd be very surprised indeed."

He looked the functionary straight in his liquid blue

eyes, unsure if he should commit his own operatives to this so-called sharing arrangement. Ever since Ukraine's independence, there was no real need for the Company to bulk up its presence there. But he did remember the new outlook and attitude the Company had to take, considering the old man's new mandate and the new hawkish President who wanted on the next great threats to national security, which, coincidentally, were the same as the old threats that had dominated the second half of the 20th Century.

"Okay," said the Deputy, after investigating the Ukranian and taking a sip of water. "You have it."

"Very good, then," he smiled. "It is, after all, a new world, isn't it? We can't afford to rest on our heels, no?"

"No," said the Deputy, already sick of him.

The Ukrainian then pulled a piece of paper out of his jacket pocket and handed it over to him. It was a list of people from Ukraine.

"Who are these people?" asked the Deputy.

"What you have there is a list of the sons and daughters of some of our assets in the Kremlin. Their children are now safely in Ukraine."

"And?"

"It would help the Ukrainian government a great deal, Mr. Deputy, if you could grant each of them citizenship here and admission into one of your esteemed universities."

"And this, I take it, would be in the spirit of our new arrangement?"

"Most of them want to go to Harvard," said the Ukrainian

The Deputy perused the list of Eastern European names and smiled to himself.

"What? Is there something wrong?"

"No, it's just that they always want to go to Harvard for some reason. But I don't see any problem with it, no. I'll arrange it."

"Excellent, Mr. Deputy. I consider this an impressive start to a new relationship between our two agencies. We look forward to receiving your operatives in our lovely Kiev. You will have all of the privileges and luxuries our government can afford you."

The Deputy simply stood and said, "don't contact us. We'll contact you." He then left the restaurant without eating anything. His driver picked him up below the well-known blue awning outside, and together they returned to Langley just as quickly as they had left. Before retreating to his office again, though, he told his assistant to arrange a meeting with the Head of Operations about the new Ukrainian deal.

"Would you be needing me for anything else?" she smiled.

He returned her smile and said, "I think you've done a good job for today. Why don't you take the rest of the afternoon off."

"Just call me at home if you need me," she said. "Oh, and don't forget your appointment with the Director this afternoon. That's the only appointment left on your schedule."

"No, I can't forget that."

He walked into his office and locked the door. Above the bar was a stereo, which he tuned to a local classical music station. It played a symphony he didn't recognize, which was usually the case. He went to his desk and pulled up the analyst's plan on his computer. He read it over carefully. He knew it was brilliant. He knew that when these geek analysts were pressed hard, they produced works of brilliance.

He remembered hearing a story about such a thing happening to a young man in Washington. The young man, fresh out of graduate school, had been hired as a up-and-coming speechwriter for then Secretary of State Henry Kissinger. Kissinger had this speechwriter work on a project, and after working very hard on it, the young man returned it to Kissinger. Kissinger flipped through its pages and then returned the speech to him.

"Do it over," mumbled the fat German.

The kid, a bit disappointed, went back home and worked on the speech again. He put way too much work into it, and when he handed it to Kissinger a second time, he knew it was much better than the first.

"Do it over," said Kissinger again.

He went home and rewrote the speech a third time. The work was grueling. He had worked all day and all night for several days straight to deliver a perfect speech to Mr. Kissinger. The young man read it over hundreds of times. He snorted lines of speed to keep himself awake. He sweated over every word, and by the time he finished his third draft, he thought he may have had to check into the hospital due to mental and physical exhaustion. He was on the verge of a nervous breakdown when he entered Kissinger's office a third time and handed over the finished speech to him.

The German simply said, "okay, I'll read it now."

The Deputy understood that by inflicting this same brand of cruelty on those who were the lowest on the ladder, he could bring out the best in them, just as he did the Jew. He pressured the weak to produce gems of brilliance. And for those who were strong? He sent them into irrelevant battles where they could easily get out alive. It built up their confidence, as winning at battle was what the Company's strong truly enjoyed. It kept them motivated. It preserved them for when they were really needed. They loved senseless missions and exaggerated challenges. They got through them without too much resistance. The thrill of the kill and the thrill of winning drove the paramilitary arm of the Company. These special soldiers needed to be put into action all the time, or else they would kill ordinary citizens in their quest for warrior glory. The weak, on the other hand, were dispensable. There was a slight pleasure in seeing them worry and sweat under intense pressure. If they freaked out under this pressure, then so be it.

Then there were the operatives themselves. They were paranoid and always afraid of dying. They used their natural, intuitive gifts of paranoia to navigate the streets of any given foreign capital. The more they learned, the better they performed. They were hungry to know more and more, always unraveling a mystery, even when there was nothing to unravel to begin with. It pushed them to greater heights. The Deputy put them in situations where they may have been caught and tortured if their cover was blown. When this happened, and it surely did happen more often than anyone knew, he wrote letters to a hungry press corps declaring that the Company knew nothing about those who had been captured, kidnapped, or executed. If a paranoid operative died, he or she died silently without any fanfare. They died in ignominy. The Company's trainers then used them as examples for new recruits, teaching them what not to do in the field.

The Deputy often sent in the sub-par operatives first to grapple with unwinnable predicaments. They were sacrifices for the greater good. He had to preserve the best, as they were the only ones valuable enough to live. The worst of them were thrown to the lions to make foreign agencies feel better about themselves. As he had learned from his Classics teacher, *hubris* led to *nemesis*. The more these foreign agencies puffed themselves up with pride for killing off sub-par operatives and soldiers, the greater the competitive edge the Company had over them. They could feast on American operatives time and again until things got serious. Then the Deputy sent in a crew of real heavy-duty commandos to deal with these foreign idiots in swift and decisive blows. After all, those who worked for the Company were numbers on a chart. Nothing more. They were chess pieces in a long-term match.

He printed the Jew's report and weighed its thickness. He wanted the copy to be crisp and clean for the Old Man. He was almost too afraid to touch it. And if the Jew failed to win over the Old Man, he would have him killed anyway. But the time had come. He took the elevator to the floor up above him. He pressed his eyes to the scanner, and the door opened. The old man was smooth-talking the new President over the phone. From what he overheard, the conversation was about the Saudis and how some of them may have infiltrated the Company. The Old Man assured the President that this wasn't the case. He baby-talked him down from a state of nervous anxiety. When he hung up, the Director offered his star Deputy a doughnut. He refused it, though, while the Director ate one himself. He then got up and poured himself a bourbon.

"You want one?" asked the Old Man.

"No, but thank you, sir."

"You pussy. You're always so fucking uptight. What's that all about?"

"It's in the job description," smiled the Deputy.

"Good answer. Well, when you're heading the

Company, you'll have plenty of time to come up with good answers. The President needs them, that's for sure. You'll also loosen up a bit, assuming our little project looks good."

The Deputy handed over the analyst's work. The first few pages were simply a summary of the plan. The details were what followed. The Old Man returned to his desk and reclined in his chair with the bourbon in one hand and the dead analsyt's plan in the other. He read through the summary, but half-way through, he leaned back, put his bourbon on the desk, and moved in closer. He raised his eyebrows at the very last page. When he finished it, he breathed deeply and put his stubby hands behind his head and looked to the ceiling. The Deputy was nervous as hell, but he made sure not to show it.

"There's a fine line between genius and madness," said the Old Man, after a time.

"Yessir."

"And you are the author of this plan?"

He was cautious here, because he thought the Old Man already assumed that he wrote it. Suddenly, he had a choice - either trust the Jew's plan or blame him for its stupidity. It was more a knee-jerk reaction than a quick decision.

"Yessir," he said nervously. "It was a lot of work, but I've been working on it since we last met."

"Looks like it, yeah? But, son, I have to tell you, it's genius! I mean, it's fucking genius! We'll take the loss, but we cut off the part to save the whole. Good work, son. You did it! You really nailed it this time!"

"Thank you, sir."

"Are you sure you don't want a drink? You definitely deserve one."

"No, thank you, sir. I'm on the job."

"Well, when you sit in this chair next year, you can drink all you want, right?"

"I look forward to it, sir."

"I'll let the President know that you're my pick."

"That's fine, sir, but if I may, I strongly recommend that we keep this on the covert level, a black box affair. Not even the President can know about this."

"What's the reasoning for that?"

"If, by chance, this thing becomes an open conflict for whatever reason, the Company has cover. There are so many variables, even though everything is already planned. So much can go wrong. If one little thing is out of place, it'll blow up in our faces."

"And that means no one in the NSC either?"

"Not even the NSC. That's the last course of action. No one else can know about this."

The old man thought it over for a couple of minutes while draining his glass.

"Okay," he said. "We'll put in a black box, as you say. We'll keep this to ourselves. Only those who are involved will know."

"But not about the whole plan, sir. We would be offering our people too much information. Each asset will have his or her own function. No one in the Company will know what the whole picture looks like, in other words."

"That way, the Company is not accountable."

"Precisely."

"And you're able to pull all the strings? There are a lot of moving parts here."

"Yessir."

"You feel confident enough?"

"Yessir."

"Alright, then. You'll fly solo on this. I'll keep it from the President and everyone else for that matter. It doesn't go any farther than this office."

"It will work," said the Deputy.

"I hope so. Otherwise, they'll have our heads."

"I'm confident it will work, sir."

"Okay, then. To victory," said the Old Man, raising his glass."

"It's assured, sir."

"And now I have to deal with the President who wants a new China policy."

"What's the new policy, if I may ask?"

"I'm advising him to break those Chinks away from the Russians. Big oil is involved, so you better start buying those oil stocks first thing in the morning," he winked. "Anyway, he wants them to cooperate in a global oil duopoly with us. He needs to get the ball rolling on this shitty economy. He wants the Chinks to dump their cheap products onto our consumer markets. They'll sell us their flimsy shit, and at the same time, we'll be stimulating trade, you see."

"Will it work? You think we'll make some money out if it?"

"Yeah, because we'll be using dirt cheap Chinese, Spic, and Taiwanese labor too. The President fucks over the unions and runs up the markets. We'll use their Third World labor to sell our own flimsy products back to ourselves. Everyone's happy, and business booms."

"That's pretty good advice, if I may say so, sir.'

"Everybody wins."

"Finally, you can get some sleep at night."

"I hope so," said the Old Man, filling up another glass of bourbon. "At least on my watch, I did the best that I could. You're going to have to do the same thing, you know. That plan of yours is brilliant. Just fucking brilliant."

"Thank you, sir."

"I guess I found the right man for the job. That's important before I leave this God-forsaken world."

"Don't talk like that, sir. May you have many more years."

"With your plan, though, the Devil really is in those details, isn't it?"

"Yes, sir. That's one huge detail in there."

"You have quite a mind, son. I can't think of anyone else better to head the Company."

"Thank you, sir."

"And by the way, send our main asshole in Iraq a case of Johnny Walker Blue and a box of Cubans, courtesy of the Bush Administration, just for Christmas. What's a war without a cute Trojan Pony and a massive diversion."

"I'll tell my assistant right away."

"Oh, and with it send him a quote from Stalin. That's the idiot's hero. I'll tell the President to have the Frogs break off ties with him. And as far as those two-faced Pakis go, we can't trust them, but we'll need them to get into Afghanistan. Get to that right away."

"As soon as we're done here, sir."

"Good. And now get the fuck out of my office before I throw you out. I want to eat my doughnuts in peace for

Chrissakes. My wife's not around to bug me about them."

"Yes, sir."

He should have thrown himself out of the window while he had the chance. He no longer wanted the shoes he had to fill. He left the Old Man's office thinking that he had gotten himself into the worst possible business a ruthless God could bestow upon a man. There was no escaping it. The degradation of his own soul for the benefit of others, as though he himself had been whipped and chained as a martyr for them, suddenly prevailed. His free will was merely an illusion, because once inside the Company, there was no getting out. No one would ever understand him either. That was the worst part. Not even his lovely wife and kids. No one would ever realize how much he suffered under the weight of the Company's universal control. Ambition was useless. He was just as controlled and maligned as the common beggar on the street.

His driver took him home to a wife he hardly knew. Neither did she know much about him, even though they had been married for fifteen years. Maybe he would sleep with her that night, simply because he wanted to. That's all he ever needed from her. His wife would give it up without any complaint. That was her job, her sole function in life. She would never know how badly he wanted to jump. Even at the highest levels of government, where he would soon take many more lives for the greater good, not even she would ever understand the dimension of his own suffering. No one would ever feel his pain. Because of this, perhaps his existence was not worth continuing, especially with the countless foreign loyalists he had already sent to their deaths. The cultivation of his own misleading ambitions brought him hopelessly close to the nucleus of power other government dingbats craved by dint of their senseless greed. Simply put, the Deputy was always controlled. He had been destined to lose, not as a bureaucrat, but as a person. It wasn't a matter of choice. It had never been a matter of choice, he thought to himself.

Chapter Six

January 2000 – Washington D.C., USA

She had no idea what to do, now that not a single medical school in the nation would give her a scholarship. She had relied on her boyfriend, and since that was over, she couldn't afford the tuition on her own. Actually, any expenses for any graduate school in the nation were massive and far beyond her reach. She needed her prescription pills, but ever since the breakup, her ex-boyfriend had cancelled her blanket health insurance. There would no longer be therapy or the sedatives that had been regularly prescribed. She took to counseling due to the pressures of being a socialite. Even though her boyfriend had no longer carted her around from party to party, she was now worse off than before. There were no pills to make her descent any easier.

She did call Harvard, though, hoping the admissions office would understand her circumstances. They said that they still would admit her, but only if she paid the full price. From a small, cramped efficiency apartment in a broken Hispanic barrio farther away from campus, she tried the cheaper state schools next. They declined as well. A full boat, she realized, was a must. She carefully weighed the option to take out student loans. Apart from her boyfriend, however, she didn't have a credit history. Even if they did give her a loan, she would never be able to pay it back. That was just the way it worked. Student loans were unforgiving.

Not even bankruptcy could take care of them. Besides, she would have to come up with some of the money anyway. She had nothing.

She collapsed on her bed, pulled her blue, woolen blanket over her head, and wept silently. She had never been so directionless before. Some thrive on being lost and directionless, but not she. Her single path had suddenly curved into darkness. She didn't know what to do next. It scared her. Her boyfriend had taken care of everything, but no longer. The fear of not knowing, the fear of not being able to see ahead of herself, left her paralyzed beneath her blanket.

She would have normally called her best friend for help, but she was no longer a friend. She would have called one of her sorority sisters for help, but they wanted nothing to do with her, thanks to her ex-boyfriend's vindictiveness. Like the idea of taking out student loans, her boyfriend was even more unforgiving. He had her excommunicated from the sorority. Sherry had pleaded with her sisters to live in the mansion on campus, but a secret committee dismissed her request. Some sisterhood that turned out to be.

After a good, long cry, she accepted the fact that she would have to return to her parents up in Vermont. She would have to vacate the shoddy apartment by the end of the month anyway. She had a mere mattress in a tiny rathole of a room. Her clothes were strewn all over the floor. A second suitcase that she dragged over the snow from campus was stuffed with more clothes. She was too depressed and lethargic to unpack them.

She fell asleep for a few hours and woke up again in the middle of the night. She wrapped the blanket around her and looked out the window. Through the frost on the windows she saw that it lightly snowed. The loneliness of the night was visceral, but she didn't fall back asleep. She collected her things and packed up her belongings. When dawn struck, she abandoned the apartment and walked to the train station to buy a ticket with what cash she had left. The sky had lightened over time, and when she returned, she made breakfast in the kitchenette. She ate slowly. She wasn't looking forward to the phone call she would have to make. Fortunately for her, though, her mother answered the phone instead of her father.

"Hi, honey," said her mother sweetly.

"Hi, Mom."

"So how are you two doing down there? I take it you're ready for Boston?"

"Mom, there's something I have to talk to you about."

"Sure, honey. What is it?"

"I'm on my way to Vermont."

"Great! Your father and I would love to have you. What time does your flight arrive?"

"Mom," she said, holding back tears, "I'm coming alone this time."

"Oh? You mean he isn't coming with you?"

"No, Mom. Just me."

"Alright. But is there anything wrong, honey?"

"I'd rather not talk about it over the phone."

"That's fine. We'll talk about it when you get here. But tell me, is there anything wrong? Are you in some kind of trouble?"

"No, I'm not in trouble. Not really, anyway. Everything's fine. I just want to come up, okay?"

"Sure. I'll make dinner. How does pot roast sound?"

"That sounds fine. And Mom, don't tell Dad that I'm

coming."

"Why? He should know about it. I'm sure he'd be more than happy to see you."

"Just don't"

"Alright."

"I'd just rather not have him know I'm coming."

"Honey, just tell me, is everything okay? You don't sound right to me."

"We'll talk more later, okay? Please?"

Naturally, she was the most beautiful creature on the train that afternoon. A redcap helped her with her two suitcases at the station, and since she took an off-peak train, she found a seat by herself and avoided being hit on by any of the young college types sitting near her. Over several hours of watching the unremarkable landscape trail by, she crafted the explanation she would soon give her parents. She didn't know what to expect, and she was afraid of how they would react to the news. Not her mother, but her father. Not only would he be floored by it, but still hours away from her destination, she could sense his utter disappointment. The rug of a future that he meticulously weaved for her had been pulled out from underneath him.

It wasn't just her own future that had been extinguished with the breakup. Her parents' future also died. They couldn't afford tuition for any graduate school let alone medical school. Her parents wouldn't be able to retire. Her father would have to put the farm up for sale. It had been in the family for several generations. While they never admitted it, her parents had relied on their daughter to become a well-groomed Senator's wife and pediatrician. Instead, they moved backwards. She might as well have not graduated with a degree in Biology or from a five-star university at all. Cosmetology would have been better. Hindsight is twenty-twenty, they say.

Aside from pondering her father's disappointment, she considered her next career move, more out of necessity than freedom of choice. A massive career shift was underway, but she had no other practical skills besides farming and skiing. Sure, she could work the phones as a customer service rep or take on an assistant's position for some ass-groping executive, but other than that, she had few qualifications other than her own undeniable beauty. Nor could she be a ski instructor or ski coach. No one survived on such wages.

Once again, the corners of her eyes leaked tears of uncertainty. Throughout the journey the barns on the snow-laden hills soon became haunting shadows in the evening darkness that returned her to a land she never wanted to see again. At the very least, her return north was woefully premature.

Practically everyone in Vermont said she would succeed. She hardly thought she would return home as a failure. She had always envisioned returning with an honorable Senator, a child in her belly, and a position at a city hospital tending to sick, vulnerable children - an admirable status in a civilization that didn't tolerate failure of any sort, even though life for everyone was replete with failures, mistakes, and disappointments of every stripe. Why her, she didn't know. God, it seemed, had forsaken her for no good reason at all, because she had done everything the proper way. Her family had used the best methods and had made foolproof plans. Yet even with these plans in place, they still collapsed. Such failures were not supposed to happen. She was supposed to succeed. Her parents had placed all their bets on it.

As the train clickety-clacked on the rails and raced

closer to the final stop on the corridor's line, her heart fluttered with every stop it made. She had spent hours thinking up explanations, but what she had rehearsed made little sense by the time the train pulled into a tiny Vermont station in the frigid darkness. Through the thick, scratched plexiglass of the train's windows, she spotted her mother's dairy farm pick-up truck with its engine running. Its exhaust fumes streamed from the back of it into the cold. Smoke dissipated above of the yellow headlights behind the truck like pneumonic exhalations.

Oddly enough, Sherry did not miss her ex-boyfriend at all. What he had done was unconscionable. She would tell her mother how he cheated on her with her best friend from the sorority. Her mother would understand. Remaining with her ex after such a betrayal would have led to even greater misery down the road. It wasn't pride that made her leave him. Instead, she imagined the many trysts he would have with countless other women. To turn a blind eye to them would have been too much for her, especially when she believed a husband and wife had to be faithful in marriage for a marriage work, not because it was a sacred or religious bond at all, but because a man and wife had to trust each other. If she stayed with him, she would have always wondered whom he slept with next. He would have screwed around as much as he pleased. She would have looked like a fool.

Maybe one day, she would meet a truly honest and trustworthy man. He might be poor, ugly, and compromised in all aspects of life, but she would look far beyond her own vanity and instead fall deeply in love with a talentless guy who didn't have a pot to piss in, nor a future, nor any direction or ambition. She would easily marry this type of man over her ex. This was what her heart now told her. She would never again fall for another winning thoroughbred, no matter how wealthy he was.

After exiting the train and dragging her suitcases to the truck, she hoisted her bags into the cargo bed and hopped into the warmth of the truck's cab with her mother. Her mother pulled her in close, kissed her on the forehead, and caressed her head. Sherry had little choice but to break out in tears. Within the glow of several headlights peeling out of sight behind them, her mother embraced her as tears bled into the collar of her coat.

"It's going to be alright," she said softly. "Whatever has happened, has happened. It's going to be alright, sweetheart."

Her mother already knew. They shared an intimate connection that usurped all other relationships. Her mother knew things about her daughter that words could not communicate – a second sense, so to speak, that allowed them to bond, not only mentally, but spiritually as well. The two were cojoined, not only by their New England beauty, but by a mutual empathic talent. Even if they were a thousand miles apart, they would still have followed each other, forever finding themselves both inside and outside of any given space. But they were physically together now, and Sherry, crestfallen by what had happened, didn't have to explain a thing. It was her father who would demand an explanation. But as soon as Sherry felt her mother's warm arms around her, she felt protected by her maternal embrace. Her mother's arms were a fortress. It had always been that way.

They drove along a dark, narrow road through a blackened valley without any road lights to guide them, and as the snow fell harder, they sped along as though the truck cruised down a runway on the cusp of liftoff. Sherry had forgotten what it was like to drive in a Vermont winter. When she lived on the farm, it was never a problem. Since living in

DC and relying on chauffeurs to drive her in and around its dense urban areas, however, she now clutched at the armrest next to her as though the truck would veer into a telephone pole at any moment. The headlights illuminated the slipperiness of the road, and the sharp curves ahead of them were typical of the rural backroads she had always been used to, but the roads were now alarmingly abnormal. She wondered if her mother drove too fast for her own good. She may have been too old to drive. She fought the temptation to ask her to slow down. Instead, she kept silent. She clutched the armrest just as tightly as she clenched her teeth. She made a mental note to discuss her erratic driving, even though it was perfectly normal for those living in the area to drive that way.

They turned onto a dirt road with white, long fences on either side of them. Sherry's father had constructed the fencing last year. The road's familiar unevenness reminded her of the cows and sheep grazing on their fields, and the hay, milk, and grain stored in their barns. The truck's tires sprayed dirt and rubble behind them, and she saw their small colonial home up ahead. It hadn't been painted in ages. The wood siding had chipped over years of disrepair. The home's foundation slanted into the snow like an iceberg on the verge of breaking into the sea. The culture shock of returning to her old home made her want to cry even more.

Even though her mother was fully present to mend her brokenness, Sherry couldn't help but feel terribly alone again. Without her sorority sisters and the fraternity boys who dated them, the farm loomed as an empty habitat devoid of any life or activity. When her mother cut off the ignition, Sherry's carved out insides had been replaced by dead air and resembled the cold quiet and the darkness of her surroundings. The wind picked up and whistled across the windshield. Before getting out, the two of them sat in the darkness and gazed at their home. A dim light shined from the second-floor window. Their eyes looked up at the same time, both wondering if the man of the house was awake or if he had inadvertently fallen asleep with an open book in his lap as he usually did.

Her father liked history, she remembered. He liked stuff about the Revolutionary War, the tragedy at Valley Forge, Thomas Jefferson at Monticello, and the Battle of Bunker Hill. He collected old colonial maps and ancient war muskets. He had an old British war cap and a bright British red officer's uniform. He polished its shining brass buttons every year for Halloweens and Show-and-Tells at the local elementary school. Her father's passion in colonial affairs was a mysterious idiosyncratic obsession that both mother and daughter had yet to unravel. They never found interest in America's colonial past, even though they tried very hard to do so.

"He's always been so set in his ways," said her mother, "but he's always wanted the very best for you."

"I really don't want to see him right now."

"I know you don't. But he'll understand. You have to give him a chance."

"I don't think he'll understand. He's never really known anything about me."

"That's not true, honey. You know that. He's always wanted the best for you, and now that you're home, maybe you can spend more time together. Maybe you can take interest in some of the things he finds interesting."

"I've tried that already, and so have you."

"He's growing old. We both are. He's not as rigid as he once was. He's softened since you were last here. You know he's been thinking about you ever since you left?"

"I'm not so sure. With what I have to tell him, I wouldn't be surprised if he just plain forgot about me from now on."

Stroking her hair, her mother said softly, "don't talk like that, honey. I know it's tough, but all of us, everyone on the face of God's given Earth, has to return home at times like these. It's that way by design, don't you think?"

"I'm not supposed to be anywhere near here, Mom."

"C'mon, let's go in. It won't be so bad."

Sherry gathered her nerve and lugged her two suitcases inside. The heat warmed her as soon as she opened the door. It opened into a wide kitchen with a wooden counter-top island stationed in the middle of it. Tarnished copper pots and pans hung above it on hooks. Old but functioning appliances filled out the kitchen's perimeter. They were brightly polished but had dimpled and dented surfaces. Designer dishware with photographs of old family members and friends pasted to their centers hung on walls that her father had repainted every few years. The house smelled of brown sugar. Her mother had just finished baking one of her signature apple pies. A full roast, a pot of asparagus, and third pot of buttery mashed potatoes warmed on the stove.

The kitchen was just how Sherry remembered it, except for an extraordinarily large and expensive plate that her ex had gifted her parents last Christmas. It featured a photograph of the young, proud couple at its center. It took up most of the space on the wall and dominated all the other plates. To her parents, it was a great achievement to have the plate hanging there. Sherry tried to ignore it, but it was just too large and ornamented to avoid. In the photograph, her ex wore a tuxedo, and Sherry looked stunning in a white, sequined evening dress. They attended a fundraiser for a Congressman's re-election campaign in Washington, and while her family's plates spoke of Norman Rockwell, the photograph on the large plate told of a life hobnobbing with the high political class in the nation's capital. The heavy flannel shirts and fleece-lined overalls of her New England relatives clashed openly with the couple's luxury partywear. To Sherry, the plate was like a boil on an otherwise unblemished rump. She tried to divert her mother's attention from it, but it was of no use. She would have to take the plate down. The picture would have to be thrown away. She could then resell the plate at a local flea market when summer came.

"Why don't you take your stuff upstairs and wash up, honey. I'll call you down for dinner in a little while. Your father is probably asleep in that old chair of his. Don't worry so much. Just make sure you don't wake him."

She lugged her two suitcases up a rickety flight of stairs to the second floor. The floorboards were weak and felt like they may collapse under the weight of the suitcases. A thin and faded carpet lined a dimly lit hallway. With every step, the floorboards sagged and creaked. Had her father been awake, the noise would have easily alerted him to her presence.

She remembered, when she was in high school, how she tried to sneak out of the house a couple of times after her parents had gone to sleep. She wanted to go to nearby house parties with her friends on Saturday nights. The weak wood within the structure of the home, however, made way too much noise for her to get away with it. Her father caught her in the hallway the only two times she tried. What followed were long, intense lectures about drinking, drugs, and what the local boys really wanted from a girl like Sherry. He said she would get pregnant before her time by some redneck, gun-toting rube living in the mountains should she venture out at night without his knowledge. It was no wonder she spent most of her high school years in her room studying, when all she really wanted was to be out with her friends. Her father promised harsh discipline if he ever caught her again. It was for her own good, he said. Since then, she always kept the music down and her telephone conversations low. Maintaining any sort of privacy when her parents were just down the hall from her was useless.

Her father had always left the bedroom door slightly ajar during his reading times. Such had been his routine before dinner for as long as she could remember. A slant of narrow light cut across the hallway from her parent's bedroom. Luckily, she didn't wake him.

When she entered her old room, she shut the door tightly behind her and locked it. She remembered when her father surprised her one night by installing the lock as a graduation present. She was an adult, after all, and they no longer needed to know where she was every minute of the day. Somehow, though, her parents had always known when she slept, when she woke up, and when she was suspiciously missing. She confided in her mother about her personal life, as she had established a deep and genuine trust in her. But the last thing her parents wanted was for her to remain in Vermont when the whole world beyond it was ripe for learning and exploration. Her father did the dreaming, while Sherry made the family dream a reality for his future benefit.

Yet he never had to convince or persuade her what was best for her after she finished high school. He outlined the path to follow, and she was ordered to follow it to the very end until it eventually led to a better life. He handled the financial aspects and all the pesky particulars, and her mother provided the emotional support and looked after her daughter's more feminine needs, like questions about men and what they really wanted from a girl like her. Her father ran the farm, and her mother ran the home. Sherry studied hard at school. It had all been working up to that point.

Her room looked the same, though. Her mother had kept it pristine for her eventual return. Despite their surroundings in a low valley of the Green Mountains, she noticed the manufactured mountain air from an aerosol can hung in the air. Everything from the floor's carpeting to the bathroom adjacent to her school desk had been immaculately maintained. A white, goose-down quilt under a light blue slipcover covered her queen-sized bed. She recalled how its thin, wooden headboard, no thicker than the wall it stood against, banged behind her when she tossed and turned at night. A midsized vanity mirror rested on a set of walnut cabinets where she had once kept her old school clothes. Her mother had since stored them in the attic for her own children, should Sherry be blessed with girls later in life. In fact, her mother kept her old toys, dolls, schoolbooks, and old awards in the attic as well. Her mother figured her grandkids would want them one day, especially once Sherry became a Senator's wife. The carpet in her room had the same thinness as the one lining the rest of the house, only that the colors didn't match. Her bedroom carpet was a darker shade of red.

She perused a wall of old pictures, her impressive high school diploma, and the several Merit awards she earned for high academic achievement, not to mention the varsity letters she won as captain of the ski team, which in Vermont was no small thing. A couple of gold-plated trophies rested on another dresser. She had won first place in a couple of major ski championships, which took her all the way to tryouts for the National Olympic team at Vail during her senior year. These artifacts crowded the small space and were junk compared to the lavish and sophisticated art pieces that decorated the luxury hotel suites, the penthouse apartments, and her ex's manor homes in Newport and South Hampton. Her old room only caged her in rather than tapped fond memories of her successful academic past. It pushed her into remembering the young schoolgirl she no longer was. Returning home felt like her big feet were being forced into tiny shoes.

After unpacking, she stripped off her clothes and took out a towel. She double-checked that the door was locked. She walked into the bathroom, the balls of her feet walking on the cold ceramic tile. Her muscles were stiff and sore from the long train ride. Neither did the train ride do wonders for her attitude. She plugged the drain in her old, heavy bathtub that had clawed feet and greenish, indelible water stains that circled the insides of it. While running hot water, she draped her towel on the sink and took a long look at herself in the mirror behind the door. Her breasts were full and shapely, its tips pink and rosy. She slowly swirled her fingers around them. They hardened and stood to attention.

The steam from the hot water battled against the cold draft of winter air seeping in from the window next to the sink. The bathroom soon grew warm and moist, like the steam room in her old DC athletic club. Through the steam, she continued examining her body in the mirror that now fogged over. Even though she hadn't worked out in days, her legs were still slender and toned, her belly tight and slim, and her arms hairless and supple. She felt the marks her panties had made on the space of skin between her navel and waist. She then stepped into the tub carefully, and once acclimated there, submerged her limp body into the warm water. The bathtub was still long and wide enough to soak it entirely. The water encapsulated her in comfort, protecting and nourishing her like a womb fit for a child.

With her legs spread apart, she ran her fingers down her abdomen and then below her waist to where a single strip of shaved blonde hair ran from the top of the source of her pleasures to the closing of it. She then opened herself up. She brushed her soft fingertips against what hid between her legs. With the imaginings of her ex on a sandy beach in the tropics, she was soon fully aroused.

She imagined him kissing her neck on the shore of this beach, his breath blowing on her earlobes, his face tucked into the well of her shoulder. His lips move ever so slowly down the nape of her neck. His warm, rough tongue circles the tips of her breasts until each is swallowed by his mouth. His teeth nibble on her breasts with a gentleness that never threatens but soothes and comforts.

She dipped her fingers into the neglected garden between her thighs. Her fingers disappeared into the wide slippery opening, moving in and out to the rhythm of her ex's girth inside of her. Her fingers then moved slightly upwards to the swollen and distressed node hidden beneath the folds of her pink inner flesh. As her fingers circled faster over it, her pleasures heightening, she was on the verge of releasing all of the stress and sorrows of the journey until she heard a sharp rap at the door, startling her out of her fantasy.

"Honey! Dinner is ready! Don't take too long in there, okay? Your father is hungry and ready to eat!"

Her ex's body returned to Hades, and suddenly she found herself back in her old bathtub, her body submerged in lukewarm water. The hot steam had evaporated and left her body cold and waterlogged in the chill of the draft that leaked through the window.

"I'll be right out," she called weakly.

Her mother had already set the table by the time she came downstairs, her delicious pot roast nestled in a bed of skinless baked potatoes and garnished with fresh carrot slices from their garden. She had piled the feast on a picturesque oval serving dish that a friend had given the family. The two of them sat in their places at their dining table next to the kitchen and waited patiently for the man of the house to appear. They were like natives waiting for King Kong arrive for his tribute. The cracking, snaping, and creaking of the old wooden floors made both of them anxious and uneasy. The house shook with greater intensity the closer downstairs he came. When he arrived, he stood in the kitchen and examined Sherry for moment. She did the same of him.

He was an older, greying man with remnants of what was once a full head of hair. He was nearly totally bald now. He had an unusually large skull, such that a quack would think him intellectually gifted. With his heavy fisherman's sweater on, he looked like a respected History professor or a retired think-tank scholar. He had gained weight considerably since she last saw him. She remembered how gaunt he used to be when she was a kid. His stomach bulged outwards from his chest down to his waist, his belt tight and hidden under a spare tube of flesh. His cheeks were plump and paunchy, and a double chin sagged over the neckline of his sweater. He had no visible whiskers on his clean-shaven face, which signaled that he still woke up at dawn and groomed himself meticulously despite the callouses on his hands from years of farm work.

He approached the table and continued his study of her. His reaction to her visit was oddly neutral. His face was blank, as though he stared through her body like a man transfixed by a ghost – no smile, no frown, no nothing. He seemed in denial that she was back home.

"Look who's here, darling," said her mother, feigning delight. "Sherry has come all the way from Washington for dinner. Isn't that great?"

Her father sat down across from her mother at the table.

As the reality of having her home set in, he looked at her with the same deep blue eyes she had. He nodded his head after muttering something, folded his hands, and offered a prayer to the Lord. Sherry and her mother followed his lead as he said grace.

"Oh, heavenly Father," he prayed, "you have blessed us once again with your bountiful food, a roof over our heads, and our livestock. You have taken care of my beautiful daughter in Washington and have given her a wonderful future with the man of her dreams to guide her and protect her. Because you have blessed her, you have blessed our entire family with your beneficence. Please guide those who have strayed from the path, so that they may find their way back to you. Amen."

Sherry had hungered for her mother's fine cooking since she first left for Washington. Her mother never cooked gourmet meals like the ones served in the many expensive restaurants she had dined in, but as far as basic, solid foods were concerned, she excelled in making down-home beef, chicken, and vegetable dishes to near perfection. Her specialty was her delicious assortment of homemade pies and jams made from scratch. She often gave these as gifts to relatives who had since moved far away and also to friends who sometimes popped in for the holidays. Whether her pies were cherry or rhubarb, most of the town knew of her exceptional baking skills. She had built a sturdy reputation over many years of baking them.

Her father stood from the table and carved the pot roast. The women passed their plates up to him. He sat down once the women had been served. He cut a large piece of meat for himself. While eating, his manners were deliberately fastidious, the utensils in his thick hands a reminder of a former New England gentility that had languished over many years of bad luck and poor farming policies at the State level.

He was rugged enough for the farm while tirelessly reserving his best etiquette for high-priced restaurants on the eastern seaboard, should he ever be invited to dine with her ex again. His manners were also useful when her ex came to Vermont. He liked showing him how cultured he was, even though the portrait he presented of himself was misleading. It was more the case that his manners reflected the type of man he wanted to be, not the type of man he was.

They ate in silence. Her father looked at her one moment and then down at his plate the next. He struggled to keep his mouth closed while chewing. Sherry waited for him to say something, to say anything, but he made her wait, perhaps as a demonstration of his power and respectability as head of household.

"Sherry, I'm surprised you're here," he said. "Where's your fiancé?"

"He's not here," said Sherry.

"Speak up, please. You have to speak louder."

"I said, he's not here," she said, almost yelling.

"That's obvious," he said calmly. "You're here alone. When did your flight arrive? He should have sent a limo, no?"

"I took the train this time."

"Oh? Traveling second class? I would think the train's no place for a woman of your stature. Why didn't you fly?"

"I came alone."

"Yes, I can see that."

"Meaning, he doesn't know that I'm here," she said.

"Well, don't you think you should call him and tell him where you are? He must be worried, and he deserves to know where you are. That's not right."

"He's not worried, Dad."

"What? Speak louder, please?"

"He's not worried!" she yelled across the table.

"And why's that?"

"Because we're no longer seeing each other!"

He spent a minute or two cutting into what was left of the pot roast. He looked down at his plate, as though the breaking news did little to affect him. He finished off the meat before responding.

"Well, you better go back and make up with him," he said. "It's probably just a lover's spat. It happens all the time, especially to younger couples. Stay here tonight, cool off a bit, get a hold of your senses, and then catch the next train back in the morning. Your mother will drive you to the station, Isn't that right, hon?"

"Sherry wants to say a little longer than that, don't you, darling?" said her mother. "She's had such a hard time of it down there. It would be much better if she spent a little more time up here with us than going back so quickly. It's so good to see her. Isn't that right?"

"I'd like to stay a little longer if I could, Dad," said Sherry.

"Did you get your fiancé's permission?" asked her father. "He must want you back in Washington."

"He doesn't want me back there," she said. "and I don't want to be back there either. We're no longer together."

"I can see that. You can go back to him tomorrow."

"No, I mean we are no longer seeing each other. We're finished. We're through. We broke up. We're not getting married.”

The dining room was a kettle about to boil over. She could only stare into her plate, her meal half-eaten, her hands slightly trembling.

“Are you saying that you’re back here to stay?” he said, looking straight at her, “because if you are indeed saying that, you might as well know right of the bat that you cannot stay here. Go back to DC and make up with him if you know what’s best for you. Otherwise, you’ll have to make your own way, this I can tell you. You’ll be just like every other nobody out there.”

“Honey, Sherry isn’t here to stay forever, right?” said her mother. “Let’s just sleep on it tonight, relax and unwind, and we’ll discuss it the morning when we’re nice and fresh. We’ll have a better handle on things tomorrow.”

“You are to take her to train station first thing,” said her father.

“I can’t go back,” said Sherry. “I don’t have anywhere to go. I don’t have any money either.”

“You best get a job, then.”

“Honey, please,” said her mother to her husband.

“How long do you expect to stay here?” he said, dropping his silverware on his plate. “What do you expect to do here? Milk the cows? Shear the fleece off the sheep? Drive the tractor around like when you were a schoolgirl? Help your mother tend to her garden? Try out for the Ski Team all over again?”

“Dad, I think you’re overreacting.”

“Am I? How the hell are you supposed to become a doctor when you’re tilling the soil? You’re supposed to be a Senator’s wife and have a respectable job in medicine for

Chrissakes. How will you afford medical school? You can't pay for it, and either can we. But what I don't understand is, why did you ever have to come back here in the first place? What did you hope to gain by coming back here? A career in agriculture? Do you want to be a veterinarian, is that it? Dr. Doolittle with all of the farm animals we have?"

"I don't want to be any of those things."

"That's because there is nothing else to be. You are going to be a Senator's wife and a respected doctor. If you don't become those two things, it's going to be Hell on Earth for us."

"How is that my problem?" snapped Sherry. "Since when was it my responsibility to support this family?"

"Oh, I see," he said, standing from the table and grabbing hold of the chair to steady his body. "You really don't care if this farm goes right to the highest bidder, do you? This farm has been in our family for over a hundred years. You know how endangered these dairy farms are around this state. No one cares about farming anymore except those Wall Street bankers from New York City who come up here and build their fancy homes on our fertile soil to impress their bosses and ski. They ski same resorts no honest family up here can afford. Land is dirt cheap to them. But now we'll have to sell this place. We'll have to work like Mexican migrants picking coffee beans just to make ends meet. We will never farm again. We're finished, Sherry, unless you take the morning train back to Washington and make up with him."

"But I don't love him."

"Love?" he smiled. "Are you serious? Like you know anything about love? You're too young to know anything about love. Love isn't the issue here. Basic survival is the issue. I don't care if you have to crawl on your knees and beg for his forgiveness."

"I'm not doing it!"

"Yes, you are! You are married to his bank account and all of his connections. Who cares if you don't love him? Who said there was such a thing as love anyway?"

"Stop it!" interrupted her mother. "Both of you."

"No, honey," continued her father, "she needs to hear this. She has to grow up. Not to burst your bubble, Sherry, but people marry for different reasons. In your case, you're getting married so that our ancestors who came before you, poor farming folk just like in our family, can finally crawl out of the rock we've been living under ever since we were cavemen. We will then take our places with a class of people who never had to worry about money in their whole lives. People like that never had to endure the hardships we Aspens had to endure since the day we came out of the cave."

"I said, I'm not going back to him!"

"Why the hell not?!"

"Because he cheated on me, okay? He's been cheating on me since the day we met. He's been sleeping around with as many women he wants to, not to mention my once-best friend. If we're married, he'll do the same thing. I'll never shame myself by marrying that adulterer, I don't care how many planes, limos, or mansions he has. It's done. We might as well forget about him."

"Sherry," he chuckled incredulously, "Sherry, my darling, naïve daughter, you weren't born yesterday, were you? Didn't you learn anything in that fancy college of yours? Your sorority sisters must have at least filled you in about how it works for men like him. He's going to be a Senator. A Senator on Capitol Hill! It's already a given that all of these politician-types, all of those guys you see on the news every night, all of those guys giving the rousing speeches and thumping their Bibles in front of these hypnotized crowds all sleep around with whomever they want, whenever they want. The last people they sleep with is their wives. All you have to do is stand next to him when they take those stupid pictures for those stupid magazines and newspapers. You just have to be his date at all of those worthless DC pig-fucks you have to attend. You don't even have to live with him if you don't want to. And suddenly, you talk about love like you really know what the hell you're talking about?

"Love is not the issue here, sweetie. If you want to love someone, then love one of those diseased children from India and nurse them back to health. But even this you can't do, because you just had to take matters into your own hands without talking to me or your mother. I mean, what's gotten into you? What did you hope to prove by leaving him? For all of that education of yours, it's a damned shame you have no common sense at all."

"That's enough!" said her mother.

"I've just about lost my appetite," said her father. "Sherry, why don't you take my piece of your mother's apple pie. You've already taken everything away from us anyway."

His plate was puddled with the blood of the roast. He dismissed himself from the table and climbed the stairs to the bedroom shaking his head and grinning in disbelief. She and her mother sat in the dining room in the aftermath of his anger. She would no longer seek his approval and didn't care anymore if she would ever get it again. His ignorance knew no bounds. Normally, she would have been heartbroken by his callousness, but now that she had been privy to what he really thought, to what he considered to be 'common sense,' she discovered the same type of innate corruption she found in her ex-boyfriend.

While it was true that children do share some responsibility in helping their parents out during times of trouble, the fact that he put it all on her shoulders went way beyond bounds. Her father might as well have been her pimp. Perhaps he was not only older but incurably sick. Being the good daughter Sherry had been, however, she resisted hating him. Yet she didn't have any sympathy for him either, no matter how twisted his mind had become. It wasn't only the money or saving the old farm that bothered him. It had to do with his inability to make proper use of her as he would have a son, had he been given one.

Even though he had pushed her every step of the way, she realized it was all an act and only a means to use her beauty and hard work for his material and monetary gain. If he had a son, it would have been much different, she considered. There would have been someone to inherit his skills as a linebacker in high school, a strong farmer, a skilled trader, and a dependable handyman. He had no one to pass these skills onto. The last thing he expected was to have a beauty queen of a daughter who ran out of a perfect marriage. And just when it mattered, Sherry screwed up, because she was always meant to screw up, just like all women who were put on this earth were meant to disrupt and obfuscate the highest aspirations of mankind. That's what her father must have seen – a curious, selfish girl who had been tempted into using her own mind instead of his.

He must have believed that it was a man's natural right to direct and govern his own family. It was his natural right alone to replicate versions of himself through the vessel of the wife he takes. But the family was now at risk, because women like Sherry prevented a man's alignment with his true, God-given nature. His nature was to hunt and dominate. Man gave order to the universe until daughters like Sherry came along and, unbeknownst to anyone, wrecked the entire plan.

And when a man's natural order fell apart, women craved the emasculation of men rather than the naturalness of revolving around the universe of a man's ever-stiffening cock. Such emasculations sentenced even the toughest to boredom, drudgery, impotence, and premature death. Women like Sherry were merely newcomers to the process. Women like her had been sucked into the vortex of those men who wanted to satisfy their basest desires. Women like Sherry avoided the multitude of solitary souls who offered them loyalty, principle, and character. Such souls were the first to be emasculated, because they utter a quiet hello to the women who pass by them. They then ignore him, step on them and abuse them. Women enjoyed exposing a man's vulnerabilities and inflicting their cruelty upon those he never had the slightest intention of hurting. This was because women were much too weak to defend themselves against men who were loud, obnoxious, criminal, and brutal, or simply put, the same men who abused women like Sherry time and again. A shy and awkward smile across a crowded room only solicited a woman's mockery, and a look from lonely eyes only gave rise to her scorn. Abuse her, and she mysteriously gives her love to you.

Her father had to achieve what he alone desired, even if it meant throwing his own flesh and blood under the bus. She vowed, once again, never to let that happen to her. She would no longer listen to men who tried to mesmerize her with their false dominance. She would defend herself against the likes of her father and the slew of men who thought they would one day rule the world on the stiffness of their erections alone.

Unfortunately for her, though, Sherry could never differentiate the good apples from the rotten ones. She may have had the will to defend herself but lacked knowledge and experience, just like most beautiful women her age. She promised to keep her eyes wide open, especially for men like her father. She had been fooled for the last time.

She couldn't stay on the farm much longer. She had to leave. She couldn't stand being under the same roof with him. He wasn't the type of man who would ever kick her out, though. He still needed to make good use of her. She was, after all, his investment. She would never lose her good looks. Sure, her value had fallen considerably now that her ex was out of the picture, but her father would find some way to profit from her by constructing another scheme or plan. Getting her married to the highest bidder and paying for graduate school seemed unlikely without her father manning the controls. She had little idea where she would go without money or contacts. Her high school friends fled their farms just as she had. There was no reason to stay in Vermont.

Her head burned thinking so much about what she should do. There must have been a way to relocate successfully. She looked to her mother for help. Her mother cut Sherry a small slice of the Dutch apple pie. She then slathered it in sweet, whipped cream freshly made on the farm.

"I can't stay here," said Sherry.

"Of course, you can," said her mother. Your father is just cranky. He'll snap out of it."

"You call that cranky? Really? He's gone too far. I don't want to stay here a minute longer if I don't have to."

"He doesn't mean what he says. He's been under a lot of pressure lately. The farm is going under. You have to take that into consideration. He's exploring all of our options. Give him some time."

"If the farm's going under, it's his own fault. Not

mine."

"It's not anyone's fault, Sherry. All the farms around here are going under. We can't keep up with the expenses when these big corporations sell cheaper milk and cream. We can't afford the taxes either. I would give it another three or four years. I know it was too much to ask of you, but marrying you off was the only option we had. We're just simple dairy folk up here. But you, you're worldly and sophisticated and brilliant and all. Naturally, your father had to use everything we had to save the farm. So don't be so sore with him, sweetheart. He means well, even though he doesn't show it very often."

"It's over, Mom. I'm not staying here."

"Where will you go without any money?"

"I have some money left. I have a degree from Georgetown. I can get any job in any city in the world."

"To get a job you need to apply and get an interview. Isn't that right? Don't think your father is going to give you any money for that. Right now, he's upstairs making his own plans for you. He doesn't trust anyone with the money he has. Not me, not you, not anyone."

"Trust me. As long as I have internet access, I'll find a way."

"We don't have such things way out here. We hear it's coming soon, but we're too far out for that technology yet."

"I know that. But the libraries have it, and once I get to a city that's really cheap, I can get a job with my degree and a place to stay through the alumni network. My degree has a lot of pull, believe it or not. And if I do get a good job, they'll pay for graduate school. I've heard of that happening before. I mean, a Biology degree? What about the pharmaceutical industry or a chemical company? Someone will take me in. I don't know why you're so worried about it. I didn't even need to come back here."

"But first you have to get to a big city. Then you can take a shot at a job."

"I can go to the library tomorrow. I don't have to travel too far for the internet. Manchester must have it. I just need your truck for a few hours."

"We need the truck, Sherry. We're running a farm here, remember? We need it seven days a week."

"Why are you always putting up obstacles? Why do find problems with everything?"

"I'm trying to help, sweetheart. We have to patch up the leaks in the boat before you ship out to sea, right? Also, you'll be alone out there. You have to be safe. You need to have a bed and a roof over your head. It's going to be very cold this winter. Can you blame me for worrying?"

"You don't need to worry about me anymore. I'm an adult. I'm a fully grown woman."

"A woman all alone without money? A young woman at that?"

"Always imagining the worst."

"It's not that I don't trust you out there, Sherry. It's other people that I don't trust. I hear about all the stuff that's happening these days. The poor farmers who can't pay the banks and have to sell their land and head into Babylon just to get a slice of stale bread and watery soup. Yeah, it's that bad."

"I've spent four years in Washington already."

"Yes, four years surrounded by smart, wealthy people with guaranteed futures. You're in another world. It won't be like that where you're headed. It won't be safe for someone like you."

"Mom, I'm not going to become a drug addict or a prostitute, if that's what you mean. I'm a lot smarter than you and Dad make me out to be. He hasn't seen me on my own, and neither have you. He says I have no common sense, which is not true at all."

"Honey, I know you are intelligent and have common sense, but you're still a simple farm girl with a simple rural upbringing. You're not street-smart like those people. They'll eat you alive."

"I'm sorry, but I have to try, come what may. You can't keep me in a protective bubble all my life. Whether it's the easy way or the hard way, I still have to learn. I don't have a crystal ball, and either do you. No one knows what's coming"

They sat in silence. Sherry poked at her apple pie but had already lost her appetite. There was no easy route to development. Nor was there any easy route to greater experience. No one got away. Whether rich or poor, black or white, people were fed into the grinder. It was a maniacal Helter-Skelter process. The higher one flew, the harder one fell. Yet she still had the nagging suspicion that those like her ex were immune to this. He seemed immune to all suffering.

And if trauma were indeed relative, she guessed she suffered just like a black kid shot in the street by a cop. What could be more traumatic that being shot in the street by a cop exactly? There must have been degrees of suffering, then, but suffering relative to the tolerance of pain a person had. She suffered easily, while the punk in the ghetto suffered greatly. Yet they both felt the same degree of suffering, even if she suffered from a broken fingernail and he a bullet to the chest. The trauma is considered the same.

Considering what her mother said, there was good

reason to stay on the farm and learn to live with her father than on the streets of a big city. But whether she stayed or left, she still lost. It would be a regression due to a fear of the hypothetical unknown. She never expected to weigh the decision of leaving or staying so intensely either. Things like memorizing how cells reproduced came easily to her. Taking long, arduous exams in large lecture halls came easily to her. But she no longer saw how the scientific method applied to the hardscrabble streets of DC. She no longer saw her friend's social lives as math problems to solve. She couldn't reify the idea of leaving home and never returning. It was an idea that was hard to tackle and deserved her complete attention and focus. Nothing she learned in college prepared her for this. She finally foresaw it without the filter of the senseless, irrelevant, intellectual nonsense they forced down her throat at school. Nothing but a starved, wounded animal came out. This was the person she now started out with.

A stream of words tumbled out of her mother's mouth. She could hardly pay attention to what she said. It was the same stream of fear and worry that said she was too sheltered to survive on her own. Her mother talked about the news stories, always the news stories - the shootings, the killings, the wars, the pandemics. A reckoning was coming.

"Just yesterday, someone killed a social worker in New York," said her mother. "The poor girl was just helping out those poor black people. And you know what? The social worker looked just like you. They slit her throat and threw her in a dumpster, that poor girl."

"The crime rate in New York is the lowest it's ever been," retorted Sherry. "Plus, I can't afford New York. It's way too expensive."

"All cities are that way. Not just New York. A young woman in a city, especially a woman like you, will always be a target for predators and rapists. I hear how those animals put those drugs in women's drinks so that they can go home with them and rape them. They call it 'the Date Rape Drug.'"

Yes, her mother had gotten old. Years of news reports, syndicated crime dramas, and fast-paced mystery thrillers left her in all-out fear for her only child. Sherry saw them etched in the lines of her face and in the white of her ghostly hair. What had once been soft eyes had now been surrounded by a permanent wince, as though a rock were forever being hurled at her face. She didn't know how to reverse it, and perhaps the best remedy was to leave her alone so she could forget about her. Her mother would stay with her Dad and drift in and out of ancient memories about what their family once was. Sherry only worried because her mother always worried – a chain that kept her bound to a father who concocted plan after plan to have her caged in when she tried to roam free.

Without having a place to go other than her roughshod apartment in Washington, she left the farm early the next morning unsure about how she'd pay for the next meal with the dollars she had left in her *Gucci* purse. Maybe this was common for women like her – runaways or escape artists fleeing domestic abuse, or fugitives of some kind, only she had done nothing wrong ever to anyone. Regardless of how sorry she felt for herself that morning, she still had to leave. Her shoddy apartment in Washington was the only place to go. Fortunately, she didn't formally vacate it.

After a light breakfast of oatmeal and strawberries, she left with her mother while it was still dark out. She hadn't slept very well. She packed half the clothing she originally came with. She figured traveling light was the best option, especially if she had to move from her DC rathole. At least the mattress that came with the apartment was already there. Even though she just woke up that morning, she oddly looked forward to the comforts of sleeping on that old, musty mattress again despite its permanent sag in the middle.

It was so cold out that she could again see her breath within the cab of the truck as they rolled out from the farm after breakfast. She didn't say goodbye to her father. He was supposed to matter, but he really didn't anymore. Why the image of the ideal nuclear family had been rammed into her at such an early age, she had no idea.

She knew America was about the strength and unity of the family, as her professor in political science class had explained, but it was much too difficult to live up to such a standard when every family fought to preserve what little it had. Having a happy and seamless family was a luxury. Only the image of perfection had been protected and dragged through time - the perfect American family that every schoolgirl wanted but could never have. It seemed useless to mirror such a model when no family but the privileged few lived up to the ideal. Had her ex still been in the picture, then maybe it would have happened, but just like much of her life, the image of a family's strength, pride, and functionality was a lie propagated over a huge expanse of time. Everything was perfect in the white American family except for the white American family. The only way not to fall for it was not to pay attention to it.

Each house they drove past on the dark Vermont road whispered to her with a forked tongue. It said that a full, happy family lived inside every cottage and ate breakfast together around an antique wooden table, side by side in the bliss that came with prosperity and traditional New England wellbeing. It was fitting that the tremendous verdancy of the rolling fields had been smothered by layers of crusted snow.

Instead of heading straight to the train station, however, her mother drove into the center of town. It was a single strip a road with two-family structures on either side of it. It housed the town's local businesses. These houses had been gutted and restored to become a couple of hair salons, a state bank, a mom-and-pop food store, and a small clothing shop. At that hour, the town was dark and empty. Her mother rolled in front of the state bank.

"What are you doing?" asked Sherry.

"Just wait here. I'll be right back. I have to run an errand."

"Now?"

"Yes, now. Just wait here."

Her mother disappeared somewhere in the bank's lobby. Sherry waited in the truck for what seemed like hours. Her curiosity flared with every snowflake that melted on the windshield. Since her mother didn't leave the truck's engine running, Sherry judged the temperature inside the truck by the puffs of warm air that pumped out of her lungs. She warmed her fingertips by breathing on them. Her fingertips were usually the first part of her body that froze up.

"Can we go now?" said Sherry, once her mother returned. "The train leaves in ten minutes. I can't miss it."

Her mother then handed her a stack of one-hundred dollar notes.

"Mom, what did you do?" she said in alarm.

"You have to be safe, and you have to have enough for at least three month's rent."

"Not a good idea. You shouldn't have done this."

"It's okay. I'll have to deal with him anyway. Might as well get it over with."

"You're really going to get it. What if he leaves, takes

all that's left, and never returns? Have you thought about that? What if he hurts you?"

"Your father? Nah. That's not him. Deep down, he's a good and decent man. Troubled, yes, and he has his faults, that's for sure. But I know he'll get over it. He won't hurt me. Not over this."

"What if he does?"

"You don't know him like I do. You're going to have to trust me. He'll get over it."

"I don't know," said Sherry.

"Just take the money, sweetheart. Start a new life. When you get a decent job and make your own way, you can pay him back. Call us once you do. That way, we know you're still alive."

She kissed her mother and hugged her tightly.

"I have faith in you, sweetheart. I've always had faith in you. You must never forget that. Wherever you go, I'll be with you every step of the way."

"I know you will."

"Keep that money carefully. Actually, put it down your bra right now. That's the best place for it."

Sherry tugged at her sweater and the blouse beneath it. She slipped the money into her purple-lace bra that her ex had bought from *Coup de Foudre* on E Street. The edges of the crisp bills were sharp. The coarse surfaces stuck to the roundness of her breast. The money would be safe there and always within reach. She could stay in Washington after all and find entry-level work using the reputation of the school she had just graduated from.

After bidding her mother a final farewell at the train station, Sherry lifted her suitcase up a metal staircase into the train car. She sat at a four-person seat and put the suitcase on the opposite side of her, just like before. As the train started moving, her mother stood next to the truck outside and waved goodbye. Little did she know that the windows were too dark to see Sherry waving back.

Sherry worried about her. Ironically, she had always hated how she had forecasted only doom and despair. Sherry found herself imagining the worst too. Yes, her parents would fight, yell, scream, beat each other, who knew? Money to her father was the end-all-be-all of life itself. It was as necessary as water or air. Maybe after one broke into adulthood, that's all America became. The money rubbing against the sides of her breasts now a carried greater emotional weight. Someone could have ripped open her shirt and stolen it. The landlord would then throw her out of the apartment. She would be homeless and out on the street in the arctic DC weather. Maybe she would have to make a deal with a thug and sell herself into sex slavery for food and shelter.

She calmed her thoughts a little as the train gained speed. She would have to cook for herself and do her own laundry for a change. She would have to use public transportation everywhere she went. One day, she might be able to afford a small, fuel-efficient car, bottom of the line, made in Japan or South Korea. It would be a car designated for those who were financially compromised. As she drives it down the street, people would look at her and think her too poor for townhouse living or the sprawling country-home splendor of nearby Chevy Chase. Maybe she would have to purchase a used car, a dented and rusted contraption that barely ran, a car that pigeonholed her as a drug-addicted mother of three in a basement apartment where sex-hungry, well-hung black men often trouped through to fuck her in exchange for a few hits of crack and a few dollars to buy some beer at the corner store.

It could have gone that way too.

Naturally, before such a scenario materialized, she would need to have some companionship, but she was too angry with men to consider ever getting involved again. She would have rather stayed alone for the rest of her life, squatting in the bush of the African jungle with her posse of gorillas and chimpanzees, feeding them milk from baby bottles, writing books about her decades-long research, appearing in interviews and documentaries on public television, loved and admired by angry, lonely women everywhere. Of course, if the gorillas knew more of her kind were on their way, they would eat her alive. But she would also have cats and dogs with her, no, female cats and female dogs, which would suit her much better than shacking up with some manipulative, adulterous sleazebag who bought his women instead of putting in the effort to woo them.

She swore she just saw one of these sleazebags down the aisle of the train car drooling over her. Funny how when pretty women traveled alone, they always kept to themselves and pretended to be busy with something. It was their only defense. Anything less than the scent of the latest *Ralph Lauren* signature fragrance stunk of arm pits, sewage, and spoiled cheese. The train was a repulsive combination of her own perfumed skin and the odors of the deranged. Even the stubby, potbellied conductor tried miserably to start a conversation with her and ended up being ignored by the brand-new feminist she suddenly became. She finally joined the women's rights movement after decades of Hollywood films, news shows, documentaries, breast cancer marches, lawsuits, and custody battles attesting to the undefeatable and indefatigable supreme power of women and their ability to pound their way into every corner of culture and society. This lasted for the rest every man's life until they were put out of their misery for not being gay, transgendered, or any other kind of new species that would never again threaten to loosen the feminine grip on their balls. She had left her old life behind, and there was something vaguely satisfying about her womanly defiance.

She did, however, have some of class dignity left. She still looked upon these Amtrak oddballs sympathetically, as though they deserved her charity and queenly blessings for being the closeted freaks they truly were. The people traveling with her had no hope. It wasn't until many miles of frozen patches of farmland transformed into signs of life that people of higher standing boarded the train. Through a stopover at cosmopolitan Penn Station for coffee and a bagel, on through the swamps and oil refineries of New Jersey, and across the flat, unremarkable fields of Delaware, slivers of nervous fear bit into her heart as she thought about spending another month in her crummy apartment. Soon, they crossed Maryland's border.

She could have made the apartment a more pleasurable place by painting the walls, buying a loveseat, or putting up prints of famous artwork. But she was too depressed to bother with such silly things. With a foggy head, she drifted in and out of sleep having thought too much.

The dream she had was brief but verismiltudinous nonetheless. In the short dream, her sorority sisters crowded around her to hear how the most important date of her life went. Her ex had proposed to her that night - in the dream, of course - and her sisters focused their full attentions on how the proposal went. In the sorority's secret inner sanctum that evening, Sherry wore a white dress, and in her delicate hand she held a long-stemmed rose her ex had given her as a symbol of his undying love and his promise to provide for her needs and do whatever it took to make her happy.

During clandestine sorority meetings such as these, there were only a few select gentlemen in the sorority's long and heralded history who were permitted access to the ultra-exclusive inner sanctum. With the white-hot spotlight shining upon her after years of unforgiving labor on her father's farm, her ex walks gracefully through the door and whisks her away to his townhouse nearby to make tender and passionate love to her. When he kicks the bedroom door open, however, the same deformed, drooling pervert down the aisle whisks her from the platform of Washington's *Union Station* and throws her in front of an oncoming express train.

She awoke with a start and found that the train shook and jostled her on its unnerving route towards a destination that seemed lightyear's away. She checked to see if the same man in her dream was still in his seat, but apparently, he had gotten off at an earlier stop. It took all of her patience to wait until *Union Station.*

It was like seeing the capital city for the very first time, as she lugged her suitcase through the subways and finally to the same efficiency apartment she had left the day before. Even though she had only been away for only one day, living in her dreary apartment was incalculably better than living with her father, even though conditions at the farmhouse were much better. Now that she was no longer tied to her ex's bank account, there were trade-offs involved. She could not have it all but settled for having choices amongst preferences instead, assuming she had the power to choose at all. Because, when poor, having a choice between two fast-food burger joints became an illusion when the view of the ghetto was the same, not to mention the unhealthiness of the food. At least when rich, the choice among views of the White House while sipping wine at *The Lafayette*, or a view from *Jose Andres* enjoying a raspberry martini, or watching the beautiful people on their way to a show at *Ford's Theater* was much more obvious. The fast-food joints merely offered the same horror, the same non-choice, like choosing one pile of shit over the other. After all, in America, there were only two choices a poor woman could make: bad or worse.

She beheld the devastation of her apartment when she walked in and from thenceforth believed that her choices had been taken away, just like the illusory choice of relocating to a better apartment a few blocks down. Nevertheless, she would have to make do, no matter how much she hated it. The first order of business, however, was to find a job as soon as possible. It couldn't be any old job, though. It had to be a job that gave her passage to much better living arrangements, preferably to the Georgetown area. She thought working at a law office was the best bet, considering that every other person in the city was a lawyer anyway. There must have been a law office in every building on every block in Washington, as though the city itself required a law degree to enter it. She may have had a problem with a degree in Biology, but a smart woman from Georgetown would still be an asset. She had a wide range of skills and talents that would benefit any law firm.

With the money her mother had given her, she bought a television and connected basic cable. She also bought a piece of crap laptop from a local computer store and hooked up the Internet. She went to work searching random job sites that took hours to download. Judging from the pay advertised for paralegal work, she would be able to move out in just a couple of months and add to the cash she already had, cash that she still kept in her bra. Soon, she saw the sun rise within the gloom and her free will hidden within ironclad destiny. Things started to look promising. She submitted nearly a hundred resumes online and waited patiently for someone, anyone, to call. Several places responded, and naturally, she chose the law office that offered the highest pay.

Much to her surprise, landing an interview took no time at all. Assuming they made her an offer, a job would net her enough to escape poverty and head out of town, perhaps to Chevy Chase with a car for the commute and a life with neighbors who had separated themselves from the animals of the inner-city. She could then call her mother, raise her fist into the air as a sign of victory, and return the cash she had given her. It all fell into place, only this time it was her own doing, her own plan, and not her father's. She saw it unfolding long before it unfolded, as though it already worked. Such a trait ran amok among the Aspens, but she was oblivious to it at the time. She landed an interview at a prestigious law firm on Connecticut Avenue just a few days after returning to DC.

On the morning of the interview, she dressed in a black suit bought by her ex for business-oriented lunches, usually involving non-profit charity work for innocuous causes most of the population already agreed with. She waited in a comfortable lobby attended by an exceptional-looking receptionist. She was a brunette with long, wavy hair and green eyes. She was foreign, no, Continental, judging by her accent when she spoke on the phone. She must have been Greek, Italian, or from some royal city-state that bordered the Mediterranean, her body an hourglass and her legs the length of the Nile. When the woman lifted herself from her ergonomic chair, Sherry nearly gasped at the light green dress she wore. It draped over her curves but was still subtle enough to hint at her capacity to seduce men of high rank and importance. She didn't appear slutty, in other words, even though the dress suggested otherwise. For the first time in a long while, Sherry was a little jealous of another woman's looks, even though this receptionist was merely a brunette and

Sherry an incurable blonde. She had never been challenged like that before.

While growing up, her blonde hair and skin had always been fetishized to the point of male obsession. Most boys assumed she already had a lover, which was the right assumption to make. The receptionist also fit this same profile. Sherry now swam in a bigger pond, played in a bigger league, competed in games other than *Spin-the-Bottle* and *Truth-or-Dare* among giggling sorority girls in bras and panties. One would think any woman would be relieved to find someone who shared the same burden of being an object to possess, but in this case, Sherry cringed at the thought of sharing the mantle with this woman. She had a lot of catching up to do. Her stint as a college undergrad was officially over.

"Come with me, please," said the receptionist, who led her into a small conference room with noise-canceling machines whirring in the hallway. "Our chief litigator will be right with you."

As the receptionist left the room, Sherry noticed how the receptionist's green dress stretched tightly over her buttocks. Again, it must have been a passive-aggressive suggestion that she was available to all men while always maintaining ethical boundaries. Sherry figured that if she landed a job that morning, she too would have to buy outfits that were sexy but with the right amount of officiousness. She would have to show that she had the scruples not to screw around with the lawyers.

She sat alone at a large oval table in the room and waited nervously for a full half-hour before the door opened. In came a tall gallant gentleman in a grey suit and tasseled mahogany loafers. He looked like an actor from an afternoon soap opera, only that he was one of the litigators for this boutique law firm to which she now applied. At first, she thought it amusing, because the room did seem like a set of a television show. But as the man opened a manila folder and took out her resume, she straightened up and suppressed her laughter. The guy was very handsome – a clean shaven thirtysomething with a square jaw and expensive aftershave.

"Miss Aspen, is that right?"

"Yes. Sherry Aspen."

"Okay, Miss Aspen. What brings you in today?"

"I'm interested in the paralegal position with your prestigious law firm."

"Yes," he said. "I can see that," running down her list of accomplishments.

"Georgetown, eh?" he smiled. "My brother went there. So did my uncle. I chose Yale, though. I thought they had a better pre-law program."

"Great. Yeah, I really liked Georgetown. I was challenged academically. I had a well-rounded education, and as you can see from my transcripts, I did really well academically."

"I can see that, yes. But why Biology of all subjects? I mean, we usually take graduates who want to go to law school. Pre-law, or at least English, Government, or History. What makes a young girl with a Biology degree want to be a lawyer?"

"I was always interested in law, especially as it relates to Biotechnology and the Healthcare industry. I feel that I would be a great addition to your team, especially if you deal with these industries or any industries related to them."

"But we do strictly government work," he said.

"True. This I know, but I feel it would be good to have someone like me for my ability to analyze cases with precision and perspective, just like a scientist.”

“I don’t quite get where you’re coming from.”

“For instance, I’m very good at getting to know a case inside and out, and I’m good at writing up documents for your clients in a very detailed and efficient manner, much like scientific case studies.”

The litigator sighed and raised his eyebrows before returning to her resume.

“Do you want to go to law school after you move on from here?” he said. “Frankly, you can’t be a paralegal forever. You’d just rot in a job like this. Are you interested in going to law school at all?”

“Yes. Yes, I am,” she lied. “I want to pursue a law degree by the time I finish my work here. I don’t expect to remain a paralegal all my life. I want to become a government or a corporate lawyer. One or the other.”

“Miss Aspen, we usually take only those who go on to law school. Don’t you think law school may be a stretch for you, considering your background? All I see is Biology here. It’s like you should be going to med school, not law school.”

“Yes,” she sighed. “I can see your point.”

“Look, you’re a Georgetown graduate, which helps. I’m your sure you are smart, so here’s what I’m going to do. We do have a position here that you are qualified for, but not as a paralegal.”

“But that’s the position I’m applying for.”

“I know, but I have another position available that may be a better fit. You may even like it much more than sitting in a drab cubicle and staring into a computer screen all day.”

“I’d be interested in something like that, sure.”

"Well, it so happens that we have room for a new receptionist for our front office. Our current receptionist is moving on to our New York office in a couple of weeks. Would you be interested in being our new receptionist here?"

"I'm a little overqualified for that."

"Not necessarily. Our receptionists are very important to our firm. Their work is indispensable. Once you take over, you will be, in a sense, our lead representative. You will be our brand ambassador. You are the first person our clients see when they walk through the door. You will be their first introduction to our firm. You have to use your high intelligence at all times to see to their needs, see that they feel comfortable in our office, and prep them to meet our staff of lawyers, or even our international partners who will drop in every now and then. Think of it this way: Laura Bush is now the First Lady, right?"

"Sure."

"Well, Laura Bush is the figurehead who has a full staff behind her. Laura Bush is 'the front office,' so to speak, the flagship, the face on the magazine cover, the face on the dollar bill. All the others are behind the scenes and in the engine room, while Laura Bush is out front in public view.

"Basically, as far as our Washington office is concerned, you can think of yourself as our Laura Bush, our Oprah, our Katy Couric, our Ruth Bader Ginsburg. And you know what else I'll do? I'll pay you the same salary we pay our paralegals. Viewing it from this vantage point, I think that taking on this position is an excellent opportunity for an intelligent Georgetown girl like yourself."

"I think I need more time to make a decision."

"I need to know now," he said more seriously. "Miss Aspen, there are plenty of bright girls out there who would kill for a job like this. I can't wait around. My time is valuable."

"I know it is. I didn't mean to imply otherwise."

"Why don't you take a few minutes. Would you like a beverage in the meantime? Coffee, water, a soda?"

"Thank you, no."

"I'll be back in a few minutes. Please have your answer by then. Think it over carefully."

In the stillness of the conference room, she thought she might have been wrong about not having choices. A choice now presented itself. When things went well, she had choices. When not, she had no choices at all. It depended on the mood and the information given at the time. Are choices made in ignorance really choices, though? Yes, because her mood was positive enough to see the new job through rose-colored glasses. She was positive enough to accept it. It paid just as much, and the pay was way above what she expected. Sure, the work was beneath her. She was overqualified. But money was money. She could have taken on more respectable work, and she wouldn't have to feel the touch of shame she currently felt. She could have been much more, if only she were born with money, like her ex and her turncoat sorority sisters. Well, take a number, she said to herself. The world didn't owe her anything. No one did.

When the handsome litigator returned, she accepted the job offer.

"Good," he said. "The receptionist will show you the ropes. It's fairly easy. Just answer phones and transfer calls to the proper extensions. Again, you are what our clients see when they first walk into the office. It's an important position, even though you may not think so right now."

"Thank you for the opportunity," she said. "You

won't be disappointed."

"I know I won't," he smiled. "Come with me."

The litigator led her out of the conference room and through a hallway that hooked back into the main lobby. There, the receptionist in the green dress busied herself making espresso. Hot steam shot out of the machine and drowed out the soft overhead music. Sherry still couldn't get over the green dress that clung to the shape of her body.

"I take it she's my replacement," she said to the litigator in her unusual Mediterranean accent.

"Yes. Meet Miss Sherry Aspen. She is taking over your position. Show her the ropes, okay," he said with a wink.

"Hi," said Sherry, sticking out her hand. "I'm Sherry Aspen. Nice to meet you."

The receptionist looked her up and down in what seemed to be an initial examination. She shook her head and said in a foreign accent, "tsk, tsk, tsk. You are all wrong."

Sherry studied the business suit she put on that morning. It was probably more expensive than her dress and perfectly acceptable.

"Why? What's wrong with it?" she asked.

"For this job, those rags won't do."

"This is not a *rag*. This is a top-of-the-line suit, you should know."

"Don't take it personally, darling. You just need clothes that are much more, oh, how should we say it, nicer to other people."

"This is a law office," she said angrily. "And besides, it's not like I can just whip out my American Express Platinum card and go to town with it."

"Oh, you are new to this, aren't you? My God, what are we going to do? Okay, darling, come with me. And take the bug out of your ass too. It will help me like you more."

"Where are we going? Aren't you supposed to show me the ropes?"

"Not with you looking like that. Just be quiet and follow me."

They donned their winter coats and took the elevator down to a small parking lot in the basement of the building. Sherry expected a simple company car, but when the receptionist pressed her keychain, the backlights of a brand-new Mercedes-Benz sports coupe flashed among a row of other high-priced cars. It was red and the latest model.

"That's your car?" stammered Sherry.

"It's for my use, yes," smiled the receptionist.

Compared to the dread of using public transportation, taking a ride in a deluxe sportscar with a driver who knew her way around the city came as a real relief. For some reason, Sherry had full confidence in her driving ability, unlike her mother or her father. Otherwise, she would have cringed and writhed in her seat, slamming on the imaginary brakes every few seconds.

After several sharp zigs and zags on the city streets, they arrived in front of a luxury building near the City Center. A valet in a red suit welcomed the receptionist personally, and in the barely tolerable cold, they walked to the mall a block away.

Sherry had been to the mall many times before, usually taking along her ex's credit card. This time, however, the mall was an oasis to a woman who had been wandering in the desert and dying of thirst. She could have kissed the marble floor and thanked heaven above for having been redelivered to a high-end shop with her new mentor leading the way.

"I haven't been here in ages," Sherry said, even though she had been there a few weeks earlier.

"Better get used to it," said the receptionist, laughing. "Just remember, the most important part of the job is looking good. You have to look good all the time."

"I can handle that," she said, smiling.

Her old self wasn't so far behind after all. Her new friend, along with the law firm's credit card, led her through the mall like a fairy godmother lighting her way from shop to shop. They giggled and laughed while trying on dresses, jewelry, and a host of accessories that the office lawyers would find 'pleasing.' And when the partners came to town, they would also be pleased.

"The sexier the clothes, the better," said the receptionist.

They whirled into one of the stores like twin tornadoes of rabid indulgence. A middle-aged saleswoman with hair that seemed unnaturally colored approached them. She had a long, elegant gown on.

"I welcome you," said the saleswoman, obsequiously. "How may I be of help?"

"We're looking for some new outfits for my friend here. They have to be good for the office but with enough sex appeal to make the bosses notice."

"My God," said Sherry, embarrassed. "Don't be so discreet."

"I think I have just the thing you're looking for," she said.

They stayed in the store for an hour and a half. Sherry

modeled dress after dress for the receptionist. She loved being back in her element. She wore the most expensive dresses with high-class designer names. The fabric felt soft and comfortable against skin that had been rough and dry from the old trailer-park wardrobe she brought in from Vermont. The restored view of herself in the full-frontal mirror returned her to the beautiful catch she had always been, as though returning to the farm was but a brief yet effective nightmare. And even though the dresses she took home with her were a little too revealing for any office setting, the receptionist assured her the bosses expected her to look that way. She no longer minded dumbing down for the job. She had no problem dating the firm's credit card instead of her ex. It came effortlessly.

"Is this a roach motel?" asked the receptionist, parking in front of her building after their shopping day was done.

"Not for long, I hope."

"You could be killed in there," she said, turning off the engine. "You needed this job. You definitely needed a change of scene. You could die in that place. It looks like someone bombed it out."

"I know. What can I do?"

"Just be what they want you to be. I'd give it a month, and you'll be out of there."

"You think so?"

"I know so. You won't stay there for long. Just wear those dresses. The rest will take care of itself."

"But what about the phones and the computer and the espresso machine?"

The receptionist laughed without answering the question. Even though Sherry had only known her for a day, she was sad to see she had to leave so soon.

"It's a new city, and a new life," said the receptionist, reflecting. "You're just getting started. Don't fuck up. The men will like you. I can tell."

"I'm not looking for anything right now," said Sherry. "I'm just coming off a serious relationship."

"That's too bad. Some very rich and powerful men in this town. You should keep yourself open to all the possibilities."

"I don't think so. I just want to make enough to move out and move on. I want a career."

"I have no time for stupid careers," she said in her foreign accent. "I go where the wind takes me."

"You mean, you don't have any plans for the future? Like raising a family or having kids? Maybe getting a better a job?"

"God laughs at plans," she said, her smile straightening. "Who knows?" she continued. "Maybe one day. But until then, I'll screw as many men as I can until I get what I want. It's the only way to go before I wrinkle up and die like a fallen leaf."

They both laughed at the melodrama in the tone of her voice. Even though Sherry was headed in another direction and didn't quite understand her need to live a sexually wild and reckless life, she wanted the best for her.

"You're such a good girl," said the receptionist, stroking her hair. "You're going to be just fine."

Her hands running through her hair felt like her mother's. Sherry fell into a mellow trance in the darkness of the car. She could have let her stroke her hair all night. She closed her eyes and allowed herself to accept the comfort of her hands, but her eyes opened when she felt a warm breath at the edge of her lips. The receptionist aimed straight for her mouth. Before she had time to think about it, Sherry tongued her newfound friend in the front seat of the Mercedes, the woman's Mediterranean fingers lost in her hair and her hand moving slowly but deliberately up her thigh. She had a tough time stopping her.

"I'm sorry," said Sherry, putting her hand on hers. "I'm not that way."

"Why don't you try it? You may like it. You want me to come up?"

"I don't think it's a good idea. I'm sorry."

"Don't be," she sighed, returning to her side of the car. "It's alright. If I were you, though, the next time you get an opportunity like this, I wouldn't pass it up. Women like us, you know, the ones who always have to look good, will never find love with men. Men don't know how to love women like us. They will never satisfy us, no matter how hard they try. You should experiment a little. Open yourself up to new experiences."

"Something to think about, I suppose."

"Good luck to you, Miss Aspen."

The receptionist kissed her one last time before letting her out of the car. The Mercedes then peeled out of sight. Barely managing to carry the many shopping bags up three flights of stairs, she collapsed on the sagging mattress once in the apartment, the bags scattering all over the floor. Perhaps being a simple receptionist wasn't so bad after all, she thought, with a tired smile on her face. Dumbing down for the position no longer posed a problem. If they wanted her for her looks, she'd give it to them, and they'd have to pay for it as well. Maybe that was how the world worked for 'women like us,' she guessed. She was more than happy to play that role if it got her back to where she belonged.

Chapter Seven

January 2000 – Washington D.C., USA

After only a week at the law firm, it dawned upon Sherry that there were no easy jobs in America. She had three examples from which to draw this undeniable conclusion.

Example One. As an adult, farm labor would have been incredibly hard on her now that she was an adult. Even though farm work and farm living were supposed to come naturally, she had grown to hate it after passing through middle school. After all, she was born and raised on a farm. Her mother and father were experienced farmers. Every generation of Aspens before her worked their own fields and sold what they produced. But because her mother was more gardener than farmer, Sherry took more after her mother than her workaholic father.

Once she entered high school, her father made sure that her mind and body gentrified out of its own atavism and latched on to the New England intellectual tradition of learning what the founding fathers learned at the great colleges and universities of the Northeast.

Her father never went to college, and neither did her mother. Her father saw higher education as an endeavor worthy of the wealthy and the elite. At the time, the rest of the population had a hard time finishing high school. She would be the first Aspen to go to college. Mix in her astounding good looks, and she became an unstoppable and serious contender ready to mate with a champion and breed a race of super-children who would work harder, calculate faster, live much better, and achieve much more than being bound to an old farm and falling in love with a farmhand of lesser value. Her father wanted her properly matched in order to save the family from extinction.

He began to get tough on her by bearing down on her study habits and lecturing about how important an education was. From her humble, young beginnings as a tomboy, she soon flourished into an attractive princess whom every boy wanted to date and every girl wanted to become, just like her father had planned. Sherry soon thought farm work beneath her and abandoned the family tradition to advance her status beyond that of a physical grunt.

Perhaps her father had foreseen the terrible future, the end of farming and the rise of the urban corporation that had never planted a single seed but knew full well how to buy entire acres of fertile land. As prescient as her father was, Sherry did appreciate how he took away her natural instincts to farm. Her life in the middle of nowhere had been reconfigured. She became a socialite beauty queen. Interestingly enough, the only difference between the lifestyle she enjoyed with her ex and the receptionist position she now had was that the money she earned was her own, and she earned it by being the same socialite beauty queen, only this time it was at the law firm's front desk. Being a receptionist at least warranted a paycheck and not necessarily a rich husband who paid for all of her expenses.

Example Two. Being a receptionist was not easy work, in keeping with her theory that no job in America was ever easy. If being a receptionist was not easy, then what job in America was easy? She had to take into account what she did on the job, day in, day out, for her new high-priced and prestigious law firm. Looking good, feeling good, and being cheerful, happy, and servile throughout the eight-hour workday did not come easily at all. She was a brand ambassador alright, but more like a model at a car show introducing the automobile of the year to an audience of enthusiasts and aficionados. Smile, be helpful, make espresso, coffee, and tea, be polite, and always, always look good, just like the prior receptionist in the green dress had said. Answering phones, making a few copies here and there, and scheduling appointments for a handful of lawyers was the easy part. Smiling without twitching, that was the hard part.

More alarmingly, everyone in the office was older than she, from the all-female paralegal staff to the all-male Chippendale's lawyers. They too smiled, spoke politely, dressed nicely, had scented skin, manicured fingernails, and worked out at the same pricey athletic club. When upset, she simply pretended to be happy and grateful to meet the next stiff who walked through the front door.

There was, however, a big difference between what the lawyers and the paralegals did on a day-to-day basis and what she had to do during the same time. The others at least kept themselves busy doing the work of the firm. Sherry, on the other hand, had a hard time staying busy at all. There would be moments, say, in a full hour, or maybe in a few consecutive hours, when the telephone wouldn't ring or the lawyers didn't need anything copied or scheduled. As Sherry confronted these huge gaps of time where these mysterious black holes opened up and dizzyingly sucked her into a universe where there was nothing at all to do except sit there and stare at an imaginary dot on the wall, her consciousness transformed into anti-matter. Bored out of her mind, she never noticed that she was still chained to her desk while waiting for something to happen and desperately hoping for the next lifeform to pull her back to earth. She had to sit at her desk, because the phone could ring at any moment. Even though the job was only too simple, it was still too difficult. She could have surfed the web, but she didn't know what to look for and didn't want to be caught by any of the lawyers chatting away with someone online. It wouldn't make a good impression. She at least had to pretend to be working, even though there was no work to be done.

Example Three. No example was more compelling and more glaringly obvious to her than this one. After her first full week of work, the firm directly deposited her very first paycheck into her bank account. It was Friday, and a rarefied excitement swept through all of the Capital City that afternoon. Everyone smiled, and the sun shone upon them all. She heard that some in the office were headed to a local watering hole for happy hour. She ran to the bank machine for cash.

In the lobby of the bank, she noticed how a black security guard, in full uniform and sitting alone at his desk, stared straight ahead at the cash machine in front of him. People of all kinds streamed into the bank's lobby through the bank's double doors. They came in off the street and walked past his desk without showing any identification whatsoever. Behind the guard were elevator doors that led to the executive offices upstairs. Yet this hypnotized guard stopped no one from entering this private area beyond the checkpoint. He sat at his desk like a statue as the cash machine in the lobby distributed its money to its customers. She also noticed how no one else lodged a complaint, made a noise, or even paid attention to this obvious breach of security. The guard never stopped anyone.

After tugging her cash out of the machine, she

approached the guard who sat motionless at his desk. His desk was without a telephone, a television, a computer screen, or even a transistor radio. Not even a picture frame, a time sheet, a newspaper, a scanner, or an x-ray machine, just nothing, not even a desk blotter, was on his desk. It was like he wasn't there at all. Sherry couldn't resist inquiring.

"Excuse me, sir?"

"Yes, ma'am. What can I do for you?" he said in a deep timbre.

At least he acknowledged her instead of sitting there like an ersatz scarecrow.

"Can I ask you something?" she said politely.

"Sure. Go ahead."

"You're the security guard, right?"

"That's what my badge says. You are right indeed."

"But everyone is walking past you. You haven't stopped one person. You're just sitting there and not watching anything. You're not doing anything either. What's that all about?"

"I'm not your everyday security guard, ma'am," he said glumly, still looking at the cash machine.

But then, out of nowhere, he raised his arm and pointed to the machine itself.

"You see that piece of equipment there?"

"Yeah. That's where everyone gets their money."

"Well, I'm here to guard the equipment. The bank doesn't care who walks in here."

She tried to make sense of this, as any science major would.

"You mean, your job is to watch the cash machine? Nothing else?"

"Yes, ma'am."

"No television or radio? No book or magazine?"

"We're not allowed to have anything on our desk or do anything for eight hours a day except to watch that there machine."

"How can you possibly stand it?" she said, losing all hope. "It's almost inhuman."

"I get paid a little over minimum wage. I consider myself lucky. I get five paid vacation days a year."

"It's incredible how much you've had to endure, and for how many years?"

"Must be going on three years now, five days a week. Let's just say it takes some getting used to. Now, if you don't mind, ma'am, I have to get back to work."

"Be my guest."

Sherry was convinced that this older black man had the most difficult job on the face of the earth. It pushed her into thinking that such an easy, simple, innocuous job such as his would drive any human being to incurable insanity. If this man's take-home pay was over minimum wage, imagine what it must have been like to be a bank teller or a bank manager?

She left the bank in a state of impending doom with the cash from her first paycheck in her purse. She was ready for a few drinks at a yuppie bar with good-looking people who liked to camp, hike, ski, take long walks on the beach, and drink shots of tequila on Cinco de Mayo. But even this was unlikely. Everything was work, forever working, even working towards the goal of having fun for a single evening. And if she didn't work at all and just had fun all the time, she would have been an open target for scorn and vituperative ridicule. She would have needed greater and greater pleasures to arrive at the same level of fun. If she didn't work, or at least didn't pretend to work, or not to be in motion and not going somewhere, always resting, not even using her intellect as labor but always having fun, then she would have never blended in. She would have stood out like the hussy-slut at a high school dance, the bearded lady talking to herself on the street with her cart of donated clothes, the whore waiting for Jesus to give her the capacity to love again like when she was a virgin. She never wanted to see the security guard again and vowed to visit a cash machine at a different location just to avoid him. She couldn't just 'be' somewhere. Such a state of 'being' was impossible.

When she returned to the office, the workday had nearly ended. After sitting at her desk the whole day and as the lawyers and female paralegals filed passed her, most likely to spend their weekends with their significant others or group of friends doing all interesting things, she at least felt like they liked her after they wished her a good weekend. At least some progress was made. The paralegals, especially, had places to go and people to see. They were incapable of spending time alone, simply because beautiful women never had the experience of being alone. They had wine parties to attend, weekend trips to take, and boyfriends to make love to. Going straight home and doing a crossword puzzle or watching a game show was not on their agenda. Neither did they ask Sherry to join them, much to her chagrin. She didn't have any new friends yet and loathed the idea of returning home so early on a Friday night. She would only stare at the walls of her apartment like she did at work.

But then, just when she thought it was all over, two attractive paralegals on their way-out asked Sherry if she wanted to get a drink at happy hour at the bar around the corner. Sherry leapt at the chance but kept her cool while pretending to check her otherwise empty social calendar. After feigning deliberation, she accepted their invitation. Just when she was about to leave with the two women and check out for the weekend, the handsome chief litigator darted out from within his office and pulled her aside near her desk. She was surprised he wanted to talk to her.

"Yes, what can I do for you?" asked Sherry, ready to evacuate.

"You've done really well in your first week," he said. "I just wanted to let you know that. We appreciate what you do here. Keep it up."

"Thank you," she said, floored by this unexpected compliment.

"Are you doing anything tomorrow night?" he asked.

"Why do you ask?"

"Well, the firm is hosting a little get-together at the Trump International. I thought you'd might like to come along."

"Do you think that's appropriate, considering –"

"Considering what?"

"You are married, aren't you?"

"Oh, no. My God, no," he laughed. "You have the wrong idea. It's work-related. You'd be paid for it. It's just a party for some of our top clients in the Northeast. You'd be there to represent the firm, just like you're doing here."

"Phew," she said. "Wouldn't want to get into any trouble during my first week."

"No, no," he smiled. "Just come to our suite at the

Trump International tomorrow night. Dress to impress, as they say, and bring that wonderful smile of yours. It's a party, so you're allowed to have a good time too."

"Okay," she said gratefully. "I'll be there."

"Eight o'clock."

"See you then."

"Good," he said, winking at her.

She took the wink to mean that he liked her. She had found someone in the working world who may have one day served as her mentor or may have helped her with a career in law. It was a real win considering she didn't have any money or any connections just a week prior. There was finally a reason to celebrate. Instead of having to go to some boring, old-timer's function with her ex, she was now free to join the young men and women of her own kind, those who were mainstream and whose parents had enough to send them to college and buy them clothes at the nearest suburban shopping mall. She was invited to mingle with new people instead of relying on an old sisterhood whose stifling conventions trapped her into being the type of woman she was never meant to be. She felt liberated and also filled with nervous excitement akin to have ridden a roller coaster for the very first time.

She donned her coat and left with the two other attractive paralegals. The weather in Washington had warmed that evening. The pedestrians on the street all seemed to smile as the city lights returned to full glow with the setting of the pinkish sun. The pedestrians on the streets seemed headed to places more exciting than their humdrum lives at home. The night was filled with possibilities. She had already forgotten about her hardcore stance towards meeting new men. All she really wanted was to hang out with a circle of friends, men and women alike. The few years she had with her old boyfriend and how her parents had continuously mulled over the future of their desolate farm grew evermore distant in her rearview mirror. A new future replete with new people and new places unfolded as she walked down the block with her two new friends. The two women were more than happy to welcome her into their circle.

She understood that, as a woman, no matter how far down the ladder she went, she must never lose faith. She must be hopeful and optimistic, especially during the bad times. There were many people in her life that had tried to steal that faith, to stomp on it, to send her into the dungeons of negativity and pessimism, and they almost always got away with it. Surely, the future isn't always so rosy, but once within that state of doom and despair, where there is nothing but darkness, she must never forget that this state of doom and despair always ends. It never lasts long enough to break her spirit. Even though she may have thought that there would be no end to it, it was merely a fallacy of thought, a careless mental error, to think that suffering lasts forever. She always falsely assumed that once crippled and blind, it was impossible to find her way out of the hole into which she was buried alive. There is always a light at the end of the tunnel.

Sherry wanted to tell every woman in the working world that she should never lose faith. It was a tired and old refrain but a necessary one. She wanted to sing this new but tired message from the apex of the Washington Monument that evening. 'Always have faith and never give up' was the new message sent from on high. She never believed it would have happened to her. Changes happen for a reason, and she guessed that some higher spirit was involved and guided her, albeit painfully, to the mountaintop of a better life with better people. There is always pain and suffering during the process of change. But once that process ends, a new life begins.

This dramatic change in outlook accompanied her on her walk to the bar. Their conversation, however, immediately turned to men.

"I wonder if he'll be there tonight," said the first paralegal.

"Isn't he already married?" said the second.

"I think he just got married. His wife's a Congressional aide."

"He's off-limits then."

"Nah," said the first. "No one's off-limits in this town. He likes me anyway."

"How do you know?"

"By the way he looks at me. He's there every Friday at the same time, talking with his friends from work. He's kind of their leader, y'know? When I'm at the bar, he'll stop what he's doing and stare into me as though we have a connection."

"The guy's still married," said the second.

"I don't care," said the first.

Sherry was single again, and even though she believed differently about marriage, she conveniently pushed these beliefs aside and made a point of it to be as easygoing and sociable as possible. She would not, however, go home with anyone. She stood firm on that. She wasn't ready to dive into the waters of a new relationship. She was still too confused about her last relationship and what the effects of another catastrophic one would have on her life, especially if she wasn't prepared to stand on her own two feet yet.

Usually, it was the pretty ones who were unable to stand so steadily. As a result, they wobbled, moving from guy to guy to keep themselves from falling. She guessed that this was the way it had to work. For a beautiful woman to free herself from such a predicament was difficult, rare, and also foolhardy. Perhaps it required the help of an entire family, assuming she had one, or maybe the help of a non-profit organization that specialized in training beautiful women for regular jobs when they had no one else to pay their bills. More often than not, though, beautiful women usually found a way out through wealthy and powerful men, as though it were their birthright. They used what they had to achieve what they wanted, even when they were born with no other talent or skill. Just looking good, as she saw it, proved to be more important than having competence of any kind.

If she recalled correctly, there weren't any ugly people at the top of the food chain. Even at the law firm, they were all beautiful, only that she didn't know exactly what it meant to be so beautiful yet. Sure, there was a need for men to have beautiful women, but she didn't know how far a woman could go on her looks alone. She was fortunate enough to be among that kind of company, but at the same time, she realized she would only be important, only be worthy of attention, only be valued by others, because of her looks. She would be envied and lusted after. She could break the hearts of the strangers who passed by her with just one look. Normally, women like these thrived on such powers, but Sherry didn't find much value in them. It wasn't that she wanted to be ugly all of a sudden, but she at least recognized that if she were ugly, she would be undervalued and unappreciated. Maybe she'd even be menaced and abused. The world was ferocious, cruel, and blatantly unfair to ugly women.

The paralegals with her weren't uncomfortable with having the privilege of being beautiful at all, and even if all three of them were uncomfortable with it, then how would it look to others if such women stood behind a soup kitchen table, pouring weak chicken broth into Styrofoam bowls for the indigent cold and hungry who confused them for white angels sent from heaven above to comfort the lowly and downtrodden and save them from starving to death as only the beautiful can? Naturally, it would look foolish for these hot women out on the town to have any conscience at all. They weren't meant to feed the poor, work with the developmentally disabled, or serve as visiting caregivers to old black men in the ominous housing projects she sometimes saw on the outskirts of the city.

The beautiful weren't permitted to do such things. Their predicament forced them into the only real role they could play, which was to find hot guys, fuck them, and reproduce. The challenge came when their children are born. Before that, might as well live it up by hopping from bar to bar, drinking, partying, and fucking, until they narrowed the list down to the guys with the best genes. As a biology major, she already knew the necessity of natural selection, but at the same time, she wanted to be much more important than that. Perhaps it was more important, however, to accept the role society had given her, only that once cast into that role, it rarely changed. It remained fixed, unless some misfortune or bad twist of fate dragged her down a few pegs. But even her misfortunes were fixed, as her destiny left little room for choice. In other words, she would always have to play the lead role and never the clownish, overweight side character. She was the type who would always be deemed desirable. She didn't even need to have a personality. The man opposite her would also have to be beautiful.

She was merely an object of desire to those who were not as beautiful, which meant most people in the world. Men wanted to own her, contain her, and have her only to themselves. Wherever she went, the ugly would be pecking at her beauty – peck, peck, pecking like pigeons at breadcrumbs.

If an ugly man came up to her and offered his hand, she knew immediately that he did so simply because she was beautiful. Maybe he wanted a one-night stand or even to own her, as though her looks and her body could be leased or bought from the previous owner. The only men who never had an interest in owning her were those men whose beauty already matched her own, because beautiful men were also objectified in the very same manner. This was why beautiful women always had to remain with beautiful men, and why all ugly men had only their own ugly kind to snuggle with at night. It made sense to her. She would never be able to relate to or trust any man who was less beautiful than she was.

She wasn't at all surprised, then, that the heavy bouncer at the door of the bar didn't check their id's and let them into a bustling neon-lit lounge where handsome men in suits and ties sat around pinewood tables, drank tall glasses of cold beer, and waited for more women who looked and dressed like the three of them did. A few of them sitting near the entrance smiled at them. Popular tunes that were easily recognizable, ridiculously overplayed on the FM radio stations, but instantly forgettable, hinted that the night would end with every guy and gal pairing up and heading home with each other. They would do it all over again with different partners the following weekend.

Most of the men seemed like they had no problem hooking up, and even though they may not have known each other, they were at least familiar with each other. They were used to hooking up with the same type of people in their former lives, and these were the same type of people they would hook up with when fully matured. But put a lone Samoan, let's say, into the white, yuppie mix, and any observant wallflower would tell that this odd Samoan man wouldn't be going home with any of the pretty women. Instead, he would hold his beer close to his chest and chat it up with his work friends, all of them men, get a little drunk, and then walk home alone shamefully at the end of the night. It was the same scenario every weekend.

The three of them, after scanning the bar's hive of activity, didn't even notice the poor soul, even though he was the biggest and darkest man in the room. Maybe the guy was too young yet to know his place in the world. Being among these white yuppies, no matter how well they liked him, would one day be detrimental to his psychological well-being. Naturally, the three women ignored the group he was in and sat at one of the booths. Sherry and her new friends could have taken home any man they wanted. Interestingly, being with the same type of men all of their lives still excited them despite its sad monotony.

After ordering a few fruity drinks that were more fashion statements than alcohol, the other two paralegals sitting on Sherry's opposite side began gossiping about the lawyers in the office. They advised her on which lawyers to avoid, like the two who were consummate womanizers, the one who would soon become a full partner, the office asshole whom no one liked despite his good looks, and the esquire materialist who showed off his latest collection of gold watches and sports cars for the other lawyers to gawk at. It fascinated her, because she didn't have to play it so nice at the office anymore. She could let down her guard a little. Not everyone in the office was so perfect and above her as she had initially thought. They may have looked like perfect specimens, but the paralegals even revealed their weaknesses in bed, followed by fits of embarrassed laughter. No, the lawyers weren't all that perfect, and she laughed along with them. A mild buzz from the alcohol and the vaguely familiar music, with the option to sing along, gifted her a good time.

In the middle of their description of how chiseled one of the lawyer's bodies were, flesh they had apparently seen firsthand after office hours, a couple of young men in nice suits approached their booth from a table in the middle of the room. One of them was heavy and the other skinny. They were also nerds. They looked smart as premature beta males, and they probably did well as bean-counters for a DC branch of government. Their expensive suits were geared more for the private sector than the public. They were clean-shaven and presentable. They also seemed harmless, quiet and shy, premature almost, but at least brave enough to walk up to them like two choirboys asking the school's most beautiful girls out to the drive-in. Sherry was nervous for them. They looked slightly too young to be in the bar. They were also way out of their league. She was surprised the bouncer even let them in.

Cheerleaders just didn't date nerds. There weren't any books or movies where the nerd gets the cheerleader either, except for unfathomable comedies, like *The Nutty Professor* or *Revenge of the Nerds*. Jane Austen's men are all fucked up, but handsomly fucked up. The two young men were asking for it, but Sherry still respected them for trying. The other two women, however, didn't let them get away with it.

"Ladies," smiled the first nerd, "We noticed you needed another drink. How about we get your next round?"

The two paralegals smiled to each other. The first then said, "um, we're having an important conversation here, so if you don't mind?"

"Yeah," said the second paralegal. "It's private. We're a little busy right now, and we don't want to be disturbed."

"Oh," said one of them. "Maybe later."

Their faces fell slack with disappointment. They looked

wounded and embarrassed before walking back to their table with their tails between their legs for everyone in the bar to see.

"That was horrible," laughed the second paralegal to the first. "That was so cruel of you."

"I know, but I had to."

"That was really bad," said Sherry. "I feel bad for them. They seemed like nice guys."

"They're little dweebs. You wound them when they're young before they end up wounding some other poor girl. But you're right, honey. They are nice guys. And nice guys finish last, as they say."

"I feel kind of bad," said Sherry.

"Shake it off," said the first paralegal. "They're not one of us."

The first paralegal summoned the waitress and sent the embarrassed men a couple of drinks. The nerds were surprised to receive them, and when they did, the two women raised their glasses and toasted them. The two nerds toasted them back wearing weak smiles. The women then broke out laughing and high-fived each other.

"Men are so fucking simple, aren't they?" said the first.

"I wouldn't worry about it," said the second to Sherry. "There'll be more bubbleheads for them to hit on. Later in life, someone will take them for all they're worth. They might as well get used to it now."

"How much do you think they make?" asked Sherry. "Really?"

"Much less than we do. I mean, look at them. Those guys are wannabe Bill Gates's. They're already too late. Good that we sent over those drinks, though."

When the topic of salaries came up, the paralegals revealed how much they made and assumed that Sherry made the same amount. Sherry downed her entire cocktail in one shot when she heard that. The other paralegals were making twice as much as she was. As casually as possible, she ordered another cocktail, and then another. Her heart sank, and her head burned. Why the sonofabitch litigator lied to her, she didn't know, but she was determined to take it up with him at his so-called, all-paid-for get-together. She imagined throwing a drink in his face in front of all of those important people in the hotel and slamming the door shut on her way out, making a huge scene and irreparably disturbing the otherwise pleasant evening. Maybe she would really do it too, because no longer did she want to work for him.

She swallowed her anger with the coolness of her cocktail and kept drinking and smiling along with the other two as they returned to office gossip and complained about the lack of virile men in the bar. These men were less-than, they complained. After an hour more of straight drinking, Sherry couldn't tolerate any more alcohol. She walked swiftly to the bathroom, opened one of the stalls, and vomited up all that she drank. The last time she had been that sick was during initiation night at the sorority several years ago. She returned to the table as perky as ever but barely able to keep her eyes open and head from dropping. The two paralegals saw this, laughed a little at her incoherence, and called her a cab. They sent her home without anything more to drink.

The poor cab driver had to escort Sherry up to her apartment, and maybe he had wild and impure thoughts before he lay her on her bed and closed her in, but either way, when she woke up dazed and nauseated late the next morning, she still remembered that the litigator was paying her half of what he had promised. The room swirled as she got out of bed.

She stumbled to the bathroom and vomited up the rest of the alcohol. She drank several glasses of tap water to rehydrate and then downed a couple of pain relievers. She hoped the torrid sickness would end by the time the get-together started that evening.

She slept for most of the day and when she awoke, had a light breakfast of eggs and toast. She could think of nothing but leaving the firm and making a huge scene about it. She wore the sexiest dress she could find. Wearing the dress, slapping the litigator, and storming out would make the echoes of her absence felt and would embarrass the hell out of a man she had trusted too easily. The night at the expensive hotel, however, didn't work out as she expected. Not in the least.

It took an incredible amount of mental energy to obsess about what she planned on doing while enroute the Trump International, but upon arrival, the obsession took a back seat to the splendor of the hotel itself. She wasn't the same person anymore. She had been out of the loop. She could have easily ordered a complimentary suite for a month, maybe two, had she been with her ex, but she now stood at the entrance knowing that she couldn't even afford a cup of coffee at hotel's café. She was also afraid that she'd run into an old friend or an acquaintance, lest she be recognized.

The hotel entrance was a series of three gaping archways, much like old train trestles that supported the heft of the hotel. A long black shelter jutted out of the middle arch and looked much like a long black tongue sticking out of a mouth. This black slab protected the guests underneath it from the harsh DC rains. Three immense Old Glories fluttered over the black slab as though a rally of the country's fiercest nationalists were caucusing there that night.

She couldn't deny, though, that everyone brought to the

hotel by limousine or taxi looked just like she used to look. She wouldn't be able to look the same again, she thought, and a certain degree of regret filled her insides, like paint coating her heart. Perhaps she was the one who was wrong in all of this, just like her father had said. There was always a price to be paid when going one way or the other, regardless of what she thought about having choices. She even entertained the idea that even the intuition used to make decisions wasn't really an option, but she left such arguments behind, as there was no use in ruminating over the unanswerable. This was where life had brought her, even though falling had made her a stronger woman anyway. She was just another nobody like everyone else, a number, a statistic on a chart, and she would have to get used to it. But through this very plain and ordinary fact, she soon came into touch with the idea that maybe she was still ordained to be important and that she was not meant to be a simple, ordinary woman on the streets to whom men would always raise their eyebrows when she passed. Call it *blondeitis*, a condition that very few women had in a mostly black-haired, brown-eyed world. They either saw her as an object of worship or a disease to eradicate from the face of the earth. At any rate, she didn't want to be ordinary and had to swallow the fact that she had been sent down a path by an indifferent, perhaps inhumanly cruel force. She prayed that this force, whatever it was, had dragged her down for good reason. She thought that this force, call it God perhaps, did this for her own benefit. Her life thus far may have been like that of a queen in disguise who must acquaint herself with the commoners before taking her throne and conquering the enemy nation.

Because what is a young woman without her dreams after all? Her dreams led her to the reality that now presented itself, not the other way around. Whatever force that pushed her from the top of the tower perpetuated such dreams. If reality was the road, then dreams were the navigators, and the force behind it all was the engine. And if this vehicle, whatever it was, ended its trip at a padded room in a psych ward, then so be it. Once there, the dream of living in a beach house on some Caribbean island, let's say, would forever usurp the reality of being forever bound in a straight-jacket and kept in solitary confinement. She returned to the Cinderella she had been before her fall from grace.

Upon entering a wide atrium with gold beams crossing horizontally and vertically above an expanse of tables and chairs below them, she noticed how the atrium had been enclosed within four high vertical walls of the hotel's sides. Each side zoomed several stories high and had floors of hotel suites that looked down upon the atrium and protected it like a fortress. Beams of light from the lower roof of the atrium as well as heavy baroque chandeliers hovering like diamonds over the seating area provided light for the guests below. The four sides of the hotel surrounding the atrium were aglow with brighter lights on the atrium's roof that fanned upwards towards the sky. A high tower graced one of these sides and faced the entrance where the arches were. It was an impressive structure but nothing new in terms of its luxuries and extravagances. The hotel was merely a reminder of what she once had, or rather, what she could have had.

Painful as it was, she checked in with guest services. A uniformed concierge directed her to a suite on a middle floor of the hotel. The carpeting below her could have been cushions for her feet. She felt like taking off her painful high heels and walking barefoot along the hallways, as though the carpeting were pillows, made in America, but of course.

When she arrived at the smooth, white double-doors of the suite, its room number engraved in gold-leaf paint, she heard the faint sound of jazz music emanating from within. Her heart fluttered. Cautiously, she knocked on the door. When no one answered, she found the doorbell and rang it several times. An older woman in an evening gown holding a glass of white wine answered. She was tall, and as Sherry expected, she was one of her kind, the beautiful kind, as though the hotel refused to do business with the ugly. Her dress had a long V-shaped neckline that tapered neatly all the way down to her hips. It exposed her breastbone and accentuated the shapes of her two manageable and symmetrical breasts. She had brown hair with golden highlights and was probably a lot older than she but naturally beautiful all the same. Her teeth were white and even, as though she had been brushing them after every meal like no one in their right mind ever did. It must have taken hours for her to do her makeup and squeeze into that tight, glittering dress of hers. A diamond neckless that must have cost a fortune hung around her neck and fell to where her calm heart radiated an aura of politesse and calm, even in the most pressurized of social environments.

Sherry had been to many parties and decadent affairs before, but this woman was one of the few who impressed her. The wealthy look much different from the gaze of a poor woman's eyes. Sherry didn't envy her, though, because she could tell that this spectacular woman admired her beauty in return and was maybe even a little envious of her youth.

"Ah," said the woman in the doorway, "and you must be?"

"Sherry. Sherry Aspen. I'm here with the law firm. The chief litigator invited me here last night."

"Of course, he did. You came to the right place, Sherry. I feel like we've already met and have known each other for years, my darling. Why don't you come in."

She opened the door wide, and this woman, who appeared to be the hostess of the party, led her into a large hotel suite with older males and a few younger female paralegals from the office chit-chatting over hors d'oeuvres and cocktails. She recognized one of the paralegals from last night cornering one of the older lawyers and making him laugh. There was a large bar with a uniformed bartender serving drinks in front of a wide window that overlooked the Washington Mall and the Capitol Building. The paralegals looked stunning, and the older men were both handsome and wealthy, much like the same ethereal soap opera of her office, but this time the show was set high in the clouds, all of it televised in the mind's eye of a wide-eyed girl who had been delivered there by a benevolent fairy. It was a reversal of what she saw in her current neighborhood and apartment, a chimera by contrast, a result of being away from her former extravagance for merely a few weeks. But she had always performed well in social situations, much like riding a bike again, and she knew already how to work the room. She followed the hostess to where the chief litigator in the middle of the room talked to one of his clients, she presumed, with a glass of amber liquid in his hand. His glass was still full, so at least he wasn't drunk so early in the evening. In fact, the party was as sophisticated as the evening parties she had been to before with her ex. Soft jazz continued to play over the sound system. A soft pleasing melody that made her tingle in places that were off-limits to all of the men that night.

"Can I get you a drink," asked the hostess, after leading her to the chief litigator.

"How about some white wine," said Sherry.

"Fabulous. I'll be right back. And you remember the litigator?" she said, smoothing his arm with her hand.

"Yes, it's good to see you," said Sherry.

"Hi," he said. "Welcome to our little soiree."

"Thank you," she said. "Everything looks wonderful."

Before introducing her to his client, he moved closer to her ear and whispered, "remember, we're working."

After the litigator introduced her, the hostess returned with the wine, and the litigator again winked at her, as though Sherry had been let in on some valuable secret that only the anointed few were told. She greeted some of her fellow paralegals, and before long, the older men in the room introduced themselves by kissing her hand and letting her in on what their relationship was to the firm. They were the big wigs.

By the time Sherry had loosened up with a couple of glasses of wine in her system, she was no longer so inhibited. She conversed freely, spontaneously, and unabashedly to the delight of the men who admired her. She was the new girl in town, so to speak. They asked where she had grown up, where she had gone to school, and how long she had been in Washington. She smartly left out everything about the farm and focused on the important elected officials she had met and the contacts she had made over the few years she had been in the limelight. She charmed these older men whose gray hair and potbellies were obvious and charmingly avuncular all the same. She never expected one of them, after introducing himself, to run his hand down her soft arm and slide it over the small of her exposed back.

She figured it was a paternal display of affection, until later in the evening, perhaps a couple of hours later, when everyone in the room was drunk and smoking either cigars or cigarettes, several of them did the same to various parts of her body, like massaging her shoulders or caressing her arms. They asked if she wanted to visit their vacation homes in exotic parts of the world. One of these men had a yacht docked in Newport and offered to sail her to Bermuda. Another wanted to fly her to his place in West Palm Beach. A third offered her full access to his bungalow in Costa Rica. Although these locations weren't anything new, their openness and generosity impressed her. It put Sherry in touch with the life she once had, and just when she looked across the room to the litigator who flirted with one of the paralegals, she snapped out of it and remembered why she was really there, especially after he winked at her from where he stood. As the old man who invited her to Costa Rica put his arm around her shoulders and then slid his hand down to cup her firm flesh below the waist, her anger boiled over.

The night before with the paralegals at the yuppie bar came barreling back. Her pleasant and flirtatious disposition suddenly turned ferocious and unforgiving. She remembered what she had originally planned. She had veered way off track because of the wine and people there. Giving the litigator a good piece of her mind returned her to the dull present and pissed on the glittering flame of fun at the Trump International from that moment forward.

She headed straight to the chief litigator who had been charming the other paralegals. For some reason, though, Sherry could not execute the plan. She was bound by social convention and didn't have the wherewithal to swim upstream from the strong inebriated currents the gathering had been swept into. She had neither the strength nor the will to reverse course and swim upstream. Better to wait until a quieter time, as specific discussions required a specific time boxed into a specific category in order to be undertaken and resolved in a specific way, much like the lines of a datebook or an organizer. A party such as this just wasn't the appropriate place. It wasn't like her to make a scene, even though she had imagined it completely before entering the hotel.

The old men there continued getting drinks for her from the bar. Already she was tipsy, but she was at least sober enough to suppress her anger from raging out of control. She walked over to the bar at the far end of the suite and ordered a shot of whiskey. She downed the first shot, banged the shot-glass on the bar, and ordered another. She was angry, yes, and even though the hot fires of her anger ignited between her ears, she expressed it under the veneer of graceful sighs, ennui, and boredom, as though the entire party were beneath her high-class sensibilities. Even if she wanted to, she wouldn't allow herself to do it. She stood at the bar with her back facing the gathering. She hoped to escape the suite without any more perverts feeling her up with their sweaty palms.

"Having fun yet?" she heard a voice calling from the far end of the bar.

She looked over and found a man who was unlike the others in the room. He dressed inappropriately. He was disheveled and overweight. He hadn't spent much time grooming himself either. His jacket was too tight, his tie too long, and his pantlegs too small around his meaty legs. Like Sherry's father, he was also bald. She studied him closely and tried to figure him out through the goggles of her inebriation. She discovered that the older man looked much like her father.

Her immediate instinct was to lash out at him and blame this man for all her troubles and the hurt she had suffered from all of mankind. But she refrained and instead gave him the cold shoulder if only to send the message that he was insignificant and inconsequential. She was good at that. The man was just another guy she had to deal with on the Amtrak.

"You're drinking quite a lot," he said.

Sherry looked away and ignored him. She wouldn't

give him the satisfaction. The other men, maybe, but not this man. There didn't seem to be anything to gain from talking to him, whereas if she talked to someone else, the litigator may have given her a bonus. No joke.

"May I join you?" he said.

"I don't know. Can you?" she said scornfully.

"You've had quite a lot to drink for one night."

"I bet you want to take me home too."

"Actually, I'm married," he said, showing off the wedding band around his plump finger.

"Like that really means anything to men like you."

"Hey, I promise I won't lay a hand on you, and I won't hit on you or ask you out. I just want someone to talk to. That's all."

"There's nothing to talk about."

"Seriously. Just good conversation. I don't bite. I promise."

He slid over with his drink in one hand and steadied himself on the bar.

"So, why are you so pissed off?" he asked. "It's a party. You're supposed to be enjoying yourself."

"Yeah, some party this is. It's more like a bordello."

"That too."

"Are you serious?"

"What else can a party like this be? Take a look around. They say the first thought is usually the best thought."

"I had no idea, but you must have known. You're here, right?"

"Not everyone is looking to sleep with someone tonight.

There are exceptions to every rule."

"Well, Mr. Philosopher, what brings you here, then?"

"I work for the government," he said, while fishing out an ivory business card from his wallet.

The card simply read, 'Department of Recruitment. US Government,' with a hand-written phone number on the back of it.

"Who do you recruit for?" she asked.

"I recruit very special people for very special government jobs. You can say that I place people where they have the most potential to succeed. Do my services interest you?"

"I have no idea what you're talking about. Why don't you try being more specific about the jobs you're recruiting for."

"I tell you what. Call me Monday morning when the alcohol is out of your system. It's better to consider the opportunities I have when you're sober."

"Can you at least tell me how much it pays?"

"If you're interested in the money, then the jobs I have probably aren't for you. But if you're interested in serving our country and protecting our homeland from threats to our national security, then maybe what I have to offer is a good fit for you. Remember, it's government work that I do. We have to be frugal in all of our ways for the taxpayer."

"I'm not going into the fucking Army," she said, raising her voice and slurring her words.

"No," he said, trying to calm her. "I can assure you that this is not the Army. It's a job that will test every dimension of your character, yes. It will test your strength, sure. It will sharpen your skills, whatever those skills are."

"Sounds like something out of a comic book."

"You're too drunk right now to see it as anything else. Take this card and call me on Monday morning if you're interested and if you remember this conversation."

Sherry placed the card close to her breast like she did the money her mother had given her.

"You better not be some kind of pervert."

"Just call me. You won't be disappointed."

"Listen," she said, "I need to get out of here. I don't want to be pressured into anything. Just pretend I'm going home with you tonight. It will impress my boss, and you'll get me out of a jam."

"You're wish is my command," he said.

The two of them said goodbye to the chief litigator who winked at them before they left. The hostess was next. She smiled in satisfaction that the party had gone exactly the way she had planned and that she had done her job as hostess well. She seemed to know that Sherry already had the right idea about how things ran at the firm. She must have thought Sherry an exceptional employee, a girl who would play ball for the team, just like the glamorous receptionist before her did. The female paralegals also played ball, as they slowly paired off with their men. Some of them had already left the party for other rooms on other floors of the hotel.

Sherry held the recruiter's hand while walking out the door, both of them ostentatiously pretending. Once they were out of the suite, they took the elevator downstairs. The recruiter immediately ordered the concierge to call her cab.

"I hope you're not lying to me," said Sherry before getting inside the cab.

"Have a good weekend. Look forward to hearing

from you on Monday."

He shut the door for her. She had made it out of the party with her dignity intact, even though everyone at the office would think differently on Monday. Already, she prepared for a new path to follow. It was an opportunity she never saw coming, because when she awoke with a dry, empty stomach, bloodshot eyes, nausea that felt febrile, and the same dress on, she felt the recruiter's damp business card deep between her breasts. She remembered him from the party. Fortunately for her, she had the weekend to recover. She planned to call him early Monday morning, assuming he answered his phone calls.

Chapter Eight

February 2000 – Washington D.C., USA

For the unfortunate man who sees Sherry walking down the everyday street, there are reasons for her ignoring him. Interestingly, women like Sherry, at least existentially, have no need to rush into relationships when they will always be taken care of. Perhaps this man may one day have the nerve to stand in her way and block her path as she walks, but this is unlikely, considering the reception he has gotten from her for most of his lonely life. But he at least tries to make eye contact, which is good, because the man at least has some hope left. His attempts fail, though, when she walks past him with her blue eyes staring straight ahead on a mission to reach those worthier than he. She may even scowl at him, because she knows no one important walks by her. She is oblivious to this unfortunate man for reasons that will eternally puzzle him.

The unfortunate man who rises above his ordinariness and contemplates the reasons for women like Sherry never looking at him or smiling or making any eye contact whatsoever is an ambition man indeed. Such questioning is like opening a door for the very first time and nervously entering it. If he reaches a solution to his own madness by finding the answers, perhaps he would have contributed greatly to his own society and would have explained the world in an entirely new way. Perhaps he is worthy of a great prize, not given by a committee that already has the luxury of sharing their seats with women like Sherry, but the ultimate prize of rebellion, which is an attempt to knock the whole system of things down just because of a woman like her. It is a beginning at least. The door has opened, and how far he goes really depends on his ability to tolerate his study and observation of this rare creature.

The question becomes then, why do such women like Sherry ignore him? We're not talking just a few times or even a hundred times. We're talking for this poor, unfortunate man's entire life. And because he has forever been ignored, he has little choice but to spot women like her everywhere he goes – in the newspapers and magazines that feature stories about her, on every television channel known to mankind, especially the advertisements and the porn flicks, the touristy and trendy sections of city neighborhoods where only the wealthy can live, and with those men who dine at the fanciest restaurants and can easily afford to bring her along.

As she walks straight ahead, her blue eyes determined and unshakable, the man thinks there must be something wrong with him. He has found no solution but keeps theorizing every time she passes. As stated earlier, he may look too poor. She knows he doesn't make enough money to support her lifestyle, let alone his own. She could do better, in other words. Maybe he's ugly in the sense that he may be too fat, too skinny, too black or brown, perhaps an immigrant who can't speak the language, a man not worth talking to, because he lives on the other side of town where there are gun shots in the streets at night. He wouldn't fit in too well with her sexually either, as this unfortunate man's phallus may be too small or too big, although the bigger it is, the more likely she will make at least some eye contact with him, or at least her one-track mind would veer off course towards and walk in his direction. She may even smile for a change.

He may have stubborn acne in middle age, or one leg may be shorter than the other. He may be an albino. He may not be as much of a human as she is. He may be some kind of creepy alien ready to snatch her body, unless she runs to her castle where her prince lowers the drawbridge across his moat and lets her inside.

Again, there may be infinite reasons, but this poor, unfortunate man will never know. Interestingly enough, women like Sherry usually share their same reasons for ignoring him, because these reasons are similar to the whole host of reasons all women have for ignoring him. Women are a collective, in other words, even though they vehemently deny they are not. Women are governed by a committee of elders who are in charge of organizing and engineering their dreams, their mates, and their children. This man sees the spawn of these elders as horribly segregated, whole cultures of women cut apart like slices of pie on a plate. They let the races mix together when they're younger, allowing them to experiment for the fleeting cause of world peace, if only their young remember such a thing exists, but beyond their young adulthood, it's time to break it off, get serious, and procreate with their own race for reasons that are penny wise but pound foolish.

It's like the tree-hugger who tries to save the environment. No one gives a shit when he ties himself to a tree to stop the oncoming bulldozers. But when the earth floods, and its people face starvation, disease, infestation, pandemics, and no one in this God-forbidden place can breathe the air or swim in the water, then in hindsight it may have been good idea to have let the tree hugger, who thought of the whole of creation ahead of time, finally let him have the woman he longs for.

While the melting pot experiment did not work perfectly, despite everyone's best intentions, multiculturalism offered no hope at all. The next stop may be the tacit acknowledgement of the coming race war when every culture looks upon the other as ugly and decrepit, Unamerican and lazy, and irresponsible to the point of parasitic. This is what the poor, disillusioned, deranged man sees as her stock market surges and a new economy is created out of the Almighty silicon microchip. Women are given even more reason to look away from him. She pursues only those she has always pursued through her flat-screen televisions and computer screens. But nothing at all has changed since time began. No matter what architecture her elders have designed for her world, the same results present themselves, as though they were forever ingrained into the American imagination. It doesn't make any sense, least of all to Sherry, but it will always be to her advantage. This is but an assumption, because maybe she gets breast cancer, or loses an arm, or part of her face, or has a hysterectomy. Either way, she will be surrounded by her beloved family on her deathbed, declared a heroine by the whole world, and smile beautifully the entire time before ascending gracefully through heaven's pearly gates. The elders will smile to each other and whisper that they have once again lost the battle with her lifeless body but not the war against her obsessive men. And for this deranged man, the pest on the corner, the Sadhu naked before his God watching this happen to her, he will be just as mean, salty, ugly, and combative for not getting her. Even in death, Sherry will still have to look and be beautiful, because that's what is always expected of her.

But she no longer wished to live up to anyone else's expectations, which is why she called the recruiter first thing the next morning. Naturally, she had tons of questions, but the anonymous customer service representative over the phone told her to be patient and that the application process could take up to a year.

"But can you put me in touch with that guy?"

"Which guy?"

"The guy who gave me the number."

"I'm sorry, ma'am, but there is no such man here."

"That's impossible. What kind of job is this?"

"Look," said the representative over the phone, "it's rigorous, but I think a smart girl like yourself would be able to handle a job like this."

"What job? Where's the guy I talked to at the Trump International? I don't even know what I'm applying for."

"Wait for the application to come, please."

"What about my current job?"

"A good rule of thumb is that you should never leave your old job before you get a new one."

"But you're recruiting me, aren't you? You think I'll get this job, right?"

"And who's this recruiter, ma'am?"

"Am I going crazy here?"

"Look," said the representative, calmly, "the process takes a while, so settle down. Don't leave your job right now until you've been accepted."

She didn't even call the litigator at the firm that morning to tell him she quit. She let the phone ring for most of the day without picking it up when he tried to call. She had no desire to sell herself. She was better than that. It was a big gamble, though. She had enough rent left for two or three months. She steadfastly believed, however, that she would get this new government job. She didn't know why she believed such a thing, but once again, her pride got in the way.

When a woman has beauty, she wants brains. When she has brains, she wants beauty. She hated to admit it, but in her case, beauty won out over brains every single time. At least when a woman is dumb and beautiful, she still has talents that get her by, just not traditional ones. After all, intelligent women usually suffer more anyway. So do women with personality. Beautiful women, though, survive as the center of attention. They attract people. A woman may start out as a poor girl in a rich man's house, but soon enough, the learning curve flattens, and soon enough, she's running the show.

Sherry knew that it wasn't right for beauty to win. Intelligence mattered to her, and it should always trump beauty. But she didn't want to become another soccer mom attending yoga classes and cooking organic meals. Women are joiners, and while the chess club never interested her, she would have rather hung out with those who had big reputations. Being smart and successful in the working world rather than becoming just another blonde driving a minivan to and from her kid's private school was the better option, because when her husband drives into the city only to return eight hours later with the scent of another woman's perfume on his neck, maybe playing soccer mom isn't always the right option. Trading sex for money was also not an acceptable way to go. Respectability was on the top of her list.

She let the phone ring all afternoon, until after the seventh or eighth ring, she disconnected it from the jack in the wall just to get rid of it. It worked. After three days of playing dead, the phone stopped ringing. Once again, it was time to start a new life with new people. She hoped it would work this time around.

Every afternoon, she waited for the postman. The application failed to arrive. She didn't want to call the recruiter again either. Sherry had very little to do, and a lot of time to do it in. She resisted the urge to spend money. She had to pinch pennies to stay afloat. The weather in Washington forced her inside. She visited a local coffee shop in another neighborhood and had so many cups of coffee each day that she could have turned into a coffee bean. The caffeine kept her hunger at bay but drinking way too much of it kept her awake at night.

She had visited all of the tourist attractions at least three or four times. She perused the stacks at the local bookstores and bought novels she never ended up reading. Nothing interested her after a month by herself, and she was soon confined to her bed, listening to music on her headphones, and eating low-fat vanilla ice cream when she wasn't completely caffeinating her system. She bathed only once every couple of days. She didn't change out of her pajamas. She had no one to call and merely listened to talk radio, the noise and static blaring in her ears. The noise became her solace from complete emptiness. Luckily, talk radio was still around.

She kept checking her weight and grabbing the folds of excess cellulite around her waist. She was changing imperceptibly. Every morning there was a new threat of excess fat under her arms, at her hips, or around her thighs. Basically, she was letting herself go. Just when she thought of calling it quits and rejoining the never-ending race for another entry-level job, she discovered a letter-sized envelope that barely fit into her downstairs mailbox one cold afternoon. Its return address placed the anonymous sender somewhere in Washington. The envelope could have contained drugs for all she knew. Nevertheless, she snapped out of her prior-ness, casted out the emptiness, and reigned it all back in. She pulled out the application sent by the Central Intelligence Agency. She had no idea that the recruiter at the party was with the clandestine services.

He looked more like a hot dog vendor or an auto mechanic than a super spy. But she was pleased because anything that declared itself intelligent was a job worth pursuing. At least she was applying for a position in a company that the entire world already knew was intelligent. This alone was a reason to cheer. If she were hired for the job a year down the road, she would never have to worry about being stupid when she tells all of her old friends who once doubted her that she was in fact intelligent the whole time and now worked for a company where she must be intelligent in order to be working there. She would be prized by important people. The important hand of government reached out to her.

By the time she filled the application out completely and mailed it back by certified mail, waiting to hear from them nearly killed her all over again. Democracies moved slowly, she figured. Like before, she had to wait it out, almost like waiting for a college acceptance letter. Any other person would have normally forgotten about it, had the person kept him or herself busy. With Sherry, though, this was hardly the case. It was back to caffeine at the coffee shop, long walks in the dreary cold, and peering into fancy restaurants where good-looking couples smiled across from each other and celebrated their fat bank accounts.

She never expected such loneliness. Considering what she already knew about those in her sorority, who were women who would end up running the country one day, she sometimes saw being alone as a freedom and a gift to be cherished. All of those men at the functions she went to with her ex, all of that adultery, corruption, and backroom dealing, all of that phoniness and superficiality made it easy to stay away from the people she had once known. She remembered she needed some time alone. She remembered thinking it a fine idea to be apart from her ex in Cambridge. Now that she had nothing to do and nowhere to go, however, the loneliness soon seeped into her porous social neurons. She tried all the lonely activities, as was mentioned, but they were soon hollow without anyone to talk to.

She could pick up another guy, but the prospect of that didn't thrill her when all she wanted was a few friends in a big wide city where the isolated never fared very well. She was a social being after all, she thought, and she never knew loneliness would ever bother her, especially for a woman who had been so popular everywhere she went. Her life was a like a current that had dammed up somewhere in the past. At first, loneliness was no problem, but now that dam needed to be released. She wanted to do something exciting. She was bored and needed to be entertained but in a safe and risk-averse way.

She thought of smoking pot for some reason or visiting the pricey art galleries, perhaps meeting a painter of sorts with his swinging dick and accolades for his substandard work, and he would introduce her to a world equally flush with class and money. Hopefully, she wouldn't leave the art scene as a drug addict. Instead, she could be a Muse, breaking her new lover out of the doldrums of depression, mediocrity, and early death by giving him the inspiration needed to finish his masterpiece. He would have to be handsome, of course, as that's how she imagined him. She would have no one less. He needed to own his own apartment or house, make a living at selling his art, and have a reputation as an up-and-coming artist to go along with the muscles he had magically put on himself. She would be the smarter of the two, and he would be the crazy talented guy who always got into trouble and fought with his rivals in the art world at all the art shows and salons. He fights when another man moves in and tries to steal her away. He wears painter's pants with streaks of yellow, blue, black, and purple all over them, and they live in a loft with unfinished artwork all around them, all of it portraits of Sherry's nude body, as he is always trying to get it just right before they make love in his loft that just happens to be all the rage in the latest architectural magazines.

The irony of Sherry's daydreaming, however, was that these dreams were actually attainable. Achieving them wouldn't take that much effort. Just go to an art opening somewhere in town, look around, wait for someone bold and confident enough to walk up to her and introduce himself, the handsome sort, in other words, because this wouldn't work for any undesirable of course. She would also have to narrow it down to a painter who had passion for his work and tons of potential, which was just not possible, considering that he just wanted his dick sucked, but she didn't see that.

Having had all the time in the world to think of these details ahead of time, she hoisted on a pair of old jeans and a thick sweater and headed to the bookstore for the hundredth time, but not to buy another book. Once there, she looked down upon the odd-sized postcards that local galleries had left on one of the tables. She found advertisements for openings in the city that week. Most of them charged admission, but paying would be much better than sitting at bars all night and dealing with drunkards wanting to get her in the sack. Cultural activities like gallery openings suited her now, she guessed, and she had always been interested in what went on in the art world anyway.

The first card pointed to a gallery near Logan Circle. She hopped on a bus to 14th Street for a gallery opening scheduled for eight that night. She arrived all too eager and way too early. The gallery doors were locked, even though there were a handful of people inside drinking wine and setting up. Because it was night, and because she was a woman alone, she was as self-conscious as a flower in a bitter tundra expecting a thief to pass by and rip her from the ground. She felt awkward standing outside of the gallery in the cold and took a walk around the area to where the trendy bars and shops with canopies and patrons underneath them spilled out into the streets. It reminded her of Manhattan's Lower East Side or Haight Ashbury after these once-terrible neighborhoods had been retrofitted and gentrified into posh residences, restaurants, and shops.

Logan was much of the same, as though every major city had such a place where the tragically hip gathered and moaned about their drug addictions and their early deaths in vainglorious attempts to create one original piece of artwork from the billions already made, until their art focuses on themselves as people, their gossip supposed to mean something important and is soon ready to be commodified, packaged, and shipped out for the next touristy sucker who can't afford such trinkets and must learn about them from a textbook. Unfortunately, a celebrity artist who does marginal work is much more valuable and gifted than an awkward, lonely soul who actually does good work.

Sherry didn't want the art. Her own subconscious led her to this new territory to get involved in yet another fucked-up relationship no matter how strenuously she tried to avoid one. She looked for trouble around Logan Circle and didn't even know it, as though she were just trying to make things interesting. Happiness wasn't the goal, only freedom before being punished for living fearlessly and excessively, like the drug addict who thinks he'll get away with it. If idleness was the Devil's workshop, then she tempted Satan hoping to avoid what she really yearned to find. She's then proven innocent when she finds herself in trouble. She had to be an active participant in the trouble she searched for, and, as usual, she would wiggle her way out of it looking as beautiful as ever.

The loneliness still clutched her as the area began to fill with the young and the hip. They had a good sense of fashion, not in a pretentious way, but in the creative way that didn't require a paycheck. They were a lively bunch of all stripes and colors. The area was the only unique section of DC that differentiated itself from cheap-suited bureaucratic homogeneity. The landlords of Logan Circle, just on the verge of selling out to the highest bidder, at least gave their cash-strapped offspring enough space to vent their frustrations against the machinery the founding fathers had built. This contrasted sharply with the artists there.

She returned to the same gallery after touring the immediate area. This time, the gallery was open, and more people were inside. They drank wine and feasted on a buffet of cheeses and crackers, carrots and celery with dip, and a cash bar for the heavier stuff. She pulled open one of the heavy glass doors that led her into the warmth of the gallery. She expected someone to greet her and introduce her to some of his fashionable guests, but no one did. She was a lone stranger who didn't like meeting others without being introduced properly. In any other circumstance, at least one man would have pulled himself away from his conversation and introduced himself, but at that point, she was no one special.

Modern artwork, illuminated by overhead track lights, adorned the high white walls and enhanced the dazzling visual acuities of each artist. Self-consciously, she moved from painting to painting to painting, studying each to find their deeper meanings. She appreciated art and those who had the nerve to create it but saw each work as a riddle that needed solving, or the colored oils on the canvases as narratives that demanded explanations. While moving down the line, she kept the eyes in the back of her head wide open for anyone bold enough to interrupt the fakery of her knowledge instead of letting her go it alone. After lapping the room, one young man had the balls to fulfill her hopes. She just wasn't good at being an unknown and lacked the experience.

"Hi," said the young man, coming up behind her. "Welcome to our show."

"Oh, hi, there," said Sherry, pretending to be startled by the man.

"How do you like it so far?" he asked.

"It's great," she said. "Really excellent work. I commend you and your group."

And then it hit her, even though it shouldn't have mattered. Those at the opening were definitely a talented bunch. They may have been artistic geniuses for all she knew. Yet the young man in front of her was missing a certain quality that made him uninteresting to her. She sensed that he was not worth knowing. She scanned the room behind him. The guests smiled, drank wine, and nibbled on their cheeses. The young man next to her must have been a friend to many others but still wasn't acceptable to her. Those in the room were stunted, she considered. They were grownups without being grownup. They were not developed enough to be on the same level of maturity as hers.

She remembered a theory she had read about in one of her Biology classes. Human beings adapt and evolve more through close and intimate relationships rather than through the vast, never-ending web of their experiences. In other words, a young man who has never been involved in a serious relationship with another woman is psychologically less mature than a young man of the same age who has been through several of them. A woman grows through her intimate relationships with men, or other women, until they move on to the next man or woman. To use a mixed metaphor, when two countries go to battle, there is something shared and something learned. A peace is born. These artists occupying the room were super-talented but psychological midgets. Like the malnourished and stick-figured children of the Third World, their growth had been stunted through no fault of their own. They had not been in enough relationships yet.

"Well, thanks," she said to the young man. "This has been a really great evening."

"But you just got here," he said, disappointed.

"I'm sorry, but I really have to go. I have a prior engagement."

"Well, at least have some wine before you go. Maybe something to eat? I'll introduce you to some of the others."

"No, I don't think so. Maybe some other time."

She left the place as quickly as she had entered it. Soon, she was back out on the street, her dreaded loneliness returning with the same biting cold that whipped through the city streets that night. She had jumped the gun. All she had to do was wait for the letter from the Company to arrive, and yet she didn't. She had to be doing something or going somewhere despite her best attempts to be contented with the stunted young man's invitation to stay. Contentment seemed impossible without having to get through torture first. She needed to squeeze more from a night that had abandoned her like an unwanted orphan.

A little perturbed by what the last gallery offered, she

moved on to the next one a few blocks down. With both her hands, she ran her fingers through her hair to loosen the blonde strands. Frustrated that she couldn't find what she was looking for, she entered another gallery that was more to her liking, her long blondeness projecting a more aggressive and predatory look. Once inside, she wanted attention from the people she saw – a Gothic mix of exposed white skin, studded leather, serpentine tattoos, spiked heels, and black fishnet stockings. Perhaps this is what she wanted, each of them an exclusive and rebellious part of a jaded artistic community.

It was dark in a large room complimented by conversation-level death metal beats pouring through precision overhead speakers. Artists of all genders, even the ones that hadn't been classified yet, discussed their disdain for society and the losing hand it had dealt them. She understood them all of a sudden but realized that this was not an underground club in New York City or a graffitied basement with beer-stained floors and half-naked men throwing themselves from a stage. For some reason, she wanted that but wasn't going to earn such a freedom easily. How glamorous it would be to put on a leather jacket, tight pants, and high black boots and throw herself into a sea of punks?

She found herself in a more sophisticated environment with Goth artists having both beer and wine and hashing things out. There was incredible artwork that harkened back to a prior era, but no one seemed to be paying any attention to it. The artwork didn't matter as much as the ongoing involvement they had with themselves, much like every exclusive, rebellious bunch. Because it was exclusive, Sherry wanted to join. She again perused the artwork, moving gracefully from the first outlandish piece to the second, and then the third, examining the outlandishness and trying to place the meaning behind each when no meaning to the show existed. But each piece must have had meaning, because the Goths assembled there were taught to apply meaning to it, were influenced by their experiences, or simply found themselves there and kept coming until they all uniformly wore black leather and tattoos. Sherry could only come up with her own ideas and opinions but wouldn't dare expose them. The Goths were simply too intimidating to approach. She was like a cop trying to hang out with *The Hell's Angels*.

Even though she had let her hair down, she in no way wanted to disrupt the flow of the showing. It was dark in the place anyway, and perhaps she could slip around without being detected. After the end of her trip around the mangled, industrial pieces nailed to the walls and sectioned off individually, she came out of the tour understanding that the junk on the wall didn't represent the quality of people there but a dialogue for those who had come before them and where they ought to be going now.

She slipped over to the bar area and grabbed herself a beer from the cooler next to a table. There were plenty of bottles in the cooler, and on the table were bottles of vodka, whiskey, and cognac. As she twisted the bottle off, a woman in black leather, fishnet stockings and tattoos on her long, white legs approached. The woman shoved crushed ice into an empty glass and filled it up to the rim with straight vodka. For a while, Sherry played at glancing at her and looking away, until the woman finally said, "I was exactly where you were once," while looking at her Goth companions on the gallery floor. "The question is, do you let yourself go? Or do you stick to what your parents taught you?"

"I already have let myself go," said Sherry. "It hasn't gotten me anywhere. And you?"

"No, it really hasn't gotten you anywhere. So, what are you prepared to do about it?"

"Nothing. I can't do anything about it."

"Is that some sort of challenge?" she said, taking a gulp of vodka.

"What do you mean?"

"Well, we can't just stand here, now can we?"

"No. I guess not. But what's the challenge?"

"If I told you that facts are not really facts but are only what you make of them, would you believe me?"

"Probably not," smiled Sherry.

"We don't have to wait here. We can do whatever we want. We can invent our own lives. We are not governed by what the facts are."

"We can't just invent facts."

"Are you sure about that?"

The woman in black leather reached into her pants and pulled out a bronze pillbox. She opened it carefully and placed a small yellow tablet in Sherry's hand.

"If you try one of these tonight," she smiled, "you'll be amazed at what you can invent. The question now is, do you stand on this cliff and just look at the waterfall below you, or do you jump in and forget about letting yourself go and waiting for things to happen?"

Sherry looked at the pill for a moment but didn't swallow it just yet.

"Still need to think about it, huh?" said the other woman. "Well, don't think too long. Before you know it, the sun will come up, and you'll be thinking about it all over again. If I were you, I wouldn't wait one minute longer."

Sherry thought that if she took the drug, she may have liked it enough never to have returned to the person she once was. It was a tempting to lead her own life instead of having life running her. Her path was so stubbornly fixed and hackneyed in her mind's eye that the means it took to arrive at the destination she had imagined for herself one day were merely crude repetitions, like walking in circles, never moving forward, neither up nor down, but walking in a straight line from Point A to Point B until eaten by worms when the body gives out and the mind degenerates to where she is unable to remember where she imagined herself to be. If a small yellow tablet could knock her off the eternal hamster wheel, then why not take the chance and see what happens when she stops running and moves beyond being such a good, smart, and responsible girl who had been guaranteed a future? Breaking loose would go against what she had learned, but perhaps the ingredients and properties to that would soon manifest itself in passageways to the infinite varieties of alternate universes that would colorfully appear and call out her name. Maybe getting through her dark hours could be easy and effortless, as finding herself while drifting through different universes, showing up at one random place and then finding herself at another without the limitations of cause and effect, these universes where she could be different types of women, shedding one and then becoming another, never having to return to the woman she once was before, and doing so without a hint of fear or care of what was to become of her, was suddenly possible.

If she neglected the black-clad woman's gift, she would forever be riding with training wheels on and never discover, not whom she yearned to be, but who she actually was. She found herself in front of the same wide table loaded with alcohol, the pill melting in her perspiring palm, still wondering if she should take it or be governed by fear as her primary motivation and play it safe instead as she had always done. She retreated to the small bathroom at the back of the room and swept the tablet from her palm into the toilet. She watched the pill slowly dissolve in the water before flushing it down.

She left the gallery as though her life depended on it, running from what she didn't understand and sticking to what was familiar – her loneliness, in other words, an illness from which she couldn't break free. By the time she returned to her apartment, took off her clothes, and collapsed on her mattress, she was too out of tears to cry anymore. She realized, finally, that she had no one, and perhaps that was how it was supposed to be. Whether or not this loneliness was her own fault, she wasn't sure. When a person is alone, there is very little room to be selective about whom she meets. But she still was lying in bed with the lights off, still trying to find her kind of people, even though these people no longer existed. They were ghosts who would forever leave deep footprints on her mind no matter how hard she tried to cover them up. She wondered if there were any use in searching for these people. She craved them, these same people who had screwed her over and sent her into exile. And yet no other type of people would do. A Catch-22 by any means, but one that only deepened her sadness. If she could snap out of it and set her head straight, she would have. Her type of people became much like a disease one is born with. They riddled her days and nights with pain and intermittent hopes of one day getting over the childishness of not moving on and not looking over her shoulder.

But such a need didn't turn itself off by any force of will. The pages of book don't turn on their own, in other words. The craving stops, and the pages turn on their own schedule. She could have undertaken any activity to distract her from the separation from such a people, but it wouldn't have worked until the separation itself decided upon itself to cleave her away from her present, leave her alone, and allow her to move on. Unfortunately, she had no such luxury.

Newfound hope arrived after a month of having nothing to do, walking around in circles, worrying, and waiting. She ripped open another letter from the Clandestine Services inviting her to take a series of tests at a location in McClean, Virginia, which was not far from the DC Metro area. She would be staying at the Hilton Hotel, courtesy the Company. Finally, a shower with decent water pressure, Turkish bath towels, clean, soft linens, and climate control instead of the constant influx of frigidity from leaky windows and the gap underneath the front door. The exposed radiator that made her apartment either too hot or too cold whenever it pleased wouldn't bother her for a little while. It was the only form of happiness she felt since being accepted to Georgetown.

She replaced her agonizing and useless sadness and self-pity with her most determined game-face. No longer would she have to accept defeat and failure. She needed exercise, new clothes, and some money, even though she was running low. In the meantime, she concentrated on excavating herself from the ruins. On that very afternoon, she hoisted on a pair of sweatpants and a heavy sweatshirt and started running again, just like she did during pre-season for the ski team up in Vermont. The running made her the talk of the neighborhood – some blonde gringo girl running in the midst of the smog, broken streets, and the noise pollution of blaring Spanish pop music, and drag racing among small Asian cars with tinted windows. No one else in the neighborhood exercised, because no one in the neighborhood had any reason to exercise. Maybe she was the only real asset in her neighborhood, like a statue of a white goddess in a blighted city park. Either way, the gringo girl kept running until she packed her bags and headed several miles over to the McClean Hilton to take the entrance exams for the Central Intelligence Agency.

She could hardly stand straight while walking into the expanse of the decent hotel. There was an abundance of heat, kind and welcoming faces, and a sanitized bathroom with a perfectly made bed. Yet she noticed something about the country she yearned to protect. America was no place for the sick or the poor. She felt the first touches of the unfairness of it all, as her first brushes with poverty left her. One needed money wherever one went. Money was what every individual needed to avoid neighborhoods like hers. Without money, on the street she went and on the street she stayed. If a woman actually had the nerve to pull herself up by her own bootstraps, she could only get farther by fucking someone richer than she. It's either that or high-class sex work for pedophiliac old men in business suits and fancy cars. The Company would take her away from the crude underbelly of her circumstances. It wasn't the case that a woman could simply move through life as happy as a clam, from one bartending or barista job to another, from one office job to another, as though nothing mattered at all except living in the moment while steadily moving into the ghetto with the other women who never had a plan and danced through life as blithely as a drunken clown on acid.

Without essential common sense that she assumed everyone else already had, she felt ignored. She had her own train of thought that kept her more occupied that what the thoughts of common people were, because she had an idea that a sense existed that was indeed 'common,' and for her common sense merely meant society's need to tolerate each other. Perhaps that was the only element of commonness that most people shared. Yet, she had lost her capacity to tolerate, though, and so she believed that if she could gain a common sense that approached an even better common sense, then maybe she wouldn't have been so ignored anymore. She had turned shy, inhibited, totally withdrawn, and lost in the wilderness of her wild, wild, uncommon thinking. It kept her searching for a better common sense that outdid mere tolerance.

Better, however, didn't mean innocent. It didn't mean that she'd be thrown in jail if she didn't walk a straight line. And Sherry had always walked a straight line and had gotten burned because of it. So, if one is innocent *and* guilty at the same time, it made perfect sense for her to join an organization that had both. The CIA had the better common sense that she searched for. A beautiful collaboration between the saint and the sinner boiled into one package.

She wanted to work for the Company, no question. She had even lost a few pounds. Her waist had slimmed, and her jeans didn't feel as tight anymore. She looked good again, as good as she was supposed to look. She was already smart, so she felt confident about taking yet another series of ridiculous tests. Even janitorial work had its tests, and so did the Company's. One couldn't go anywhere anymore without taking a test. Call it population control, or the resurgence of the processes of predestination, she figured. Nevertheless, tests had to be taken, and she had to prepare at least mentally for the series of aptitude and psychological exams necessary for the job.

First, she was directed to Building X, a square block of a maniacally constructed complex that stood close to the hotel. Finally, she saw her own kind there – the top of the heap, the best of the best. They were apple pie-eating Americans through and through, all of them white with a few Asians who had been fed the same apple pie. Most of them were fresh out of the Ivy League, their bodies cut and chiseled through the sponsorship their respective elite and exclusive fraternal and sisterly orders. The women were just as beautiful as she and just as ferociously competitive when it came to taking exams. As far as her exams were concerned, everyone had at least one unguided tour of Hell anyway, and for that there are no tests required, just enormous costs to escape.

In Building X, she waited in a small antiseptic room before being ushered to a nurse's station with an examination table, a blood pressure machine, and a scale in it. A nurse came in and handed her a plastic cup. She went to the women's bathroom. She returned it to her half full. She was relieved that she didn't swallow the yellow tablet from the art gallery the month prior. She had forgotten all about the mandatory drug testing. Once this was completed, the nurse gave her a thorough physical exam, her rubber hammer hitting the precise spot below the kneecap, a steely edge running straight down the middle of her foot. The nurse soberly recorded the results. She had had a busy morning testing all of the applicants.

Thus far, it was easy, but the other exams were a completely different story. These were difficult and alien, even to smart people. She was smart, so she felt she did fairly well, especially with Calculus and the weird puzzles that only closeted entomologists invented. She made her way through them with time to spare. She read paragraphs meant to put any rational person to sleep. She thought she had answered most of them correctly. She had always been a good test-taker, she affirmed, but not much good at anything else. But the real problem came with the psychological testing. Such questions put her in bizarre foreign or ethical situations and asked her what she would do in them. She found this part difficult, simply because of the old dictum, 'know thyself.' Sherry had little idea who she was except for a farmhand-turned-beauty queen who had lost her way in the world. She didn't think she did very well on these sections, but once she completed all of them, what came next was even more grueling – the polygraph test.

In another small room in the middle of Building X, they hooked Sherry up to a standard polygraph machine and asked her questions so personal, that she didn't know how to answer them appropriately. They asked her pointed questions about her sex life, for example, or whether or not she ever had any lesbian affairs. They asked if she ever cheated on any school exams or plagiarized any papers. They asked her detailed questions about her family history and if any of her relatives ever abused her or sexually molested her. By the end of being totally intimidated and then turned loose to return to the hotel, she felt barren, as though the examiner had scooped her insides out. She did, however, answer every question honestly. She just didn't know what they were looking for. Whatever the case may have been, they were unable to catch her in a lie, even though they did try to trap her into lying. She felt like she had been probed by a group of space aliens. She was exhausted, and she fell asleep early. She had to be out of the hotel at noon the next morning but had no desire at all to return to Metro DC. She would have rather stayed at the hotel instead of her apartment. It was comfortable. She felt at home among the thick towels, soft bedsheets, luxury soaps and shampoos, the bath beads, the skin lotions. She snuck them in her bag before she left, intending to replace the generic shampoo she bought at the corner convenience store in her neighborhood.

She then waited patiently to hear from the Board of Examiners. She placed all of her eggs in this one basket until she couldn't imagine doing anything else with her life except working for the CIA. She could have found another job to bide the time, but she refused even that. Working with the Clandestine Services was all that she saw. Perhaps such tunnel vision was the result of not having anyone to talk to and the hardships she had endured. Either way, she checked her downstairs mailbox daily only to find it stuffed with junk mail and notices from her landlord that the rent was overdue and that she needed to pay it to avoid further action. She had tried to save as much money as possible but had leaked it everywhere she went. She didn't know how to economize and saw her money supply deplete like water slipping between her fingers. She didn't eat dinner or breakfast, only lunch. It kept the pounds off, even though she ate her lunches at outside restaurants and avoided the more plebian tasks of going to the supermarket and cooking her own meals. Regardless, the junk mail kept collecting with persistent demands that she pay her past due rent.

Normally, a person late on their rent would at least try to negotiate with their landlord, but by this time, Sherry had shut herself in so completely, that she was a prisoner in her own home, unable to communicate except to say quiet 'thank you's' when she purchased things she could barely afford. It was a result of her ongoing isolation. Neither did she call her mother. She avoided her calls no matter how close their relationship had once been. She could sense her mother's worry and anguish and even gave into it, which made her worry even more about her worrying.

The need for companionship reared its head every now and then, but that head wasn't necessarily so ugly. She couldn't convey to anyone what she had experienced thus far anyway. But even in her desperation, she only wanted to associate with her own kind and not anyone lesser than that. It was pointless to go searching for her kind. Her ideal man still had to be a blonde-haired, blue-eyed demon emerging from the water on a beach of white sand, his body bronzed and his abs ripped. His muscles still had to be in all the right places. It was an Aryan tribalism akin to the old films of Leni Reifenstahl, the perfect male body made for the perfect female body, such that even those who were off-color by the tiniest of margins were forced into looking like the perfect white male. Such tribalism never ended when the Jews were liberated from Auschwitz and Treblinka. The need to have an Aryan man who complimented her good looks continued up to the present. God-forbid her man to be shorter or fatter or blacker or browner or poorer. Whole populations bought cosmetics that whitened their skin, continuing to buy into the same ideal while never being able to achieve it, because they were never meant to. Instead, they were bled dry. After all, no one ever saw skin cream on the store shelves that promised to make a man look blacker, now did they? And even if such an item were found in the hands of a black or brown man, those products would always be of lesser value.

Even Sherry's once-cheery and welcoming landlord was Hispanic. Maybe he started off that way, because Sherry's presence, all on its own, increased his property value, assuming that more single white women like Sherry were to stay there. Wherever the young, white, hot women went, the money followed. The short, aging Hispanic guy with twisted teeth and a scar on his chin from a gang-related knife fight years ago in his South American city of origin, however, suddenly gave her notice that she either pay the past due rent or vacate the apartment. Sherry had no intention of leaving, especially when she had no place to go. She was holed up there, unable to get out of bed on some days, unable to clean the place, unable to do her laundry except when her clothes ran out. Despite how many times the landlord knocked, Sherry wouldn't answer the door. If she left for food or for a trip to the bank, she avoided him at all costs. She was successful, even when the poor guy filed a complaint with the local court.

She was tremendously nervous. She imagined the worst, like being thrown out into a horrendous DC winter with nowhere to go. She was relieved, then, when another note from the CIA arrived. She had been accepted and invited to join, but they told her that she couldn't tell anyone about it, which she found highly peculiar, because she wanted to climb a mountain and shout out loud to all of the world. Nevertheless, she was so happy and relieved when the note arrived that she went to the dive bar down the block and drank herself silly with her Hispanic neighbors. Not a gringo in the room. She was a Clandestine Services Trainee and was informed that someone from the Company would pay her a visit sometime soon. She had no idea what this visit would be about, but the letter said that it was standard procedure for all new trainees. The landlord still left menacing notices that he pasted to her door, which she peeled off so that the Company's representative wouldn't see them. The last thing she wanted was for her new employer to discover she couldn't afford the rent.

The Company's representative knocked on her door the very next morning. The incredible drinking spree from the night before left her with bloodshot eyes, body aches, fatigue, a terrible headache, and a general queasiness that she tried valiantly to hide from the mystery guest. To her surprise, the mystery guest just happened to be the very same portly bald man who had originally recruited her at the Trump International. Her apartment, though, was a disaster zone. Her heart nearly jumped out of her chest she saw him standing in the doorway in what seemed to be the same suit he wore that night. She had her pajamas on, and her blonde locks, tangled and frayed, stood on end.

"Good morning, Miss Aspen," said the recruiter. "I hope I'm not interrupting you."

"No, of course not. Please, come in."

They could only sit on her mattress – a ball of bedsheets and a blanket.

"I'm really sorry about the mess, really I am. I didn't expect you to come so soon."

He looked uncomfortable sitting there, but there was nowhere else to sit. And yes, the place was a mess, especially with the landlord's torn notices scattered all over the floor and her clothes in one corner of the room in one big heap.

"Interesting place you have here, Miss Aspen," he said. "I hope your habits will be, well, a little more hygienic when you get up and running at McClean."

"Oh, I am normally the cleanest person in the world. It's just that you caught me at a bad time. I had no time to prepare."

"As a CST, you should always be prepared – for anything. You have to be aware of everything around you, just as I was aware of you when I found you at the hotel that night."

"I agree totally."

"How are you getting by these days?" he said, his eyes wandering around the apartment. "Are you working now?"

"What do you mean? I'm working for the Agency now."

"No, no. It's 'The Company.' The Company is what we call it. It's a nickname. But before you can call it that, before you can own it, you are simply a CST, or a Clandestine Services Trainee. You still have a long way to go before you are an Operations Officer."

"Absolutely. I understand."

"Good, then. So, as I was saying, are you working now?"

"No, I am not working."

"How are you supporting yourself, then?"

"I have some savings that I'm living on."

"I hope it's enough to last you a couple of months at least."

"What do you mean?"

"We do a reinvestigation of your file, and that can take anywhere from two to three months."

"Two to three months?! You're kidding, right?"

"No, Miss Aspen. That's why I'm wondering what your financial picture looks like. You have no need for work?"

"I think I can just make it."

"You think? Or do you know?"

"Is that a trick question?"

"No. Just answer the question. Do you believe, or do you know?"

"I don't know."

The recruiter sighed heavily and rolled his eyes.

"It takes three months, Miss Aspen. It might be a good idea to return to Vermont."

"I can't do that."

"My suggestion is that you better think of something. And besides, you can't tell anyone you're a CST anyway."

"I was going to call my mother and tell her the good news. No one else."

"It's good that I'm here, then. When I mean *nobody*, I

mean *nobody* at all – not your parents, your boyfriends, your friends, your future husbands, should you have any, nor your children, no one. Absolutely no one can know. No strangers, bums, drunks at the bars, no one. Understood? Also, and this is equally important, so listen carefully. Absolutely, positively, no relationships. Seriously, you are not to have any relationships, sexually or otherwise."

"Not even sex?"

"Masturbate, if you have to. That's what we all had to do. Trust me, you'll do it a lot. Seriously, no fooling around. I hope you get to camp safe and sound, Miss Aspen. Training is pretty grueling for everyone involved, so you should be prepared. You'll be hearing from us. And clean this place up. A CST shouldn't be living this way."

"Of course. I'll see you at McClean, then."

"You won't be seeing me anywhere, Ms. Aspen. That's our specialty."

"Got it."

"Good. If your living arrangements change, let us know immediately."

A couple of months later, a summons to appear in court came in. She was more bewildered than frightened by it, because getting evicted just didn't happen to women like her. She was completely unprepared for it. By this time, she was maladjusted to certain realities and had no idea how to live properly. She had to choose between waiting for the Company to contact her, getting a job, getting a wealthy Aryan boyfriend, or getting the hell out of DC. Perhaps the only real choice she had now was to marry and breed well. Climbing the corporate ladder would only get her as far as marrying and breeding well anyway. She might as well have taken the plunge and picked up another guy who looked like her, behaved like her, and was probably a total scumbag too. But this didn't matter as much as making sure her rent was paid and that she made herself over within established parameters of legitimacy, health, and prosperity. She had to put herself out there again, and it wouldn't be hard for her. The first man she saw who fit the profile would serve as the dog she walked down a boulevard that caters to her every dream and whim. Pain and suffering would be artifacts of a lonely past.

Just after the landlord slid the summons under the door, however, she checked her mailbox downstairs. It hadn't been checked in a week. It overflowed with utility bill warnings, cheap clothing catalogs, charitable appeals, and credit card offers with usury-level interest rates and annual fees that were way out of any poor woman's price range. She was tempted to take all of it out in one big handful and dump it in the trash. In the back of the mailbox, however, was a thin envelope addressed to her by an anonymous sender from McClean, Virginia. It looked like junk, but she opened it. It was a short letter ordering her to camp for training. The other junk mail fell to the floor.

She almost fainted upon reading it. The recruiter must have heard her cries for help, and help just happened to come from an organization imbued with importance, respect, and even a little danger thrown in, not to mention a bona fide position inside the US government. It was like a star in the nighttime sky, dead or not, beaming its immortal shine right into her very core. She couldn't have been more relieved or delighted. She still had more than enough time before the cops would have to break in the apartment and forcibly remove her.

Chapter Nine

March 2000 – McLean, VA, USA

When one of the employees at the CIA showed her to her room, she was surprised to find that her new roommate was one of the same pretty Asian women she saw on the first day of testing. The woman looked at her quizzically, as though she were judging how well she would fare during training, considering that it was fiercely competitive. CSTs were let go if they couldn't cut the mustard. The Asian, a striking creature to behold, had firm legs and smooth skin, translucently pale. She had thin red lips and jet-black hair tied at the back of her head with a scrunchy. She looked like an exceptional prep school student.

"You must be Sherry," said the Asian, walking up to her like a soldier prepared for bootcamp. She then stuck out her hand.

It was soft, like Chinese silk. Sherry could yet tell the difference between Chinese, Japanese, and Korean women, but if they became friends during training, she'd be sure to ask. The woman had already taken the bed closest to the window. It overlooked a larger building with satellite dishes, radio antennae, and other objects protruding from its flat rooftop and scraping the passing clouds. The building was not much to look at, at least aesthetically, except that her roommate's window did face the rising sun. She had already unpacked and put away her clothes. She was already prepared for the initial orientation meeting to be held in an auditorium in the main building. Sherry had arrived on the late side.

"I don't think we have much time," the Asian said. "We'd just better head on over. All the others are probably there already."

"I'm not late or anything, am I?"

"Not really. You'll just have to wait to unpack your stuff until later tonight or before breakfast tomorrow morning."

She spoke perfect English with a noticeable southern twang that placed her somewhere in Texas, Louisiana, or Georgia. It was weird, as she had never heard an Asian with a southern accent before. Perhaps it was typical of how far Asians had assimilated into mainstream American life, even going so far as to adopt more provincial traits that made them more fiercely American than some of the girls in the sorority she had known. Nevertheless, she guessed she would always have to work harder, just like blacks had to work three times as hard to be rewarded with the same entitlements whites had already been born with. Either way, Sherry found it hard to claim any superiority over her. She could tell she was highly intelligent and stunningly attractive enough to have any boyfriend of her choosing, even a guy with cowboy boots and a ten-gallon hat on, assuming her parents allowed her date outside of her race. The woman could have been a candidate for a space mission for NASA for all she knew. That's how impressive she was. She was all business, it seemed, and maybe that's what CIA expected of all of its trainees at the camp, because after all, this wasn't the typical dormitory. McClean was much different and much more austere than a dormitory full of freshmen preparing for their first day.

Sherry knew she had to straighten up. She was already

insecure and intimidated. The Asian may have been given the training manual prior to the start, she mused. She followed her new roommate out of the room, down the hallway, and out of the building. The Asian even knew where they should have been, as though she had been given a map of McClean beforehand. She followed her sheepishly in the wintry air. It started to drizzle, now that night had fallen. If only they had some kind of meet-and-greet mixer before plowing into training. Sherry didn't even bring a pen or a notebook with her. Her new Asian rival had both.

When they got there, they entered a large auditorium only a quarter full. The other CSTs were scattered in the seats far apart from each other, all the men white. Two exceptionally-looking brunette women who sat next to each other, their eyes following Sherry and her new roommate, most likely sized them up. They didn't seem too friendly or welcoming. Neither were they as nervous or anxious as Sherry. Fangs grew out of their incisors, or at least Sherry imagined them that way. The dozen or so men in the room were well-dressed in collared shirts and slacks, notepads and pens in hand. They were a handsome and well-kept bunch whom she guessed were from well-connected families within the Washington establishment. Some of them may have had relatives already employed by CIA. A few of them even turned to notice Sherry's attractiveness and perhaps even had secret longings for an Asian rub-and-tug if they got to know her roommate better. Several of them even smiled in a show of collective relief that two more women in the program showed up.

The trainees were mostly seated in pairs, each according to whom they bunked with. She snuck a quick peek behind her where the brunettes sat, and with their fangs out, they too rated the other trainees. Childish but natural all the same.

After an unbearable period of waiting, a middle-aged, slim, and athletically-framed gentleman in a short-sleeved shirt and tie walked calmly across the stage to a podium with a microphone jutting out of it. He turned it on and addressed the incoming trainees.

"First of all," he began, "I want all of you to fill in the first two rows and sit together. Do that now, please."

The trainees looked at each other bewilderedly, but then the instructor said, "let's go. Get moving. This isn't English class. You're employees of the Clandestine Services. You're being paid for this. Get up and get into the first couple of rows, please."

They did what he ordered. Sherry's roommate took the lead. Sherry followed her for a few rows to the front of the auditorium. The other two brunettes took their seats in the middle of the first row within the swell of masculinity that filled in around them.

"That's better," said the instructor. "Yes, you are competitors, and each of you should strive to be the first in your class, but at the end of the day, we're playing on the same team, and that team is the United States of America. You have been selected to protect and defend her, even at the cost of your own lives. I hope you know what you signed up for, because if you don't, the door is right behind you. We won't take any offense if you leave. In fact, if you have any doubts, then we would consider it a great favor if you left McClean now rather than wasting your time and ours. Staying here and wasting the taxpayer's dollar is even more offensive than getting up and leaving.

"I'll give you a few minutes for all of you to think it over. When I return, I can assure you that those who remain will be here with the goal of completing the training."

As quickly as the instructor walked on the stage, he walked off of it. A low murmuring in the auditorium followed. The trainees looked to each other to see if anyone had the balls to flinch. But everyone stayed in their seats, including Sherry.

"That was a little harsh, don't you think?" whispered Sherry to the Asian.

"It's that serious," she replied with that stubborn Southern twang in her voice. "He's not exaggerating either. Too many have died already."

"How do you know?"

"You mean, you don't? It's the first thing we have to know. This is why we have to put our best foot forward right from the very start. We have to give our training one-hundred percent, nothing less."

Sherry's insecurities deepened. She did consider bolting from the room but instead stayed pinned to her seat. She had nowhere else to go, which made her plant herself there like a fawn frozen in front of a truck's headlights.

When the instructor returned, he held a small Styrofoam cup of coffee as he scanned the trainees. His eyes seemed to bore right into her own soul, searching for anything valuable to feed on, as though he knew already she would be the first one to be cut.

"Good," he said. "I would like to welcome you to the Central Intelligence Agency. You were chosen, because you're the best of the best. Each of you brings qualities to the table that thousands of other applicants didn't have. These qualities will be of great value to our national security. But let me make a few things clear to you right off the bat.

"The job of an Operations Officer is probably not what you expect. I'm not going to stand up here and spoon-feed you what I know. You're going to have to figure it out on your own. Let it be known, though, that this training will not be easy on you. We will find what you lack and stab it to death to make you stronger, if not invincible, out in the field. You will be tested, but should you make it through the three phases of training, you will be the best our country has. You will have both the pride and the status to do whatever it is you want to do, whether you stay with the Company or not. It all starts here. It's not enough to do your best. You have to do better than that. And with that, I will say a few words about how the guard has changed here at CIA.

"Well, the last Administration didn't care too much for us. They saw us a bunch of reptiles. They didn't trust us. We said the Russians killed Kennedy, but they still think we did it along with the mob. It took the bombing of the USS Cole and two of our embassies in Africa by Osama bin Laden and his *Al-Queda* organization last year for them to wake up, smell the coffee, and come crawling back to us. And now we're playing on a totally different ball field. The pot-smoking hippies are out. The real warriors have come back to the table. That's why this year's trainees are so important. The country's priorities have changed. The Department of State, the Department of Defense, and Central Intelligence will no longer operate separately. We will no longer be 'compartimentalized,' in other words. Because of the Ames and Nicholson cases during the Cold War, we will soon be 'decompartimentalized.' This means that CIA will work with other state agencies from this point forward.

"These terrorists are a ruthless and uncompromising bunch. They're fanatics. Their sole allegiance is to their God and to their extreme brand of religion. And when I say *their* God and *their* religion, I say it to differentiate theirs from *our* true God and *our* true religion. These people have no God.

They are poor, illiterate, uneducated thugs. But they know how to make bombs. They know how to scare people by strapping these bombs to their chests and blowing themselves up. Terrorism, as all of you should already know, is a highly effective weapon against all that we hold dear. They see us as the enemy because of our steadfast support of Israel, and how we, as a Christian nation, encroach upon their lands. To them, there is no Jordan, Saudi Arabia, Iran, or Iraq. To them, Islam is one nation, and the whole of the Middle East is that nation. To them, Islam knows no borders and no separate nationality.

"Ever since Israel's creation in 1948, these Arab terrorists have been royal pains in our asses. But our new President and his Administration believe it has gone on for too long. Along with our allies in the Middle East and, believe it or not, we do have our Arab allies fighting with us, our job is to take the fight to them before they take it to us, like that blind sheik who bombed the World Trade Center in New York City. Just remember that the enemies of our enemies are our friends. Intelligence also has to recruit the dregs of humanity to combat those who are even worse.

"For the first two weeks, there will be an overview of all aspects of operations. After that, there will be a two-week orientation period. Once you have finished orientation, you will be assigned to your respective offices for your first Interim. The Interim period will last three months. That will complete Phase One of your training. And then comes the fun part, which is Phase Two, or Paramilitary Training. All in all, each of you has a very long way to go from this point forward. Assuming you make it through, this particular class will have the task of fighting terrorism on all fronts.

"This is why you are a special class. You will be the next salvo against these barbaric savages. These are the same fanatics stone women if they suspect them of adultery.

These are the same barbarians who kill innocent children to further their cause in front of the television cameras of the world. These are the same monsters who infiltrate peaceful communities in Europe, snort their coke, screw their whores, and then blow people up when they don't pray to their God or insult their prophet. I don't like them, an either should you. Every one of you should be mad as hell that these guys bar us from the world peace we all want. We should be angry that these guys threaten the safety and security of our servicemen and women who have already chewed so much Arab dirt that it's coming out of their ears and noses just to protect innocent Jewish and Christian lives. Well, I, for one, am mad as hell, and if you aren't mad as hell by now, maybe you should reconsider joining our elite organization. There's the door behind you. I'm giving you one last chance. Leave now, and none of us will hold it against you. But if you stay, let it be known that you are now charged with defending our country against these horrible ingrates who deny us peace time and again. With that being said, all of you should be getting plenty of rest tonight. I want you up early and ready for classes tomorrow."

The instructor left many of the trainees dumbfounded as he walked off the stage. They sat in their seats, not knowing what to make of his speech. Eventually, Sherry shuffled out on the heels of her roommate. She had no idea how serious joining the Company was. Her roommate was right. She wasn't prepared for how hard-hitting it would be. She would have rather preferred coffee and doughnuts or at the very least a panel discussion with other Company employees and not something as dreary and defiant as hunting down terrorists in Arabia and slaying them before they wreaked havoc all over Europe and America. Her Asian roommate, however, seemed emboldened by the talk.

"Better get to bed early tonight," said her roommate when they returned to the dorm room.

At lights out, Sherry pulled the covers over her head but heard some of the other trainees socializing down the hall from where they slept. Her roommate kept her there in bed, readying herself for tomorrow. It was only their first night there, but Sherry wanted to talk to the other women.

"I wish they would quiet down out there," said her roommate.

She then heard a few male voices as well, most likely visiting the other two brunettes down the hall. She wanted to let her hair down and have a little fun, a redux of college life just one more time before they fed her into the meat grinder. But she would have no such pleasure that night.

"I don't think the men are allowed in here in the first place," said the Asian. "It's lights out already."

Sherry liked hearing the laughter down the hall. It meant she shouldn't take things so seriously. She fell asleep ruminating on whether or not she'd get through the training. She also thought of her mother whom she wasn't supposed to tell about her involvement with the CIA. She should at least call her and tell her that she had found a good government job in Washington and that the money would soon be rolling in. She would pay her mother back in spades, and with that final thought, she fell asleep and woke up the next morning a little exhausted from not getting enough rest. It was the first day of 'CIA 101,' as the CSTs liked to call it.

Training, however, didn't begin in a very conventional manner. Quite the opposite. They ate breakfast together in the employee cafeteria, but it was a subdued breakfast. Apparently, some of the men and the two brunettes were up way past lights out. They looked hungover, actually. Sherry suspected that the men must have smuggled in alcohol. They were the typical Alpha variety, or more appropriately stated, the kind the Company favored. They could do no wrong. Already, the party clique had formed, and Sherry felt left out. Once again, a dull feeling of loneliness overcame her as she faced her uncool Asian roommate who ate breakfast methodically, clearing off all the bits of scrambled egg and crusts from her toast, not letting a single packet of butter or salt go to waste. If she could have moved to the other table where the partygoers sat, she would have. But it would have been out of line, and she didn't want to hurt her roommate's feelings. She did admire her, though. She worked incredibly hard, even though it was only their first day. She made eating breakfast seem effortless.

After breakfast, they all convened in the auditorium again.

"We sell our souls for our country," continued the tinsel-haired instructor in the same vein as the night before. "Just as we predicted, Afghanistan, which is the territory our President wants us to focus on, is in the hands of radical fundamentalists. What was once a no-man's land of isolated feudal warlords trafficking heroin has been infiltrated by the fanatics of the Middle East who never left after they drove the Soviets out. These same Arab belligerents never left Afghanistan after the Soviets left. They have taken over the place. It was those pussies from State that ran policy from the Oval Office. If anyone did anything to prevent the Arab heathens from running riot over Afghanistan, it was us.

Since the end of the Soviet occupation and Soviet communism, the terrorists have overcome the very same fighters that we had trained. In other words, once the Soviets pulled out, a bloody civil war resumed in Afghanistan and also a good part of the Northwest Frontier of Pakistan, where the

Pakis, and our on-again, off-again ally, President Zia Al-Huq, set up *madrassas*, funded by the Saudis to radicalize Afghani exiles who had bled the Red Army to death. This same exiled population now wants to fight the West, this in spite of the sacrifices we've made. It wasn't Zia's fault exactly. It's just that those Paki clerics just can't get enough of their Islamic shit for one lifetime. Anyway, the situation in Afghanistan is dire. Our analysts predict that Afghanistan will soon be a launching pad for these Arab fanatics to send their destruction all over the Middle East. This includes our Israeli friends…"

The instructor continued on like this for some time. Sherry listened attentively. She didn't know too much about the Middle East other than she never wanted to go there. She had studied European History more than any other subject other than Biology. None of the trainees wanted to be stationed in the Middle East either. They affectionately called the whole of the Middle East 'Ickystan.' The trainees never wanted to deal with anything remotely Islamic. They thought these places most unfashionable and suited primarily for fierce CIA paramilitary units ready to kill and destroy everything within their paths. That was the only way to deal with them.

Her Asian roommate, however, had nothing to worry about, because the Administration wanted stronger trade and much stronger political ties to China. She would be sent into Beijing to live in the lap of luxury, posing as some kind of Embassy official or translator with a cushy desk job. The question became, then – which one of them would have to go to Ickystan? As the lead instructor discussed the issues that affected Afghanistan, Sherry casually glanced around the room and noticed how nervous the other CSTs were as they listened to him. Even Sherry had illustrious and farfetched daydreams of being stationed in London, Paris, Vienna, Florence, or Geneva, having wild love affairs with James Bond-types who drove stylish sport's cars, bought her expensive jewelry, and took her to lavish Embassy get-togethers where foreign dignitaries hobnobbed with European royalty. Despite her best attempts to fight back such grand fantasies, she couldn't help them. It distracted her from the possibility of being stationed in the Middle East. Even remaining stateside would be preferrable to being sent to Ickystan. Undoubtedly, all of the CSTs hoped to be stationed overseas, but there was nothing worse than Ickystan. Sherry almost sighed out loud when the instructor ended his lecture.

Before language classes commenced that afternoon, however, the CSTs were scheduled to meet individually with the camp's trained psychiatrist for one-on-one sessions. Although Sherry welcomed the idea, her session didn't turn out like she expected. She thought the session would be much better than listening to the instructor drone on. Unfortunately, she was sorely mistaken.

She found herself sitting in an uncomfortable metal chair across from a short, frail doctor in a lab coat. His coke-bottle glasses made his beady eyes look extraordinarily large as he looked her up and down, examining her shape and the tone and suppleness of her blonde skin. He didn't say anything at first. He had a yellow legal pad in front of him, but he neither looked too interested nor too upset about who she was or the type of girl she represented, although there was something subtly calculating and exacting about him, as though he appreciated dissecting her just like dissecting harmless animals at medical school. Sherry averted his gaze as he judged her body, or perhaps it was her mind that he judged, considering he was a psychiatrist. She looked all over the room to avoid connecting with his beady and steady eyes.

"So," he said finally, "how are you settling in here at Intelligence?"

"Fine, doctor. Just fine. I've found everything quite comfortable so far."

"'Comfortable?' That's an odd choice of words. Why do you say, 'comfortable?'"

"I dunno. I guess that's how I'd describe it, I guess."

"Do you expect to find things 'uncomfortable?'" he asked.

"No. Everything is fine, doctor. Really, it is."

"But there is something that you must have imagined to be uncomfortable about staying here, no?"

"I see your point," she said, trying to be friends with him. "To tell you the truth, I don't know what to expect, but so far, I have been pleasantly surprised."

He took down some notes and said, "surprised by what?"

"For one thing, our lecture on Afghanistan and also the other CSTs. Everyone's so accomplished here."

"Just accomplished? What are some of your other thoughts about them?"

"I don't really know any of them yet."

"Okay, let me rephrase – how about some first impressions. How do you find the other women in the class?"

"My roommate is very prepared. She's highly motivated and intelligent. She'll do really well."

"You mean she'd make a good Operations Officer, in other words?"

"Sure. Why not?"

"Because she's intelligent and motivated, yes. But how about attractive?"

"Sure. She's attractive too."

"In what way?"

"She's slim, strong, and athletic."

"Continue."

"Continue with what?"

"Continue about how you find your roommate attractive."

"Okay," she smiled. "Just for shits and giggles, she has nice strong hair, smooth skin, a nice body."

He scribbled this on his legal pad.

"So," he continued, "if she approached you in the middle of the night and made an indecent overture towards you, what would be your response?"

"Like, what do you mean?"

"She approaches you in the middle of the night, slides her hand underneath your sheets, and rubs the tips of your breasts, let's say. Would you welcome that or not?"

"No, of course not! I wouldn't welcome that at all. I'd tell her that I'm not interested in that kind of thing."

"But how would her hands feel on your breasts? Would you be aroused by that? Or would you not be turned on at all?"

"Well, umm, naturally I'd be aroused, but I wouldn't let it continue. I mean, we are training to be Operations Officers here. I wouldn't reciprocate, if that's what you mean."

He wrote a couple of paragraphs in silence. When he finished with his scribbling, he said, "but her hands upon your breasts would feel good. That would feel perfectly normal?"

"As I said, it would feel good, but I wouldn't permit it

to go any further."

"So let's say, for shits and giggles, as you say, she slides her hands from your breasts down between your legs. If her hands on your breasts feel good, as you said, then her hands between your legs would also feel good, if not better, no?"

Sherry didn't know how to answer him. His eyes through his glasses probed her facial expressions for any hint or clue that she might indulge in such a deviance.

"It would feel good," she said, "but again, I'd never let it get that far. I'd have to explain to her that I'm not here to have sex but to train at the camp."

He again jotted down a few more notes.

"How about with one of the male trainees?"

"No. Absolutely not, I can assure you, doctor. I'm not here for that. I'm here to learn and do my job."

"But if your roommate's hands feel good on your breasts, and they feel even better your legs, then a male's hands upon you would also feel good, am I not right?"

"Yes, you are, but I would never indulge in that sort of thing here at CIA."

"Tell me, then. When was the last time your touched yourself?"

"Excuse me?"

"Just answer the question, please."

"A few months ago."

He jotted down a few more notes and made a check mark on the side of the page.

"Did you achieve an orgasm when you touched yourself?"

"Excuse me?"

"Just answer the question."

"Yes, I did."

"How long did it take you to achieve an orgasm?"

"About ten minutes, I'd say."

He took more notes and surrounded them in a box at the side of his notebook.

"And what did you fantasize about?"

"What?"

"Just answer the question, please."

"What did I fantasize about?"

"Yes."

"I guess I imagined being with a man."

"Be more specific, please."

"Be more specific about what?"

"Elaborate, please."

"Well, he was a well-built man. Handsome, bronzed, tan."

"What about his size?"

"He's a little taller than I am, I suppose."

"No, I mean the size of his phallus. Was it large, small, or medium-sized?"

"Doctor!"

"Just answer the question," he said firmly.

"He was well-endowed, I would say."

He wrote for a minute or two and then asked, "and he was inside of you, this well-endowed man?"

"Yes, he was inside of me."

"Was he thrusting in and out of you or just rocking inside of you back and forth?"

"He was rocking, I suppose. You could say that, yes."

"And I would be correct in saying that you prefer men who have large phalluses?"

"I don't get the question."

"You like men with large phalluses?"

"Yes, I do."

"So, you wouldn't accept men who have smaller phalluses?"

"I didn't say that."

"But you clearly prefer men with large phalluses. So, can we assume that men with smaller phalluses are out of the picture?"

"It depends."

"On what?"

"If I cared about the guy, it wouldn't matter what size his phallus is."

"But as far as achieving orgasm, you require a man with a large-sized phallus."

"Yes. You're right."

"I see," he said, taking more notes. "So, if a man with a small phallus opened his heart to you, showed you his weak side, you would reject his love in favor of a man who showed less emotion but had a large-sized phallus, is that correct? As far as achieving an orgasm is concerned?"

"Yes, I would. I need a large phallus. There's nothing wrong with that."

After a few unbearable moments, he asked, "let's say you were romantically involved with a man who had a small phallus. Am I correct, then, in assuming that you would still need an emotionless man with a large phallus as well?"

"Maybe."

"And so, the man who opens his heart to you and who has a small phallus would never satisfy you for very long. It would cause you to be unfaithful to him."

"No! I didn't say that! I would never be unfaithful to him!"

"But it is likely that you would cheat on him and have a relationship with the man who has a large phallus to achieve a robust and satisfying orgasm."

"Doctor, please! I can't answer these questions anymore."

"Just answer the question. Would you cheat on him or not?"

"Yes, okay! Yes, I would cheat on him! Are you satisfied now?"

"Okay, I think that's enough for today."

He handed her a box of tissues that sat next to his notes on his desk.

"I may be calling you in again for further review in case I need to, just for you to know. But you're done for now. You can return with the others and to your other appointments."

"Thank you," she said, wiping a tear away from her moist eyes. She left the room and returned to the dormitory where she found her roommate lying on her bed and reviewing a Russian textbook.

"Hi," said her roommate in her usual Southern accent.

"My God, what happened? Is everything alright?"

"Just having a hard time of it," she said, wiping away the residue of her tears.

"What on earth happened?"

"I just had an appointment with the psychiatrist."

"The psychiatrist? And it was that bad?"

"Yeah, it was bad."

"What on earth did he ask you?"

"I'd rather not get into it. Why? You didn't get the same treatment I did?"

"No, not at all. My appointment went really well. He even complimented me on how focused I was on the training. He gave me high marks."

"Did he ask you back?"

"No, why?"

"Wait. What?"

"Yeah, it went really well. I also talked to some of the others, and they had no problems with him either."

"The other two women too?"

"No. Just a couple of the other guys."

"Fuck."

"C'mon, we have language training, and then dinner. Let's head over to the main building. We don't want to be late. Better to be early. After dinner we have another lecture or two. A really busy day, this was."

The chatter at dinner had picked up considerably. It was their first day, and they eagerly shared their opinions on how it went. Two men from the male side of the dormitory joined Sherry and her roommate unexpectedly. Sherry welcomed talking to men again, but her roommate was a little shy and reserved around them, as though she never had the chance to look up from her textbooks all her life. The men were a welcome addition, even though Sherry still kept tabs on the popular crew sitting at the table behind her. No longer the center of attention, Sherry monitored both what was in front of her and also what was behind her. The man who sat next to her had flaming red hair. The second man across from her had brown hair. The rarity of sitting next a redhead threw her off a little. Never had she seen a redhead so up close. Yes, he was handsome in his own right and built well, but her eyes focused on the brown-haired man who talked cheerfully with her roommate. The Asian and the brown-haired man were getting along. Perhaps because the red head appeared so strange to her, she just wasn't interested in getting to know him. Her uninterest was just another conditioned response to someone who merely wanted to say a few words to her.

"How do you find the training?" said the redhead.

"Fine," said Sherry.

"I find it really interesting so far, especially the stuff on Afghanistan. You never know if any one of us has to go there."

"Yeah," she said.

"So, where are you from?"

"Vermont."

"Wow. Great skiing up there. Do you ski yourself?"

"Sometimes."

"Really? That's great. I've skied there a bunch of times. I like Killington the best. How about you?"

"It really doesn't matter."

"Oh. Well, how long have you been skiing?"

"A while."

"I've only been skiing a little while. I'm just a beginner, but I do like it a lot. I took a few lessons up there, and you wouldn't believe how hard it was. I could hardly stand on those damned skis. It was so funny. I fell so many times, especially right before getting off the chairlift. It was really funny. You should have been there."

"Great."

Sherry then interrupted the enjoyable conversation that her Asian roommate had with the brown-haired guy.

"So, where are from?" interrupted Sherry.

"Virginia," he said, pulling away from her roommate.

"Wow, that's really great. I've been to Virginia plenty of times. I really love it there. Does your family live there?"

"Richmond. They live in Richmond," he said in an unsuccessful attempt to bring all four of them into the conversation.

"I've never been," said her roommate.

"I've been there once," said the redhead. "Just passing through."

"Do you like the Dave Matthews Band?" asked Sherry. "Aren't they from Virginia?"

"I love the Dave Matthews Band," said the redhead enthusiastically.

"I've heard a few of their songs on the radio," said the brown-haired guy. "They're okay."

"I love them," said the red-haired guy again.

"I don't listen to them much," said the Asian. "I'm into classical music mostly."

"Me too," said the brown-haired guy excitedly. "Who's your favorite?"

"You've probably never heard of him."

"Try me."

"Rachmaninov," said the Asian.

"Seriously?"

"Yes, seriously."

"I love Rachmaninov," said the brown-haired guy. "He's one of the toughest composers to play."

"I think we better head over to the auditorium," said Sherry.

"I'll head over there soon," said the brown-haired guy, wanting to continue the discussion.

"I'll head over there in a little while too," said the Asian.

"I'll go with you," said the redhead to Sherry. "Better to get there early."

"Well, I have a few other things to do at the dorm before I get there," said Sherry. "I'll catch up to the rest of you later."

"See you later, Sherry," said the redhead.

Sherry headed straight for the auditorium after clearing her tray and eating, what she considered to be, a lackluster meal after a lackluster conversation. At first, the auditorium was empty. She sat alone, wondering what the evening would bring. She didn't want to hear anything more about Ickystan. She suspected that they wouldn't station her there anyway. She would be more valuable in Europe or Australia. She would blend in more easily, she figured, like a real operations officer had to in order to collect intelligence. She even imagined herself there again, as she had been to both places before.

She stays at a chateau on Lake Lucerne, or in a large

flat overlooking the Thames, or maybe even in the heart of gay Paris at a jazz club in the middle of the night, slow dancing with the brown-haired guy who is stationed there with her. Her reverie doesn't last too long, however, as the other trainees slowly filled in the seats around her.

Interestingly enough, the two brunette women, escorted in by a cadre of men, sat down behind her and made it conspicuously clear that they were among the partying bunch. Nevertheless, they wanted to know Sherry better.

"Hi," the two brunettes seemed to say simultaneously from behind her.

They vaguely reminded her of her sorority sisters, and she felt familiarly comfortable talking to them.

"Oh, hi," said Sherry.

"That guy you were sitting with at dinner is pretty cute," said the first brunette.

"Which one?" asked Sherry.

"Don't play dumb," said the second brunette. "It definitely wasn't carrot top over there."

"Yeah," she said. "He's really cute."

"Some of us are getting together after the meeting tonight in our room. Maybe you'd like to join us."

"Sure," said Sherry, relieved to be asked. "Sounds like fun."

"Why don't you bring him along?"

"Who?"

"The cute guy."

"Oh, I don't know. I don't know him well enough."

"Ask him," said the first brunette. "You never know

unless you ask."

"Okay. I'll ask him."

The instructor then marched on stage and took his usual place at the podium.

"Good evening, all of you," he began. "Language training continues tomorrow. You will also be taken through other types of training. This will all take some time, but just be patient until you reach the end of the first phase. Follow our instructions carefully, and as always, we'll evaluate your performance, so all of you should perform to the best of your abilities. We know you are capable of getting through this. The question is, do you believe you'll get through this? If you don't, then you better find that belief here and now. You won't be able to complete training without it. And with that, there are a few things we have to discuss before training continues in the morning.

"First of all, the primary job of an Operations Officer is to target people whom you think are in a position to reveal highly classified information, which you, in turn, will turn over to your appointed Station Chief. You will also write up a lot of reports, and when I mean a lot, I mean a lot. You target those people whom you know have information that can be valuable to us. For example, say there's a conference attended by international nuclear physicists, and there's some scientist from Lebanon who's attending it. We make you an attendee of that conference. You attend the conference and approach your target. You get to know him. When you do, you ask the target to reveal information relevant to our national defense and security. Once the target is hit, in this case the Lebanese physicist, this physicist is now an acquisition. You have acquired him. You are the asset. You are not agents, and if any of you here is stupid enough to call yourself an agent from this point forward, we'll throw you off of this campus. You should get it into your heads that you are *assets*, not *agents*. Some of you may need to rehearse it before bedtime. There is no such thing as a CIA agent. You are CIA assets, and your title within CIA is that of Operations Officer. That's all you need to know right now.

"You also need to know about relationships, and by that I mean romantic ones. Women, you are absolutely not to fall for anyone overseas who isn't an American. If you need to have sex with someone, they must be Americans, and it must be seldom. This isn't the fucking *Love Boat*. An asset who is too loose gets a bad reputation and that can affect your career at CIA. Our research and experience show that women will betray their country if they fall for a foreigner who may be an asset from another country. So, women, stick with American men. Many successful assets have relationships while here at CIA. It is, however, not acceptable to fall for a foreigner who may be Russian. Always guard your heart. Guard it with your life. Otherwise, it may be taken with the country you swore to protect.

"For men, guard your hearts too, assuming you still have them, but you are free to have sex with working girls both here and abroad. Just don't have sex with the same girl twice. If you get in trouble, don't expect us to bail you out. You should already know when to keep it in your pants. We are not you parents. If you want your parents again or if you want to have children with some farmer's daughter in Iowa, then get up right now and go there. Don't do it on our dime. Make sure you keep it in your pants when you need to and keep your noses clean, But you function in the same way the women do. Collect human intelligence always.

"Now does anyone know what human intelligence is? If so, you were born a very long time ago, and you should be old, grey, and impotent by now, because CIA was told to take a hike for a while and come back when human intelligence became trendy again. We need HUMINT, or human intelligence. CIA is the Rumplestilskin who has just woken up. You are always acquiring targets, or 'scalping' them, and you are building a portfolio of acquisitions from whom you extract information. You deliver that information to your Station Chief. Lie, cheat, and steal if you have to, but just don't get caught."

"Always protect your cover. Your targets are oppressed or in trouble in their home countries. Throw them a lifeline. If they fall for your romantically, say that you are already involved. Any romantic interaction with a target or acquisition must be cleared through your Station Chief first. You are not permitted to have sex with your targets or acquisitions unless authorized to do so. So, women, you do not have sex with some idiot without prior authorization first. If you don't preauthorize it but still get the intelligence from him, that's not a win. First, get authorization. Don't rely on your own mind but the Company's mind. Never do anything without prior authorization. Your souls belong to the United States of America, and your hearts and your sex lives belong to CIA.

"For the men, it's the same, but CIA likes to save its women from trouble and not its ugly-looking men. Why? Because men should already know better. Women don't know better. If you fuck up out there, the consequences may be severe. If a woman fucks up, we save her. Whether you like this or not, that's your own business. If you take that anger out in the field, then it becomes CIA's business. And if that's the case, we're sending you back home…"

Sherry sat in her seat like a fighter pilot about to be ejected. Her Asian roommate steadily took notes. The two brunettes behind her seemed completely apathetic. They slackened in their seats with their pencils in their mouths and looked as though they were on the verge of self-destruction if they didn't get to the after-hours party that night. They seemed not to care about anything the instructor said. Like most women of their cultivation, they often used what was prominent about themselves and did what was natural within their own range of talents, and that meant partying after lights out, their highest priority of the day.

Sherry was an independent. Unable to belong to any clique in the CST ecosystem, she still was shy and a little scared. She looked to a destination somewhere in the distance. She pictured a beach with warm ocean water, a strawberry marguerita in her hand, and no worries on the face of the earth, living her life as she wanted to live it without any of the concerns that reality shoved her way. Her imagination developed beyond the theories in her Biology textbooks. Despite her best attempts, she may have bitten off more than she could chew. It involved getting through training without cracking. Being an independent wasn't so bad, though. She didn't need to be in first place in order to make it through.

It felt as though she were purposely sent there, perhaps monitored all along by some external force that made her boyfriend cheat on her and made her father disappointed in her. She had come to CIA by design. Someone determined that she had to apply, and this was where she had to be placed. She had no clue about Ickystan, the brothels, the restricted relationships, and the prior authorizations that the instructor spoke of, but she learned gradually.

After a few short weeks, the brunettes' attitudes appealed to her. She should have some fun before all the new restrictions were set into place, and yes, she wanted to ask the brown-haired guy to the after-hours parties. After the last few words tumbled out of the instructor after another one of his intense lectures, Sherry made sure to find the brown-haired guy who by this time had broken off from his usual laughter-filled conversation with the Asian at dinner and headed towards the quad between the main building and the dormitory for the night. Sherry watched him, making sure he didn't get too far ahead. Once outside, she ran up behind him and patted him on the shoulder. He was startled but more than happy to answer any of her questions.

"Oh, hi," he said. "Nice to see you. What's up?"

"Nice to see you too," said Sherry, a little out of breath. "Are you doing anything tonight?"

"Tonight? No. Just going to sleep."

"Sleep? Don't do that. There's a party in the women's dorm tonight if you want to go. How about it?"

"Nah, I don't think that's such a good idea. Got a big day ahead of us tomorrow, and I don't want to get into any trouble. I want to be well-rested and all."

"Not even for a short time with the other CSTs? C'mon, it will be fun."

"I'm sorry, but I can't. My roommate will probably want to go, though. Why don't you ask him?"

She remembered the carrot-top at the dinner table.

"Maybe some other time then," she said.

She fell behind him as her Asian roommate raced ahead of her on the outside. When the Asian and the brown-haired guy caught up to each other, they laughed and chatted about God knows what. Suddenly envious, Sherry resolved to go to the party anyway and thought up a few explanations for the brunettes as to how she let the brown-haired guy get away. Apparently, the brown-haired guy was now what the female CTSs wanted all of a sudden. They wanted him for no other reason other than that's what they all wanted. There was no explanation, no reason, and no suitable logic. The dynamic and interplay at work put this very plain guy at the center of their feminine attention. They were likeminded greyhounds chasing the same rabbit. The guy just wasn't interested in them. He only took interest in the determined, conscientious Asian. Sherry had no idea what he saw in her either, but it was clear that he was the primary target she needed to acquire.

While her roommate slept, Sherry slipped out of the room wearing her red, silk pajamas. She made sure not to wake her. She tiptoed out of the room and over to the other side of the dorm where the two brunettes played alternative rock tunes out of a small boom box in their room. They smiled when she entered and pointed to a small cooler. Sherry fished out a cold beer from it.

"Where'd you guys get all this?" asked Sherry.

"Perks," smiled the first brunette, lying on her bed.

"But how?"

"That's classified information," said the second brunette.

The beer was cold and bubbly on her tongue. She hadn't had one in ages and looked forward to getting a little buzzed. She took a seat on one of the desk chairs.

"Where's your friend?"

"She's asleep."

"Not her. The one you were going to bring with you?"

"He needed to get up early tomorrow."

"That's strike one," said the second brunette.

"Just don't strike out," said the first.

"There's still time," laughed Sherry.

"Not with that Asian in the way."

"What do you mean?"

"Like you don't know?"

"What about her?"

"She's your competition. Seems like she has him in a vice alright."

"A real tight one," said the second brunette. "The kind that squeezes him nice and good, I bet."

"Oh, I think they're just friends," said Sherry.

"Don't play the dumb blonde. She's all over him. Don't you want him for yourself?"

"Well, if she wants him, let her have him."

"Wait a second," said the second brunette. "How are you going to be an effective Operations Officer with that kind of attitude?"

"What do you mean?"

"God, maybe you are a dumb blonde," said the first brunette.

"We always have to get prior authorization," smiled Sherry, trying to be smart and then taking a gulp of her beer.

"I don't think you get it," said the first. "The Company wants women who take a more initiative than that, and that goes with our targets. They just say they want prior authorization because everything has to be legal. But out in the field, we do anything we can, and that means sleeping with our targets if we have to."

"And how do you guys know all this?" asked Sherry incredulously.

"We have friends," said the second brunette. "We're

the type they want, not the wiz-kid. You can't be very good if you can't get a guy like that. He's not that difficult. Just shake it a little, and he'll follow your tail. Don't let your roommate get to him first, because once these Asian women get to our American men, the men never turn back. It's a national security risk, actually."

"You guys are funny."

"You think we're joking?"

"C'mon. Let's change the subject."

"Okay, but you'll find out soon enough.

"Give it some time," smiled the second brunette, licking the curve of her upper teeth with her tongue.

"You're kidding me."

"We're not joking. You have to give it up to get the things you want in here."

"I would never do that."

"Suit yourself," said the first brunette, "but don't tell us we didn't tell you so first."

"How do you guys know these things?" asked Sherry.

"We know people both inside and outside the Company."

"What about the rules? You heard the instructor."

"At the end of training, come back and tell us we're wrong."

"I guess I'll have to, because I'm not giving it up for anyone."

"We'll see."

They talked for a little while longer before two men from the other side of the dorm arrived. They dressed in tee-shirts and sweats. As before, Sherry thought them handsome.

The brunettes made room for them on their beds and handed them beers. The five of them together seemed well-matched. The women were beautiful, and the men were handsome, such that it would be totally permissible for them to be shipped off to an island where they could mate and form their own colony of beautiful people, if such uncharted territory didn't exist already. They were the same type of people in a world where they had been crushed together and then passed through their respective lineages until they were unable to disentangle themselves, break out, or overcome what lied beyond their own kind.

At the camp, it was the brown-haired guy's turn to be joined with the popular crew who happened to know more about the Company than any of the other trainees. Sherry found herself in good company. She cracked open another beer, but once she finished it, the first brunette said, "I guess it's time for bed."

"So soon?" said one of the men. "You're kidding, right?"

"At least it's time for Sherry to go to bed," said the second brunette.

"Yeah," said the first. "She's a little wet behind the ears."

"She doesn't know how this works yet," said the second.

"I can show her," said the second guy.

"Not a chance," said the first brunette. "Three's company tonight."

"Why?" asked Sherry. "You guys planning a party after the party?"

"Let her stay," pleaded the first guy.

"No, not tonight. Sorry."

"Maybe some other time, Sherry," said the first guy.

"I guess I'll be going to bed, then," said Sherry. "You kids have a fun night."

"Oh, we will," said the first brunette. "And Sherry, bring your cute guy here next time, and maybe you can join us."

On her return to the room, she opened the door slowly and slid into bed making as little noise as possible. Unfortunately, her roommate was awake.

"Where were you?" her roommate said drowsily.

"Don't worry about it. Go to sleep."

"Listen, it's not a good idea to do anything after lights out. They can kick you out for that."

"Just go to sleep. There's nothing for you to worry about."

The Asian turned her back and tried to fall asleep again. Sherry saw her as a developing pest, watching everything she did. Why she cared, Sherry had no idea. Maybe it was an extension of the congenial politeness and servitude she had learned in the prep schools she went to, the bill paid by her wealthy parents in whatever Southern city they had immigrated to. Sherry's new policy was not to tell the Asian anything. But at the breakfast table the next morning, as Sherry sat side-by-side with the carrot-top and faced the Asian and the brown-haired target laughing heartily at something they had both discovered in one of their textbooks, she knew she had to be more aggressive in separating the two soon-to-be lovebirds. She deflected all attempts from carrot top to hold a decent conversation. Her sole objective was to nab her brown-haired target and join the others for their after-after party. It was intelligence work at its most critical. This stuff was not in any of the textbooks, language labs, or code breaking seminars they had her attend. Sherry followed that thread.

When she was told after the morning lecture that she would be studying Pashto, Farsi, Arabic, Urdu, and Russian, she didn't consider how she may have needed them one day. She studied them because she was ordered to. She also continued to focus on the afterhours parties and how she needed a third guy to make these parties balanced with the same ratio of men to women. It wasn't until a couple months later that the Asian and the brown-haired guy were a definite couple, and even though there were a few other guys who tried to hit on Sherry during those first few months holed up at the camp, her only interest remained with the target, aided, of course, by the coaching and coaxing of her brunette friends who guided her.

Chapter Ten

July 2000 – McLean, VA, USA

At three months, Sherry didn't know how she fared in the program. The instructors and the several specialists who taught her classes didn't tell her how she did thus far. They took copious notes evaluating her performance, but they hardly said a word to her. Even though she asked them from time to time for suggestions on ways to improve, they were more annoyed by her questions than pleased that she asked them. It had been nearly three months of grueling work, and none of the trainees knew where they stood. Naturally, this caused her concern.

In one of their last classes before the Interim period, the trainees sat at their desks in a classroom in the main building and observed an older Arab professor dressed in a brown tweed jacket and crimson bowtie. He arranged his notes at the front of the room. The professor's salt-and-pepper hair, trimmed black moustache, and light olive skin placed him as a Lebanese or Syrian national. The trainees, however, couldn't tell which country he hailed from. It turned out that he served as a tenured History professor at American University, its main campus in nearby Washington. He had been imported all the way from that university's campus in Cairo and was an expert in Middle Eastern affairs. To Sherry, he seemed like any other foreigner in a Westernized outfit, but when he introduced himself, his acted perfectly American. It made her and the others unsure of exactly how to categorize him. He didn't even mention his name. Perhaps he kept his name private to refuse giving the trainees the satisfaction of thinking him anything other than a full-fledged American devoted to American values and his truly American family as well. He seemed to them the future of all Arab-Americans in the United States. He was a citizen way before his time. He was the prototype of perfection, always in a state of striving.

Sherry thought, however, that such a man, no matter how valiantly he tried, would never shake or outrun his own ancestry. Either way, Sherry paid attention, even though she, along with the rest of her fellow trainees, prayed that they wouldn't be stationed anywhere near Cairo. As the training moved forward, that reality became increasingly apparent to them all. Some of them would have to go, but no one knew whom. Sherry prayed that she wouldn't be one of them. Iceland would be far better than the rubble of Lebanon or Syria.

He first asked the class a simple question in an erudite American accent. He even wrote this same question on the porcelain whiteboard behind him in bright red marker, underling each word.

"Who is Osama Bin Laden?" he wrote in bright red marker underlining the name.

Whether it was too early in the morning or if the trainees were still too reticent to respond to the question was beside his point. The Asian's hand shot up in the grim silence. With pleasure, the professor called upon her. It made his job much easier when the students he taught participated instead of sitting there like frogs on lily pads.

"Osama Bin Laden is the founder and leader of the Al-Queda terrorist organization," said the Asian confidently to the chagrin of her other trainees. "He was expelled from Saudi Arabia for being a militant Islamic extremist who went against the Saudi royal family."

"Very good," said the professor with a smile wide enough to show his brown, tea-stained teeth. "Can anyone give me a history of the man, how he came to power, and where he is now?"

Again, there was silence. The Asian refrained from answering so as not to anger the other trainees.

"Actually," chuckled the professor, "I'm glad you don't know the history of Mr. Bin Laden yet. It would give us nothing to talk about for the rest of the class. But from what I've been told, all of you need to know who this man is and what he believes, but not before we discuss what inspired this man to make the United States and all of our European allies the object of his hatred.

"You see, the young Osama was once an exceptional Islamic scholar, and they all start out that way, don't they? Born to a billionaire construction industrialist, Osama at one time had close ties to the Saudi royal family, a relationship that had been cemented by his father. Even though his family hails from Yemen, Bin Laden was born in Riyad as a Saudi national. His family raised him as a devout Sunni Muslim."

The Asian's hand shot up again.

"Just to make sure," she said, "the Sunnis and the Shias have always been fierce enemies, right?"

"Excellent," smiled the professor. "Yes. The majority of the Muslim world is Sunni, and the minority of the Muslim world is Shia. They have always been at odds, ever since the Prophet passed away, because the Prophet never left a successor. The Sunnis elected their leader, while the Shias appointed the Prophet's closest blood relation. That's the essential difference. Over generations, though, these two sects of Islam grew far apart. The Sunnis take up most of the Middle East, while the Shias are mainly Persian. Persia, as we all should know, is now Iran. Thank you for making that distinction. That was excellent.

"But to continue, the young Saudi studied economics and business administration at King Abdulaziz University but turned to religious studies instead. He somehow found great interest in interpreting the Qu'ran, Islam's holiest book. But when the young Osama left the university, he used his vast monies from his father's construction company to funnel guns and weapons to the *mujahideen* in Afghanistan to fight the Soviet occupation there. Interesting, isn't it? An ally of the United States one decade, and our terrible foe the next? This happens constantly in the Muslim world, as Islam is the constant, while our democracy is always changing, whether we are moving backwards or forwards. Anyway, Osama was fiercely against the Soviet invasion, so he supported the rebels against the Communists there. Afghanistan is his current base of operations.

"With his help, the Soviets were thrown out. He has now taken *Al-Queda* to a new level by organizing smaller groups of *jihadists* against the United States under the umbrella of *Al-Queda*'s leadership. Our intelligence points to slow alliances forming between *Al-Queda* and other terrorist organizations in Iraq, which places our Armed Forces in grave danger.

"But now that America is so heavily involved in the Middle East, whether oil is our interest there or our strategic defenses, it is actually very easy to see why Osama bin Laden and his organization are such threats. For Bin Laden, it has always been a religious question, not a question of political or economic reality.

"The history of Bin Laden notwithstanding, does

anyone know who inspired Bin Laden into believing in his militant brand of Islam?"

Sherry knew she had to defeat the Asian. She couldn't let her get away without answering another question. The Asian had always been the front-runner, the superstar to beat, and while no one else was up to the challenge, Sherry had to stop this inexorable trend and compete where no competition had been before. Maybe she would be admired for it – the genius who could party like mad and yet was talented enough to beat the frontrunner. She raised her hand despite her doubts.

"Considering that he was brought up as a devout Muslim and studied it in depth at the university he went to," said Sherry, "it follows that his work at Abdulaziz led him towards militancy."

The professor held his chin between his thumb and forefinger. He pondered her answer. He looked at the floor confusedly before saying, "not really. Your analysis is logical, but not wholly correct. While it is true that his upbringing as a devotee of Islam and his religious studies at university certainly influenced him, you are not being specific enough. Also, you need to use 'King' before using the name 'Abdulaziz.'

"Anyway, to continue, somewhere along the line, Osama lost interest in his father's construction business and began studying the Qu'ran in depth. Anyone who knows the Qu'ran understands that such an enlightenment that comes about through its careful study can be all-encompassing and perhaps all too powerful for any one man to bear. You see, as a youth, Osama was trained to follow Islam and the Qu'ran to the letter. To the letter!" he said, suddenly raising his voice. "He believed that the laws and the history written in the Qu'ran had to be followed and appreciated literally and without compromise. There was little room for interpretation. He believed in the inflexible rule of Sharia Law and rejected all forms of secularism in government. This includes democracy, communism, and even socialism, even though many Western scholars have linked socialism and communism to the Islamic way of life.

"He hated democracy most of all, especially its Judeo-Christian foundations. He subscribed to the *Athari* school of Islam, which propagates the full restoration of Sharia Law and that the Islamic world has been on a slow, continuous decline towards eventual but certain extinction. This decline has to be prevented by devout Muslims all over the world, especially since Israel uprooted the Palestinian state at the end of the Second World War.

"Now here's a question that should stump all of you: what or who turned a young and conscientious Osama bin Laden into believing in the *Athari* school of Islam? The young lady here tried to answer it but couldn't. Does anyone else want to try?"

Even the Asian didn't know the answer to this question. The buzzing of the fluorescent tube lights above them filled the void as the esteemed professor waited for a response.

"I guess we have a lot to discuss, then," he said disappointedly, "but don't despair. If you knew this already, I wouldn't need to be here, now would I?"

The class merely sat there like swollen sponges trying to classify this very strange professor.

"Before World War Two and also during it, the nation of Palestine was actually a British colony. The Balfour Amendment established the State of Israel after the war, as we should all know by now. We should also know from our history books that the British Empire had colonized huge swaths of land that had stretched and impacted almost every territory on the face of the globe. Palestine was no exception, and either was Egypt, its next-door neighbor. Actually, the whole of the Middle East was under British control, and out of this cruel occupation of the Middle East came a single Muslim who defied the British Empire, fought it tooth and nail, and helped free Muslims in the Middle East from unrelenting British oppression. That single Muslim was perhaps the only man who could inspire Osama bin Laden to become the international terrorist he is today. This man was an Egyptian named Sayyid Qutb."

The professor's eyes widened as he annunciated his name. His eyes glowered in frenzied thought as he paced in front of his desk, the trainees watching him apprehensively.

"It's really no surprise that no one has heard of Sayyid Qutb and his vast contribution to our current state of affairs. Such a man never really mattered to us, because Americans never considered such Arabs a threat as great as the Russians or the Chinese. He didn't matter to us until recently. Because in order to understand the motivations behind Osama bin Laden, we must go through Sayyid Qutb, which is why all of you are here today. It is Sayyid Qutb's writings that are more threatening than Bin Laden's terrorism. Osama is the realization and the fruition of Qutb's ideas, and the time for those ideas have finally come.

"Qutb was born in 1906 in a small town known as Musha in Middle Egypt. He was the eldest of five children. At the age of ten, this young prodigy memorized the entire Qu'ran line by line. Can you imagine it? Instead of playing baseball, chess, or Pin the Tail on the Donkey, a ten year-old memorized the whole of the Qu'ran, every verse of its sublime poetry, every Sura, every fucking historical figure!"

"Because no one at that age could possibly memorize such a large book. It's not even humanly possible. I mean, who cares about these snot-nosed kids playing cricket, right? He was a kid who sat indoors on hot sunny days and memorized one of the world's holiest books.

"In 1922, when Qutb was just twenty-two years old, a man named Hasan al-Bana created an organization that he affectionately called *The Muslim Brotherhood*. Interestingly enough, the socialist Gamel Abdel Nasser, Anwar Sadat, and Hasan al-Bana all knew each other in military college in the 1930s. Qutb joined the *Muslim Brotherhood* right when it formed. Realizing that their son was indeed a prodigy of the strangest kind, Qutb's bewildered parents sent him to the great *Al-Azhar University* in Cairo. The university is considered to be the pinnacle of all learning in all of Islam. Armed with full knowledge of the Qu'ran, Qutb studied hard, gut-wrenchingly hard, until he finally graduated from *Al-Azhar* in 1947, which is near the end of World War Two. Can anyone guess where the young Qutb went next?"

"The little fucker goes to the United States of all places! Can you imagine that? From memorizing the Qu'ran and rigorously studying Islamic theology, he is sent to the most immoral, lascivious, and promiscuous land in the world? He is sent to the University of Northern Colorado in 1948 to pursue a Master's degree in Teaching. What the hell were his parents thinking? A man in Middle Eastern garments praying five times a day, having studied in the most prestigious university in all of Islam, is suddenly walking around campus in his pajamas while the students there drink their beers and party all night? No, I say, no! Bad decision! Bad move!"

The professor pounded the table and then steadied himself at his desk with his teeth clenched. He calmed himself before continuing.

"And what does the young man see there," he said more quietly. "Half-naked women dancing, baring their naked shoulders and flaunting their protruding American breasts and uncovered legs. He hears young Americans fucking in their dorm rooms late at night, his ears unable to drown out the squeaks of the bedsprings next door, the unbearable torture of the moans, groans, and giggles seeping through the walls in the middle of the night. Can't you hear it now? Just think of the young Qutb trying to sleep, or the young Qutb saying his evening prayers. He tries to study for his exams, but meanwhile, there's an orgy next door, the sounds of merging flesh, the heat and sweat of mad humping slowly driving him insane.

"Maybe one night he thinks, 'if you can't beat 'em, join 'em.' Fine. The innocent Qutb, influenced by the corruption of the Western world buys a single rose from the campus store and dares to ask one of those campus sluts on a date, only that the comely harlot rejects him. And do you know why he's rejected? First, because he is a foreigner. No one can understand him, and no one likes him. He's ugly to these Americans. Second and more importantly, he's a poor foreigner at that, a poor foreigner in a land without any money to spend on a date. The women on campus laugh at him. Perhaps he dreams of marrying one and then taking her back to Egypt to live in holy matrimony. But he finds that, in America, he needs money wherever he goes just to get a smile or a few words out of the women here. He discovers that everyone in America is devoted to money. What a shock it must have been to find out that the love of money even crushes the power of God. Even though he chooses God, he understands that he will never have enough money to buy an American woman. He can't possibly afford the Barbie doll on the store shelf.

"He grows so isolated and insular in his own thinking that this social pariah, trapped in Shitsville, Northern Colorado, must rebel and rebel hard against everything American and whatever the Western world stands for. Perhaps he is compelled to masturbate every night and is caught by his peeping dormmates, plunging him into a shame so deep that it necessitates a complete rejection of the Western capitalist machine. As a result of his complete humiliation, he must be morally and intellectually superior to them just to bolster his own withered ego. His self-esteem has been pummeled. He has no women, no money, no nothing. With this detritus in his weakened psychology, Qutb returns to Egypt angrier than ever before. He returns with a seething hatred for America and the British rulers who spawned them. He is ready to fight for Egypt's independence and the creation of a new Muslim state where women can never hurt, degrade, or reject him ever again. Is it no wonder why, then, that this young Sayyid Qutb, having witnessed white promiscuity and the worship of their green money, is inspired to fight? Quite a common tale, I'm afraid. Such a tale still reverberates to this very day, even as we speak."

The professor's eyes burned straight through Sherry. She avoided his gaze by taking notes furiously, but she couldn't help but feel vulnerable, his spittle flying from his lips. She seemed to be the object of all his ire and hatreds. Whether this was a misperception on her part or not, she refused to believe that attractive and promiscuous white women were the primary cause of the conflicts in the Middle East, even though the thought fleetingly crossed her mind. She forced her head down into the pages of her notebook and tried not to look at him. The professor continued his strange lecture. He again had to calm himself, as he moved on. He then discussed Qutb's return to Egypt after his disastrous stint in Colorado.

"When Qutb returned t Egypt, he also returned to the *Muslim Brotherhood* which he had first joined in 1928. It was

1951, and the Brits were still in control. He became Editor of the newspaper *Al-Ikhwan al Muslimin,* or the *Muslim Brotherhood Weekly.* In it, he railed against British rule, and with the *Muslim Brotherhood's* direct assistance, the Muslims in Egypt staged an impressive, full-scale revolution in 1952. It sent the British back home to their pubs and large country estates. Egypt had finally become an independent nation. Qutb played a large part in that. He also continued to write his philosophies on Islam and its future in the newspaper he edited.

"After the 1952 revolution, a man named Gabdel Abdel Nasser came to power. Nasser became the first president of Egypt. As I mentioned earlier, Nasser, al-Bana, and Sadat all knew each other in military college in the 1930s. These men now held most of the cards in Egypt. But Nasser was a socialist who believed in pan-Arabism in the Middle East. He advocated the joining of Arab nations regardless of how secular or devout they were. He advocated a unity of nations but not the unity of all of Islam, like Qutb. Nasser introduced many popular reforms in Egypt and nationalized the *Suez Canal,* the major waterway that the West used for trade. The canal was now in Egyptian hands. The US was not too happy about that. Nevertheless, Nasser gained a huge following as his pan-Arabic and anti-imperialist stances against the colonization and occupation of Arab nations solidified his role as the strongman of socialism in the Arab world. Now I ask of you, what was Sayyid Qutb's reaction to Nasser's politics?"

Sherry knew she had the right answer. Just to appease what she perceived to be the professor's inexplicable anger towards her, she raised her hand and simply answered, "Qutb and his *Muslim Brotherhood* must have been against Nasser's regime and his belief in pan-Arabism. Qutb didn't want secular nations in the Middle East. He wanted a full and religiously-cohesive Islamic state, not a secular or politically socialist one. So, he must have resisted Nasser when he came to power."

The professor was silent for a few moments.

"Is she right?" he asked while scanning the classroom.

No one in the class responded.

"Yes, she is right," he said disappointedly. "Qutb and his *Muslim Brotherhood* did not support Nasser because of his anti-religious stance. Nasser was, after all, a socialist. In 1954, the *Muslim Brotherhood* went so far as to try to assassinate Nasser. They failed, and Qutb, the primary leader of the attempted coup, was sentenced to twenty-five years in prison in Tera. In fact, all of Qutb's brothers were all thrown in prison at the same time for aiding and abetting him. In 1957, prison guards in Tera massacred his brothers in their jail cells.

"While in prison," continued the professor emotionally, "Qutb was beaten and tortured to no end for his defiance of Nasser. He spent most of his time there in the prison infirmary recovering from his injuries. The prison guards allowed him to write, and write he certainly did. In prison and in the prison infirmary, his writings became increasingly radical. He fought against any society that wasn't Islamic. He envisioned a true and unified Islamic state, an *umma* like none other that applied Sharia Law fully. Any nation that did not apply unfettered Sharia Law must be overthrown through *jihad*, or what he thought to be, not traditional Islamic struggle or striving, but a full-scale holy war against infidels who diluted the strength of the Islamic way of life.

"Can anyone tell me who Qutb's audience was as he was writing these things?"

Sherry again thought she had the answer. She raised her hand bravely and said, "Qutb wanted to rally his fellow Muslims to continue the fight against Nasser. His writings were meant to inspire them into action."

"Is she right?" smiled the professor.

Her Asian roommate took a stab at he question.

"No, she is not," said the Asian. "Actually, Qutb's wanted to scare Nasser and the political elites who had taken over Egypt at the time. He was also saying that if these elites sided with any other superpower, say Russia or China, or any force that went against Sharia Law, then that superpower must also be overthrown. The only way to overthrow these forces is through Islam and *jihad.* It would make no sense to rally the the *Muslim Brotherhood* again. Most of them were wiped out anyway."

"Correct!" smiled the professor, exposing the brown stains in his teeth. "His goal was to threaten, or to terrorize, the Egyptian political class through his writings. Excellent.

"But to continue, in his seminal work, *Neglected Duty*, he directly presented these radical ideas. Many years later, it turned out that Qutb's work inspired the likes of Osama bin Laden and his right-hand man, Dr. Ayman al-Zawahiri. Qutb had created what is commonly known to scholars as 'Qutbian Islam.'

"In Qutbian Islam, all Muslims are called upon to transcend flimsy national boundaries and create a world community of believers, a worldwide *umma* that is not isolated within fictitious national borders. In Islam, there are no borders. The whole world must submit to Islam to be truly free. More importantly, however, Qutbian Islam says that there is absolutely no separation between church and state. None!" he barked.

"No longer would young virgin maidens get to fuck without punishment! Everything is governed just as the Prophet decreed and that is only through Sharia Law. Thus, Qutb has created the concept known as 'political Islam.'

"Imagine that? No borders? No other law, religion, politics, or economy other than what has been decreed by the Prophet in the *Qu'ran*, the *Hadith*, and the *Sunnah*. His version of Islam says that the false concepts of politics, economy, and national borders are all unholy constructs of Western colonizers and Chinese and Russian Communists. Without worldwide Islamic submission, the world is in a condition of reckless anarchy. And in Sunni Islam, the *Fitna* plainly states that 'an evil ruler is better than anarchy!' In order to stop these infidels who would rather have their way with Islam, Muslims must fight them by any means necessary. Hence, we have what is known today as 'terrorism,' a legitimate resistance against anarchy.

"For the likes of Bin Laden and his close associates, Qutb is nothing less than a sanctified martyr. It gives bin Laden and his *Al-Queda* the wherewithal to overthrow and defeat those who do not submit to Sharia Law and a total Islamic society.

"In 1964, the President of Iraq convinced Nasser to release Qutb from the Tera prison. There, he had been beaten to a pulp. But in 1964, Qutb is jailed again after being accused of armed revolt and terrorism against Nasser and the Egyptian state. His entire family and the remaining members of the *Muslim Brotherhood* are also jailed for anti-government activities. Qutb, the poor soul, is finally hung in 1966.

"Can all of you understand now why Qutb is seen as an Islamic martyr. I hope so, because the key to understanding the motivations of Bin Laden is through understanding the writings of Sayyid Qutb. Now that you know why these people kill themselves in the name of Islam, you at least have a general idea of how to defeat *Al-Queda* as well – not through militant Christianity or a Jewish reactionary response, as the Company has practiced in the past, but by knowing that the all-encompassing totality of any religious state will put all of us back in shackles and chains. Our world of today and the freedoms we have now will cease to exist. Instead of wanting to live, we too will want to die for the same cause Qutb died for. Bin Laden and his followers are more than willing to die *for* a borderless Islamic world. It is we, on the other hand, who desire to live for the freedoms we have *from* the major religions, one of them being Islam.

"And therein lies the key that will ultimately lead to *Al-Queda's* demise. We are not dying for an ideal. While we live and fight for what we already *have. Al-Queda* fights for a concept, an idea, or a world they imagine *may* one day exist in the future. Can I make myself any clearer? We fight *Al-Queda* to live, while *Al-Queda* fights to die for an imaginary goal that kills themselves off. I ask you, then, defenders of our nation, who do you think has the upper hand here? Who has the advantage? I would place all of my bets on the United States, no matter how entirely fucked up and corrupt this God-forsaken place is, no matter how vulgar all of you are. We preserve our freedoms so that we can live. Let the zealots blow themselves up and die for a figment of their own overactive imaginations."

The trainees in the classroom were stunned by the professor's lecture. Some of them were even afraid of him. They sat in silence as he took slow, long breaths to steady and calm himself after such a display of emotion. With a more peaceful demeanor, he said, "I know all of you have a week off before your final examinations. Allow me to give you a little hint as to what your instructor may test you on next week. It is a question of great interest to many scholars who have studied Qutb and his writings.

"The great British historian, William E. Shepard, theorized, and I quote him directly,

> *'Qutb's prison experience hardly provided any training in moderation, and the isolation from outside political society must have encouraged the tendency toward the theoretical and radical consistency that marks his later thoughts.'*

"In other words," he continued, "we must ask whether or not Qutbian Islam is a product, not of any breakthrough in philosophical thought or genius of intellect, but of his intense isolation and the tortures he endured in the Tera prison. Was he tortured so badly that he birthed Qutbian Islam through intense suffering and pain? Or did he have a healthy and properly functioning mind when he invented his radical ideas? Osama bin Laden and his associates must have also felt the pain and the suffering of isolation when their homelands cast them out for their devotion to their imagined way of life. Remember that Bin Laden and many Arab radicals like him were sent wandering into the far reaches of the desert without any family or country. Their respective governments exiled them. So, is the psychological makeup of bin Laden similar to that of Qutb's in terms of the pain he suffered as an outsider ripped apart from his own people and his own family by the ones who governed his homeland?

"That's the question I'm going to leave you with. You have been schooled in the many methods of torture and interrogation through your several months of training here at Langley, I'm sure you can at least begin thinking about this question as you head into your final exams. I sincerely hope you defeat these people before they defeat you. It will be better for us all."

After the professor dismissed them, Sherry noticed sweat beading on the professor's brow. She left as quickly as possible and waited for the two brunettes in the hallway. It was time for lunch. She was hungry enough to eat a small salad in keeping with her strict dietary habits. The red-haired trainee caught her waiting there and complimented her on how bravely she fielded the professor's questions.

"I'm surprised you even answered him," he said. "He looked like he wanted to plunge a saber into you."

"Thanks," she said, rolling her eyes. "I'm glad you enjoyed it."

"But it's great how you responded to him. That guy had some sort of grudge against you, that's for sure."

"I guess so," she said.

"Your answer didn't seem wrong to me, though. To differentiate Qutb and Nasser? You took a real risk. I admire that."

"Thanks."

"Your assessment was close, but no cigar," he chuckled.

"I know," she said. "I've got to run."

The brunettes passed her, and she ran ahead to catch up. She joined them on the slow walk to the cafeteria through the biting cold. The trainees were thankful to be given a clue as to what would be on the exam the following week. The exams would test language ability, psychology, decoding skills, and the many other terms and subjects they had learned in the months that had passed. They were all at the end of Phase One.

At the time, the Asian and the brown-haired guy had a close affinity for each other that wasn't too hard to see. They were now the star couple at the Camp as they headed into the Interim period. They sat apart from the others at meals. They only needed themselves within their own, tiny cocoon of mutual admiration and common interests. They delighted each other will babble that made no sense to anyone but themselves. Sherry only saw them as a couple that needed a good breaking apart. She couldn't stand to see them together, and after more advice from the two brunettes that night after hours, she decided to visit the lead instructor in his office after her final Pashto class the very next morning.

The tinsel-haired instructor sat at his desk and reviewed some papers there. They were stacked in front of him, and he looked extremely busy and optimally productive, a quiet machine that never broke down. He dressed the same every day – a white, short-sleeve shirt, a tie that looked like it had been bought at a garage sale, and the same Styrofoam cup of black coffee always within arm's reach. He didn't stop his work when Sherry came in. He seemed uninterested in her petty problems. His main concern was the top performers.

"What can I do for you?" he mumbled, his eyes fixed on his papers. "I have a busy afternoon."

"Sorry to bother you, sir, but an issue has come up that I need to address."

"Oh? Better be good."

"Yes, sir, it is. It's my roommate."

"Yeah? What about her?"

"She's disturbing the other trainees."

"Why's that? Because she's the best in the class?"

"No. It's something else."

The instructor looked at her and asked her to take a seat.

"What about her?"

"My roommate has been carrying on with one of the other trainees."

"And how does that affect you and the other trainees exactly?"

"She's making all of us restless, and now everyone wants to get involved. I, for one, can't focus on my work, especially when she doesn't stop talking about this other trainee and discussing specific details about their illicit relationship. We're not in college anymore, sir. My work is suffering, and it's bothering the other trainees as well."

"How do you know they're romantically involved?"

"She talks about him every night. I think they're in love, and it's really dangerous for that kind of thing to happen, now that we are so far along in our training."

"Does your roommate remember that she can be thrown out for something like that?"

"That's why it's bothering the rest of us. It's like she's rubbing our noses in it."

"I see."

"Also, it's not fair that she gets to see someone when the rest of us can't. It's only natural to want to be with each other, sir."

"Okay. That will be all. You can return to your next appointment now."

"Aren't you going to do anything about it, sir?"

"Whatever I do is none of your concern. Get to your next appointment."

At dinner, Sherry sat with the popular crew while peeking at the Asian and the brown-haired target aloof in their own blissful world. She was desperate to score a win, and now that the Asian would surely get the boot, a woman like Sherry would slide in to seal the hole in his heart. She looked forward to bringing him to the late-night get-togethers, having a few beers with him, kissing him, leading him on, and then dumping him once Paramilitary Training started after the Interim training ended.

When Sherry returned to the auditorium later that night for the instructor's lecture, though, she noticed that the happy couple was missing. The other trainees also noticed it. She heard someone whispering that the two may have quit the Camp and run off together. It caused a bit of a stir, because the couple was usually the first ones in the auditorium every night. With perfect punctuality, the instructor marched upon the stage and took his place at the podium again. He didn't look too happy.

"We had to let someone go tonight after a full two months of training. When I mean no relationships, that's exactly what I mean. Any of you goofs who thinks you can get away with it is sorely mistaken. Absolutely no relationships. Get it through your heads. Relationships easily dilute the rigors of the training. If you have a problem with this, we may have to get rid of all of you in one swoop. No relationships here at Camp."

What Sherry did had its unique, irrevocable effect. It wasn't a game, and at the same time, it was a game. This idea had been reinforced by the popular crew. She didn't know which was which exactly. She took it upon herself to play the good asset and play dirty at the same time. It was the best route through training, she believed. Cutting corners and working on the more advanced aspects of CIA suited her better than the boring fundamentals that the Asian had painstakingly learned. She no longer relied on her heavy textbooks. She knew better than that. Just like the others, fangs grew where her teeth ought to have been.

When she returned to her room after another lecture, she found her roommate in tears weeping, sniffling, curled up in a ball on her bed.

"What happened?" asked Sherry. "You didn't make it to the meeting tonight."

"People are cruel," said the Asian.

"What happened?"

"Someone told the instructor that I was romantically involved with the guy I've been seeing. But it isn't true. We're just good friends."

"I expected something like that would happen sooner or later. You have to be really careful around here. You two were pretty close."

"We weren't involved. We were just study partners and friends, and now they accused us of having a relationship when we knew there are no relationships allowed at Camp."

"What did they do?"

"They threw him out and kept me, because I'm the best in the class. He didn't do anything wrong. If anything, I'm the one to blame for all of this."

"They threw him out? Shit."

"Yeah. And they never told me why. They don't tell anyone anything unless we need to know."

"I'm sorry. I'm really sorry. I guess he was a good friend."

"I ruined his entire career. He has nowhere else to go. CIA was his whole life."

"I'm sorry."

"Don't trust anyone in here, Sherry, and I mean no one. There are snakes in here."

"Who do you think it was?"

"Those two women down the hall. Who else?"

"Maybe you should get some rest for now."

"Is it almost lights out?"

"I'm going over to the other room for a while."

"After what just happened? After what I just told you? Are you thinking straight?"

"Worry about yourself. I'll be fine."

"I guess that's we all have to do around here, right? Worry about ourselves?"

"Get some sleep, okay? You've had a pretty rough day."

The Asian sniffled and wept in her bed, and Sherry left the room. She found the two brunettes and the same two guys drinking beer and listening to the radio.

"Didn't get the cute one, eh?" said the first brunette.

"Strike two," said the other.

"They threw him out," said Sherry, grabbing herself a beer.

"Strike three."

"I'm playing it safe for a while. They're not fooling around. I don't want to be thrown out of here. I think we have to buckle down."

"There'll be other targets," said one of the men.

"I'm sorry, Sherry, but until you get a third guy, we can't have you over."

"Don't be that way," said one of the guys. "Sherry's not doing any harm here. Plus, I'm sure we can accommodate her," he smiled.

"You can roll your tongue back into your mouth," said the second brunette. "She needs to find another guy. Our parties go late, Sherry. You're welcome to come over every now and then, but we have enough here for now."

"I think so," said the first. "I guess you have to get up early tomorrow morning, right Sherry?"

"Yeah," said Sherry, taking her last sip of beer. "I guess I better get going."

After she slipped into bed for the night, she wondered whether she could play on the same field as her two brunette friends. She didn't want to abandon her regality and nobility – the old Sherry Aspen who once had integrity, had always played by the rules, did what everyone else told her to do, had an irrational sense of responsibility, attended all of those charity fundraisers, and believed in just causes much larger than her own mortal and humble life. The remnants of her younger self placed checks on those older, worthier parts that sent the brown-haired guy packing when she had meant to send the Asian packing. The Asian even slept politely, her breathing soft and soothing, like a wave machine that gently pushed Sherry into sleep as well.

She fell asleep having no remorse but only holding on to the steadfast belief that an asset had to play dirty to get what she wanted. Perhaps there would be others to drag through the mud, she wasn't sure. But the light of her conscience, purity, and innocence dimmed. She did it for her country, she thought, just like the instructor had said a valuable asset always had to do. She was getting better at it. Little by little, she was getting better.

At the cafeteria the next morning, a general hush ruled over the Asian who sat alone within her own aura of mourning. Sherry saw it so well that she could have cut it open with the plastic knife she sliced her muffin with.

"She's really angry," said the first brunette sitting across from Sherry.

Sherry had officially abandoned her roommate-refugee to fend for herself. As she had a better look at the Asian from across the room, she didn't look so much as sad and depressed as intensely angry from within. She must have faced the same injustices dealing with the same system that had always been too domineering. Her parents must have imposed such a system on her. They subtly pressured her while refusing never to stop caring and worrying about her, fusing their intense emotional connection with such silent pressure, as though they had seen a fatal flaw at birth before she ever recognized it in herself.

"I bet they make her the President of Taiwan," said the second brunette, laughing. "Just look at that face. I bet she ends up conquering the Chinese Army one day."

"She's the best trainee in the program," said one of the guys.

"That's because she's really a supercomputer," said the first brunette. "Her family put a chip in her brain before they immigrated here."

"Holy shit. What if she really is an android? With a Southern accent, no less?"

Hushed laughter soon followed, but Sherry wasn't in the mood to laugh. She didn't know what to think. She had trampled her roommate's spirit.

Thankfully, they had the week off before Interim, an immediate cause for celebration. The three of them planned to go into DC and party all night long, hopefully without the superstar Asian who would most likely spend the night reading or playing board games with the redhead. Sherry wouldn't miss their company. All of them would be staying at the dorms during the week, but they no longer had to stay together like a chain gang breaking rocks on an empty road.

That night, Sherry and the two brunettes dressed provocatively and took a hired car to the outskirts of the vast metropolis. By nightfall, they knew exactly where to go. They visited a lounge closer to Langley. The brunettes heard that some of the employees from the State Department hung out there after hours, and as CSTs, it was their prerogative to rub their status as CIA in their faces. They aimed to make fools of out them as the paralegals once did at Sherry's old job at the law office. The two agencies had traditionally been fierce competitors ever since the CIA's founding. Off-duty FBI officers would also be in attendance. From what the women had learned, the FBI were no more than a horde of glorified cops. They never could hold a candle to the elite Operations Officers at Intelligence.

The car dropped them off at a swanky spot strewn with handsome, attractive men in suits who engaged in the business of getting drunk and disorderly without the stern supervision of their bosses and the paranoid pubic that they served. The place was a stable for government toughs who were usually under extreme duress and bound by strict codes of conduct. Blowing off a little steam by drinking and hitting on the women there were rare occasions but high on their list of priorities.

The few women in attendance were overweight crew-cut types who wore long pants and tee shirts that advertised the emblems of their respective agencies on their chests.

Sherry and the brunettes looked good in their revealing dresses. Their made-up faces and shapely bodies stood out as they passed through the lounge like a Juggernaut of nymphs on a mission. They attracted stares from all of the well-groomed men. Their entrance was so conspicuous that the brunettes even waved to a few of the men on either side of them. They looked like contestants in a beauty pageant. All they needed were silk sashes over their shoulders embossed with the states they represented.

They took their seats at an empty table in the middle of the room. As music played, they soon became the center of attention, the objects of the male gaze. A group of young State Department officials huddled at a table in one corner of the room, while the FBI guys stood as wallflowers waiting to see which branch of government had the balls to approach the three of them. For a while, no one did. They drank long enough to loosen their tongues and build up their beer muscles.

After an hour or so, a young, brash State Department official made first contact. He was slick and handsome. One of the brunettes spotted him coming from miles away.

"My God," she laughed. "Look at the stick in his pants."

The official sauntered over and casually introduced himself. He was no pushover. He was confident and seemed to be well-established, even as a young adult. He was impregnable, should the three of them try to ridicule or make a laughing joke out of him. He could have taken their barrage of insults in stride and laughed it off like fingers poking at his ribcage. Any attempts to belittle him would roll off his fine suit as though it were waterproof.

"May I?" he asked before taking a seat.

He did so without being invited, but the women were too surprised to put up any resistance.

"Where are you guys from?" he asked. "I've never seen you around here before."

"We work for the government," said the first brunette.

"Yeah," said the other. "The Office of Protocol. You ever hear of it?"

"Hell, yeah," he said. "The friendliest girls in Washington. What brings you way out here? The White House is a few miles down the road."

"We wanted to check out the local stock," smiled the first brunette.

"Yeah," said Sherry, participating in the fun. "We wanted to see which one of you had the most talent."

"Talent where it counts," said the second brunette.

"Ah, I see," he said. "Well, I can tell you that I'm the most talented one here. You'll definitely know by tomorrow morning when you make me breakfast in bed."

"No, silly," said Sherry. "Talent in terms of how fat your wallet is. Aren't you going to buy us drinks, or are you just going to sit there and flatter yourself all night?"

"I'll be right back," he smiled before making his way to the bar.

"God, Sherry," said the first brunette after he left. "I never thought you had it in you. You've come a long way."

"I start out slow," she said, "but once I get going, my engine doesn't stop."

"What do you think of him, then?" asked the second brunette.

"He has possibilities. He needs to be tamed, though. Broken in. Which one of you will do the honors?"

The brunettes pointed to Sherry. She could only smile in return. They put her through another test, and she wanted to pass it this time around. Despite her cavalier attitude, inside she was just as nervous as when she first met her two friends.

"Okay," she said, finally. "I'll do it."

"Just as you said," said the second brunette. "A man that good-looking has to be tamed. He has to learn the hard way."

The official returned with three bottles of cold beer in his hands. He placed the bottles in front of them. Together, they drank as his State Department buddies goaded him on from their table in the corner. He was the stud of the night, the champion who had won the day. The FBI wallflowers, however, wore straight faces, jealous, perhaps, of the official's success. The four of them were soon drunk and engaged enthusiastically in conversation so superficial that no one would believe they could have discussed such topics with the abandon they exhibited. It wasn't until near midnight that the two brunettes stood from the table in a move to leave.

"Well, I guess we better get back to the White House," said the first brunette, "but Sherry here will keep you company, isn't that right Sherry?"

Sherry was too drunk to care. She laughed it off, thinking her two friends were joking. But they were being serious. The two brunettes donned their winter coats and left her there with the official. But again, she was too drunk to care very much. She knew her mission had already been determined, and yes, she would make the cocky official learn the hard way. There would be no way around it for him. She then asked him if he could drive her to a location close to Langley but not in sight of it. She was fortunate enough to have remembered never to reveal who she worked for or where she stayed. Just as she intended, Sherry now played the real intelligence game. She was careful enough not to blow her cover, even though the official insisted on driving her all the way back to the White House.

Instead, they drove in his BMW down Dolly Madison Boulevard in the middle of the night. It was all a blur until he parked the car near the blaring lights of a gas station close to the complex.

"Are you sure you want to be left out here?" he asked concernedly. "I have no problem driving you into town. It's on my way. There's no one out here."

"I'm staying with a friend tonight."

"Let me drive you, then. It's really no problem."

"No, I don't want you to drive me home. You might be some crazy stalker."

"I'm no stalker. Let me drive you to your friend's place. It's cold out there."

"No thanks. Right here is fine."

"Give me a kiss at least. It will reassure me."

"Of what?

"That you'll be okay, and I won't have to worry."

"No. I don't want to lead you on."

"Don't you *want* to kiss me?"

"I don't want to give you the wrong impression."

"Then why the hell did you ask me to drive you home? You could have taken a fucking cab."

"Listen," she said, placing her hand over the bulge in his pants. "I don't want to lead you on. If you really want to see me, you'll call me tomorrow at the Office of Protocol, and we can try this again. Don't think I'm that easy. It's only the first time you've met me."

Sherry massaged the bulge in his pants. She felt it grow hard in her palm. The guy practically panted in desire, his bulge emitting a pulse that throbbed painfully in her hand. He could do nothing but breath heavily, hang his mouth open, and pray that she took enough pity on him to unzip his fly and go down on him. But Sherry was too clever for that.

"Sherry is your name, right?" he panted.

"Call me tomorrow. I'm listed in the White House directory."

She left his car having completed her mission. She wanted nothing more than to gloat to the two brunettes over her conquest. She figured that the two of them were most likely screwing their boyfriends in their dorm room by now. As she walked from the gas station towards Langley, the State Department official opened his passenger side window and yelled, "you're a real bitch you know that, Sherry?"

He then peeled out of sight.

Chapter Eleven

June 2000 – Washington D.C., USA

They permitted Sherry to move on to the Interim training. They didn't tell her how she did on any of her exams from Phase One. They told her only what she needed to know, which was nothing, as per Company policy, so she had little idea how she scored. Either did any of the other trainees know what their scores were. She made sure to avoid the pot some of the up-and-coming government employees passed around and encouraged her to smoke at a few of the small DC house parties she attended with the two brunettes, but she did allow herself to drink whatever she wanted at the many bars they dragged her to during their week off. The Interim Training began after a week decadence and abandon.

Sherry had rinsed away the stresses and insecurities she had absorbed during Phase One and entered the Interim with a better attitude and stronger capabilities. No longer did she play the victim or wallow in self-pity. That part of her life had ended. Her confidence and enhanced instincts made her an even more attractive and valuable trainee, not necessarily to the men in her class, but also to those who were older and more established in the Company. If she didn't know what to do, she faked it until she supplied what they demanded of her. No longer was she a hurt, naïve college sweetheart. The dresses she wore exposed a little more cleavage, bare shoulders, and legs. Her talk was more carefree and casual. She learned how to joke around. No longer was she so apprehensive about ridiculing others for a laugh, playing head games with other men, or having gossiped with the two brunettes over cocktails at popular city watering holes, dive bars, and pubs during her week off. After the brief vacation, though, the trainees were then separated and assigned work locations away from the McClean campus. Welcome to the Interim.

The Company planted them in non-descript, inconspicuous office spaces that purposely looked either abandoned or defunct. At some spots, fake signs hung over battered entrances representing a fake telephone company in one location or a shoelace manufacturer in another. These places easily fooled anyone who may have been curious enough or even remotely suspicious of who or what really occupied these run-down, aesthetically debilitated buildings. An employee of the Company in an unmarked car drove Sherry to such a location near the intersection of the Trinidad and Atlas Districts of the city. They hung a right on a narrow, potholed lane off of Maryland Avenue and stopped in front of a lonely brick edifice on which blue spray-painted grafitti had been scrawled on its boarded windows. It denoted the area as another forgotten and blighted section of worthless abandonment where squatters fought for sleeping space under leaking roofs and within frigid walls. Luckily, spring slowly unfolded upon the city. The sun shone over the drunken and drugged-up derelicts in garbage-strewn corridors between crumbling structures that had once been a prideful industrial center decades earlier.

The driver directed her towards a vacant alley that stretched several blocks north towards the more hospitable and habitable sections of the district. She bundled her coat's blue, woolen collar. The ends of her blonde locks danced along her shoulders as gusts of cold wind chilled the blood in her cheeks. She walked quickly before discovering a heavy steel door on the side of the building. She pounded the door with her fist, but after several minutes of doing so, no one answered. She also tried pressing the buttons on a small digital combination lock, but to no avail. She almost gave up, until someone from behind the door struggled to force it open. The door scraped against the fractured pavement below it. She likened the sound to nails scratching against a chalkboard.

A shadowy figure waved her into a dimly-lit hallway, its flickering overhead lights caked with the husks of dead insects. It was much like a bomb shelter with but a few survivors left after a nuclear apocalypse. The shadow led her through a maze of wet corridors until the last one opened into a large, synthetically bright room without windows but with all the trappings of a busy office. The workers within sat at shoddy, aluminum desks and hovered over banged-up laser printers carelessly used over many years of unsung service. No one noticed her. They kept on working without any greeting or introduction. The brightness of the room, however, unveiled the shadow who brought her to this hidden den of efficiency and production. In keeping with the standard Company uniform, he too wore a solid-colored shirt and tie. He introduced himself as the Station Chief of that particular area.

He was a balding white man who approached retirement, unusually tall and harboring a bulge at his belly, probably due to having a few too many beers after working hours. Unlike her father, the Station Chief was cheerful and avuncular. He shook her hand and welcomed her as though she were a close relative.

"Welcome, CST Sherry, to your Interim," he smiled. "Let me show you around."

There wasn't too much to see. A dozen interconnected

desks with computer monitors and files on them filled out the front of the room, while a dozen more high-speed laser printers continuously spewed out documents and brazenly hummed in the back. The Station Chief introduced her to the other officers there one-by-one. Too discombobulated by the journey through the bowels of the warehouse, Sherry couldn't remember any of the names but only shook their hands like a captain of an opposing team meeting on an athletic field. She promised she would get to know their names during the course of her three-month stint trapped in this bunker of unappealing commonfolk. She bid farewell to the dreamy, handsome spies she had hoped to run off to Europe with. The prospect of spending three months with such dull and average people disappointed her. Already, she missed her fellow CSTs, especially the two brunettes with whom she had celebrated her prior week with juvenile and fun excitement. She hoped to avoid the sins of boredom in such a cave where a quietude and palpable lack of spirit confined these officers to lives of drudgery without any complaint or protest. It was a real let-down, to say the least.

There must have been something more to it, but the Interim demanded nothing less than to be exposed to the tedious and mundane side of intelligence work. She hoped to avoid the mummification of being buried alive in a tomb with ant-like unknowns crawling around in mindless collective activity. She already sensed they were not only bored to death with their appointed functions but also bored with the vapidity of their personal lives after they were freed from the building as well.

The kind station chief showed her to a small empty desk next to the printers at the back of the room. It was loud enough there to be annoying. Nothing was on the desk except a blotter with an unopened package of black magic markers.

She wanted a computer with Internet access, but she would be given no such joy.

"The Office Manager will be right with you to show you what you should do. Until then, make yourself right at home."

Although she waited for close to half-an-hour, no one noticed her sitting there. She merely observed the same mind-numbing activity she had first seen when getting there. She felt like a customer at a restaurant whose waiter forgets her order. Just when she reached her maximum level of tolerance, however, a slender man of medium build and a pockmarked face walked up to her and introduced himself. His portly wife followed him. She wore a used flowery sundress that looked purchased from a flea market. The pockmarked man introduced himself with a cordial smile as the Office Manager. His portly wife, however, didn't smile at all or offer any words of welcome. Neither did she shake her hand in any show of comradery. She looked her over menacingly for a few moments until she grunted an 'uh-huh' before pulling her husband back to their adjoining desks away from the printer area. Sherry's place was in permanent isolation away from the other officers.

Without having any idea what she should be doing, as the man and wife discussed something that may or may not have concerned her, Sherry took the initiative. She waited for the pockmarked Manager to end his conversation and asked him directly what to do.

"You mean they didn't tell you?" he grinned.

"No, they didn't tell me a thing. They didn't give me any training or instructions or anything."

"That's so typical of them. Of course, they didn't tell you. I guess I'll have to show you then."

They entered the printer area next to her desk. The machines cranked out intelligence reports from all over the world. They never stopped printing. They remained turned on for twenty-four hours, seven days a week.

"These reports are coming in from our stations at all hours of the day and night. We joke around here these printers work harder than we do. Some of these reports are quite long, as you can see. Your job is to make sure there is enough paper and toner in all of these printers. That's the first part. The second and more important part is to desanitize each report that comes in. Once you do that, you bring each desanitized report to my desk. I then give them to the officers who check them over and upload them to Langley. The reports are then sent directly to Congress and officials in the White House, courtesy of DI.

"What does 'desanitize' mean?" she asked confusedly.

"You mean, they didn't tell you that either?"

"No."

"It figures. They make us lackeys down here do all of the work, when it's really their job to train you before you get here. It's the same bullshit. They always leave us with the annoying shit like this. You're going to make mistakes for the first couple of weeks, but I'll help you with that," he grinned.

She distrusted him already.

"And if you don't desanitize the reports accurately, the Station Chief will have your ass, that I can tell you. You can't afford to make any mistakes, which is why I have to work closely with you, even after hours if we have to. We have to make sure you do everything perfectly."

"But how do I desanitize reports? What does it mean?"

"The concept is the easy part, but doing it is a royal pain in the ass. You can't fuck any of them up."

"So can you tell me what it is, so I can start doing it?"

"Of course," he grinned again, one corner of his mouth pushing high up into his cratered cheek. "Desanitation is just as it sounds. The reports you receive out of these printers are rough drafts. They contain raw intelligence that come in from our stations all over the world. Nothing is left out, and all of the information is classified, top secret shit that no one else on earth knows about. You basically scan every line of these reports and make damn sure you remove any revealing information that can screw up our operations. You're basically making a classified document unclassified. You are protecting the privacy of our operatives in the field and their targets and acquisitions by using those black markers to black out all the classified information. You then give those desanitized reports to me. If you make a mistake and some shithead finds out what they're not supposed to know, it can put our operatives in grave danger. You do have to redact information, because the reports are then sent over to DI. From there, they're forwarded to Congress and the Oval Office as unclassified documents. If DI finds you screwed up on any of these reports, you'll be reprimanded for it. It will go on your record. A poor evaluation will get you thrown out of the Company just like that," he said, snapping his fingers.

"So read carefully, and for the first week or so, I'll be working very closely on them with you. You don't want to be reprimanded or written up, do you?"

"Of course not."

"Then I'll help you through it. Think of me as your mentor."

"Thank you so much," she said.

They discussed specific techniques on how to desanitize the reports that pumped out in a steady stream through the printers. The next few hours bled into quitting time. The night shift had come in, and most of the office day shift had left. Her new mentor, his heavy wife, and Sherry sat near the back of the wide office. It was odd being there. The machines were louder than their voices. She didn't want to stay, but she had to. Her mentor's overweight wife, however, didn't look upon her husband's mentorship so favorably. When the wife finished with her computer work at her desk, she walked up to them as they desanitized a report that came in from Nigeria involving a planted operative in an oil company. The operative's name appeared some fifty times, and it was nearly a sixty page report. Sherry had to read the report at a snail's pace and remove all revealing information using the techniques her mentor showed her. She was uneasy of her new mentor's guidance, especially his weird grin reminding her of the ghouls she traveled with on the Amtrak trains to and from Vermont.

"Time for dinner," announced his wife to her pockmark-faced husband.

"You'll have to eat without me. I've got to break her in. Otherwise, they'll nail her to the wall."

"They should have done that at McClean. Why do you have to do it?"

"Wouldn't ya know it? They didn't. They always leave the shit work for us."

"How long will you be then? I have to eat. I'm hungry."

"Don't wait up, okay? This is going to take a while."

"We can continue this tomorrow," interrupted Sherry. "We don't have to stay too long, do we?"

"At least a couple of hours," said her mentor. "Otherwise, it's your funeral." And then to his wife, "just go home, okay? I'll try to keep it brief."

After his wife grunted at her one more time and left the building, her mentor continued where they left off. He was right. Desanitizing reports was tedious work. After a short time, the words blurred on their voluminous pages. Her eyes had grown red and tired from all the reading, every line packed with detailed information that had to be redacted. After finishing each report, she ran it by her mentor who watched the Nationals' ballgame from his desk.

"You've made several mistakes," he said, after reviewing the Nigerian report.

"Where?" she asked.

"That's for you to find out. It's not going to do you any good if you don't find them yourself. You'll never learn that way. You better go over it again."

Disappointedly, she returned to her desk and read the report a second time. She scrutinized every line in the lengthy document. When she finished, she couldn't find a single mistake. She edited out all of the classified source material with an exactitude that astounded even herself.

"Better," he said, after reviewing it a second time.

"What do you mean 'better?' What's wrong with it?"

"Just what mean," he said. "It's coming along. You need more practice, and maybe you'll have to stay longer after work every night, but you must understand, Sherry, that lives are on the line. If you reveal any piece of intelligence that's classified, heads will roll around here. You'll be risking the lives of our officers in the field and our paramilitary units.

You'll be handing them a death sentence. Desanitizing these reports requires a lot of patience. It sucks, because 99% of the population can't handle the work you're doing. That's why you're a CST and not some corrupt politician on Capitol Hill. Rise to the occasion is what I'm trying to say."

He handed the same report back to her, and once again, she reviewed it until her bloodshot eyes felt like they were popping out of their sockets. She handed the report back to her mentor for review.

"Better," was all he said. "We can continue this tomorrow. You have to move much faster, though, because the reports come in a mile a minute on those horrible machines. Believe me, when there's no more paper or the toner runs out just when a report is coming in from South America or some other part of the world, you'll want to kick those things. Sooner or later, though, you'll learn. But go home and rest up for now. I just want to watch some more of the game. See you tomorrow."

She could hardly make her way back to the dorm that night. She had a vicious headache, and her watery eyes were moist with the blood of dizzying exhaustion. She found the Interim training much harder than Phase One. In fact, she breezed through Phase One and never expected to be working at something so monotonous and tedious to the point of aggravation. When she finally got back to her room, she forewent rendezvousing with her two friends and went straight to bed. She didn't even take off her clothes. Even the Asian hadn't returned to the room yet. With the light still on, she covered her face under the sheets and fell asleep almost immediately.

Unfortunately, she awoke in the wee hours of the morning. It was still dark out. The rising and falling hump of her roommate's back, flush with pleasant and uninterrupted breathing, found her totally awake and wondering what she should do to fill in the few hours before she had to be at the office. The entire campus still slept, save for the sentries guarding the gates. She showered, donned a dress, and asked one of them at the front checkpoint to call her a taxi. She took it to a small diner near the site, had a bite to eat, and read the *Post*. Even after finishing her meal, she admitted to herself that she was afraid to go into work that morning. She had never encountered such a fear before, because for her, working always came effortlessly. She didn't want to make mistakes that would jeopardize the lives of others. The pressure built up slowly, because she didn't know how so many mistakes were made. She never had a problem reading carefully before.

Nevertheless, she sat at the diner until she forced herself to go to the warehouse. She must have had ten cups of coffee by the time the greasy spoon filled with its morning customers. With butterflies in her stomach, she left and made her way to the warehouse on yet another lukewarm day.

She knew the combination to the door, so she let herself in. Workers on the night shift manning their computer terminals and tending to the nonstop hum of the printers were more than happy to be relieved by the daytime staff. With a sadness that bordered on depression, Sherry bid the woman she replaced farewell and filled all of the printers up with paper and new toner, the dry ink from the plastic cartridge staining her clean dress. Already, it was a terrible start. The thought of calling it quits right then and there loomed attractively in her mind. But while intimating this impetuous response, in came her pockmarked mentor gleefully accompanying his upset wife for another day of drudgery. The work they did would kill any man, she thought, as she desanitized the first report that came in.

Despite reading carefully and remaining paranoid with every line of text that came at her, she still made mistakes that her eager, grinning mentor refused to point out. But as the hours dragged on, she didn't care anymore for his weak pedagogy and cared less and less about her performance. Every report she turned in had mistakes, said her mentor, and once again, they would stay after work to find a remedy for her new disease. Nonetheless, she tried as best she could as the seconds hand on the analog clocks on the walls slowly swept around dials that she checked every few minutes. Time dragged as though she had been shot into a black hole and sent backwards through time to when she first walked into the warehouse that first torturous day. Finally, however, after her mentor's encouragement through several grueling hours, the day ended. She had the displeasure of confronting her mentor's angry wife again. By this time, his wife had grown suspicious of her husband's newfound relationship with a flawless hot blonde. When her mentor went to the restroom, the obese woman took her aside and whispered through her teeth, "I'm watching you. You make one false move, and you're outta here."

Sherry was too tired to lend any credence to the threat. Actually, she hardly paid attention to what she said. She only saw the woman's bulging eyes above a sour scowl, her cracked lips moving but muted all the same. When her mentor returned, his wife stormed out of the office, steam blowing out of her ears. He offered another wanting pep-talk to tackle yet another sixty-page report, this time from a station out of Estonia. The reports had long and complicated names, and she confused the unintelligible document. Her confusion notwithstanding, Sherry still went over it thrice and returned to him.

She waited patiently standing next to him at his desk.

He checked every page for errors. It took him almost ten minutes. When he finished, he stood from his chair and sadly shook his head, indicating his disapproval. But it was all for his own cruel amusement, because just when Sherry was about to weep, he said, "Sherry, I hate to tell you this, but....you did it! You finally fucking did it. A perfect fucking report!"

She nearly fainted on top of him. She nearly lost her balance when she heard the news. The pockmarked mentor anticipated this and rushed to her side and pulled her body in close to his. He wrapped his slender, perspiring arms around her in a tight embrace.

"You did it," he whispered into her ear. "You did it. I am so proud of you."

Sherry almost wept into the collar of his shirt, and they hugged each other long enough for her to reconstitute and return to the person she was before the nightmare of the Interim began. She wiped her eyes, and her mentor dismissed her. The same driver came and brought her back to her dorm where she slept soundly for the night, only to repeat the same eye-popping and brain-draining process over again the next day and then the next. After a straight month of flawless work, her mentor walked into the office one spring morning as the room hummed with its usual activity.

"You're doing well," he said, approaching her desk.

"Thanks," she said. "It's all due to you."

"Oh, c'mon. You're doing it yourself. I hope you're more confident now. You'll never have to stay after work again."

"I can only hope."

"I'll let you get to it, then."

Over the course of a couple of weeks, she used the

same techniques of checking the reports. She checked them over three times. After each report, her mentor simply turned around and gave her a thumb's up. But as the last month marched on, the reports seemed to get longer and more copious for some reason. Everyone chalked this up to the change of seasons. Once again, though, her vision blurred the lines on the page. She submitted the latest report, but this time, her mentor frowned at her from his desk. Again, she made mistakes.

"You were doing so well. What happened?"

"You're not showing me what I'm doing wrong. Can't you at least point out the errors?"

"We've been through all of this, Sherry. You were right on the ball, but now, your missing it."

Sherry again stood next to him as he sat in his chair. It was after hours again. He made her stay late. She wanted to head back to McClean, but instead of setting her loose, her mentor wrapped his arm around her waist with the flawed report in front of him. He pulled her in close.

"What are we going to do about this, Sherry?"

"I don't know," she said, exasperated. "You're not going to write me up, are you?"

"If you want my honest opinion, you really shouldn't be making these kinds of mistakes so far into the Interim. I'm not sure if you can handle this type of work."

"So, you'll tell the Station Chief?"

"Oh, Sherry, of course I won't. But I'll have to desanitize some of these reports myself. Your pace is slowing, and there are glaring mistakes. I'll have to work harder."

"But that's not fair to you. You have enough of a workload."

"Yeah," he said, ponderously. "But maybe we can help each other out?"

The hand that clung to her waist slid ever so slowly downwards.

"If we're going to get through this," he said softly, "I'll need a little help."

He squeezed his hand there. Sherry knew exactly what he meant. She was more frightened by the gesture than angry over it. She wondered how far he wanted it to go. After two and half months, this sick man had cornered her without the knowledge of his even sicker wife. She reached behind her and removed his hand from her backside.

"I'm going home," she said.

"See you tomorrow," he said, "and just so you should know, we'll be staying late again until you get things right."

Naturally, many more mistakes were made, and through it all, she put up with his wandering hands – first her ass, then his hands made their way to her breasts. She stopped him from slithering anywhere near her crotch, which he reluctantly agreed not to go near. The touching lasted until the end of the Interim. When she threatened to tell the Station Chief on several occasions, he merely grinned as he always had the habit of doing and said he could make her life very difficult unless she cooperated, which she did to avoid poor evaluations. It wasn't until the last week that Sherry tried an experiment to confirm one of her relentless suspicions.

On one blue weekday, she desanitized a report that came in from Syria. As usual, the names, identities, and places were long and complicated. The raw intelligence also proved to be complicated. As her mentor and his wife went on a lunch break, Sherry had another worker review the report after she had checked it over three times, as usual.

"Just please take a look," she plead with him.

"Do your own work. I'm already behind."

"Just this one time. Please."

It took the guy ten minutes to read. Without any emotion he handed it back to her and said, "this is fine. Put it on the Office Manager's desk, and he'll upload it to DI."

The pockmarked mentor had been lying to her all along. She felt like slitting his throat or putting a bullet through his brain but settled for confronting him after work. Once everyone left for the day, her mentor, on schedule, felt her up. This time, however she grabbed his hand and pulled it away when he went for her breasts.

"I know, you fucking scumbag," she said. "I know."

"Now Sherry," he smiled, "I wouldn't do anything rash right now. It's your word against mine, and I have much more clout and seniority around here than you do. I'm valued here. You're just another CST who's been a quiet working girl for good evaluations. Guess who's gonna win that battle? You're the one who went along with it anyway."

"Touch me again, and I'll break your fingers off," she said, before leaving.

Too bad that there were only three more days left of Interim. She let the pockmarked man handle all of the reports from then on. She left early and went to bed at a reasonable hour for a change. Humiliated and spent, she figured that she had received a satisfactory evaluation from the area Station Chief. The Company invited her to Paramilitary Training without reservation. She had no idea what the station chief wrote in his report, but he probably didn't note what went on between her and her mentor. Just like before, she adamantly swore never to let anyone take advantage of her in such a manner again. Little did she know that Paramilitary Training would be the hardest phase of all, not in terms of the demands it would place on her, but for a different reason entirely, which turned out to be the same old reason.

Chapter Twelve

June 2000 – Camp Peary, VA, USA

For many, nothing is more exquisite than a blonde woman's body. If a man, through graciousness of luck or divine providence, meets such a woman, either in the workplace or in an educational institution, then approaching her while she basks in the spotlight of continuous attention might prove to be one of the most lonely, painful, and hellish experiences he can ever endure. Imagine, then, a woman in the center of a room with some tough men around her. These men are thugs, but they can't help it, because the observing man who sees all of this at the edge of the room would have also circled her, if he were of such size and build. A foolish man he would be if he decided, in his own time, to pursue this woman at all. But he can do no more, since he has been secretly observing her for eons. She is surrounded by mighty warriors. Perhaps they have guns, knives, and other weapons to bludgeon him with. But these men have minds too, as that is how the course of their lives has developed. A lethal combination for any man to have - both brains and brawn.

There are many such men, and all of them are suitors, but within this room they number only four – four men ready to kill for her just as the observing man would. She will choose one of the four, but for now, she is content tantalizing them in the social setting she is in. Eventually, she will have to choose after close counsel with her family. That's the way it has been done traditionally. Perhaps these four men are even her friends, like gaming friends in their own ways. But after the woman chooses, there are no hard feelings amongst the warriors. The selection is made, and she will marry whom she chooses.

But the observing man, however, still sees her from that infinite distance, not because the distance is so infinite, but because there still has to be some strategy to maneuver through that distance to gain her attention. The damage will be severe, but it still has to be done. The room she is in is crowded with bodies stronger than his. Her suitors have wit, persuasion, cunning, and defenses potent enough to bury a poor, atrocious coward like the observing man, as that's what he thinks of himself. Maybe he needs a little liquid courage, but it never worked in the past, and all he has to show for it are terrible memories, broken relationships, asylums, jails, punches to the head, horrendous temper tantrums, the worst of his humanity for all the world to witness. He no longer drinks with others. He is sober and a sober coward at that. He is not bored at all, because all he can do is come up with the same ridiculous, stupid, knuckleheaded, farfetched, know-one's-place-in-this-world strategies that will never win her heart. At the end of the day, he remains in a constant state of strategizing, standing in this room at the edge of oblivion watching her dance and then watching her when she leaves. He may even get a few looks from other women while there, but he is not interested in them. He is tempted by them, but really, if the man has a brain cell left, he should bolt from the place without trying. Instead, he stands there watching the blonde at the center of his solar system surrounded by thugs of every stripe, protected by an homuncular array of pure white muscle just waiting to pounce upon someone like him, just waiting for him to reach for a drink and get out of line. That's how it has to work with this woman at the core of his fascination and stupefaction. He can't help it any more than her protectors can. He may try to become like them in size and build, but this is a long process that is possible for him only far beyond the grave. It's just not easy.

So, he continues to strategize, as he is used to going through the same bullshit he's always gone through - the bouts of prolonged staring, his never-ending, oblivious staring. That's all he can do. Nothing else works. At least in his own life he has the courage to drift from failure to failure in his own routines without any loss of enthusiasm, provided he doesn't grow old enough to lose such enthusiasm. But at every stage of his life, it is the same woman at his center, and his failures are his only real guide to her. After so many failures, perhaps this is the only true pathway to her heart.

Interestingly enough, it is far worse for the observing man when he does not observe her. One would think it easier for him to cross the infinite distance then, but even though she is alone, she is still surrounded by the formidable gates of Langley, the guards girdling the perimeter and their waiting for any anomaly that will give them good reason to fire their weapons. The man, however, observes her from the outside while she is under the protection of the Company. She gets ready for the last phase of training, which will prove to be the most difficult of them all, both in terms of the man's valiant attempt to win her and in terms of her final attempt to brave the worst of it.

Somehow, he doesn't fear for her. He only lives to watch her and hope that she falls one day so that he may be alive to catch her. He almost hopes she falls, just to be there when she does. But he will always wait, just like the many others who came before him. It is far worse now, because suddenly, she is one step closer to her goal, and his observations are just as dangerous and fraught with suffering as hers are.

Behind Langley loomed its dark evergreen forest that spread for several acres in all directions. The leaves had grown on the branches of its shorter bushes and shrubs ever since the winter's slow thaw. Instead of a skeleton of trunks and bare branches, the leaves and the grasses, the flesh and blood of the forest, had grown to fill in the lush spaces below the tall evergreens. It was well past midnight when the trainees stood at the edge of the dark forest with their instructor at the lead. They wore CIA-issued sweatsuits that felt new and comfortable on their skins. It was much better than being trapped by the formality of their dress clothes in the Interim offices. The breeze was much like an oxygen tank for lungs that hadn't breathed enough outside air. The lawns and the forest, freshly mowed by CIA landscapers and wet with overnight dew, scented the area with the arrival of the new season. Strange wildlife shook the trees, and every few moments, an owl's hooting interrupted the shrill of nighttime crickets.

Before the official start of their paramilitary training at Camp Peary, the instructor stood before them with a hot lantern at his feet at the Langley campus. He gave each trainee a couple of fluorescent nightsticks and a small compass that looked like it tumbled out of a gumball machine. Before being thrown into the forest, the trainees searched amongst themselves, wanting to find someone to identify with their general confusion and ignorance of the what the instructor wanted.

The trainees who feared the most were afraid of the exercise itself, their imaginations milking a darkness so profound that they could not advance into the forest without assurances that they would make it out without injury. They would get what they'd get at the Camp and only on a need-to-know basis. Their fear of what they'd get eventually governed their lives. Whether or not they'd succeed at Camp Peary also became a major concern. Nevertheless, they had enough knowlegde that Intelligence would end their tenure, and even their own lives, when it was best for the country, kind of like playing Russian Roulette and waiting for that one bullet reserved especially for them. Which shot would kill them inspired their nightmares. These fearful trainees, in other words, had to be pushed off the ledge in order to swim. They froze before moving.

There were several too who didn't care how they did. These particular trainees would come out wherever they came out, and there they would be, for better or for worse. The brunettes espoused this kind of attitude. Their inherent cultural privileges eliminated whatever fears they would have normally hidden. They felt frustration and pain only when they didn't get what they wanted – the lucrative job, the vacation home, the new car, the hot boyfriend. There was little reason to fear but many reasons to be venomous when they desired something, like a new toy or that one dress in the store that many other customers chased that day. They fiercely competed but without the ethics and morals required of basic sportsmanship. Anything and anyone in their way was fair game, just as long as they cheerfully served themselves.

The determined and confident ones, such as the Asian women, always had something to prove or someone to prove it to. They weren't necessarily afraid of life but had enough insecurity to know that relying on their own natural talents and cultural privileges would never get them very far. What they lacked naturally they made up with practice and assiduity. These were the cornerstones of their successes. They worked hard, studied hard, and lived the hard way even when it wasn't necessary to do so. They gripped the handle too tightly. They always found themselves climbing without the fun of coasting down the other side of the hill. When the road went uphill, they pumped their legs and lungs even harder. Perhaps a low self-esteem had plagued their younger years and had since followed them into adulthood. If they didn't get what they wanted, they hadn't work hard enough or lacked good judgement. Their mistakes were justifications for shame but also opportunities for improvement. Faith had very little to do with it. If something went wrong, it was their fault alone, as though some internal circuit went out of order and needed immediate repair.

Sherry had all of these qualities combined. She never pulled to one side or the other. Her qualities depended on the situation. So, at the edge of the forest with two unlighted nightsticks in hand she wasn't afraid, cavalier, or determined. She observed the forest and projected what it would be like without having entered it yet. Her imagination didn't drift into fear as her mother's did, and neither did she imagine the best possible outcome either. The forest was another question mark that had to be answered with a modicum of confidence, some hard work, and some talent. The trainee to beat, of course, was the determined Asian. She knew better now not to use such twisted means to defeat her. Had one of the brunettes gone after the same brown-haired man, the brunette would have burnt up with jealous rage and given it another go. Sherry had no desire to compete that ferociously.

"Listen up, CSTs," called the Instructor. "You have your compass and your nightsticks. That's all you're getting."

He then pulled out a map, and the CSTs huddled around him.

"You are to start here and exit here," pointing to a wide clearing where the forest ended on the Western side of the complex. "You will be timed. The person with the best time wins. Remember that you are competing against each other, but all of you will finish, even if we have to come in to find you. The CST with the best evaluations will go first, and we move on down the line. You'll each go in one at a time in fifteen-minute intervals. Is everyone clear?"

"What if there's an emergency?" asked one of the trainees.

"Tough," said the instructor. "No matter what, you'll make it through. It you take too long, we'll know something's wrong, and we'll come in and find you. So, if you are mauled by a bear, you'll have to remain a bleeding carcass until we discover your body and take you home to your parents. It's as simple as that."

"You're kidding, right?" asked another trainee.

"Do I look like I'm kidding? I'm not here for your amusement. I'm not your friend, your teacher, or your cheerleader. You should already know you're the cream of the crop. If you guys don't believe in yourselves by now, that's your problem, not ours. Also, you'll be doing this exercise again during Paramilitary Training."

"But isn't this PT?" asked a third trainee.

"Not yet. This is only a drill. The real PT comes next. You'll be evaluated on everything you do. Drill or not. You have to succeed at everything to become a member of this Company. Hopefully, we won't have to send any of you home. You are not to fuck up, because you are not permitted to fuck up."

"Yessir," they all seemed to say at once.

"Okay, we're starting with you," he said, pointing at the Asian.

He then announced the starting order. Sherry would be

the third to go in. Carrot Top was second.

"Wow, Sherry," said the enthusiastic redhead. "Maybe we'll be working together once we're done with all this."

"Yeah, sure," she said.

The instructor gave the go-ahead to the Asian. Even though they raced against each other for the best time, the CSTs clapped for her in support. Once she entered, the glow of one of the fluorescent nightsticks slowly faded deeper into the bush. In fifteen minutes, Carrot Top followed her amidst another round of clapping. Sherry had a fifteen-minute wait. She tied her hair in the back, did some stretching, and made sure her compass worked properly. The instructor then released her into the forest.

The temperature dropped as soon as she took her first steps inside. In just a few yards, she bumped into the bark of a large tree. She cracked open one of the fluorescent nightsticks. A bright green glow lit up the space around her. She checked her compass and moved straight ahead, which was north. She then planned to head West once she reached the center of the forest. All around her, amongst the tall evergreens and lower lying trees, the forest burst open with the rustle of critters scampering along the forest floor and on the tree branches. They had made the forest their own village. She stayed alert for bears, prowling wolves, even snakes. The forest floor was damp with insects. It breathed on its own, its lungs pumping out an overload of oxygen and thereby energizing her. She didn't dilly-dally, though. Within the radius of what little light she had and while moving ahead, she accidently tripped on the stubborn root of a tree. Her chin hit the ground when she fell. She cut her arms on the prickly bushes and stray branches when she dove. She didn't think the forest would be so unrelenting in that way, but the cut under her chin trickled some blood, and the scratches on her arms stung and burned, even under the protection of her sweatshirt.

The compass still pointed her in the right direction, but she didn't know where to turn west. She trotted north, and with each step her nervousness became her chief instinct. The more nervous she was, the closer she came to turning. She remembered this mostly due to her studies in Biology. She had to wait until her nerves reached a fever pitch. The emotional map, and not the topographical one, made the decisions for her.

The faster she ran, the more times she fell upon the damp Earth. She sweated in her sweatpants and sweatshirt. She took off her sweatshirt and abandoned it at the foot of a tree. Such a shame to lose the exquisite souvenir on display in the CIA store, but she ditched it anyway to avoid overheating. At one point, she had to work harder to maneuver around the tight spaces between the evergreens and the small bushes that no longer provided the same level of nutritious oxygen. Panting amongst the shrubs, she felt her mind expand with hot anxiety. She rested for a bit and caught her breath. Her thirst for water was acute, her tongue dry, sticky, and stale-tasting. She raised her hands above her head to facilitate breathing, but she didn't find this very effective. She preferred bending over and resting her hands on her knees. Even the scratches on her arms leaked blood. For some reason, she imagined pouring rubbing alcohol over them. She wiped the sweat from her face, spat on the ground, and turned west. Just when she thought she headed in the right direction, her fluorescent nightstick lost its luster and died in the darkness.

She tried reviving it by shaking its contents, but to no avail. The lack of light left her in near pitch-blackness. The forest suddenly revealed several shining eyes watching her from the behind the bushes, as though they had been watching her all along. She heard the hoots from a nearby owl and the wind swaying the evergreens. Other strange movements followed her. The eyes were fixtures in the forest, almost like apparitions that would not stop haunting her. She quickly shook her second and last nightstick to life. Her pace adjusted to the risks of tripping over the bushes and their gnarled, arthritic roots that dug themselves into the Earth. All kinds of bugs and parasites attached themselves to her skin. They made her scratches itch. Nevertheless, she kept moving, always moving, her heart racing, her lungs burning and muscles weakening with every step. She thought that if she kept on her present course, she would make it out of the forest in reasonable time, but just as such an optimism surfaced, she saw a large, darkish creature scream in the night and swoop down from one of the forest's infinite branches. She had no idea if the wide-winged owl intended to hit her or not, but she dove to the ground to avert it from smacking her straight in the forehead. She had fallen so hard that it knocked the wind out of her.

She lay on her back trying to regain her breath while tightly clutching the nightstick. She forced herself to breathe, but she couldn't no matter how hard she tried. Like a heavy weight upon her chest, her suffocation squeezed her like a python wrapping itself around her body, until, after a few moments of lying there with tears leaking from her eyes, she lifted her pelvis off the ground to take in more air. Soon, her lungs sucked in intermittent pockets of oxygen. She began to breathe normally. She quickly picked herself up and headed west again until finally making it to a clearing with only a little juice left in her nightstick. After sprinting to where the instructor timed her with his stopwatch, she fell at his feet in pain and exhaustion. Little did she know that three other CSTs had already beaten her to the finish, even though they had started later than she did.

Lying in her bed that night with the scratches on her arms and legs and the cut under her chin, she didn't know what to expect of paramilitary training anymore. She again feared and thought the worst. She didn't think she'd make it through to graduation, all of her misery at the Camp wasted on yet another pointless endeavor to strive for something better than she really was. Ever since breaking up with her boyfriend, she saw herself as a bird flying with a heavy stone tied to her foot, her wings flapping wildly but unable to lift higher into the air. No matter how wildly she flapped, she steadily lost strength until hitting the ground. And there the bird faced starvation, unable to untie the stone from its foot. Soon, the circling vultures descended upon her and ate her alive, fighting over her entrails. She slept that night with these images and dreamt of her inability to make it out of the forest. She awoke just when one of these vultures picked at her plump flesh.

The CSTs moved their stuff from the McClean Campus over to Camp Peary nearby. The instructor called it, "The Farm", and visions of grain-fed hogs and cattle building muscle for their eventual slaughter came to mind. The CSTs would spend several months at the Farm undergoing a tortuous physical transformation that they may have one day reminisced over in admiration or dread, depending on the outcome. The instructor told them nothing before they departed. Once there, they were shown to ramshackle barracks – the men in one cabin and the four female CSTs in another. The seasons had changed into Spring, and slowly the heat stretched towards Summer. The barracks were hot and humid. Just by carrying her athletic gear to her bunk, she already broke into a sweat. The Asian parked herself in the bunk right above hers. The two brunettes bunked together a few paces away. Several empty bunks filled out the remainder of the barracks, as the number of women CSTs in her class had been cut considerably to establish a new breed of female asset ready to tackle the tough threat of terrorism. They donned their sweats again and reconvened on a wide, grassy field that led into the veins of rough dirt trails that burrowed deeply into another lush forest. The acreage on the Farm was massive. Its fields and forests stretched for miles.

A number of CIA personnel accompanied the lead instructor when he addressed the trainees. He made it clear that he would no longer be sticking around to see them train. He left their collective fate in the hands of a new crop of tough and gifted trainers who would break them down only to build them back up into perfect beasts ready for assignment. Before the instructor took off, though, the mischievous smiles that these new trainers wore told them that they would enjoy taking them to the edge of death and have them return as totally different people. Sherry could only gulp when the trainers ordered them to get in line and ready themselves for a five-mile morning run along the road circling the grounds. Sherry found herself running in the middle of the pack until conking out at the third mile. Only one or two trainees made it to the five-mile mark. They panted heavily and clutched the sides of their ribs to tame the cramping. Sherry's shins broke in pain. She was unable to run very far with unnerving shin splints. A sorry display, barked one of the trainers, while a second shouted in their faces about how horribly they had performed. They slowly limped to the finish line with frothing mouths and bent backs. Sherry went almost deaf from the volume of their shouting, the venom of their insults making it clear that it was only the beginning and that they were the worst idiot bunch of trainees the Company had ever recruited. They would never make it to the end.

The start of the day, then, proved painful enough to

dread the coming months of intense physical toil that would test their resolve to the hilt of their humanity. They didn't call it The Farm for nothing. It was a place where the trainers fattened them up until they metamorphosized into animals ready to be released into the never-ending glut of sacrifice.

After a full day of grueling and injurious conditioning, Sherry went straight to her bunk to lie down. She recalled the five-mile run that found several of the CSTs vomiting on the road, the obstacle courses, both on land and in the Farm's Olympic-sized pool, a timed two-mile sprint, and sit-ups and push-ups bringing them to the edge of seizing like an epileptic would. She didn't know if she'd be able to wake up the next day at five in the morning or not. But her Asian bunkmate shook her awake after she dozed off for a couple of hours. She reminded her that dinner would be served in the mess hall. Only two hours had passed, but it seemed like only an eyeblink to her.

Their daily routine wore them down like a bruxer does his teeth. Slowly but surely, they were reduced to nubs of their former selves. Tired and angry, they soon got the hint that they weren't supposed to be happy campers. The only person who maintained at least a little determination and a positive attitude was the Asian. She cheered on all of the others after she completed every drill and exercise better and faster than the rest. After running for five miles every morning and sprinting for two, the Asian consistently appeared at the top of the list. Her Southern drawl no longer charmed any of the CSTs. Of course, for Sherry and the two brunettes, the Asian became their primary object of scorn and ridicule. The Asian was much like the only player on a team who makes everyone work harder than really necessary. If she would just slow down and take it down a notch, PT would have been much easier. But through a couple of months of hardcore conditioning on the sweltering fields of Camp Peary, no one spared the Asian of their silent hatred. They never showed it. They grinned, bared it, and kept their complaints to themselves. It was only a matter of time before their anger boiled over.

Even though the CSTs had synched their schedules, their performance continued to differ widely among them. The Asian, of course, had always been the top contender. Sherry was in the middle of the pack. The two brunettes trailed behind with the stragglers. The brunettes had used the simple strategy that they could straggle but only as was commensurate with the Asian's performance. If the Asian performed well, the brunettes picked up the pace and threw more energy into their exercises. If the Asian had a less than spectacular day, they slowed down and hung in the back without the exertion it took to perform better. Either way, they cut corners wherever they could.

Sherry played it safe too but did her best at every drill, even though her performance had never been a cause for celebration. She disliked being average, but her averageness would get her to graduation without rendering her paranoid every morning if she somehow had to outperform all of the CSTs in fierce competition. She didn't need to do anything but stay in the middle.

Once in the barracks, the women readied themselves for the shower room. Once again, they were exhausted. Sherry thought the training would get easier, but instead it stayed unbearably level if not steeper than that. The tough-as-nails trainers cursed at them at all times, but the CSTs had gotten used to it. Sherry could still hear one of them shouting 'Bitch! Bitch! Bitch!' while wiggling out of her swimsuit, her long limbs wet with her sweat and the chlorinated water from the pool. The wetness dripped from her arms, her full, moistened breasts, and over the flesh of her Valentine buttocks. She had shaped up considerably since first arriving at The Farm. She would have liked to have looked at herself in a mirror, but there was no such luxury at Camp Peary. She imagined what she looked like by running her hands along her taught body – her firm and nicely-proportioned breasts, the natural flatness of her stomach, the bit of excess flesh between her thighs. While her measurements didn't tell the entire tale of her fitness, she felt that the muscle around her waist were tight, her thighs were all bulked up, and her backside was as firm and flexible as a stress-ball when grabbed from behind. The other women also removed their swimsuits, their bodies coalescing into a singular feminine shape, as though the trainers had meant them to have similar bodies.

Like the others, the Asian's body looked firm and toned, if not more so. Her slick, tanned skin and the dark teats around her breasts dripped with the dew of the day's challenges and victories. She entered the shower room with the poise of a leader, followed by the other three. As warm water spilled over their bodies like waterfalls, they didn't say a word to each other.

Interestingly enough, only Sherry and the two brunettes knew why they stayed quiet. The Asian did not. With a handful of pearl-liquid soap from the dispenser, the Asian massaged the viscous fluid into the pores of her supple skin, making sure not to leave any part of her body untouched. She placed a dollop on her fingers and reached below her waist, cleaning the stretch of her pink bounty between her legs, circling its lips and then plunging them deeply into her tight and narrow canal to restore and purify her femininity. Her method didn't anger the three others. The work she put into it did. Even while showering, the Asian outperformed them. They could only stand under their showers without the energy to move a single part of their bodies while witnessing the Asian's striking shower routine. The perfection of her movements, her natural beauty, and the overall accuracy of her intellect throughout several months of torture angered them. Her perfection taunted them into believing themselves inferior, even though they already knew they were superior by default, at least in their own country. It gave them unspoken ideas on how to shunt her precious development. They only discussed their ideas openly after an occurrence that finally pushed the three women over the edge.

Another two-mile sprint around The Farm on a hot afternoon. Even the Asian showed signs of fatigue if not all out boredom from physical labors that hadn't changed for a few painful months. They were ready to move on, their muscles tearing and slipping from their bones like well-cooked pork. Yet the women appeared beautiful and had an image of themselves that said the same. Anything less would have diluted their power and the effort and sacrifice it took to handle the work. By insulting them, the trainers actually made them immune to their insults.

Yet this one Asian pushed them to ridiculous heights of overachievement when they could have coasted by, the men included. So, when they lined up and readied themselves for another two-mile sprint, there was little question that every person on the field that afternoon wanted another woman to beat the Asian.

That responsibility, however, didn't fall on Sherry. The Asian even beat out most of the men, but it was high time that the brunettes took up some of the slack and finished her off. They were due, as they had been the consummate under-achievers. Everyone knew it. Even though they had their strategy, small fissures appeared on the surface of their plans. If the Asian took on the bulk of all resentments, the brunettes shouldered what remained, especially now that the trainers made examples of them that morning and made the entire crew work harder just to compensate for their lackluster performances. The trainers drilled the rest of the group even harder often enough to make them more aware that it was time for the brunettes to end their loafing and pick up the pace. It reflected poorly on them, and the brunettes knew it. Being scapegoats didn't sit well with them, even if the Asian was the most obvious scapegoat amongst them.

The whistle screamed at the starting point, and off they went like a pack of wolves chasing fleshy legs of prey. Right at the outset, the two brunettes set the pace and ran ahead of the Asian in an explosion of energy that seemed forced but necessary. The rest of the pack lost time just by witnessing this freak phenomenon. The brunettes wanted nothing to do with being unpopular or scapegoated, even though they readily dumped it onto others. It pushed them harder, especially at the first mile marker where the three of them, the two brunettes and the Asian, ran neck and neck. Even at the midpoint of the run, three of the trainers took the time to run alongside the brunettes and sprinted with them for a full half-mile before the finish.

"You gonna let that bitch defeat you?!" yelled one of the women trainers. "Pick it up! Never accept defeat!"

The second brunette received the same treatment.

"You're a fucking loser if you don't win this time! You've been fucking around for too long. Don't think we don't notice it! Let's go! Move!"

The Asian, however, didn't get any such treatment. It was as though the trainers wanted one of the brunettes to defeat the Asian, and yet the Asian pressed on for the last quarter mile, huffing and puffing and gasping for air in an all-out sprint for the finish line.

Right beside the Asian sprinted the first brunette, the second brunette right on her heels. For some reason unbeknownst to anyone, however, the Asian veered out of her lane and slammed into the first brunette beside her. What Sherry saw from behind confused her, because she didn't know if the Asian purposely blocked the first brunette or not. Either way, the Asian's shorter legs cut into the first brunette's and tripped her up so badly that it sent the first brunette tumbling onto the roadway and diving upon it with her hands stretched out in front of her. She rolled on the pavement like tumbleweed in the wind, her short-lived yelp heard even by those in the way back. The Asian, however, continued her mad sprint. She finished the race in record time behind two other men who worked as hard as they possibly could to avoid the disgrace of being beaten by a woman.

Sherry and the second brunette stopped to attend to their fallen friend but were only met by the antagonism of the trainers.

"Don't stop for a loser!" yelled one of them into Sherry's face. "She's a loser. Look to your own damn self, you got that?! Don't waste your time on her! Once you're dead, you're dead! Now, move it!"

Sherry and the second brunette jogged calmly to the end behind the rest of trainees who didn't stop at all for their fallen teammate. When they crossed the finish line and their times were recorded, the second brunette caught her breath and immediately went for the winning Asian.

"You fucking little bitch!" she yelled. "You did that on purpose! We saw you, right, Sherry? We saw you, you fucking bitch!"

One of the male trainees had to hold her back.

"I never tried to trip her!" yelled the Asian, defending herself.

"Don't lie! You're a fucking liar!"

"Shut up, the both of you!" shouted one of the trainers. And then to the furious second brunette, "you're the loser! You're pathetic, you know that? You think one little drill is gonna excuse you and your idiot friend for your laziness? Get going and hit the showers. You are a both goddamned disgraces! I doubt you'll make it, you twits! You and that other friend of yours."

Sherry observed all of this in horror, but she too wanted to confront the Asian. In a few minutes, the first brunette who fell finally made it across the finish line, her knees and hands bloody but her cosmopolitan face saved from any damage.

"You, too!" yelled another trainer to the bloodied brunette. "How pathetic was that? Let's go. Hit the showers. And next time, you think about how badly you want to blow things off, because the next time we see anything like that, we'll boot you outta here, you got it?!"

The Asian approached the fallen CST attempting to reconcile and declare her innocence, but she only received a cold, angry glare in return. The first brunette didn't utter a single word to her. She only limped to the Infirmary with Sherry and the second brunette on either side of her, their arms wrapped around her shoulders as though she had been wounded in battle. By this time, the Asian had returned to the barracks. The men branched off and headed to their barracks as well.

On their way to the Infirmary, the three of them didn't exchange any words but only recognized what a disappointment the day had been. The first brunette entered the Infirmary like a lame animal, further establishing her status as the most inferior of the bunch. She stayed at the infirmary after Sherry and the second brunette returned to the barracks. Perhaps it was inevitable, then, that the Asian had to be held accountable for this.

When Sherry and the second brunette returned to the women's barracks, they heard the Asian showering in their common shower towards the back of the room. The two of them, however, didn't undress. They looked each other in the eyes and made sure that what they were about to do was right and just. The second brunette grabbed her towel from her lockbox. Sherry, uncertain and nervous, followed her into the shower room. Under the showerhead, the Asian soaped her skin tamely and shut her eyes to resist the rush of warm water cascading down her body. For a minute or two, they watched the Asian wash herself. The second brunette, however, then took her towel and slung it tightly over the Asian's face. With the Asian covered by the towel, unable to see or call for help, she yanked her down to the tile floor and landed punch after hard punch to her face in rapid succession. The Asian tried to yell, but her yelling was muffled by the wet towel. No one heard.

"Do it!" yelled the second brunette to Sherry, who froze after watching her friend land several more blows.

"Do it!" she yelled again.

Succumbing to the pressure, Sherry landed several hard blows. The Asian's blind screams fell on deaf ears, as Sherry kept on punching her until she ran out of breath. With the Asian's limp body prone on the shower room floor, the second brunette added a final blow and whispered into her ear, "and stay down, you fucking chink."

When Sherry left the shower room, all she could see was the pink, puss-dripping swill from the Asian's pummeled face swirling into the drain along with whatever confidence she had left.

Sherry sat in her usual spot in the mess for dinner later that evening. She took her regrets with her. She had been told at the Farm that a soldier in battle can either fight, flee, or freeze, as those were the only essential reactions in any confrontation that really mattered. Where she fell along those lines, she didn't know. She wasn't proud of what she did, but from that day forward, the Asian's performance dropped dramatically. The bruises on her swollen cheeks and the splits in her lips made it clear to all that they would no longer get any more trouble out of her. They were right.

Sherry came in first in the second Land Navigation Exercise. She also did well during driving training where she completed an obstacle course in a banged-up government car. She successfully rolled out of the car just in time during a simulated crash and burn scenario, where a bomb had been planted under the hood. The car subsequently exploded into a ball of flame. Neither did she injure herself slamming the car into hard objects and other barriers. The Asian, however, remained silent, as she had finally understood her place in the world. She continued to perform poorly the further on she went. She stayed out of the way and let others participate in their own successes. Although there was no mystery to her poor performance in the eyes of trainer and trainee alike, her challenges were just too difficult to overcome. The CSTs kept away from her and perhaps rediscovered her from time to time sitting in the mess hall by herself, languidly eating every morsel of food off her plate.

Luckily, after that timed exercise, the field conditioning had culminated in a short rest for a day only to break into more exercises that tested their abilities in completely different ways. The trainers were satisfied that the trainees had performed ably on the physical drills. Now it was time to add in the more serious intelligence work that assumed the CSTs were in good enough shape to withstand even more torture.

They stuffed them in a glass building where they learned to assemble bombs out of C-4 plastique and Clorox bleach. They had them march in single file into a tiny gas chamber in which they could hardly fit. They then assaulted them with blasts of pepper spray. Sherry blamed herself for joining the CIA voluntarily, as she alone had signed up to be treated in such a way. There was no fun or excitement involved anymore. Nor was there any hope for the future. They became human punching bags that had their minds, bodies, and collective spirit broken. They witnessed their own demise, a mirrored perspective of their dwindling selves sinking into the dust from which they primordially sprang. The trainers treated them like bacteria.

In another exercise, the trainers interrogated each of the trainees in a small concrete room. A hot, white spotlight blazed into Sherry's face, and when the trainers didn't believe her phony answers, they doused her with hot water until she made her answers believable. When she later emerged from the hot cement box, she was near-deaf from the volume of their yelling. Slowly, Sherry became a machine that lost touch with all of the lofty ideals she carried as a functioning person. There was no such hope of making it to graduation anymore. As far as she was concerned, the training would last for the rest of her life, and the only way to deal with the radically different lifestyle at the Farm was to adapt until all of her feelings and sentiments had been hollowed out and scraped clean, leaving her insides as barren as a body without a soul. Insanity was the only return to her humanity, but before cracking, they pushed her into a motorboat on another crash and burn mission that found her swimming for her very life to escape a strip of fiery water where the boat had skidded into another ball of flame.

It was a game, and it wasn't a game. She was no longer sure if the trainers provided a safety net or not. If she didn't fight for her own life, no one else on the Farm would. But the trainers didn't let her forget that there were some life-affirming options to choose from, like remembering her nautical distances, water navigation techniques, and tidal storm patterns just before the waters almost swallowed her up. Or another life-affirming activity of putting her on the firing range with heavy submachine guns, Barretta revolvers, sawed-off shotguns, pistols, hunting rifles, and AK-47s firing at targets dressed as Arabs, the faces on these targets wearing black Van Dyke moustaches, their scowls reminding her of old propaganda drawings of Dutch Devils that the British defeated in war. The trainer who oversaw this exercise praised her when she blew the heads off most of them. There were reasons to hate Arabs, even if she gave up her own life doing so. She killed off as many of them as she could. It was the unspoken rule, and it made perfect sense after a short time.

She made her way through five full days of hand-to-hand combat with both male and female CSTs alike. She no longer saw her fellow CSTs in terms of those she got along with and those she didn't. She no longer distinguished her fellow CSTs in terms of personalities to manage or circles of friends she wanted to be a part of. They became a robotic army inflicting blows upon each other, exhausting the use of their limbs and bones until they fell to the mat like scraps of junk metal ready to be recycled and returned to the showroom floor. At least before bedtime, the trainers allowed them to tend to their wounds and bruises. They then had to check their bodies over for lice, chiggers, and ticks – a side effect of living in the barracks. So, there was a humane quality to the Farm after all. The Company protected the taxpayers' investment, as the trainees discovered their own net worth, like a CEO would or a head of cattle on the range.

Slowly but surely, they had been transformed into assets as uniform as factory widgets. And then they moved onto the simulated border crossing into unknown hostile territory. This required a mile jog to another side of the Farm they hadn't seen yet. These acres of field that the trainers hid from them revealed an environment that came as close as possible to a real Middle Eastern desert - rocks, rubble, and all. How the Company managed to furnish such a landscape, they had no idea. Nevertheless, in front of them lay acres of desert and sand that funneled up into the slight breeze like miniature tornadoes. How it became that way puzzled them but not consciously. It no longer mattered that the camouflaged soldiers who dotted the rocky soil would hurt them in this exercise. Sherry had been through too much to be concerned by such a threat. Perhaps they would abuse her on the sands of this mock desert, among the sharp misshapen rocks strewn around low-lying desert shrubs. But visions of such abuses no longer accosted her.

The thick pieces of her mind, like slices of pie, merged together into a whole person who now stood where she stood. She started the border crossing not worrying about the dangers. A simulation. A test-run. A drill. DEFCON-4. A big red button about to be pressed. Wires clipped just before the big bomb went off. All of that stereotypical mockery in those television-show doomsday scenarios were now artificial, if not altogether silly. They were remembrances to laugh at. In other words, her mind achieved a wholeness that made her projections of tackling any of these challenges unimportant. Pain had marked her progress, and pain would be the end result.

'Just shut up,' she thought. 'Fuck this place and these people.'

They directed her to a car with two other male CSTs inside and gave her the keys. She would be the one driving, and the two male CSTs would be her passengers. For this mission, they didn't carry weapons. Briefed as they were, they were to make their way through the desert and miraculously find their way out. The American personnel on their side of the line, however, weren't the real danger.

"Sherry, you're to drive a few miles up this road, make the border crossing, and then get the hell out by accelerating your vehicle as fast as you possibly can to avoid any casualties. You'll drive straight through, right to the very end."

"What are we looking for, sir?" she asked.

"That's not for you to know," said the trainer. "Just do as you're told."

"Yessir," she said. And then to her two CSTs, "you guys ready?"

"What are you? Our mother?" said the CST next to her. "Just get going."

She slammed the car into gear and rolled passed the soldiers who represented the Company's paramilitary wing. They soon arrived at a lonely checkpoint – a warped shack in the sand. A tough, bald-headed soldier in military gear and an automatic rifle ordered them to show their visas. They handed over their passports one-by-one. He checked the passports carefully, gave them an evil eye, returned them, and waved the CSTs through.

While hearing the tires of their out-of-shape vehicle running over the rubble, she rolled up the windows as a defensive measure. The interior of the car grew warmer the further on they went. Before long, a small village appeared, its dwellings made of the same weak lumber the checkpoint was made out of. Clearly, the inhabitants who lived in this village looked and dressed like Arabs in Muslim turbans and black robes. They had brown skin and long, wiry beards that fell to their chests. When they saw Sherry's car, they immediately rushed towards it, brandishing long, wooden bats.

"Holy shit," said the CST next to her. "These guys don't look too friendly! Let's get the hell out of here!"

Sherry tried to outmaneuver the angry mob, but at every turn more of them moved in. They soon surrounded the car and banged their bats and batons all over it, glass from the car windows shattering and spilling into their laps. One of the Arabs shattered the front windshield as well.

"Holy shit, man, they are not fucking joking! We gotta get out of here! Run them over if you have to!"

But before Sherry could break through the crowd, rapid fire from an AK-47 interrupted everything. The sounds, while startling, were less of a priority than the moist, calloused hands of a mock Arab reaching into the driver's side window wringing her neck.

The CST shouted, "let's go, Sherry! These fuckers mean business! Move, now!"

With black-cloaked Arabs banging on the car and shouting obscenities in their language, Sherry slammed on the accelerator and surged through the antagonistic mob, the Arab's sweaty hands slipping from her throat. She maneuvered around the Arab horde just like the obstacle course she trained on. She floored the car to the hilt. The tires spit out plumes of rock and dirt behind them. The car filled with the choking debris of dust and sand. With all of the windows shattered and the body of the car banged up, they reached the other side of the desert. One of the trainers took notes for their evaluation and clocked them out. By the time the three of them exited the vehicle, they knew they didn't do well on this particular exercise. They had underestimated the hostility of their environment. The trainer, however, didn't say a word to them. He only told them to wait by the side of the road and observe the other CSTs speeding to safety from the treacherous village through which they had just passed.

Interestingly, none of the CSTs really cared about how they scored on any of the exercises anymore. Scoring and evaluations and reports were the stuff of the Ivory Tower. They had forgotten about these trivialities, because even though the exercises on the Farm were only mock simulations, they were real-life events that birthed new creatures who had gone through real tests of courage. The trainers had physically and mentally worked them out of themselves, as though there existed a separate entity inside each of them that finally permeated the nucleus of invincibility. Their subsequent five days of rest and relaxation were well-earned, even though they neither cared nor remembered any such vacation ever being granted or enjoyed. Now that they had finished all of but one of the exercises, the CSTs couldn't tell the difference between training and real life. Like a rug being pulled out from under them, their jolting return to the world beyond the Farm and Langley challenged them to carry on in what may have been another simulation.

Still though, it was the world of July 2021, and that was not a simulation. Totally transformed, the CSTs were sent out by the Company, not necessarily as maniacal specimens ready to kill for their country, but as persons within the bounds of normalcy who suddenly had the misfortune of returning to a civilization that required them to be every-day people. After five days of rest, they would return for skydiving with kettles tied to their feet, and the *piece de resistance*: the infiltration of a terrorist base camp to rescue American hostages, collect as much intelligence as possible, and get the hell out before they lost their lives. Was the 'life or death' scenario real, imagined, or simulated? Not one of them knew. Fantasy and reality blended. Not even the lovely and persecuted Asian, her petals reincarnating into the sweetly scented rose she had always been, knew whether or not she was still alive or dead, in Heaven or in Hell, or in the next life or in this one.

Neither were they cognizant enough to reflect upon or analyze how they had changed or what they had changed for. Their five days of rest and relaxation loomed ahead of them like an entirely unknown universe where every variable had to pass grueling guidelines created by their own suspicious and skeptical minds. They had been trained to spot all anomalies, to look beyond a simple shop window and see if there were any terrorists hiding within, ready to detonate a bomb in the name of their God.

The Company, however, gave Sherry her own path to follow. After the Border Crossing exercise, she showered and was immediately ordered to the residence of one the trainers near the administration building at the front gates of Camp Peary. She didn't know why she had been called there nor did she care. The other women in her barracks didn't care either. They did what they were told without so much as a single raised eyebrow.

Sherry dressed in plain civilian clothes when she went. She would soon be relocating to McClean for her short vacation. The trainer she had to see lived in a sturdy brick house with a small garden and a tree flushed with cherry blossoms on the front lawn. These blossoms stirred in the early evening breeze and floated to the grass like feathers off a bird, the lawn and garden splashed with soft hues of pink and red. The trainer greeted her at the front door and let her in.

A man of strong build in his middle age, the trainer showed her into his home office and shut the door. It smelled of thick cigar smoke. Sherry remained standing, as he didn't give her permission to sit. He too remained standing, his well-cut body leaning on his desk, his arms folded, and his thin lips straight, as though he had only the most serious of intentions.

"CST Sherry," he said, "I've been personally monitoring your progress, and I have to admit, I am impressed by your performance. Soon, you will be moving on, and I hope we had something to do with that. Myself in particular."

"Thank you, sir," she said, staring straight ahead.

"I hate to tell you this, though, because I'm not sure if it's obvious to you, but there is a lot more to intelligence work than just getting through training and getting to graduation. I hope you know that. There are other facets to the job that you haven't been exposed to yet."

"Sir?"

"It's about dealing with your emotions, Sherry. According to your evaluations, you handle pressure really well, but it's the emotional component that we are most concerned about. It's not your fault, really. It's just that you, as a woman, are not as capable of taming your emotions as men are. Sounds logical, right? You are not as capable taming them in a way that will best serve your country to the greatest possible extent, when that time comes."

"I don't understand, sir."

"Well, your reports say that you are able to kill without emotion. This is the first thing we want out of our CSTs. But what about relationships, Sherry? What about other men out in the field? What if you had to have a relationship with one of them in order to carry out an assignment?"

"I would need prior authorization – "

"Yeah, I know all that. But can you actually handle it? Can you have a relationship when it is required without getting too attached? Can you do it when and where it is necessary?"

"That shouldn't be a problem, sir."

"Are you sure about that? Better be, because you may be called upon to perform services for your country that may compromise your emotions. You may be called upon to do things you never expected to do."

"I don't understand, sir."

"Well, let's take sex, for example. Are you able to have sex with someone, foreign or domestic, man or a woman, when you least expect it, or when you are not prepared to have it? I guess what I'm trying to say is that having sex, like in all relationships you may have abroad or here at home, is a science. You must look at sex as a biological, scientific occurrence and not an emotional one. From what I understand, you were a Biology major before getting here, and you even wanted to go to medical school, am I right?"

"Yes, sir."

"Can you see a man as just another number who needs to fulfill certain shallow impulses and desires, and not as a person who will care for you or as a person you should care for, should you have sex with him?"

"I don't know, sir. I haven't really gotten there yet."

"You have to know, Sherry. You *must* know before we send you out there."

"Yessir."

"So, just as an exercise, I want you to take off your clothes."

"What?"

"What, *Sir.* You heard me. Take off your clothes."

"Right now?"

"Don't question me, Sherry. Just do as your told. Take off your clothes."

She did as he instructed. She first removed her pants, then her bra, and finally her cotton panties until she remained totally in the nude in front of him. The trainer removed his clothes as well until they both stood in front of each completely naked. His chest was hairless and smooth, and his muscles from his thighs bulged above the knobs of his kneecaps. She could see that he was fully aroused below the waist. He throbbed with the same impulses and desires he spoke of. He moved in closer and rubbed the front of his body along the softness of her back from behind.

"It's a science," he said into her ear. "It's a biological necessity."

He wrapped his sturdy arm around the front of her waist, and reaching between her thighs, he spread her lips with his warm fingers.

"That wetness that you have is a science too," he whispered. "There shouldn't be any emotion involved, you see."

Her sweet juices flowed freely, and although she tried to muffle her gentle moans, she felt his fingers probe inside of her. Within moments, she shuddered, and once she did, the trainer pushed her over the desk, leaned her blonde body over it, and penetrated her from behind.

He thrusted in and out of her. She tried not to think.

She buried her emotions – whatever feelings of violation and shame she had – the faster, the more powerful, and the deeper his thrusts became. She shuddered a second time, as he fell on top of her body stretched over the desk, his warm hands cupping her hardened breasts, thrusting in and out of her until he released all he had inside of her, his length and girth pushing up into her as far as it could possibly go. He stayed within her for a few moments before slipping out of her wet and limp, his impulses and desires satisfied. He rubbed whatever wetness remained on her backside and gave her a little spank. He then ordered her to take a shower in the next room.

After making sure the door was fully closed so that he could not enter, she ran the shower. Once inside, she closed the glass door, slid down the cold tile wall, and sank to the shower's flooded floor. She coughed up tears of welled-up uncertainty and confusion, her whimpers not necessarily cries for help but reminders that she had to control her emotions and that she shouldn't emote too expressively over an initial exercise that trained her for future missions. She suppressed her tears, because she understood the nature of the job and how the trainer had to do what he did to make her aware of her weaknesses. It made her a more capable asset. She squatted below the running water until she brought herself under control. It wasn't long before she heard a sharp knock on the door. The trainer told her to hurry up, which she did. She dried her body off, dressed again in her civilian clothes, and returned to the trainer's office.

"You did well," he said, sucking on a cigar and working at his desk. "You are ready to move on. When you return to McClean tonight, you're to go directly to the Main Building, to the Office of the Deputy of Intelligence."

"But what about my five days of R and R, sir?"

"Consider yourself trained. You're moving on,

Officer Aspen."

"I don't understand, sir. What about the rest of the training?"

Annoyed by the question, he sighed and said, "just do as your told. Return to McClean with your stuff, and when you get there, go directly to the Deputy's office. He's waiting for you now."

"Yessir."

"And Officer, make sure you wear that same dress when you go in. He'll like that."

"Yessir."

Chapter Thirteen

December 2000 – Washington D.C., USA

Admittedly, especially after her time at The Farm, Sherry was ready for any challenge. Even though they may have sent her to Siberia, Tiera Del Fuego, or Death Valley, she would have served her country just as admirably. The Company made her such that she could ground nails between her molars and swallow them. She could take a geek's neck between her bicep and forearm and crack it like a walnut. She could drive a car at top speed without ever getting caught. But her nerves sprang to life when she met with the Deputy of Intelligence for the first time.

While her mind didn't wander so much anymore, mild anxieties still resurfaced. The Farm didn't kill her off completely, in other words. Although the Company produced what looked and seemed like perfection, humanity never survived on perfection. Sherry would never survive if she were perfect. Perhaps there were other elements at work, and even though she busied herself with her calculations as thoroughly as ever, she still couldn't find the solution to any internal problems that may have existed. She made it a routine to check herself for her own imperfections if only to make them perfect, thus becoming the solution to the lives that weren't so perfect. Now that she had been trained to kill whenever and wherever she needed to, she could neutralize those who presented problems with a squeeze of a trigger.

It would help, though, if she could for just one night alleviate the suffering of mankind. Or at least relieve the fierce burden placed upon men maligned by cruel fate, men who never had the chance to talk to her, never had the chance to touch her, men who were unable to be seen walking hand-in-hand with her, because such a radical change would send shockwaves through the orderliness of the universe. This would manifest in the jealously of other men as well as their fierce anger and ridicule, as they see this maligned man walking with the beauty for their avaricious eyes behold. It invites conflict, mayhem, and other forms of humiliation. Cowardice rules the day, not Sherry's cowardice, (because the Company had already beaten it out of her), but the cowardice of the man who fears retaliation by the same world that places his sorry soul on the altar of womanhood for his eventually slaughter by the angry mob of culture she had helped create. Arrest records, prison time, and psychiatric hospitals are where such men wind up. They have fought hard for her and have been left to rot in these places. The key to getting Sherry, then, relied on subtle persuasion, like propaganda working its way through the television screen, or the bird with broken wings who sings to her in the middle of the night and assumes she hears his call either to be with him or free him from his cage.

The bird's faint pleas notwithstanding, Sherry only heard the call of the Deputy of Intelligence that evening. Too soon out of training, her rigid movements, her stoic countenance, and directed gaze appeared deliberately officious while walking into the Main Building at Langley, she a product of perfect protocol - more disciplined, refined, and sophisticated than the most decorated officers of the Armed Forces. The combination of learning and physical conditioning produced a woman more capable than most of America's men. The meeting with the Deputy in his 6th Floor office reflected this undeniably. After picking lice from her scalp and pulling chiggers from her hair in training, the cool comforts of The Deputy's office welcomed her with luxuries she no longer recognized. Only what the Deputy wanted from her mattered and not the polished oak paneling on the walls, the fully stocked minibar, the classical music playing on the stereo, or the fine leather sofas and chairs. She had been trained to collect intelligence, but in his office where much more important people usually gathered, she didn't have the wherewithal to think, regardless of what she had been trained to do. The Deputy commanded her full attention as well as her blind faith. She might as well have been in a tent somewhere in the forest, feasting on strange insects and accepting them as parts of her daily diet, perhaps even preferring them to other forms of nutrition.

The Deputy's pressed suit and country-club tie, artifacts of his former life, didn't yank her back through those prior times either. She vaguely remembered those times and chalked them up to youthful indiscretions. As soon as she stood in front of him, she knew she had to listen and not think. But still, the touch of anxiety she brought with her snuffed out any such ideal.

After all, an asset can't merely press her ear against the wall all of her life. An asset must also process what she hears from the very maniacs who threaten national security. It is not enough just to listen. A listener would rather hear his or her own thoughts and line of reasoning than pay attention too long to someone else's. Collecting intelligence doesn't absorb like a sponge but participates in its own enterprise. It gleans greater truths out of the vague and confusing voices it hears. An asset, to be effective, must interact with those she loathes, finds unsuitable, finds ugly and unworthy, or those with no passageway or escape from lives to which only the damned have been sentenced. She must interact with the underbelly of life – not to record it on tape or film it on video – but to squeeze out the rotten pulp from its sour rind to reveal the most desiccated and spoiled flesh of its fruit.

Sometimes, though, an asset finds herself skinning an onion, layer upon layer, in the hopes of finding the center of truth that is never there in the first place. Sherry believed she knew the difference between real intelligence and an endless enigma, now that she had advanced from CST to Company Operations Officer. Sorting out verifiable information that mattered was one of her many new talents but was perhaps the one talent that mattered most. But even in the Deputy's office she couldn't rest her mind. Perhaps therein hid the tragedy of every Operations Officer – the inability to pause, even while at ease.

"Officer Sherry Aspen. Well, well, well," said the Deputy standing from his seat and approaching her after she entered the room. "It's a real pleasure to finally meet you."

He held out his hand, and she shook it.

"I've heard a lot about you," he said. "All of it good. Welcome to our Company. It's good to have you on board."

"Thank you, sir."

"Oh, you don't have to call me 'sir' anymore. You're training days are over. You're not in uniform, are you? No. You have a good-looking dress on, which is how we like our best assets to dress."

"Thank you."

He drifted over to the bar area.

"How about a drink? To celebrate your success."

"No, thank you, sir."

"Okay, but from here on in, you are not to call anyone

'sir' anymore. Our Company serves itself and not anyone else. For that privilege, we protect the interests of our country. It's okay to have a drink if you want one, Sherry. It's not passed your bedtime, is it?"

"I guess not, no," she smiled a bit.

"That's what I like to hear. Your smile brightens the room. We need more smiling out of you."

He poured himself a whiskey and one for her as well.

"Please, have a seat."

She preferred to remain standing, but the Deputy led her to a comfortable chair facing his. The informality was awkward, but she played along with it despite her own judgment.

"I'm impressed," he said. "We've been waiting a long time for someone like you. With the bombings of our embassies in Africa, it's high time we put you to work. How's that whisky working for you? Good stuff, right?"

"Yes, sir. I mean, yes. I like it."

"Only the best here at Langley. Trust me, though. You won't miss this place much. Being trapped in an office all day? Nah. That's not for you. What you need is a challenge, but a challenge with benefits. Training challenged you alright, but now that you're out, things are just beginning for you."

"Thank you."

"Sherry, and I'll speak with you honestly, it'll be an adjustment, I'm sure, but you'll have to start speaking normally again. Take your time with it, but I don't want you to be so stiff anymore. I want you to be your lovely and pretty self."

She had forgotten who that person was, and to restore her to that former woman required even more training. But she wouldn't have the chance to be retrained in social dynamics, charm, and manners. She made a point of it to socialize as much as possible from thenceforth and get a better handle on blending back into the ordinary world, but while being extraordinarily clandestine at the same time.

"As a result of these Arab monkeys bombing our people and our stuff," he continued, "things have changed around here, as I'm sure you've already been told."

"It's a welcome change," she said, sipping her whisky.

"Damned straight it is! The Cold War folks are all laid out in their hospital beds, shitting in their diapers, sucking oxygen out of their tanks, transfusing their blood from all of that alcohol they've been drinking all their lives. We need new blood to tame those Arab animals."

"I hope to be a part of that."

"I have no doubt that you will, which is why I needed to see you right away. It's why I needed to cut your training short."

"Is there a specific reason why you did so?"

"Sherry," he said, "you're no *nouveaux riche* priss like most of our female candidates. You have *always* been one of us. You are one of a rare breed, and we need more like you. We need to restock this place with people just like yourself. We've needed you back since the very start, and now that all this Cold War garbage is over, we need your kind back all over again."

"But why do you need someone like me?"

"It's tradition, Sherry. Because in the Company, and I'm sure they didn't teach you this at the Farm, we're not only in the business of collecting intel, stealing secrets, and scalping targets. All that shit is boring. A girl like you needs something exciting, which is why assets like yourself really are the first true feminists there ever were. We're the real speakers of truth to power, not only at home, but all over the world. A girl like you needs a big bone to chew on, meat you can really sink your teeth into."

"Let me guess," she smiled, "you're sending me to Europe."

He chuckled at this, but said, "oh, Europe's for pussies. You know those two other women in your class? They'll be stationed in Europe. The Chinese woman in your class will be stationed at our Embassy in Beijing. But you? We have plans for you, my dear. Big plans."

"May I ask what those plans are?"

"We're bumping you up, Sherry. Way up. Europe is boring as hell. How many times do you have to see the fucking Sistine Chapel for Chrissakes? Or the Mona Lisa at the Louvre, am I right? You want to go where the real action is. You don't want some kind of *Let's Go Europe*, fuck-me-in-a-hostel experience anyway, do you? Plus, you're not to have relationships abroad anyway, but that's your own business, if you know what I mean," he winked. "I want to put you in Black Ops, and there are non-disclosure agreements for the level you'll be on, you understand."

"Black Ops? I mean, thanks for the opportunity, and I'm glad that you have that much faith in my abilities, but do you really think I'm ready for something like that? I didn't even finish training, technically speaking."

"I pulled you out early, because you're more than ready. And when you're done, we'll set you up as a high-ranking member of this Company with a big fat salary to go with it. We're talking the highest pay grade. How does that sound?"

"That sounds great, but are you sure about this?"

"I've never been more certain. I've read all your evaluations, all the recommendations and reports. You're more than ready to go."

"I don't know. It seems a bit, well, capricious."

"Capricious? Sherry, do you think a man in my position ever acts capriciously? I am very careful about whom I choose for operations like this. I know you're the one. I've always known. The operation I'm putting you on is not beyond your talents. I wouldn't have called you here if I believed that."

"Thank you for placing so much trust and confidence in me. So, what's the operation?"

"Okay, Sherry. Terrorism is now Public Enemy Number One, and that's where I'm putting you. Right in the belly of the beast. Right in the eye of the storm."

"I hate to say this, but don't you want someone else for this? Maybe I can assist a more experienced asset?"

"I'm sending you solo on this one. After a few days off, I want you on a plane with one of our best paramilitary units. I want you in Afghanistan."

"Afghanistan?" she laughed. "You *are* joking, right?"

"The hell I am. Only for a short time. I want you to travel with one our paramilitary teams and find out where these Arab pricks are hiding. I want to know who the actors are, where they're located, and where they'll strike next. To do that, you'll have to command the unit I'll assign you to. You will not be out there alone, okay? I want you to make as many friends and contacts as possible wherever you travel in Afghanistan, and I want you to collect what we need by any means necessary. I want you to acquire and get intel from the Afghans you turn. Now, from what I understand, you're fluent in Pashto, Farsi, Urdu, and Russian, right?"

"Yes, I am."

"Good, because these fuckers thrive on hearing their own language spoken back to them by foreigners like us. All you need are appropriate clothes, a weapon, and your paramilitary team. Together, you will infiltrate Afghanistan from the South, from Pakistan, and make your way northeast to Kabul. The more Afghans you turn to our side, the better.

"I hope this sounds acceptable to you, because rarely do we give an asset such latitude. No one will edit or desanitize your reports either. You are the boss. You are running your own classified operation. You're to transmit your reports directly to me here at Langley. The only people who will know what you're doing is the unit you're traveling with and our Station Chiefs throughout the Middle East in case you get in trouble. They will be watching out for you, so don't worry. And I'll be monitoring you from here at Langley. Do you understand all of this?"

"Yes, I think so."

"You can't *think* so. Before you leave this office, you have to *know* so. You see, these terrorists are killing our Case Officers, and we have to stop their attacks like a goalie does a hockey puck. At this time, you are my star goalie in Afghanistan. Kabul is your final destination, and by the time you leave, you will know who our enemies are, where they are hiding, and which Afghans will help us fight them, because sooner or later, we got to smoke these mother fuckers out when the President gives the go-ahead."

"I understand."

"Because this is a Black Ops mission, you cannot divulge a thing to anyone except those in the know. If you do, the consequences will be severe. You understand that too, don't you?"

"I understand."

"Excellent. Then let's toast to a nice, few days off and a really successful operation in Afghanistan. When you return to Langley after six months, you can expect a high post along with all the perks."

"Thank you for this opportunity, sir. I won't let you down."

"I know you won't. And don't call anyone 'sir' anymore. You're one of us now. I expect you to take the lead and like it. And I want you take advantage of the next five days to brush up on your social skills. Go to nice places and talk to people – bars, restaurants, you name it. You'll leave from Bolling in five days. My assistant will give you all the details – where you'll be staying as well as a list of places you may want to visit around town before you leave. We'll also give you some spending money for new clothes and whatever else you'll need. Enjoy yourself while you're in town."

"I'd appreciate that."

The Deputy leaned back in his seat, sipped more of his whisky, and said, "y'know, Sherry, I do want you to return in one piece, but it's not going to be a cakewalk, that I can tell you."

"In Ickystan? I understand."

"Ha! That's funny. Ickystan. You'll be challenged there, and you will be duly rewarded too. You shouldn't forget that when you're out there. It'll motivate you."

"I won't," she said, finishing off her glass.

"Good. My assistant has all the paperwork for you to sign outside. Can I count on you?"

"Definitely."

"Then I'll see you when you get back. Six months, no more. I promise."

"I won't disappoint you."

"I know you won't. Here's to a successful operation, Officer Sherry Aspen. And when you return, a successfully career at the Company."

In the middle of signing the non-disclosure agreements with the assistant outside, she overheard her on the phone taking instructions from the Deputy to send platters of Moussaka and grape leaves to the DCI upstairs. Sherry figured she would soon be in that upstairs office herself one day taking instructions from this same Deputy who would one day be appointed Director.

But if only it wasn't Afghanistan. Of all places to be stationed, the Company had to send her there, a perilous journey across another Ickystan and living amongst the Ickystanians, eating all of that under-cooked, viral goat meat. How horrible. As the Deputy said, though, she would be amply rewarded for it. The other motivating factor came from the fat wad of cash the attractive assistant handed over to her. She signed all of those ridiculous papers that didn't mean anything. She was above the law. Only the mission mattered as well as the very next task ahead of her, which was to check in at the Ritz-Carlton hotel on Embassy Row. The Deputy wanted her to brush up on her social skills by being around an international crowd, this after a short but effective shopping binge at City Center to buy clothes.

From the Gucci store to the Bustier Boutique, she bought all the dresses and lingerie needed to look attractive and professional for the ugly Ickystanians. Of course, the thought of their eyes wandering all over her disgusted her, but in order to collect intelligence and turn every terrorist she would have to be prepared for it. She was given the latitude to do anything in her power to find out when the next attack would come. Despite her thoughts of the dirt and grime that would stain her journey to Kabul where the mission would end in six months, she grew excited by the idea of mingling that very evening with the wealthy international types at the Ritz, but this time not as some blonde bimbo on another man's arm but as an independent operator with a purpose about which no one but she and handful of others knew. Despite leaving the Farm earlier than expected, the rarified nightlife of DC brought the pink back to her cheeks.

When she checked into her hotel room with overloaded shopping bags dangling from her fingers, her new life as an Operations Officer opened the same trap door to the young girl she used to be, but this time she was a woman of extreme importance with steady control, if not superiority, over all she surveyed, including all of the actors therein. She was now capable enough to manipulate her surroundings into any outcome she desired. She laughed to herself when she beheld the decadence of the hotel room, its king-sized bed, the whirlpool in the bathroom, its fine collection of Turkish towels and bathrobes. It wasn't an arrogant laughter but a stark discovery of how easily pliable her environment had suddenly become, whereas before she left Langley, she was trapped, smothered, and hemmed in by the rigors of the training.

The transformation felt incredible. The fierce solider who left Langley surrendered to the lovely blonde killer in a dress, a killer who no longer concerned herself with the consequences of killing. She could hold a gun at the temple of someone she didn't want alive or even looked at her the wrong way. It was a sublime power fit for a goddess who now gripped a lightning bolt in her fist from atop Mount

Olympus ready to disintegrate anyone who crossed her. A swell of happiness filled her. She returned to the woman she once knew but was pumped up enough to kick any man in the balls if he got out of line. What woman wouldn't want to be a member of a Company that gave her that kind of license?

With her gun slipped into the small of her back, she indeed pierced that nucleus of invincibility, a nucleus that would never pop and spill its juices all over the rest of its living parts, because she was too adept at entering it, like a needle moving in and out of an area too delicate for any ordinary person to permeate. It separated her from all the ignorant. It was her first taste of real power and the need to gain even more power and control, to want more and to have more, to experience pleasure more, everything more to an exponential degree just to rid herself of the despair of being a nothing, a nobody, a ghost on a dark street corner, another human being who didn't matter, just another oppressed female nearly dead only to emerge as content as any great woman needed to be to survive on a despicable Planet Earth. It only took a half-hour conversation with a high-ranking Company official who had faith in her inherent skills and natural abilities to be used, even in a place as unbearable and unforgiving as the hot furnace of Afghanistan.

And then it hit her. Amidst of all that glory, she remembered she had only five days before she had to leave. There would be no Trump Internationals or Ritz-Carltons in Ickystan. There would be no alcohol there. Maybe she could buy some on the black market under the protection of the paramilitary men who would be traveling with her. She wouldn't have to try very hard, just have one of them threaten some brown, gapped-toothed villager in a *kishlak*, a dirty Muslims in a mosque to fork over a six-pack from his private stash. Yeah, they must drink beer too, she guessed.

She beheld the view of the lighted Capitol from her window. Her muscles were still sore from completing the last exercise on the Farm. Filled with happiness, regardless that she had to leave soon, she could have wept with gratitude. Before long, she was down at the hotel bar looking for someone to talk to. She looked good in a new blue dress, even too good-looking for the bar itself. She impressed the bartender who placed a napkin in front of her. A woman of class and importance ordered a vodka martini.

"Shaken, not stirred?" he smiled.

"Excuse me?" she asked uncertainly. It couldn't be that her cover was already blown.

"Just kidding," he said. "We get a lot of those types in here. It is Embassy Row after all."

"A real international crowd, eh?"

The bartender gracefully poured her the martini. He selected his best brand of vodka.

"A lot of diplomats too," he said, placing the martini on the napkin. "They come from all over the world."

"I bet. Even you look like you come from the Continent. Are you?"

"Yes, but that is all I will say for now," he grinned. "When you get to know me better, I'll let you know more. After all, everyone's a spy around here."

"What did you say?"

"Just drink up, madam. I hope you enjoy your stay at the Ritz-Carlton."

"Thank you."

The bar, emptied and hollow, offered the only hope of getting tipsy after a long period of abstinence. She could drink without consequences, just as long as she kept her mouth shut. The Company's money had her bar tab covered. She no longer had to be concerned with living a pedestrian life with pedestrian things, like having a budget, spending more than she had in the bank, or maxing out her credit cards. Only the ecstasy of the moment mattered. Drink up and be merry was the prevailing attitude. Now that she was free and alive and looking fair and fantastic, her skin tingled all over from taking the first sip of the bitter intoxicant, her thin, soft fingers twirling the olive in the chilled glass. The drink kept her company along with the soft overhead music. That was all she needed until a well-dressed man in a black suit and red-striped tie sat near her at the bar.

"The usual?" asked the bartender to the man.

"Please," he said in a British accent.

To Sherry, the man with the accent seemed like he needed a release from a rough day. Not that he dangled over a precipice and stared into an abyss. He didn't seem depressed at all but rather absorbed in thought. The British are often like that, she remembered, especially the educated ones. They always asked questions that had no answers, always wondering 'why' or 'how come,' questions that had blank spaces next to them along with a glimmer of hope that these questions were leading them in the right direction, to places where they didn't have to ask any more questions, to places that felt more like home without ever having a home, as though the man had sailed too far off course and yearned for land while staring and waiting in quiet desperation to snap into something that felt as loose and carefree as America but had little chance of ever being that. Perhaps it was the English rains that did it to them.

She didn't feel sorry for him, though, because he wasn't sad exactly. He only searched for a fulfillment way beyond his reach, a luxury problem, which is why he must have looked over to her through the uninhabited and cavernous space between them, hoping to fill the vacancy that would lead either to their ship dashed upon the rocks or watching the sun set from an island in paradise. And, yes, he was handsome, just as most young, British men were handsome. Maybe he liked English football, cricket, or rowing on the Thames, she didn't know. But when their eyes connected, she tacitly invited him over.

For Sherry, it was a mere exercise in conversation, just as the Deputy had instructed, but she admitted that it wasn't only that. No matter how much she hated to admit it, his aquiline features and slim body, his meticulously clean-shaven face smoothed by lotion, she presumed, and his black hair, slicked-back and exposing just the right amount of receding hairline at the temples, attracted her to him. She begged him to say something instead of probing too deeply into the question marks that kept his mind rotating in never-ending circles, like dogs chasing their own tails.

"May I join you?" he finally asked in his British accent, an accent too polite for the United States. "We can keep each other company while we're here, if you'd prefer some company, that is."

"Sure," she said.

He picked up his drink by the stem of his glass and moved over to the seat next to her.

"My name is Phillip. Pleasure to make your acquaintance."

"Sherry. Nice to meet you. What brings you here so late on a work night?"

"I should ask you the same," he smiled, revealing a straight row of pearl-white teeth, unlike most of the teeth in

Britain.

She didn't want to get too close to him, though. She would be leaving in a few days, and as far as what she did for a living, well, she worked out of an American Embassy overseas, say as an assistant to the American Consulate General in Saudi Arabia? Sounded good enough.

It turned out that the handsome Brit also worked in government, for her Majesty in the United Kingdom, an assistant as well, but he wasn't more specific than that. Perhaps he was one of many assistants. He must have heard of T.S. Eliot, as all Britons must have heard of him.

"So, Saudi Arabia. How do you like it there?"

"Well, it's strict, and it's hot. Very hot."

He had a good laugh over this, even though her life really had been strict and hot without being anywhere near Saudi Arabia. Confinement at the Farm and also at Langley for so long had made it so. She craved release from what she had been through, and her attempts at conversation unexpectedly took an incredible amount of effort, as though every word she uttered had to be forced of her, even though the handsome Brit couldn't tell the difference. She fought hard to hold the conversation, while he held his beautifully. She desperately hoped he wouldn't discover how hard she had to work. Before long, however, verbal communication alone didn't do a good enough job of it. Words failed her, not because she had nothing to say, but because there existed a communicative distance between them that she wanted to bridge, so that she could cross over to his more casual and nonchalant side.

And then she felt the alcohol taking effect, her skin still tingling, and communication that wasn't verbal at all but a connection with the handsome Brit as though he were getting inside of her. True, she hadn't been with a man in the longest time, at least legitimately, most unlike the trainer at Camp Peary. To have him inside of her, not akin to the empathy she shared with her mother, but to have him inside of her physically, liberated her mind and provided for the sweet and generous psychic release needed to feel better and more complete, more confident and capable in her womanhood. She knew full well there wouldn't be another attractive man in sight in Afghanistan. At least the polite, gentlemanly, and attractive Brit made her body shiver with his glowing skin and imperial accent. Hearing the guttural language of the Pashtun goat herders would hardly suffice. She needed his British length inside of her, deep inside of her, up to the hilt inside of her, entering and touching the womb inside of her, so that she could emote all over his body as a woman sometimes needed to do. Twice in one day wouldn't be so bad, she guessed.

He was a temptation to say the least, but then she suddenly remembered her role as an Operations Officer and stopped her imagination from drifting too far off course. Sure, the Deputy gave her free reign to do what she needed, but this handsome Brit could have easily been a spy, seducing her for an exchange of intelligence later down the road, intelligence that may have wound up in Russian or Chinese hands, or perhaps in the hands of the next terrorist who blows up yet another Navy vessel in international waters. How foolish of her to be so self-serving, especially since she just left the Farm only a few hours ago. Their conversation, as forced as it was, marched on, however. In the end, they were just two lonely people longing for company. The Brit would be just another lad slaughtered on the altar of another beautiful woman. Her ebullience lost out to the duty and sacrifice her job required. Even the bartender noticed that these were two exceptional people ready to take one another to bed.

Most likely, though, it was just another grand pig-fuck in the guise of gentlemanly and romantic courtship. For the ghoulish, the lame, and the decrepit, the more obvious pig-fucks were on the hard nighttime streets of DC, as these unfortunate people were the real sacrifices slaughtered by the feminine executioners for hoping for one last shot at touching a beauty that they would never feel, taste, or penetrate. Although the beautiful didn't necessarily have the best of lives either, being beautiful sure did program these unfortunates to bow down to women such as she.

The Brit who sat next to her was buzzed enough to make an advance, but he kept smooth-talking her in a way that Sherry found pleasurable instead, as though she received a bouquet of roses from an admirer who had been masking his true feelings. When their eyes connected again, however – hers a soft, clear blue and his a deep brown – she knew it was time to pull away. She played it cold when he asked for her room number. She refused him. Under the fog of disappointment, the Brit had the bartender charge both drinks to his room and politely said goodnight. Satisfied that she had protected herself, she regretted that she spurned him as well. He could have done wonders for her.

"Is it always this slow?" she asked disappointedly after the Brit had left.

"Weekdays are usually slow," he said. "Weekends are much busier, although sometimes on nights like these, we do get a few late night stragglers. Here comes one now."

Sherry swiveled around on her barstool and witnessed a tall black man enter the bar. Like the Brit, he also wore a dark suit but with pinstripes. He also looked like someone important. His skin wasn't as dark as someone's from Africa, so she assumed he was an American just like her. She was right, because when he ordered a light beer from the bartender, his accent was perfectly American. His voice sounded educated, perhaps a policy analyst or a Congressional aide, but definitely not someone from Embassy Row. Why he visited the Ritz-Carlton that night on his salary, she wasn't sure. Neither did she want to know too much about him.

Again, he was handsome but only for a black man. Many black women would have found him handsome, she was sure of it, but he wasn't a part of Sherry's culture, as there were many different cultures, and he belonged to his and she to hers. So, when he had the audacity to ask if she cared for a drink, she politely refused and left it at that.

She imagined being another white woman at the bar fielding the same question from the same man. She imagined too that this imaginary woman was actually interested in this black man at the bar. Considering a black man's voracious appetites, he must have wanted this white woman for a one-night stand and nothing more. If anything, the white woman she imagined was probably married already, wanting to cheat on her boring husband or spend one night of sin with a man such as he in tabooed ecstasy. She might have been curious what it was like to sleep with a man of such size, or maybe she enjoyed being with a man who had a certain animal prowess that satisfied her more than her small, limp husband did, no matter how rich and successful her husband might have been. She may have only wanted to use what a black man had been abnormally endowed with for one night of fulfilling and satisfying pleasure. But in no way would this attractive, educated, albeit imaginary white woman want anything other than that, and certainly not a relationship of any kind. She would have never left her upper-crust husband and her polo-clad children to become a part of his world. There were differences after all - she a rich housewife in the suburbs with her kids accepted to the prestigious country day school, and he a black, low-level civil servant working a dead-end job.

Unfortunately, love never proves strong enough to cross class lines, let alone racial ones. It never does. Maybe in college, some experimentation between the colors is permitted, but such relationships usually don't survive beyond the utopia an idyllic youth provides. When society gets serious for the couple, they naturally go their separate ways, back to their own racial corners, because they are too uncomfortable and threatened to be living out amongst the rabble-rousers who continuously threaten them. They return to their positions of fetal comfort, to their families who raised them and who had initially warned them of such risky moves.

All the money in the world wouldn't bind them together for very long. Too focused on her own bloodlines and having the indignity of a black man muddying it up with his inferior history, her love would prove to be too dangerous no matter how much wealth he possessed. After all, what would her parents think? If they didn't disown her outright, they would at least drown in their own disappointment, as their own adorable, white starlet whom they had raised with all of their love and attention with all of their resources and sacrifices chose to mix the family's blood with a black man's of lesser value. The black man's family would have probably been overjoyed, now that they had moved a step up on the racial ladder, while the white woman's parents would have plunged into eternal despair, her All-American, trophy-winning brothers whispering 'nigger' under their breaths at the Thanksgiving dinner table, her forefathers turning in their graves like roasting pigs on sticks.

Not that it bothered Sherry very much, because she was far from being interested in the black man who had asked if she wanted a drink. The black man belonged in his world, and she in hers. She politely said that she was too tired without showing the slightest hint of emotion and left the bar soon after he arrived.

Nevertheless, her stay at the Ritz-Carlton on Embassy Row for the next few nights was successful in the sense that she developed her conversational skills amongst an otherwise auspicious crowd of handsome men looking either to cheat on their wives or for a quick route into the Central Intelligence Agency through a green asset who may not have known any better. She visited many watering holes around Washington, met many men, but slept with none, even though she was tempted to every step of the way. She handled herself well, all the way up to the day of her departure from Bollinger Air Force Base. She almost cried when the car came for her on that dreary wet morning. Visions of Afghanistan's giant spiders, centipedes, and poisonous scorpions came into full focus before she even got on the plane. Yet Afghanistan remained a land too foreign and outlandish to contemplate with any degree of accuracy by the time she boarded the aircraft.

Chapter Fourteen

December 2000 – Baluchistan Province, Pakistan

Sherry found it odd that only a handful of paramilitary men traveled with her to Pakistan on a cavernous C-17 Globemaster jet meant to carry hundreds of soldiers and heavy cargo to and from far-off destinations. The Deputy must have thought it too expensive to fly them on an Air Force C-40 Clipper or a similar airliner. Despite being an official Operations Officer, Sherry wore Army fatigues, which her paramilitary unit found particularly offensive, firstly because she never saw active combat, and secondly because they saw her as a fragile elitist who couldn't withstand any actual combat at all. She wasn't like them. They were the muscle, and she only the brain.

Within the long hull of the aircraft, an American flag hung high above them, and the roar of the engines drowned out any communication between her and the soldiers on the opposite side. She held a letter-sized envelope that instructed her to read its contents only when beyond American airspace. It was for her eyes only. One of the Deputy's men left it in a drop box at the airport prior to takeoff. She opened the dossier that read the C-17 would fly them to a secret airbase in Pakistan otherwise known as Shamsi Airfield in Baluchistan Province, Northwest Frontier. The airfield, near Afghanistan's southern border, had been leased to the Company by the ISI, the Pakistani Intelligence Services. Their mission was to change planes at Shamsi after a brief, two-night stopover and then fly a much smaller passenger plane to an even more clandestine airstrip in the Helmand River Valley, Afghanistan. Their mission would begin there. They would then head north to Herat and then journey all the way east across the length of Afghanistan's dangerous terrain, moving from village to village to collect intelligence on terrorist cells operating in these areas. At each village, Sherry would transmit her reports to Langley detailing the location of any terrorist actitvity. The mission would end in Kabul.

While the route was simple enough, the mission itself wouldn't be . They were sure to meet enemy fire, especially from Bin Laden's men and perhaps the Taliban, the newest force to occupy Afghanistan after the bloody civil war that maimed and butchered thousands of Afghan men, women, and children. They would be confronting hundreds of hidden minefields that had already blown apart both Soviets and Afghans alike. Their dried, blackened blood on the desert's otherwise rust-colored floor, their dead sinew that once quivered like the tentacles of jelly fish, and jutting bones from their severed arms and legs were omnipresent reminders of the war's unending continuation. The dossier also contained a report about the Taliban, their history, and the events that preceded their recent conquest of the country.

The dossier reported that the CIA quietly backed the Taliban with its Saudi and Pakistani allies. From what she had learned in the classrooms at Langley, the Afghan economy functioned in roughly five different ways. Four of the five were opium production, heroin processing, gas and oil, and various smuggling operations carried out by tribal warlords. The fifth was no less important: wheat and barley production on agricultural farmland that the Soviets destroyed using Mao Tse-Tung's 'scorched earth' tactics. What fucking animals.

Because of the destruction of these fields, the rural poor of Afghanistan had to resort to growing opium to make their money back.

The Sunni Pashtuns populated the Southern regions of the country. This tribe, fiercely independent and religiously conservative, fled south across the border to the Northwest Frontier of Pakistan after the Soviets had invaded. Another tribe, known as the Ismailis, once occupied the Northeast of the country but fled west into neighboring Iran as refugees. The Ismailis were Shias and so were the Hazaras, another ethnic Shia tribe that populated Central Afghanistan. The Hazaras were an oppressed and harassed Shia minority that had been marginalized both culturally and politically by the Sunni majority for hundreds of years. Even in a place as unforgiving as Afghanistan, the sad and brutal enmity between Sunni and Shia still continued, especially since the Sunni Saudis and the Shia Iranians fought their brutal proxy wars in the region using these respective tribes as pawns.

But Afghanistan's tragic history truly rested in the attempts made by many rulers, both inside and outside of the country, to conquer it. But it was a country that somehow evaded being conquered, as though Allah had decreed that Afghanistan would never be conquered and those living within its borders would suffer a thousand years of death and destruction. Even Alexander the Great built a great city near Herat only to have it destroyed by the resistance of fierce tribal leaders.

By the time Clinton took office in 1992, a *mujahideen* government had taken hold of Kabul. Just four years later in 1996, the Taliban captured Kandahar in the South, Jalalabad in the East, and Herat in the Northwest. Eventually, the Taliban took Kabul away from the *mujahideen*. Not bad for the children of the same fighters to whom the Company funneled arms and provided training a generation earlier to counter the Soviet invasion. When many of these freedom fighters died while fighting the Soviets, their fatherless offspring fled south into Northern Pakistan, filled up new orphanages, and studied in new *madrassas* funded, no less, by the Saudis. The only book studied was the formidable *Qu'ran*, taught to them by demanding mullahs who rejected liberal Western values as well as the Persian liberalism of the Shia Iranians next door.

The Taliban had overwhelming Pashtun support. They had common interests of remaining dedicated to conservative Islamic traditions and codes. The Pashtuns also wanted the Taliban to stop the corruption of Tajik and Uzbek leaders and to restore law and order in a country where mass killing was a daily way of life. The dossier said that the Taliban wanted to help the Pashtuns assert full dominance over the whole of Afghanistan and drive out the Ismailis and the Hazaras within it. Interestingly enough, the Pakistanis also wanted the Pashtuns to rule Afghanistan with the help of the Taliban, not only because the Sunni majority in the cities of Pakistan resorted to a religious fundamentalism of their own. Rather, the Pakistanis, ruled by President Zia Al-Haq, desperately wanted lucrative trade links with the newly formed and liberated former Soviet states of Turkmenistan, Uzbekistan, and Kyrgyzstan that abutted Afghanistan's northern border.

Iran and Turkey wanted these same trade links too and vigorously competed with the Pakistanis for them. The Pakistanis even staged a publicity campaign by sending one of its ministers through Afghanistan. Sherry couldn't help but raise her eyebrows when she read that the Taliban protected this very same trade Minister and his convoy on behalf of the Pakistanis. In return, the Pakis supplied the Taliban with arms and the military training to help the Pashtuns take over Afghanistan.

It followed that the Company also supported the Taliban. With regards to the Company's involvement, though, countering Iranian influence wasn't the only reason for forming this alliance. As with any Company operation, countering Iran couldn't move forward without a profit motive. Enter the California-American oil and gas corporation UNOCAL. With the Company's full approval, UNOCAL began to build a vast oil pipeline from the former Soviet satellite states in the north, only to end at the Arabian Sea in the Middle East. To follow through with such an ambitious project, the Company and UNOCAL needed the Taliban's protection from Afghanistan's terrorist elements. Since the Taliban already had Pakistan's full support, the Company also supported the Taliban. With the Saudis funding the orphanages, religious schools, and fundamentalist Islamic movements along Pakistan's northern border, the oil was sure to flow, money would be made, and the Iranian and the Turkish competitors would be sent packing. The Pakis, the Saudis, the Taliban, and the United States, therefore, formed a four-point alliance. The Iranians and the Turks formed an alliance between themselves to counter competition for these same trade links.

One of Sherry's main objectives was to get to the Company's Taliban allies before Bin Laden's Al-Queda organization did, find out where he was hiding, and prevent another attack. Bin Laden and the Company were once on the same side fighting the Soviets. But not anymore. Having American troops protecting the House of Saud on Muslim lands didn't help matters. As she recalled, Bin Laden despised the House of Saud as well as the loose values that America had spread throughout the holiest lands of the Islam. If Sherry could turn some of the Taliban and Pashtun leadership to the American side before Bin Laden did, her operation would be a success. Fortunately, the Company trained her to speak

Pashto, which further confirmed her belief that the Deputy knew exactly what he was doing by sending her there. She now knew never to doubt the integrity of the Company when it came to furthering the interests of her country.

The final note in the dossier read that her host at Shamsi would be a high-ranking Pakistani Commander who wouldn't know anything about her intention to forge a stronger alliance with the Pashtuns and the Taliban to counter *Al-Queda*. Unfortunately, the Pakis also threw their weight behind Bin Laden, considering the precipitous rise of Islamic fundamentalism in Pakistan. As far as the Pakis were concerned, Sherry and her paramilitary team were there on a diplomatic mission to visit UNOCAL construction sites and cement the friendship between the United States and the Pakistani leadership. Nothing about Bin Laden would ever be mentioned.

After reading and re-reading the dossier, she tried to sleep on the plane but her shaken and jostled body was met with loud disruptions of the jet engines on either side of the cavernous aircraft. She looked over to the men on the opposite side of the hull. Three white men and one black man looked like they came straight out of a Hollywood war movie. Clearly, the Black one was the strongest of the bunch. She had no idea how she would spend six full months wandering around the villages of Afghanistan with these boneheaded beasts. Naturally, she would have to put up with their adolescent humor, childish pranks, and vulgar language. When push came to shove, though, she had no doubt that this group of toughs would take a bullet for her if they had to. After all, they were there to protect her.

Each one of them was a killing machine. She could only speculate how many Ickystanians they had already wasted, especially in Iraq and other horrific parts of the world. She thanked God that these killers were on her side and not the Ickystanians. They were uncultured, heathen animals, yes, but they were uncultured, heathen *American* animals. What a relief. Hopefully, none of them would get funny ideas while traversing the lonely deserts of Afghanistan with her, especially the ferocious black one. Traveling for so long with a woman like Sherry might have twisted their minds, no matter how disciplined they were. But these guys had been trained to live without food, water, or sex in the worst conditions imaginable for prolonged periods of time. That's how Langley wanted them. Again, she had faith that the Company knew what it was doing by sending them along with her. She put her own paranoid ideas aside, even though as an asset she had been trained to sleep with one eye open. She had to be suspicious of people, places, and events she hadn't even seen yet.

The plane shook them so badly that by the time they landed at Shamshi after the seventeen-hour flight, she couldn't help but feel thoroughly nauseated. Her body bounced up and down as the C-17 touched down on a broken airstrip. Thankful that the horrendous flight had ended, she immediately darted for daylight when the ass of the plane opened up like a pregnant whale giving birth. She ran out into the hot, acrid air only to have the food from the rations she ate on the flight tumble out of her gut. The men behind her laughed in hysterics.

"Fuck off!" she yelled at them after vomiting.

"Oh, poor baby," said one of them. "Daddy couldn't afford a vomit bag for his Queenie."

"Alright," said the black soldier. "Leave Queenie alone. We need her to test the minefields. We better keep her happy."

"I know how to keep her happy," said a third soldier. "I

can show her later on tonight."

"Yeah, right," laughed the black soldier. "Ain't no fucking in Pakistan. Ain't no porn here either. They'll put you in jail just for beating off around here."

"That's enough," yelled Sherry, wiping her mouth with her sleeve. "Mind your manners, or you'll be on the first transport back to Bolling."

"Yes, ma'am," said the fourth soldier. "Don't get your panties in a bunch, princess."

"Must be that time of the month," said the first soldier.

"Go get the equipment," she ordered angrily.

The black soldier disappeared inside the hull and pushed out two large crates on rollers filled with anti-aircraft missiles, long-range sniper rifles, night vision goggles, plastic explosives, and electronic communications equipment. Once these crates rested on the tarmac, the third member of the team unpacked one of three Predator drones. Each drone was equipped with infrared cameras. With a remote, the soldier turned one of the drones on, its low-noise wooden propellers whirring close to the heads of the others.

"Put that fucking toy away," said the second soldier. "That thing's worth three million bucks!"

"We should have used this thing against Quadaffi in Libya," said the soldier flying the drone. "We could have killed that son of a bitch."

"Put it away!" yelled Sherry, relieved of her nausea but still in bad shape from the flight.

She was relieved enough to see land through the haze of blazing sunlight that already burned her skin. On one side of the airstrip sat a row of ramshackle barracks similar to those at the Farm. They were spread out alongside the airstrip and looked thoroughly uninviting. The two pilots commanding the C-17 then strolled out of the back of the hull from the cockpit inside. They closed the wide opening by pulling a lever from outside the plane.

"Now that was one rough ride," said the black soldier, smiling.

"Too bad they could only break for lunch and have to fly seventeen hours back to Bolling," said the third soldier. "What chumps."

By the time the paramilitary team took stock of all the equipment, an A-1Z Viper helicopter came within sight. Its chopping rotors muffled the wisecracks the men made. The futility of disciplining them dawned upon her as the helicopter, with its splotches of green, yellow, and black camouflage, settled on the broken tarmac adjacent to the giant C-17. The Globemaster dwarfed the small helicopter.

The A-1Z had once been used in the Vietnam War and was American made. The helicopter had been retired, refitted, and resold to the Pakistani military by the Defense Department, which had rendered it obsolete. The Pakistanis often bought obsolete arms from the US for its defense against India, its archenemy. The Pakis could always count on the Americans for financial and military aid, even though Pakistan remained a weary and fickle ally. The Pakis had always been two-faced in their foreign policy. They complained that the US would start a conflict but never see it to its conclusion. Many other countries also offered the same complaint. The Americans came and went when they pleased, usually when it was politically advantageous for their leaders to do so. No wonder these countries hated the US so much.

The Commander on the A-1Z wore mirrored aviator sunglasses and a green military uniform. He stepped onto the runway and approached the team with a wide smile. His balding scalp with a few whisps salt-and-peppery hair refracted the bright sunshine. He was out of shape for a soldier of his rank, his belly protruding above is belt buckle and his thin legs barely supporting his top-heavy body. As he moved closer, Sherry also noticed his splintered teeth, as though he had been punched in the mouth one too many times. Interestingly, the Commander knew beforehand whom to meet. He marched directly to Sherry and extended his hand to show his immediate friendship. Sherry assumed he would approach one of the men first, in fitting Islamic fashion.

"Miss Sherry Aspen," said the Commander. "Welcome to Shamsi, our little palace out here in the desert."

"Thank you, Commander," she said. "On behalf of the US State Department, I thank you for your hospitality and your permission to stay here."

"Come," he said. "You and your men must be exhausted. Our servants have been waiting for you."

He pointed to the row of barracks on the side of the dusty airstrip.

"You will be staying in the barracks next to mine," he continued. "It is has a comfortable bed and a nice shower. The same goes for your men. I want your stay to be as comfortable as possible here. On behalf of the Government of Pakistan, I humbly welcome you."

"We are grateful, Commander. "I'll have my men store our equipment near the barracks right away. We'll need to take it with us in a couple of days."

"Of course. You should make yourselves at home. I will personally provide whatever it is that you need. You must be hungry, yes? Our servants are preparing your lunch as we speak. Settle in and freshen up. We'll meet in the dining hall in a couple of hours, yes?"

"That will be fine, Commander. Thank you."

He did an about-face and headed towards his makeshift residence next to where she was supposed to stay. When he was far enough away, one of the soldiers said, "God, what a shithole this place is."

"Hey, keep it down," said Sherry, annoyed. And then more forcefully, "Listen, we are here as their guests. Whatever you do, be on your best behavior. You do remember how to behave, don't you? That means I want you to mind your manners and be presentable. Watch your language. We're supposed to be on a diplomatic mission here. Just smile a lot, eat whatever food they give you, take your showers, and keep your mouths shut. Pretty soon, we'll be out of here."

"Yes, ma'am," said one of the soldiers, saluting her.

"Glad I brought my *Hustler* along," said the Black soldier.

"When do we get to see the whores?" asked the third soldier.

"Paki whores?" said the fourth. "No such thing."

"Glad, you took the *Hustler*," said the first solider. "I'm going first. The outhouse is behind the barracks."

Once again, Sherry could do nothing to stop them. Their job had always been to kill with impunity. She wanted them to stay away from the Commander at all times. Besides, they had landed in the middle of nowhere without any other landmarks, buildings, or Paki villages around them for miles. The Commander wouldn't be able to show any of these men the wonders of his country. Only this shitty part. The last country to leave Shamsi had been the United Arab Emirates. Technically, while the Company now leased the base, Sherry only needed it for two nights before crossing the border. If she could keep the team in line for that short a time, the better her chances of making a good impression on the Commander. Yet she knew she had to go beyond that to make sure they could count on his help after leaving, should they need it. There was nothing like Pakistani assistance when something went wrong. Hopefully, nothing would go wrong. All she had to do was stick to the plan as outlined in the dossier.

She didn't expect much of her living arrangements. Her barracks contained a single straw-filled mattress facing a dirt-stained window that let in some of the intense sunlight. A standing oscillating fan whirred in a distant corner. The sunlight would be intense at sunrise, so she dragged the mattress to a shaded area to prevent overheating in the early mornings. There was a shower stall and outhouse in the back, but no toilet paper in either. The outhouse had a rusty faucet on the bottom side wall and an empty plastic jug below it to clean herself off. The area reeked of unraked sewage that must have been rotting there for months. The shower next to the outhouse functioned by filling up a large, rusted tank with water that hung above an equally rusted showerhead. By flipping an electric switch, the water slowly heated. But as soon as the water hit her dry skin, a variety of fat cockroaches scampered over her toes and then darted in all directions. Compared to the insects at the Farm, though, the roaches weren't nearly as bad. Afghanistan's wildlife would be much worse.

After a lukewarm shower, she slept for several hours to get over her jet lag. She awoke much later in the darkness. She flicked on the lights and dressed professionally while remaining attractive enough to rope in any man who had the privilege of looking at her. By the time she looked her very best, she checked in on her paramilitary team. In the small dining room their barracks afforded, the soldiers fed on large bowls and platters of spicy Haleem and buttery naan with a similar fan pushing warm air through the room. They had been famished since they left Bolling and lapped at their food without utensils or napkins. In Pakistan, and all over the Middle East and Southeast Asia for that matter, people ate with their hands and washed them off with cold water. The soldiers hardly minded it at all, as they had been used to eating and living in conditions that were much, much worse. The buttery naan, which they dipped in the brown, oily Haleem, dripped from their fingers in gobs before they stuffed it in their wheat-smeared mouths. They ate like pigs at a trough while the Commander's Pakistani servants bustled around them loading more and more naan onto their plates.

The men were in much better spirits, even though they didn't converse like earlier in the day. They were too busy eating to look up when Sherry entered the room. She preferred them tame and quiet this way. She didn't have to deal with their childishness.

"Gentleman," she said, "we leave in a couple of days, so rest up and be nice to our hosts."

In typical fashion, the soldiers waved her off as an annoyance.

"I want you guys in bed early, and I want you up early. We're on the other side of the world here, and you'll have to adjust to the time zone and our new environment."

"We know all that!" yelled one of the soldiers, chewing his food and waving her off. "Just do your job, and we'll do ours. Keep the Commander happy!"

"Right," she said, her authority and leadership meaning nothing to them. "Just making sure we're clear. Goodnight, gentlemen."

They didn't even notice her loveliness when out of her military fatigues. She needed the Commander to notice her, though. She would get on his good side and make a good impression, which was essential to the mission. It took only one slight insult or one typical act of American condescension for him to deny them of any help. While she didn't look forward to charming him, she knew she had to. She loosened the elastic band at the back of her head and let her blonde, luxurious hair fall all about her. With powder, lipstick, and eyeshadow on her face, she looked dynamite. A brown man with a brain half the size of any white American would crave her companionship without thinking twice about it. Women like Sherry easily attracted these Third World types. She was a magnet for them.

While walking to the Commander's residence, she remembered that she should never tell anyone about her employment with the CIA, no matter what. Not even a future husband could know, should she ever have the luck of finding one. At the time, though, she did ruminate on having a family in the future, a family with strong, healthy white kids and a McMansion in the suburbs, sure, but she knew it would be difficult if the Company ever sent her overseas again. While she had no need of settling down immediately, she especially wanted to fall in love like all couples did. Yes, she still carried these incurable fairytales with her to Pakistan. She thought she had been cured of them years ago.

Whether she liked it or not, she did believe in love. She never felt it with another man, but she still believed it would happen one day. Many a night she lay awake wondering when love would find her and what it would feel like when it did. Her wandering imagination, the foundation of her disease, only took her so far until it hit a wall in its attempt to go further. Love, she figured, was a gift that she would feel one day, like how a caged heart beats from a chest when a man sits across from her and looks deeply into her blue eyes, and then Boom! she just knows love has arrived, and he's the one. His love from his own beating heart connects directly to her soul through the medium of his sorrowful eyes. To her, love wasn't a process, though. It wasn't something that could be explained, analyzed, or taught. Rather it was an intuitive knowing that confounded and confused even the most infallible of minds. She would know it and feel it simultaneously. That's all she knew. Once she returned to the States after the grueling six months out in the field, she would begin a new mission to find love and hope when it struck her. Suddenly in the Pakistani heat, she couldn't wait for that day to come. It couldn't come soon enough.

Once in the Commander's lair, however, thoughts of finding love dissipated in the musty heat. His residence had luxuries and other amenities that all of the barracks did without. A servant in a starched, white uniform greeted her and escorted her to the Commander's table in the middle of the room. The servant was a smallish, kind soul whose brown face sweated profusely. The insides of his teeth had blackened with old tea and tobacco stains, his demeanor obsequious under the calculating watch of the Commander. The servants of Pakistan were treated as personal slaves yet were happy enough to be employed in a land where most people went hungry. The Arabs treated them the same way in the Middle East, no matter what jobs they did for them. It must have been a great honor for the servant to be taken in by the Commander, his sandals revealing bent, crooked toes and fungal-infected toenails. Sherry guessed that the servant must have spent most of his life barefoot in the service of others.

She couldn't help but feel homesick and culture shocked in the Commander's presence. He stood from the small dining table draped in a thin table cover. Several cooks in a back room, also in white uniform, prepared a meal imbued with coriander, parsley, cumin, chiles, and wild mustard. These heavy spices flooded her nostrils as she readied herself for a traditional Pakistani meal. She was relieved to spot plastic eating utensils on the table as well as brown paper napkins. She wouldn't have to eat with her hands after all. A bottle of Boerl and Kroff Brut chilled in a tin bucket of crushed ice. Maybe the experience with this man wouldn't be so bad after all. If only the Deputy had instructed her to learn the nuances of Indian and Pakistani cuisine instead of learning how to flirt well, she would have been better off. Her sensitive stomach would have appreciated it.

The Commander stood from his seat. He came around to her side and held the chair for her. Holding the chair impressed her, but the more sobering thought entered her mind that this man would have otherwise been pumping gas at a Haji Mart in Jersey had he not been a decorated Commander in the Pakistani military.

"Thank you," said Sherry.

"Ah, Miss Aspen," he said, "might I say, you look absolutely wonderful this evening. It is so good to see a representative of your venerable State Department in our small corner of the world. On behalf of our government, I officially welcome you to Pakistan."

"Thank you, Commander. The United States Secretary of State humbly accepts your greetings and sends you his fondest regards."

"Yes, the guard has changed in America," he said. "But what's with all the weapons? That's usually not State Department protocol."

"I wouldn't be concerned with it, Commander. That's

just for the soldiers. Not me. You must send our regards to the General."

"Absolutely. Would you like some champagne?"

"I would love some. Thank you."

The servant filled both glasses for them. The Commander remained standing. He then toasted her.

"To a successful diplomatic mission," he said. "We will assist you in any way possible."

"That's very kind of you, Commander. Thank you."

An open window in his residence overlooked the airstrip where the C-17 had taken off on its return to Bolling. It was dark out, and the runway lights were off. Only the light of the moon cast shadows over the Commander's helicopter that squatted on the airstrip. The obsequious, thin-legged servant carried plates of salads and dishes of lamb and beef *terkari* to the table. After she finished off each plate, he inquired how she liked it, to which she nodded her head in appreciation. The beef and lamb were smothered in rich, curried masala and cooked in tomato paste. The hot spices nearly blew a hole in hole in her stomach, but the lamb and beef dishes were indeed spectacular, especially when taken in by the garlicky and buttery naan that came with them. Thankfully, she wasn't obligated to eat hand-to-mouth as her paramilitary team sloppily did, probably with the same exuberance of flipping through pages of the *Hustler* they brought with them. The Commander made sure that Sherry was well fed and satisfied with every part of her meal. The soldiers, she thought, must have felt right at home.

She excused herself for a moment after the sweating servant placed a small, silver bowl of pistachio *kulfi* in front of them after clearing away the dinner plates. She wiped her lips off with her napkin and quickly walked outside to where the Commander's outhouse menacingly stood. She closed the wooden door in on herself after squatting on an open hole in the pitch-black darkness. For ten minutes she remained in the outhouse doing her business as flies hovered above and below her. Like before, the outhouse fumed with the stench of rotting sewage. And there was no toilet paper to be found, only a rusty faucet next to her legs and a plastic jug below it to clean and rinse herself off. She washed thoroughly before returning. Her rectum burned from the spices she ate, and her stomach turned sour. But it was important not to show any discomfort. Luckily, the servant had boiled all the water, so there was little chance of catching a stomach bug.

After returning, the Commander refilled her glass of the expensive champagne. Having another American sitting across from him must have genuinely excited him, especially a female American who was so strikingly attractive. Sherry guessed that he must have thought himself important to be having dinner with her. Apparently, the rundown, Third World environment usurped her own imperial vanity. Nevertheless, Sherry happily drank with him. She was more than tipsy by the time they polished off the bottle. The Commander then leaned back in his chair and offered her a *Silk Cut*, which she politely refused. He casually lit one up and seemed relieved to be smoking after the long, drawn-out meal.

"So, your friends at UNOCAL are building the pipeline," he said, "but I'm left wondering why they sent you all the way out here just to see how they're doing. I mean, why you of all people, and why now? We all know about the bombings of your Embassies in Africa and the terrible calamity it caused. It's surprising you don't need our help in any way. I mean, why go it alone with you and just a few men with weapons? Afghanistan isn't exactly the easiest place in the world."

"It's just to check on things and to make sure our

UNOCAL executives and workers have adequate protection. We have to make sure all their needs are met. We'll only be in Afghanistan for a week or so."

"You'll be flying into Kabul, I take it?" he smiled. "Or will it be Kandahar?"

"Kabul. We'll need one of your passenger jets for that."

"It's on its way as we speak. It's my pleasure to provide you with one. But why not fly to Kabul directly from Cairo or Karachi? Why do you need Shamsi of all places?"

"Since this is a diplomatic mission, we wanted your government's kind approval, in case we need your assistance in Afghanistan."

Without warning, he reached his dry hands across the table and placed them on top of hers.

"Miss Aspen," he smiled, "you will definitely need our help since you are flying into Kabul, and since you value our mutual friendship here and now, maybe you can let me in on why you're really here at Shamsi."

She slipped her soft hands from underneath his and said, "Commander, whatever do you mean? I am here on a diplomatic mission. I am here to make sure our Americans are safe. To do that, I have to speak with the Taliban leadership that governs Kabul. That's all I'm here to do. We stopped here because it is a matter of convenience and also because we wanted to keep a low profile."

"But why so much equipment? You could kill off a small army with what you brought here."

"What if we were ambushed by the very same terrorists who bombed our Embassies in Africa? It can easily happen in Kabul."

"But all of that equipment? Please, Miss Aspen. I'm no fool. You are here for something entirely different."

"I can assure you we're not, Commander. We're heading straight to Kabul."

"So, if I call your State Department tonight, they'd tell me the same? That they sent you, a young woman barely out of university, to lead a ruthless group of marauders into Kabul to check on a bunch of oil executives? Something isn't right about this. Maybe I should call your Embassy in Karachi and inquire as to what your Ambassador thinks."

"Go right ahead. But you know very well that you are not authorized to make such an inquiry. It would get you into a lot of trouble, to circumvent authority like that. Wouldn't it?"

"I have enough pull to do whatever I want here in Pakistan."

"Commander," she smiled, "we both know that's not true. You can't just call an American Ambassador without going through the proper channels. That just wouldn't be prudent of you."

"So, it wouldn't bother you if I called him, then? It means nothing to you if I did?"

"It's a moot point, Commander, because I already know you won't be making that phone call."

He surrendered a wide smile and said, "I tell you what. You tell me why you're really here, and I'll tell you something you can't possibly ignore."

"You're going to tell me anyway," she smiled, propping her elbow up on the table and resting her head in the palm of her hand.

Her new posture was suggestive, and right away the Commander knew what she implied.

"I can work with you that way too, Miss Aspen. I do have information that will make you a very popular girl back in Washington."

"Then you can tell me all about it tonight."

"Don't worry," he said. "I'll tell you once we get to know each other better."

She parted her lips slightly and ran her tongue over the curve of her upper teeth, her usual go-to for situations like this. The gesture worked. She didn't want him pestering the US Embassy in Karachi. He may have called and could have gotten into trouble for it, but if the State Department got one whiff of the CIA's running another Black Ops mission in Afghanistan, there would be severe repercussions, both for her and the Company. She had to make sure the Commander's attentions were redirected towards having her in bed, but hopefully not so soon. She would string him along, not only to prevent the phone call, but to extract the intelligence and transmit it to Langley. She would impress the hell out of the Deputy with it and maybe even the DCI himself.

He was hungry for her, though. This she knew for sure. Stranded at a secret airbase without anyone around for miles must have affected his judgement, especially with a woman like Sherry within his reach. She felt the maddening pressure of his libido from his side of the table. It demanded relief, and in return he would reveal what would soon make her a superstar back home.

She brushed her leg against his underneath the table, and he smiled his wide, welcoming smile again. Sure, he was a pig, but he was her first acquisition from abroad — and an extremely useful acquisition at that — a high ranking commander in the Pakistani military whom she could press whenever she liked, provided she satisfy him in ways most unconventional. It was part of the job. It was only sex. There would be nothing emotional about it. Nor would her actions impede on her vision of love. Rather, love and sex would always be separate. Love was personal, and sex was business. She would never confuse the two nor would she be ashamed of having sex with him. On the other hand, she would be praised for it and knew full well that she did it to protect her country from the Islamic menace. Yes, the Deputy would be thrilled indeed. She made a new ally in the middle of Shitsville, Pakistan. The more she pleased him, the juicier the intelligence he would provide.

The shadows in the Commander's residence couldn't compete with the cumbersome flies that buzzed around the light above their table. She was close enough to his face that she could smell the halitosis on his breath. Nevertheless, the Commander made no moves whatsoever, even though his bed hid in the darkness behind her in the corner of the room. Under the half-light of the dining table, though, the Commander not only looked like a demented child, but one stricken with paralysis. In other words, Sherry would be doing all the work. She smiled knowingly, walked to his side of the table, took his hand in hers, and stood him up. He was significantly shorter than she was. She reached her hand below his waist and unbuckled his belt. His green military khakis slid down his thin legs. He wore white jockey shorts that caged in his small stiffness. She rubbed her hands over the tent of his shorts. His heavy breathing and the ongoing swelling beneath his shorts implied that he liked what she was doing.

Her fingers stretched his waistband and uncovered the creases on his skin. She slid his shorts down to his ankles. It revealed a throbbing, swollen phallus surrounded by a moist, musky tangle of black hair obstructing its direct view. She knelt below him and brushed the jungle of black hair aside. His manhood was dark brown and thin and reminded her of a pencil a school kid would have otherwise used. She then took him into her mouth. Fortunately, the next move of taking him into her throat was easy. The Commander clutched the sides of her head as she moved him in and out of her mouth. Every few moments, she circled the rim of it with her tongue. His breathing became increasingly heavier as she slipped him in and out of her mouth with swift, rapid motions. His open shirt flapped in the breeze that the fan blew on their bodies, but despite this, sweat beaded on his chest and coursed down his round belly onto her cheeks and the bridge of her nose. The faster she went, the tighter his hands gripped her head, and within a few moments, the Commander shuddered and released his heat inside of her mouth.

Like an exceptional asset, Sherry swallowed instead of spitting it out as she had done with her ex. His fluids tasted salty and reminded her of oysters she once had with her ex at Boston's Quincy Market many moons ago. After licking him clean, she wiped her lips off on his open shirt, pulled up his shorts and belt, and buckled him up. After she stood to face him, the Commander smiled sweetly and hugged her as a child would a mother. She finished what little champaign was left in her glass and quietly returned back to her barracks.

Apparently, the Commander must have cherished her actions much more than she did, as though he may have already fallen in love with her as most ugly men were prone to doing. Before falling asleep that night, Sherry knew she had him right where she wanted him. He would do whatever she wanted him to do. By dropping propitious hints, she could manipulate him. Sherry could press anything out of him, provided he behaved and was a good enough boy. In return, the horny Paki would finally get to sleep with the quintessential American Barbie and live to tell the generals about his divine experiences.

After waking the next morning, Sherry put on sweatpants cut off at the upper thighs as well as a crop-top that clung tightly to her breasts, exposing much of her lithe body. Her paramilitary team hardly got over it. They stared at her all morning. The same went for all the Commander's servants. She was the star of Shamsi. Surprisingly, the soldiers commented about her looks only in the privacy of their own barracks, and they did so in secret. They refrained from their usual loud and obnoxious catcalling. They knew full well that the more Sherry turned on the Commander, the more protection and assistance he would grant them, should anything go wrong. They didn't want to act up, appear ungrateful, or waste the Commander's graciousness just before they catapulted themselves into terrible danger across the border.

Even though Sherry prided herself on roping him in, she was also in a state of calm dread. For her, the reason was obvious. She didn't want to sleep with the Commander in the least. She didn't want to go any further than the blowjob she gave him. The prospect of sleeping with him repulsed her. It would be like having intercourse with a wild and uncontrollable macaque.

She remembered seeing a few of them with her ex-boyfriend. They restlessly climbed up and down the bars of their cage at a fundraiser they attended at the Smithsonian's National Zoo. Her boyfriend had taken her to see them many years ago. Macaques and Pakis looked alike, just like the countless iterations of King Kong and Blacks looked alike. There always had to be monkeys involved when whites doted on persons of color. Considering the course of events over millions of years of evolution, she knew human beings were all primates once, only that she didn't know what sort of primate her own white race had once been. Such information on her own origins had been censored and conveniently suppressed from prying eyes for the express propagation of the idea that whites were immune to evolution's pull and were, in fact, heaven-sent to tame and dominate the brown and black primitive beasts that had already existed on God's green Earth. They had to be tamed to prevent misbehavior and bad table manners. Her own logic led to this conclusion despite her majoring in Biology and her earlier desire to practice medicine in the best of hospitals to bring sick, primitive children back to life.

Considering that the Commander looked like a macaque, acted like one when his dick was in her mouth, and given his all-too-easy emotional attachment to her, it may have been a good idea to pretend to be on his same level, pretend to rely on him emotionally, and attend to him by just fooling around with him instead of going all the way, the whole point being that she wanted more than protection from him. She also wanted the information he withheld. So, she once again found herself much like a woman in the bush, teaching a chimp sign language, and serving him as an intimate maternal figure who would one day leave her dear macaque lonely, abandoned, and angry when the time came for her white American Superman to rescue her from the other monkeys who were jealous of her, who would attack her, and who would otherwise take their own long-lost baby macaque back their own part of the jungle where he had been born.

Naturally, the Company paid handsomely for that type of research and would promote her once her dashing white-American superman carries her kicking and screaming all the way back from Pakistan to Washington. On her way up the career ladder, she would feign love for her husband while reserving her charms for the more important Company men who look like her and make more money. She would achieve an optimal amount of happiness this way and transcend any childish idea of love that had once been given to her by just another idiot-monkey swinging from vine-to-vine miles and miles away in the Third World. Maybe the Commander was that monkey, she wasn't sure.

In her crop-top and cut-off sweats, she returned to the Commander's residence for a light breakfast. She didn't want to be judged for what she wore that morning, assuming her team judged her negatively at all, which was hardly the case. Anything and everything had to be done to get information, whether that meant killing thousands of people or fucking the Commander that day. It was a tough but necessary job no matter what anyone thought, because if someone from the Company didn't do it, an asset from another country would. It didn't try her soul.

She decided to imagine herself in the arms of a white porn star when the time came. Only then would she get through it. This porn star would leave her exhausted and satisfied. She had just fucked for a cause greater than herself and protected the greatest number of Americans from being bombed to bits by foreign terrorists. Doing her duty, no matter how dwarfish and inadequate the Commander's animalistic prowess, replaced whatever hang-ups she had about sleeping with him. She forced her eyes to sparkle when she sat down in front of him again.

The same servant placed a fruit cup in front of her, and from there, she started pretending to be attracted to him. The All-Mighty had sanctioned such an unusual bond between a macaque and a goddess from the heavens. Even Atheist

Russians were spared monkey-hood, considering how they looked like white Americans to a far greater degree. Perhaps she would one day have to pretend in front of Osama Bin Laden or whatever animal the Company now made of him. The fruit in her cup, however, tasted bland. It was handpicked from orchards in the Pakistani countryside and packaged in crates that were flown into Shamsi from Karachi. The eggs, awash in ghee, tasted good but were fattening and encouraged acne. She could have made a breakfast burrito from the eggs and the flat, brown bread that had been served with them, but she mimicked the Commander by scooping up both with her fingers and stuffing them into her mouth. No longer would she eat with utensils.

"I like the way you look this morning," said the Commander in between bites. "I really enjoyed your companionship last night. You must have enjoyed it too. It's not every day you get to be in the company of a Commander, no?"

"It was my pleasure," she said, wiping her hands off. "Now, what was it that you wanted to share with me?"

"All in good time, my sweet. You are going to learn a lot from me before you leave for Kabul."

"Oh, I see," she smiled. "Another Playboy I get to seduce. I bet you do this to all the girls. Love 'em and leave 'em, right? But I'm just not any girl. I'm sure I won't have much trouble getting what I want out of you."

"You underestimate me. It may take a long time and a lot of work."

"Not for me. It shouldn't take very long, especially when I have you right where I want you."

"Later tonight, yes, but for right now, I have plans for us."

"Pray, do tell."

"I want to take you on a little ride. I want to show you a bit of the landscape you will soon be visiting."

"Now you know I can't do anything without taking my team along with me."

"No, not by ground. By air. I want to take you by helicopter over Helmand Province. I want you to see some its spectacular terrain. This may be the same terrain you and your team may one day have to travel if you're not careful."

"Only if you have me home by midnight," she smiled.

"I never knew beautiful women like you ever had a curfew."

"I may have to be back by midnight, but I never said I had to go to sleep by then."

"Fair enough. I'll have my servant pack a basket lunch for us then. I guarantee that you will love what you see. I'll have what you've been waiting for first thing in the morning. You have my word on that."

"I know I will," she said, "because by tomorrow morning, you'll be begging for me to stay here with you instead of flying off to that cruel Kabul with all of those hungry men around me."

The runway scorched the soles of her sneakers as they walked to the A-1Z attack helicopter. By the time she boarded the helicopter with it, sweat had dripped from between her cleavage, across the oval of her navel, and onto her cotton sweatpants. Her crop-top was wet from within. She tugged it away from her to avoid exposing herself, even though the Commander liked seeing her that way. An old headset dangled from her hand. She needed it to protect her hearing in the helicopter's cockpit as well as communicate with the Commander while up in the air. Waves of blurry heat rose from the dirt-ridden runway which the Pakistanis had routinely tried to smooth over for impromptu takeoffs and landings.

The doors of the A-1Z opened from the bottom to the top like an insect's wings. After Sherry carefully climbed into the passenger's seat, lest she bang her knees on the console in the middle of the aircraft, she wrapped her warm, perspiring legs around the cyclic in front of her. It was a tight squeeze to say the least, but she saw the Commander had no problem with his position in his seat. They donned their headsets, and with a flip of a switch on the console, the liquid crystal control panels dazzled her with an array of colorful and complicated numbers and navigational designs. Once the rotor blades stirred, the Commander said that an automatic flight control system would fly them over Helmand after they were fully airborne. While she disliked spending more time alone with him, she was genuinely thrilled to be viewing Afghan territory, finally, from above. It sure beat humping through it.

The missile launchers and the gun turrets on either side of the A-1Z had been stripped of ammunition. The pilot who flew the Commander to Shamsi had unarmed the aircraft, thinking he wouldn't be flying it until he returned. Plus, the military valued the Commander too much to have him fly off by himself. Soon, the rotor blades turned at full force, and with a hoist of the cyclic, the Commander lifted the aircraft from the runway and headed north towards the Pakistan-Afghan border.

The Commander flew at low altitude so Sherry could see the vapidity of the northern desert. The A-1Z cruised at one-hundred and eighty miles per hour. Through his headset, the Commander spoke about how lonely and quiet the desert was for simple men who spent months at a time away from their wives. Sherry then placed her hand upon his thigh and gradually moved it higher the further on they flew. Filled with more confidence now that Sherry professed her willingness, he ramped up the speed and lifted the aircraft's altitude to get a better view of the sheer breadth of the Helmand River Valley, which they approached after crossing the Afghan border several miles behind them.

Having crossed Pakistan's Ros Koh Hills and moving on to the grassy plateaus and rocky slopes of the Chagai Hills of Southern Afghanistan, its numerous, jutting peaks blanketed by frozen snow, they flew above another lonely desert until miles of poppy plants in bloom sprang up in all directions, their bright-red bulbs sunning themselves in the arroyos of the hot valley. These poppy fields were untamed and would have otherwise led to the Helmand River itself where many of Afghanistan's rural folk resided, but the Commander chose not to fly over the river and instead kept their joy ride closer to the Pakistani side of the border.

Sherry could barely make out the long, slow-moving river from afar. It flowed in from Eastern Iran and ran westward towards Kandahar. The Commander had shown enough of the land for her to remark how large and lonely a place Helmand province must have been. Even though they were far from the river, they flew parallel to it. The farther west they flew, the more populated the land became. The poppy fields soon turned into empty but functioning plantations where warlords and other tribes harvested opium and sold it to Iran. The Iranians, in turn, refined this opium into heroin which they distributed to wholesalers in Europe in the hopes of addicting the masses there. The Iranians used Afghanistan's poppies to stage narco-terrorist attacks against the West.

Of course, Sherry had known this from her education at Langley. She didn't want to dwell on the geopolitical ramifications of all this but instead focused only on the Commander. She moved her hand over the bulge in his pants and messaged him.

"So, Commander," she said through her headset, "what was it you wanted to tell me?"

"How can I deny you anymore? I take it we won't have to wait until tonight?"

"No, Commander. You won't have to wait once we land. You'll feel a lot better if you told me now rather than later. You already have me, if that's what you want."

"Yes, I supposed you're right," he sighed. "I shouldn't be telling you this. It could get me killed if my superiors found out. But it's the Iranians, those damned Iranians always causing problems. Just because they think their different from everyone else, they give themselves permission to do whatever they want. Granted that your CIA drew first blood with their foolish caper against Mossadeq ages ago, but we've always been suspicious of them, and soon, in a few weeks, in fact..."

"Tell me?" said Sherry, taking his hand from his cyclic and moving it beneath her crop-top, his hands clammy upon her breasts, his moist palm circling and squeezing her soft firmness.

"I don't know if I should be telling you this," he continued, as the helicopter flew on its own, "but it's the Russians too. The Iranians are expecting a huge shipment of arms that they purchased from Russia. The Iranians plan to ship these arms to their Hezbollah counterparts in southern Lebanon and launch a full-scale attack against the Jews in the coming days..."

Even though he kept talking, it was all she needed to hear. But the more he spoke, the faster her hand rubbed over the bulge in his pants and the firmer he gripped her breasts. From beneath her shirt, the Commander subtly slid his hand down her exposed belly as though he knew what he was doing, and just when he arrived at the delightful garden to which she had promised him costly admission if he were patient and good enough boy, a deafening bang disrupted their romantic exchange.

The helicopter veered to the side and dove down towards the vacant poppy fields below. The truncated wing on the Commander's side of the A-1Z blazed hot orange as they fell at face-rippling speed. Sherry let out a piercing Aryan shrill after grabbing hold of the Commander's cyclic in her futile attempt to level the aircraft. But it was of no use. She only remembered the poppy plants and how they swayed tall and languid as the helicopter slammed its undercarriage into the field. She blacked out when they crash-landed several miles north of the Pakistani border and several miles south of the Helmand River in rural Afghanistan.

Chapter Fifteen

June 1983 – Helmand Province, Afghanistan

"No, no, you don't do it that way," said the Older Brother to his Younger Brother. "You take the *nastar* knife and score it like this, not too deeply. The *sheera* mustn't drip to the ground. Otherwise, you'll waste it."

"But I *am* cutting it right," insisted his Younger Brother, an eight-year-old child half his height.

"No, you're not," his Older Brother said in his native Pashto. "You can't attack the bulb. Tap it gently. Take the three blades and cut it vertically, until the *sheera* drips out. The milk should stay on the bulb."

Tired from tapping raw opium all afternoon, his Younger Brother couldn't listen to him after a time. He wanted only to return home to a hot meal with the family. But they had hardly finished their work on their small plantation that afternoon. In the hot sun, the two brothers had a few hours of tapping left. The *sheera*, or the raw opium milk secreted from each bulb, will have aged and formed a dark-brown resin, called the *taryak*. The two brothers would return to these same fields the next morning, collect this resin, and bring it back to their yurt not far from the edge of the field they worked on.

Naturally, this work would have broken anyone's back, but to feed their family, maintain their enterprise, and protect their string of connected yurts, the *taryak* had to be collected every other day without fail. Once scraped from the sides of the bulbs, they placed the *taryak* in plastic containers at their sides and took it to a storage tent to be packed into bricks. The family then sold these bricks of resin to refineries that processed them into morphine. The refineries finally processed the morphine into heroin, which they sold to buyers in Iran and Pakistan. The family depended on their opium harvest ever since the Soviets destroyed their irrigation systems once used for wheat and barley farming. Without water to grow their crops, they resorted to harvesting opium, since the poppies required little water to grow. The plentiful poppy fields stretched for hundreds of miles in all directions.

"No," chided the Older Brother. "You're not allowed to lick your *nastar* knife."

"Why not?" cried the Younger Brother.

"Because you are not old enough yet," he laughed, licking the *taryak* himself.

Interestingly enough, the poppies, ready to be scored, bulged alongside those bulbs that the two brothers had already tapped the previous afternoon. Both the *sheera* and the *taryak* existed side by side in the open field, which was why the older brother had been able to scrape some of this resin from nearby bulbs onto his knife and lick it clean, the effect being a joyful high like no other. At least this made the hard work much more enjoyable and offered him a just reward for his labors. His Younger Brother, however, learned the hard way, just as he had learned when he was a boy tapping the bulbs with their father watching over him.

"You can't lick it," said the Older Brother again. "Once you become my age, then you can partake in the true majesty of what we grow. Until then, you put your head down and work. Clean your knife off with water if you get any *taryak* on it."

"It's not fair!" cried his Younger Brother. "You get to eat it all the time!"

"That's because I'm older and much stronger."

"I'm just as strong as you are!"

"Besides, do you really want to be licking opium all your life, cutting these stupid bulbs and getting high off of them, licking your knife and staring off into space when you could be doing something important with your life?"

"What else is there?"

"There's a whole world out there, my brother. There are places we haven't seen yet, and I'm going to see them. I'm not staying here for the rest of my life. This I can tell you. I'm going to be a great and famous man one day."

"Keep dreaming," said the Younger Brother. "You've been licking your knife too much."

"C'mon," he laughed, scoring the next bulb. "You will one day see how great I become. Now stop wasting time. We have a ways to go before dinner."

"But I'm hungry now!"

"You've got to earn your next meal. No one will give you anything for free. We have to fight for everything we've got."

Their parents had plans for them. The two brothers would one day manage the plantation on their own, but first the father wanted his eldest son to marry a young Pashtun girl from the next *kishlak*. The Older Brother had already found this girl strikingly attractive, and she was already in love with him, even though they hadn't exchanged their wedding vows yet. But the Older Brother had other plans too. He wanted to travel the world before settling down and raising a family.

The last thing he wanted was to tap opium for the rest of his life and raise the goats, sheep, and cows that grazed on his farm. Farm life he could do without. Frankly, it bored him. He yearned for adventure.

The bride's family also ran a poppy plantation. They harvested opium soon after the Soviets destroyed their irrigation systems. Not only were the bride and groom a perfect match, but the two families had known each other through many generations and were the best of friends. They were kin, in other words. The marriage of the two love birds would thereby expand and strengthen their clan and bind close friends and allies who shared, not only the same Pashtun values, but also the same business interests. Many had already said that the Older Brother and his bride had a wonderful future ahead of them. Opium production had become the most profitable industry in Afghanistan for these once-poor farmers, ever since they could no longer grow their wheat and barley on their droughted fields.

Although there were rumors that some of the area's militant groups, like the *Taliban* and *Al-Qu'eda*, didn't approve of opium harvesting, these groups reluctantly permitted it provided the Pashtuns pay a tax for their protection against other such groups that may have muscled their way in and destroyed their fields, just like the Soviets did when they had passed through Helmand. The *Taliban*, in other words, promised to protect these Pashtun farmers and were seen as a welcome addition to an area that had been through terrible times and its fair share of violence and corruption by its country's supposed leaders. The *Taliban* protected them from local governments to whom they had little or no allegiance, and they also permitted harvesting opium despite their militant adherence to *Sha'ria* Law, which meant absolutely no drug use, no drug smuggling, and no refining of opium.

The Pashtuns hardly cared for Islamic ideology, though. Family and kinship ties, as well as the revenues gained from their opium, mattered much more than prayer or *Sha'ria* Law. Even though the Pashtuns were spread out all over the southern parts of Afghanistan, their community came first and mattered much more than any widespread Muslim *ummah* did.

To the Older Brother and his family, Afghanistan was hardly a country. It did not hold any national value. It was an area of land fertile enough to harvest opium. His family rarely consulted a map to see where they had lived before and after the Soviets moved on to destroy other parts of their territories. The Pashtuns lived as a disconnected people apart from the rest of the world, apart from any conception of country or whatever Afghanistan was called at the time.

While homeless several years ago, the family slept underneath the canvas tents of their neighbors for nearly a year before returning to their smoldering farm. They remembered the humiliating imposition of staying with their neighbors, how the destruction of their fields had haunted them, and how their own hopelessness slowly and painfully eroded like the fierce sands of the desert when they had the strength and courage to rebuild. Like their father, the two sons were equally depressed and woebegone for a few years. They spoke little and toiled hard, even during Eid, which was just another reason to sleep early without its usual fanfare and celebration. They hoped they didn't starve again or were forced into migrating with all of their belongings packed high on the Missouri mules that mysteriously populated the flat plains and the green zones of Helmand.

After the sky darkened, the two brothers returned from the fields famished for their evening meal. After a warm bath and dressing appropriately, they prayed with their family under the tent of the common yurt. The men prayed in the front with their father facing Mecca in the west, and their mother with their sisters prayed behind them facing the same direction. The Father, a thin man with sallow, pitted cheeks, wore a white turban that hid his close-cropped, tinsel-white hair. He wore a white cotton *kurta* that draped over the shoulders of his body. His bony knuckles protruded from otherwise long and thin hands. One could see that the father had not only worked hard all of his life but had suffered through his work as well.

The women that night wore green *duppurtas* with white *hijabs* wrapped loosely around their heads. They ran and managed the household. The Mother advised her girls on marriage and supervised her daughters' cooking and cleaning, while the Father ruminated over the difficulties of marrying his giddy daughters off to good Pashtun families, some of whom were already interested in them. The girls were as fetching as the bride his Older Son would soon marry.

"Father, stop staring," said his Younger Son, laughing while waiting for their food at the *thali*.

"He does that a lot," said the Older Brother. "Must be old age."

"Maybe you're right," said the Father. "I am getting old, and you two will be running the farm soon, once your mother and I go senile. All of my white hairs are because of raising the two of you."

"You're already senile," laughed the Younger Child.

"Like a desert fox, I'm senile," said the Father.

"Uncle is taking a long time," said the Older Son.

"He'll be here soon," said the Mother emerging from the tent adjoining it. "Dinner is ready. We're keeping it warm."

They patiently waited for close to an hour for the Uncle to arrive. They milled around the common yurt. After overhearing a car parking next to theirs outside, the Uncle walked through the flapping canvas entrance. He looked like he had gained some weight, which meant that he prospered for some unusual reason. The family, mystified by this change in fortune, ran up to him and embraced him, especially the Young Child who squeezed him extra hard. The Older Brother hugged him too, and the Father of the family kissed his cheek, hugged him, and welcomed him to his home.

The Mother and the daughters soon followed. The Uncle placed his hand over his heart and bowed to them in a show of the highest respect for his sister-in-law. He also bid her heartfelt *salaams*, making sure to avert his eyes from hers in a show of modesty. Once they all sat at the *thali* for dinner, their legs tucked smartly under the weight of their bodies, the women of the family served up a meal that consisted of several courses.

To celebrate the Uncle's arrival, they began the meal with *sheer khumar*, a sweet, solidified yogurt dish, colored light brown, with an assortment of dates and noodles within it, topped off with a sprinkling of saffron. *Boranee bangar* followed the first dish, fried eggplant topped off with white yogurt. The daughters kept serving the men as they finished off each dish they had placed on the *thali*. Once they finished each plate, the men stored them under the *thali*. Plates of *ashak, lavash,* and *korma kofta* filled their empty stomachs. They still had plenty of room for the main dish, *kabuli pulao,* cooked lamb and steamed rice mixed together and piled high on several large silver platters. The men ate heartily, and after the women finished serving them, they ate separately at their own *thali* apart from the men.

The men didn't talk while eating. They simply munched and pulled food from the middle of the *thali* to their respective places around it. Once they had finished and were fully satisfied, the women removed both *thalis* and the plates from underneath them for cleaning in the adjoining yurt. The men leaned on pillows at the edges of the common yurt as the daughters served them hot *chai*. The family didn't have the luxury of serving such a grand meal very often. Only because of the Uncle's impromptu visit did they prepare such an incredibly large meal. The Younger Child also settled on the side of the yurt. He sat in amazed interest, being allowed for the first time to take part in this high-level meeting among the leaders of the family. The men sipped their tea and went right to business after the whole customary affair had ended.

"What brings you here, my brother?" asked the Father. "It is unusual for you to travel all this way without much notice. Is there anything wrong?"

"I apologize for that. I didn't mean to alarm you in any way, but I had to come. Something has come up that you should be aware of right away. It demands your immediate attention."

"Good or bad?"

"Neither. It's an opportunity."

"An opportunity? For us? Oh, you shouldn't have. Opportunities are rare in these terrible times. But speak of them, if you must."

"You've been struggling here, dear brother," said the Uncle solemnly.

"And from what I can tell, you have not," laughed the Father, patting his thin stomach. "You've obviously grown more prosperous over the last year. You will retire well."

"Yes, but it's only because we have a new buyer for our product, which is why I am here. These buyers want to connect with you. They want to buy from you. They will increase your sales and output ten-fold."

"These people came to you, or did you go out looking for them?"

"They came to me, and now they are coming to you."

"Rich men from Iran? Pshaw! There aren't any rich men in Iran anymore. Nor are there any rich men left in Pakistan. Not many of them anyway."

"The buyer is not Iranian or Pakistani."

"Then where are they from?"

"They are from America. The person who contacted me is an American."

"An American?" piped up the Older Son, sitting to the right of his Father. "Wow! A real American? Here in Helmand?"

"The American contacted you, did he?" continued the Father.

"Just a few months ago. He's been buying from us regularly."

"Well, what does this American propose?"

"He wants to buy three times as much as you sell in a single month."

"Three times? Are you sure?"

"Yes, brother. At least that much. If your dealings with him go well, he promises to buy even more."

"And they contacted you? Did you ask them why they're here buying our product? What do they need it for?"

"Well, dear brother, that's the catch. That's why I'm here. I want to convince you to sell them your product."

"Of course, there's a catch. Why shouldn't there be a catch in this ravaged land of ours? There always has to be a catch. Nothing has ever come that easily to us, dear brother. There is always a catch when our own wellbeing is involved."

"The Americans are here to help us. They are friends."

"Really? We don't even know them. After all, they came to you."

"Not only do they want to increase our profit by huge margins, they also want us to help them fight the Russians and expel them from the region. They are here to save our lands. My brother, the Russians are their sworn enemies, just like we are."

"But what does that have to do with us? Let them fight them if they want to."

"They want to pay for the product, not only in cash, but in weapons. They want us to aid them in the fight. For the weapons and the cash, we trade them our opium."

"Are you out of your mind? Have you completely lost it, brother? You made a deal like that with people you don't even know?"

"Finally," interrupted his Son, "we again have a chance to fight those damned Russian bastards! Look what they did to our lands."

His excitement and enthusiasm even reached the women in the next yurt.

"You be quiet," said the Father to his headstrong Son, and then to the Uncle very calmly, "have you lost your mind, brother? You're dealing with strangers."

"We're not, dear brother."

"Who's 'we?'"

"Not only me but the rest of us across the whole of Helmand. It's time for us to stop the Russians from ruining us. It's time for us to fight, and fight we must. Otherwise, they will come back again and again."

"That's all garbage," said the Father. "Let the Americans fight them if they want to."

A common tale for the Pashtuns, and everyone else in the region for that matter, who had been lured into bloodshed by powers much greater than themselves. The Father never cared about money or living the life of a king. He only cared about being left alone.

"You obviously don't see the bigger picture," continued the Uncle. "We don't have to use all the weapons they give us either. We can sell the ones we don't use back to the Pakistanis across the border. The Americans will also supply us with cash, not only weapons. We'll make ourselves a fortune, and we can finally build fortresses where our stupid tents and mud-packed hovels now stand."

"Where are they getting this cash from?" asked the Father, standing up from the his side of the room.

The Uncle and his Son also stood as the Young Kid watched on in amazement.

"The American people, of course. Why do you ask? What does it matter?"

"What are the Americans going to do with all that opium? Did you ask them that?"

"Who the hell cares?!" said the uncle, irritated by this line of questioning. "That is not our concern."

"Of course, it is. I do care," he said, turning his back to him. "Obviously, they want to dump all of our opium somewhere. That's a lot of opium. What are they going to do with it, I wonder? They'll refine it into heroin and sell it off somewhere else. Don't think me a fool, dear brother, because you already know all this. You're not dumb. You're too smart *not* to know. You're not fooling anyone. Even my youngest here knows."

"Knows what?" asked the Kid.

"You be quiet, you," said the Father. "Let the adults in the room talk."

"I *am* an adult," cried the Kid.

His Older Brother stood next to where the Child sat and calmed him down.

"Fine, brother," said the Uncle. "They are selling the heroin back to the Russians in the hopes of addicting their army and their people. What a better way to cripple them."

"Oh, please! You trust these Americans that much? They're just going to waltz into Russia and dump all of that heroin onto the highest bidder in the middle of Red Square on November 7th?"

"Obviously not. That's not what they said."

"Then say it! They can't push that much onto the Russians when they're their own enemies. They have to make a good enterprise of it. They too have to make a profit. They'll sell it all over the world."

"Who the hell cares, is what I'm saying. Why is it so important? We get our guns and our cash, and we get even more cash selling the weapons to the Pakis. What's wrong with that? Can't you open your mind a little? See the bigger picture? We make out like bandits, and we defeat those fucking Russians at the same time. We win twice. No, three times, if you count it. Everyone wins."

"So, these Americans not only addict the guilty but also the innocent? Of course, I care where our product goes! How can you trust the very same people who addict the innocent? Maybe they'll sell it back to their own country? I mean, we'll be using American-made arms. They'll sell the heroin back to their own countrymen, right? You can't trust these people. You should never have made any dealings with them. I want nothing to do with them or this war they're fighting."

"You're assuming things."

"No, I am not. They can addict the whole world with our opium. We'll be buying American weapons. They'll sell the heroin back to their own people and many innocents around the world. How else will they raise the cash to buy the weapons? It's a sick cycle you've gotten yourself into, brother. We can't trust these people. Maybe they'll burn our lands. Maybe they have their own designs on our lands. Have you thought about that? We can't trust anyone in this war, period. Enough said. My family chooses to live in peace. We have suffered more than enough. We'll continue to sell what we have to our buyers in Iran and Pakistan. At least we know it has some medicinal value over there. At least we know who we're dealing with. At least we can trust them. With the Americans selling it, we'll be the target of every civilized society throughout the world.

"Father," said his Older Son suddenly from the edge of the room, "Uncle is right. We must prosper, and in order to prosper and defend ourselves, we must fight with the help of the Americans."

His Father, taken aback by his Son's interference, approached him next.

"Your place is on the farm. Know your place in the world, my son. I make the decisions around here. You and your brother will continue to work."

"I'm not staying here forever, Father."

"You will stay here until I say you can leave and not before!"

"I will fight," said his Older Son defiantly.

The Father moved closer to him until they stared each other eye-to-eye. The Older Son's heart raced like it had never raced before.

"We must fight," said his Son, trembling.

"What did you say?" breathed his Father.

"I said, we must fight. *I* must fight, and I am going with Uncle to fight alongside the Americans. I'm not staying here any longer than I have to. I have a life to live, and it is out there, not here."

"Say it again."

"I will fight, I said," his whole body shaking.

The father raised the back of his hand and smacked the side of his Son's face, not once, but twice. He hit him so hard that he fell back, his body hitting the floor.

"You will know your place, boy!" yelled the Father. "You hear me?!"

Summoned by the commotion, the Mother entered the tent and gasped at the sight of her Son, blood trickling from his lips.

"What's going on in here?" she asked.

"Nothing," said her Husband. "Go back to the kitchen. Mind your business and leave us be."

"Why is my son on the ground?" she asked.

"Now's not the time," said the Father. "Go back to

your work in the kitchen."

The Uncle went to help his Nephew off the floor. A welt grew on his lower cheek. The Son brushed off his garb and still would not yield.

"I'm joining the fight, Father. Finally, it's time for me to fight the Russians, since you are too much of a coward to."

The Father lost his temper and lunged at his Son, but the Uncle came between them. The Uncle pushed him to the other side of the tent and far apart from his Son.

"Stop this now!" ordered the Mother.

The daughters, hearing their Mother's voice, also ran into the tent. As the whole family stood there, the Son defiantly reaffirmed his intention to leave the farm and join fight. The Father, seething in anger, stood at the edge of the room, his breath hot and heavy.

"You will do no such thing!" he yelled. "We are a family of peace."

"I'm going, Father! You can't stop me either."

"You are not going! You'll be dead in a year. Your place is on the farm."

"Let him come with me," said the Uncle, holding his Brother back. "He can join us. We'll put him to good use."

"You keep out of this. His place is with us, not with you. He's not fighting anyone."

"You can't keep him here," said the Uncle. "What a waste of talent, tapping *sheera* all of his life. You really want this for him? He can be a *mujahideen*. You can't prevent him from doing that. He will never grow up if he stays here. He will never be a man. He'll be an ingrate farmer. He'll be a nobody. A nothing."

"Yes, just like you and me, and our father, and our grandfathers, and our great-grandfathers before them."

"He can be so much more, but you're turning him into a retard."

"Shut up!" yelled the Father. "My son is not going anywhere."

"I can make my own decisions," said the Son on the other side of the tent.

"You leave with him, and you are not allowed back here."

"Don't be so stubborn," said the Uncle. "He is your son. Your firstborn. He deserves a chance to better himself."

"You will no longer call me 'brother' either. Maybe not in your family, but my family has suffered enough. I'm not letting my own flesh and blood fight in a war that will never end. I don't care how much profit we make from those damned Americans. They're probably worse than the Russians."

"I'm sorry, but that's not your decision to make," said the Uncle.

They both looked to the Older Son. They could do no more but wait for his answer. It dawned upon the Father that his Brother intended much more than to make a profit. His Oldest stared back at them. His decision wasn't a hard one. He always wanted to fight, ever since childhood. And now he was a man, as though he had grown up right in front of his family that evening.

"I'm going," he said quite suddenly. "I'm going with Uncle."

With his Father's anger unabated, the Older Son couldn't help but hear his Younger eight-year-old Brother shout, "I'm going too! I'm going too!" leaping from the edge of the room and running to him.

"See what you've done," said the Father quietly, his voice breaking.

The Mother caught hold of her youngest son.

"Let go of me!" struggled the Young Boy.

The Father held his head in his hands, trying not to weep in anger and frustration, his usual sympathetic response. His Older Son then left the yurt with his Uncle.

When the Son marched outside with him under a red setting sun, its pink light stretching its rosy fingers endlessly above the rocky land, they headed towards an old, beat-up GMC pickup truck next to the family's connected yurts. It stood next to the family's beat-up car as a reminder of years of intense warfare, its wheels without hubcaps, its body beaten but strong enough to protect a group of militants inside of it and withstand the many crashes and collisions it would repeatedly endure. An armed, fifty-caliber rifle sat on the truck's back bed ready to be fired against any Russian tank or jeep that it came across. On the desert roads of the Middle East and on the dirt roads along the poppy fields of Helmand, the GMC truck and its metal-jacketed rifle had become the cheap, agile, and effective weapon of choice. The militants who used them now included the Father's Older Son. He climbed into the back of the truck with the gleaming, American-made rifle next to him. The gun swiveled after he inadvertently bumped into it.

The Father, however, gave it one last shot. He ran out of the yurt with his Wife in tow. The Younger Brother followed them, even though she held him back again as soon as he ran for the truck.

"I forbid you!" yelled the Father. "Leave now, and you

are never to come back here again, the both of you. Do you hear me?"

"I must go, Father! Don't you understand?"

"You leave now, and you will never set foot on this farm again!" And then to the Uncle, he said, "and because you are sentencing my son to death, you are never to call me your brother again. You hear me?"

The Uncle started up the truck, and said, "fine. Your son will be protected by his new family. He is doing God's work. You needn't worry about that, since God's work is all you've ever been interested in. One day you will realize what a hero he is to the cause."

"Never come back here again!" yelled the Father.

"Please, my son," called the Mother, weeping. "Listen to your Father. Think about what you're doing."

The Uncle put the truck in gear and slowly pulled away. As he did so, the Younger Brother broke from his Mother's arms and chased the truck as it picked up speed and tore down the dirt trail that cut through the fields of the plantation.

"I'm fighting too!" he cried with his hand stretched towards his Brother on the truck. "Take me too! I'm old enough! I'm a man too! I'm coming with you…"

The Young Child tripped over a rock and fell to the ground as the truck sped away and headed south. They had to drive two hours in the night to get to the Uncle's farm. The Child rolled in the dirt as the truck drove onwards, his small, brown body a dot in the distance, and his Older Brother already bereft of the welcome nuisance his Younger Brother had always been.

Chapter Sixteen

December 2000 – Helmand Province, Afghanistan

The side of her face rested on the loins of her ex-boyfriend one early morning, the patch of his hair as coarse and as rough as sandpaper. Her head rested on the flaccid bird beneath her cheek as his belly rose and fell and branches of yellow sunlight stretched over them. All seemed right with the world. The placement of her head at that exact spot guaranteed her tuition for medical school and an engagement to the love of her life. She would never have to worry about anything else ever again. The part where her head rested mattered as much as his heart, said her ex-boyfriend to her on a number of occasions, until of course, he said his heart really didn't matter at all at that stage of their romance. She prized his heart, though, and had always tried to break into it by resting her head there, his soft member an extension of his heart, a muscle flexing, its heat and perspiration comingling with the side of her face, the fragile eaglet growing stronger as she brushed her soft cheek against it.

They may have been on a secluded beach overseas they had visited or on their yacht anchored offshore in a blue sea, sand stuck to their bodies, the eaglet rising and pointing to the sun. But suddenly, there was something uncomfortable that intruded on their interlude. While his patch of hair was still as rough as before, the eaglet had gone missing. Maybe someone had kidnapped it, she wasn't sure. Without the eaglet there, however, her sense of security and potential access to his heart grew futile. No longer did she rest on his loins. The side of her face pressed upon something entirely different. It felt almost like damp hay or a doormat made of twine upon which acrid boots that had just trekked through a swamp had been placed or a pile of wet leaves after a thunderstorm. Something had gone horribly wrong with the dream of her ex, and she longed for the dream to return.

She struggled to open her eyes into which sweat dripped and stung, the side of her face bumping against the meat of someone else's shoulder. She craned her neck and saw the back of his head, his curly, black hair, his sweating muscles moving to the beat of his steady gait, and the crabgrass tangle of growth on his back, a body odor so strong that she needed to pull her neck away just to avoid it.

"What the fuck?" she mumbled drowsily.

She gathered her strength and looked over the stranger's shoulder. This strange man walked on a rocky trail between two rubble-strewn hills through a narrow and rugged canyon. Unbeknownst to her, this stranger had slung her on his back with a wide strip of cotton cloth supporting her bottom, her body piggy-backing his, her body bumping against his back, and her arms swinging at her sides.

"What the fuck?!" she yelled suddenly.

The stranger, however, didn't respond. He kept walking on the trail at a steady pace, a walking stick tapping the dirt as though he didn't hear her at all.

"What the hell is this?" she asked.

Someone had pushed her off the ledge of her dream into the hole of a nightmare.

"Who the hell are you?" she yelled again.

Her drowsiness and the slack of her body gradually receded.

She yelled, "what the hell is this? Where the hell are we? Who are you? Where is the Commander?" and a number of questions that elicited no response at all. Then, she tried yelling in his ear, for twenty straight minutes as she rode his back. She even taunted him, not by any interrogation method she learned at Langley, but because she felt like it.

"Do you know who I am?" she yelled. "Hey, you! Yeah, you. Hey, Mohammed, or whoever you are, I'm talking to you! Put me the fuck down! I don't think you know who you're dealing with. Put me down, or I'll put your dirty Arab ass away for a long time. We have places for people like you!"

After yelling at him for what seemed like an eternity, she noticed, though, that this stranger had cleverly plugged both of his ears with beeswax. He couldn't hear her at all. His *poostin* coat and lambskin hat kept him warm in the cold as her exposed body shivered on his back. She also saw a green canvas sling of a grenade launcher, most likely an RPG-7, hanging over his shoulder. And then she figured it out. This stranger who now carried her had shot down the helicopter she and the Commander had flown on their romantic getaway that afternoon. It also meant that he had emptied the RPG-7's steel tube of its booster and destructive warhead.

"Where's the Commander?" she asked desperately.

She tried yelling in his ear again and even shrieked so loudly that it could have raised all the hair on the man's arms. She taunted him again with epithets such as towelhead, sand-nigger, terrorist, Haji, and the like, but still no response from whom seemed like a very dangerous man. Who knew if he carried another warhead on his body for another attack. It was too difficult to tell. She then readied herself, gathered all of her strength, and with a force she never knew she had, she bit down hard on the stranger's exposed back. She bit him and didn't let go, but the man merely grunted a few times, dropped his emptied RPG-7 to the ground and used his hand on the opposite side of him to swat her head away, and when that didn't work, physically unhooked her clenched jaws from his back. Sherry couldn't bite down forever, and when she paused, he punched her in the head. Her head swung back in pain, but at least she had bitten off some of his flesh, his wound now bleeding. But the stranger only grunted, as though her bite was only a minor inconvenience, as though he were impervious to pain. Blood streamed down his back and colored her cheek that rested against it. He hit her so hard, that her vision blurred. Perhaps he gave her a slight concussion, she wasn't sure.

"Take that, you piece of Arab of shit! If you don't put me down, I'll do it again!"

He tore off a piece of his cotton garb from the lower end of his body, balled it up, and stanched the flowing wound on his back. It also provided a protective barrier between Sherry's ferocious jaws. Since the man hardly responded to the attack, Sherry forwent biting the other side of his neck. It would have made little difference. With her body still hoisted upon his and supported by a tight sling under her buttocks, they traveled through a gorge that grew progressively deeper between two heightening mountains, its high peaks covered with ice and snow. She wouldn't be getting any answers out of him, especially with his ears plugged.

She didn't fear this man, though. He may have killed the Commander, but he spared her life, maybe because of her status as an American and the chance that her team would come searching for her. Neither did she know why he had the nerve to shoot her helicopter down in the first place. It worried her most, however, that she couldn't feel her body from the neck down. She may have been paralyzed, or at the very least, so badly injured that she couldn't feel the rest of her body in any way for the time being. The arms at her sides felt like rubber bands. The blood on his back bled through the cotton cloth over which he stanched the wound. After an hour of walking, the blood on his back congealed and clotted. After the wound scabbed, dried blood stuck to the side of Sherry's face. She was helpless dangling on his back. Only he had control of where they were going.

The mountains gradually receded, and their march through the gorge ended. Night soon covered them and shrouded them in darkness until the stranger took out a flashlight with a strong beam that lit their way before the mountains eroded into manageable hills. They walked on a flat plain for a spell. At its conclusion, they entered a lush forest replete with larch, aspen, and juniper trees. They followed a well-worn trail through its dense forest. The trail meandered below the trees, the forest emitting new oxygen that her near-desiccated body readily absorbed. Renewed energy returned, but her body was still numb. It relieved her that they at least walked on a route that many had taken before. While she could hardly make out the beauty of the trees surrounding her, she rested a little easier knowing that they headed to a clear destination instead of being lost.

It grew much colder as well. She hoped he would offer her a blanket or a coat. He carried much more equipment on his body than the grenade launcher. The clinks and clanks of his equipment rhythmically sounded off in the silence. She considered that this stranger had already prepared for such an event with the exception of finding a blonde woman with a crop-top and cut-off shorts at the crash site. She guessed she was still in Pashtun territory. Naturally for her, just when she needed a compass, she didn't have one.

In the time she had, she tried to make sense of it, but why the man shot down the helicopter made no sense at all. Neither did she know why the stranger didn't do away with her. It made no sense, for instance, why a Pashtun would want to take down a Pakistani helicopter when the Pashtuns and the Pakistanis were allies, albeit uneasy ones. These questions turned in her head, the side of her face plastered to the cloth that staunched the wound on his back.

Sherry had the urge to urinate. She held it in, hoping that he'd stop soon. Miraculously, the stranger sensed that she had to go. It may have been her body pressed so close to his, or perhaps he had an empathetic second sense, just like her mother. Oddly, the stranger's sensitivity to her swollen bladder and subtle shaking may have alerted him to it. Perhaps he had a thin skin to match. He may have taken things too personally, like disrespect and insults. No wonder his ears were plugged.

She had learned at McClean that when the British colonized the Middle East, they had often thought of the Arabs as effeminate. The Arabs became bellicose soon after World War II, when the British could no longer sustain its colonies, and the Palestinians fought the British and then the Jews who remained in the same territory. At present, though, the Arabs had the reputation as nutcases and zealots hell-bent on blowing themselves up to be with their seventy-two virgins in heaven. To male freaks and oddballs, this, perhaps, was not a bad way to go, as they couldn't possibly get laid down on earth, unless they paid through the nose for it, of course. But disability didn't pay very much back home, and there were no entitlement programs in the Arab world, she believed.

For a woman, though, it seemed utterly ridiculous for the

Arabs to conceive of a heaven this way. She knew the virgins scenario to be propaganda that fed the ignorant American mindset, but considering the threat of terrorism ever since the creation of the State of Israel, the Arab reputation for savagery wasn't hyperbole. Furthermore, the way the Company spoon-fed the terrorist-Arab caricature through endless news cycles on television and radio indicated that terrorism may have been too difficult to defeat. Ever since Munich, terrorism scared Westerners senseless, mostly because it worked. A defense that worked demanded a negative stereotype just to justify Congressional funding, defense contracts, and the clearing of land and property for oil pipelines and stronger Israeli defenses.

Apart from her mind drifting, the stranger's flashlight revealed an opening in the forest that served as a makeshift campsite for travelers on that route. Sherry silently rejoiced. The stranger stopped and dropped all of his equipment. He then moved the cotton sling above her buttocks to the small of her back. He pulled down her sweats from behind him. She shivered now, because her backside was fully exposed to the cold. Slowly, the stranger backed into the forest until the leaves brushed against her back. Sherry took this as her cue to let loose. Much of her urine wound up on the man's clothing, but he didn't seem too concerned about this. It seemed he had done this type of thing before.

She finished, and the man returned the cotton sling to its proper place, left her sweats behind, and headed back to the center of the campsite. He pointed his flashlight to a long log that someone had cut from a Juniper tree. It lay on the ground for travelers to sit on. He seated himself on the log with Sherry's legs wrapped around his waist. Carefully, he untied the string from his front. Just when the sling slackened loose, he extended his arms behind him as far as they could go and caught her before her body fell back. He seated her on the log and slid his hairy back down between her legs. She gasped, thinking that she'd fall back, but by the time he was sitting on the ground with his back to her, she rested on the log with his hands holding her up from behind his body. He then disconnected himself from her. In the nick of time, the man turned around from where he sat and caught her forearms, thereby preventing her from falling backwards to the ground. He kneeled in the wet ground in front her. The lack of adequate lighting gave the man only an outline of what most men would have died, or killed, to see, as her body was fully exposed below her breasts.

She again gasped, now that he held her in place. She still couldn't see him, though, because the flashlight on the ground beamed in another direction. Now that he faced her, his hands slid from her forearms to her wrists. The man stood, tucked one of his arms underneath her knees, and with his free arm around her back, he skillfully carried her to the middle of the campground, much like a knight carrying a distressed queen over a puddle. He lay her on the cold, wet ground. And then it became obvious what he was about to do to her. His intentions were as cold as the dew that now soaked her back.

The man ran his flashlight up and down her body. He didn't touch her as of yet, but Sherry knew what he wanted. When the light finally hit her face and blinded her to the man who seemed much like a doctor examining her on an operating table, she again screamed as loudly as she could. She screamed until her voice grew hoarse. The stranger let her scream. No one could hear her. The forest offered deaf ears and offered no help. She prepared for what would come next. He placed his hands on her bare legs and massaged them slowly, squeezing them, possibly to determine how firm and toned her muscles were. He liked women's legs.

"Don't you dare, you mother fucker," she said, remembering now to utilize her fluency in Pashto as her last defense. She had been speaking English all along. "Don't you touch me, you disgusting Arab pig! Can't get a woman on your own, eh? Well, bring it on, asshole, and then you can kill me, because there is no way I'm living with the shame of a dirty, smelly Arab fucking me."

After examining her legs, the man placed the spotlight on the ground, and from its angle, Sherry saw him remove the beeswax from his ears. Finally, he could hear her. She screamed again, until she lost her voice near-completely. She demanded that he kill her rather than violate her body, but the man stayed silent. Soon, however, she found herself begging him with tears in her eyes, begging him to kill her. She wanted his God to descend from the heavens, slit his throat and cut off his balls for what he was about to do. His family would be cursed for a thousand years, and Sherry's offspring with this man would be none other than the child of *Iblis* bathed in blood, setting the world on fire, sentencing them both to the lowest plane of Hell for an eternity, unless he curbed his urges and stopped touching her legs.

The man was below human, and she a tight hole, a plaything, a sex toy, a doll that he would force himself onto, straining to penetrate her with all of his might. He was as ugly as they came – a leprous, lecherous loser, a freak, a circus geek, the type with a cut off nose and ears eating the heads off of chickens, a black sand-nigger freak, the kind no one on earth would ever fuck or could ever love, not even for a moment. Nor would she ever agree to a drink at a bar with him, have coffee with him at the local diner, or take a ride home from work with during a thunderstorm. He wasn't worth the time, because this man was as pitiful as they came, lower than life, not even valuable enough to spit on, but hideous in his features, black of heart, a repulsion of life, straining with every last muscle and breath to claw his way to the surface of the living. He had made it his mission in life, from the day of his own consciousness to the night when the caretaker buries him in the soil, to chase her through the annals of time until finally catching up with her just after the chauffer drops her off at her ex's townhouse, and from a dark, wet alleyway, he springs upon her, grabs hold of her shoulders, and wrestles her to the pavement to do what he had always wanted to do. The stranger would stop at nothing to get what every freak roaming the earth had wanted – a piece of her without consent, the plundering of what little innocence was left of a white American beauty queen, violating her, sentencing her to the hollow existence of wandering amongst the ghosts of those who have forever been shamed, she disempowered, forever corrupted, made unwholesome, like fresh milk turned sour, her body dirty, diseased, and ultimately, decaying.

"It's funny," she laughed sardonically in his native Pashto, "once my team finds you, they'll put a bullet through your thick, Arab skull. They will hunt you down, you and your family, and they will avenge my death by slaughtering the lot of you. So, go ahead and get it over with, you dumb fuck."

The man then stopped massaging her legs and walked over to the log to rest on it. He cleared his throat and said in his native Pashto, "it's such a shame that a woman so fair has such as sick mind. Many of you will be coming into Afghanistan, I take it. I suppose Americans haven't changed one bit ever since they left."

"What do you mean?" she asked bewilderedly. "What did you do to me? Why is my body numb? Why can't I feel anything?"

"Because both of your legs are broken. I shot your

helicopter down from the sky. And when I found that your legs couldn't stand on their own, I pumped as much morphine into your veins as a cow's. Too bad it didn't numb your brain as well. Your vitriol still remains. Your body will be numb for quite some time, unless, of course, you want to feel the pain of having two broken legs."

"Why did you shoot us down in the first place? We weren't doing anything wrong."

"In Afghanistan, no one knows who people are anymore. We are in a constant state of war. You could have been anyone. You could have been a rival warlord spraying our fields to kill off our poppies. Maybe you were the ISI flying in to take our children, deliver them to orphanages in the Northwest Frontier, and training them to inflict terror on my family. Who knows who you are? You look, sound, and talk like an American, but maybe you're a Russian agent? The pilot who flew in with you, the Pakistani soldier, he died in the crash. You, however, survived."

"You took pity on me?"

"Not really, no. I couldn't give a damn about you. I once liked Americans, but now I don't. I want to know why an American, such as yourself, is here in Helmand, and if there are any more of you on the way. I can't imagine what for. The people of this land have already suffered enough. Most of the land is mined. I can't imagine why you came back here. Either you need to build more pipelines or exploit us to fight more of your enemies. I really don't know. That's why I saved you instead of killing you. Trust me, it wasn't an easy decision."

Relieved, Sherry cleared her head of all of the fearful images she had of him.

"I need a blanket or a coat or something. I'm freezing.

I don't know how much more of this cold I can handle. One minute we're in the desert heat, and the next we're in the cold."

The stranger sifted through his sack which he kept at the side of his waist. He unfurled a blanket made of lamb's wool. He spread it over her mostly naked body. He took off his shirt, folded it, and placed it under her head.

"I should have done that sooner. I will make a fire now."

He disappeared into the bushes. She heard him breaking off branches for kindling. He returned with an arm's full of it, gathered it in a pile on the ground, and cast a flame underneath it. Thick smoke blew in her direction at first, but after a few minutes it blew upwards and away from her. He had been used to building fires, living outdoors, and traveling the countryside. He traveled the forests and the green zone, where thick trees, long vines, crops, and tangled vegetation grew in the wild. He traveled through swampy terraces, rice fields, rivers, ridges, and valleys. He crossed bridges, looked out on observation points, and hid in harsh canyons. He traversed dams and watched out for Soviet brigades from the high peaks of ice-capped mountains. Hailing from Helmand, this stranger also spared her life. Still, she didn't think it reasonable enough to have shot down her helicopter. A high-ranking Pakistani Commander had been killed, and naturally, the Americans would take the brunt of the anger and mistrust from the Pakistanis.

Fortunately, she still remembered the intelligence the Commander had slipped her: an arms deal from Russia to Iran with those arms would then be funneled to Hezbollah in Southern Lebanon. She had to inform either Langley or the Station Chief in Karachi right away. Out in the wilderness, though, there were no phones. She would have to wait until the Pashtun stranger took her to one. She had no idea where they were. She didn't have a compass, a map of the terrain, or a gun for protection. Instead, she looked like a dancer at a strip club on break.

Too bad she was way out in Afghanistan and not in the arms of the type of man who needed her, the type of man who deserved to be with her – the honest man, the nice guy, the quiet one, the introvert, the pilgrim, the kind one, the sweet one, the man who always watches her and sees her crossing a city street and is angry and irritated that she reminds him of a beauty he can never capture for himself. It never stops. It's ingrained in his head, woven into the flesh of his brain, flowing within the bulging vessels that strangulate his grey matter until they tear and patiently yearn for the hand of God to cauterize its ruptures. He is unable to separate himself from her image. She is planted within him, merged within his consciousness. He could escape to anywhere in the world, yet she'd still be there. He could hate her for an eternity, and it would do no good. Day in, day out, the torture consumes him no matter what stunts he pulls to get as far away from her as possible. Without any remedy, he wastes his life walking in circles with her body on his brain, laughing to himself at what his life has become because of her.

The stranger, however, didn't see Sherry in the same light. She knew this full well. He cared neither for her looks nor her body. Her beauty had no use where they were. He needed to know if there'd be more Americans coming. If Americans were coming, it would make the bloody civil war even bloodier. The Americans would once again arm them, exploit their poverty and enmity of each other, let them do the dirty work of getting maimed, butchered, and blown up, and then fly off into the great blue yonder after dropping their bombs and then taking their own children to Disneyland when they got home and other such corporately-sponsored destinations that would ultimately dictate their lives, assuming they made it back home at all.

When the Soviets left, radicals from the Arab world remained in Afghanistan. The Pashtuns were overwhelmed by them. Even though they had once fought side-by-side, those who flooded in from abroad treated the Afghan natives as *kaffirs* – farmhands, retards, and idiots who lacked an Arab's genetic superiorities, lavish traditions, and glorious empires. The Pashtuns had bird legs, wrinkled brown skin burned by the sun, dirt-poor yurts to live in, just like their Pakistani brethren south of the border. Yet these Arabs conveniently forgot how many Soviets the people of Afghanistan killed and how many of them had suffered. The stranger had killed many after he left his own farm against his father's wishes and trained with the ISI and the Company's paramilitary commandos. He had joined the *mujahideen*.

That was almost twenty years ago. Now as an older man, war had exhausted him and yet would forever outlast him. He wanted nothing to do with war but still had a toe in it. His father may have been right after all. A hothead no more, The Pashtun stranger wanted to live as his father and his family once did, before he ran for the Pakistani border in his Uncle's *ahu* and joined the freedom fighters.

The fire he made warmed her body. The heat penetrated her wet skin, eased the circulation of her blood, and reddened her cheeks. After several minutes of having her feet close to the fire, she felt whole again, even though she couldn't wholly feel the gift of the fire's restoration. Her body, still numbed by the morphine, felt better.

"When does this stuff wear off?" she asked.

"Not for a while," he said. "You need medical attention.

We can't stay out here for long."

"I need to return to Pakistan, to Shamsi Air Force Base. Have you heard of it?"

"I've heard of it, but I've never been there before. It's far from here. You'll need a car."

"And you don't drive? Where are you taking me exactly?"

"I'm taking you to my farm. From there, I can transport you to a hospital. Possibly to Lahore or Karachi."

"I'd rather go to Shamsi."

"Not in your condition."

"From there I can be flown in."

"I see."

"Or they can fly me in from your farm."

"Sounds like a plan, but first I need to know why you are here in Helmand."

"I'm with the US State Department. We were on our way to Kabul to meet with company officials who are building a pipeline through the country."

"Why is it always oil with you people? Is it really that important?"

"It heats our homes, fuels our vehicles. We can't do anything without it."

"Oil is the curse of the Arabs. Have you ever heard that one before?"

"Many times. It's true. But oil, to us, is a necessarily evil."

"Much like war, I suppose."

"Why do you say that? I still believe in peace, and yet

we still have people attacking us."

"And they attack you just to attack you, eh?"

"I'm not that naïve."

"Why were you flying in a helicopter with a Pakistani soldier dressed in what you're wearing? Doesn't seem like an official US State Department visit to me."

"He wanted to show me the countryside. We didn't mean any harm."

"You were in an attack helicopter flying over my poppy fields. You could have destroyed them like the Soviets did."

"An assumption made on your part."

"I'm not wrong to assume things. Now the Pakistanis will send more people looking for him and for you. We'll have an international incident on our hands. You've entered a civil war. Now's not the time for a diplomatic visit."

"Still, it will take time before they start searching. The sooner I get to a phone, the better."

"Why don't I believe that you are here to visit oil executives in Kabul? Maybe you plan to infiltrate Afghanistan from the south. Maybe you want to get involved in the strife, plunder our resources, enslave our people like the Russians did. Why even bother with our people?"

"I told you. I am here on a diplomatic mission. I'm meeting with a group of oil executives and a few government officials in Kabul. That's all. What are you going to do? Torture me until I confess something that isn't true? You'll just have to trust me."

"I can kill you and get one step ahead of the Americans who are on their way here now."

"Do that, and they'll bring an army in here to find me.

Get me to a phone, and I'll be airlifted to a hospital nearby, to Lahore or Karachi, just as you said. The choice is yours."

He paused for a few moments and kicked the fire to give it more life.

"You're right," he said, finally. "It's better that I get you to a phone. I don't want my lands to become a battlefield. Once the Arabs hear there is an Americans from the State Department here, they'll send all of their fighters within range."

"Why would your farm become a battlefield?"

"Plenty of people would like to do away with an American State Department official."

"Like whom?"

"A number of armed groups that can't stand anything about you. If they get word you're here, they'll come to kill you. Najibullah's men? Ali Mazari's people? They would love to find someone like you out here. You're lucky a local Pashtun found you."

"Are you an enemy or a friend?"

"Neither. I believe your story, and I believe you will do no harm here, provided I get you back to your people before they come looking for you."

"How do you know I am telling you the truth?"

"Because I used to work with Americans years ago, but I'm no longer so sure you are the same people you once were. There are many here who believe you have turned rotten."

"Like whom?"

"Plenty of people."

"Like whom? What groups?"

"*Al-Queda*, for one."

"Yes. They're trouble for us. Do you know where they are? Do you know where Osama Bin Laden is?"

"They'd kill me if I knew, and besides, I don't know anyway nor do I care to know."

"How about the Iranians?"

"There are many Pashtuns who fled to Iran, but many of them have returned with Iranian help. They want a piece of this land too."

"And the Russians?"

"Still licking their wounds. I have not heard of any Russian activity in the area."

Something distracted him then. It must have been a distant memory, as his thoughts seemed to drift elsewhere. He sighed heavily and took out a small brass pipe from his sack of equipment. He stuffed the pipe's bowl with a dark brown powder and smoked it. It relaxed him. It smoothed the edges of their conversation as he began to trust her more. He then waxed philosophical for a time as Sherry followed along and tried not to fall asleep. The morphine kept her in a perpetual state of drowsiness, but she tried hard to listen to his words. He seemed like a natural born historian and had a keen interest in other worldly philosophies. These genuinely interested her, which was why she strained to stay awake.

"I went with a group of Bin Laden's men to blow up the Salang Highway. Have you heard of it? It's the main road that connects Afghanistan with Russia. We used Buffalo guns to raid Wreshman Gorge on the highway between Kabul and Jalalabad. We blew up bridges to obstruct the advancements of the Russian armored divisions. The Americans had armed us, and I worked with Bin Laden's men at the time. Apparently, circumstances between the Americans and Bin Laden have changed, or that's what I've heard."

"Are you still allied with Bin Laden's men?"

"I stopped fighting after the Russian's left. They've left all of us to starve. My family perished, all except my younger brother. When I returned to the farm, my parents and all of my sisters had been executed. I now run a plantation with my younger brother. Ever since then, my brother and I vowed never to have families of our own. It's just too risky to raise our own children here. Instead, we take in the children whose bodies have been maimed by the landmines scattered all over countryside."

"When do you think all of this will all end?"

"You mean war?"

"Yes."

"Never. War never ends."

"I'd have to disagree with that."

"The *Taliban* now protects us from other armed groups. We are in a state of constant anarchy. There is no law and order here."

"At least you have the *Taliban*."

"They protect us, but we are not friends because we like each other, if you know what I mean. My brother, myself, and the children are easy targets here. We need *The Taliban* to protect us. The ISI, The Muslim Brotherhood, Hekmatyar, and *Al-Queda* all want a piece of our land. It's as bloody as it gets."

As the Pashtun stared into the fire, Sherry fell asleep for a little while, but then popped awake a little while later. Still dark out, the man now ate from a small tin of food. He ate with his hands. These were dinner rations left over from the Soviet war given to the Pashtuns by the Pakistani army. She was very hungry but had little idea how she'd eat with a paralyzed body and had even less of an idea how to ask him for food.

"How do I get some food around here," she asked, half-jokingly.

"You'd like some food?"

"Yes."

"When was the last time you ate?"

"Yesterday morning."

"Well, you did take a big chunk out of my neck, but you could use some more food. We'll have to remedy that."

He fished out another tin of rations from his sack and peeled the top open with his finger. Sherry eyed him suspiciously but accepted that he would have to shovel whatever food he had into her mouth by hand. But she no longer feared him and no longer thought of him as so dirty. In fact, she found him quite polite, pleasant, and somewhat sophisticated. She felt sorry for calling him all those names and made a mental note to apologize to him. Maybe she did have a sick mind like most Company assets inevitably did. The sickness developed over years of playing the endless game of outwitting enemies, games of whom could out-sicken whom in order to defeat the other. While she didn't fully trust the stranger yet, she had no problem holding her mouth open for his food.

By the light of the fire, he walked over to where she lay and sat beside her. The tin contained white rice with lentils in a pool of clear yellow liquid. *Dhal*, it was called, Sherry remembered. Nervous without the use of utensils, she opened her mouth. The Pashtun expertly gathered the wet, sticky rice with his fingers and shoveled it in her mouth. She gulped it down readily, like an infant in a highchair, and opened her mouth for more. The Pashtun even wiped her lips off when some of the liquid ran down the sides of her mouth. Because she hadn't eaten for some time, she cherished the taste of the meal, regardless of its simplicity.

"This is what most of us eat," explained the Pashtun, slipping another load of rice into her mouth.

"A simple meal," she said, chewing.

"You think so? Any food is a luxury around here. These tin rations are left from when the Pakistanis trained us. I've stored crates of them at the plantation. It's survival food for when we have to fight again."

"You're no longer the type to fight again, are you?"

"Never again. I stay clear of that garbage. Stare at it too long, and it will drive even the strongest mind mad."

"How can you avoid it, though?" she said, accepting more of his rice and *dhal*.

"I try not to pay attention to it. That's half the battle. Ignorance is bliss, they say. And suddenly you show up, and I know there's trouble coming."

"I'm with the State Department, remember? I'm a diplomat."

"Flying around half-naked with a Pakistani commander? I can't imagine what will happen next."

"I'm sorry," she said.

"For what? I'm the one who broke your legs."

"I'm sorry for what may come, if anything comes."

"Well, thank you for that, but I'm used to it. We trade our opium until we're dragged in. We don't go looking for it. I was an idiot fool when I was younger. A real hothead. I always wanted to fight. What a dope I was. Everyone already knows that no one wins a war. Convenient how we forget that right before we start fighting it. But there's no alternative. There will always be war. Just ask Sayyid Qutb and his protégé, Osama Bin Laden."

"Wait," she said, energized by this. "You know Sayyid Qutb?"

"Who doesn't? Why do you think Bin Laden and his men are now fighting the Americans overseas? It's because he studied Sayyid Qutb in that pathetic university of his. It filled his mind with craziness."

"Terrorism is crazy. All they want to do is blow themselves up for martyrdom."

"You really would think that, wouldn't you?"

"What do you mean?"

"Americans have the wrong idea about terrorism. I'm surprised your State Department hasn't taught you better."

"I don't understand."

"Terrorism is a political strategy. The people who carry it out aren't necessarily madmen. The reasons for using terrorism are mad, but terrorism as a strategy in war isn't mad at all. You shouldn't buy that martyrdom crap."

"But you believe in martyrdom. You consider Qutb one of the great Islamic martyrs of all time."

"Yes, but the use of terror itself accomplishes more than shipping radicals up to heaven. You know that right?"

"Hey," she said, "I was taught to fight against terrorism. Don't think for a moment there's anything rational about terrorism."

"You see, in a civil war such as ours, there is no government. No one is in charge. There is no central command structure. People have always had to rely on their own culture or community. People fostered group cohesion for their own welfare. Terrorist groups can accomplish great things. They can take down the strongest of armies. Just ask the Russians. No one needs large armies to wage war anymore."

"There's strength in numbers, though."

"Not really. A small number of terrorists can accomplish greater things."

"Nothing great about it."

"You know what I mean. Terrorism is terrible, but it can defeat armies and scare civilizations to death. To terrorists, America is seen as an imperialist oppressor."

"Israel too."

"Which is just another extension of the United States."

"But these terrorists hate the Jews."

"Naturally. They hate anything that goes against Islam, doesn't matter if they are from the North Pole, South America, or Mongolia. Qutb hated the British, and so Bin Laden hates America and Israel."

"All I know is that these are very dangerous people who hate other people. They're disturbed."

"Not so. In fact, terrorists are supported by all foreign governments. A small group can rarely fund itself. No one knows what countries are really behind terrorist attacks."

"Like the Russians."

"Maybe. We don't know."

Sherry knew better, though, given the intelligence the Commander had given her before he perished. Connect the dots, and Russia would soon instigate the next string of attacks against the Israelis. Karachi Station had to be informed. She had a long way to go before she got there.

"There are benefits for the group," continued the Pashtun. "Whoever claims responsibility gets their name shown on every news channel in the world and printed in every newspaper. Fear rises. It invites more members to join the cause. They are famous all over the world with their sympathizers and enemies alike."

"They attract all the crazies."

"You talk to these people, and they'll sound as normal as you and I. They are not mentally disturbed at all. See, you in the West merge the good and evil elements of your mind. Good Terrorists make sure to keep them distinct and separate."

"What's that got anything to do with it?"

"Because the Prophet knew the difference between right and wrong, good and bad. Westerners know the difference, but they shrug their shoulders when they sin. Muslims and by a greater degree, terrorists, do not. It matters a lot, because it makes the Muslim more determined to succeed. Westerners already know they are sinners. For Muslims, it's a battle they must win all the time to keep themselves holy."

"So why keep these elements separate? That's no way to live a life. We all sin. You kill just as we do. Even worse. What Muslims do is dishonorable. You kill innocent people."

"The people who are part of these terrorist groups have been orphaned by prior wars all of their lives. Their parents have been killed in war. One parent dies, and the other parent starves. The children have to watch it as it happens. The terrorist, or any good Muslim for that matter, will never blend right and wrong, the good and the bad. There is no justice in a boy watching his mother die or starve to death. In fact, we have a saying amongst our people, 'he who never knows hunger in his life cannot understand the cries of hunger.' Neither are these terrorists cowards for killing innocent people. Just like a soldier takes the life of an enemy soldier with his gun on the battlefield, so the terrorist takes lives on the global stage of battle, just not directly as a fighter would do on a battlefield. You are all enemy soldiers to them, guilty or innocent."

"Still doesn't make it right. All Muslims are savages. Fanatics to the core. Heathens."

"Terrorism is much more intelligent than plain savagery, fanaticism, or evil. Terrorism is the most powerful groupthink on earth. It's an example of the collective mind at work. For instance, people in the group can sense when someone disagrees. When that happens, they cut out his heart and show it to everyone in the group so that everyone stays in line. The group is a success if it goes on until everyone in the group dies. That is the end goal, not killing or destroying the enemy. Terrorism is much more practical than that. It's a brotherhood, much like Islam is supposed to be. Muslims crave brotherhood."

"Unity. Just like the *Qu'ran* says."

"But the smaller the terrorist group, the more productive it is."

"So how do we stop these people?"

"I have no idea. Terrorism will always be here. It will never go away. It is effective. It is proven. It is impossible to stop. Like anything else that is impossible to stop, it can only be managed. If one group fails, another takes its place. Simple as that."

"So, another Bin Laden will rise up?"

"The difference between the average terrorist group and Bin Laden is that Bin Laden actually believes in his cause. The princes of Saudi Arabia want him dead, and the Iranians want him to be their next Supreme Leader. His men are probably the only terrorists in the Middle East who actually do believe. The *Taliban* also believes. Most other groups just want what the West already has. But Bin Laden, he wants an Islam just like in the days of the Prophet, and he'll stop at nothing to get it. Then you ask what we Pashtuns want? Nothing of the sort. We want our farms, our women, our children, our food, our livestock, and our lives. Nothing more."

"I guess the Saudis don't make things any easier. They come to us for all the things they can't get. Sex, cocaine, Ferraris, luxury hotels. They have none of these things in Saudi Arabia. They only give their citizens Islam."

"That's because of the *ulema*. Many, many terrorists, though, want what the Arab princes have. They want what the West has. But Bin Laden and his crew want Islam back to its purest form to root out these political elites, such as the House of Saud. That way, the corruption of the elite is exposed. The Saudi elites love their cars, their gambling, their jewels, and their white American prostitutes. As for most terrorists, they want the same, but in order to get it, they just want to move one step ahead. One move forward. They don't want virgins in paradise and all that bullshit. Only dumb Americans would believe all of that propaganda from their own government."

"So, Bin Laden is the only fanatic in town, is that what you're saying? Interesting. He's a true believer amongst terrorists who don't believe?"

"It is the difference between *ijtihad* and *jahilyyah*. *Ijtihad* is what most terrorists have. They have independent analysis and reasoning. Most terrorists do have *jahilyyah* as well, which is the state of ignorance of God. They are smart, but they are Godless. Bin Laden and the *Taliban* have one but not the other. They have analysis and reasoning, *and* they have full knowledge of God. That's why they're such a threat. They have a community that survives and thrives on political Islam as though there is no difference between politics and religion. They have *ijtihad* without *jahilyyah*, two weapons that will defeat anything in their way."

"You haven't told me how to stop them."

"Out-analyze and out-reason them. You may do that. But you're never going to out-God them. Remember, you blend light and dark. Bin Laden keeps it separate."

The stranger, tired of their conversation, drew another blanket from his sack and spread it on the ground on the other side of the fire. He lay down and gazed up at the thick forest canopy that shielded them from the stars.

"We leave at dawn," he said. "We still have a few hours walk before we get to the plantation. Once there, we need to get you to a phone."

Her body still numbed by the morphine and her belly full of *dhal*, Sherry dozed off.

Sharp spikes of intense sunlight broke through the canopy and bathed her in warmth the next morning. Even though the morning's light brought relief from the cold, it also brought great pain. Her broken legs, now awake from the dwindling effects of the morphine, forced her to cry out, thereby awakening the Pashtun stranger who slept on the other side of the smoldering fire. He sprang to life, rummaged through his sack of equipment, and pulled out a syringe filled with clear liquid. He injected the morphine into both legs. Within moments, her pains went away, and her legs were numb as before. She no longer cried out.

"We need to get you to a hospital as soon as possible," he said. "Fairly soon, the marrow in your bones will find its way into your bloodstream. You'll be dead in a couple of days."

"Where's the nearest hospital?" she asked.

"I would say Lahore."

"How about the nearest phone?"

"We'll have to drive you to a phone as soon as we get to my farm. The phone is near the border, just north of Pakistan."

As long as the morphine kept her pain in check, Sherry knew she would get to the hospital in time with the help of this Pashtun stranger. But whether she died no longer mattered as much as it did before. Afghanistan became this horrible nightmare where everything had gone wrong. The morphine soothed her to such a degree that she lost the hard will to survive. She had never felt a pain so acute before. It was much like a tortuous crescendo that opens to an incredible symphony leading her out of the horrors of living. Aside from her legs' soaking up the morphine, the stranger brought out his pipe again and pressed its brass end to her lips, which she readily sucked on. Having done this, the struggle to live lifted. She was on a plane to the eternal everlasting soon enough, to the joy and bliss of all creation. It hit her in waves. The blissful energy came on so strong that she wept with gratitude for the God who undoubtedly saved her life. When the stranger looked down upon her, she smiled up at him like a gleeful child.

"Don't get too used to it," he said plainly. "If we don't get you to a hospital, you may die before nightfall."

"If this is how I have to go, then I'm all in," she said, smiling. "The universe is so whole and complete. It's a vision of pure beauty. I'm floating on clouds of beauty."

"I bet you are," said the Pashtun.

It took him some trouble, but he wrapped the blanket

tighter around her body and again hoisted her on his back. The wound at his neck had dried. Sherry remembered biting him when she saw it in her line of vision.

"Sorry about biting you," she said.

"Trust me. I've been through much worse."

"I can do it again, if you like?" she laughed.

"This is no time for jokes."

Soon, they were on their way again. Out of the dark forest, they entered a wide, sun-drenched field full of blossoming poppy plants, many of their green stems limp with swollen buds.

"So, this is where you work every day, eh?" said Sherry. "Not too bad, if you ask me. At least you don't follow Bin Laden. At least you have sense enough not to get involved with that menace. You would lose all of this."

"What makes you think that? Maybe I'm really with Bin Laden, and I'm taking care of you to extract more information from you. Morphine and heroin are effective for that kind of thing."

"You wouldn't dare," smiled Sherry, wagging her finger. "C'mon, you and I? We're almost best friends. 'Best friends forever,' as they say in the US!"

"You know nothing about me."

"You believe in God, don't you?"

"Yes, I do. Why do you ask?"

"I dunno. I guess I'm wondering why Bin Laden has so much sway over the people who follow him. He's a cult leader, really."

"Like your Julius Caesar."

"Caesar? You mean, like the Roman Julius Caesar?"

"Yes, Julius Caesar. Don't you all worship him where you live?"

"Worship Julius Caesar? Of course not. A great man he was. He was the Emperor of Rome."

"Only God was the Emperor of Rome."

"No. Caesar was the Emperor of Rome."

"I have to disagree with you," said the Pashtun, clearing their way through the poppy plants with his walking stick.

"What are you getting at?"

"Let me explain something to you, and this will give you some insight into Bin Laden. You see, man can never rule over man. Only God can rule over man. If a man rules over man, that man is usurping that which is an attribute of God. This violates the oneness of God. Don't you say in your country, it's either Jesus or Caesar?"

"Not really, but please go on. I'm curious."

"Jesus is not the same as Caesar. God is not the same as the state. What the state has is God's. To leave something to the state is to take it away from the oneness of God. Bin Laden believes that there will never be a political leader here in Afghanistan or anywhere else in the world. We are all a people ruled by one God, and the laws have already been written in the *Qu'ran*. If one submits to a leader, then one is submitting to multiple Gods. That is paganism, not monotheism."

"You think you're smart, don't you? Well, in my country, nobody serves anybody. There is no king or ruler. We elect people who represent us. There is no way to make laws and legislate them when three-hundred and eighty million people are in charge at once. So, we elect leaders who represent the people, organize our society, and create just laws that protect us as a nation *and* as individuals. The state is not a deity. The state is an apparatus that serves its people. So, put that in your pipe and smoke it, my brown Pashtun friend."

"But that's not how it really works, is it? What about the temptations of greed, money, and the lust for power? And if people rule the state, aren't these people playing God over the state? In Islam, there is no difference between the state and its people or faith over the state. It is simply one people, under one book, under one God, whose Messenger is Muhammad."

"And if you don't believe that, you should have your head cut off, right? In my country, people defer their authority to the state. The state and the people are one. The one and the many are really the same thing. From many, one."

"In Islam, there is no few and many. There is just one indivisible God, and because there is no authority but one God, one must resist submission to the state and defy any existing secular political authority. In order to do that, a man must act and not merely invent theories, constitutions, and philosophies. That is the essence of what Sayyid Qutb thought. That is now what Bin Laden thinks. There can be no discussion or diplomacy. Only action."

"Ha! So, you are a follower of Sayyid Qutb after all!"

"I said nothing of the sort. I'm just telling you what Qutb wrote. See, if people have sovereignty over the state, then people are playing God over the state. It's either the people who control the state, or faith in God that controls the state. According to Qutb, it is simply all one people, under one book, under one God, whose Messenger was the Prophet Muhammad."

"Says him."

"Says Bin Laden too."

With Sherry hoisted on his back, the Pashtun continued to meander through the tall poppy plants on the resplendent field that tumbled ahead of them for several miles. She didn't notice how long the journey had been, considering the influences of the morphine and the heroin. Her high spirits made the discussion of Qutb easier to learn and process, especially while feeling the urge to spread her arms and brush her hands over the tops of the reddening poppy petals, thanking them for her newfound bliss after the initial tumult of acute pain. No wonder people tolerated living in such a place. Nevertheless, her arms were just as numb and useless as before. Even though she could not lift her arms, she still felt them spread like wings all on their own while slumped over the stranger's back. It was a triumph of the imagination over the corporeal. He senses flew skyward on an otherwise mundane trek. She didn't care whether the conversation continued, but she forced herself to listen. No matter how exuberant her outlook, her instincts as an asset still clung to this stranger's knowledge of Qutb. She hoped to find the answer to defeating Bin Laden, because when she finally returned to DC, she would be the shining star of the Company with all the awards and accolades that came with it.

"Christianity and Judaism are both parts of Islam," said the Pashtun. "It is all the same plan for humanity. Testimony for God's faith itself is the *action* a man makes to align himself with God's plans, rules, and laws. The return of mankind to God is a revolutionary project. It is a wide-ranging political project. It is all encompassing. This is what Qutb says."

"We do have choices," retorted Sherry. "A person, man or woman, doesn't have to submit to authority. We don't all have to follow the same laws. There are different laws for many different people. Islam is just not practical – "

" - but the claim that man alone has the right – "

" - and women – "

" – that *man* alone has the right to create his own values and legislate rules and dictate the terms of collective behavior is, in fact, a rebellion against God, because it presupposes that this authority rests with mankind and not with God. Because man has relied on himself to create all of these things, the result has been the oppression and misery of all of his creatures."

"The *madrassas* are teaching you this? They also teach you how to make bombs to kill the Jews and all of that shit."

"Judaism is just one part of the procession. So is Christianity. According to Qutb, there must first be a complete takeover. Once everything is taken over, then those who remain will be led to God. All that man has created so far is a rebellion against God's sovereignty on Earth. Reasoning is man-made. Reason makes some men Lords over others. Truly, if we all believe that there is no deity except God, all rulers, kings, presidents, and princes in any place and in any age will find this a direct threat to their power, which is why they will always try to suppress God. Remember when Jesus says, 'render to Caesar the things that are Caesar's and to God the things that are God's?' Well, Jesus was not the perfection. Jesus was part of a procession of prophets. He was holy for his time. But it was Muhammad who put all of the prophets together and brought the message from God that there is no deity but God, and that no man or group of men rules this earth. Men should do only what is set down in the *Qu'ran*."

"But Jesus allowed mankind to love, to find peace, to be individuals. Islam doesn't do that. Islam is a communist dictatorship. Everyone has to be the same, follow the same book, pray in the same way."

"In Christianity, God is many but also one. Even

mankind's own reasoning has contradicted mankind's own reasoning. How can many be one? Remember, there can only be one God here, not many Gods."

"We're all different people, though."

"Which is why Qutb thought that everything and everyone must be conquered first, a complete takeover. Then, we are led back to God. One God rules all, not many Gods ruling many individuals in many different ways."

"You know nothing outside of Islam, do you? You have no idea how liberating America is. A person can worship anything he or she wants in America. It is a right of being a citizen."

"Which is why, according to Qutb, the Western world is Godless. Qutbian Islam has God, but it is also totalitarian. I'll give you that. But he says, *"where legislative power and sovereignty belong to human beings, there is a kind of slavery of people to other people. But in Islam, and only Islam, all people are liberated from such slavery and serve the Creator alone."*

"It's only a kind of slavery if you look at it like that."

"It *is* slavery, according to Qutb. Your president can put you in jail if he wants to, even if the reasons are dubious. That is a kind of slavery, no?"

"We have a court system."

"Search your heart and tell me if your word would weigh more than your President's. Islam and the West both want freedom from tyranny, but you choose man-made democracy, while we choose Sharia Law, which is something that God has made."

"Hey, whatever floats your boat."

" – because *jahilyyah* cannot be compromised with in

this day and age, and because it cannot be fought in theoretical terms or in terms of reason, the ignorance of God can only be fought against through action. It must be conquered through *jihad*, or *jihad bin saif* – striving through fighting. *Jihad* is the only reaction that can ever come from *jahilyyah*. The obstacles that put men in the servitude of other men must be removed by force and force alone. There is no preaching left to be done. There is no one left who can be persuaded anymore. Only force alone can do this, says Qutb.

"And once those who rule are removed by force, *then* the people will be free to make up their minds. When that time comes, they can either accept Islam or reject Islam with a clear and open mind.

"In Qutbian Islam, *jihad* is always on the offensive. It is never a defense. Its aim is to free all men from the oppression of others, to free all men who are forced to serve other men. Qutb, then, is a liberator, and if Qutb is a liberator, so is Bin Laden. Bin Laden wants to liberate Americans, while your Presidents, Senators, and Judges are slave owners and slave merchants oppressing their own citizens. Not only Muslims but all men have the right and the duty to take action and annihilate these man-made systems of government."

"There is no slavery in America," said Sherry. "We fought a civil war over that. Ask anyone. Arabs were once slave traders themselves. We have freedom of choice. We have the right to weigh our options. We don't have a single book that tells us what God wants."

"What you have is all man-made. It is not the work of God. You have made a rebellion against God, and in order to break the chain of those you have oppressed due to your rebellion against God and the slavery you have put your own people in, Bin Laden is now fighting for you. Ironic, isn't it? As Qutb says, "any system in which its final decisions are referred to human beings defies human beings by designating others than God as Lords over men."

"So, once we lay all of our governments to waste, all of our human methods of reasoning, all of our human-made laws to where where people are able to serve only one God and not other men, then all the people will finally be free to choose whatever religion they want?" said Sherry. "You must be fucking kidding me?"

"I think you're beginning to understand," said the Pashtun. "You see, Bin Laden has no problem with Judaism and Christianity. He does have a problem with secular governments and theoretical, political, and economic laws created by human beings that make people slaves to other men."

"Many will die," she said, gazing into the blue sky and waxing philosophical, just like the Pashtun. "Wow. I have come into contact with the insane. Bin Laden is trying to take over the world, so that we can all be free?"

"For freedom from slavery, wouldn't you want to fight?"

"It's all how you look at it, my brown, Pashtun friend. But we will always have to serve somebody in this world. Yes, we are obedient, but we Americans still find life worth living than dying over. We create our own laws to be free, happy, and alive. Too bad you don't see that. We're not slaves in the least."

"When Islam stives for peace, this is not a shallow peace that requires only some of the people or the greatest number of people, or even just the followers of Islam. The peace that Qutbian Islam promises is one religion, or the laws of society, purified by God. Society's obedience is reserved for God alone, not by some men who are Lords over others, like in an American democracy, no matter how much happiness and freedom are dispensed by those Lords. Even in Islam, there is no compulsion in religion. No one is ever forced to change their values or beliefs. Rather, it is through Islam that the chains of man's servitude are broken, so that men can finally have the freedom to choose how to worship God and how to live their own lives."

"Saved by Zero."

"First, purity of the entire world. Second, the people will be free to choose where they want to go. In order to purify the world of all its corrupt toxins, many will have to die. Bin Laden's fight against the West's rebellion against God will not be easy. I ask you, then, what would a purified world look like to you?"

"I have no idea," she said, her mind in orbit. "I guess it would be something like being a totally blind person seeing for the very first time."

"War, says Qutb, is the only practical solution. Writing books, creating theories, and using our own reasoning doesn't contribute at all to the freedom Qutb wants. War, then, is eternal for Qutb as well as Bin Laden. War may rest, but it never ends until the point of complete purification. So, for most people living, it will be that way until God takes us. But while you in the West fight for gold and status, Bin Laden fights to free others from obedience to other men. By committing acts of terror, he at least begs the question – which cause is the greater cause? His or yours?"

"But if we serve under the same God, then why are we fighting each other and not fighting together?"

"Because you follow human beings and not God. Bin Laden hopes to save American citizens from their own perverse government, the people in charge, and those respected officials who enslave you. He's the one who is trying to free you. He's fighting your government, and yes, innocent people will have to die, so that those who live can be free. Otherwise, absolutely no one can be free. At least their children have a chance to be."

"Oil, territory, money," pondered Sherry. "Fast cars, easy sex, high-pillared mansions. Bin Laden wants to bring us back where we really belong. The fucking Stone Age! Don't get me wrong, though. He does want everyone to be free. But give me a fucking break! Regressing us back to caveman status is not the way to go. I understand, though. Plenty of people want to be monks. Bin Laden is more of a warrior than a monk. He's a monk with a bomb strapped to his chest. We'd have to fight *Al-Queda* until we kill every last one of them."

"Because you can't stop Bin Laden without taking action against him, killing him is the only way out. It's the only way to stop him, even if you have to torture him first. He won't stop until he's dead. His followers believe the same. As far as war is concerned, it is an eternal fight. First Bin Laden, and then the next one, and the then next one, until the next one takes his place. It doesn't end."

"That's the harshest idea I've heard yet," she said more seriously.

"It is harsh. It is baffling and ridiculous as well. That's what you, as an American, are up against. Bin Laden says that the enemies of those who undertake *jihad bin saif* want to change the struggle into an economic, political, or racial one to confuse the true nature of the struggle. Democracy is really a man-made imperialistic attempt to destroy God. Just as the British colonized Egypt during Qutb's time, so the Americans are colonizing Arabia, the Crusades all over again, as a rebellion against God. So, until the world is finally pure, the cycle of war and peace continues. Peace is only a rest from war. Peace is merely temporary. War will always last until the point of liberation. Then comes peace on Earth."

"Once the Earth is purified. Our side has forgotten God, in other words."

"Wrong. You are trying to take over God and put man in God's place. Bin Laden believes that he will free you from the corrupt rulers who are causing you to fight him and his followers, these same rulers who are forcing you to rebel against God. The goal in Qutbian Islam, then, is one God, one land, and one people, but before that happens, the earth needs to be totally stripped of its corrupted rulers. I wish you good luck in stopping him, because you will have to kill him and every one of his followers to save your own country as you know it. As he sees things, America has the most corrupted men in government that the world has ever known before."

They remained silent for some time after that, the profundity of his words hanging in abeyance above the poppy plants surrounding them. It echoed in her ears as the sun's heat intensified on her face and shoulders.

"Mmmm, the sun feels good," said Sherry, as they waded in another large field of poppies overlooking the family's plantation that magically appeared in the near distance.

Although the plants stretched for acres in all directions, she spotted a set of interconnected yurts fixed to the middle of a flat field. These yurts were surrounded by dirt trails running around the Pashtun's farm. Plumes of smoke rose from a couple of these yurts, and as they approached, Sherry caught sight of another space of flat land behind the property where a hundred or so tents stored what looked to be a couple hundred families with children tossing frisbees around and small groups of them kicking soccer balls, much like how kids play on sunny days in any given American park. As they approached, though, her view widened, and what she at first thought of as a pacific, idyllic playground of running children and their cheerful parents supervising them soon discovered a makeshift refugee camp where half-naked children ran about and their elderly grandparents sat listlessly warming tea in tin pots and smoked tobacco from foil pipes. These children, most of them filthy and caked in mud, ambled over the flattened landscape with crutches, their bodies severed of arms and legs, a few of them with only one appendage dangling from their shoulders and waists. They clung to their crutches while trying to free themselves from them at the same time, like boisterous cubs trying to chew themselves out of their steel traps but unable to do so, as though their missing body parts would miraculously regenerate from the nubs of their shoulders and knees, these parts blown off by the thousands of scattered landmines that had been dug into the countryside like ankle-deep, surgical lacerations in the soil forever reminding them of the ongoing bloodletting.

"This is my home," announced the Pashtun proudly, his arm extending in front of him like a magician finishing off his show.

Even though Sherry couldn't see his face, she knew he must have smiled at the sight of his home and the memory of the many people he housed and fed there. The ghastly sight of the maimed orphans and their atrophied guardians, however, astonished her. They had nowhere else to go and waited for their savior to free them from their misery. The same Pakistani outhouse scent wafted through the air and tickled her otherwise perfumed olfactory senses, and she confirmed the plantation to be a place of intense suffering where this Pashtun and his chosen people barely had anything to eat and barely got by, no matter how many acres of poppies they owned. They could have had heroin by the truckloads stashed there, and it still wouldn't have made the slightest bit of difference. His family was still as disenfranchised now as they were when the Soviets burned their wheat and barley fields twenty years earlier. From the beatitudes of the fields to the pestilence of the camp, the joy of her journey ended abruptly when she spotted a neon orange frisbee embossed with the UNOCAL logo thrown amongst several of the crippled children as they splashed their bare feet in glistening puddles of sewage. Luckily, the refugees considered the oil company to be on their side rather than allied with the despicable old Soviets.

She didn't want to insult him by exposing how the conditions at the camp disgusted her. She had flown at the height of ecstasy only to tumble now into the bone-crushing pit of despair. She had looked forward to a soothing bath in a tub full of hot water and poppy petals but instead confronted the smell of human decay, the slow and steady kind that insects bite away at only to impregnate newborn bowels with their larvae. No wonder assets do themselves in early, she thought. She looked upon the shithole of his world and thought that there was absolutely no God in what she witnessed. Those she had sworn to protect back home were the biggest, whining bunch of pink, pansied, spoiled, filthy-rich, yuppified scumbags she had ever known.

It wasn't so much anger at the sight of the camp than the deep-seeded resentment of the ignorant, pompous, and condescending snobberies and luxuries of the glittering world she had been cast out of that brought her to the brink of her own unique madness. Sympathy non-existent and empathy nowhere to be found, she had the queer premonition that she would never return to the country to which she had once sworn allegiance. The camp absconded her heralded past. This was not what she signed up for. The morphine and the heroin were better substitutes, but the high was wearing thin. It was a hard smack to the face that returned her to the Company and the mission at hand.

The Pashtun was proud of his shithole when it could have been so much more. He could have made them work for that food instead of having them sit there with their grubby hands out for their lentils and rice that they ate with the same hands they wiped their asses with. Make them work for it, because that will free them from their own natural misery. They can then build their own housing made of bricks that they themselves bake. They will assemble the wood for their dormitory bunks all on their own, and when they are finished scraping the raw opium from the plants in the fields, they will still have enough strength before lights out to stitch their own uniforms and emblazon them with gold badges that will forever define them as proud refugees from the camp of long ago, because they must never, ever forget, or else history will repeat itself if they do.

But in the meantime, they will construct their new and improved camp out of nothing, and the Pashtun himself with run it. He will accept help from the hierarchy of worldly powers that provide for their gruel and the extra comfortable pillows on which he shall sleep at night, until the time comes to blame all the world's problems on the refugees. The Pashtun must then ration his supply of gruel, and with the help of these same worldly powers, he erects fences of barbed wire around their cluster of brick dormitories. He forces them to take showers together to make them clean and fresh and more worldly, like the powers that put him in charge. They need to be more presentable and look more human, because the world declares them even more vile than they really are, until, of course, they equate them with simple insects and corrosive parasites who thrive on the backs of the hard-working family as well as their corporate overlords who employ them, these same corporations that provide meat for their children, provide for their schools, and heat their homes in wintertime.

The refugees hoard whatever they can scrounge to save their community and the camp they built together. They hoard to save whatever food they are given and whatever traditions remain. At last, they look upon their dormitories with pride and smile at their children who amble to and fro within the encampment. Altogether, they are ushered once more into the common showers. The Pashtun throws the switch. And they are never allowed to leave again.

Sherry regained her composure. Soon, the field dipped, and the Pahstun's yurt obstructed the view of the children, the appalling sight of them, stumbling and limping legless and armless, their eyes bright and cheery, as every child still has a childhood, she figured.

As new immigrants, they learn to get along, gather in ghettos, and try to integrate, to assimilate, to love their neighbors, but remember their fallen forefathers all the same. They love their new homeland, read their holy books, share their knowledge, take care of the sick, sometimes build hospitals, cherish peace but fight hard in war, become notorious gangsters, dentists, film moguls, and financiers. They defend the unjustly incarcerated, teach incorrigible thugs in crumbling city schools, join struggles for social justice, play the violin, dance in the face of tragedy, try to run away from themselves until the same footfalls of the same old history come around again, the same grainy documentaries of their time at the camp, the same visions of their old, dirty, grubby, starving children being jabbed in the ribs with sharper bayonets that force them to work again, to clean themselves up again, to stop their hoarding again. As a result, they shunt their own intelligence to prevent this from happening. And so, as citizens of the new empire they carry these same bayonets to arrest another nightmare. Everyone gets it, thought Sherry. No one is spared. Not even these sorry children. Soon they will become what their enemies once were.

The sight of them and her own visions notwithstanding, the Pashtun carried Sherry to his own yurt where he unhitched her from his back and lay her on his bed with the blanket still covering her body. Angry and bitter but still numbed of pain, she lay there and heard the Pashtun stranger summon another person to the room. It was the Pashtun's younger brother.

He looked much younger than he did. He was very handsome but hot-headed and inexperienced as most younger brothers tended to be. Built more modernly than the Pashtun, his garb draped over his sturdy body more appropriately, his disposition more domesticated than his elder brother who worked mostly in the fields. Sherry encountered how shocked the younger brother became when he saw her lying there. Then came his fiery anger as he scolded his older brother in his native Pashto.

"Are you fucking nuts?! What were you doing out there? You were supposed to be surveying the land, and you bring home this? They'll kill us for sure. We're as good as dead. You brought suffering to our home. You brought destruction to our home. First, the Russians, and now the Americans? Did you have to do it, brother? We have to kill her. We should kill her here and now. Just wait here. I'll get my gun."

"You aren't going anywhere," said the Pashtun sternly. "Get a hold of yourself. We're not killing anyone."

"Have you lost your mind? They are already coming for her, friend and foe alike. I know you like to turn the other cheek every once in a while, but this is fucking ridiculous. Your head is not on straight."

"I didn't do anything wrong, brother. I shot a helicopter out of the sky that flew over our fields. It could have been anyone. This woman is all who lived. You see, she's here on a diplomatic mission. That's all. She means no harm."

"She's an American, you idiot! They were born to do harm. Look at her. She's a menace just by the way she looks. We have to get her out of here. More will come looking for her. Arab militants too. I say we do away with her and bury her out back before it's too late."

"Will you shut up for a second, please? Try to understand how this will work."

"We cannot trust this woman!"

"Just shut up and let me explain. Sit down on the bed next to her, and she will listen too. Isn't that right?"

"Yes," said Sherry, trembling.

"All we are doing is getting this woman to a phone near the border. Say Chaha Burjal. From there, she will be picked up and taken to a hospital in Lohore or Karachi. No one knows where she is right now. Settle that imagination of yours, my brother. All of your thinking has your head full of hot air. Focus on we're doing, and don't think so far ahead of yourself."

"Fuck you! It's mind over matter!"

"Before I slap you hard," said the Pashtun angrily, "just listen."

The younger brother shut his mouth and held in his anger. His face red with rage, he tightened his lips to avoid his older brother's discipline.

"Good," said the Pashtun. "We carry her to the truck,

take her to the phone in Chaha Burjal under the blanket so that no one will see her. We'll make a stop at Uncle's place. And then, at sunset, we'll depart again from there. Better to travel at night, so we're not spotted. At Chaha Burjal, she'll call her friends to pick her up. And that's it."

"And that's it, huh?"

"Yes, easy as cake."

"If you say so," said the younger brother incredulously.

"Just accept it, brother. You are not as experienced as I. You are hyper-intelligent, beautiful, and with a mind of a *djinn*, but you haven't lived as long as I have. The old are always right, and you are always wrong. Understood?"

"Fine, but I object."

"Noted. So, let's do this the right away." And then to Sherry, "are you hungry or thirsty? Because it's about an hour before we reach my Uncle's, and a few hours before we reach a phone."

"I'm fine," she said, relieved. "We might as well get going."

The older brother took her legs, and his younger brother carried her under the shoulders. They brought her back to an old Toyota flatbed truck and lifted her in. A slight hump in the middle of the flatbed marked where a rifle had once been bolted. They covered her with a second blanket. The sky had dimmed since she last saw it. Then, everything went pitch black after they covered her face, her nose and cheeks itching under the rough wool. And then she heard another round of arguing near the back of the truck.

"Go back inside with the others," she overheard the older brother saying. "Someone has to watch the plantation.

By the time I get back, our hands will be washed of all this, we'll sit down to a nice meal, and forget this ever happened."

"It doesn't work that way," said the younger brother.

"I'll be back before dinner. Go in and get the sisters started. Don't start eating until I get back."

"Is this a game to you?" asked the younger brother.

"I don't know what you mean."

"You're about to get your head blown off."

"Settle down, okay? I'll be back before you know it."

"Not this time, brother. I'm coming with you."

"No, you are not. You are seeing to the plantation and the children. That's where you are needed."

"I'm needed, because the entire region is looking for this woman!"

"I think I can handle this on my own, thanks. And she's not just any woman. She's a US diplomat. She's on a mission of peace. Get your head straight."

"I'm coming with you!"

"The hell you are! Get back in there and make dinner!"

"Gentlemen!" said Sherry from underneath the blanket. "We need all the protection we can get. We don't know who's out there."

"There you go," said the younger brother. "The American actually makes sense."

"I said get back in there!"

"We need him," said Sherry a second time.

"Would you stay out of this, please!" And then to his

younger brother, "you really don't need to do this. I can make it by myself. I can move faster that way."

"You'll need another gun. You'll be ambushed out there. Don't you realize that?"

"Brother, don't make the same mistake I made. Do you really want to fight everyone and everything for the rest of your life? Do you want war to never end? Are you prepared to take someone's life and never be able to repay that person bac? Or his wife and children? Think about it. Fighting doesn't make you a man, my brother. You are already a man. You are responsible. You care for the people on the farm. You run the plantation. You are much more of a man than I will ever be. And it's too dangerous out there. Much too dangerous."

"Then why are you going it alone?"

"Good point," said Sherry, her voice muffled under the blanket.

"Stubborn you are," said the Pashtun, but after thinking about it, he said, "fine. Go to the storage and get our Enfield's. Those are all we should need. I didn't think we'd need you, but the American makes sense. Might as well listen to her."

She heard the brother's feet scamper out of range. She muttered a few choice insults for the Pashtun's younger brother for wanting to kill her, but now that that was resolved and her journey to a phone near-certain, she relaxed a little. She liked the older Pashtun just then. He took her advice. He accepted her analysis. She reasoned her way into protecting the three of them. Her self-esteem returned to where it belonged. The black ops mission would continue, and the intelligence she had gained from the Commander trumped everything else. More important than locating terrorists, she rose to the height of protecting an entire country, Israel, both ally and friend, from a Hezbollah attack.

They wouldn't merely give her a pat on the back for this. Accolades awaited her. A promotion and a grade up in pay. Chief of Station anywhere in the world. In crisis, there is opportunity, she once read in a book about a famous American. Knee-deep in crisis, the opportunity presented itself. She won for a change.

She then heard them return. They jumped into the truck without much conversation and drove away from the plantation. As they drove, her back hurt from the rapidity of the bumps, dips, and ascents in the road. Her body slid in the back from side-to-side, even over where the machine gun had once been bolted. The pain in her legs slowly returned, and she craved another shot of morphine. But they were well on their way, and she wouldn't be heard amidst the junkyard melody of loose vehicle parts, rocks spitting from behind the truck, and the whines of a tinny *ghazal* at high treble squawking out the front windows.

As the minutes passed, so did her anxiety. She measured minutes in upticks of pain that came more frequently. Piercing pain soon shot through her lower legs, and soon her body was alive again and attuned to the real medical condition of having two broken legs and the marrow slowly emptying into her bloodstream. The brothers couldn't see her winces underneath the blanket. She knew they were short for time. Neither could they hear her screams. The truck's engine and the tires on the dirt road were louder. It made no difference anyway. She endured, until, of course, to her relief, the truck slowed and came to a standstill at a turnoff in the road. They were in the middle of nowhere.

The two brothers tumbled out of the cab and cursed in their native Pashto.

"Here they come!" said the older Pashtun.

"We're totally fucked," said his younger brother

"Get in the truck and head back to the plantation," he ordered. "I can at least negotiate a release."

"What negotiation? They're coming right at us. They're sending the biggest trucks I've ever seen."

"Get back in the truck and return to the plantation. I can save us both if I negotiate with them. At least we have the American, and we have taken good care of her."

"Please help me," cried Sherry from the back. "More morphine! Please!"

"Shit," muttered the Pashtun. "Get in the truck and head back. Take the American with you. There's no time to delay."

"Please!" she called again. "I can't stand it any longer! I need a shot!"

"Give her a shot just to shut her up!" barked the younger brother. "Hurry up!"

Another round of scampering feet, and within moments, the Pashtun uncovered her. He held a syringe in his hand. He stuck the needle deeply into both legs.

"Try not to scream," he stammered.

He again covered her, and with the injections a slow warmth fanned up the broken lower half of her body.

"Oh, thank God," she sighed.

"Get the guns out!" she heard the older brother say to the younger brother.

"What's happening?!" she demanded to know.

Then came the cracks from the shots fired from their

Enfield's. In between the shots, she heard the two brothers pull the bolts of their rifles to load in the next ones. Their rifles were old as sin, as they fired against what sounded like rapid-fire AK-47s. American voices drew closer and broke her dalliance with the Pashto language. Odd languages yelled back and forth, barking and commanding, cursing and ordering. It soon slowed to a calm silence. She then made out American soldiers chatting amongst themselves. Everything beyond the truck slowed to a tenuous calm.

Within minutes the blanket was stripped from her body, and she faced the Black member of her paramilitary team looking down upon her menacingly.

"Fucking bitch," he said, and he quickly covered her up again.

"Hey, wait a second," she yelled through the blanket. "Get back here! You are still under my command! And I mean get the fuck back here right now!"

"Get her out of the truck," she heard the Black soldier say.

They ferried her from the back of the truck to the hard ground where sharp rocks on the road jabbed at her back.

"You're not to touch those two," said Sherry, sweating and breathing heavily, her now face uncovered.

She craned her neck to see the two Pashtuns on their knees, facing away from her, their hands behind their heads.

"You lost this damned mission as soon as it started, Princess," said the Black soldier from above, kneeling down to her. "You fucked up. We're not supposed to even be here, and we come out here and risk all of our lives looking for you? You're supposed to be back at Shamsi sucking the Commander's cock, and now he's dead. Every asset in

Pakistan is looking for you two. Yeah, you fucked up big. Our cover is blown. You don't get to say one goddamned word to anybody. You're relieved of duty by order of the Karachi Station Chief. So, just shut the fuck up and lie there until we airlift you to Karachi."

"I said, don't touch them."

"I wonder, Officer," said the Black soldier in response. "Whose side are you on?"

Two of her men covered her face again and hurried her into the back seat of an enormous Hummer. She then heard two sequential shots race across the desert plain. She heard the bodies of the two brothers fall lifelessly to the ground with two soft thuds, one after the other. With her mind still confused and her body completely numb, her paramilitary team climbed into the Hummers with her, turned around, and headed back towards Shamsi across Pakistan's northern border.

Chapter Seventeen

October 1982 – Northwest Frontier, Pakistan

If the great powers can't make destitute refugees work their food, and if they can't scapegoat them for their greater political gain, then the very least they can do is teach them how to fight for themselves while aiding them in defeating an enemy they have in common. Might as well make use of them if they're just standing around, scratching their balls, and taking up space. They need to catch the fish instead of being handed one. After all, no one will do it for them, and if someone did, wouldn't that make them forever dependent on those who gave them something for nothing?

A mosque may give them food, but the price is their full conversion to Islam. The Christian churches and Jewish synagogues also use the same technique. They can have food, just make sure they pray to God for his beneficence and join his army when the time comes. Yes, even charity of this kind has its trade-offs, because nothing is free. Have them pay, fight, or starve, and when they do, religion is always an exceptional motivator in times of doubt.

Although his assignment had been handed down on short notice, the young ISI Officer for the Pakistani Intelligence Services found Headquarters' plans for Afghanistan unique and cleverly conceived. It put Pakistan in control of the resistance against the Soviet invasion and not the United

States. The Officer felt superior now as the United States needed Pakistan, a role reversal that moved his country closer to the front lines.

The ISI alone trained the Pashtun refugees pouring in from southeastern Afghanistan as well as the many Arabs from the Middle East to fight the atheist Soviet infidels. More importantly, if the Soviets managed to take over Afghanistan, then Pakistan would be their next target. Although President Zia Al-Haq remained the outward public figure of Pakistan, the ISI ruled Pakistan and, by one degree of separation, so did the Pakistani Armed Forces.

He reviewed what he learned from Headquarters in Islamabad. To aid the Pakistanis, the Company dumped loads of cash and arms on top of the ISI's heads to train the Arabs and the Pashtuns. The Saudis funded the Pakistanis to build *madrassas* and orphanages along the border for the children of these fighters, thereby inculcating Islam into the next generation of Muslim warriors. The Pakistani military procured ancient weapons from US arsenals to fight its greatest foe, India. In this arrangement, everyone made out, even the ISI Officer who dipped his beak into the strong currents of cash for his own benefit. Nothing was better for business than a war he didn't have to fight himself.

And so, with the common people of Pakistan leading the way, Iran soon joined the Pakistanis in their mutual love of Islam, and of course, their mutual hatred of the Hindus. If the Hindus of India hated Islam, it followed that the Ayatollahs of Iran hated the Hindus. Iran and the ISI combined forces to fund Bin Laden to wear down the militant Hindu threat in the disputed territories of Jammu and Kashmir, a steady and ongoing conflict Pakistan had with India. The Saudis directly funded Bin Laden to crack down on the Marxist revolutionary movement in Saudi-controlled Yemen. And as far as the ISI could tell amidst the confusion of who funded whom, the ISI used the money and arms from the United States, as well as from American enemies Saudi Arabia and Iran, to thwart the Soviet advance. Bin Laden served as a great asset to everyone involved. He gladly did a lot of the dirty work. Since the Soviets hated the Iranian Revolution that put a radical cleric in charge, the Ayatollah Khomeni, strange bedfellows were made, and the ISI was at the center of it all. Lucky them.

Standing above his trainees, he observed his group of ragtag fighters of Afghan-Arabs and native Pashtuns crawl through the mud with Chinese AK-47s lassoed on their backs. The Chinese also loved their Pakistani brothers, especially since they both hated India. But seeing one of the Pashtun refugees with his ass too high in the air annoyed him. The guy's ass was always too high in the air. He walked over to the barbed wire cage under which they crawled and stamped his boot down on the guy's boney bottom, thereby making sure his torso sank deep into the cold mud.

"Next time I see that ass that high up, I'm going to shoot it off, you dumb *kaffir*," he snarled. "Now keep moving!"

"Yessir," said the humble Pashtun, struggling to keep up with the others.

To him, they were just children who needed discipline. The Soviets wouldn't be as kind. The harder he worked them, the more Soviets they would kill, and the safer Pakistan would be.

He had been at the camp for nearly three years. Pakistan's top brass couldn't have been more nervous. News of the invasion had sent shockwaves through the leadership of the ISI. To properly defend themselves, the ISI needed full control over the flow of arms and money coming in from the West. They insisted on full autonomy when it came to training the freedom fighters. They did not want US forces on the ground, either in Pakistan or Afghanistan.

Fortunately for him, the ISI Officer joined the military early on in his career. He moved up the ranks until recruited by the ISI. Surely, torture and murder were tools of the trade, but to amass power, wealth, status, and to see the expressions on other men's faces when he told them whom he worked for made committing those unspeakable acts worth every scream and cry that echoed in his ears at night. It wasn't always that way, though, and even while observing his men crawl through the viscous mud on that cold, wintry afternoon, he remembered the woman he almost married several years earlier.

But he refocused on his men and confirmed that the training had been going horribly thus far. He trained an equal number of Arab volunteers alongside rural Pashtun farmers who defended their lands and their way of life no matter how primitively they lived. Even though they fought together, the ISI Officer found it difficult to maintain any sort of comradery between the two. He often observed them eating in separate sections of the camp. The ISI Officer even housed them in different quarters, as fights often broke out in the evening after they trained all afternoon. The ISI Officer always made it a point to break up these fights before they grew too out of control, thinking that his fighters wouldn't be able to confront the massive Soviet advance if they were at each other's throats. After all, the two groups needed one another. Lately, though, he had grown tired of how the two traded insults back and forth, especially after the training day had ended.

To the Arabs, the Pashtuns were second-class, useless *kaffirs* without an education. To the Pashtuns, the Arabs were foreigners who had no business meddling in Pashtun affairs and defending what was rightfully theirs. The Pashtuns thought they could have easily done it themselves. The Arabs and the Pashtuns looked different, wore different clothes, spoke different languages, and had different stakes in the war.

When it came to Arab involvement in the struggle, the ISI Officer knew that his country walked a fine line between the religious fundamentalism *against* the West and the ISI's need to procure both money and arms *from* the West. Since the ISI played with countries who were enemies of each other, the line between Islam and the West became dangerously thin and even overlapped through the hub of the ISI.

Regardless, if Pakistan's double-dealing between the United States and the fundamentalist elements of Iran and Saudi Arabia put it in the middle of all things, its relationships opened the door to all kinds of corruption. The ISI Officer's bank account had grown ten-fold that year just on the money he siphoned off from the funds that were supposed to go towards training the freedom fighters. Also, the ISI sold its arms to other militant groups while stockpiling arms meant for Afghanistan for their fight against India. They were blinded by their hatred of their Hindu neighbors next-door.

After another afternoon of training, he couldn't help but notice again how different the Arabs and the Pashtuns were. Although the Pashtuns lacked natural ferocity, he admired their stamina and their profound sense of respect for themselves and others. Even in the camp they tried to dress well in earth-toned turbans, trimmed beards, and heavy coats that withstood the frigid Afghan cold. The Afghan-Arabs, however, were bellicose, rude, and pompous. They fought for martyrdom with the likes of Bin Laden and other militant groups while praying to die in the process. At one point in the conflict, they had set up white tents in the flight paths of Soviet MIG-17 fighter jets over the border just to be bombed by them. They celebrated the killing of their own fellow

Afghan-Arab freedom fighters. Bin Laden and his *Al-Queda* organization held the same attitudes, but while Bin Laden and the US worked together to thwart the Soviets, the Afghan-Arabs didn't care for the infidel Americans at all. To them, Americans were also their enemies. They wanted only the austere and most righteous Muslims to fight with them in the war, and this didn't include the Pashtuns or the Americans.

The Pashtuns were mostly a secular lot and looked upon their Arab brothers-in-arms as crazed zealots hell-bent on destroying each other. Because the Afghan-Arabs came to die, they filled themselves with self-importance and sanctimonious disregard for the Pashtuns, as though the conflict represented an alternative pilgrimage that rivaled Haj season. Organizations like Bin Laden's attracted such men, and the poor Pashtuns wanted nothing to do with it.

After dinner that night, however, the ISI Officer sensed restlessness in the camp. The two groups had reached their limit of disdain for each other. They ate a dinner of lamb *biryani* in their separate sections. When one of the Afghan-Arabs jokingly referred to a Pashtun fighter's mother as a disgusting whore and also muttered that she had a vagina of a grandmother, the poor Pashtun overheard this slight and took matters into his own hands. Instead of breaking them up as he usually did, he let them fight until the Arab beat the poor Pashtun to a bloody pulp. He could have broken it up, but once in a while, fighting solved what spatial separation couldn't. The ISI officer washed his hands of it. Training would continue the next morning regardless.

But the Officer was never born a cruel person. The ISI made him one for his own benefit, or at least that was what they told him at the end of his training. Born in Orangi Town, one of the world's largest slums in northwestern Karachi, he was raised by an overprotective Punjabi mother who kept him away from the cutthroat gangs that fought over turf just outside their ramshackle cardboard dwelling. The gangs of Orangi Town reflected the several different ethnicities that carved up this slum-megacity of some two-million people. Sindhis, Bohras, Mahajirs, Punjabis, and Ismailis all ran their own sections, and the Officer would have otherwise been a childhood member of a Punjabi criminal enterprise had it not been for his mother who closed him in and prevented him from ever leaving her embrace.

While pregnant with him and half-starving, his mother thankfully found work as a servant girl in a large household on the outskirts of Clifton, a posh seaside neighborhood replete with ornate mansions and lavish retail shopping malls. His natural father abandoned his mother just after he found out she was pregnant, this in keeping with how babies often grew up in Orangi Town. At least being abandoned while pregnant protected his mother from being raped all the time, especially since her belly started growing. In fact, the majority of women in the slum had been raped, usually late at night before they fell asleep in small, cramped dwellings the size of a typical one-bedroom apartment. These small dwellings usually housed a dozen or so people.

Smartly, the Officer's mother carried her baby to work every day in a sling wrapped around her breasts. Once at work, the servant-mother stored her child in a small closet with several of the other children who were also taken to work by the other servant-girls. Call it daycare for the very poor. Interestingly, the baby Officer spent most of his early days in a dark closet while being fed between breaks during the servant's overloaded cleaning schedule. Brushing away dust and dirt from marble floors all day with a long straw sweeper and squatting on her haunches, however, didn't provide for enough rice and formula to satisfy the baby Officer. While sweeping the other rooms, the servant girls heard their children forever crying, sometimes screaming for more food.

Each of the servant girls took turns feeding their children, but they were forever in need of something more than that. Perhaps they needed sunlight or the caresses of their mothers. Regardless, the girls worked with the full knowledge that their children restlessly starved each day in that dark closet. Once paid, they then bought them as much food as they could after taking them home to Orangi Town.

Slum living, with its lack of sanitation and clean drinking water, didn't do wonders for the baby ISI Officer's health either. Sick with diarrhea and having large, pink blotches on his chest and stomach, the Officer might have looked into the eyes of his servant-mother for the last time had she not determined that her precious child was indeed dying in the crowded dwelling where they slept and in the closet where she stored him while at work. He slept endlessly and cried during the short times he was awake. At night, her dwelling-mates threatened to throw them out. They did so each night, until she had little choice but to approach the man who employed her.

She begged the owner of the mansion on her hands and knees, "please Doctor, *sahib*," after ten hours of straight cleaning, "I need to discuss something important with you."

The practicing physician, sitting on a large, plush couch imported from the United Kingdom, watched a Pakistani drama on his black and white television with his pretty wife and his two teenage boys next to him. Clearly, he didn't want to be bothered. At first, he didn't respond, but after the servant-mother persisted, he finally responded.

"What is it?" he asked, sucked in by the events on the screen.

"I need to speak with you, Doctor *sahib*. Please."

"What is it?" he asked, annoyed.

"It is about your home. There is something wrong in the kitchen."

"What is it?" he asked a third time.

"I need to speak with you, *sahib*. Please."

"Can't it wait?"

"No, *sahib*. It is important."

"Just tell me what is wrong, woman!"

"I can't explain it, *sahib*. You have to see it for yourself."

"Damnit!" he said, thumping his fist on the armrest.

He followed the servant-mother who darted down a long hallway made of marble like the rest of the mansion. It led to a kitchen where several of the younger servant girls washed pots and pans and scrubbed the floors on their hands and knees.

"Please leave us," said the servant-mother to the other girls.

"What a second," said the Doctor. "What is that noise? Do you hear it?"

"*Sahib*, I can explain, but you must promise not to be angry with me."

"Shhh. Can you hear it? It's somewhere close. It sounds like crying, but at a very high pitch. Very subtle. Can you hear it?"

"I can explain, *sahib*, but you must not get angry with me."

"It's too late for that," he said. "I've already missed my show. But where's that sound coming from? Obviously, you know something about it. Tell me now, or you'll get a beating."

"Please, *sahib*, take pity on us!"

The other servant girls had vacated the room already, leaving the servant-mother pinned with her back to a closet in the kitchen. The other servant-mothers had already moved their children so as not to get into trouble. They also didn't want to risk infecting their own children by storing them in the same closet with the diseased child.

"Sounds like someone's crying in there," said the Doctor, pointing to the closet.

"Please, *sahib*. Don't be angry with me, please."

"Open the door!" he commanded thunderously.

By this point, the mother held the owner of the house by meat of his arms and begged him not to erupt in a furious rage, but he had had enough of her and pushed her aside. He yanked the door open. The crying was much louder now that he had discovered the child. He flicked on the light and gasped at the sight of him. He had encountered several children hidden away in his mansion before, but never did he expect to see one so diseased. The pink splotches on his chest and face, the sweat beading all over his febrile body, and his toothless mouth from where the high-pitched and incessant screaming came disgusted him. The room smelled of fresh feces.

"My God," he exclaimed, waving his hand in front of his nose. "What the hell is *that* doing here?! Who brought this into my house? Whoever brought this thing must leave with it at once and never come back with it."

He closed the shrieking infant inside and headed back down the long hallway shouting, "we're not a charity! I'm a doctor!"

But the mother maneuvered in front of him and blocked his path. Tears from her eyes fell in thick, heavy droplets, and as she wept, the awkward curve of her open lips revealed large, yellow teeth and black, malnourished gums. She had no one else but this child, the only light in her world, and the immediate impulse to save him ruled over all other considerations. If they were sent back into Orangi Town, they would both starve, even if she sold herself to every man she saw.

"*Sahib*," she cried, "he is my son. He is very sick, *sahib*. Very sick he is. He needs your help."

"My help? Get that damned thing out of my house! I want the both of you out! How dare you bring a half-dead child into my house without asking me. How many children are stored in here? I want all of them out. They're dirtying up the mansion!"

The mother fell to her knees in front of him, clasped his legs, and buried her face in his trousers.

"Please, *sahib*, take my son. I will do anything you want of me, anything you ask. He is very sick, *sahib*. Don't send us away. You are a kind and generous man, most merciful and beneficent. Have mercy on us. Please, help us now, and I will do anything you ask of me for the rest of my life."

The servant-mother braced herself to be beaten, but instead the Doctor stood there in silence as she continued her weeping. In fact, as the infant continued to wail in the closet, he allowed both mother and child to emote tearfully in front of him. Apparently, he already knew what to do about them. His pause gave the mother a flicker of hope that the Doctor might treat her sick child instead of throwing the two of them out.

"Can you at least shut that thing up?" he sighed,

defeated.

"*Sahib?*"

"Just shut it up, turn it off, whatever, just stop the kid from crying, please. It's giving me a bad headache."

"Right away, *sahib.*"

She ran into the closet and shut the door behind her. There, in the small room, she took her child in her arms, opened her blouse, and held him close to her breast. The child tried to suck his mother's milk, but her breasts had dried up. They were useless and empty vessels. But the act at least stifled the infant's crying. No matter how furiously the child sucked, he survived on the illusion and the promise of milk that would have otherwise nourished his underweight frame.

A gargantuan, horrific vision came to her of the both of them wandering pennilessly and aimlessly through Orangi Town, trying to find a place to sleep between the dense, cardboard-lined alleyways where rotting garbage served as their pillows. She couldn't handle standing and waiting in the closet any longer. The walls narrowed in.

The door then swung open from the outside, startling her. At the entrance stood the Doctor's pretty housewife. Rather than anger, the housewife gave the servant-mother a look of knowing concern. She then called in the male servant of the household who handled the family's more personal and intimate affairs.

"Take the child to my husband's office while it's still open," she said. "Do it right away."

"Yes, madam," replied the male servant obsequiously.

"Oh, God bless you, madam," cried the servant girl after handing over her child.

She fell to her knees, and just as she did the doctor, she

clasped her arms around her legs and cried into the skirt of her *duppurta*. The pretty housewife ordered the other servant-girls, who had been eavesdropping the entire time, to make two cups of tea for them both. The servant-mother, awestruck by this display of pity and grace, continued to weep into her *duppurta* and bless the housewife who said, "your baby is being looked after as we speak. We are showing him to one of my husband's colleagues for treatment."

One of the servant-girls brought in two cups of hot char and left them alone. The servant-mother stood up, and the housewife handed her one of the cups.

"So," said the housewife, "I take it you are not able to take care of your son, considering the condition he is in?"

"Yes, madam," she said. "I fear he is dying, but you saved his life."

"You are from the slums, yes?"

"You mean, Orangi Town? Yes, my son and I are from there."

"That's no place for a child. You live in squalor. A child deserves to be healthy, eat healthy foods, go to school, learn how to read and write, make friends, all of the things he can never get in Orangi Town. Let's face it. You can't provide for your child, and either can we. He definitely can't live here, and he'll die living with you. What will happen the next time this all happens? It will happen again and again, you know, until it has stopped for good. What we did for you today is only a temporary fix."

The servant-mother carefully slurped her tea to avoid spilling it over the edges of her cup.

"How's the tea, by the way?" asked the housewife. "Are you feeling better?"

"Yes, madam," said the servant-mother. "It will always be tough for us. When my son grows up, I'm hoping he will get a break somewhere. Maybe he can learn a trade. I can tell he's such a strong child, and God has blessed him by keeping him alive through your beneficence."

"But what kind of life would that be? You don't have a home. You don't have any money. And if he lives in the slums, he's going to get sick again. You have to start thinking about his future. You don't want to lock him in closets all of his life, do you? What I did for you was rare. I've never done that before with the other servant-girls, but I do have experience with children and knowing what they need."

"I'm so very thankful to you, madam."

"Listen, I don't think you are prepared to be a mother to him with the resources you have."

"Madam?"

"I'm just being straightforward and honest with you. If you want your child to survive and do well, it is far better that he lives somewhere else and not in that disease-infested slum. You can't bring him here anymore. You know that, don't you?"

"I agree, madam, I agree!"

"We cannot afford better housing for the both of you either. After all, we can't house everyone who asks us for it. But your son deserves a better life apart from the cruelty of the slums."

The mother sipped her tea slowly, trying to understand the housewife's point.

"I guess what I'm saying is," continued the housewife, "that I don't think it's a good idea for you and your son to continue living together. In order to ensure a better future for your poor child, you should give him up."

"Madam?"

"I think you should give up your son to another couple who can better take care of him. It's obvious to me and my husband that you are unable to care for him."

She absorbed what she said and combed through her statement, studying it to verify that she actually suggested such an outrageous solution to the problem. The housewife, however, was serious as she could be. The servant-mother, even in her humbler position, couldn't help but defend herself.

"I don't think that will be necessary, madam, but I thank you for the idea. My son is well now, thanks to you, and he will be fine living with me. Our lives are not easy by any means, but a son needs his mother. I should also add that in Islam, adoption is forbidden."

"We're not talking about adoption here," she said. "We're talking a trade of sorts. You see, I belong to a women's organization here in Karachi that specializes in cases just like yours. We give children better lives, a fighting chance to become productive citizens of our society. It's really very easy, you see. You give up your child, and for that we give you a place to live and a suitable job. In your case, you would be living nearby and continue your work as a servant like you are doing right now. Everything will be taken care of – your food, your clothing, your rent – all the things that you need to live a carefree life with us as a servant. You'd be keeping your job here and living in a nice, clean place."

"And my son? What about him?"

"We'd place him in the home of a married couple who, for whatever reasons, are unable to have children. We only deal with select couples who make a good annual income and can afford to give a child a fulfilling life. Many of our kids go to school and then go on to college. They become doctors, lawyers, and important government officials. We have a success rate of ninety percent as far as careers are concerned. Our couples are well-vetted, screened, and selected from the very best of applicants. I can assure you that your son will have a shot at living a very important and fulfilling life."

"But will I be able to see him? Will I get to talk to him or know him at all?"

"No, there will be no contact. You will not know where he can be found either. Also, our organization aims to reduce that alarming rate of poverty in Karachi by making sure that you don't have any more needless children yourself. Pakistan is already overpopulated with poor people as it is. For a woman in your position, it is very risky for you to have more children. No one is able to bear the costs of any additional children that you may have in future. Therefore, you will have to go through a small operation at my husband's office. That's part of the deal."

"I don't know, madam," she said, trembling. "It would be quite a change, and I would never see my son again. I don't think I can go through something like that. I would always need him with me. I would always worry about him and wonder how he's doing. I would be missing his entire life."

"Yes, but you'd be giving him a much better one, a life he could have never had living with you. Don't you see? He'd be getting the best of everything. He'd be placed with a loving, caring family with status and position. You would be free from worry knowing that your child is being well taken care of. And you'd be working here and living in your own flat. It's an entirely new start for you. And not to mention you'd be helping poor people like yourself by reducing the overwhelming number of hungry mouths to feed in the city."

"I appreciate the idea, madam, really I do, but I don't think I can go through with it. My son needs to be with me as hard as our lives are."

"Well," said the housewife more forcefully, "we can't risk him getting sick again, and we can't risk him infecting you, and then you infecting the rest of the household. I have my own children to look after. You won't be able to work here. You have to find employment somewhere else."

"But madam, I can assure you that – "

" - no, you can't. As long as you are living in the slums with that child, a child you will always have to carry around with you, you are both a health risk. My husband will never allow it, and neither will I. If you can't give your son a better life through us, it would be best if you left and found employment somewhere else. I'm giving you a choice. I am giving both you and your son an opportunity. I think it's clear what you should do. I think you should free yourself of the burden of childbirth and give your only child a life any child would only dream of. Think about it over your tea. I will be back shortly."

As much as the servant hated to admit it, the madam-housewife had a strong point. Lumping in tubal ligation did seem odd, tangential, and a bit extreme, but she understood that the good doctor was not willing to shoulder the costs of saving another child of hers, should she be raped all over again in Orangi Town. A kind of feudal sterility seemed to be the right approach, as she would be living in a nice, secure place, working a decent job with servants she already liked working with, and living a life without risks, troubles, dangers, or problems, only years of calm contentment where she would find inevitable happiness in her small compact world. On her days off, she'd walk to the ocean nearby, bask in the sunshine, cool herself off in the warm tides, and watch the shipping vessels dock and unmoor, transferring precious cargo from one ship to another, ships from all over the world headed to exotic ports of call.

She may even make enough money to afford telephone service or buy a sparkling new wardrobe from one of the fashionable stores in Clifton, stores where she would have never been able to go had she been stuck with her diseased child. Her dreaming took her all the way to her marrying an older man who had never been married before, or a recent widower from Clifton who looked for a mistress or second wife but didn't want any more children. There must have been many a man like that in Clifton. Traveling to Haj, learning how to read, and taking dancing lessons also filled her mind with visions of the good life, the good life far away from Orangi Town and the vermin that bit at her toes at night, the scumbags who rolled on top of her, held her down, ripped off her garments, and plundered her with their sweaty, malodorous bodies in the dwellings she slept in, those cardboard shacks that stank of shit, rotten fruit, spoiled milk, and fresh corpses being eaten away by poisonous, grotesque-looking insects that made Orangi Town a worldwide nest of pestilence.

Damn straight she took the deal, and on that very day, she left her child to the good housewife who gifted her a clean, vacant apartment down the street. She would never behold her own son again, never hold him to her body again either. No longer was there anyone to care for, worry about, or love. From living for her son, she now lived for herself, a novelty she would have to get used to, as the only part of her life that had any meaning had been replaced by blissful security, stability, and freedom. So be it, she thought, so be it. All she had to do now was to forget about him.

His fits of diarrhea ended after just a few days in

Karachi's main hospital where the doctor had stored the sick child. The pink splotches on his skin disappeared. He cried and slept at regular intervals. He smiled to the comely nurses who took turns brushing their fingers against his plump cheeks and cradling him in their arms before putting him down in his crib for sleep. The nurses loved their new child and pampered him with an overflow of maternal affection. Tempted to breastfeed him themselves, the nurses made sure he ate too much for his own good and drank an over-abundance of formula so that he burped and pooped loudly enough to elicit delicate rounds of their Sylphic giggling. When they changed him, they held his tiny, circumcised penis between their fingers, moving it up and down and flipping it from side to side, sometimes taking it in their mouths in private to witness and record his responses, adding his reactions to their wardrobes of feminine knowledge, only to apply it when the time was right. Their illicit behaviors rouged their cheeks with virginal bashfulness and playful wantonness.

From a near-certain death, the child had been returned to the living and passed on to a couple who were friends of the pretty housewife's. They paid a considerable sum for the child. The couple couldn't have any children of their own, the barren wife weeping for at least a year straight because of it. The new adopting father, also a doctor and fellow colleague, worked on soldiers in the military. The government requested him to do this, because he also had his own successful medical practice. Treating soldiers in the military and working as a military doctor was an honor bestowed only upon the most gifted citizens of the country, the select few who earned their medical degrees in country, passed military loyalty tests, and proved themselves to be avid patriots of Pakistan.

His barren wife worked as an accountant at a well-known shipping company. The couple lived in the Clifton area and were even wealthier than the family to whom the servant-mother surrendered the child. The ISI baby bound his new aloof and hapless parents together just like when they were first married, and their lives brimmed with the joy of welcoming a new child into their magisterial home. They never told their new adopted son how he came to them. Once they purchased him, they never mentioned his origins again, even while alone.

They took a vacation for a month to Kerbala, Iran, and told their close friends, family, and associates that the child had been born while traveling there. The couple's family welcomed the child with open arms, because, finally, their seed would flower and give birth to new generations of their offspring. Naturally, the couple sank all of their parental love into their new child, giving him everything he ever wanted – toys and more toys, the best clothes in the best styles from the best shops, a flurry of other wealthy children to play and associate with, and of course, the very best education at Karachi Grammar School. There, he learned how to be a good boy and a good student, dress well in the standard uniform of blue shirt, striped school tie, polished black shoes, and navy-blue blazer.

In his third-grade year, however, the Headmistress of the School, a plump elderly woman with a shock of white hair on an otherwise grey head, set up a conference with the couple regarding their son. She had large plastic, oval spectacles, and the stern voice of a seasoned disciplinarian. She explained that the entire third grade had taken a series of aptitude tests recently and that she was meeting with all of the parents to discuss the results and how their children fared academically at the prestigious school.

The adoptive doctor-father, a tall and lanky fellow in his mid-thirties, had high hopes for his only son, given the money he had been shelling out for his education. So did his adoptive accountant-mother, a petite, comely woman in her late twenties who liked to wear fancy clothes to her corner office at the shipping company. By all accounts, the couple exemplified what was best about the professional class in Karachi. They had important and influential friends on whom the doctor counted as clients. This included city politicians, government officials, and of course, high-ranking friends in the military, some of them well-known and others buried within the mountain of its enormous bureaucracy. The couple was well-respected, gave generous *zakat* to their local mosque, and were considered to be, not only talented, but socially conscious as well. The good doctor saw himself as Pakistan's primary Health Minister in the not-too-distant future. He had strong enough connections to be considered for this top position in Islamabad one day.

He had similarly high hopes for his son, if not higher hopes. Just like any father, he wanted his son to be an even better doctor than he, as medicine was the career he wanted him to pursue from the very start. So, when the portly Headmistress called his parents into her office with numerous diplomas and certificates of her own striking academic and civic achievements hanging on the walls, she didn't look too happy with them. She had a stack of papers sitting in front of her which she leafed through briefly. The couple sat quietly on the opposite side of her expecting to hear that their son, with the elite education they had given him, had done exceptionally well thus far.

"Thank you for coming," said the Headmistress dispassionately.

To them, she looked like she hadn't smiled since she first started teaching at the school some forty-five years ago. Her black eyes, set in pools of membranous white cataracts, alternated between looking down at the papers and then looking directly at the doctor and his wife.

"Your son needs a lot of improvement," she said. "His aptitude tests are less than satisfactory, and his grades are barely passing, which is better than failing, of course.

Her eyebrows narrowed, and she cleared her throat. She then returned to the boy's test scores.

"But we need to see a lot of improvement, especially in the sciences – mathematics, biology, and chemistry. He's adequate in reading and writing, but he doesn't seem to have any arithmetic acumen, which is a bit strange, seeing that both of you did so well in that field – being a doctor, sir, and your wife an executive accountant. Yes, it's mighty strange indeed."

"What are the subjects he's good at?" asked the doctor. "Where does he show the most promise?"

"Oddly enough, the only real potential that I see so far is for manual labor. He is good at athletics. Your son is a budding field hockey player."

"Field hockey?" said the doctor. "You can't be serious?"

"Oh, I am being quite serious. While he doesn't seem to have much talent academically at this point, he does love his field hockey. He's pretty good at it, actually, or so says the report from our athletic department."

"This can all change, though, right?" asked the accountant-mother, worriedly. "I mean, he could do better academically when he goes into the higher grades. That is possible, of course?"

"Of course, it's possible. It's very possible. He is still in his formative years, and with the right help he can overcome what his teachers call a wandering mind. From what his teachers write about him in their comments, your son has a difficult time paying attention. He's also lazy when it comes to his schoolwork. He is often unprepared for class, and he lacks discipline at home, which is what he sorely needs. Have you been helping him with his homework and making sure he has good study habits?"

"We've kind of left him on his own," said the doctor, looking to his wife. "We haven't done that yet. We leave our son to his nanny who watches him after school. The both of us are so busy, that we haven't really had the time to monitor him at home. We assumed he was self-reliant enough to study on his own."

"Ah!" said the Headmistress. "Then you've found your answer. Most of our students usually do well when they are left to their own devices. But your child does not fall into that category, now does he? You can't expect your child to do well here at Karachi Grammar without your direct involvement in his studies. But not to worry. I have seen other parents in my career here who have made the same miscalculation with their children. While your son has average intelligence, as indicated by his scores on his aptitude tests, he can do well academically, provided he has the right support from you both. You can't send him to us and just hope he does well. Your son is not some message in bottle that you can simply throw out into the ocean of education and hope he reaches the shore of intelligence. It doesn't work that way. You have to be pro-active with him. You have to get involved. He is in the third grade, so I'm glad that we caught this in time."

The doctor put his lean hands on his wife's, the callouses on her fingers the result of long hours on calculators and keyboards. Equally surprised by this revelation, the wife looked at him with wide eyes, wondering how to go about making their average son as smart as they once were. As they looked into each other, they wondered if anyone or anything could change his intelligence, as his was the intelligence of another mother. They couldn't hide the easiest and most tempting solution to their problem, which was to give the boy back to the pretty housewife, and she would, in turn, return the boy to his birth mother. They shared this thought silently and felt ashamed of themselves for it. Their son wasn't a defective appliance that could be returned to the manufacturer for a refund. They did love the kid, but at what cost? His dimwittedness may have one day stained their untarnished reputations, especially since the government had since considered the doctor for a more prestigious appointment in Islamabad. There had to be a solution.

"Can he take those tests again?" asked the wife.

"There's no need to at this point," said the Headmistress. "His intelligence has been accurately measured. We can deduce that he will always have a less than satisfactory intelligence. Nothing can change that."

"But how can you be so sure?" the doctor fired back. "There is no scientific evidence of that. From what I understand, people bloom at different times. He may be highly intelligent when he moves on to college. Who's to say? His genes are malleable, aren't they? Everyone knows that."

"Depends how you look at it," she said, consolingly. "It is my experience, and through our research corroborated by all of the best universities in Pakistan, that that's just not true. Your child, unfortunately, is stuck with the intelligence he was born with, which is why it is so hard for me to believe that he has such a lower intelligence than you have. Maybe it comes from your grandparents or perhaps an uncle? It may have skipped a few generations?"

"So, what are you saying exactly?" asked the doctor. "Our son has no future?"

"I'm not saying that at all," she said. "What I am saying is that the knowledge that I am giving you today will help reshape your son tomorrow. If you know that he is not particularly bright, he can at least be highly educated, or better yet, overeducated to such an extent that he will seem highly intelligent on the outside but remain mentally weak on the inside. I've had several students like yours before, and they have all done extraordinary things with their lives. After all, intelligent people don't really do that well when their own happiness is concerned. Being intelligent can also be a curse. I mean, how unfortunate it must be to have a world of morons surrounding you? On the contrary, I would argue that your son is in a better position to find happiness than many of our most gifted students."

"I can't believe you're saying this," said the accountant-mother. "He's not going to understand what he's studying."

"Correct," she said. "He'll be mimicking the intelligence found in his books and the words he hears from his teachers. He will master the art of regurgitation. So, when he leaves college and has to work and earn a living in the real world, he will appear just as educated as the smartest of students. His mind will also appear the same, but he won't be able to apply any of what he's learned. He won't understand anything intuitively. He won't be able to process what he absorbs logically. I can only get him to the finish line of his academic career. I will get him where he needs to be. If you want him to be a doctor, he can get through medical school on the wings of his education alone. After that, he may have to take a break to recoup, learn a bit more about the world and his place in it, and then return to medicine as a simple, every-day, average doctor. He can do that and live with whatever assets and materials you bequeath him.

"You see, your son does have a good future in store for him. His lack of intelligence can be a gift too. At least he'll be happier than the more intelligent men his age who have to think and brood all the time. His gifts in athletics will win him many admirers. For now, though, things will have to change for him if you want him to move ahead. We can help him at Karachi Grammar, if you are willing to accept our help."

The couple looked to each other again and thought their situation hopeless. The wife's eyes teared up. The Headmistress offered her a tissue. Her husband continued to comfort her.

"Honey," he said to her, "this is not as bad as it seems. So, we have son that's not the brightest in the world. He'll still be like everyone else. He'll be an average person. A regular person. There's nothing wrong with being average, regular, and happy."

"I don't know," she said, wiping away her tears. "I just thought he'd be so much more. I just want what's best for him."

"And he will get the best," said the Headmistress. "You simply follow my recommendations as outlined in my report, and he should be on his way. He'll improve academically, that's for sure."

By the time the doctor and his accountant-wife returned to their home in Clifton overlooking the rolling, sparkling sea, their son had already returned from school. Once again, he watched the television with rapt attention as though it were the only educational device he ever needed. His books were still zipped up in his backpack. He hadn't even taken them out since coming home.

Seeing this, the good doctor walked in front of him and

blocked his view of the television. Judging by how red his face was, the doctor suppressed his rage and spoke slowly and methodically to his child, thereby avoiding beating him. His kid was an embarrassment to them both. The Headmistress and the teachers at the school must have been laughing at them, laughing that this married couple, with such a squeaky-clean and city-renowned reputation for excellence and achievement, gave birth to such a mediocre and dimwitted son.

The doctor felt like suing the housewife and the organization from whom he purchased him, she and that whole corrupt crowd with whom they hob-knobbed at holiday get-togethers, weddings, and birthday parties, the same crowd that championed reducing the birthrate of the poor people of Karachi, so that the best would outbreed the very worst. It just wasn't responsible for the poor to have children, and now he knew exactly why. The population of slums like Orangi Town had grown by leaps and bounds over just a few short years, because the dirty people housed there lived like animals, unclean and diseased, fucking all day and all night, pumping out children every chance they got. Even though the good doctor had little idea where his son originally came from, as that was part of the bargain, never in a million years would he have thought that a child who had crept in and taken his family name could be so, well, unintelligent.

They fought their immediate instinct to throw him back. They kept him instead and followed the Headmistress' plan. They both tried to love him as a deficient older boy, as it had been easy to love him as a cherubic new infant when they had first bought him. They were not a cruel people. They thought it better to be good and moral and nurture the child through his difficulties than to be reckless, throw him back, and live for themselves instead. They buried their resentment for him from that day forward, a resentment he never earned but still sensed as his father shut off the television, grabbed him by the arm, and pulled him into his room, locking the door from the outside until he opened his books.

In his room, he lay upon his bed wondering what he did to upset his father, but he couldn't figure it out. His father's anger had surfaced for the first time. Normally, his parents were all smiles. They showered him with affection by buying him anything he wanted. Little did he know that from thenceforth this trend would radically change.

They placed him in special after-school programs and paid the most notable tutors in Karachi to sit with him and teach him what his teachers and new after-school programs missed. They forbade him from playing any field hockey until he picked up his grades, and what's more, they hired a hoard of specialists to whom they paid thousands of rupees to bolster his knowledge and augment his lagging aptitudes. They claimed that great men are not born but made, and so these specialists made their money feeding his parents that philosophy.

Over several years of merciless and endless study, these schools, programs, tutors, and specialists built a boy who not only achieved but overachieved. By the time he reached high school, he excelled in all of his subjects, joined the cricket and field hockey teams, and attracted so many young women to his corner that this young, dull child who once had no hope at all of succeeding became a young man of high stature and a student whom every peer in his class thought the most likely to succeed. He enjoyed immense popularity. Just as he loved Karachi Grammar School, Karachi Grammar School loved him. The doctor and his accountant-wife had turned a sure loser into a potential winner.

He scored average on his medical school placement examinations, but his doctor-father had enough connections and enough of a foothold in his profession to allow him to squeeze into a much-coveted spot at a medical college. He graduated from Karachi Grammar cum laude and entered Army Medical College where his own doctor-father had earned his medical degree twenty years earlier. Apparently, his father's influence went a long way. Once his parents secured his admission to medical school, the happy couple chased the one last item on their list that would guarantee his incredible success down the line. They wanted to marry him into a good family with similar social status. They wanted this to happen before they shipped him off to medical school. That way, he wouldn't do anything stupid, like fall in love with a girl of whom the family did not approve.

Naturally, it was the accountant-wife who searched for the girl, and she soon found one – a homely, plump, wealthy girl with a well-established family who were heirs to a shipping conglomerate in Karachi. The boy's parents were overjoyed at their good fortune. Whether he liked her or not, the young man, taking direct instruction from his father, proposed to the plump girl one night in a swanky restaurant in the Clifton area. All of their family members and friends already knew that he would propose to her that night. It was hardly a secret. Even the diners at this expensive restaurant also knew, but everyone played it cool as they watched the two from the corners of their eyes and pretended not to notice them eat, drink, and smile. Then the boy popped the question over a dish of butter chicken and platters of lamb and goat with spicy masala over sticky saffron-infused rice.

The plump girl, with glittering gold jewelry all over her pear-shaped body and in a *duppurta* made of mirrored sequins, accepted immediately. His proposal was a silly question to ask of her in the first place, a mere formality considering that they both knew the answer to the question already. Clifton's social newsletter posted their engagement prominently the very next day. They would be married once the boy finished pre-med at Army Medical College. They would not only be marrying each other. Their marriage fused two wealthy families together.

The time soon came for the engaged couple to pack their things and move to Rawalpindi, the Punjab. Yet even though the boy's future had been fixed and his parent's plan had been near-foolproof, he still had a very vexing concern that continued to bother him ever since the night he moved to the college. The boy searched himself again, and he would marry her, no question. Getting married wasn't the problem, because he didn't really have a choice but to marry her anyway. His problem on the cusp of his marriage, however, loomed as a private matter that he kept fiercely to himself and far from the ears of anyone he knew, even from his best friend whom he loved and cherished as the older brother he never had. They had graduated together from Karachi Grammar School. Normally, he would have confided in him, but when it came to this particular problem, he kept his mouth shut.

One night in the sticky summer heat, while in his room in his parent's home in Clifton, the young man, after a night out of snacking with friends, couldn't hide his urgent and pressing need to address the all-too-frequent erections paining him every few hours, even in his sleep. Of course, he had had them before, but no longer could he tolerate their severity, as they now interfered with his daily life. Everywhere he went, at every sighting of a pretty Pakistani girl on the streets, in the shops, or at the restaurants he frequented, he couldn't control his fierce, throbbing, painful, and rock-hard erections. Unable to relieve or arrest these erections hurt him so badly, that he first thought it a strange medical condition. But his reticence prevented him from discussing it with any of his father's colleagues or with any doctor in all of Karachi for that matter.

In his bed that night, he could do nothing to stop it. He rolled onto his stomach and rubbed it against his bedsheets, but to no avail. Only after lying awake in the dead of night for a couple of hours did he turn over and let his phallus stand free. He needed to cure what ailed him in the most logical way possible. He held it and then stroked himself hard and fast until the grandest, most pleasurable release of pain and frustration shot like cannon fodder from out of him, the load so terribly suppressed over many moons of suffering, that he could have sworn he heard the cannon firing itself.

Having committed the sinful deed, his body sweating and limp, he no longer suffered. He found out exactly what to do. He enjoyed a summer of self-love, telling no one of the cure to his ailment. The act soon became so commonplace, however, that he grew bored and tired of it by the time summer ended. There were only so many ways he could imagine the overly clad women of Pakistan. It took too much effort to imagine what they looked like underneath their clothes and to visualize their breasts, their bellies, their legs. They covered themselves so completely that he had nothing to feed on but wild speculations of their bodily dimensions that were too difficult to discern. He also found it equally unsatisfying using their green-hued *duppurtas* as objects of his twice daily, and once nightly, habitual practice of relieving himself.

When the long summer ended, he and his fiancé finally made their unprecedented move to Rawalpindi.

"Excited?" he asked his plump fiancé over snacks at an outdoor café by the train station.

"I wonder what it'll be like?" she said, chewing the last bits of a meat-filled samosa.

"Rawalpindi sure is different. I'll be studying most of the time. You'll be at home."

"Sounds boring," she said, the dimples around her mouth and on her chin pinching her face as she dunked a large piece of samosa into a small bowl of lime-green chutney.

"My, you're really hungry tonight. I hope you won't miss all of this too much."

"Probably," she said, focused on her food.

"I bet you can't wait until we're married, eh?"

"There's no rush. It'll happen anyway. You first have to work on getting through pre-med. After that, we'll be able to go ahead with it."

"You don't mind waiting, you mean?"

"Why are you asking me all these questions?" she said, still focused on her food. "You know what our plan is. What's the rush?"

"But you don't mind *waiting*?"

"Waiting? Waiting for what? I just told you. It's no problem. You have to finish pre-med."

Missing his point entirely, she ate her meal as though nothing else on earth mattered. He didn't press the issue again until after they settled into their campus living arrangements on the college grounds.

Rawalpindi is Islamabad's lesser-known twin city. Because the boy's father wanted to be appointed to a top position at the Ministry of Health, the Army Medical College became the ideal place for his son to live. Their living on the campus curried favor with key bureaucrats in both the army and the Ministry of Health. It showed their loyalty to the school and its tradition of feeding its graduates to important government posts in the next city over.

Because of their engagement, the Dean at the medical college permitted them to reside in hostels adjacent to each other. After all, they came from good families, both of theirs well-known and well-connected. No one foresaw any problems with their being placed side-by-side. The bride-to-be stayed with the more mature graduate women, and the young man resided with the graduate men who would soon move on to earn their doctorates in medicine. The men stayed with the men, and the women stayed with the women. No exceptions meant no problems.

The older women taught the young bride how to cook and clean, while the young man devoted all of his time and energies to the pre-med program with his older male colleagues who set fine examples for him. Both of their families agreed that their children moved on a faster, more advanced track. That way, it allowed them to mature at a faster rate than the average incoming student. They thought of it as advanced placement for a couple soon to be married. In turn, their living arrangements would make them the shining stars of the college. Because they would remain in Rawalpindi instead of returning to Clifton, except for brief visitations during holidays, the couple's lives would be fixed and stable. After med school, the couple would return to Clifton to be married formally amidst a whirl of rose-petaled fanfare, festive parties, countless feasts, and colorful dances – the entire Clifton aristocracy reveling in the union of two of their own.

Wherever the young man went, however, so followed his most private of problems. In pre-med, he did marginally well, as he had strong study skills and a hardcore work ethic, but at nights in his room all alone, he couldn't help but succumb to the same pressures and pains that plagued him, especially after attending several concerts sponsored by the female cadet chorale after long hours of intense study. None of the older men in the hostel ever caught him in the act, though, as he rigorously applied the cure late at night after everyone fell asleep.

He saw his fiancé every day when he was not studying and then relieving himself of his strange, invariable malady. Countless times, the young man used the power of suggestion and strong, unwavering hints to his fiancé that he could no longer wait. He feared he would soon get caught in his room by the other men if he continued for much longer.

And so, after dinner with his friends in downtown Rawalpindi one evening, he returned to the hostel feigning fatigue from the enormous meal they ate. His colleagues expressed their unanimous disappointment that he declined to attend a lecture given by a well-known army veteran who spoke at Ayub Auditorium that night. Instead, he found himself dangerously alone in his hostel room after his housemates left for the well-attended event.

He made sure no one saw him when he snuck over from his emptied hostel to the shadowy side of the women's area where the campus spotlights didn't shine. On the cropped lawn below her fiance's window, he saw that she was alone in her room, doing what, he wasn't exactly sure. Needless to say, while watching her move to and fro, his pains exceeded even that which he thought possible. Without further delay, he whispered hotly into the stillness of the crisp nighttime air, hoping to dear and precious God that she heard his cry for help from beneath her window. He must have called her name for an eternity, it seemed, until he called it out so loudly that it broke the barrier of whispering and entered the realm of an all-out, frustrated yelp. He found himself suddenly resentful of his fiancé who only had to learn to cook and clean while he struggled with his exacerbating condition. Surely, cooking and cleaning wasn't all she was suited for. What he needed from her didn't require any real competence on her part, only her natural duty to save mankind, a quality that all women possessed. Men killed, and the women saved, even though there were mostly male students at the college since its founding. By the time she opened the window above him, he was almost shouting her name.

"What the hell is it?" she exclaimed, looking down on him from the second floor. "You know you're not supposed to be down there."

Her plump, dimpled face looked more angry than surprised by his intrusion. They could get into big trouble if they were caught. Incidents such as this were rare, so the guards on campus generally didn't look for this kind of infraction. Their situation also differed from many of the other disciplinary ones, like cheating, failing grades, and insolence towards professors. Most cadets assumed that no man would be dumb enough to sneak into a women's hostel at night.

"I need to come up," he whispered hotly.

"Certainly not," she called down. "Go to your room, before we both get in trouble."

"I'm coming up. I have to talk to you."

"The hostel-mother will catch you, stupid."

"She's asleep by now. I'll be quiet. I swear."

"No," she said, but she did find his overtures cute.

"I'll be up in a minute. Just wait right there."

He made it to her room without getting caught. Most, if not all, of the graduate women had left for Ayub Auditorium already. But he and his fiancé were alone on her bed, a single reading lamp casting its circle of light over their warm bodies.

"What are you doing here?" she whispered. "We could

both get in a lot of trouble for this. We could be expelled. What the hell is so urgent?"

"I think I have a problem," he admitted, finally.

"And what's that?"

"I don't know how to express it. But I think I'm very sick."

"Sick? What do you mean, sick? You don't look very sick to me."

She held her chubby hand to his forehead and felt for a temperature.

"Well, you don't have a fever of any kind. Did you eat something bad? What's making you sick? Describe it to me."

"It's hard to describe, really," he said, cozying up to her. "I can let you feel it."

"Feel it? You can't 'feel' a sickness, dummy. You're the doctor. You should know."

"Here. I'll show you."

He took her hand and pulled it into his chest. At first she pulled away not knowing what he'd do, but soon enough, his hand forced hers from his chest to the throbbing bulge between his legs. Her hands felt his manhood through the thin layer of his pants and, almost as an after-effect, she understood his monumental concern and the insurmountable odds of healing his sickness before they were married. Still, she gripped it in her palm.

"Is this where it hurts?" she whispered softly in his ear.

It took him all but a few minutes to relieve himself inside of her, both of them willing conspirators. When he departed for his hostel a half-hour later, his symptoms had been replaced by both new knowledge and new fear. Each time his symptoms resurfaced, he turned to her for the same remedy. It also cured stress during test times, anger and frustration from losing several important field hockey matches, and boredom on weekend nights when everyone went to an old movie in the auditorium. Neither of them knew of the consequences.

As soon the young man confessed to the administration that he had impregnated his fiancé, however, the unmarried couple had a serious talk with the Principal and with the Dean of Students of the medical college who pulled him off the athletic fields. Never had the Principal been so shocked to learn of a couple copulating before marriage. He thought they were better than that. What they did went totally against the values and traditions of the college. The Principal imparted a stern lecture that cast a pall of shame upon them before summarily throwing them out of the prestigious college in Rawalpindi. They returned broken and humiliated to their respective families in Clifton.

With his fiancé pregnant, the boy had nowhere else to go but back home. In fact, he expected to be disowned. His future wife, of course, would be taken in and coddled for having to fight off the predatory impulses of a deviant, perverted teenager who forced himself into her room and committed an unspeakable deed.

"You have shamed our family," said his doctor-father, thoroughly disgraced. His son had been expelled from the very college that would have confirmed him as Minister of Health. "What the hell were you thinking? All you had to do was wait. We could have married you sooner if you had said something, you damned fool!"

"Father," he said, "the situation was critical. I had no choice but to take matters into my own hands."

"No choice? Are you joking? You expect me to believe

that?"

"I'm telling you the truth, father. I had no choice."

"Explain it to me, then. How did you not have a choice in the matter?"

"You have to believe me."

"Then explain it to me? Why couldn't you have just tied it in a knot?"

"You want me to explain it now?"

"Yes, now, you idiot! When do you think I want you to explain it to me? Tomorrow?"

"It's hard to explain. I lost control. I was in serious trouble. I was not feeling well. I was very sick, feverish almost. I was in great pain, terrible pain. I couldn't sleep at night. I was sick, I'm telling you! Sick!"

"And that's your excuse? That you were sick? Give me a break. You just couldn't tough it out until after you were married. You're weak, plain and simple. You have always been a weak man with a weak mind. You cornered her in her room of all places, and you forced yourself upon her in the most awful way. You are very lucky the college agreed to keep this all confidential or else this entire family would be finished, I tell you! Finished! All because of your stupidity and your selfish impulse to screw before your time. How senseless, selfish, and stupid you are!"

"I'm sorry, father. I'd reverse it if I could, but I can't take it back. Now what do we do?"

His father stood from his chair, put his hands on his hips, and let out a heavy, foreboding sigh.

"We have to get rid of this child of yours."

"Wait. What?"

"The child will be born out of wedlock, and yes, the child has to be born, no doubt. Anything else, and we could easily wind up in jail for the rest of our lives. We can't take care of the child ourselves. Imagine what our friends in town will say? Imagine what my colleagues will say? I'll be run out of the profession. The only people who know of this is our family, your fiance's family, the Principal and the Dean at the college. The problem is contained, in other words. Nothing has changed except that you two are home, and the child is safe inside of her, waiting to be born.

"But it's our child, father."

"Of course, it's your child! Who else's could it be?! I thought all that schooling and tutoring taught you something, but I guess I was wrong. Maybe you need even more of it!"

"So, what are we to do?" he asked, hoping to steer him back on track.

"Just give me some time, and I'll have to think of a solution that is best for our family and your fiance's family."

"We're still to be married, right?"

"Oh, I don't know. You're just a couple of stupid kids who have gotten us into big trouble. Big trouble. You just couldn't wait? What got into your head?"

"I was sick, I tell you! Dear God, I swear it. I was sick! There is no cure for it!"

"Quiet down! Don't blame this on modern medicine, please. I don't want to hear any more of it. And you're blaming science for your idiocy? Just shut up until I find a solution. You are not to go anywhere. You are not to see or speak to any of your idiot friends either. You got that? You understand that at least?"

"Yes, sir. I am sorry, father."

"It's a little too late for that," he said, breathing heavily into the musty air. "I just hope you didn't ruin us all."

It turned out that the young man didn't ruin his family. Instead, they sheltered the young fiancé and hid her from public view. When the time came, she gave birth in the doctor's office in Clifton in the middle of the night. They used the same organization to which the madam-housewife belonged to auction off the child to the highest bidder. Another childless couple up north became the proud new owners of a child who never was to be heard from again. Nameless and without a background, the frail, blanketed parcel fetched a handsome sum for both families. The marriage of the couple had been postponed indefinitely, if not altogether scrapped. They decided the two didn't belong together.

The father, not knowing what to do with his son, exercised the only option available. He sent him to the Pakistani military, as that would be the best and the safest place for him. Pursuing a career in medicine had been too tall an order for this simpleton. A career in the military suited him much better. His son used his athletic prowess to learn how to fight instead of the more maudlin and empathetic art of healing the sick and caring for the infirm. After all, he could never rightfully claim his family's cultured breeding and high intelligence as his own. He never delivered on what his father had dreamt for his family. A good education only went so far, he figured. It only did so much when he hadn't really been his son to begin with.

With his fiancé still in seclusion and his career in medicine terminated, the young man left Clifton for the nearest recruiting station deep in the urban fray of chaotic Karachi. He carried a lifetime of shame when he arrived there and signed on the dotted line.

Now as an older man in the ISI, he gazed upon these

Pashtuns and Afghan-Arabs left in his charge while they meandered through the mud. They slid on their bellies through the obstacle course, the sun setting under the mountains and casting its blood-red colors on their makeshift training camp. Most of them would die. Some of those who had been sent across the border had probably already been killed. Not that it mattered much. Neither did he care if the Russians took Afghanistan. He would have sided with any power that had the audacity to hold a gun to his head no matter what country it was. That's what he had learned about survival after training with the ISI. The ISI wanted him, because he at least had an aristocratic background. He at least had some experience in medicine before choosing the ultimate patriotic path. Just like in most countries, he found good company in the ISI. He earned a spot on their roster, as though his kind were already meant to be an officer.

He took to his rifle and fired a loud, startling shot high into the horizon. All activity at the camp stopped, his platoon stilled while plastered in the cold mud.

"I said keep your asses down, or I'm going to shoot them off!"

Once the echo of the shot drifted over the immediate hills below the mountains, the platoon continued to elbow its way through the obstacle course they had built by themselves. After firing the shot, the Officer thought only about getting assigned far away from the bleak, cold oblivion of the training camp, hopefully out of the country and away from the Muslim world, so that he could live a little at the very least. Instead, the ISI gave him the shit work of training fanatical zealots wanting to be blasted to kingdom come on one side, and on the other these toothless, beggar refugees who had nowhere else to go.

He spat on the ground as the fighters took their turns.

He hated what he saw in them. He hated what he himself had become, even though he had the power and prestige of being an ISI officer. He could have been a doctor with a family in Clifton. He could have been raising a brood of his own who would have then gone on to become doctors successful enough to immigrate out the fundamentalist shithole that Pakistan had become. He could have been living in more prosperous countries where even these Pashtun fighters could have earned top-dollar and driven around in Mercedes-Benzes all day.

And in his sights, he saw another ass too high off the ground. He took up his rifle for the third time and aimed it at the very same ass who had always kept his ass too high off the ground. He wanted to fire it badly and kill the man who ignored his instructions time and again. It would teach his platoon a valuable lesson if he simply squeezed the trigger and blew the Pashtun's recalcitrant ass right off the face of the earth. Another dead Pashtun or Arab wouldn't have made any difference in the war.

He almost pulled the trigger, but just before doing so, he paused before making another terrible mistake, a mistake made on impulse, another mistake made because he was sick and in pain again. Yes, he wanted to kill the fighter, but he threw his rifle to the ground and knelt in the same muck these fighters had been crawling through all afternoon. He couldn't hack it in Northern Pakistan anymore. He couldn't hack the war anymore. A few screws had fallen loose. At least he realized it.

Leaving his rifle stuck in the ground, he marched to his commanding officer's tent not far from the barracks that housed some of the worst fighters he ever had the dishonor of training. He marched in to find his Commander staring into the stone hearth of a crackling fire, sipping from a dented tin cup filled with dry British gin.

Drunk as usual, the commanding officer turned to his runt of an adjutant next to him and ordered him to pour his sick Officer-friend a drink too. The Officer needed to loosen up anyway and tell his commander that he was leaving the Northwest Frontier for good, never to return. Obviously, his commanding officer wanted him to speak freely, not that it had ever stopped him before. His commander already knew what was on his mind. It was the same thing he had always wanted. The ISI officer wanted to return to Karachi, to live out the rest of his days in unceremonious peace and tranquility.

"You don't think I know how it feels?" said his Commander, taking a swig of his gin. "You think I like it here too? Why don't you have a seat. You're making me nervous."

"Permission to speak freely, sir?"

"Sure."

"Sir, I think I am really losing my mind this time."

"You want out?"

"Yes. I want to return to Karachi, to my family home in Clifton. I need immediate psychiatric help. I can't handle it up here anymore. I have to return to civilian life before I do something I'll regret."

Chortling from this admission, the Commander took another swig of his gin.

"It's funny," he said.

"What' funny?" asked the ISI officer.

"That you think there's a way out."

"I'm walking this time, and you can't stop me either."

"Oh, my dear friend, you can globetrot all around the

world if you wish. But if anyone asks you – and you heard it from me first – they'll always find you and drag you back your black ass back here no matter where you go. The harder you try to leave, the harsher the place they'll station you after they grab your hairy, Pak balls and put you in a place worse than they had you in before. You should know that by now."

"I have put in way above and beyond the number of years required of me here. I need out, and I need out now. You can't deny me that."

"Oh, yes I can. You don't leave until I say you can leave. Remember who you're working for. You are owned by the government of Pakistan. You are an instrument of the ISI. You might as well have it tattooed on your balls. We tell you where and when you can go, and what, if anything, you can do and where you can do it. But this time, it is obvious to me that you do need a break. But to be relieved of duty? To retire? None of us has that privilege, my friend. Your presumptuousness astonishes even me."

Lightly buzzed, the ISI officer stared into the fire with his commanding officer, both equally entranced by the dancing light and both trying to find their way out of the war through the flames. While the fire's hypnosis captured the ISI officer, his commander was still sober enough to order him out of the Northwest Frontier.

"You'll still be on the job," he said, "but I'm sending you home.

"To do what?"

"It's not your job to know. Your job is here – to train these fighters. But not anymore. Islamabad needs someone in Karachi."

"I'll do it. Tell Islamabad right away."

"Don't worry. I'll tell them. I guess you're a lucky man today. In many ways, I envy you."

"So, what do they want me to do. I need specifics."

"They want you to liaison with the Americans."

"Americans?"

"How's your English?"

"I don't know any."

"We need you fluent in a month."

"Wait a second. Just hold on. I'm not some desk-jockey flake. Why don't they take me over the border? I need some action. I'm not just going to sit on my ass, eat sweets, and get fat all day."

"You? In Gujarat? Pshaw! We don't need another one of ours terrorizing Dot-heads all across India. We have plenty of those."

"I'm not made for that spook shit, sir. I'm a soldier."

"Oh, I think it's time you learn something new," he said, smiling into the fire. "You are tired of it here, aren't you?"

"Yes, but – "

" – but nothing. Take it, or you'll do another three years here, maybe four."

"Then I'll take it. Why wouldn't I take it?"

"Good. I'd say you've done your time here. You've paid your dues. Karachi is where you're going from here. But don't you dare let anyone outside ISI know what you're doing. You're not there on a social call. Quite the opposite, actually. We're putting you in the Embassy. You're to get in tight with the Consulate there. Find out all you can. Report it back to Islamabad. You'll receive further instructions when you get home."

More mystified than overjoyed by this tremendous turn of events, the ISI officer wondered if they'd even let him carry a piece with him anymore. Either way, he did look forward to catching the next transport to Karachi, and maybe sleeping around with the whores for a week before his time came to work again.

"And sir?" he said.

"What?" grumbled his commanding officer.

"I'm not so sure if I should thank you for this."

"Oh, just get on your fucking way, will you? I hope I never have to see you again."

Chapter Eighteen

January 2001 – Karachi, Pakistan

For the man who peers into the vacancy of his own future and foresees those same years haunted by shame, torment, and folly, those same years that he sees in advance that he in no way can recover what has already been lost and severed, such as the women he had once known, the ones who had left him, and the ones he had wanted for himself but could never have, the same women who blinded him with longings so acute that he had known nothing else but resentment while in their presence, he may otherwise in his present state imagine a young Sherry Aspen alone in her bed at Jinnah Hospital in Karachi with her thin eyelids closed, her skin fleeced in soft blonde down, and her blonde hair strewn all over the pillows upon which her tender head rested and shudder at the thought of beholding his princess whom he had once so reviled and think differently about her while she suffered.

He must ask himself what a man so beaten down as he, a man so isolated and worked to the bone, still wants with this *fraulein*, the cause of his sorrows and impairments, the reason for the placement of his kind in the workcamps and the torture chambers where this blonde, blue-eyed menace has stored him, the woman who has never cared for him, who has never wanted to know him, who has never thought one iota about his welfare, as he must pick his axe into the ground below for a slave-master who oversees his work while she waits at home for him after his hard day of slave-driving, his arms sore from whipping, tired from shouting commands and witnessing his lower legions routinely shirking their duties, routinely performing shoddily, unable to work up to his expectations, never making their quota of earnings, as this is the man she wants and truly cares for and not the man who cares for her by default.

Instead, this *fraulein*, in keeping with her same traditions, only follows what makes sense to her, unable to see or avoid the ugly, avoid these same people she never wants to associate with, these same people who carry her luggage, hail her taxis, and shovel the shit from the sidewalks in front of her house. These are the men she will not fuck or marry, because, in a sense, she cares not for the sacrifices they have made on her behalf, as those sacrifices have given her the best of everything. Instead, she shares the sum of their labors with the slavedriver who claims that he alone has toiled and struggled, as his arms are too sore and his mind too frustrated from being the only man alive responsible for delivering her happiness in a world of ugly and lazy peasants.

But how long can such a resentment last as he sees her lying there with her legs encased in heavy plaster, knowing too that if she had her way, those two Pashtuns would have still been alive instead of executed by those bastard paramilitary goons. Because Sherry Aspen has suffered. She has paid her dues. Yes, she is beautiful, but for the man who knows that his life is going nowhere, he can no longer hold her beauty against her. He can no longer look upon her in anger and claim that the world has given him nothing and at the same time assume that the world has given it all to her. She has sacrificed herself for the greater good. She is also a human being who is neither so privileged nor so prone to privilege as he had once thought. Because after he looks back at the nonsense of his own petty wants and desires, he realizes, then, what a terrible industry it is to blame and resent the only woman he loves just for being born into beauty and at the same time assume that she never feels pain or will never know his kind of suffering.

It may be difficult indeed to make the crossing from a man who resents her to a man who forgives her, but it must be done to unveil the truth of what such a woman is and not what she seems to be as presented by those who use her for their own advantage and gain. Because those who use her are too expert at presenting her image alone without any substance behind the woman who endears others to her own image. Her image becomes a sign of privilege and success rather than the substance of what it takes to build privilege and success. The sign wins over the substance of her, because it takes too much effort and time to investigate the woman's truth underneath the veil of her image. In this sense, for the man who is riddled by his own failures, Sherry Aspen can no longer be a sign but instead a woman of substance and therefore worthy of his forgiveness and worthy of being deemed innocent for the hatreds he holds for his own existence. He must admit to himself that while he may be a nothing, she is not to blame for it, as she is not a nothing like him. There is, in fact, no one to blame for his own nothingness, because her eyes cannot possibly focus on the nothing he is. It forces the issue into the realm of God and not her own innate trait of seeing the nothing he is when there is so much around her, so much possibility, so much life.

She is no longer chained anymore to the inevitability of the man's slow decent into death when he must understand that his life is headed in that direction. Perhaps the man is acting like a child demanding some attention and for damn good reason, but he cannot blame a woman's beauty for not paying attention to him when his path leads to nothingness and hers to all of the abundance a good life affords.

Letting her go is the order of the day, and he must consider this carefully, because the energy within him that allows him to blame her for all of his troubles is the only element of his sordid days that keeps him alive, as though blaming her is the only reason he stays alive, so that she may hear his plaintive call and pray to dear God that she pays attention to him and not coddle the same slavedriver whom she has had the misfortune of associating with. In other words, if he lets her free, he loses his identity, and to lose his identity would mean to lose his history, and perhaps his history is worth preserving, and so, he cannot let this particular woman go, because otherwise he would negate all that he has learned, the miracle of what he has learned, even though it still amounts to nothing.

If one should lose his grip on this amazingly beautiful woman, then perhaps he is truly lost. She is not to blame for his troubles, but she is at least the guiding light beyond his own death. Good luck to her, because she is what he desires before he grows lackluster, infirm, and unimportant. She is unable to see beyond the slave-master she loves and unable to latch on to the one who truly loves her. At least he is trying to save her as she fucks the man who abuses her. So be it, Sherry Aspen. At least a lonely man can no longer blame her for all that has gone wrong with his life. He can only look after his sweetheart and hope she outwits her terrible fate and makes it out alive.

She is free now, and this is for the best, because by setting her free, he is also setting himself free. He accepts his own inadequacies and faults and also accepts that such a woman was never meant for his sole embrace. She was never meant for him. Call it the cruelty of the world, the system of how things really work, or the fascism behind the beating heart, but he cannot label her cruel and continue to cage her by insulting her and continually hoping that she'll respond to his insults. Such behavior only hurts himself and not anyone else. In the end, she deserves to be freed from his anger and his gaze that searches her out, zeroes in on her, and snuffs her by aggrandizing his unending fascination. Still, he wonders if she has ever known what it is like to look upon a beauty such as she and crumble at the sight of her. Perhaps she will never know, and maybe it's best that it remains that way. It is best that she not see him there looking upon her as she lies in her hospital bed, her body draped in a flimsy blue gown, her legs broken, and her consciousness swimming in the ether of pain killers that keep her drifting in and out of sleep. Yet she feels someone near her. She hears a voice, not a consoling one, but one that is sharp, like a lieutenant, and constrained, like a judge at sentencing.

"You really fucked this one up," he said, standing next to her bed.

When she came to, the blur of the Karachi Station Chief's face condensed and sharpened to show an unusually tall man with a well-cut build in a grey business suit that fit tightly to his body. He was upset with her, that was obvious, and even though she had been recovering at Jinnah Hospital for the past several days, the Station Chief didn't have much sympathy for her. She blinked at him a few times and confirmed that he wore a fierce expression. She then remembered what brought her to the hospital in the first place and the two Pashtuns her team had done away with.

"You're going home," he said curtly. "Your time here is done."

"What are you talking about?" she asked drowsily.

"You nearly caused an international incident with the stunt you pulled. What were you thinking?"

"It's the information I was after," she said, becoming fully alert.

"And what's that? What did you find out?"

"If you're sending me home, then why should I tell you?"

"Don't play cute with me, missy. You're lucky you're still alive. Spit it out. What did the Commander tell you?"

"I have no idea what you're talking about."

"Fine. You want to play games? Go ahead, then. But you're on the next flight out of here tomorrow. Your mission is over."

"What I know is important. You scratch my back, and I'll scratch yours."

"What a second. Who the hell do you think you're talking to?"

"The man who ordered the deaths of two innocent Pashtuns who saved an asset's life."

"I can beat it out of you, if you like."

"You wouldn't do that, because what I got out of him is good, and I don't squeal too easily. I also have a nasty habit of forgetting things."

"Hey, if I wanted you dead, it'd be no skin off of anyone's nose. Not even the Deputy Director whose mission you completely fucked up."

"But what I have trumps all that. If you want it, you can have it, but only if you're willing to keep me on. Last thing I want to do is go home with my tail between my legs and be the laughing stock of the whole Company."

"God, you really are a vain little cunt to be talking that way to me. A Pakistani commander is dead, and you're lucky our own men got out alive without the whole world finding out about it. You think you're in a position to bargain with me when all you care about is not looking like an idiot when I send you back?"

"I have my reasons for not wanting to leave, and now you have your reasons for keeping me on. Do we have a deal or not?"

By the way his jaws clenched, she knew she had him.

"First," she said, "put me on another assignment, since the one I'm on is dead."

"You're really pushing it."

"Give me something to do other than pack my bags and head home."

"If I put you on assignment again, you are to get authorization for every little move you make. If you take a shit near a foreign embassy, I want to hear about it. You follow orders. No straying outside the lines. I want reports for every Goddamned thing that you do. Am I making myself perfectly clear?"

"Yes, I give you my word."

"You know better than that. An asset's word means nothing out here. I want a guarantee."

"The information I'm giving you is my guarantee, and if I fuck up again, you can send me packing, and you won't hear a single word of complaint out of my mouth."

Once again, he clenched his jaws. She didn't know if he was busy deliberating or restraining himself from ripping her throat out.

"Lemme call Langley, then. Even I need authorization for the things that I do. Give me a moment."

He pulled away the blue nylon curtain that separated her from the rest of the hospital and made a phone call a few feet away. She heard him murmuring but couldn't decipher what he said. He returned a few minutes later wearing the same lock-jawed and tight-lipped expression that had added weight to his solemnity.

"You have strict instructions this time," he said. "It's to meet with an ISI Officer here in Karachi and get on his good side. You're to come on to him and make sure that he wants to be with you. When the time is right, I want you to give him the message that Langley wants the ISI to begin moving Afghan emigres out of Northern Pakistan and return them back home to Kabul, Kandahar, and the other Pashtun areas of Afghanistan. We want them to resettle them out of the north. In return, we'll give them more weaponry. Believe me, he'll like the idea, and his ISI chiefs will approve of it. They have to start moving them back there anyway. These Taliban types are more radical than the Mujahideen that killed themselves after the Soviets left. We want them out. It's too risky to have them destabilize Pakistan, especially since we are still on good terms with them.

"You let him know you're an asset when he admits he's ISI. The fact that you'll be in relationship with this man is the only reason we have that he'll bite, and you're the bait. First, the sugar. Then, the medicine, when the time is right."

"Yessir."

"And now your part of the deal. What did the Commander tell you?"

"It's the Iranians and the Israelis again, sir. The MIOS wants to buy from the Kremlin, and what they buy will go right to Hezbollah for an Iranian attack from their north."

"Are you certain about this?"

"The words came straight for the Commander's mouth."

"Good. I'll call it in to have it verified. In the meantime, don't fuck this up, Sherry. Don't you dare fuck any of this up. Play nice with this guy until he's ready to take the deal to his bosses. Understood?"

"Yessir."

"And I want reports filed into my office every day – from the first day you meet him to the time you bid your farewells. Is that understood?"

"Yessir."

"Good. You contact me in Karachi if we have any fuck-ups, but there won't be any fuck-ups, right?"

"No, sir. I am on it."

"Good. Welcome back, Sherry. You get to live twice."

"Thank you, sir."

"And I mean what I say. Don't fuck this up. All you're doing is giving him a message and adding your persuasion to it. That's it."

"I understand, sir. Thank you, sir."

For the next couple of weeks, Sherry took a room at the *Hotel Intercontinental* in Karachi until her legs fully healed. Aside from obligatory doctor's visits, she didn't go outside at all. She went downstairs to the restaurant for her meals and then back up to her room where she read the newspaper, *Dawn*, and wrote several letters to her mother in Vermont, letting her know that her position with the State Department had been the best career move she had ever made. As soon as she was promoted, she'd send even more money back home to help out with the farm. She didn't inquire about her father, though, thinking that he'd rather not remember her for leaving the farm in peril. At least with the money she had been forwarding them, the farm still operated. Her father, however, wouldn't be able to retire for another year, or until the Company bumped her up a pay grade. Considering what had transpired in Helmand, that was a remote possibility.

She tried to think of how the Deputy of Intelligence reacted to what had happened in Afghanistan. She was tempted to write him as well but didn't know quite what to say or how to word things. She didn't think an apology were necessary, especially when her two Pashtun friends had been shot dead. This sore point explained what intelligence work involved. Assets usually did have to sacrifice the ones who helped them, and while it didn't sit well with her at all, such sacrifices were necessary for the job. An asset, though, never really got used to it. The Company took everyday people who wished only to feed their families and make a decent living and led them into grandiose daydreams of Western decadence. When the time came for the Company to deliver, however, it reneged and watched as these everyday acquisitions languished in jail cells where their captors starved and tortured them, eventually putting a bullet between their eyes.

Her body resting against his back as he carried her over the perilous terrain of Helmand and the rich smell of hashish and tobacco on his skin haunted her at night. Sometimes she woke up sweating and hearing the shots and the thuds of their bodies fall to the ground. Between fear and shame for what had transpired, there was also anger at what the Company did to cover its tracks. What's more, she wasn't sure if the Company did wrong in killing the two brothers. They did what she would have done. But the more she reviewed what took place, the more she inured herself to their deaths. The more closely she analyzed each and every snippet of the scene, the more her mind became a buffer that separated the ideation of what had happened with the reality of their being killed for no good reason. As long as it wasn't she, she figured, it was better to mourn the loss of life and force a tear out than be the next one to die as needlessly as they did.

While secluded in the hotel room, she took baths almost twice a day. The bathroom had a heavy ceramic tub, much like the one at the farmhouse in Vermont. She had no desire to please herself in the tub, though. She let the warm water envelope her lean body up to her neck and unfurled her taut muscles to where it soothed the fissures of her healing bones, like a hallucinogen that untangles a knotted psyche. Sometimes she lay in the tub for prolonged periods of time, letting her skin flake and wrinkle. The warm bathwater comforted her like a womb does a newborn. When her body was waterlogged enough, she lifted herself out and walked on the balls of her feet to the newly-made bed and fell on the cool bedsheets while stark naked, staring into the ceiling. But within those walls of security into which no one could pry, she felt the Company tugging at her. She heard the clock on the nightstand ticking. Such freedom in doing nothing, she thought, the door to her room tightly secured without any noise to be heard, only the mellowing Karachi sun creeping through the curtains with the air conditioner on, her time of peace and contentment, her time of idle nothingness in which her own consciousness slipstreamed into infinity. With both legs fully healed, with a steady gait, she reported for duty by calling the Station Chief and announcing her intention to make first contact with this ISI Officer.

No, she did not know what to expect, only that initiating a romantic relationship with him, while not a pleasing thought considering how the Commander had looked and behaved, would come fairly easily and quickly. She was never too fond of Pakistani men. They thought they were smarter than everyone else and had volcanic tempers that erupted when least expected. They preferred their women uneducated and submissive, another unpalatable feature of these short, brown egomaniacs, especially those in the ISI and the Pakistani military. She had no idea how he would respond to her, but given how black and brown men responded to her kind, it should be a walk in the park, an easy assignment to deliver the message and then persuade him to pass on the request to his bosses.

She understood, however, that she was irreversibly American as well. She wouldn't be trusted as an equal or capable partner. She needed something to trade besides amazing sex, but sex alone wouldn't do it. She could offer him citizenship in the United States, but his chiefs wouldn't accept the deal if they lost one of their assets to the US. She would have told him of the Russian arms deal to the Iranians if he didn't know that already. And when she realized it, her heart plummeted into the pit of her stomach. She wasn't supposed to do anything of value.

Well, he would never take her heart. No one could ever have her heart. And yet her country owned it, and her country used it, and her country could trample on it if it wanted to, and she'd allow it. She could lie and say she loved him, cared for him, wanted his children, but she would never surrender her heart, not to any man. Another nail in the coffin of a Company asset. Fine, she thought. Fine. Her diminishing heart would remain locked and chained in the iron chamber she placed it in, dwindling into a cold, dry, lifeless, worthless, overused artifact of what it could have been. Femininity in reverse, like a blazing hot poker carving out the hollow of her chest leaving a gaping cavity of charred flesh and bone, a once-beating organ singed into uselessness. The mission demanded no less.

The *duppurta* she wore to the Consular function at the

American Embassy fit tightly enough to alert all of those in attendance of her milk-white exquisiteness and uncommon kinship with the people of Pakistan. She had to pretend even this, as the goal was not to impress other Americans at the gathering, but the private appetites of the Pakistani men there. The Station Chief had given her the photograph and a near-complete dossier of the ISI Officer's tireless work with the Pahstun and Arab fighters during the old Soviet invasion many years ago. Predictably, the bloody Afghan Civil War ridiculed the same country the Russians had abandoned.

She knew when to look at a man and then to look away, if only to get the man to look at her and then follow her around the room, to have ideas that upended the gentility of the display, like teeth biting into the skin of an apple and tasting the forbidden flesh that hid beneath its sour surface. All parties were about the allure of sex after all, and this one was no different, only that when she walked into the room at the Embassy, she already had her prey in mind, if only she could find him there. She was the daughter of a State Department worker stationed in Karachi, an underling to be taken advantage of, to be misled, to have her young heart gutted and reduced to pulp. She carried herself with an air of innocence as a prop for her act, another young white American floozy wanting to be important if only she found the right guy to take her through the never-ending maze of parties, dinners, and diplomatic soirees, to one day dine with exiled kings and Third-World strongmen who had too much wealth to know what to do with in mock-democracies that starved its own people but still gave them free reign to travel the world, flirt, and dance with other deposed leaders who lived in mansions built on the backs of slaves from the deep South, starving refugees, and noble feudal peasants, only because their power allied itself neatly with the interests of the Stock Exchange, real estate speculators, venture capitalists, and asset managers who forced open markets, extract resources, and sold them wholesale to the highest bidder.

Yeah, that kind of innocent, naïve, fuckable girl that every dark-skinned animal from a foreign country hanging around a Western embassy wanted. She would be the woman all-too-easily entranced by a man's position and status, the woman whom a man takes under his wing so that she can avoid the memory of the broken down, cancer-stricken Dad she abandoned back in East Bumfuck. He'll slip jewels on her fingers and hang pearls around her neck. Yeah, that kind of top-shelf woman to be picked up and thrown away until the next good looking young thing comes around. She knew he'd fall for her submissiveness right away. He could take this bright-eyed, bushy-tailed blonde bunny as a mistress to compliment his lifeless marriage to the Pakistani woman who actually cares for the bastard. Another Third-World dummy to be toyed with.

A woman as readily astonishing as she could not be left standing alone for too long. Rubbing up against her, another fat State Department bureaucrat, part of another envoy hoping to get something out of these worthless Pakis, who, because they were on their own turf, were actually worthy of being talked to, for what reason, she didn't know, nor did she care, only that she should find her target, the next acquisition, and dispense with the useless automaton who asked her the same mundane questions that had been asked of her too many times before, yielding the same tired outcome: that she wouldn't give him her phone number to where she stayed in Karachi, because she would never be lonely enough to call him just in case she wanted to ruin his life with the beauty she had been born with and took for granted.

She had a few sips of champaign with him, since alcohol

was allowed at American-sponsored functions, and then on to the next worthless obstacle, nothing but mostly white State Department lackeys wanting to take her to bed, her *duppurta* on white skin in keeping with the fair up-and-coming, go-getting, ass-kissing, cock-sucking consort to the powerful and those pretending to be powerful. Another American obstacle, and then another obstacle, like a fullback breaking tackles and stiff-arming helmets. It happened all night long until she finally broke through to the Pakistani side of the tracks, to a close cadre of brown men in suits laughing along with a grey-haired older gentleman with pineapple chunks taken out of cheeks.

"Who's that?" she asked the white American in a suit standing next to her.

"That guy over there?"

"Yeah. He seems important."

"That's because he is."

"Do you know him?"

"Yes. Why?"

"Can you introduce me to him?"

"Sure. He's the Consulate General of Pakistan."

"Really? Yes, please. I want to meet him."

"Sure. No problem. He's not too hard to meet."

She followed his lead, moving around those chatting in groups of two's and three's. They sipped wine, beer, champagne, and any alcohol they could get their hands on. The man who escorted her nudged them into the circle of Pakistanis surrounding the Consulate General. Up close, the Consulate General's jowls sagged, and the scars on his face cut deeply against the grain of his skin. Nevertheless, he commanded the respect of those surrounding him as they walled him off from the rest of the party as though imperceptibly protecting him from an assassination attempt. But when they made it within earshot, the group of brown men in suits opened their circle, their arms spreading wide to welcome a couple of curious guests into their home. For all of their posturing, getting to the Consulate General wasn't very hard at all.

"Ah," he said, "what have we here?"

He had been drinking, and this put him in jovial mood. He seemed to be too august of a man to hit on her that evening. His avuncular smile and the slight hump on his back told her that he was happily married with children, domesticated, and had no need for an extramarital affair. He just wasn't the type.

"Sir," said the American escorting her, "may I introduce Sherry. She's the daughter of one of our State Department officials out here in Karachi."

"Ah, Sherry!" said the Consulate. "What a wonderful name you have. I like to drink it from time to time."

His cronies smiled along with him. These were four men who most likely served under him.

"I really love your country," she said. "This is my first visit here. There are so many sites I want to see."

"Oh, yes, there are," he smiled happily.

"Can you give me the names of a few places, so that I can visit them tomorrow?"

"There are too many places to count, but I'd start off with *Quadi's Mausoleum*. That's where our great leader Mohammad Ali Jinnah is buried."

His cronies nodded in agreement.

"Or how about the *National Museum*?" he continued, "and then to *Empress Market* to buy a few souvenirs for your family back home? How long will you be in Karachi for?"

"For at least a month."

"Wonderful! I would hire a driver for the day, and he'll take you around to all of these places, to eat out at *Do Daya*. That's not bad, or how about *Port Grand* right on the sea? You can buy a tourist guide from a bookshop and explore all of the beauty our beloved country has to offer."

"But I don't want to go alone," she pouted. "I need someone to come with me. It's not right for a young girl to travel all alone in a big city, is it?"

"Especially someone as beautiful as you, Miss Sherry."

She went down the line of workers who flanked the Consulate General, studying their features until she found the man whose photograph hung prominently in her memory.

"How about you?" she asked.

She faced an older man with a completely bald head and wearing a black, neatly-trimmed moustache. His skin was much lighter in hue than the dense black hair that covered his upper lip. He must have colored it with black dye to hide the grey. His slim athletic build suggested that he exercised as part of his daily routine. He had shaved closely that morning as the stubble on his face hardly showed. Only his smooth, fair skin that he may have saturated with lotion shined in the glow of the ceiling lights. He wore cologne, the scent of which she couldn't determine. With all of these features combined, Sherry faced a surprisingly handsome gentleman whose brown eyes darted back and forth nervously when she picked him out of the lineup. He didn't answer her question, though. All of the workers waited for the Consulate General to make the decision.

"Oh, sure, why not?" he laughed jovially. "Go ahead, you two, why don't you. Show this young American flower around Karachi. You need a break anyway."

"Sir," said the man, "with all due respect, I'm not properly suited for this assignment. I have too much work upstairs, and – "

"Tut, tut," said the Consulate General holding up his index finger. "Nonsense. I won't hear another word of it. When such a fetching woman is a guest in our country, it is only proper that she be chaperoned by a man so protective as yourself. I won't have her traveling alone looking as she does."

"But sir, I – "

"No buts. You work too hard already. Show her around town, will you?"

"Yes, sir. Of course."

The man bowed his head courteously, acquiescing to his demands. Sherry stood in front of the same man in the photograph whose features she knew so well: the ISI Officer with whom she had just made first contact.

"It is my honor," he said to Sherry.

"You don't have to lie," she said teasingly. "That's not a good way to start, now is it?"

The Consulate General roared with laughter.

"And a sassy sense of humor too! How wonderful! My top man has finally met his match."

The ISI Officer smiled weakly. Obvious to her, showing her around Karachi was more of a chore he would have rather passed off onto someone else. This made him all the more attractive. He was not one for entertainment. There must have been something special about him. She wouldn't mind his company in the least.

"How about ten o'clock in the lobby of the Hotel Intercontinental?"

"Yes, madam," he said, "that would be fine."

"Great," she smiled. "See you tomorrow, then. I'm looking forward to it."

"I as well," he said.

"I'll make you mean what you say by the time our day is over."

"Yes, madam," he said perfunctorily. "I look forward to it."

He placed his hand on his chest and bowed his head slightly, trying not to make such a big deal out of it in front of his friends who tried admirably to hold in their laughter. She left their company and walked to the other side of the room with the same white American who had introduced them.

"Hey, you could have asked me," said the American. "Why didn't you?"

"I wanted a more authentic Pakistani experience."

"Yeah, but you have nothing in common with them. I could have taken you around."

"Maybe some other time, sweetie," she said, holding her hand to his cheek.

"Well, at least let me take you home. Wouldn't want you to get kidnapped out there."

"I'm a big girl. I'll be fine on my own, thanks."

Relieved that she had found the ISI Officer, she had no other reason to stay at a party whose guests were slowly filtering out anyway. She had an immediate urge to get as drunk as possible to celebrate the victory but then remembered that she first had to file a report into Karachi Station. Still, she had a couple more glasses of champagne and listened to an emotional *ghazal* by Nusrat Fateh Ali Khan playing on the overhead speakers before leaving. The champagne made her a little lightheaded, and when she looked behind her towards the back of the room where the ISI Officer stood deferentially next to the Consulate General, she couldn't help but become more mystified by him. She figured he hid his wounds behind a cloak of reverential respect, but to a fault. She liked the idea of loosening him up, as that was her first order of business – to get him not to brood so much and not to be so concerned about his chivalrous Pakistani honor and all the bullshit that went along with it. She'd get to him. She was sure of it. Piece of cake.

She met him in the hotel lobby the next morning. He was freakishly punctual, and she made him wait for a full half-hour downstairs before calling the concierge to make sure he had arrived, hoping to stoke his curiosity and anticipation. She dressed in another *duppurta* that clung to the curves of her body, but instead of donning a headscarf, she wrapped the transparent fabric around her shoulders, leaving her blonde hair long and exposed. When she came out of the elevator, he stood from his seat. He dressed traditionally in a white *kurta*, and when he saw her walking towards him, he froze up, his eyes darting from side to side again, not knowing what to make of this woman who wore her clothing so tightly and let her hair fall so loosely upon her shoulders. The sleeves of her *duppurta* were short, and her exposed skin illuminated the room like a second sun. She had meant to frighten him, to put him on edge, to have him come to terms with her female confidence, her swagger, and an allure he had never been used to before.

The ISI Officer was taken aback, she could tell, by the power of her beauty. Sherry had little problem using her beauty to her advantage, as this was hardly the time to be modest. Instead, she flaunted this attribute in front of this lonely, quiet, and closeted older man, just for him, as though she chose him above all others when she could have easily gone with the typical white American she was with. He must have been wondering, 'why me of all people?' It made him think specifically of her, accosted by a blonde anomaly in a hotel lobby, erasing whatever strategies he had taken there from his office.

"Why, hello there," said Sherry. "Thanks for meeting me."

She offered him her hand to kiss, but instead he shook it indifferently, not showing the slightest bit of interest but silently wearing his poker face like an iron mask, his eyes still darting in an attempt to make sense of her motives.

"You are most welcome," he said softly, his Urdu-inflected accent suggesting a humility that she knew would recede once she penetrated the surface and touched the ISI lunatic he really was.

"So, where are we off to first?" she asked cheerfully.

"Well, there are a few sights we can see," he said unenthusiastically. "I thought I'd first take you to the *Quadi Mausoleum*. It's quite a sight to behold. It is the pride of our country, madam."

"You don't need to call me 'madam.' Call me Sherry."

"Sherry it is, then," he said.

"And I'd rather walk there than take a cab. It's such a nice day, don't you think?"

"It is not wise, madam. It is very hot outside, and walking in the streets can be a bit intimidating for a woman from another country. You may be more comfortable taking a cab to the places we visit."

"You mean, *you* would rather be more comfortable.

But don't worry. I'll protect you. Besides, I'd rather walk anyway. I want to take in some of the street life while I'm here in Karachi."

"You can just as well see it from a taxi, madam."

"Please, call me Sherry, and no, I'd rather walk."

"If you insist, we shall walk then."

She found his social awkwardness rather cute and almost endearing, even though he was really a killer in disguise. She couldn't tell if his reticence was part of the act or not. He had trouble determining if he should lead her through the streets first, or if he should walk behind her as a sign of respect. He had little sense of protocol while walking amidst the chattering of salesmen in vending stalls while weary old women with broken teeth crowded in the shoulder of the roads selling overly ripe fruit in wicker baskets, casting the street in a delightful swirl of multitudinous color – the red of the pomegranates, the richly dark figs, the copper-yellow apricots, and the bright orange mandarins. Within the stalls along the sidewalk, the tall, rolled fabrics of textiles and the outdoor bookshops where British and American classics had been stacked one on top of the other in cramped spaces soon led to a small, open-aired restaurant where brown, pajama-wearing men crowded around large, circular skillets and waited patiently for their hot tea, *dosas*, and other Pakistani street snacks, the sizzle of roasting spices floating up high into the air and tempting everyone within range.

Throughout their walk towards the mausoleum, she sensed his nervousness. Somehow, wherever they walked, the eyes of the street were upon them. These onlookers, men and women both, couldn't hide their fascination of one of their own touring their city with a hot, fiery Westerner. It was a rare sight to behold, his nervousness bordering on a bewitched social anxiety. He didn't want to be the object of the crowd's fascination, the stares of strangers sucking them into their logic and, perhaps, their misguided judgments. He treaded carefully, his body as stiff as a board and poised to defend, like a terminator protecting her from their perceptions and thoughts of the street people, guarding her from anyone who may have veered into the indecent as they all gazed at the star couple and imagined what they did behind closed doors.

Since he led first, she grabbed his arm and slowed him down.

"Hey, wait up," she said. "Is something wrong?"

"No, madam. It's just that out here in the streets, it can be overwhelming for a tourist."

"For me, or for you?"

"I don't understand what you mean."

"I'm mean, I have to catch my breath. You're walking too fast. I can hardly catch up. You've got to relax and enjoy yourself. Let's not rush our time together."

"You are right, madam," he sighed. "I am sorry to be so preoccupied, but the streets can be dangerous for a woman, well, or your kind and stature."

She pulled his arm towards her so that she could look at him face-to-face.

"Hey, look, I can take care of myself. I may be a tourist, but I know how to defend myself."

"Then why do you need me? I'm telling you that it's important that we don't attract too much attention, which is why I'm walking ahead of you. I know these people, and I know these streets. People get ideas when birds of a different feather flock together."

"But why? Are you embarrassed of me?"

"Of course not, madam," he said irritably. "I just don't want to invite trouble."

"Don't worry so much, okay? No one here cares who we are or why we're here."

"I am sorry, madam. I will walk slower."

"It's Sherry. Call me Sherry."

"Yes, Sherry. I am sorry."

They arrived at a tall, white-domed mausoleum that looked like a mosque. It honored the late *Quad-e-azam*, or the late Mohammed Ali Jinnah, the founding father of Pakistan. Underneath the high white dome, a Pakistani soldier, dressed in his green khaki uniform and a black beret, stood next to Jinnah's tomb with a long rifle in his hands, like the British soldiers who guarded Buckingham Palace with care and respect. A small crowd had gathered in front of the tomb.

"You should watch this," whispered the ISI Officer. "It's quite incredible."

But just as the soldier high-stepped and changed positions around the tomb, the stomping of his feet loud and its echo reverberating below the high concave arc of the white dome, Sherry pulled her headscarf from her shoulders and let it fall to the floor of the mausoleum, thereby exposing her supple white shoulders for the entire crowd to see. Even the soldier whose duty it was to concentrate exclusively on his task had little choice but to steal a glimpse of Sherry's skin upon which the caresses of soft light that entered the archways of the mausoleum touched and graced. The ISI Officer quickly grabbed the scarf from the floor and covered her shoulders again.

"Ooops," she smiled, "didn't mean to drop it. Thanks."

The ISI Officer, clearly shaken by this display, looked

like he was about to have a heart attack.

"We've seen enough here," he said. "We should go."

"But we just got here. Don't you want to look around?"

"There's nothing more to see here. We should get going."

He ferried her out of the mausoleum, and they went back out into the streets at which point Sherry broached the subject of his employment with the Consulate.

"Hey, would you slow down? It's like you're clearing the way. You're acting like a bodyguard. Is that what you are for the Consulate General? A bodyguard?"

He slowed down and said, "you can tell? Is it easy to tell?"

"For me it is. I've been around plenty of bodyguards, soldiers, and secret service types all my life. You forget that my father works for the State Department."

"I never knew this. I am sorry."

"And stop being so sorry all the time. It gets annoying after a while."

"I am sorry, madam. I will not say I am sorry any longer."

"And my name is Sherry! Not madam!"

"I understand. You want me to have a more informal relationship with you."

"I mean, you're not on the job now, are you?"

"I am always on the job," he said.

"What do you mean by that?"

"Nothing," he said quickly. "Come. You must be hungry. Would you like something to eat or drink?"

"Sure."

While walking through the bright streets teaming with old Japanese efficiency cars driving like cornered mice through thickets of brown-skinned stick-figures in the middle of the road, Sherry intentionally leaned into him on their way to a small restaurant he directed her to. Each time she did, he pulled away and made sure that his body had been properly cleaved from hers. At one point, she held his arm pretending to want to see a young child selling dirty brown finches in a bird cage, but he again pulled away in an obvious effort to avoid touching her. Even after their lunch when Sherry had again made the point that 'he wasn't what he seemed' and that he may have been more than just a bodyguard and a foreign service officer, her attempts to touch him proved fruitless.

After entering the lobby of the Hotel Intercontinental, they both stood face-to-face within the luxury of the place, and she asked him to take her to a movie, because she had nothing else to do and had no one else's company in such a large, lonely city. He declined the opportunity.

"I have work to do. I am sorry, but I cannot."

Yet she persisted. She didn't stop pleading, because this woman never stopped, as that was her duty. She pursued the idea and asked to see him after every hot, ungrateful day. But he wanted nothing to do with her, which made him even more mysterious and more attractive. All he wanted was to attend to his work back at the Consulate, and those duties didn't involve being goaded into activities with such a persistent woman with whom he had no interest being around. It ruined his stability, ruined his content and complacent routine. She continued to pick at him, tickle him, bother him, and provoke him. She kept pushing him to reveal more about himself, about his upbringing, his schooling, his family life, his professional career, but he remained tight-lipped and said very little. But he was ordered by his boss to chaperone her, especially after she called the jovial man at his office each day and complained that her chaperone didn't like her. His boss came down hard on him and ordered him to see to the poor lonely girl's safety in a foreign land until she felt safe, as the State Department would only do the same for the Consulate General's own daughters if they ever visited the US.

When they went out, she did most of the talking. He simply nodded and shook his head at her questions that attempted to get to the heart of what his true function was at the Consulate. After dropping her off at the hotel lobby after yet another tremendously hot afternoon, she wanted to see another Lollywood movie, the same Lollywood movie they had seen before, a long three-hour one, the one he fell asleep to.

"A second time?" he asked incredulously. "I'm sorry, madam, but I really have to work."

"Oh, come on," she teased. "Don't you like my company?"

"Yes, I do, but I still have to work."

"Let's just see it one more time. Please? It's such a wonderful romance. I'm sure the Consulate won't mind, will he? I can call him again. After all, I am the daughter of a State Department official in Karachi. My father is away, and I don't think I can handle it all alone."

"I'll see if I can, madam."

"Well, how do I contact you directly? I'm always talking to that stupid secretary of your boss'."

Getting a personal contact number was essential, because then she could bother him at all hours to take her sightseeing. What kind of man would leave his own daughter alone like that, he hadn't the slightest idea, and perhaps the ISI Officer started to get suspicious, but she called him right after he left the hotel after their movie and convinced him to take her out again the very next day. But first, another street-side restaurant around which vendors, loud rickshaws, beggars, and taxicabs flowed with the steady noise of engines, horns, yelling, and chattering within a continuous fog of exhaust fumes from ornamented transport trucks.

In the restaurant, while the ISI Officer sat across from her eating sticky Basmati rice with his hands, she extended her arm across the table and placed her hand upon his.

"I just really want to thank you for what you're doing. I know you don't have time to do all this. A guy like you must get a lot of girls who want you to take them out, no?"

"Why do you ask?"

"You mean, you don't have a girlfriend? You're not gay, are you?"

"No, I don't have a girlfriend, and no, I am not gay."

"Not even a girlfriend? I find that really hard to believe."

"My work takes up all of my time. There is no time for a family, I'm afraid."

"That's quite a sacrifice you're making for a position so, well, a position that's not so high up. You know what I mean? It's like there's something you're not telling me."

"Like what?"

"Oh, I don't know. It's just that there is something very strange about you. You're a tender man, but not all of you is so tender."

"I have no idea what you mean."

"Maybe it's just my American sensibilities," she laughed. "Do you even like Americans, by the way?"

"I have come into contact with a few. They are an interesting people."

"Men or women?"

"Men. I've never known any American women."

"Well, now you do. And what do you think of American women, if you use me as an example?"

"I would say that I don't know them well enough to judge."

"Good answer," she said. "When do you think you'll know?"

"I'm not sure that I'll ever know. There's too much other work to be done to be chaperoning them around Karachi all the time. I don't have the luxury of spending my time so frivolously."

"Let me ask you something. Why are you always so serious? You don't have to be so serious with me."

He looked down at this plate of rice and meat and continued eating.

"You don't have to be so rigid with me too, y'know. Don't you ever just let your hair down and have fun?"

"I don't have any hair to let down, madam."

"It's Sherry. My name is Sherry, damn it, and that's not what I meant!"

"I know what you meant, and the answer is no. I have to be vigilant at all times."

"But why?"

"It makes me better at my job."

"No kind of job demands that much seriousness. Unless there's something you're not telling me."

"Like what?"

She paused and picked at her butter chicken with the tines of her fork.

"There's something very strange about you. There's something you're not telling me."

"What is it that you want to know?"

"How did you come to work with the Consulate General? How did you become his right-hand man?"

"I moved up the ladder, just like any other civil servant."

"You went to school for it?"

"Yes, in fact, I did."

"Y'know, I'm going to medical school in the States right now."

"Oh. I didn't know that."

"Does that surprise you? That you're sitting with a soon-to-be doctor?"

"No, but I find what you want to do admirable. I too wanted to be a doctor before I entered public service."

"What happened?"

"Plans change."

"And God laughs at plans."

She didn't want to press him here. She could see that he was becoming uncomfortable with her line of questioning, but at least he revealed much more than usual. For the rest of the afternoon, even during the intermission of yet another Lollywood drama that that they viewed at a local cinema, Sherry fished out bits and pieces of his history but not enough for him to let on that he was indeed an ISI Officer. By the time the long and insufferably boring movie had ended, the sky had darkened, and she had the nerve to ask him to take her out to dinner. His reluctance to divulge anything of importance followed them, but she still fished out what she could while hoping not to push him too far. Obviously, being an ISI Officer was his well-guarded secret, but the pointed questions she asked only led them to that conclusion. It wasn't until after they had dinner that the answer finally hung over the officer's head like a bright neon sign flashing in the darkness.

While walking back to the hotel, she again leaned into him and lightly touched his arm. She told him about her past. He did not do the same. Their conversation turned out to be one-sided. She asked questions that came closer and closer to his truth.

"So let me understand something. How does a man in the military wind up in the Consulate General's office? Shouldn't you be out in the field? I don't think being trapped in a building is the right place for a soldier."

"We have options after we serve," he said.

"But don't you want to be out there in the field doing something important? You fought against the Soviets, right?"

"No. I trained *mujahideen* to fight against the Soviets."

"But then a desk job? Shouldn't you have risen in rank in the military?"

"War is its own kind of hell."

"I just thought they'd give you something a little more important to do, or that you'd stay with the military and not move on to a crummy desk job, which is really a front for being a bodyguard? There's something I'm not getting here."

She could tell she got to him. He ground his teeth at

this remark but maintained his silence. If he couldn't admit that he was an ISI Officer, then she couldn't admit that she was a Company asset. They had to be on the same page to make a deal. He had to suspect there was something extraordinary about her too, something he hadn't discovered yet. Nevertheless, the more she questioned him, the more irritated he became. She alternated between asking him these pointed questions and then flirting with him openly, the good-cop, bad-cop duality that produced the greatest possible outcome, a two-pronged attack that proved she wanted a romantic relationship with him as well as an affirmation that he was ISI. She pried into places she shouldn't have gone.

"How about a drink?" she asked him when they returned to the hotel.

"I'm sorry," he said. "It's late, and I really must get going."

"Oh, come on now. Just because you're a low-level state employee doesn't mean that you can't have a drink every once in a while."

"I can drink any time I want to," he said.

"Well, come on, then, grumpy," she smiled. "Have a drink with me."

They sat at the far corner of the hotel lobby which also had a small bar and café. They ordered tall glasses of cold American beer.

"I wouldn't worry about it," said Sherry. "You'll get a promotion eventually. Maybe you'll even get better clothes out of it. It must be hard to be someone else's assistant."

The Officer's eyes darted back and forth again. It would only take one more senseless and silly question that pointed to his lowliness to push him over the edge.

When a little tipsy, she said, "well, I guess you'll never get out of Karachi. You deserve so much more. If they'd only notice what a kind-hearted man you are. You need more confidence to make it in this world."

He could take it no longer. He pulled out a Glock from beneath his *kurta* and pointed it at her head across from where she sat.

"Now you can tell me who the hell you *really* are," he said angrily.

Sherry didn't stare at the gun. She only looked him in the eyes while placing her hands palms-down on the table where he could see them.

"Okay," she advised, "take it easy. Calm down. You don't want to do anything foolish."

Her face expressionless, she told him to calm himself a number of times until she was sure he didn't intend to fire his weapon.

"You still haven't told me who you really are," he said, holding the gun steady.

"I'm a friend. That's all. Just a friend."

"What kind of friend?"

"Put the gun down, and we can talk more."

"You better start talking right now."

"The bartender will see us."

"Then let him see. It's of no consequence to me."

A moment of silence passed. Sherry didn't say anything. But just when she spotted the killer within the depths of his brown eyes, finding his instinct to kill hiding behind the tender, shy, and social awkward man she was with each day, she pulled his wrist holding the gun towards her body in a sudden, jerking motion, and with her other hand, she pushed the gun out of his grip, the celerity of this push-pull method sending the gun flying out of his hand and sliding across the floor to the other side of the room. It came to a rest underneath one of the café tables. With a free hand, she grabbed her own gun that she had been carrying at the small of her back and aimed it at him squarely between the eyes.

"Not bad," he smirked, wondering where his firearm had gone. "I guess I'll go first. It shouldn't be such a mystery to you now. You've already known what you wanted to know."

"Quietly get up and move to the elevator. Hurry up."

With the gun pointed at him, he did what she instructed. Within a few moments, they stood in the hotel elevator with her gun to his back heading up to her room.

"I have no idea why you're doing this," he said, as the elevator climbed to her floor. "You don't need to."

"Just be quiet. Don't say a word."

When they got to the hotel room, she opened the lock carefully and shoved him inside. She then pushed him against the nearest wall and frisked him to make sure that he wasn't carrying any other weapons.

"There," she said. "Now that wasn't so hard, was it?"

She turned him around, removed her headscarf from her shoulders, slammed him against the wall, and kissed his mouth heatedly. The ISI Officer surrendered his reticence and dropped his inhibitions, and no matter how alien and awkward his hands felt upon her skin, he moved up her arms and lost his fingers in her hair, his thin lips sucking her neck, and his hands then slipping down her back. She knew she had him right where she wanted him.

From thenceforth, the two knew each other as assets

from different agencies who were now on the same side for however long they would remain together in Karachi, long enough for her to convince him to take her message to his superiors and having the ISI clean out all of the radicals from the border. She conveyed the message after making love to him.

"We need this to happen soon," she said, her body wrapped in his.

"We can't just uproot them," he said, "and order them to return to a homeland that has been torn apart by a bloody civil war. Kabul is destroyed. Hekmatyar, Massoud, Dostum, Najibullah, Sayyaf, the Hazaras, and now the Taliban and Bin Laden? They won't go willingly. What you're proposing is absurd. Only a fraction of them will go without a fight. The rest of them will stay. How absurd I'll look. I'll be a laughing stock requesting such a thing."

"But don't you agree that Pakistan is at risk if they stay? You don't want Pakistan to fall to the radicals, do you?"

"It has fallen already. There's no reversing it."

"We're prepared to compensate you generously for this."

"How generously?"

"Enough for you to drive those Afghans out of Northern Pakistan?"

"They'll just join the Taliban. Is that what you want? And the Taliban will protect Bin Laden, who's the one you're really after."

"Let them join them, then. What they do after they leave is beyond the scope of what I have to do. Let the higher-ups hash that out amongst themselves. All you have to do is take my proposal to the ISI and convince them to do as we say."

"If I'm to do this, I need a full list of what you're prepared to exchange. And I need you to follow through on it."

"I'll get you the list. Give me a couple of days."

"I can't do anything without talking the specifics to them."

"I said, I'll get you the list. Don't worry. And in the meantime, you can stay here with me."

"Why should I trust you? Like every American, you just want to use us and toss us aside."

"It's a trade we're making. We're not manipulating the ISI. You need something, and so do we. And I need something else from you besides the deal."

"Like what?" he asked, staring into the ceiling from his prone position on the bed.

She slipped her hand from the middle of his chest to the stiffness in his loins. She had to admit that it was a lot larger and more powerful than she expected it to be. Without delay, he rolled on top of her, and they made love a second time. After expending whatever energies they had, Sherry still wanted to know more about his work, specifically why he worked as an assistant to the Consulate General.

"It's a cover," he said. "Just like being the daughter of a State Department official is a cover of yours."

"But why are you at the Embassy?"

"If I told you that, I'd probably have to kill you."

"Hey, we're in this together, aren't we?"

"That doesn't mean I have to tell you everything."

"Is it something involving India?"

"Everything involves India in one way or the other. I

wouldn't be working in immigration otherwise."

"Y'know, the longer we stay together in Karachi, the more we can help each other."

"I'm already helping you."

"But we can help each other in more ways than one."

"You're too young to be fooling around like this. You should just do as you're told. You've already got me to do your bidding. Why take it further than that?"

"Oh, don't be such a spoiled-sport. I'm just saying that we can help each other in other ways too. Not just this one."

"Fine. A few weeks ago, someone shot down one of our helicopters in Afghanistan. Whoever did it killed one of Commanders. Not only was he a high-ranking Commander, but he was also venerated by some of the ISI's top leadership. Now this guy's dead. Any idea who shot him down? And if you don't know, do you know where I can find out? The military is all over us about that."

"See, that's what I mean. We can do things for our own mutual benefit."

"Well, what is it that you want?"

"I want to know where and when the terrorists will strike next."

"What makes you think there'll be a next time?"

"C'mon."

"Okay. As you know, there will always be a next time, but if you can find out who shot down the helicopter and killed our Commander, then maybe I can help you find this Osama Bin Laden."

She rolled into his sturdy body and kissed him, her full, moist lips melting into his thin, dry ones.

"It's a start," she said. "Let me see what I can do, just as long as you'll do things for me too."

"You find out who shot down the helicopter, and I'll do a lot of things for you. You can be certain of that. Oh, and I almost forgot. Let me call downstairs. I've got to get my gun back. I don't want the bartender to find it and call the police unnecessarily. I guess the Company, as you call it, trained you well."

"We're the best in the business and at your service. If you're my friend, I'm your friend."

As predicted, the ISI Officer left in the middle of the night. She found him gone when she awoke early the next morning and felt for him on his side of the bed. Pleased that he would at least take the deal to his superiors, Sherry called the Karachi Station Chief after a light breakfast downstairs and announced the success of the mission.

"Good," said the Karachi Station Chief over the phone. "Tell him that you'll slide him some cash for his trouble. Make sure that he tells his bosses that we'll sweeten the deal by giving extended visas to qualified Pakistani men who want to work in Saudi Arabia for a few years. We'll arrange that with the Saudis."

"Both good ideas, sir. He'll like that. But he wants a list of weapons."

"If you'd give me a second, I'm getting to that."

"Sorry, sir."

"I'm sending a courier with the list. I think he'll like what we're offering, especially since we haven't sold them anything since they launched their nuclear weapons program. Remember that? They tested their bomb in '98, and Congress broke off all arms deals with them? But this time, they'll finally get what they want if they help us."

"You mean, *when* they help us."

"I find your optimism troubling. 'It ain't over 'till it's over.' You can't trust these people. They'll take weapons from you one minute and quietly sell them to our enemies the next. Hell, they may not even do a very good job sending all of those Afghans in their *madrassas* back to Kabul either. Just give him the list, and you're done. You can then report back to Station for your next assignment."

"Which is what?"

"I've got to find out from Langley. Just hang tight and wait for the courier. Once you give the Officer the list, hightail it out of there. You don't need to deal with him again. They know where to contact us."

The courier arrived a little before lunch time. She opened the door to him and discovered a short Paki who addressed her in a perfect British accent. He wore a crew-cut, a new suit, and he was armed. She found it unusual that they sent someone who addressed her so formally. She took the envelope from him, shut the door, and spilled its contents onto the bed. It read:

- 1,500 Sidewinder missiles and bombs for the F-16 Aircraft.
- 300 15mm Self-Propelled Howitzers
- 1,000 Harpoon Anti-Ship missiles.
- 10 AH-1F Cobra Attack Helicopters.
- 10 412EP Utility Helicopters.
- 20 Mid-Life Update Kits for the F-16 Aircraft.
- 10 Phalanx Close-in Weapons Systems for Naval Guns.
- 200 AMRAAM Air-to-Air missiles.
- 5 C-30 Military Transport Aircraft.
- 10 Surveillance Radars.

- 1,500 TOW Anti-Tank missiles.

Also included was a breakdown of how much all of this weaponry cost. It amounted to millions.

She called the ISI Officer at his contact number directly afterwards and said, "do I have a surprise for you," tauntingly.

"Good," he said. "I'll be right over."

It took him only a half-hour. After he came, he read over the list carefully, his eyebrows raised as his moved further down the page.

"And some cash for you," she said. "Work visas in Saudi Arabia to help Pakistani families. That should give your economy a little kick."

"I think they'll like this. I think they'll like this a lot."

"See, I told you we'd work well together."

"And you'll find out who killed the Commander?"

"I'm working on it as we speak."

He let the list and the rest of the paperwork fall to the floor. He took her in his arms where they again locked lips. He then undressed her.

"Yes, you're right," he said while unhooking her bra. "We do work well together."

Chapter Nineteen

January 1979 – Teheran, Iran

They treated him like a king. He remembered that much. He had worked for the Shah's men running guns to the Kurds in Iraq next door, the Kurds being another oppressed minority group who just happened to squat on two-thirds of Iraq's oil fields. The Iranian Shah saw Iraq as an opportunity. Fund and support the Kurds to destabilize Iraq so that his country, Iran, could become the sole superpower in the Middle East. With the full sponsorship of the United States, Iran could become 'The Guardian of the Gulf,' as the Shah coined the term over the airwaves of Teheran. It was the Shah's hope that Kurdish separatists would overthrow Baghdad and form their own independent nation as they had so craved for generations. With Western help, with the Company's help, it all seemed so possible. For his allegiance to the Shah and for his dedicated service, the King of Iran gave him a mansion, a couple of Rolls Royce's, all the money he needed, and all the women and whores he desired.

Those were the good times, he remembered, when Iraq went to the Soviets and Iran went with the United States, thereby maintaining a balance of power that kept the planet from nuking itself into oblivion, the same story of the proxy wars, each small, desperate country mere playthings of the Superpowers. Iran wanted the region, while the US and the Soviet Union wanted the entire globe. In the meantime, the

Shah's Intelligence Officer indulged in Western products, and when the big corporations moved in and told the Shah how to run his country, how to suck the nationalist's oil right out from under them to give them the leverage to create a permanent underclass of Muslims who, in turn, served the Iranian elite, the result being the rapid division of the rich from the poor, the gaping divide growing wider and more volatile, all the money going to the top while the bottom three-fourths of the country starved and succumbed to the humiliation of poverty, no one saw the turning of the tide coming.

The luxuries heaped upon him, perhaps, blinded him to the windstorm of change that blasted through the open desert that soon overthrew the Shah's bumbling regime. The cars, the women, the nice suits, the women, the booze, the women all over again, the decadence and the excesses were at the expense of the majority who served him his drinks, polished his shoes, made his bed, and swept his floors. The poor waited patiently for the right time to strike. All they needed was a leader, a supreme firebrand, to straighten the gate and level the playing field, to throw these corrupt Iranian elites, backed by their equally corrupt American corporations, out of Iran, confiscating their mansions and Rolls Royce's, and burying them in the fiery chemical pits set ablaze by the nation's devout. Once again, America had wanted another gas station. For attempting to build one and ship its fuel westward, the Iranian Revolution on the 26th of January 1979 couldn't be stopped. The Intelligence Officer figured that his nose was too deep in pussy to notice that the Shah would be ousted.

A common tale, but not common enough, as he found himself in dire straits once the news of the Shah's exile trickled over the airwaves, the tinny Arabic, Islamic voice of an unfamiliar newscaster pressing into his ears, until that same Arabic Islamic garbage showed up on his doorstep one morning, pulled him and his family out of bed and held them up with their rifles on their dirt field near the garden where his wife often worked.

The Revolutionaries were a volatile and unruly gang of illiterates. He didn't know if fighting back would provoke them into firing their weapons, so instead he remained cautiously still, did what they told him, and stood with his family a few paces ahead of them. For close to fifteen minutes, they withstood their litany of grievances and their commentary of eternal anger and frustration for what had been done to them. Because they exhausted themselves in this manner, perhaps they wouldn't be so cruel and spare their lives, or at least the lives of his children who had nothing to do with the rapacious sins of their father. Out of all the dissidents in his own country whom he either tortured or killed, he never imagined his family would be next. But these zealots knew full well who he was – a stooge of the Shah's, a hooligan responsible for a thousand deaths, his mansions and his cars purchased by the blood and broken bones of the faithful, his rank in the regime earned by preying on the misfortune of others. He had hoped to build a great financial empire that never materialized and neither included nor valued the most vulnerable. For the first time, he realized that he had little in common with the common Iranian who now relied on a stone-faced, black-turbaned cleric to boot all Western influences out of his country, except to take hostages from the Embassy when America opened her arms and embraced the exiled Shah instead of letting the masses stone him to death in a public square. Khomeini's return from his lonely exile in Iraq put the power of God into every Iranian's head. From thenceforth, the Iranian Revolution stood as a symbol to all that Islam could rule under the spell of the right leader and that the undeserving elites could no longer withstand the eternal anger and frustration of the meek.

Right there in the dirt in front of their newly-built mansion did they get on their knees and bow to a God they knew nothing about. He could hardly remember how the prayers went.

"Recite!" they shouted with their rifles pointed at their backs. "Do *sajjda*! Do *sajjda*!"

Together while muttering fake prayers, he and his family bowed and kissed the dirt as they had seen and heard countless times before. But it was useless for any of the Shah's men to pray, they said. Secularism and Western materialism had clouded their judgment. Useless for his wife and children to pray too, as a clear division between church and state had only recreated an America in the Middle East, which ought to have led to prosperity, as that had been the blueprint for Iran, up until now. Unfortunately for him, such a vision fell short and died when these revolutionaries had radically different ideas.

They bowed and kissed the dirt a second time, and when his wife and two young children came up for air, the thugs riddled their bodies with bullets. He screamed into the sky when his wife's blood splattered over his clothing, the same torture he had inflicted on others suddenly reciprocated. Apparently, they had use for such a man ripped from a vision of what could have been and then thrusted headlong into another vision altogether, a new vision of endless prayer and martyrdom. He wanted to kill them, for sure, but he would have no such opportunity. Instead, one of them butted his head with the end of his rifle, tied his wrists together behind his back with rope, and dragged his body to the truck into which they dumped him and drove him off to Evin, the resting place for the new breed of political prisoner, or the thousands who had defied the Government of God by aligning themselves with the Shah. For him, a special cell awaited where they stripped him down and bound his wrists to chains affixed to the ceiling, the balls of his feet barely touching the concrete floor.

He must have hung there in the cell for several hours, the joints between his shoulders and arms weighing him down, his mind ruminating on what awaited him and why they had spared him. Perhaps they wanted information about the whereabouts of the Shah's inner-circle, the people he had once confided in, the others he called close friends, the ones he would now rat out. Not that he wanted to surrender this information, because he really wanted to spit in their faces. But when push came to shove, rarely were there any heroes doing heroic deeds after a violent coup comes to town. Just like any confused insect, he only wanted to get out alive, as he was much like a fly who is captured by a curious child who then rips its tiny, transparent wings off, letting it scurry around fearing for its life.

He heard the gate to the cell swing open. The footsteps he knew to be one of Khomeini's Inquisitors. This Inquisitor stood behind him. The Officer could not see him while dangling there, his shoulders on the verge of snapping out of their sockets. He only heard the gravity in his voice, the seriousness of it, the many accusations of war crimes against God that he had committed. Sex with many women, for one. Drinking alcohol excessively, another. Living a lavish lifestyle on the backs of the faithful, of course. Finally, killing and torturing people just like the Inquisitor had been doing since the Government of God takeover.

The Inquisitor called him sick. A rare sickness he had. Such a sickness, he said, could not be healed with time, prayer, or medication Western medicine could have provided. Rather, his sickness had to be purged. It would be like a surgical operation without any anesthetic, a phantom pain when his limbs had already been severed. In the end, though, the purge would be for his own benefit. It would move him closer to God and the new government that had supplanted a the Shah's Satanic regime.

He remained quiet, even though he desperately wanted to argue in his defense. But it would have been pointless to do so. The corruption, said the Inquisitor, was in his own mind. The negative pattern of his own thoughts, the inchoate anger towards his own people, his allegiance to pleasure and not for the dry and naked submission to God who wanted him as he was and not the pleasures that he reaped. Stark, naked, clean, and unencumbered was how God wanted him. To stand naked below God with nothing but the corruption in his brain, because the Inquisitor had found it and isolated it, because the Inquisitor already knew of his corruption, and it had to be purged or the greater sin would have been never to have known God, and no man could ever live without knowing God. *Jahilyyah* on steroids. It was premeditated and carefully planned, and this was not his fault but the work of *Iblis*. Only through a proper purging could he be rid of such ignorance, because whatever failings he had and the happiness he had shared with his family was not the way God had wanted him to live. He had experienced only a synthetic form of happiness, all of the gratuities of sin for doing nothing at all. The Inquisitor accused him of getting away with happiness and pleasure without paying an exact price.

The first lash against his sweating skin became his first installment of this repayment. These installments came one by one, his back on fire until he could no longer feel the skin on his bones. The Inquisitor whipped the skin from his back and left a bloody pulp in its place after many successive rounds. As he cried out, his backside a sanguinary mess of tissue, exposed muscle, and tendon, he had fleeting thoughts of his children again and how fair they looked, how successful they'd be, how smart they already were. But these thoughts passed when the Inquisitor dropped him from the ceiling. He fell to the floor into his own cesspool of blood. He could not keep his eyes open long enough to catch a glimpse of the Inquisitor who then pulled him to another side of the cell where a strange, antiquated machine had been waiting for him. It only took a moment or two for it to warm up.

It had wires coming out of it and a control panel that resembled an old engine he had seen in an encyclopedia once, but he soon remembered that he had used the same machine himself to pry many a confession out of a high number of dissidents many times over. And now the Inquisitor hooked him up to the same contraption, electrodes affixed to his toes, fingers, nipples, and finally, his balls. He then put a large aluminum can over his head so that he could hear the echo of his own screams.

Together, he and the Inquisitor would learn and memorize the first *sura* of the Qu'ran. They would go through it line by line until he memorized it. The Officer would repeat after him. They would then return to the very first line, and he would have to remember the lines he had just recited. If he didn't remember or said anything incorrectly, the Inquisitor would jolt him with increasingly higher voltages of electricity.

The Shah's intelligence Officer followed him for the first few lines, but when asked to recite many of these lines at once, he faltered. Apparently, the Inquisitor forced him to admit that he knew more about the Christian Bible than the Qu'ran, at which time he shocked his body at longer intervals, black currents cresting through every electrode, his balls on fire, his toes and fingers phantomly singed from his hands and feet. Still, the lesson continued, his entire body burning from being shocked every time he didn't remember something or said something incorrectly, until he burned with the glory of God in his veins, passing out intermittently from the pain and the anticipation of even more of it, a never-ending continuum of pain, like a spliced tape reel that runs on forever. Just when he thought every last nerve in his body - from head to balls, from ears to toes - had been completely burned off, and just when he thought he had taken his last breath, the Inquisitor stopped after a half-hour of shocking him senseless and asked, "you will learn the Qu'ran now, yes?"

Tears flooded his eyes at the Inquisitor's tender mercy for not shocking him anymore, for not flogging him anymore, for making him forget about his wife and children and the old Godless life from which the great Ayatollah had now delivered him. He would be of great use to the Government of God, he shouted up to the ceiling, at which time the Inquisitor untied the rope from his wrists and unhooked the machine from his balls, fingers, and toes. He removed the aluminum can from his head, his own screams implanted menacingly like a loud stereo embedded deeply between his ears, the deafening sound of the ringing barely allowing him to discern what the Inquisitor said to him. Finally, he heard what God sounded like, and his conversion to Islam was complete, or so he assumed. But for the final step an ablution would be performed. He had no idea what that meant. Perhaps the Inquisitor would permit him to take a shower, dress in decent clothes, and eat something to fill his belly. But he still had no idea what he meant.

As he sat in his chair unhooked from the machine, his head free from the can, and feeling blessed for being saved, the Inquisitor brought a pot of boiling water over to him from a small stovetop at the edge of the room. The Inquisitor smiled graciously as he disinfected and sterilized his body of his old ways, the pores of his skin opening up and accepting the scalding holy water that flushed through him. Again, he screamed, as he no longer knew the difference between pain and joy, ecstatic exuberance and horrific nightmare, heaven above and hell below, but fully planted into the earth with God high in the heavens rinsing his body clean of all the corruption that had wasted his days. The healing waters scalded his scalp, arms, and shoulders as the Inquisitor refilled the pot and rinsed him repeatedly with it.

"You work for us now, yes?" asked the Inquisitor.

With his body a bloody mess and his skin peeling off, he screamed, "yes, dear Lord, I do!" the scalding of his head so complete that it congealed into a wet, rubbery gelatin with a long flap of his former skin folded over his ear. At this time, three men from another section of Evin came to carry him to another, second cell into which they threw him and where he lay on another concrete floor. They locked the gate with a skeleton key and shut him in.

He passed out for many hours, it seemed. When he came to, he couldn't return to sleep, as the burns all over his body hurt too much. He also hungered for something to eat but was too weak to pick himself up, call out through the iron bars of the cage, and summon one of the guards patrolling the hallway. He couldn't lift himself up for days. The cell lacked windows, so he could neither measure the sunlight nor keep track of time. A small electric light that never turned off kept the cell dimly lit for every conceivable hour. His stomach growled for anything edible. The cell reminded him of the machine. But food never came. He had barely enough strength to call out, but when he did, no one came as though he were in an isolated, soundless chamber where they stored the most egregious cases. He curled up into a ball to withstand the pangs of hunger, these pangs great strains that impinged on the walls of his festering stomach. The guard patrolling the hall offered no relief and kept him awake at all hours with his footsteps. He didn't know if it were day or night, and in a strange way, he no longer wanted to know or cared, neither did he know if he was still alive. He again saw brief images of his wife and children in their mansion in Teheran and how happy he had made them, but all of this corruption from his former life had been burned and doused clean. Now nearly starved and emptied, his mind newly formatted, the damaged sectors of his memory smoothed over for a rewrite, he sensed death knocking at his door. Just when he thought the scythe-bearing creature cut out his heart, he heard the gate of the cell unlock and swing open.

In the blur of his failing sight, he made out a black-turbaned Mullah wearing flowing black garb over his portly body. He had a black beard of medium length, and his eyes shined like slick onyx in the dim light of the cell. He brought a cushion in with him with which to seat himself against the wall closest to his curled body. Beneath the folds of his clothing, he pulled out a soft piece of pita bread and tossed it to him. The Officer hardly believed that this angelic Mullah nourished him, considering the corruption of his past. Slowly, he sat up and chewed on the bread, forcing it down his throat. He took small bites, each stale morsel sliding down his esophagus and dropping into the empty well of his stomach. He felt like vomiting, but he dutifully held it down, hoping not to insult the Mullah.

After finishing all that he could, he crawled to the bearded Mullah, kissed his hands, and wept on his knees.

"You are one of the fortunate ones," said the Mullah, like an indifferent father who knows his child's fever is only passing. "You have killed and tortured many, I am sure, and now you weep, because you have found God, and you have been saved from a calamitous fate. But you have only been through a fraction of what hell is like. Yet it's God's will that you suffer no more, unless of course, you are foolish enough to take your own will back."

The saved man buried his face into the Mullah's thick, black garb, his tears moistening its folds. The saved man, baptized by the new government, shook his head upon his knee.

"As our great Ayatollah has decreed," said the Mullah, "Islam declares monarchy and heredity succession wrong and invalid. Do you adhere to this same decree?"

"I have nothing, my father. I am not a king, and I have no family. I adhere to the great Ayatollah's decree."

"Do you agree that victory is not achieved by words. It can only be achieved by blood. It is achieved by strength of faith?"

"Yes, I do. I would never think otherwise, my Lord."

"And now that you have entered the light, now that your mind and body have recoiled against corruption, do you agree that revolution must come before victory?"

"Yes!" he cried. "First comes revolution! Then comes victory!"

"Good. I hope you remember these decrees before you have to be taught another lesson on how to be a devout Muslim again. The guard will bring you more food. Until then, eat, drink, and wait here patiently. We shall decide where you go next."

When they released him from Evin after several weeks, he learned that nearly 12,000 men in the Shah's former regime had been executed. For some reason, they spared him, because he submitted to God, they said. He also learned that all across the Middle East, those who supported the Ayatollah Khomeini mirrored his revolution and conducted terror campaigns of their own in places like Saudi Arabia, Bahrain, and Kuwait, the poor rising up against the wealthy kingdoms that served the interests of the Christian West rather than the souls of millions of its own devout. No wonder so many people worshipped the Ayatollah. The Twelfth Imam had finally arrived and urged the great minority of the Islamic world to overthrow their majority Sunni oppressors and the Christians they now served. It pitted the new Islamic Government of God against Saddam Hussein's *Ba'ath Party* for supremacy in the Gulf.

Saddam soon declared the fragile peace between Iraq and Iran null and void when he took over the *Shatt al-Arab* river at the mouth of the Gulf. The Intelligence Officer who once worked for the Shah was ordered to work as a soldier for the Revolution, swearing allegiance to the Ayatollah Khomeini and his Government. He became a member of the MIOS.

He beat his chest on the *Tenth of Muharram* and marched through the streets forcing tears out of his eyes for the sheer sadness of Hussein's tragic story and his ultimate sacrifices. And despite all that he endured, still a small sliver of counter revolutionary mistrust intruded into his otherwise obsessive loyalty to the Ayatollah. It whispered in his sleep that something was very wrong. He awoke every morning in his cramped, one-room apartment in Teheran sweating and daring not to tell anyone about this new shard of doubt that demanded more and more of his attention as the war between Iran and Iraq commenced.

When Khomeini announced to his people that Iran's foreign policy was to eschew both the East and the West, that shard of doubt grew into a more widespread skepticism about his cherished leader's mental fitness. But to tell someone meant getting hauled off to Evin to be whipped, shocked, boiled, and starved into submission all over again. He kept quiet and told no one, even when he read in one of the local papers that the entire world conspired against the will of the Government of God. This included the Soviet Union and France who sent billions of dollars in arms to Saddam. The United States, reeling from its own hostage crisis, also worked against the Ayatollah, until Iran, a country that declared it was neither East nor West, stood alone as a sole revolutionary republic hell bent on fighting a holy war with all of the world. No one was ready for a radical Islamic country built on the shoulders of a poor man's revolution. Even the old Bolsheviks in the Soviet Union denied Iran and needed to stop its religious fervor from spreading too far.

Still, he heard the *muezzin's* call from the minarets towering above him. He prayed dutifully for Iran's ultimate success. Iran alone was the underdog here. Every Iranian on the streets wore his underdog status like a badge, the Indo-European race of Persians so low, that the lowliness had molded them into an undefeatable fighting force against the superpowers, if only they achieved it by blood and their strength of faith in God alone. Yet again doubts crept into his dreams at night. He awoke startled by these doubts about the Ayatollah's strategy and the victory he had hoped to achieve against Saddam. What followed was even worse.

He met with the same benevolent Mullah who fed him his first piece of pita bread before being saved and rescued at Evin. This Mullah, now a few years older with a streak of grey in his once-black beard, sat down with him for tea at a location near his own small apartment. Now that he was one of the newest members of MIOS, most of his head burned off as his initiation into this secretive and most loyal of all organizations, he listened to his superior, not only with a disciplined ear, but with an affectionate one as well. After all, the man who saved him from Evin sat right in front of him sipping his hot tea, a gold nugget of a ring on his plump finger, as he explained the challenges the country suddenly faced as a result of being boycotted by and isolated from the rest of the world, Iran being its own isolated desert island with very few resources for its masses to feed on. Nor would anyone buy its oil.

"We don't have much ammunition left for our holy war," said the Mullah, staring into his cup of black tea. "No one wants to buy our oil in exchange for weapons. Instead, we are getting spare parts and ancient rifles as acts of charity. They are intent on destroying us. They are funding the Iraqis, sending them arms, food, money, anything they wish. And now we are low on equipment, ammunition, and food. The US has even opened up a new Embassy in Baghdad.

"Now do you see how much they fear our leader?" the Mullah said suddenly. "They are so scared of us that they are sending army's all around the world to fight us. That's how petrified they are of us. We have the power of God on our side, and God is a force so strong that he alone will bring the rest of the world to its knees before the revolution takes a back seat to the materialism, greed, and corruption that pays for the pleasures of the profiteers. We are the inheritors of God's will and God's sword and not these evil empires who conspire against. Don't you agree?"

"Of course, I do, my father. We will shed our own blood to defend ourselves. That is how we are saved. Blood is the strength of our faith."

"Do you really mean that, my son," said the Mullah with even wider eyes.

"Yes, I do," said the MIOS Officer. "I believe in my heart that only our own blood and our faith in God above will grant us victory, just as our leader has prophesized."

"I am overwhelmed with joy that you have said this, my son," he smiled. "You have come a long way from where you started. You have emerged as a man of faith who understands that blood must be shed if we are to gain victory and continue our Imam's revolution. The revolution must continue, and we must bring it to every corner of the globe. To do that, we must subdue our enemies with all the Islamic blood in our veins."

"I wholeheartedly agree," he said, not quite sure what he was getting at.

The MIOS Officer soon found out.

"You are ready to fulfill your first duty to the Government of God. Are you ready? This is the question you must ask yourself. It is obvious to me that the corruption has been exorcised from your mind. All of the *djinn* of *Iblis* have been expelled, and you are ready to move forward with our Supreme Leader's plan and strategy for God's government."

"Yes, my father. I am ready to receive my assignment."

"Good. Our Leader has decreed that you will take part in mobilizing a fighting force that will work alongside our professional Iranian military. This will be a youth volunteer force whose movement the Ayatollah has named, the *Basij e-Mustazafir*, or 'The Mobilization of the Depraved.'"

"How young are we are talking about?"

"No one older than fifteen. You will serve them as a teacher and motivator before we send them into battle against our Sunni Iraqi foes."

"That's good," he said excitedly. "Someone has to show them how to use guns and rifles against those *Ba'ath* party bastards. It would be an honor to teach them these things. I excel at weapons training."

"I don't think you understand, my son. I just said that we are low on ammunition, weapons, equipment, and food. We cannot spare them in the slightest except for our own professional army. The *Pasdaran* will have to use other means to subdue the Iraqi forces."

The MIOS Officer took a deep look into his black tea.

"So, what is it that you're asking me to do, father?"

"Victory can only be achieved by blood. It is achieved by strength of faith. These are the children of our Supreme Leader, and they will use these two weapons alone to defeat the Sunnis of Iraq."

"I don't understand."

"The *Pasdaran* will only be using their blood and their strength of faith, just as I said. Nothing more, nothing less. They will employ these two elements of victory alongside our own army that cannot afford to spare the smallest pistol or the slightest bullet against the Iraqis. You will be one of their teachers and motivators. You will be the one who sends your group of depraved sufferers into battle. You will be the one who mobilizes them. Do you understand what you're assignment is now, my son?"

He again gazed into the blackness of his tea, searching for a way out. Once again confronted by doubt, the MIOS Officer held his tongue and fought the urge to question his superior and mentor, the same man who saved him from Evin and granted him new life, so that he could serve what God had intended, only now those doubts grew in size and dimension. It made him want to flee the country before accepting such an assignment. But he knew he had no choice. Just when the silence between them exposed the doubts that swam in the soup of his newly reconstituted brain, he dunked them below a beatific smile and said, "when does my Supreme Leader want me to leave? I am ready as soon as he is."

At first, they sent the MIOS Officer into the religious middle schools in and around Teheran. For the assignment, they provided him with flowing black robes and a white turban to hide the scales and burn marks on his hairless scalp. He grew his beard in keeping with the standard size for teachers set forth by the Ministry of Religious Affairs and his own Mullah, who even measured it before he sent him off to teach the children. On black and white Iranian television, he witnessed Khomeini addressing a group of young *Pasdaran* ready to be launched into battle. The Supreme Leader placed plastic gold keys around their fledgling necks as a symbol of their assured entry into paradise once slaughtered by the Iraqis.   The children had been selectively picked from the most devout of Shia families.

The children wore red and yellow headbands attesting to their Supreme Leader's greatness and their ultimate unshakable loyalty to the All-Mighty.   And finally, the Ayatollah pinned a strip of white cloth to their uniforms, a symbol of a funeral shroud, each child taking his own dead peers fighting side by side with him through death and into eternal life whom God alone would grant them, each death a representation of how each child carried the deaths of the other children with him into paradise.

When the first crop of school kids gathered before him in the school's grimy auditorium, their clean uniforms pressed against their young skinny bodies, their bright headbands ready to absorb the sweat and blood of battle in the name of their Supreme Leader, their faces were angry, fierce, and glowing with the innocence of passionate devotees in whom God above had already placed his trust. He began the rally using the knowledge the Mullah had given him at Evin and their talks at teatime.

"Victory can never be achieved by words. In the end of time, words are hollow and meaningless coming from the lips of all human beings. Victory can only be achieved by blood and strength of faith. In this instance, the blood and the strength of faith are yours. Because of this, you, and only you, are the true army of God. Go ahead and look to your brothers around you. Look at how they are dressed, the golden key around each neck, the gleam in their eyes, knowing full well that the next time you will be seeing each other is in heaven above, where you will achieve even greater victories. God alone will treat you like the most exquisite jewels to have ever been offered at his feet. You are an offering for his enduring beneficence, charity, and light. This is who you are. You represent victory, your martyrdom and entrance into heaven assured by the blood and guts you are willing to shed and how much faith you have.

"So, say it with me now, will you? Shout it in the name of God: Death to Israel! Death to America! Death to France! And Death to Saddam! Shout it so loud that God in heaven hears you!"

The children, riled by his instructions and ready to be sacrificed, rose from their seats and chanted the mantra as he waved his tight fist into the air, hammering along to the cadence of their chanting. It must have gone on for a straight hour, the most devout of the children shouting the loudest, beating their chests, shedding tears of rage, ready to bleed for victory against the Evil Doers. They knew they were blessed compared to the hell that awaited their enemies.

The MIOS Officer beheld his creation from the stage of the auditorium. No longer did he have to shout. The children took over and did it for him. They had no fear, and when

Khomeini ruled the very next day that all of Iran's children did not need parental permission to join 'The Mobilization of the Depraved,' thousands of young children ran away from home and joined. The MIOS Officer thought his job complete, until the Mullah appeared again at the front door of his apartment and told him, in no uncertain terms, that he would be joining the *Pasdaran* in a week's time, directing the very same children he had motivated in the auditorium on the field of battle against Saddam's army.

Doubts again raced within him, but he bit his tongue, because he had no choice. He affirmed his allegiance to the same creeds with which he indoctrinated the children. He would lead them to their premature deaths. The Mullah said that it was one of the highest honors ever bestowed upon a member of the Party of God – for a teacher to manifest the lessons taught to his students and to witness their victory.

The MIOS Officer stared into his black tea like many times before, agreeing with the Mullah and at the same time wanting him to leave, so that he could gather a few things, stuff them in a small bag, and leave the country. After his mentor left the apartment, however, he did pack a bag, only that he wouldn't be leaving the country at all. On the next morning in the city's center, buses waited for him and the children he had taught and motivated. He boarded one of these buses and rode for several hours to the border town of *Qasr-e Shivin* to challenge the Iraqi forces.

Once on the road, they sang a variety of holy *ghazals*, much like a happy family on a camping trip. They chanted endlessly. The buses carried bicycles on their roofs, most of them donated as gifts by parents who wanted their children to use them in battle so that they too could enter paradise. The *Pasdaran's* ascent into manhood was guaranteed by their martyrdom, and so these parents were pacified. The children were proud and fearless. The MIOS Officer had made them so. He had motivated them to be even greater than what they thought capable. Not only were they fearless, but their rapture surprised even him. None of the children on the long journey slept despite the intense heat and the dry desert winds that blew in through the half-open windows caked with soot. They were too excited to close their eyes, like kindergarten kids who refused to be dragged into naptime. They were too excited to think of anything other than facing the Iraqis on the battlefield. Even at their age, their lives in heaven mattered much more than any joys or achievements their lives on earth brought them. They had no use for their pasts, shrugged off the present, and put all of their faith into the certainty of their futures.

After taking them through the desert, the bus ended the journey at a small, ramshackle outpost near the town of *Quasr-e Shivin*. They could have been a football team playing an away game against a much-despised rival, but this was very different. Once unloaded, the uniformed children formed neat rows, one after the other, many of them standing with their bicycles. The MIOS Officer peered through his binoculars and saw that the opposing army in their military fatigues and their machine guns, jeeps, and tanks headed straight in their direction. Once the children had readied themselves, he launched the first human wave of attack. The most devout of the children went first, shouting, "God is great!" They ran for miles in the direction of the Iraqi border, until the Iraqi soldiers, stunned by this offensive, fired bullets into them.

After the first human wave came the second, and then the third, each long column shouting, "God is great," and being gunned down by the Iraqi troops. Through his binoculars, the MIOS Officer saw the bullets breaking through their backs, staining their uniforms with blood, their young bodies falling to the floor of the desert, still shouting "God is great" even after they were shot, and the most devout of them lifting themselves up to have another go at the Iraqi battleline. Once all of the children had been sent and by the time the carnage had ended, all of them had perished. He looked through his binoculars a final time to view their bodies scattered all over the desert. In the farther distance, he saw Iraqi soldiers bent on their knees and weeping for what they had done. If anything, thought the MIOS Officer, the deaths of the children weakened their morale.

His thinking again reverted to the former military strategies he had learned under the Shah. They had always been there somewhere. While the children made the enemy feel bad, they at least died for a heavenly cause. It was a loss of manpower, but a spiritual gain. He soon craved a drink, a cigarette, and a whore to celebrate the victory. Iran had won morally, and this alone had been worth the deaths of his students. He at least could be of more use to the government, now that the doubts he had been having all along didn't feel so foreign or intrusive anymore.

After a final ceasefire between the two warring countries had been declared during constructive talks in Geneva, the MIOS Officer knew he had moved on to bigger and better roles in God's government. Even Khomeini had loosened his grip on the minds and hearts of his people.

"Happy are those who have departed through martyrdom," said Khomeini. "Unhappy am I that I still survive. Taking this decision is more deadly than drinking from a poisoned chalice. I submitted myself to Allah's will and took this drink for his satisfaction."

As Khomeini had to live with his decisions, so did the MIOS Officer. The Supreme Leader had admitted that he was weak now, and so too was the fury of his rule and government.

Maybe now the MIOS Officer could drink in some of the old pleasures that Khomeini had banned. The war had ended. No one really won. But the martyrdom of the flower of youth had delivered a revolutionary victory.

Chapter Twenty

February 2001 – Teheran, Iran

Iran had loosened up, and the MIOS Officer had loosened up with it. What's more, a Pakistani physicist slid them notes on how to enrich uranium in the hopes that the rest of the world would leave the embittered minority alone as well as have the same revolutionary mullahs maintain their hold on power. While times were much better for him than when he had mobilized the Depraved for the Ayatollah, the inconvenient hatred from the Christian West, and by extension, the Jews who occupied Palestine, still isolated Iran and squeezed them slowly. The Iranian leadership placed all their hope on building a bomb before the Christians and the Jews squeezed them out entirely. Their relations had warmed, however, with the Chinese and the Russians after the Ayatollah's death and the end of their bloody, chemically-infused war with Iraq.

The MIOS Officer emerged from his one-room apartment and met the resplendent sunshine, the late August heat unyielding and uncompromising, the sweat breaking through the edges of his turban. He had a flittering thought that he should have shaved his beard, like in the times of the Shah, but those days were over. The Shah's smooth-shaven face and imported silk suits were relics of the past that had flown to the other side of the world, leaving him with his faith but with enough of his doubts and corruptions to have landed him a star promotion in the MIOS. He was on his way to meeting a popular Iranian General and a representative of the GRU, or the Russian foreign military agency.

The GRU eyed the west with skepticism ever since Putin strengthened his hand and prepared his men to do battle again with his old nemesis, or the same gang of countries that had embarrassed the old Soviet guard by splitting their great empire apart, the most humiliating turn of events in Russian history. Gorby might as well have handed the entire Eastern Bloc over to the capitalists, the end of the old Soviet Union an unnecessary miscalculation by a foolish, do-good lawyer, mostly due to insignificant events, like Afghanistan and Chernobyl. Given that the second Bush would also strengthen the CIA, like his father did, and the Pentagon, like US Republicans had always done, it only followed that Putin would do the same and look to square off against the Americans before they came to close to Russian borders. What's more, their populous neighbor to the south, China, had been granted most favored nation trade status, the olive branch originally offered by Nixon now a great big bear hug to the Far East, or in Putin's view, a blatant attempt to wedge the Chinese away from the Russians, the wave of change tumbling over the entire hemisphere and dragging out the Russians in the undertow. Not only was Putin humiliated by the loss of his old empire, but the new relationship between the Americans and the Chinese insulted Putin's intelligence. In no way would he let the Americans peddle their soft power anywhere in the region, especially the countries he traded with. Even without the power he once had, Putin still had to keep Chechnya and Georgia in line. In order to survive, Putin needed a wider sphere of influence, and he never trusted the Americans to stay within their borders anyway. Globalism was just another word for imperialism, the same game only with different players, the repetitive process of history recycling right on cue, such that the Russians already had it timed down to a science. The time had come to act, and a GRU representative had a vital message to carry to his Iranian friends who would always hate America and do anything to eliminate it.

By the time the MIOS Officer arrived at the appointed meeting place, a drab office space in a state-owned building, he knew the Russians wanted to deepen their ties. The Iranians, of course, had no other choice but to embrace any country that wanted to deal with them, considering that high gas prices and inflation peaked that summer. As always, food supplies were low. Although the people remained tame, any ripple of dissent may have shaken the very foundations of the Revolution, an ever-present theme running through the fabric of Iranian life. Things had loosened up in Iran but not by much.

By the time the MIOS Officer opened the door to the non-descript office, the popular General had already arrived. He sat in a chair at a polished oval table with nothing on it. The room had no telephones or computer screens, no file cabinets or desks, no wall hangings or windows. Only the *shwoosh* of the air conditioner filled it with cool relief from the dreadful heat outside. The General, in a green uniform with red and gold epaulets on his narrow shoulders, didn't bother standing. He was already too important and popular to show any outward respect. Rather, it was the MIOS Officer's obligation to greet him and kiss his ass for a little while until the GRU representative arrived. After all, the General's giant portrait had been pasted on the sides of Teheran's most notable buildings, the same man who fought the Semites, not with the delirious religious passions that had crippled an earlier Iran, but with guile and cleverness, two qualities that the Iranian people opened themselves up to and enthusiastically supported. No longer did they have to be guided by religious rage, especially since the war ended and normalcy had been restored. The Death of the Ayatollah gave the country new life, even though the West still pushed for regime change by slapping on sanctions and hoping the Iranian people would rebel due to high prices and the looming threat of starvation.

The MIOS Officer sat near the General, and normally one would think that the two of them would greet each other cordially, but this wasn't the case. In Iran, an antipathy between the army and the MIOS made the General act coldly, mainly due to the competition over who got what or who suffered more. Due to the MIOS Officer's position and rank, the General had the clear upper hand when it came to dealing with the Russians. The MIOS Officer, especially due to his former association with the Shah, played a more supporting role. The General would be calling the shots, and while this did not sit well with the Officer, considering the grunt work he endured with the Pasdaran and witnessing the horrors of those unwinnable battles, he would still have to keep his mouth shut and begrudgingly accept the General's pomposity and dominance. The General was, after all, one of the most popular figures in the Iranian government.

"It is an honor to finally meet you," said the MIOS Officer to the General. "I hope this meeting is productive and advances our divergent interests against the Semites and the Saudis."

"Just let me handle things," said the General abruptly. "You just watch, listen, and take notes if you wish."

"Yes, General. While I do agree that you and the Russian have a lot to discuss, we also have an interest in adding our comments to the discussion as well. After all, we are a partner in this too."

"Not much of one," he said curtly. "Only those who fight are my partners. Those who play games, sit on the sidelines, and observe don't command much respect in my book."

"While you may have some grievances with our organization," said the MIOS Officer, "you must still consider that we are the eyes and ears of military. Without us, you wouldn't be able to see more than a few feet ahead of you."

"Oh, I see a lot farther than that. We know who you are. You're snakes, plain and simple. You dodge conflict, live in debauchery and excess, and demand reward while we do all the dirty work. Don't worry, Officer, because I know your kind. We may have to work with you, but you are not to be trusted or respected."

The MIOS Officer took the General's criticism in stride. Sure, he felt like smacking the older man for his disrespect, but again, he was the lesser partner here. To insult the General would mean to anger the Mullah and those above him who supervised his work. With so much support from the people, the General could pretty much say what he pleased, no matter how condescending or insulting. If anything, the conversation he tried to have with him merely filled up time and space before the GRU representative arrived, if only to avoid the awkwardness of having to sit there alone with him and remain silent as he stared him down. In Iran, however, whatever functioned on a lower level demanded the higher respect. So, the butcher merited more respect than the landowner on whose property the cattle roamed. The man in the trenches merited much more respect than the strategists who put him there.

They sat in the silence uncomfortably. Making any more conversation with the General would be pointless, if not a sign of weakness. It became a test of wills to see who could remain uncomfortable the longest, until, of course, the GRU Representative barged in like a noisy kid running through a quiet library, surprising them both and breaking them out of whatever random ruminations consumed them.

"Gentlemen!" announced the large and burly Russian.

He wore a tan suit in keeping with the latest European fashion and lugged a bulging leather satchel around his shoulder that seemed much too heavy for him to have carried all the way from the taxi to the office.

"My God, it is hot as hell out there. Oh, get me near the air conditioning, please!"

He dropped the heavy satchel on the floor, threw off his suit jacket, and made straight for the air conditioner on the wall. The red-faced Russian cooled his sweating face in front of the vents. The MIOS Officer thought he may pass out had it not been for the trustworthy machine.

"How do you guys take it here in Teheran?" he asked. "There must be something about Muslims and the heat that go together. There's no moisture here whatsoever. In Russia, we bond with the cold."

He dried himself off in the cold air and shook the sweat off of him like a dog who had been playing in a pond, the sweat dripping from his brow and balding scalp. Only when he significantly cooled off did he finally pick up his suit jacket from the floor, fling it over one of the chairs, and sit himself down at the table. The sweat stains on his shirt still hadn't dried yet. From his satchel he pulled out an enormous bottle of Russian vodka and three shot glasses. He poured each of them a drink, but when it came time for them to toast to their good health, the General abstained.

"I'm sorry, sir, but I am not permitted to drink," he said.

"Even a little one?" asked the Representative. "Don't worry. No one here will tell on you."

"God sees all," he said. "Let the Officer here drink with you. I already know where he's going."

"Ha! Ha!" said the Russian. "So be it."

The MIOS Officer and the GRU Representative shared a couple of shots of vodka as the General looked on in disgust. The MIOS Officer liked that he watched. The General would get no such pleasure. He laughed along with the Russian about the heat in Teheran compared to the frigid temperatures in Moscow.

"I almost melted when I got off the plane," laughed the Russian, slapping him on the back. "For some reason, the fucking sun is so close to the land here. I need a glass of water every step I take."

"It makes our women nice and dark," laughed the Officer. "I know how you Russians like your women dark, our Iranian women especially."

"And you can't get enough of our white Russian women too, I know. And so we trade, no? We do that best."

The Officer laughed with him, the two quick shots of vodka seeping into his bloodstream.

"You should have brought a couple of them here with you," he said. "The General and I would have liked to have met a couple of your Moscovites."

The General cleared his throat and said, "gentlemen, if we can get down to business? I have another appointment to make."

Like a record skipping, the General put an end to their brief spasm of fun. The Representative poured himself another shot and took a seat across from the General. The

MIOS Officer sat at the middle, a mediator between the two main power brokers. He wasn't expected to say much, only listen to what both of them had to say and report back to the Mullah, hopefully later the next day when he was not so inebriated.

"Well, yes, General," said the husky Russian, also clearing his throat, "it is an honor to have finally met you. And with that, I carry a few messages and ideas from Moscow, as well as our President's warmest wishes. Now that the war has ended, we have a new set of security arrangements we would like to pursue. We think we can be of great help to you and that you can be a great help to us."

"How can you be so sure?" said the General. "You never gave us the support we needed against our Sunni oppressors. Why bother with us now?"

"But times have changed, General, wouldn't you say?" interrupted the MIOS Officer. "The Iran of today is much different than the Iran of yesterday."

"That is true," said the Russian. "A new sun rises for us all, and we want to advance a few new ideas that you may find very interesting."

"Like what?" asked the General sardonically.

The Russian paused, not knowing how to confront the General's sourness, his jovial expression frozen like a kid caught with his hand in the cookie jar. But he broke from it a few moments later, grinned, and said, "okay, I guess business means business. So, let's get down to it, shall we?"

"Let's," said the General.

"Yes, well, General, see here, we both have a mutual problem, and that is the United States."

"You mean, you have your own problem with the

US," said the General. "The United States has always been a problem for us."

"Right, of course. Well, we know you have been developing your relationship with the Pakistanis, and we would like to see that relationship deepen."

"We do have a good, friendly relationship with them, yes," said the General, "at least culturally. We both have common interests, like our faith, for one. We also like what they are doing for Bin Laden and the Taliban."

"Bin Laden is an independent operator. He goes where Islam goes, yes?"

"Bin Laden is a believer. We funded him to fight the Soviets, and now he is using our funds to fight the US. The US has way too much influence in our region. We must continue the fight, so that it does not imperialize and confiscate our lands, our heritage, and our culture like they have tried to do so many times before."

"We agree," said the Russian, "which is why I am here. Apparently, the Americans want Bin Laden dead after he bombed one of their warships and two of their Embassies in Africa. That friendly relationship between the US and Bin Laden is no longer. Together, I hope we can seize upon that opportunity."

"What do you propose, Mr. Representative?"

"For starters, we must deal with Pakistan. The Pakistanis are angry as hell that the US abandoned Afghanistan after our old empire withdrew. They left the Afghan population to rot, a bloody civil war, and also left the Pakistanis with thousands upon thousands of Afghan refugees to deal with. With the second coming of President Bush, it is likely that the US will renew its ties with Saudi Arabia, and that means trouble for you."

"Yes, it does," said the General. "The Christians now occupy Saudi soil, offering them protection. The House of Saud needs the Christians to defend themselves against the *ulema* most of all, whom we support. That means, the Royal Family will turn against us. The Saudis and the Americans will work together, which is also why you are here, I suppose."

"And the place is Pakistan, where all the roads meet," said the MIOS Officer.

"You are right, comrade," said the Russian, pouring himself another shot, but this time the Officer abstained in deference to the General's parochial tastes.

"If we supply you with arms, will you sell some of them to the Pakistanis in return for their help? We need their intelligence as far as what the US is doing on the ground in Pakistan and maybe even across their border."

"More arms?" asked the General. "We hardly have enough food to feed our own people, and you want us to buy more weapons from you?"

"I hate to say this, my friend, but if we don't get the Pakistanis on our side, the Americans will. And if the Americans have the upper hand in Pakistan, the Jews and the Pakistanis are strange bedfellows, no?"

"We can go on like this forever," said the General. "I'm not a strategist. I'm a soldier. We leave strategy to the weaker sides of government."

"Right," said the MIOS Officer, trying to calm the tension. "I would say that we can use more arms. Our people are used to hunger. They have small appetites. We must remember that we are still a country much alone in the world. We have to defend ourselves against a very powerful force."

"Bush the Second," said the Russian," throwing another

shot of vodka down his wide throat.

"The Pakistanis will always take more arms, no matter where they come from," said the General. "Anything to defeat the Hindus. Bin Laden helps them with that too. But in return, the MIOS can get better intelligence from the ISI, and we can get more weapons for our Hezbollah friends in Syria."

"We need to know about troop movements in the region, certainly," said the MIOS Officer. "We don't want the CIA to show up at our front door again like they did with the Shah."

"No, definitely not," said the Russian. "But I also want to propose something important that you should consider. You see, there are a number of steps the Americans will take next, or at least that's what our intelligence tells us. We believe that Bush wants another proxy war, just like we had with the US in Afghanistan. But, and I hate to say this, but Bush's next target is Iraq."

The General laughed and said, "you're joking right?"

"This is no laughing matter, General. We believe that the second Bush will continue where his father left off, but this time he will stay behind in Iraq to rebuild it and install his own democratic government."

"How can you be so sure?" asked the MIOS Officer, also in disbelief.

"Not only is Iraq rich with oil, but it also puts America's footprint in the heart of the Middle East – a wise political decision as well, if we consider how Bush will use Iraq to protect the Jewish state. Two birds with one stone."

"No wonder you want to help us," laughed the General again. "You need us to fight the Americans in Iraq."

"Right, but this can only happen if you can see your

way to aligning yourself with Saddam."

"Now I know your joking," said the General. "That's the most absurd thing I've ever heard. Maybe you're too drunk, Mr. Representative. We just destroyed each other, and now you're suggesting we help each other? The bastard killed thousands of our own. Our children our fatherless, our mothers childless. That's the last goddamned person we would ever help. The chemicals he used? The underhanded tactics? The bastard can rot in Hell for all I care!"

The MIOS Officer remembered how the Iraqi forces wept when they killed off the last of his students.

"I think we should at least listen to him, General," said the MIOS Officer. "No matter how preposterous this may all seem, it may lead to something."

The General continued to chuckle and said, "okay, okay. This should be entertaining enough. Why don't you explain it to us, Mr. Representative?"

The Russian lifted his heavy body from his seat and paced in what little space the small room afforded. The MIOS Officer heard the gears of the old Soviet mind turning. His reasoning had to be good enough to convince the General. More than any one person, the General despised Saddam Hussein. And yet the Americans and their Jewish friends came in at a close second. The Officer wanted the Russian to convince him. It meant more arms for Iran to fight the Jews, more arms to protect themselves from the imperialists, more money for the MIOS from the money they would take off the top from selling Russian arms to the insatiable Pakistanis. Let it ride, dear Russian, let it ride, he found himself thinking.

The Officer poured himself another shot of vodka despite his better judgement, and within a few moments visions of mansions and Rolls Royce's came to mind, the tortures he endured in Evin reversing on themselves and offering what the Iran of the present day sorely lacked. If the people continued to go hungry, that was acceptable, just so long as the MIOS padded its wallet and gave itself a solid, long-overdue pay raise. He would have gladly traded his cramped one-room apartment for another chance at a larger house, a big luxury sedan, the women, more booze, and again the women, the whores, this time white Russian women wearing next to nothing, his hands running over their smooth backs, his palms full of flesh, the doubts and corruptions he once had percolating and awakening him from the nightmare of the religious blindness that darkened Iran's past.

He placed his hopes in this Russian to convince the hard-ass sitting to the left of him. While the General would agree to send Russian arms into Pakistan, having him work with Saddam was a tall order. Even the Officer bristled at the thought of it while dreaming of the Russian girls he'd have in his bed if the Russian got what he wanted.

"How would we be working with Saddam?" asked the General.

The Russian rubbed his hand over his face as though he were rinsing off in a washbowl. He then said, "Bush II will invade Iraq. If he takes Iraq, he will take Iran next, no question. Even if he threatens to take Iran, we will have no other choice but to step in and help you fight him off. General, you need our help. Now that Bush II is targeting Iraq, it is high time that you mend fences with the Sunnis next door. Otherwise, the US will do away with the Iranian clerical order in an eyeblink when they topple Saddam, which they can easily do. As soon as Bush takes Iraq, it will give him greater access, not only to Iran, but to Afghanistan, Tajikistan, and finally, to Russia. Iraq is not only their footprint in the Islamic world but also a gateway to the East. They will say it is to fight terrorism when they are really like a vacuum sucking up oil and land on their slow march towards Moscow. And this includes Iran. With the Jews, the Americans will take one country at a time. Afghanistan is our red line. If they manage to take Iran, then we will confront them in Afghanistan, a place we have no desire to ever see again, but if we have to, we will. Do you understand where I am going with this, General?"

"These are interesting ideas, and you certainly have a vivid imagination, Mr. Representative, but working with Saddam is out of the question. The Iranian people won't accept it."

"But our people don't have to know about it," said the Officer. "And the Iraqi people don't have to know about it either. We have to agree to help each other out when the time comes, an alliance of sorts in case Bush continues his father's campaign in Iraq. I know Bush must have a lot of unfinished business there."

"Maybe they are just after Bin Laden?" said the General. "Maybe they just want to protect the Jews from terrorism in general? Why wage a wider war?"

"Why not help the Jews by containing Iran?" said the Russian. "Why bother with a small potato like Bin Laden?"

"A war on Iraq is a hard sell to the American people. How will Bush convince them?"

"That's what we don't know," said the Russian. "But whatever Bush does, his intention is to get closer to our borders and not necessarily to stop Bin Laden. He's a puppet figure to them. This we know full well. He will tell his people that Bin Laden needs to be brought to justice, but he will need a good reason to convince his own people to invade Iraq. We don't know how or what Bush will do to convince them, but mark my words, he will do it."

"How do we start, then, Mr. Representative?" asked the General.

"You don't have to do anything yet. We will open a channel to Baghdad and propose this alliance. Saddam will have to be open to it if he is to protect his power from the US. In the meantime, steer the Pakistanis in our direction and away from the Americans."

"But the Pakistanis are already helping the Americans find Bin Laden, no?" asked the MIOS Officer. "They are helping them hunt down Bin Laden as we speak. The Pakistanis will be taking arms from us and money from the US at the same time."

"Pakistan is in the eye of the storm," said the Russian, returning to his seat a little wobbly. "They are taking money from the Americans to hunt down Bin Laden, and they are taking money from Iran to protect Bin Laden and the Taliban, am I right?"

"Yes," said the General.

"It's important, then, that we keep the Pakistanis on the right side. Arrange our arms deal to keep them loyal to us with the stipulation that they limit US interference in their own country. That means Bin Laden stays alive to fight against the Americans and the Jews when we need him."

"I will have to take these ideas through the proper channels," said the General, "but I'm beginning to understand what you mean. I will tell the Prime Minister that we need Iraq's and Pakistan's help, under your sponsorship, to challenge the Americans and the Jews. I will let you know what they say."

"And I will approach Baghdad," said the Russian.

"Okay," said the MIOS Officer. "At least we now have

a plan.”

“A toast, then,” said the Russian, standing and pouring another shot for himself and the MIOS Officer. “To our own defenses, determination, and self-preservation. *Za Zadarovje*!”

The vodka slid down his throat like liquid ice and coated his stomach in warmth. It felt good to be drunk again after such a long time. After shaking hands with the Russian, who even gave him his own bottle of vodka, in a black bag, of course, he left their company without saying a word to the General on his way out. He stumbled along the streets of Teheran, getting lost in his own thoughts and reveling in the day despite the stubborn heat and the sweat that seeped through his flowing robes and tightly wound turban.

He studied the faces of the women who passed by him, their heads wrapped in *chadors*, their eyes dark and mysterious, their curves guarded by black garments that flowed to their ankles. They appeared like bells hovering over the sidewalks, dark shadows in the blaring sunshine, their stares blank, even though he wanted them to smile with him, say something to him, pay attention to him, because he could have used their attention then, his heart wide open and ready for one of them to inhabit it. His inebriation permitted his beatification to blossom like the ancient *Nowruz* flowers against the sun’s continuous rays, his head light, his stomach warm, and his eyes adjusting to the other women’s eyes, if only they didn’t look the other way as soon as their eyes connected. The women of Teheran exhibited a profound sense of shyness. Eye contact was too personal for their reserved sensibilities, their lives guarded and preserved like exquisite dolls that had never been taken out of their boxes, their mocha skin translucent with a hint of white porcelain, as though they were a separate species entirely, like a tribe that had yet to be discovered, their communication severed from the rest of the world. Of course, he had noticed these women many times before but not against the magnification of their beauty, their naturalness unblemished and radiating as they walked.

He even considered marrying again, his family buried in another time, stuck in the recesses of his memories, sealed by thick strands of silk spun by spiders that had caught them in their cobwebs, crawled upon them, and finally devoured them. He did not remember them anymore, and the day itself, new and fresh and alive, sprung with new possibilities and a manner of thinking that came as naturally to him as his aboriginal state that had crafted him to do what he did before the war, before the Ayatollah, before he had joined the Shah and tortured all of his enemies to death. He floated along those streets effortlessly until he found his apartment building, climbed its tan stone steps, and found the Mullah unexpectedly waiting for him at his front door.

"My father," he stammered confusedly, "I did not expect you until tomorrow. Do what do I owe the pleasure of this visit?"

Nerve-wracked, the MIOS Officer kissed his hand and welcomed him into his apartment as he plummeted down to Earth, his bed un-made and yesterday's clothing strewn all over the floor. He offered him a seat and immediately put the bagged bottle of vodka in the ice box. He then boiled water for tea. The Mullah sat there like a statue within a funnel cloud. The Officer kicked aside the clothing, embarrassed by how filthy his apartment was, and handed him a piping hot cup of tea when it was ready.

"It is good to see you, my Lord. What brings you here so soon?"

"Your talk with the Russian. How did it go?" he said

matter-of-factly.

"It went well. They have a proposal that will interest us."

After he related what went on in the meeting, the Mullah looked at him quizzically.

"I hope you're joking," said the Mullah. "This is no time for jokes. And there's something a bit off about you, like you haven't slept all night."

"I am excited by the idea. It is an exciting idea, don't you think?"

"An alliance that includes Saddam is no reason to cheer. It's disgusting, actually."

"But my Lord, times have changed. A new day has come to Iran. It's a new day for Islam. The Christians, they're scared to death of us. Bin Laden has done a great deed by provoking the Americans. He fights where Islam leads him, no matter where it takes him, no matter who were once his friends, no matter who were once his enemies. He believes, and now we have the Russians who want to help us. Alliances shift with changing circumstances. Yes, our children's blood is still fresh in the desert, but it will dry. We must focus on the living now, not the dead. It is a new day, if only we have the courage to bury the past and seize the day."

"It's unforgivable what those unruly *Ba'ath Party* bastards did to us. Unforgivable!"

"Sir," he said calmy, "we all have grievances. We all feel the pain of how many Saddam had slaughtered, but that is the past, and this is the 'now,' the everlasting 'now.' We have to adjust to new realities. We have to manifest the new vision for our national defense, for our faith, to continue the Revolution. We are only at rest. Soon, we will have another opportunity to strike against the Americans and the Jews. I would seriously consider the Russian proposal. You can see it happening, can't you?"

"I can't see anything."

"Let me help you, my Lord. Let's take the Russian arms deal to the ISI. They will eagerly accept it. That means a full Islamic alliance against the Americans and the Jews. Pakistan, Iran, Iraq, Bin Laden, and the Taliban. The most faithful force ever assembled with Russian backing against the greatest of the Evil-Doers. You can see it, can't you? A Sunni and Shia holy alliance – all the elements of our faith working together against the Great Satan?"

"But the Pakistanis too? They have no idea what friendship and loyalty means. They'll kiss your hand one minute and stab you in the back the next. At least we know where we stand with Saddam. But we can't trust the Pakistanis as far as we can throw them."

"The deal will swing their second face towards us. With Russian backing, we can't go wrong."

"I don't know, my son," he sighed. "I just don't know. But I will advance the idea and take it to the leadership. In the meantime, sweeten the deal with the Russians. If they want to arm the Pakistanis so badly, then they will give us even more weapons for our Hezbollah friends. In return, we can suspend our funding of the Chechens and the Georgians, since Putin is so inclined to work against the Christians and the Jews. Do you think that would be acceptable?"

"Oh, yes, my Lord," said the Officer, noticing tea spilling from the sides of the Mullah's cup. "That's an excellent idea."

"Then the Revolution continues," said the Mullah. "I'll give you an answer in a few days. Let's see what the

General's people decide. If it's a go, prepare to depart for Karachi. I want the ISI informed as soon as possible. I guess you have really done it this time. Let's hope the arrogant General feels the same way you do."

"Just give me the word. It would be nice to see Karachi again after so much time."

"If you go, I want you well-rested. Your eyes are too red, and your smile is too wide. Take better care of yourself. I want you fresh for Karachi, if that's what God wills."

After the usual ceremonious hand-kissing and good wishes, the Mullah departed. The MIOS Officer then went straight for the ice box. He took out the chilled bottle of vodka and filled his empty teacup with it. He would rest alright but not without getting as drunk as possible before he passed out.

Chapter Twenty-One

March 2001 – Karachi, Pakistan

Considering that she is free to do as she chooses, assuming choices do exist, which is a questionable assumption at best, and considering her obvious beauty that perplexes even the noblest of us, a beauty forever beyond any man's reach as we are already well aware, if such a beauty is unmoored from the shoreline and afloat within battle-infested waters that are not of her own making, would this be better for her country or worse?

It's a moot question, really, because once she has been granted her freedom from whatever instruments that had first chained her to the rock as bait for the Aethiopian monster, there is no force that man can create or build or purchase to reclaim that freedom, a reclamation that would guide her towards the best possible outcome. Such is the cost of freedom, or better yet, the cost of setting her free and letting her make the same mistakes many a wise man has already made.

Understandably, no two women are alike. After all, a woman such as she is free to do as she wishes, but when considering what works best, what would be good and right and just for the seemingly insurmountable tasks that she must overcome, one must ask if any man could ever let a woman like Sherry Aspen free when other lives are at stake. One must ask whether what benefits Sherry Aspen exclusively outweighs what benefits the collective whole. And yet there she floats in battle-infested waters - gun boats, warships, aircraft carriers, nuclear submarines, the oil tankers that fuel them, and the fighter jets that dart overhead poised to bomb the innocent, all of this suddenly at her command like Washington crossing the Potomac. It begs the question whether her freedom and the command that she has merited leads us to an end that has never been manifested before, or will it lead to the same tired old paradigm that instructs the fair queen to send her armies into the warzone if only to keep her afloat and not anyone else.

There is no need to call her freedom selfish when freedom, by definition, is a selfish construct to begin with. She is free and blameless at the same time, and since she is so, one can only hope that it is for the better and not the worse. Although no two women are alike, the power entrusted to every woman and the freedom she has forged with it is the same and perhaps has always been the same. It is as beneficial as it is destructive. Within the fog of gun smoke and artillery fire, the future, after she has been set free, is just too hard to see. If it leads to the same old world, then maybe it's better to let the monster have its way with the innocents who want nothing to do with the drama that follows her wherever she goes.

As is usually the case with such a woman, the attraction is still too powerful to tolerate, a senseless attraction, to be sure, among those she will always ignore, maybe even despise, or what's worse, find particularly annoying. But she is free now and in service to her country, never to be seen again except within a dull man's memory, or better yet, a dull man's vision, as though such a woman is all but an illusion, a meme on a computer screen, a pic on a website, a robot implanted with the latest software, far advancing the airbrushing of yesteryear, eyeball to skin and perhaps some crystal-clear audio going along with the deluxe package, as though whatever the best and brightest have developed, this tactile, sublime entity, may indeed force a man to commit dreadful deeds that skyrockets him into a higher tax bracket just for a chance to sit next to her on a park bench in a swanky neighborhood to see her smile once more. If he is to be a man, he must say goodbye to all of that, even though whatever stunts he pulls to escape her beauty leads him closer and closer to her heart, that inexorable, ineffable tug that breaks him slowly. If only she makes it out of this war alive…

In media res, Sherry cozied up to her lover, her new ISI lover who visited her at the hotel daily without fail, their only activity taking off their clothes and sliding under the cool sheets, their dialectical bodies merging into each other's, taking comfort there, sleeping for an hour or two, and then he'd leave and return to the Embassy, to do what she wasn't sure. Every afternoon, he'd ask about the downed helicopter in Helmand Province, and she'd reply in kind that she still didn't know but was working on it. Their relationship, however, wasn't producing the kind of shared intelligence she expected. Also, he was growing tired of her, or so she felt by the way he made love to her, his need for his hands to touch her body, much like taking medication in the morning but without enough of a copay for her to be satisfied. There had to be something more to it, she thought. He had to give her something more, any new intelligence at all, to justify the relationship.

She dutifully submitted her reports to the Karachi Station Chief, each report getting lighter with nothing much to say. If the Station Chief weren't aware of the pointlessness of it, at least she was. She decided, then, after one more afternoon session of making love, to terminate the relationship. But first, authorization. Always authorization. Never should she act alone, or else she'd be sent packing, and so she requested to be pulled, only to be ordered to keep him in bed, in his arms, his manhood parked within her body just as he liked it, his body on top of hers, his head buried in the crook of her neck, his thin lips occasionally kissing the divot above her collar, until further notice.

When he rolled over, he said he had to leave, to return to the Embassy and scrutinize the foreign actors who were being let into the country, to determine if they presented a national security risk. There was something about the ordinariness of his work that demanded greater suspicion, or at least more curiosity.

"There's something you're not telling me," she said.

"What do you mean?" said the ISI Officer who lay next to her. "Nothing has happened."

"Why do I get the feeling you're not telling me the truth? We're supposed to be trusting each other, remember?"

"You mean that we're not supposed to keep secrets from each other. I already know that. But what we're doing isn't done every day. We all have secrets we have to keep. Don't be so naïve. I'm sure there's a lot you're not telling me too."

"I don't know what you mean. I've shared whatever I have."

"And the helicopter?"

"I need more time."

"And I say the same."

"Oh, bullshit. Don't lie to me. I'm good at picking out liars, remember? I'm not a fool."

"Hardly," he said, turning into her. "I know you're not

a fool. Did I ever say you were a fool? No, I never said that. In fact, you're the most intelligent person I've ever met."

"Seriously?"

"Hey, I thought you could pick out the liars?"

She punched him in the arm and said, "that's not funny."

"How could I resist?" he laughed. "I'm sorry, okay? But you're right. You have a right to be suspicious of me."

"So, there *is* something you're not telling me."

"I have nothing to tell you."

"Oh, come on," she smiled.

She reached below his waist and brought him back to life. She pulled off the covers and wedged herself between his knees and bent down to take him into her mouth. Her blonde head bobbed up and down, but every few moments she stopped, leaving him breathless and begging for more.

"Nothing to tell me?" she asked.

"Nothing," he said.

She went down on him again, stopping a minute or two later.

"Still nothing to tell me?"

"Nothing. Please, Sherry."

And then a third time, bringing him to the breaking point. She knew his body well enough to stop before pushing him over the edge.

"I guess you better go now," she said.

"Don't be this way, Sherry. Please."

"You're giving me no other choice."

"I swear I have nothing new to tell you, except..."

She wrapped her mouth around the tip of it.

"Stop playing with me, Sherry," he said. "Just get it over with."

"Except what, then? What haven't you told me yet?"

"Does it really matter that much to you? Every little fucking thing that I do?"

"Yes. Every little thing."

"Fine. I'm meeting with an Iranian tomorrow night."

"That's better," she said.

She went down on him for a final time and finished off what she playfully started, if only the game weren't so serious. If only it weren't a game within the framework of a larger game, a game with real consequences for losing. She had won through trading, as tacit as the trading could have been. At least she recognized it in keeping with her ascent into cleverness, guile, and a new self-awareness that she could still guard her heart while trading away everything else, her heart the only asset worthy of protection, and sex just another, everyday transaction. You get what you pay for, and his meeting with the Iranian would produce the kind of results with which could cover up her past mistakes and remake her image as a top asset in the eyes of her superiors at the Company. She should have recognized it sooner – that the search for puppy love, for a connection from her heart to another man's, was as worthless and pointless an endeavor as wishing upon a star.

Relationships, then, were based on trade – I scratch your back, and you scratch mine – a stock exchange now the center of her universe until she collected all that she wanted and squeezed out all the juice, sucked out all the marrow, of life itself. This was what her freedom led to. So be it. No wonder her freedom breaks all men. It amounted to a teaspoon of her sophistication and a tablespoon of disappointment for the rest of humanity. Better to get married young like the Hindus do. Being the freed woman that she was, however, she didn't know if she should inform the Station Chief of the Iranian visit or not. She didn't inform him, because she wanted, more than anything else, to see where the new information led, or how she could capitalize on this new development to find the terrorists protected by countries like Iran. Like waving a metal detector over a deserted beach, perhaps she'd discover a nugget of gold, like a list of terrorists and where they were hiding before they killed more Americans. Her enhanced trading skills had led to something after all. And so, she asked him. No, she implored him.

"Take me with you," she said, after she finished him off and licked him clean.

"Now you're talking crazy," said the ISI Officer, too out-of-breath to argue.

"I'm serious," she said. "I want to go with you."

"To what?"

"To meet the Iranian. I know what you guys do when you meet. Two friendly countries, sexless and boozeless?"

"I can't take you," he said. "You're easily an American."

"I'm fluent in Russian. I can be Russian."

"He'll figure it out. One knows an American when he sees one."

"That's the most asinine comment I've ever heard you make."

"He'll know the difference. This guy's been dealing with Russians for years. How long have you been dealing with Russians?"

She rose to her knees on the bed, her tan breasts facing him, the sheet that separated their bodies wrapped around her waist. She started speaking fluent Russian with an authentic Russian-inflected accent. Her impeccable delivery barely moved him, though.

"Convinced?" she asked.

"No. It's too dangerous. He'll be carrying a weapon. He may kill us both."

"No, he won't. We'll both be armed."

"That's not the point. These relationships are based on trust, or at least the semblance of it. You break that, and it ripples across the Middle East. I have no idea what this guy will tell me, but whatever it is, it's probably too important for me to fuck it all up, and bringing you along will fuck it all up."

"How do you know that? I can get more information out of the guy than you can."

"I said it's too risky. Besides, you haven't told me anything since we met. There's no point in taking you along."

"How about the helicopter?"

"What about it? You still don't know anything."

"I do know something about it."

"You mean, you've been withholding it all this time?"

"It was only for our own benefit. We're partners, after all, aren't we?"

"You're a real bitch, you know that? You should have told me."

"Aww, sweetheart, don't be so angry," she said, stroking his leg. "I tell you what, you take me along, and I'll tell you what I know."

He grabbed her wrist and placed his thumb on her radial artery.

"I'm not playing games with you," he said. "You want our partnership to last? Then, you better start talking."

"You're cute when you're angry," she said. "I hear Pakistanis have terrible tempers. Is it true?"

"What? You want me to fight you over it? I'd rather leave and never see you again. It's not worth the effort."

"What's it worth to you, then? Take me along, and I'll tell you what I've learned."

"Fine," he said. "Go ahead, then. Talk."

"It was the Russians. The Russians shot down your helicopter."

"How? They need permission to fly over Pakistani airspace."

"They hired a couple of Pashtun plantation workers to do it."

"For what?"

"In a civil war, who knows what anything's for. The Commander must have been doing something they didn't like. But from what I've learned, the Russians killed your venerable Commander."

He held his thumb to her wrist as she sat above him naked and grinning.

"Can you trust me now?" she asked.

He removed his hand and fell back into bed.

"Fine," he said, "I'll take you along, but absolutely no fuck-ups, and you follow my lead. Is that clear?"

"Yes, your highness."

"Good. No fuck-ups. I need to report this to headquarters right away. Now if you don't mind, I have to go."

"When will you come to get me."

"I'll give you the address tomorrow. And I hope you know how to dress. Arabs like the bare minimum. Wear your best lingerie."

"I'm not doing anything like that."

"Then prepare to get nothing out of him. The more we make him feel comfortable, the more likely he is to open his mouth and tell us something we're not supposed to know."

"Got it," she said.

Thankfully, she knew how to lie without accelerating her pulse. Otherwise, he might have tried to kill her. But after a quick shower, the ISI Officer left the hotel for the Embassy. She lay in bed, her body tangled in sheets. Using her trading skills, she won again. Until she uncovered something significant, she wouldn't inform Karachi Station. She'd keep it to herself for now, if only to dredge up her reputation. Finally, sleeping with the Pakistani had produced results, if only she didn't have to sleep with the Iranian too. Because she protected her heart above all else, it really didn't make much of a difference if she slept with another towelhead or not. She'd been dealt in again, knew how to play, and she'd play to win. She committed herself not to fail. With even one terrorist's name and where he set up camp, she'd emerge victorious. No way she could lose.

On the next morning after a breakfast that tried to resemble a buffet in Vegas but failed miserably, she returned to the hotel room and carefully selected what to wear. The ISI Officer wanted her sexy. So, after a mellowing shower, she shaved what little hair had grown on her body. By the time she finished, nothing but her blonde locks remained, her skin as new, smooth, and clean as a ripened peach ready to be bitten. She wore a black bra and panties set of silken lace, no panty hose or other accoutrements necessary. She studied herself in the mirror and knew she looked good, her body a commodity to be traded, even though she would never let it get that far. If the ISI Officer had any feelings for her whatsoever, he'd take her back home before the Iranian tried anything. But she didn't know what to expect. She then called the ISI Officer, and reluctantly, he surrendered the address.

He directed her to a part of the city she had never been to before. It was night already, so there was no point in tracing the scenery or the route. The streets at night were all the same without adequate lighting, many slumping bodies sleeping on the sidewalks relying on the natural warmth of the region to shelter them until sunrise.

Before leaving the hotel, however, she visited the bar in the lobby and had a couple of drinks. A German businessman hit on her, but it wasn't too difficult to brush him off. European businessmen hailing from abroad carried their manners and civility with them, as though an upright character and well-heeled ancestry lent them more than any fiscal acumen that landed them their jobs. His pressed, worsted-woolen suit and horned-rimmed glasses in the summer told her everything she needed to know about him. Even if she weren't working, she wouldn't be duped into being a wealthy man's sex toy, as that would have been the end result. She was smarter than that, and wiser too. Once these types broke out of their stuffy habitats, their libidos followed in kind. He bought her a drink, tried to make easy conversation using his best English, but after a few minutes of trying to impress her, she shut him down. She had places to go. The skilled trader reared its head. Charm, charisma, and a loving, open heart were immaterial. These useless traits and emotions had been swept to an unimportant and neglected side of the room and replaced by what was ideally practical. What she gave someone else had to be worth its weight and reciprocated in kind. In her case, only information mattered and not the suave introduction, the originality of the pick-up line, or the pleasant conversation for conversation's sake. Even in her leisure time, the clock ticked. Every minute mattered, and if she wasn't gleaning information, she wasted her time. She soon left the bar and the disappointed German and took a taxi into a dark, foreboding neighborhood in Karachi.

"Are you sure you want to be left off here, madam?" asked the concerned cabby.

Again, she thought it useless to investigate her surroundings. With a gun in her jacket pocket, she had no reason to worry about her safety. She readied herself to kill any strange man who laid a hand on her, her weapon so small and compact that it wouldn't ever be detected. In a way, she almost hoped that one of these Paki bums attacked her or tried to kidnap her. The high heels she wore would have walked all over his corpse, should the creep be so bold.

"I'll be fine," she said in her best Urdu, and she tipped him well.

She thought about asking the cabby to wait for her to take her back to the hotel once all of this was over, but the night reeked of unpredictability. She had no idea where she'd wind up that night, hopefully in bed again with the ISI Officer. She stepped into the hot air with nothing but a purse in which she stored her gun, a short overcoat, her skimpy dress, and the lingerie underneath it. The rats on the street picked at the toes of the humped backs of those sleeping on the pavement. They shooed them away, and aside from a few bits and pieces of their whispered conversation, only the weak lights hanging over the street buzzed as though a transponder nearby were ready to blow. Fortunately, she didn't have to walk very far.

She made sure to be in character before knocking on the door, an old colonial door meant for a Duke or a Duchess but rotted for contemporary use. She noticed a small camera on the doorframe. When she knocked, someone on the other side mysteriously buzzed her in. She walked through a dark hallway where she immediately heard the festive din of mingling, glasses clinking, music playing. She recognized the music as a favorite Iranian pop tune. She entered a room filled with brown Pakistanis and several light-skinned Iranians lounging on modular cushioned chairs, young women in short black miniskirts and high crop-tops barely covering their youthful bodies dancing in front of them and sharing their drinks. In the air hung the familiar scent of hashish that her olfactory senses pinned to her time with the Pashtun in Helmand Province. She gathered up her nerve and reminded herself that she was there to work and not to play. Abstaining from the hashish and the alcohol would take discipline, but she knew it important for the information to be accurately recorded and then dispatched to Karachi Station. Not that she requested prior authorization or anything, but she had the feeling that the Station Chief would be more than happy with what she'd procure. After all, she at least had information that the Pakis may rid themselves of all the radical Afghans at the border and send them all back to Kabul. This alone would excite the Iranian MIOS Officer whom she hoped to find through all the tobacco and hashish smoke, heavy clouds that hovered over the room and cloaked their bodies as though the oily residue of the smoke had been rubbed into their skins, the few ceiling fans in operation unable to clear the way for any fresh air. Just sucking it in made her a little high.

And yes, the dancing women were just as good-looking as the models she had seen on the television in her hotel room, the international cable networks connecting them to Islamic centers all over the Middle East, as though these women were the only creatures gluing the region together, their bellies tight, their navel rings shining in the track lighting, the hips swaying to the electronic beats of the pop tune, the talk of the men, and the giggles of these women seated next to them barely audible. Even with her luxurious blonde hair, she couldn't make a dent in distracting any of the men who were either too drunk or too stoned to notice the ray of sunlight entering an otherwise dark room, female hands touching the arms and thighs of the important men she had to meet and press for information. It wouldn't be as easy as she thought. She had competition.

Nevertheless, she put on her best Russian in both the accent of her voice and the somewhat innocent, seductive demeanor of her attitude, as though she knew her place as a comfort to these men from abroad, her body loaned to them by Russian mobsters and their worldwide network of sex traffickers. She entered like a lamb in a den of wolves, but wolves who were drunk and high nonetheless. She almost wished she wore something sluttier, her dress hiding too much of her body, unlike the other women who brazenly let themselves hang out. The women there were an assortment of brown women in different shades, some of their skins lighter than others. Some of them even looked white, but from what she could see through the haze of smoke, no other blondes took up residence there. Again, one would think that any of these men would run up to her and offer her something to drink or at least grope her ass before doing so, but this didn't happen. Somehow, she had to make herself noticeable. She had to be proactive within this crowd.

And then she saw him, the ISI Officer sitting next to a man whose entire head had been burned off, leaving red scars and slices of skin where his scalp should have been. Still, the dancing women leaned over this man and giggled at whatever came out of his mouth, comforting the burned man as though they had been born and bred to do so. It amazed her how a man so disfigured attracted such beautiful girls. Perhaps Kissinger was right when he said, to paraphrase, that a man's power is his greatest aphrodisiac. As ugly as this man was, he enjoyed himself while talking with the ISI Officer.

She approached them carefully, the shy, innocent Russian girl used to taking orders from whomever shoved her around the most. She interrupted their discussion by bending down to kiss the ISI Officer, the soft women magically parting the way for her like Moses did the Red Sea. Competition among these women for the powerful men in the room had been condemned. The women hanging around them made room for her, as she squeezed in between another half-naked beauty and the ISI Officer, her evening dress out of place for an in-door beach party such as this. In Karachi, no less.

She put her arm around the ISI Officer, her hand dangling from his shoulder and barely touching the MIOS Officer who sat close to him.

"And who is this?" asked the MIOS Officer, in Urdu.

"Why, this is *La Femme Nikita*," laughed the ISI Officer. "Don't you know that already?"

"Of course," smiled the MIOS Officer. "Whoever you are, welcome to our little party."

"Thank you," said Sherry in her best Russian. "What do I have to do to get a drink around here?"

"How about some vodka? For old time's sake."

"That would be lovely, yes."

The MIOS Officer whispered into the ear of the half-naked girl next to him, his finger grazing her thigh. The girl left for the bar and returned with a vodka martini with a plump green olive swimming in the middle of it. The girl handed Sherry the drink, which she sipped slowly.

"When I was in Moscow last, I had a full head of hair," said the MIOS Officer across the vacant face of the ISI Officer who had thrown the party for him. "How do you find the heat of Karachi? You must find it difficult, no?"

"I was raised in Cuba," said Sherry in Russian. "I rather like the heat. It reminds me of home."

"A lucky woman," he smiled. "You grew up in Havana. You have a tan to show for it. It is both natural and contrived. Come, let me see more of you."

Sherry, always on guard, rose to the occasion. She left the ISI Officer over whom her arm draped and stood full-frontal in front of the MIOS Officer like a mannequin in front of a seamstress.

"Go ahead, then," he said.

"What would you like me to do?" asked the Russian version of Sherry.

"I want to see more of your tan."

She understood what he meant, and she complied, but not before glancing at the ISI Officer penetratingly, as though removing her clothes had to amount to something. And so, she removed them, and soon she stood in front of him with nothing but her black lingerie on covering very little of her bare body.

"Stunning," remarked the MIOS Officer. "Just stunning. You are a true Russian beauty just as I remember them. Just make sure not to put your dress on again while you're here. You won't be able to fit in otherwise, am I right?"

The girls near him giggled at this comment, while the ISI Officer smiled politely, prompting Sherry to giggle as well, a staged giggle meant to attract him.

"Please," he said. "Come sit next to me."

She squeezed in between the MIOS Officer and her ISI partner making sure to monitor any communication shared between them.

"So, how did you two meet?" asked the MIOS Officer to the ISI Officer.

"She's on loan," said the ISI Officer.

"Oh, I see," laughed the MIOS Officer. "Well, you can now loan her to me." And then to Sherry, "you'd love Teheran this time of year. There's only so much to do here in Pakistan."

"Unfortunately, my good friend," said the ISI Officer, "she stays in Karachi for the time being."

"Until someone takes her home to Moscow. Or is it Havana?"

"Neither," smiled Sherry. "St. Petersburg."

"Ha! Even more beautiful of a city. Good for you. The most beautiful women in the world come from St. Petersburg."

"And how do you know this?" she asked.

"With you as their representative, how could I ever think otherwise?"

"That's very sweet. Thank you," and she leaned into him and kissed his Persian cheek, causing the ISI Officer to stir in his seat.

"Okay, my dear friend, we should get down to business, before we're too drunk to talk."

With the music blaring, they shouted to each other with

Sherry in a privileged seat between them, the other brown women hanging from their sides and smoking hash like there were no tomorrow.

"Let her dance first," said the MIOS Officer.

"My dear friend, the night grows old. We must discuss what we have to discuss before we both pass out."

The ISI Officer nodded to Sherry, and like a trained seal, she got up again and faced the MIOS Officer in her black lingerie. She then danced to the electronic beats of the Iranian house music. Surprisingly, she was good at it, swaying her hips and raising her arms, writhing them together like hypnotic snakes, and then stretching her hands below her waist, running them up her thighs, her hips, and then her ribs, and into the air again, an innocent Russian angel fully aware of her devilish side that she only showed to those who commanded her, only to the criminals who controlled the world and the beautiful women whom the Good Lord had dumped there.

The MIOS Officer, in a moment of exuberant spontaneity, reached out and placed his hands on her hips just above her panties. As she swayed, his hands swayed with her. His smile widened, and his eyes brightened. When his head moved in on her navel, the ISI Officer put a stop to it.

"Please, my friend, time is of the essence. I'm glad you're enjoying yourself, but we should get to work."

Sherry broke away from him and sat between the two once more but not without the MIOS Officer's hand patting her on the ass *en route*.

"Thanks for the dance," he said, the glare of the track lighting refracting off of his ruined scalp. "I am at peace now, but not for long. Maybe we can have a drink later?"

"Maybe," she said.

"Okay," said the ISI Officer, slapping his hands on his thighs. "So, what brings you to Karachi all of a sudden? What does the MIOS need from us?"

"We need you to be with us," said the MIOS Officer. "We need you to be on the right side of history, my brother."

"And what side is that?"

"Let's talk about Afghanistan first."

"What about Afghanistan?"

"The Taliban and Bin Laden. Don't you agree that they are the ones best suited to rule Afghanistan, now that the civil war is cooling off?"

"It's hardly cooling off," said the ISI Officer. "Massoud is still alive in the North. How could it be cooling off?"

"We know the ISI supports the Taliban and Bin Laden. You also support Hekmatyar. We know as well as you do that the US won't support any of them, even though they are in combat with the Taliban over finding Bin Laden."

"The Taliban will never fork over Bin Laden to the Americans. They consider him their guest in their homeland. That's just not going to happen."

"What if the US sent more money to the Taliban just to keep them honest? After all, Bin Laden is the bigger fish. They want him now more than ever. What is he? Public enemy number one right now? A most enviable position for any Muslim to be in."

"The Taliban will never hand over Bin Laden to the Americans no matter how much they're given."

Sherry, hearing this all, simply played dumb and listened to the information roll from the MIOS Officer's thin lips, a gushing waterfall of it. All it took was an electronic dance for the MIOS Officer to open his mouth. That and a lot of whiskey and hash that had numbed his brain. Or was it her touch that did it?

"That way, the US is suckered out of their money like they usually are," said the MIOS Officer. "Tell them to fund the Taliban, and when the Taliban refuses to surrender Bin Laden, we can save some of the money we always give them. Our coffers are nearly empty anyway. Only dumb Americans would think that they could win the Taliban's loyalty. Let them try if they want to."

"An idea worth considering. I'll think about asking my superiors."

"Good, but I didn't travel all the way from Teheran to tell you that. A simple phone call would have sufficed."

"I know. Why are you really here, then?"

"An arms deal. What else what I would be doing here?"

The news of this was like a splash of cold water in her face. She immediately perked up. Anything involving arms shipments to the ISI deserved her utmost attention.

"I'm all ears," he said, taking a sip of his drink and massaging Sherry's thigh, his hand rough and dry on her skin.

"Again, we want the ISI on the right side. Forget these dumb Americans. They will always be there when it best suits them, whether you work with their enemies or not. We'll give you some first-class Russian arms, more advanced than the Americans will ever give you, for the low price of working with the MIOS and the GRU instead of the CIA and the US State Department. When was the last time you were offered a deal like that?"

Knowing full well that the US had already brokered an arms deal with the ISI to move radicalized Afghans out of the Northwest Frontier, Sherry waited for the two faces of Pakistan to emerge, accepting arms from all quarters just to defeat the Dotheads. Pakistan would never stretch itself too thinly doing exactly what it had been used to doing, she thought. Their faces multiplied when offered arms from any nation, friend of the US or not. They played all sides while flashing the nicest smile to those they made deals with. It hardly mattered, though, because Sherry had already captured this particular ISI Officer, the free flow of their trading amounting to trust and a certain degree of faithfulness.

"But what do we have to do for you in return?" asked the ISI Officer.

"When the time is right, you side with us."

"You and who else?"

"You, me, the Russians, the Taliban, Bin Laden, and the Iraqis," chuckled the MIOS Officer, reaching around Sherry and slapping his back. "Now that's a New World Order, wouldn't you say?"

"What are you doing in bed with Saddam of all people? Won't the Americans come after you?"

"As long as we have Russian support, it's a new day, my brother. We are in the driver's seat. Not the Americans."

"I see. Well, here's to it, then. Let's see how this all plays out."

The ISI Officer raised his glass, and the MIOS Officer followed suit. Sherry smiled sweetly again playing dumb and delightful, the MIOS Officer again putting his hand on her thigh, the taste of vodka in her mouth like liquid metal cascading into the warmth of her stomach.

"How about you let me take her for the night," asked the MIOS Officer. "I'll bring her to you in the morning."

"I wish I could, my dear friend, but she's wanted at the

Embassy tonight."

"Oh, I see. She has already been reserved for the evening. That's too bad." And then to Sherry, "wouldn't you rather be with me tonight?"

Sherry giggled and used her best Russian to say, "I'm sorry, but I have another engagement. Maybe some other time?"

"I tell you, you can always come back with me to Teheran," he said, moving his hand between her legs. "I will show you all around town."

"I'll have to take a rain check on that," she said, removing his hand and taking another sip of her drink, "but when you return, it would be lovely. Thank you."

"We go now, my friend," said the ISI Officer.

"At least leave her here to enjoy the rest of the evening. I'll have her back at the Embassy after the end of the night."

"We really must get going."

Sherry slipped on her dress in front of the MIOS Officer and asked him to zip her up from the back, which he did. She then bent down and kissed him on his scarred scalp, the ridges of his torched skin awkward on her lips.

"A pleasure meeting you," she said.

"Enjoy the night," said the MIOS Officer. "The next time I'm in Karachi, you're coming with me."

Sherry and the ISI Officer escaped into the late evening air, the dark streets silent save for a few random rickshaws traversing the closest avenue. They hailed one down and hopped inside. The hot breeze caressed her face as the loud rickshaw motored in the direction of the hotel.

"What? You're not coming up?" asked Sherry,

converting her speech to English again.

Once they arrived at the hotel, the rickshaw's motor sputtering, the ISI Officer said, "of course not. I need to get to the Embassy. We have a deal on the table."

"You're not actually going to take it, are you? It's garbage. We'll make you an even better offer."

"So now we're in the middle of a bidding war?"

"Damn right, you are," she said. "Take that deal, and there will be consequences."

"Oh, yeah? Like what?"

"To be determined. Don't fuck around. Convince your leadership not to work with the Iranians."

"That's not for me to decide. My work is done here. Stay out of it. You got what you wanted. So did I."

"First tell me that you won't take the deal."

"That's not for me to decide."

"But you are the one delivering the message."

"I report what I'm told to report. Nothing more."

"Then I guess I'll do whatever I have to do."

"It's nothing personal, Sherry. It's just business. It's the business we're in. This is how it works. There are no goodbyes. Do whatever you have to do, then. Don't think for a moment we ever had any control over this."

"Says you."

"Don't be foolish. And don't do anything stupid. You collect the intelligence and hand it over to your Station Chief. Seriously."

"Like you even give a shit what happens to me. Like you ever cared."

"We all have a job to do," he said. "You have yours, and I have mine. And no, I never cared about you. It's just business."

"Fuck you, then."

"I'll miss you, Sherry. Believe it or not."

"I'm telling you. Don't take the deal."

She stepped out of the rickshaw, which then motored into the night with the ISI Officer inside of it. It left her off outside of the hotel lobby all alone. As the hot Karachi breeze coursed through her body and lifted the skirt of her dress, she couldn't help but feel the loss of him, even though she wasn't supposed to care either.

He was right, though. It was business. Just business. Just trades of sex, of information, of jockeying for better positions within their respective agencies. It harkened back to the basic functions of the human animal she had once learned of in her Biology classes, how a man and a woman swapped sweat, saliva, and come for their mutual survival. Otherwise, it would have been pointless. Emotions had to be removed, as their pointlessness only interfered with the tasks at hand. Collect the intelligence, take it directly to Karachi Station, and maybe she'd get a pat on the back, or even a promotion for a job well done, her body an empty sack of flesh, blood, and bone in the pursuit of what she now truly needed – more and more information that would eventually lead to her own self-respect while undermining it all the same. She'd have to live with this duality, and hopefully it wouldn't destroy her like it did other assets in the field. It could have easily been murder, extortion, or the mass genocide of an innocent tribe. The thin fabric of Old Glory that shielded her soul sometimes ran thin.

Despite justifications for doing anything and everything

for her country, the emptiness within her had been carved out by a ruthless scalpel that had operated on its own volition and knew no boundary, caring neither who she was nor the future she would have born but only the information she was going to deliver, which is exactly what she intended to do after rushing into the elevator and waiting patiently for it to carry her up to her room. Once securely inside her room, she picked up the phone and dialed the Karachi Station Chief at home.

"Yes, what is it," he answered groggily on the other end of the line.

"It's Officer Aspen, sir," she said.

"Do you know what time it is? It's fucking three in the morning. What do you want?"

"I have a lot to tell you, sir. It's important."

"At three in the morning? It can wait. Call me tomorrow at the Station."

"It can't wait, sir. It's important."

"Shit. Alright. Just hold on a second…"

She heard him fumbling the receiver on the other end and then a long pause. She heard her own heart beating in her head, her pulse quickening.

"This better be good, Sherry," he said, more awake. "Go ahead."

"Sir, the Iranians have offered the Pakis an arms deal."

"Who? The Iranians?"

"Yessir. And there's an alliance forming between the Iraqis and the Iranians. The Russians are putting this together."

"What? What the hell are you talking about?"

"Sir, there's to be a Muslim alliance with Iran, Iraq, The Taliban, and Bin Laden."

"I still have no idea what you're talking about."

"Just as I said. You heard it right. The arms deal, the Islamic alliance with the Russians. It's all happening as we speak."

"Where did you get this from?"

"I went to a meeting with the ISI Officer you assigned to me and an Iranian MIOS Officer."

"You did what?"

"That's right, sir. I infiltrated the meeting, and that's what the MIOS Officer disclosed to the ISI Officer. I was right there. We have to move on it fast or we'll lose Pakistan. And any plans for Iraq that DOD may have may be compromised."

"And you did all this, you figured this all out, without prior authorization, am I right?"

"Sir?"

"You did this without notifying anyone at Karachi Station, especially me, right?"

"Sir, I can't see how…"

"Are you fucking crazy?! How many times do I have to beat it into that thick skull of yours that you never do anything without prior authorization?!"

"It's the information, sir," she stammered. "Whatever happened has happened. New information has come to light. We have to act upon it, immediately. We can't get caught up in regulations right now."

"Bullshit! We're not doing anything."

"Sir, we can hardly sit on this."

"Just hold on, okay? Hold on. Let me breathe for a second, before I freak the fuck out. Hang on…"

She heard his heavy breathing on the other end. After a minute or two, he was calm.

"Alright, Officer, let me explain a few things, and I am going to be as calm, cool, and collected as I can."

"Yessir. Go ahead."

"These Paki and Iranian fucks are born liars. They will do anything to steer us in the wrong direction. We have absolutely no evidence that corroborates anything that you've just told me. Actually, what you're saying sounds totally preposterous. It sounds like some conspiracy theory generated out of a Karachi nuthouse. We are not in the business of pursuing conspiracy theories, Officer. We deal in cold, hard facts, raw intelligence, that leads to tangible outcomes. You have been the object of a sweeping disinformation campaign only meant to obfuscate what your real assignment is – to fuck the idiot ISI Officer until further notice. And did you follow through with that? Of course not. Did you get authorization for any of this, the kind of authorization that could have verified this? The kind of authorization that could have supplied you with backup, in case someone took a bullet and fired it in your head? You could have been killed. Is there something fucking really wrong with you, Officer?"

"Sir, respectfully, I went in using Russian cover. Iranian Intelligence had no idea that an American was in there."

"Horseshit. Like the fucker can't tell the difference between an American blonde and a Russian blonde? My teenager back in Washington can tell the difference. You've got to be kidding me."

"I think you've got it all wrong, sir. I really do think we have to stop this deal between the Iranians and the Pakistanis.

That's the first step in all of this."

"You sound like a lunatic, you know that, Aspen? All you were supposed to do is stick with the ISI Officer until further notice, and now you've blown your cover to an Iranian asset, and you've come up with some stupid fucking conspiracy theory that has probably already made us the laughing stock of every Iranian terrorist cell from Karachi to the Kremlin. I tell you, Aspen, you're lucky I don't come over there and strangle you myself."

"Sir, I really don't appreciate – "

"Fuck you, because I don't give a shit what you appreciate. You fucked up, and I'm sending you back home, and you're lucky you're not flying home in a body bag, for dear Christ."

She slammed down the receiver and sat on her bed panting, her heart beating out of control, her brain swollen with anger, frustration, and confusion. Not only was the Station Chief a prick, but he was a stupid prick as well. And who was he calling stupid anyway? She didn't sleep with the ISI Officer for nothing, and how long did he expect her to sleep with him exactly? She had little idea what 'until further notice' meant. She could have been stuck in that hotel for months, a slave chained to a bed only to be freed at the whim of a Station Chief so dense, that he wouldn't know a piece of good intelligence if it fucked him in the ass. That fuckhead didn't know what he was talking about. He didn't understand the preponderance of what she had learned. If Karachi Station wouldn't listen to her, then perhaps someone else would. And it wouldn't have been anyone in the Middle East or Pakistan.

She thought of calling Langley to relay the intelligence, but then Karachi Station must have already called Langley and informed them that one of their loose cannons had been fooled by the MIOS and the ISI into coming up with a scenario so outrageous, that her next assignment should have been in an asylum teaching art classes to a bunch of mentally insane retards on Haldol, as they would be the only ones receptive to such a wild, bogus theory. She felt like throwing one of the chairs in her hotel room out the window. The Station Chief pissed her off that much. But in order to continue where she started, she had to calm and steady herself, which she did. She took very general and slow deep breaths as the telephone suddenly rang and rang, her anger abating and a sense of her surroundings returning. Perhaps they were coming to get her and force her back home. What a bunch of scumbags.

She had to move quickly. She waited for the phone to stop ringing, the echoes of it rifling through her head. She then called the ISI Officer when it stopped. Thank the Good Lord that he was there and picked up the phone so late at night. He must have been in a meeting at the Embassy.

"Hi," she said breathlessly, "I need to speak to you."

"Sherry, I thought you understood. We're through. I can't see you anymore."

"It's not that. I need a ticket to Tel Aviv. My time is up here. I think I'm in trouble."

"Trouble for what? You don't sound alright."

"That's because I'm not alright, shithead. I need a ticket to Tel Aviv right away."

"Just calm down, okay? Just tell me what's wrong."

"I don't have time to explain, okay? Can you get me to Tel Aviv or not?"

"Shit, Sherry, what's wrong? You're not communicating. Maybe I can help you if you told me more."

"I can't right now, okay? Can you help me out or not?"

"PIA doesn't fly to Tel Aviv. You'd have to fly out of Mumbai, transfer there, and then fly on to Tel Aviv."

"Well, can you get me fucking there or not? I don't have time to mull over travel arrangements!"

"Okay, just head to the airport. A ticket will be waiting there for you. Remember Karachi, to Mumbai, then on to Tel Aviv. You may have to wait for a while, but you'll be booked through to Tel Aviv."

"I'll get you back for this, you know that, right?"

"Consider never seeing or hearing from you again payback enough."

"Fuck you," she said and hung up the phone.

She stuffed whatever clothing she had in her suitcase and ran out of the hotel after calling a taxi. By the time she told the driver to step on it for a few extra rupees, she knew she had gotten out before Karachi Station reeled her in. Once again, she had to calm herself to cross the necessary checkpoints traveling on her American passport. She banked all of it on the Tel Aviv Station Chief believing what she had learned, no matter how ludicrous it may have sounded.

Chapter Twenty-Two

September 2000 – Jerusalem, Israel

It troubled him that he may have been one of the only Israeli cops dispatched to the Temple Mount that morning who believed that peace with the Palestinians may have been possible. He didn't hate the Arabs for their crude ways, their guttural language, and their staunch chauvinism in defense of their God. Not that he knew any Arabs to begin with. He just hated the political process that provoked violence when none of it had been necessary. Not that he had any solutions to what haunted Jerusalem, but he knew provocation when he saw it. And when ordered to stand guard over a fat man in a suit whom the Arabs called 'the Butcher of Beruit' as he announced to the world the Temple Mount had always been open to Jews and that he came in peace when all he really wanted to do was win an election, the whole affair stank of corrupt politics that won out against any peace initiative the Americans proposed at Camp David that year, which failed, yes, but still marked a significant turning point that would, one day, remove him from the line of fire.

He didn't read *Haaretz* much. He hardly found the time. From what he had heard from members of his own troop, though, the Likud Party opposition leader's visit that morning easily tabled any talk of peace, considering what many of his fellow officers had said and what they would surely witness after he spoke. But the Israeli Cop still believed that the Camp

David talks would lead to something, like one small step in the right direction despite their failure. Perhaps the firearm at his side and his green policeman's uniform trumped his wishful thinking and youthful naivete.

Israel had become too big of a problem to solve when surrounded by the millions who hated her, those rock-throwing Muslims on the edges of the city claiming that Jerusalem was theirs, if only to counter the claims made by Jews that they were the rightful guardians of the city and the ridiculous rock where Abraham offered up Isaac as a sacrifice to God. Granted that this shit went back thousands of years, but how on Earth could a just God ever intend for two of the major monotheistic religions to be at each other's throats over it. If anything, the solution to the entire Temple Mount may have been to desecrate it before he had to wake up another morning, put on his uniform, and brace himself for another day of the same threats that kept his eyes monitoring every black Arab and kept his finger tapping at the trigger of his gun.

And here comes the fat Likud Party fucker in his suit and his smile, sashaying up the narrow stone path to the doorway of the Temple Mount, surrounded by his followers who really knew what this visit would amount to after the garbage that came out of his mouth claimed that he was on a mission of peace and yet at the same time declaring Israel's sovereignty over one of the holiest shrines the world has ever known, the place where God eternally dwells and only the highest priests are permitted, the same place where millions weep at the Western Wall while even more millions are slain to claim ownership over it. It sounded completely ridiculous to him, and in many ways, he resented having to defend it.

Not that he hated himself as a Jew. Hardly the case at all. Rather, he took issue with how an entire religion mattered more than his own right to direct and determine his own morality based on his own experiences, no matter how many precedents had been set, no matter where the religion had guided people like him who wore the same olive tan and spoke the same language based on the same genocides that had forced them to wander the Middle East, until men like Cyrus the Great permitted them to return from Iraq to rebuild this temple and protect this rock enclosed in a golden dome, while he and the rest of Jerusalem, long vulnerable to suicide bombers and random acts of violence, set him on edge every morning while walking to work. The opposition leader's visit typified any other day in Jerusalem, only this one had been purposely arranged to provoke the seething warrior-anger that hid at the heart of every rock-throwing Muslim and the inevitable response of unloading a few sharp-tipped bullets into their chests, sparking international outrage and condemnation, when really they ought to have condemned the entire city for putting him and his fellow police officers at risk and arming them to the teeth to begin with. For a city reputed to be so holy, Babylon would have been a much safer bet had he the privilege of serving there.

He had grown so sick. His sickness went beyond all arguments and all postulations of what was right and what was wrong, all the facts of history as to who owned what, beyond the Prophets who would have been rolling in their graves at the sight of such horrors. Not that he could do anything about them, but at least he had a right to complain. Neither could he lead his people out of this conflict had he been as powerful as the old fucker speaking in front of the television cameras. It took two to tango, and both sides were at fault, no matter how many of his brothers and sisters pointed their fingers at the despicable Arabs and their natural violent tendencies. Like apes they were, wrecking the holiest place on Earth when they really should have gone back to Mecca and done their wreckage there.

And his own Jewish people, if they were really Jews at all, pretended to be the chosen ones but chosen only to evict those who inhabited the land of the people they just couldn't get along with, until they ultimately extinguished the Palestinians, and when the Jews got what they wanted, a land of their own, they merely extinguished one another over time in the same fight for territory, until no one remained but one man and a thousand of his wives, like the great Pharoah of old, making slaves of some but enriching his own inner-circle, like any adept and psychopathic dictator.

His captain ordered him and his fellow officers to follow the Likud opposition leader with careful eyes, just to make sure no one shot him in the head or that the Arabs didn't rise up in revolt and kill the supporters he took into the Mount with him. If anyone should have risen up in revolt, it should have been the common Israeli taxpayer who paid him to protect a man like that and the political system that kept the conflict continuing. It was the same as any democratic political system, only worse. At least in the West their leaders lied to their people before sending them to war, as war was usually the first item on the agenda once a leader takes office. They might as well have funded an entire party based on war, until there isn't a choice anymore but war, until war becomes ingrained into the daily lives of its own people, until slowly but surely, the war ethic takes over their intellect, their reasoning, their dreams and fantasies, until an entire race of people become war incarnate, and then another generation evolves into better and more capable warriors just like the Arabs, only fiercer and nastier, forever remembering the day a thousand years ago when a fascist madman tried to extinguish their entire species from the face of the Earth, which they use as justification to defeat their Arab neighbors, until one day they turn against themselves and defeat each other, their monochromatic visions of utopia destroyed by the very men elected to defend them and their vision to expand their small parcel of disputed land into an empire built for kings.

His vision for his own country notwithstanding, the police officer did want a wife and children of his own like most Israelis his age wanted, but far away from Jerusalem, far away from any place where a Jew didn't always have to remain a Jew, and a Muslim a Muslim, as though he had to wear his Jewish status as openly and boldly as the badge tagged to his officer's uniform, as though such a distinction actually mattered when a real flesh-and-blood human being hid behind the ramped-up version of him paraded around by opportunists like the Likud Party fucker who would simply incite other fat, opportunistic mullahs, who would then, in turn, incite even wilder lunatic Arabs to fire their limp-wristed rockets into Israel in the hopes that they may kill a few Jews, until the Israelis army responds by killing a few thousand Arabs with their missiles.

He thought he'd be better off marrying a Wiccan or a woman who practiced Voodoo than marrying another Jew from Jerusalem. Even if he married a Muslim, he still had a chance of a narrow escape, but this time at least he found a solution to the problem rather than the perpetual prolongation of it. If only these Arab women didn't cover themselves up, then maybe there'd be a chance at some divine compromise, or perhaps they had already invented such a thing in the secret labs of Tel Aviv where they spliced Muslim and Jewish genes together in the hopes of progressing towards a peace deal somewhere in the future, until the war hawks get a hold of those embryos and stamp them out under the heels of their government-issued boots like the last cigarette they smoked that day.

If miscegenation paved the only real road to peace, then all other negotiations and methods of diplomacy would never come close by comparison. Some crazy Jew had to initiate it. All of the history books, political abstracts, polemical arguments, and speeches past and present would never hold a candle to an idea as revolutionary as Muslim/Jewish speed-dating. As of yet, not even that one interesting idea made its way through daily Jewish life. Instead, Jews and Muslims both created novel theories, unique methods, and clever reasons to utterly destroy themselves.

He remembered hearing the old stereotype that Jews were very smart, but no one ever mentioned how many stupid Jews there were in Jerusalem, one of them being the Likud opposition leader, poised in front of the microphones and television cameras, sending his message of peace and goodwill to the masses by invading the Temple Mount, the same leader responsible for the massacre of Arab refugees in Lebanon's earlier civil war. What was sadder still, the Likud leader would probably win the election for what would happen after he descended from the Temple Mount to rejoin the same political system that birthed him.

The Cop had time before he had to move. He lit up a cigarette and leaned against one of the ancient walls where a great prophet must have once stood. A clear dereliction of duty, but for a setting so derelict, no one would have really minded. If only he had something stronger to numb him and all the people around him, he would have been in a better mood, but not today. It was the same bullshit, the cigarette making him sicker, and the hot, dry air making him perspire, his body slack and the sky flashing red and blue as though he were in the throes of a fever.

He could have been many other things – a doctor, a lawyer, a banker, or even one of these archaeologists who sifted through the sewage to uncover the same old battles, the same old wars, uncovering the same tired shit to justify who we were, to do exactly what the great books had said for us to do and hopefully make it out alive, if only the rules contained therein had been followed, if only they all could have gotten along, while the artifacts dug out of the ground only proved that the only real animals in the universe were the idiots who made them. They were guideposts on what not to do, like highway markers that ought to have been taken down to make the universe stumble a little, so the same cycles stopped repeating themselves.

He knew that today was not that day. Hie entire life was not that day, and when that day came, he'd be the first to jump on board the slingshot aimed directly at the sun, ready to launch and never looking back at the horrors this place had caused, the place he would never find, as though such a concept had never been explored here, all of Israel crying out for it but unable to imagine it, unable to conceive of it, the school children having even greater wars built into them, the learning of their own history self-defeating, their fragile, insane minds unable to cleave the past from a future that didn't have to deal with any of it. It only made sense when it stopped making sense.

He crushed the stump of his cigarette under his boot. Perhaps there would be day when he didn't have to deal with it, if only that day would come quickly. No, immediately. The Muslims were too impatient, but he understood. If he had any balls at all, he'd do the same and tape dynamite to his chest, set the timer, and get what he wanted right away. Ironically, he wouldn't feel a thing. It wouldn't matter whom he took with him. If it took out the fat man at the microphones, then maybe it would have led Israel in the right direction, not that he cared anymore anyway. He had a job to do, a function to perform. He brushed the stray ashes that cluttered his uniform. The gun at his side seemed to sweat along with him, an inevitable extension of him. A depressed Israeli was the last kind of killer they wanted on the force. He stiffened the slack of his body, the slack of his mind, a new determination to shut the hell up and do his job, no matter how thoroughly it disgusted him.

A lawyer, doctor, a banker, a father of a better version of him, a husband of a woman more beautiful than him, someone who gave of himself time and again to those who asked of him – these were the people he wanted to be. But a God so great hadn't been found yet. Everyone on the Temple Mount that morning waited for it, and each morning, they returned and waited for it again. Call it mandatory conscription at the age of eighteen that kept him wanting and hoping for more, and if the spirit struck him there, maybe he should have taken off his officer's cap and uniform, collapsed to his knees, and uttered some small prayer. But in a city full of prayers, some obviously more important than others, some as old as the day man had emerged from the primordial ooze, he couldn't say if any of his prayers mattered.

So, when the organization of the rally upon the Mount grew even more unstable, unstable enough for him to locate the Likud Party opposition leader after he finished addressing the cameras and the photographers for the entire world to behold, his message of peace delivered unequivocally in terms of the language he threw at whatever events would follow, the Cop joined the rest of his unit, muttering faint hellos here and there, and followed the rarefied procession of politicos, religious leaders, and Jewish right-wing fanatics down the Mount where an angry mob of black Arabs awaited them, their stones from their nearest abused mosque ready to be hurled at the crowd.

He had a job to do, and it made sense again when it stopped making sense, which was why he took up his handgun and aimed it right between the eyes of the same dirty Arab he killed last week and the week before that. He saw neither chaos nor confusion in it, just an organization that had crystallized and made sense, like sliding his foot into an old shoe cobbled especially for him alone.

Chapter Twenty-Three

June 2001 – Tel Aviv, Israel

She needed Tel Aviv. She missed medium-story government buildings made of glass and steel that modernized the ancient into workable forms that she at once recognized as the architecture of the homeland she left behind. The calm, sedate setting could have been Geneva or the Hague compared to the beauty of his brown body and the disorder of Karachi, or at least her experiences with him. If anything, she was glad to get out of there and away from him, glad as hell to leave the old world and enter the new. She enjoyed the serenity of being amongst like-minded colleagues, almost like Georgetown, but again, not ancient in the least but advancing into an era that resembled sanity. Unlike Langley, she had nothing to achieve in Tel Aviv. She had already achieved it to have wound up there.

Aside from coming to a place of comfort and rest, she relished in the familiar faces of Tel Aviv's people. She found respite in a government building that she vaguely remembered, even though she had never been there before. She studied people's faces, some of them with yarmulkes on and walking towards a destination but not knowing where their journey ended.

A plan of action presented itself, but the plan of action didn't lay out a destination for her either. She wouldn't let herself go in Tel Aviv, she thought. Walking a straight line had its benefits. Having limitations and the discipline not to let herself go made a great deal of sense, even though she had little idea why.

She had dressed appropriately that morning. Her long, black suit with long straight legs covered her entire body in the extreme heat, as though the heat were its own welcome. More than anything, though, she was tired and a bit shaken. She knew that another meeting with yet another Station Chief warranted her anger more than the malaise and fatigue that accosted her after she entered the revolving doors of the government building. Tributes to Jewish history streamed down from the ceilings in vertical banners that recounted the travails of Israel's short and perilous history. She didn't even need to show an identification card or passport.

"Yes, Miss Aspen," said the female security guard. "They're expecting you."

She looked into the eyes of the female guard hoping to find some clue as to what the future held, but she found no answers there. The security guard did what she was told. She had a family, deposited her weekly paychecks in the bank, prepared meals with her children, lived so simply that it went way beyond Sherry's own petty understanding.

"Miss Aspen," said the guard. "Please, they are waiting for you."

"Thank you," she said, and she found her way to the elevator doors as though a rope pulled her inside.

She spotted the black dome of a small camera affixed to the ceiling, even in a place as confined as an elevator. In Israel, they could never have been too careful. She could have been carrying a bomb, after all. But the suit she wore hung loosely around her, bringing immediate recognition to all that she was unarmed. Unless the supreme freakdom of paranoia seized her, she didn't have to worry too much about killing another person or killing herself in a building that had its climate control set to perfect room temperature, as though the climate itself could monitor her own body and make adjustments to suit her needs all on its own.

The elevator doors opened wide to the Station Chief's office. Tel Aviv, apparently, had treated him well. He sat at his wide desk while on the phone glancing up at her and then trying his best to get off the phone. At least she mattered that much to him. She didn't feel the need to ask him for a seat. She dropped her purse, sat down in front of him, and uncoiled her legs like a spring that refused to hide its own tension. She wouldn't bounce around the room unless provoked by him, in other words. By the manner in which he tried to end his phone call, she could tell that he didn't want to provoke her. By the looks of him, he seemed like a caring man in some imperceptible way, which was nonsense, because caring in the Company was its own dirty word. If anything, he pretended to care, and he would probably do a good job at it.

"Officer," he said finally, after hanging up the phone. "Langley is not too pleased with you."

"Well, you can tell Langley that I am not too pleased with them," she said.

"To be quite honest with you, Officer, it makes little difference to Langley that one of its officers is not pleased. What matters here is that Langley is not pleased, which means we have to remedy that."

"Let's stop wasting our time here," said Sherry. "I'm not a bureaucrat, and either are you. I'm here to tell you what I've learned."

"All in good time, Miss Aspen. Sherry, it is, right?"

"Officer will be just fine."

"Okay, Officer. Sometimes we forget that there is an actual human being inside, but Officer it is. How about something to drink?"

"I really don't feel like being picked up today, sir. This is not a hotel bar."

"Tea. I was thinking of tea. Would you like some? I have some very wonderful green tea that a friend of mine sent in from Japan. How about having some with me?"

"If you insist," she said resignedly.

His hands shook while picking up the receiver. He ordered the tea from his assistant downstairs, it must have been. Barely audible, the Station Chief's voice concealed a system at work under extreme duress. After ordering the tea, he returned to his same, hospitable self.

"The tea will be here soon, Officer. How was your flight, by the way? I trust you found the accommodations suitable?"

"And what accommodations are those, sir? I changed my clothes in a Mumbai water closet."

"Ah, I see," he said even more delicately. "Listen, Officer, I sense that there are a lot of issues that you'd like to talk about, or a lot of anger you'd like to get off your chest. Maybe we should do this at another time, when you are more settled in."

"Why wait? I still haven't tried your delicious tea from Japan yet. After all I've been through, why not have a cup of Japanese green tea in Tel Aviv? Actually, it's the only reason I came to Tel Aviv in the first place, to sample some real Japanese green tea. So, no, I'll wait for the tea."

The Station Chief sighed and leaned back in his chair.

The elevator doors behind her opened and in walked a lovely Israeli assistant, cute as a button, handing her a saucer of green tea, the service impeccable. She felt like throwing it against the wall.

"So, Sherry – "

"Officer."

"Yes, Officer. Well, I know some things are upsetting you. When we're out in the field too long, sometimes we don't know how to put things into proper perspective. Langley has filled me in, and I know you have some information to share, but I'm thinking you need a little break instead."

"Like a psychotic one."

"Ah," he laughed, "there's that old Company sense of humor. All of our finest assets have it. You are no exception. How's your tea?"

"It's the Russians, sir. The Russians."

"Always those Russkies. Aren't they a funny bunch?"

"This is not a joke. I'm not here to play games with you. The Russians are forming an alliance with the fundamentalists. Bin Laden, the Taliban, Iran, and Iraq. The Pakis are in the middle of it. That's why I'm here."

"Y'know, Officer, sometimes when we're out in the field too long, we tend to get too far ahead of ourselves. We need time to digest what we've learned."

"I've digested enough sand for now. This information came straight from an MIOS Officer."

"That's good. That's certainly a plus. We meet all sorts of people on the road. Assets generally find each other, even when they are supposed to be traveling incognito. Call it one of the seminal phenomena of the work that we do."

"Apart from the philosophy lesson, the question now becomes, what are we going to do about it?"

"Sherry, if I may, let me just get down to the point of the matter, okay? You need a vacation. Even the best of the best needs a break. I can't send you back out there like this. You are not effective like this. You need some rest."

"I've had plenty of rest, but thank you for caring. Did you tell Langley of my findings? I mean, they need to know right away, and then I need to get back out there. I need a team. I have to return to Afghanistan. We have to find Bin Laden. We can find where all of these terrorists are, but we don't have much time."

"Sherry," he said, shaking his head, "this is lunacy. It really is. Whatever you learned is all being taken care of, okay? Don't worry about it a second more."

"I'm not worried about it," she said pointedly. "That's *your* job. I need to get back out there fast before this alliance is fully formed. Otherwise, the entire homeland is at risk."

"Sherry," he sighed.

"Officer."

"Officer," he sighed again, "I'm sending you home."

The silence among them hung over the office like a brilliant theory that had been proven wrong. She looked at him in that silence while trying to interpret what the Station Chief said.

"I have to send you back home, Sherry. Don't make this any tougher on me than it already is."

And then she said, "it's not going to be tough on you at all, because I'm not going back home. I can't believe you would even think such a thing."

"Officer, sometimes when we're in the field too long –

"

"I know what happens when an officer is out in the field too long. You don't have to remind me."

"There's no need to raise your voice in here."

"I already know what happens, and that's not what's happening. Now I have a lead on something here, and you damn well better get on the phone with Langley and let me follow it."

"You have been reassigned, Officer. I'm sorry. You need a break. You need rest. You need to return stateside for now. Just take it easy for a while. We can set you up there, no problem."

"Doing what? Training a bunch of snot-nosed CSTs? Absolutely not."

"It's just a vacation, Officer. That's all it is."

"And then you'll keep me there like some museum piece? Fuck that. You will not send me back, because I am not going back. We've come too far for that now."

"Listen, I sympathize with you, Officer. I really do. But to make things plain, your orders are to go back, and whether we like it or not, we all have to follow orders. That's the way it is in our line of work."

"If reports are what you need, I have no problem filing them, but I have to remain out in the field. You have to put me back in Afghanistan or even Iran. I'm more than willing to do that."

"Tell me something," said the Station Chief, sipping his tea. "Have you even thought about DC lately?"

"DC? I'm not going back to DC. *Ergo*, there's no reason to think about it. Now look, we have to follow this through. We can argue back and forth about what we ought to be doing, but I already know that you have to send me back in there."

"That's just not possible," he said.

"Then, I'm not going. I'm just not going."

"You're not going rogue on me, Sherry, are you? Please don't tell me that. I may be a Jew, but the Company has very little tolerance for rogue officers. While I can understand your feelings, the Company won't."

"Well, be a good Jew, then, and let's find a way out of this, because the last thing I'm doing is returning to DC with my tail between my legs and our national security at elevated risk."

"You're too wrapped up in it, Officer. Can't you face that? You're obsessed with this alliance idea for some reason. Yeah, the Karachi Station Chief told me. It makes us less effective, which is why I can't send you back into Afghanistan."

"I'm definitely not going back to DC, so we have to work something out. The last thing the Company needs is a rogue asset on their hands, wouldn't you agree?"

"But first you need a break."

"I just said I am not going back to DC. What part of that didn't you understand?"

"I didn't say DC."

"I hope the next word out of your mouth is 'Kabul', then."

"Not Kabul. I'll put you on a break with a limited assignment. It will give you enough time to pull yourself together. It will give Langley enough time to explore what you've learned and figure out where to place you."

"But I'm not going home. We have an understanding on that, don't we?"

The Tel Aviv Station Chief hung his head in his hands, clearly exhausted by the discussion. Maybe there was an ethic of care in the Company after all.

"You're putting me in a terrible position here, Officer."

"Hey, if the Company can't trust one of its own, I guess there's no trust to be had anywhere. I don't fuck up. I have never fucked up. I take what I'm given, and I hunt it down. That's what I do."

"Understood, Officer, understood."

He reached under his desk and, after a careful search, pulled out a file. He licked his thumb and flipped its pages.

"You've never worked with Mossad before, have you?"

"It would be a first, sir."

"This is a friendly mission. You understand that, don't you?"

"Yes, sir, I do."

"Meaning, there'll be no combat here. No conflict."

"I understand, sir."

"Meaning, you'll be working with someone who works with us too."

"A double-agent, you mean?"

"Not exactly, no. He's still Mossad. He used to be an Israeli police officer stationed out of Jerusalem. But you are not playing spook on this one, Officer. You're just delivering a message."

"Which is what I usually do anyway."

"But there's no trouble waiting at the end of this

assignment, if you know what I mean."

"Yes, sir, I do."

"As long as we have that understanding, I want both of you to get to know each other, but you are not to have any romantic relations with this man."

"Understood, sir."

"It's just a light assignment, in other words."

"Yes, sir."

"Officer, do you know much about Hezbollah, or the situation Israel has in the Golan Heights with the Syrians?"

"Apples and oranges there, sir."

"Yes, I know, but see, Mossad is about to deliver arms to the Christian South Lebanon Army to fight against Assad. You know all about him, right?"

"Yes, sir, I do."

"So, as far as the Company's interests are concerned, we don't want our Mossad friends making that delivery."

"Why's that?"

"Sherry, I mean, Officer, you should know better than to ask that question. You are on limited assignment here. No digging. No coming up with things that will confuse this very simple mission. Don't maximize the minimum."

"Sorry, sir. I understand. Please continue."

"Tell the Mossad asset that they are not to deliver those arms. Instead, Hezbollah in the Biqua Valley must think that's what they are doing. Naturally, once they uncover this plot, they will blame Israel and hold rallies, but they will only know about the plan before it happens. Once the news spreads among their ranks, they will attack Israel."

"They are already going to attack Israel, sir. Langley should already know about this from the reports I filed in Karachi."

He again held his head in his hands, shut his eyes tightly, and sucked in his breath.

"I'm sorry, sir," she said. "Please, continue."

He exhaled slowly and said, "well, anyway, the Company wants Hezbollah to attack, but after they do, Israel is not to retaliate. All you have to do is deliver that message. You are also to take a break with your Mossad contact. In other words, just hang out with him for a little while. Don't convince him of anything or press him for any information. After a week's time, I'll see you here for another tasting of this Japanese tea. Understood, Officer?"

"Who's my contact?"

"Thank you for letting me continue, Officer."

He pulled out a black and white picture from the file. The Mossad asset she studied had short black hair, beardless, olive skin, and natural good looks, the look of a soldier, and hidden feelings behind his dark eyes that she couldn't read from a single photograph.

"Another hotel bar?"

"Yes, Officer, another hotel bar, but I want you to take it easy. He's already your friend, and you best see to it that you remain that way and conduct yourself accordingly. For an asset of your experience, this should be a walk in the park. Nothing more."

"And what are we supposed to do for a full week?"

"That's entirely up to you, but stay put with him for at least a week. After that, please return to Tel Aviv Station, and we'll take it from there. You'll then be reassigned."

"Yes, sir. Thank you for this opportunity, sir. Thank you for not sending me home."

"That's just it, Sherry. This is not an opportunity. This is a job. Just do the job and take a little leisure time for yourself. You're not to fuck this up, so don't fuck up."

"Thank you, sir. I already know that I don't fuck up, sir."

"Enjoy yourself on this one. Good luck, Officer. My assistant downstairs will fill you in on some of the details."

Along with directions to the hotel and cash for her expenses, the assistant also gave her several brochures for a trip to Mount Sinai.

"Have a good time," said the assistant with a polite smile, as though she had already found the last piece of the puzzle that Sherry lacked.

"God, they get younger every day," she said before taking the elevator down to the lobby and leaving the building.

Little did she know that they'd be heading to Egypt, the Sinai Peninsula to be exact, for some bizarre and outlandish reason. She knew better than to return to the floor above her and question the Station Chief. She guessed the trip served a good purpose. Instead of trying valiantly to figure it out, the landscape would lead her to conclusions that were unfamiliar, randomized, and non-strategic. She wouldn't have to plan for it. Perhaps that was what the Station Chief meant by leisure time, or at least to have a good time, which was a condition or a state of mind that had never found her before, as though such conditions floated in the air and had been waiting patiently to seize hold of the hard wiring embedded in her mind if only to find a new set of wires to connect with, a mind that learned how to enjoy itself instead.

When she left the government complex, she couldn't imagine how to enjoy herself. When she tried, she couldn't get around her own self-image as a Company asset who never fucks up. Even while sitting in the taxi and riding towards the hotel, she couldn't see beyond that.

When she walked into the hotel, she looked for the ex-Israeli cop she had studied in the photograph. A man sitting in the lounge area read *Haaretz*, but the pages hid his face. She saw the brim of an Australian trail hat sticking out above them but nothing else. If he was the Mossad contact, he didn't look very interested in finding her. She couldn't resist the temptation to walk across the carpeted floor to where he sat.

"Excuse me, sir," she said, "I was wondering where I can get a copy of the paper?"

When he folded the paper up, she unmistakably recognized him as the good-looking man in the photograph. The man was her Mossad contact dressed as a common American tourist. Not only did he wear the Australian trail hat that looked like it was purchased from a mall, but, true-to-form, an old-fashioned Kodak camera hung around his neck. The kind with film in it.

"A paper, yes," he said. "Follow me, and I'll show you."

He tucked the paper under his arm and headed towards the elevators. He said nothing to her on the way up. Only when he securely shut the door in on themselves did he remove his hat, toss it on the bed, and said, "you must be Sherry."

"Yes," she said.

"Pleasure to meet you."

He had an Israeli accent but one covered up by an American one that he must have learned during his training.

After all, a Mossad asset could play just about anyone, not only an American, but an Arab as well. But on this occasion, they were going as tourists on a camping trip to Mount Sinai.

"Should we get it over with now or later?" he asked.

"What do you mean?"

"You mean, you don't know?"

"Of course, I know. I just don't know what you mean by your question."

"You wanted to tell us something. The mission, remember?"

"Oh, yes, of course," she smiled. That's what you meant. Don't you want to wait a little while first?"

"You mean, until we're on the trip?"

"Yes, let's do that. We can talk more when we get to Egypt."

"When do you want to head out?"

"Soon. Let me freshen up a bit first, and then we can leave."

"Be my guest."

She didn't mind showering in his hotel room. She was way beyond the point of finding it awkward. But while underneath the showerhead with the hot water running down her body, she doted on the Mossad asset who patiently waited outside. She had little idea how to approach him, because there was no information to extract from him. She had little idea what she ought to be doing with him.

She liked his face, the squareness of it, and how proportional his clothes fit to his body. She missed being in the presence of men who looked and talked like him. She soaped her body, but there was no rush, and nothing left to run away from. She could take her time and ease up. It wasn't so much liberation than the simple need to relax, as though the Company had mandated her to slip her hand down her slick, blonde thigh and just let it rest there, if only to feel herself again. With the Mossad asset in the next room, her shower soon became a slow and well-guarded garden of safety.

Like any garden, it needed to be replenished, as though the Tel Aviv Station Chief handed her a prescription to inch her slim, supple fingers over to her inner thigh and massage a part of her physique that had been ignored for centuries, eons of time, ever since the Christian Dark Ages when the Muslims ruled most of the world. In no way could she ignore the flowering orchid between her legs anymore. Such blooming demanded immediate rescue and intervention, her soft, pink petals wet, warm, and open for discovery, and in the orchid's center she felt an only child that needed better mothering, the mothering her soapy fingers lent to a frightened, nervous, and neglected seedling. Such an orchid would give rise to so many other rare and exceptional orchids just like it. To touch its center meant the end of all warfare, the manifestation of goodwill towards men, a ceasefire, the transmutation of a thousand rifles into a thousand orchids, if only she took the plunge and committed herself to unlocking the pleasures she had always been entitled to.

But her seedling needed time to develop, the soap on her body dissolving, and her reasoning replacing the need to emote with the sudden awareness that the Mossad asset waited for her outside, his handsomeness another routine. While the mission hadn't a clear definition yet, she always had to be going somewhere and doing something, even though she had already been there and done that.

The water from the showerhead turned lukewarm. Realizing that water in the Middle East shouldn't be wasted, she awoke from what could have been a radical restoration and returned to the gates of her garden as an asset who needed to do her job. Her mesmerizing notwithstanding, she turned off the faucet, dried herself off, and donned the clothes she had placed at the sink. She looked too good to bother with checking herself in the mirror and met the Mossad asset on the other side of the door.

"How long do we have to camp for?" she asked him.

"We'll go for a week. That should be good enough."

"How are we getting there?"

She didn't feel like getting on a plane again, but the best way to the Sinai Peninsula involved taking a short fight from Tel Aviv to the Red Sea resort town of Sharm El-Sheik, which they did. Her Mossad contact packed a tent and hiking boots along with warm clothes, courtesy of Mossad. The contact said that it would be cold in the mountainous areas that not only included Mount Sinai but also Saint Catherine's Monastery, a local Muslim mosque, and a Greek Orthodox Church.

"Maybe we'll just camp out for a few days and then head back home," he said. "I see no reason to stay in Sharm El-Sheik for long."

"Either do I," she said, after dropping her bag at the foot of a queen bed in their hotel room near the sea.

Both of them had separate queen beds. Even though Sherry wouldn't have minded having an orgasm, she was still too weary of having sex ever since she left Karachi. There was a vacancy about having sex that she couldn't put her finger on. Sex with another man hadn't been fulfilling, even though it had been pleasurable. Also, the mission forbade having any romantic or emotional attachments to her contact, which was what she thought the Tel Aviv Station Chief intended by placing her on limited assignment.

In many ways, it was a relief to be away from Karachi and out of the arms of the ISI Officer. He was no longer worth thinking about. He was just another stranger with whom she had shared her bed with and nothing more. Perhaps the vacancy of having sex manifested itself in the lack of emotional attachment she had to him and a new start with the Mossad asset.

Her new relationship would be strictly professional, of course, as though they worked for the same corporation in America after she crossed the great divide between Heaven and Hell, not sharing which one was which with anyone. She missed the stability of professionalism, the simple routine of waking up in the morning, brushing her teeth, showering, and putting on a clean dress before heading to the train station for work in the city. She saw her visit to Mount Sinai in much of the same way, as though they were both American yuppies on a brief vacation from the world of high finance, with the exception of being a target on the firing range for men hunting for beautiful, high-climbing women. Some women just cost too much money, and Sherry fit the part perfectly.

The Mossad contact did too. They looked like typical Americans at the top of their game, although no one would really know why they wanted to visit Mount Sinai of all places. At least they both used American accents, but still, Sherry looked like she belonged at a Caribbean resort with very little on, or at least that's what everyone in Sharm El-Sheik who beheld her must have thought.

At the hotel, she instead decided to wear modest clothes that reflected spiritual values, which she hadn't developed yet. Going as a pair of archaeologists suited the scenario better. They ditched the idea of going as a corporate yuppie couple, in other words. Then they ditched the idea of going as archaeologists. In the end, they both agreed to create the illusion of two pilgrims journeying to Mount Sinai on some quasi-religious trek to supplicate God in a world of decadence and eventual ruin. From what she read in the newspaper she took along with her, the world of Internet start-ups and IPOs had already bubbled and burst back home. Because the new President preached the importance of having spiritual values and good character, perhaps acting like Evangelicals wouldn't be such a far reach. It would have been more believable had she worn a crucifix around her neck and her Mossad contact the Star of David, on a gold chain no less.

But when in the field, wearing such indulgences so close to the heart may have scalded and scarred their skins. They found the idea of wearing these symbols too outrageous. It would make them feel too uncomfortable since they were at one of the holiest places on Earth. Even disguises had ethical and moral boundaries. They went as secularists in search of God.

The amber mountain itself, when they had arrived by car, stood almost eight-thousand feet tall. In order to reach the summit of the massive rock, they trekked up the mountain with a Bedouin guide, which they had to do. A skinny older man who had been roaming the deserts of North Africa and the Middle East, the guide was too solitary a figure to have a conversation with. Once they left Saint Catherine's Monastery, where monks still dwelled, they had little choice but to take the Steps of Penitence, which were a set of uneven steps hand-carved into the bare rock by those who believed, she figured. They took this difficult route to the summit, because they felt the need to exercise the hard way. They tacitly wanted to see who had the most breath left when they reached the top.

The Steps of Penitence were a tough climb, and they

had to stop a few times to drink their bottles of water. They then proceeded cautiously. The closer they came to the summit, the colder it became. With this dramatic shift in the temperature, the wind blowing and the sky darkening, she hoped she wouldn't catch a cold or fall sick. Being raised in Vermont had its advantages, though. She may have been immune to it, but her Mossad partner wasn't. Like a caring mother, she advised him what to put on and what to take off. They could have been any other married couple, which amazed even themselves and fooled the inquisitive eyes of the Bedouin who led them up to the summit.

Of course, the views at the top were spectacular. The peaks and valleys of the mountain range unfolded and stretched out for miles in all directions. Oddly, but not unlike the other couples at the mountaintop, the Mossad asset put his arm around her waist. It reminded her that God still had a place and purpose in her life, but she had little idea why or where.

While training at Langley, she remembered running into a trainer who was a strict atheist who didn't believe that God existed. And how could she blame him, considering the things the Company asked him to do? She figured that the more time spent in Hell, whether just visiting or desiring assistance from darker forces, the harder it was to find a way out until one own's existence became the embodiment of that Hell. The only release was upon death when the real decisions were made.

Some in the Company identified themselves as ruthless Christian warriors and held on to God that way. That identification created a unique sect within the Company and dovetailed with many militant Christians all over the world. It provided the necessary justification for many of the things they did. Sherry searched for such justification while on the top of Mount Sinai. As the Mossad asset took pictures of the crimson sky and hulking landscape, she didn't know what God thought of her. She wanted good advice from God, because she may have been doing things the wrong way. But no advice came except for the brief spark of a miniscule idea that maybe she could, one day, fall in love, not using her eyes but her heart. But like her spiritual values, her heart hadn't developed yet either. Her heart thumped in her head and rarely did she feel anything at her chest. But on the mountaintop, she felt the hand of some strange puppet-master rescuing her heart and bringing it back to life from the nothingness of sleeping around for scattered pieces of information that no one believed.

Ironically, she never willed her heart to come to life. It had to be coaxed out of its shell by the strange marionette only God used, until her own heart grew a mind of its own. Freak obsessions and wandering eyes had to be relegated to the past, only that they wouldn't be put to rest if she alone willed it. Perhaps God had to do this for her, and she prayed upon the mountaintop that maybe God would do this and convert her nothingness into meaning, so that the mind could turn off and the heart could beat freely without restraints, parameters, rules, regulations, and authorizations.

"C'mon," said the Mossad asset, when finished with the photos. "We have a few things to talk about."

His voice jarred her out of her trance. She had forgotten he was there. She rubbed her eyes, as though waking from an important dream that was too vague to make sense of.

"Okay," she said. "Let's go."

"Hold my hand," he said.

They climbed down the Steps of Penitence together until they connected with the Camel Trail that then led down to a natural basin where the Prophet Elijah experienced his revelation of God. Old chunks of ancient rock from churches and chapels once used to worship and venerate dead saints and prophets were scattered all over the mountainside. They held hands whenever the Mossad contact reached for her. Otherwise, she may have wandered dizzyingly off somewhere, lost in the prayer she had quietly made on the top of Sinai.

After arriving at Elijah's Basin, they took out their tent and set up a small camp before the sun sank. This set up included a small fire, some black coffee, turkey and cheese sandwiches, and various snacks, such as cookies, pretzels, and potato chips – basic fare for basic American tourists. When night fell, they made sure that no one was within earshot before talking.

"You have to halt the arms delivery from Mossad to the Christians in Syria," she said.

"Okay. What else?"

"Instead, Hezbollah will foil the plan, and they will attack you, at which time you will not retaliate."

"Is that all?"

"Yes."

"I'll take it to my Station but let me tell you something plainly and clearly – Israel is no colony of the US. In all likelihood, we will retaliate."

"What if we were to sweeten the deal, say with technology or advanced weaponry?"

"You are not authorized to negotiate," he said. "That's not why we're here. Is there anything else you have to tell me?"

"No, that's it."

"Well, I, for one, am exhausted," he smiled. "I'm going

to bed.”

“Me too. I’m tired as hell.”

“Tomorrow, we’ll go for a camel ride. What do you say?”

“That sounds fine.”

They wedged themselves together under the frame of the tent, their bodies wrapped up like cocoons in their down sleeping bags. The Mossad asset fell asleep quickly, but Sherry couldn’t sleep. After an hour of tossing and turning, she nudged the Mossad asset next to her. He sprang to life, thinking it was some kind of air raid.

“Whoa,” said Sherry.

“What the fuck?” he said. “What’s going on?”

“Easy. Sorry to wake you.”

“Holy shit, Sherry. Don’t fucking do that.”

“Light sleeper?”

“Just don’t do that.”

“I wasn’t sure how to wake you.”

“Next time, wait until morning.”

“But I had to ask you something.”

“Now? It’s the middle of the night.”

“It’s something that I wondered about while on the mountain.”

“Like what, for Godssakes?

“It’s hard to explain, really.”

“I can’t read your mind, Sherry, so you’ll have to start explaining it.”

“I felt something up there.”

"What do you mean? Felt what?"

"I can't explain it. I was touched by God, I think."

"Sherry, do you have any idea where you are and what you're doing here? We're on assignment. That's all it is. Don't be naïve."

"I'm not naïve," she said. "I really think I felt something up there."

"Well, get it out of your head," he said, propping himself on his elbow. "You can't be involved in any of that shit. Stay as far away from God as possible, especially with what we do. Now let's get some sleep, please."

"But don't you ever think about God? As a Jew, I mean?"

"To me, it doesn't matter if I'm a Christian, a Muslim, or a Jew. All I know is that I am a function of my government. All I know about God is that people like us need to be shielded from him."

"What do you mean?"

"Think about what we do. We murder people. We assassinate people. We rig elections. We install puppet dictators. We wipe out whole villages. We pledge our loyalty to a person, and then we stab him in the back. We do God's dirty work. In order to do that, we have to stay as far away from Him, Her, It, Whatever, as possible. The only difference between the Muslims and the Jews is that the Muslims do it with more passion. We steal for God. We lie for God. We kill for God. We destroy for God. We are the foot soldiers of God. In order to do these things, we cannot let whatever you felt on the mountain distort or cloud our judgement. This is how we survive and do God's bidding. Otherwise, God's creation fails. So please, stop thinking so much and get some sleep. I want to be up early in the morning."

"I have to ask you a few more things, now that we are friends."

"I'm not your friend, Sherry. I don't want to be your friend either."

"Do you know anything about the Russians?"

"What I don't know, I don't want to know. What I do know, I don't repeat. What I don't remember is worth forgetting. That's the extent of it."

"I'm asking, because I believe the Russians are setting us up."

"What are you trying to do here, Sherry?" he said propping himself up on his elbow again.

"The Russians may be forming an alliance with Iran, Iraq, and the fundamentalist elements in the Middle East. Have you heard anything about this?"

"What I know is none of your business."

"Can you at least give me a lead here?"

"I don't want to get killed. Why would I tell you anything? I hardly even know you."

"Our agencies are very close. We've often worked together before. Why can't we do the same now?"

"You don't work for the State Department, do you? No, you don't. You work for the CIA, and I for Mossad. What our relationship is or isn't is none of our concern."

"Listen, whoever you are," she said angrily, "I have to know. I have to know if you've learned anything about this."

"I don't want my dick sucked tonight, Sherry. You're not getting anything out of me."

"Okay. What is it that you *do* want?"

"I want you to shut your mouth and go to sleep."

"I'm not doing that."

"You're threatening me, is that it? What do you think you'll do to me?"

"I'm not threatening you. I'm not trying to bully the information out of you. I just want you to share with me what you know."

"If it will shut you up, then, yes. The Russians are forging such an alliance, but no one in Mossad is fully certain. We think that's what's happening, though, given what we've learned. We're just not certain. But what's most important for you to know is that the Iraqis will go with the Russians and not the US. Any money or arms that CIA is funneling into Iraq won't be used against any of the terrorists or Iran. It is useless. It will fail."

"For what reasons?"

"Because the Russians and the Iranians both know that the Second Bush will invade Iraq a second time. That's what the Russians and the Iranians are telling Saddam. He will betray the US. The Arabs always key in on the different political families in power and none of that foreign policy bullshit. Saddam will easily believe that the Second Bush will invade again. And all three of them, the Iraqis, the Iranians, and the Russians, don't want this for obvious reasons. This is what binds the alliance you are referring to together. How did you find out about this?"

"I learned it from a meeting between an Iranian MIOS Officer and a Pakistani ISI asset."

"Keep it to yourself then. Otherwise, they'll send you back to the States."

"No one believes me anyway."

"They'll believe you, but it'll be much too late by then."

"What do you suggest?"

"We head back to Tel Aviv. You tell your Station Chief that you successfully completed your assignment with Mossad, and then you move on like everyone else."

"But what about the alliance? If I don't act, who will?"

"That's not your concern."

"The hell it isn't."

"Sherry, do you actually think that I can go to my Station and convince them not to retaliate against Hezbollah after they attack us? No, I can't. We're going to bomb those fuckers back to Najaf. Israel won't stop until we take Lebanon and the Golan Heights, and there's not a damn thing I can do about either. I have to do what they tell me to do."

"You can easily contact someone in Hezbollah who wants peace with Israel and pre-empt the attack with what we know."

"Don't give me your glib insights into how we should deal with our enemies. We already tried that with Fadallah."

"Who's Fadallah?"

"Probably the strongest and most pious man this region has ever known. He's with Hezbollah, and yet he persuades them to make peace with us. But if he goes against the wishes of Iran, they will kill him and his whole family. Their clerics know better than to expose him to Mossad. We've tried to extract him before, but our assets have been killed and tortured to death trying to get him out. No one wants to take Fadallah out of Biqua anymore. It's too risky."

"These fucking people."

"Iran just makes sure Hezbollah gets their arms. They store weapons in different countries and get licenses to import and export them in roundabout directions to avoid detection. They're damn good at it too."

"You think we can defeat them?"

"The terrorists? In my view, terrorism itself is unbeatable. The Muslims have perfected it, and the oppressed will always use it. It's a fact. All a terrorist has to do is show that the Superpowers are afraid. The leaders in the US, however, are not afraid of their people dying because of a suicide attack. They're afraid because the insecurity that their population feels may lead to mass revolution, or better yet, being elected out of office and replaced by someone who handles it better."

"A small act can cripple whole countries."

"If the US bombs one of these small Muslim countries due to a terrorist act, the Muslim people in that country will see the US as evil aggressors. Terrorism is the most brilliant idea ever invented. And guess who invented it? The fucking Jews!"

"How do you figure?"

"C'mon, Sherry. You should have studied the history books more closely. Think 1940s Palestine, remember? *Eretz Israel, The Stern Gang, The Irgun*? These were all Jewish terrorist groups who drove the Palestinians out. And now the Muslims have perfected it and use it against us. The fighting hasn't stopped since the British left."

"That's fucked up."

"It's all fucked up! We say terrorism is cowardly and cruel, while the terrorists say our cruelties are on a much higher level. My only fear is that they might be right. Either way, we have to defeat them, you hear? That's what we're employed to do."

"Someone has to act upon the formation of this alliance."

"That's not your fucking job. Your job is to do as you're told. Otherwise, people die. You have to understand that."

"Understood," she said.

"No more talking then. We've said too much already. We'll spend the day here tomorrow and then return to Tel Aviv with a successful assignment under our belts. Agreed?"

The Mossad asset fell asleep that night well before Sherry did. She thought up various permutations of how to pre-empt the formation of the alliance, even though she had no business doing so. She wouldn't let go of the thought.

She returned to Tel Aviv Station a few days later. She sat in front of the Station Chief in a state of disbelief.

"How does that have anything to do with what's at stake here?" she said. "I don't see any relevance here whatsoever."

He didn't try to calm her down this time. She had a right to be floored by what the Company asked her to do next. The limited assignment he had put her on grew distant in the rearview mirror, but her ambition to continue her work on the Russian-Terrorist alliance was as pointed and high-throttled as ever. The Station Chief didn't have an explanation for her about the preposterousness of the new assignment, only that the Deputy Director back at Langley had intervened. She would no longer pursue the terrorist cells she had been hell bent on finding. It took her out of the action. She demanded to know why, but the Station Chief only sat there and took the brunt of her ferocious questioning and extreme disapproval.

"Are you sure the Deputy wants this? It doesn't make

any sense. It sounds ridiculous, actually. Did you tell him I said that?"

"He has noted your objections, Officer," said the Station Chief, already tired of discussing it with her. "You either do it or go home. That's what he said."

"Let me talk to him, then," she said.

"That's not possible. He has other concerns to attend to besides your own."

"Bullshit, because it sounds like I'm being taken off every important case and being put out to pasture, all for retrieving the most important information that everyone keeps denying. Did you tell him what I've learned?"

"Yes, Officer. As I said, he has noted it."

"I can't believe he would do nothing about it. Now listen, I am your best asset out there, and if you don't let me finish what I've started, we're all going to pay a very heavy price. This I can tell you."

"It is already being taken care of. It is no longer your concern."

"Oh, I get it. You think I'll fuck up. You think I'm either too dumb or not tough enough. Is that the issue here? Because from what I'm hearing, you want me to play another dumb blonde. Well, Chief, I've already played that, and I've found it wanting. I've been through too much shit to have to play princess to some dumb Arab. You can tell that to the Deputy too."

"Officer – Sherry, I think you are confusing what this new assignment is all about. You are no dumb blonde. We all know that. The Deputy and I have the highest respect for you. He knows how valuable you are to the Company."

"Then why are you putting me on the sidelines? Look,

now that we know that the Russians are behind it, you can send me in there. I've got corroborating evidence. Both the MIOS Officer and the Mossad asset, both are saying the same things. Put me in the fucking Kremlin if you have to. I have a really bad feeling about this if we let this go. I mean, don't we want to stop the smaller conflicts before the bigger ones start? Isn't that what we're supposed to be doing here? I see no point to this."

"If you don't do it, the Deputy wants you back home. It's as simple as that. You don't really have much of a choice here, Officer. That's straight from the Deputy's mouth. Now, you are one of our best. We need you on this one. We have no one else who fits. Take it or leave it. I'm sorry."

She still couldn't believe it. For all of their posturing, they really were sending her on a meaningless assignment, after all the hard work she had put in, after all the information she had uncovered for the purposes of saving her reputation from the Helmand helicopter incident and protecting the country. And now the new, irrelevant task at hand was a far cry from dismantling the Russian alliance before it formed. They didn't take her seriously. Was that it? She needed to be taken seriously, because she had earned it. She deserved to be at the center of the action, because she belonged there and nowhere else. While she understood the concept of 'decompartmentalization,' what they were having her do sounded like a task for some bimbo ditz at the State Department and not for a Company Operative who had learned that her country's security was at serious risk.

"Take my advice, Sherry," said the Tel Aviv Station Chief. "This is a long-term undercover assignment that you are perfectly made for. You are hardly being put out to pasture. You are not being blamed for Helmand Province. This is long-term duty."

"But I don't want to get married."

"Any asset would die for an opportunity like this."

"I'm not a princess. I'm just not. I'm not ready to be someone's wife."

"A wife of a member of the Saudi Royal Family. Not just any wife."

"So what information am I supposed to get on this one, eh? What kind of intelligence am I supposed to gather? How he likes his blowjobs? How wet and tight he needs me to be before he falls asleep? Really, sir? Is this what the Deputy wants to know?"

"You really are being a little childish about this, Officer. You are probably the only female asset in the Company who doesn't want to be courted and married by an Arab prince. That's what I find hard to believe, not any of this Russian stuff that you can't seem to let go of."

"I'm not riding away into the sunset with him on an Arab charger, sir. That's not what I signed up for, sir."

"And that isn't what you signed up for. It's a long-term assignment and an important one. We need you in there. The Administration wants to strengthen its ties to the Royal Family, and through that, the House of Saud will be more closely aligned with Israel. The Palestinians are finished. Even the Saudis are giving up on them. If anything, the Princes want to crush their own *ulema*. Think of your assignment as a blow to those fanatics who are always at the Royal family's throats. We'll have another American paired with the House of Saud. This is a great opportunity here, because if the Royal Family continues to lose ground to the Saudi clerics, we're all in big trouble. The Administration needs you. You must not forget who we work for. This comes straight from the Oval Office, not only from the Deputy but from the damned

President himself for fuck's sake. Now, you do it, or you're going home. I'm through explaining it to you, and I don't see what the problem is. It's like you want to chew dirt the rest of your life instead of operating on a much higher level. I mean, how much torture do you want? You're defeating yourself, and you're taking the Company down with you."

"You'll take my objections to the Deputy, then?"

"Yes. He will duly note them, Officer."

"Fucking fine. I came all this way to become someone else's fucking princess. Maybe I should have never left home. I would have been much better off."

"Better leave that attitude here before you head to Jeddah. You wouldn't want it to blow your cover. Do your job, and do it honorably, or don't do it at all. It's impossible for you to lose. You and your children will be set for life. Has that fact even dawned upon you? This is an American's wet dream!"

"No, I never pictured being married off like this. Is the Deputy going to walk me down the aisle too? Or how about President Bush? Will he be at the wedding? Or how about you, although I don't think they allow Jews in Mecca yet, or do they?"

"At least you have a sense of humor about it. It's a good sign, Officer."

"What if I can't stand him?"

"Always remember that you're on assignment. A long-term one. I'm sure you'll get along anyway. He's a loyal friend of ours, and we need the Royal Family on our side. You should know that already."

The flight from Tel Aviv to Jeddah, Saudi Arabia was just about the longest and loneliest flight she had ever taken.

She never imagined she would be marrying an Arab no matter how many riches he and his family had. Most other female assets would have considered it a high honor, but what really lay at the heart of her objections, other than being out of the action, was that she didn't know how to let go of the image of the perfect American husband with whom she wanted to fall in love, a wedding with her full family present, the toss of the bouquet of flowers into a throng of giggling girls, smearing wedding cake all over her husband's face, and then making love to him on their honeymoon, a white American husband and not a brown Arab one who probably didn't know how to make love to a woman of her caliber. Sure, she would do it for her country, but she never thought that the Company was in the business of arranging marriages too. It must have come from the Oval Office after all. That's where the buck stopped. Of all things, she'd become a Muslim wife. She would have to learn how to become one, and do what with it, she had no idea. Talk about being a fish out of water. The equation, if there ever was one, didn't make any sense.

While up in the air and occasionally glancing upon the shelving of the desert sands below from the airplane window, she even considered returning to DC and marrying someone she naturally fell in love with instead. And yet, these were fairy tales she had to grow out of, those old images from American apple-pie-eating propaganda that she found impossible to eschew. Some vague prevaricating force kept her looking for them, as though her dreams of an ideal white American life were still possible, the ones she read of in those silly romance books and the romantic comedies she saw on television, because when it came to marrying a man, only the clone would do, the typical clone who sat beside her at a chain restaurant in any suburban mall, its patrons looking over to their table and remarking that the beautiful blonde woman, her just-as-tall man, and her perfect two children were the ideal representation of the All-American family, as all families ought to have aspired to touch that height of total, all-encompassing conformity, their home the only one on the block that didn't need blood smeared on its door to avoid the plague. They were the only human beings Noah would take in when the next flood covered the Earth, their family immune to pain, suffering, and tragedy.

Naturally, she'd be kept in a perpetual state of luxury. All of her needs and wants would be met. With the Prince's money, perhaps she could become the pediatrician she had always wanted to become, a First Lady in a way but in Saudi Arabia. Oddly enough, her new life wouldn't seem too different from the one she knew at Georgetown, just in another country with a completely different set of people about whom she knew very little. Then she wondered if she'd ever see a white face ever again, as though her removal from white America and her total immersion into another culture pushed her into a corner of loneliness so profound that marrying even an Arab Prince didn't seem tenable without a prolonged period of abject depression following it. At least remaining in the field in places like Iran, Afghanistan, and Russia would have kept her hopes alive of returning home to a hero's welcome, a big fat promotion, and a handsome white American husband, until the President appoints her Secretary of Something-or-Other on his Cabinet.

No, even marrying an Arab Prince didn't fit into her ultimate, idealized plan, not only because such a marriage might have been unpredictable, but more so because she would be severing her connection to her white tribe and her white past. She didn't know what she'd tell her mother, even though her father would be more than happy to have her Arab Prince over to the Vermont home for Thanksgiving dinner.

At least her father now had ample reason to celebrate, as she single-handedly saved the farm from going bust and would have more than enough money to buy plenty more farms in any country in the world if she so desired.

She'd have to learn and adapt to a feeling as precious as loving another man, like being ordered into a long-term reeducation camp that recalibrated her entire cognition. She didn't know if she could do it, but since the order came from on high, not carrying it out would mean being just as lost. Either way, she'd be separated. Perhaps if she had more time on her inevitable march towards maturity she could have made a few adjustments. But young and beautiful was how these wealthy Princes wanted their women. There'd be no more grace periods. Jump she must, or otherwise she'd be forever searching for a contentment and serenity that would have never materialized.

Chapter Twenty-Four

June 2001 – Dubai, United Arab Emirates

He owned one of the fiery black thoroughbreds that competed in the Dubai World Cup that year. The purse for the prize reached ten million dollars. Not that he cared. He neither needed nor wanted the prize money. That's the last of what the race represented to him. Rather, he wanted bragging rights. Horses and jockeys from all over the world met at Nad Al Sheba Racecourse every year to compete, and this included thoroughbreds from Europe and the United States. It didn't matter if his horse didn't win the entire race, just so long as he beat out those damned Yankees and Europeans who always toured from race to race and captured all the attention from the international media who deemed the race worth covering because of the endless Western participation.

With his entourage of playboys in tow, he rolled in from Saudi Arabia that year unwilling to lose an inch of ground to them. For some reason, the higher-ups in his family granted equal respect to these white Yankees and Europeans. Even common Saudis had been placed on a lower tier, followed by Pakistani and Indian Muslims who did the Kingdom's grunt work. Black African Muslims rounded out the bottom, a racial hierarchy at work due to American and European hegemony all over the globe and also due to Saudi Arabia's sole natural resource that kept these rich, privileged countries coming back for more, the precious black gold that the Saudi Royal

Family begrudgingly allowed them to suck out of the ground.

Even though he was indeed a member of the Royal Family, he felt less of himself, which was why he needed his horse to win. His need to defeat them took on majestic proportions, and when his family had sent him to Harvard for a truly Western education several years back, the women whose looks he fell in love with cared neither for his wealth nor the family from which he came. He ran into many of them on the university's campus, and they showed little or no interest in him. He spent his years at Cambridge cordoned off in one of the library carrels on carnival Saturday nights quietly and uneasily studying his textbooks instead of going to parties or dating the pretty women he dreamt of taking back to Mecca. He left university with a chip on his shoulder due to his inability to connect with any of the women there. It's not like they mistreated him. They just ignored him.

After university, he only stayed in Mecca for short intervals. His father gave him some money out of the graciousness of his heart, and he used a lot of it to become the Western playboy he deserved to become, all of those Ivy League scumbags coming to him for oil contracts and connections to other members of his own family. When they came to him searching for deals, then they paid attention to him and wanted to be close friends, as their basic level of respect for him had to measured by his net worth, if only he traded away what he owned for a shot at the same pretty women who had always ignored him. He witnessed their fakery during back-door business meetings, after which they invited him to exclusive get-togethers in New York and Los Angeles, or when they gave him lavish gifts in their show of appreciation and affection for a valuable friend who continued to supply them with the oil they needed. He knew, though, that if Saudi Arabia had only grown carrots, the whites would have gone the other way.

Only the Americans and the Europeans had worked their fingers to the bone and had earned what they owned, in contrast to Arab princes like him who had inherited their wealth like spoiled children with little talent for anything else. They sat on their oil fields and sold whatever bubbled out of the ground to the highest bidder, or at least to his closest friends. Naturally, the whites won out every time, and this heightened his suspicions and mistrust of them.

And now his family went so far as to want American protection from the radical threats emerging out of Teheran, a radicalism so infectious that even Saudi commoners found the slow and simmering turn to what was really important about Arabia, its religion and not its oil, worthy of preserving than the gradual surrendering of its religious and cultural heritage to a foreign civilization hell-bent on swallowing up everything within its range. Gradually, out of his need to compete with the Americans and whatever allies they brought along with them, he needed to drive them away.

He lost out to the American and European horses that year at the Dubai World Cup. When he greeted their owners and their families at the after-race parties, he took his defeat in stride and smiled along with them, congratulated them, tossed back a few glasses of champaign with them, and even took a few photographs that were placed in the local newspaper and went to those Western media outlets that reported nothing other than more spectacular American victories.

One day, his father showed him a photograph of the woman he wanted him to marry. She was a beautiful and exquisite white American creature, the same type of American woman who had ignored him ever since his early days in Cambridge. His heart leapt out of his chest. But when he examined her visage many times over, he couldn't hide his resentment of her as well. Due to his wealth, he had landed the golden trophy. His family had paid for it, and as a result, his marriage would also enrich America's own business interests while depleting the oil reserves that his family sat on and accumulated.

Aside from his role as a Prince, he didn't know why he deserved her. Nevertheless, he had a need to control her and rinse her of her American ways. When the time came to meet her, he sent a long white Mercedes limousine to fetch her from the airport in Jeddah. It took her to his home in Mecca, a stately mansion worthy of his position and title.

He remembered how the women in America had ignored him to such an extent that he had hired sex workers there to comfort him at his loneliest moments. He frequented strip clubs looking out for the best ones. Even though their beauty nourished him when he needed it most, the fact that they wouldn't have a decent conversation with him without payment again made him feel less of himself. He didn't think himself ugly or physically compromised in any way. Even when he had told these sex workers that he had royal blood flowing through his veins, their interest in him ended when he had stopped paying.

When he saw young American couples his age ready to build their lives together, he also saw that they had found true value in each other, not because of how much money their respective families made or what they would one day take in, but because they saw a certain beauty in themselves that they could not resist, and that vision of whatever they found beautiful did not include him. The woman on her way to his Meccan home that afternoon had to be coerced into finding the same beauty within him, which was why he was determined to make her a devout Muslim stripped of her American ways. But even having her submit to his Islamic way of life didn't ease his resentment of her. He exacted his own revenge by molding her into that which most American women ignored or even resented about Arabs, because Americans were made to resent everyone but their own kind.

Interestingly enough, his father agreed with this approach. She needed to enter the Royal Family through the slow and painful conversion of what she found naturally beautiful about a man into relearning what was beautiful specifically about the man she married. Eradicating her conceptions of American beauty and replacing them with strictly Arabian ones would be the only way to make such a marriage work. Because when the international press takes their photographs of the new alloy of their marriage, at least they would have to admit and recognize that the most exquisite blue-eyed, blonde American girl their readers had ever seen had found supreme value in spending the rest of her life making love to an Arab Muslim just like her new husband.

Her rigorous training began as soon as she disembarked from the plane. The limousine brought her to his home. She unpacked her things in the spare room where she stayed, as living in the same room with him before marriage was improper. But after having her settle in for a few days, the Prince immediately enrolled her in one of the many fine Islamic schools that taught the *Qu'ran*. She'd learn how to pray. Her rigorous and comprehensive training took nearly a month and not more, since his bride-to-be already spoke Arabic fluently. After she formally converted to Islam, the two of them married with the full blessings of the Royal Family, or in her case, the full endorsement of the Prince's friends at the US Embassy.

But after they married and she became a genuine Muslim wife, the Arab Prince refrained from speaking to her or even interacting with her outside of the bedroom. She dutifully stayed at home while he traveled on business to Bosnia for his work with the Saudi High Commission there. He would return to his wife in Mecca more miserable than before he had left.

Nevertheless, he still yearned to frequent the bars, the night clubs, and the restaurants that his European male friends invited him to, but never did he shake off the visceral loneliness into which their girlfriends and their wives cornered him, as though they purposely kept him apart and isolated him from the rest, or at least this was what he perceived to be the truth while having lived the high-life in those wealthy and fashionable European cities where he paid for everyone else's booze and cocaine. He missed those days, albeit painful ones they were. It seemed pre-planned, as though Allah had ordered it. It wasn't because he was now married and had reached the age of settling down. Rather, he had been cast out for reasons only known to women. He turned them off wherever he went, as though they knew of his dalliances with sex workers of all kinds and knew of his penchant to sleep with as many beautiful women as possible, thereby rendering him a particular kind of foreign sleazebag whose only value was his inherited wealth and the privileges his Saudi Royal Family had doled out to him. At times, he even mused that these American and European couples that he considered friends acted much like parents to a worldly orphan who was always lost and homeless. After all, these overseas women couldn't be pried away from the shallowest and most meaningless relationships with the men they dated. His tears through Europe, then, had been more of an exile. And now he was stationed in post-war Bosnia. When he returned to Mecca to his lovely, submissive wife, she looked like the same American and European women who had damagingly cast him out.

Luckily, after traveling to and from his work for the High Commission in Bosnia, his new Muslim wife had progressed marvelously. She prayed in the Grand Mosque five times a day and even continued more advanced Islamic study at the religious schools nearby. Praying became second-nature. He often saw her in the expanse of one of his many living rooms dutifully bowing towards the House of God. He didn't feel the need to talk much to her or get to know her. She functioned only as a Muslim wife to be gazed upon for her unparalleled good-looks and to sleep with on demand. He treated her like the other women he had met over the years treated him. With this reversal of fortune came a satisfaction like no other. Finally, he neglected her as he had been neglected, his resentment of her unshakable and his continual need to flee the house and attend to some unimportant family business locking her out of what could have been a fulfilling marital arrangement, had she known about what he did overseas.

Her sole purpose was to serve him, and it worked to his satisfaction, until his work had him return to Bosnia. Then, back to Mecca where he ignored his wife except when he needed her in bed. This cycle ran its course, his new wife remaining silent and emotionally irrelevant.

Chapter Twenty-Five

September 2001 – Mecca, Saudi Arabia

Contrary to conventional wisdom and popular belief, the total absence of thought may have been the key to finding an entirely new utopia. Thought and all of its processes do nothing but tax the mind and may not necessarily lead to the happiness she needed. Thinkers past and present are so revered throughout the annals of time as though they have touched the divine or have at least stolen from the heavens that which can better explain the world in which we live or provide creative solutions to age-old problems that never really had any solutions to begin with. Thought, if anything, is labor. In a world that demands action above all else, thought pays too little and requires too much. Both great men and women often have to narrow their thinking and focus their minds on mundane tasks and duties that avoid, not new ideas that are promulgated through action, but the reliance on their own minds that generate the detritus of ideas that are mostly worthless, as though one good idea requires a million ancillary thoughts, thereby crippling the mind before one miraculous idea is discovered. What's more, the mind is hardly self-contained. As Sherry had learned, all thoughts come from God.

After studying the *Qu'ran* in the *madrassa* in which her new husband had enrolled her, Sherry believed she had found a mindless and hypnotic utopia that demanded nothing of her but her full submission to God without the burdens of thought that the Company required of her. Whether she prayed to the *Kaa'bah* five times a day, read a total of three books – *The Qu'ran, The Hadith,* and *The Sunnah* – that told her exactly what to do and what to think with a complete history and background included, or submitted to the whims and fancies of her new husband, the absence of thought along with the absence of any other goal or plan produced a nether-world of mind that stripped her of fear, anger, insecurity, and other useless emotions that had held her back and had sent her headlong into places she shouldn't have been and shouldn't have contemplated, lest she damage herself to an even greater degree.

Her full submission to God and the instructions of his Prophet simplified and reduced the complexities of the unending expanse of the great mysteries that had always besieged her. Always wanting to get out merely meant getting all the way in, a direct link to God that required His will and not hers, His customs and traditions and not her individualized ones. The collective mind operated at the same time and on the same schedule without the clutter of mindless divergence that had driven her into dreadful states of corruption and dismay, her life unfulfilled, the guidance she had found in the *madrassa* a wondrous equation that made sense. The answer as well as the problem were both inductively and deductively wholesome and complete, never needing revision and never accepting contradiction, just straightforward strings of logic that relieved her of worry and doubt, if only she repeated the same routines that everyone in Mecca had already repeated.

Her husband, however, was usually away on business, he said, and when he returned from his trips to Bosnia, he went to work in one of the Saudi Ministries with his father, whom she hardly ever saw either. Sherry kept to the home when not visiting the Grand Mosque. The expanse of his home, with its many rooms, servants, and lavish furnishings, kept her delightfully occupied, content, and serene.

She even reestablished a connection with her family in Vermont after being away from them for what seemed like years. She told them the good news of her new marriage, and to their surprise, she regularly sent them the Prince's money. With it they paid off the bank and retained full ownership of their family farm. Her farther started speaking to her again, satisfied with her change in fortune. All rested in abeyance, as though time had halted its unruly progression and delivered an eternal present that kept her where she stood, knelt, bowed, and prayed. It all seemed to be rolling along so smoothly, her splendid isolation near-complete, the earlier corruption of Company work sidelined for the comforts of non-thought. The absence of mind provided comfort and relief with a constantly multiplying community she had promised to serve.

From the simplicity of wearing black garments that covered her charms from head to toe to the halal food she served her husband whenever he showed up at home, everything flowed along like the flatness of a calm river. It seemed almost unreal, until, of course, her Western curiosities seeped in. These were stubborn remnants of her nagging ability to think critically, a skill that had been pounded into her as a Company asset and her time as a student at Georgetown. Too bad. Such experiences planted an indelible mark on her otherwise hypnotized mind.

Even though her mind had been structured and simplified into routines that she practiced each day, she searched for a husband who had never been present. She knew very little about the work he did in Bosnia. Like a good Muslim wife, she did not want to concern him with her questions, especially when he mentioned that he was suddenly taking a trip to Moscow.

"Really?" she said, her ears perking up at this slip of the tongue over a dinner of lamb and sticky rice. "Why are you going to Moscow?"

"Just business," he smiled.

"How long will you be away this time?"

"Not long. About a week."

"That's not long at all," she said. "What will you be doing out there?"

"Just business as usual."

"But you hardly travel to Russia. It's usually Bosnia, right?"

"Usually Bosnia, but this time it's Russia."

"Strange, because why would the Royal Family be involved with Russia?"

"We have some business there."

"Oil, you mean?"

"Do we deal in anything else? Of course, it's oil, not that it's any of your concern. Now stop asking so many questions. Pay attention to your duties here at home."

"No, it's just that it's interesting that you are working with the Russians, even though I have no idea why."

"It's a new world, Sherry. We are all friends. Now stop asking questions and eat your dinner. Afterwards, you can make my bags ready for the trip. It will be cold in Moscow, so make sure you pack my things accordingly."

"Yes, of course."

She ate the rest of her meal in silence, her eyes pinned to the remaining morsels of stringy lamb's meat on her plate. After dinner, her husband adjourned to his study, a place that he kept under lock and key. He let no one inside. He was always in there when not away, and this had always piqued her mad curiosities. Even though her mindlessness was near-complete, she couldn't help but recall all she had learned about Russia and the alliance that had probably already formed with the fundamentalist elements in the Middle East. But that wasn't her job anymore. Her job was to remain a dutiful wife and a faithful Muslim. She wasn't about to engage in ideas and thoughts that didn't concern her. Yet while servicing him in bed on the night before his departure, the machinery of her mind kept turning. She couldn't turn the damned thing off, especially when he said that he'd be away two weeks this time and not just one.

"Business must be pretty good between you and the Russians," she said, after rolled over her moist body and pretended not to hear her. "I mean, you've extended your trip. Must mean you've made important contacts there."

"Leave me alone, will you? Just go to sleep. I've had enough of you for one day."

His reluctance to tell her anything only made her think more and more about the alliance that may have already formed, an idea she had dropped when she had married him. She tried to dismiss it, but she couldn't let go of it.

While he was away in Moscow, she remembered how the formation of such an alliance had been confirmed by two sources, the MIOS Officer and the Mossad asset. The remembrance of them interrupted her devotion and strict reliance on prayer. It jutted into everything she did, a knee-jerk, involuntary intrusion that popped into her head the longer her husband stayed away. She even felt like calling Langley and having a word with the Deputy, if only he would take her phone call. She needed to know, her old life as an asset barging into the new one that had blinded her to all facets of operations work and the life she left had behind.

Her desperate need to know took her into the kitchen in the middle of the night where she pulled out a small knife from one of the drawers without any of the servants noticing her. Little did anyone in the household know that she knew how to pick a lock and do it well from her days in training as a CST. After her first few attempts, she picked the lock to his study. It was fairly easy. She didn't know why she didn't break in earlier. The heavy mahogany door opened to a large room with an immense Afghan carpet on the floor, several file cabinets, a computer on a desk, and bookcases lined with old cloth books, some of them antiquated enough to be considerably valuable. A wide window overlooked the quiet lane to the household outside.

She had never been in his study before. After closing the door, she locked herself securely inside as her husband had always done when he returned home from Bosnia. For the next hour or so, she rifled through each file in the cabinets, looking for clues as to what her husband and the Princely Royals wanted with the Russians. And then she found a file nestled in between many others that her husband specifically marked as classified.

She read that the Prince and his father had operated independently while dealing with the Russians. Apparently, the Prince had been colluding with the Russians to manipulate international oil prices to the detriment of Europe and the United States. They worked to set prices to eliminate competition among other foreign oil companies. But what's more, the Russians provided sophisticated weaponry, not to the Saudi Royal Family, but to the *ulema* and other groups through her husband and his father. Sherry put two and two together. With the *ulema's* help and the arms provided by the Russians, her husband planned to stage a coup against his own family so that he and his father could rule the Kingdom. As a result, in his new reign as King, he could then ally with the Russians and join the coalition of terrorist organizations that the Russians had sponsored.

Another file contained the names of Saudi nationals. One name caused her to think more critically than ever before. Ali Ahmad Ali Hamad, a Mujahideen fighter who served the cause in Afghanistan and was now suspiciously stationed with the High Commission in Bosnia under her husband's employ. And then she remembered. This was the same man who had set off a car bomb that attempted to kill off many non-Muslims there, the overall goal being the reignition of the same Bosnian civil war that had previously torn the country apart. The list of employees at the Saudi High Commission in Bosnia such as Hamad spanned several pages. These were all terrorists who worked under her husband. The supposedly innocuous Saudi charity, by employing these terrorists, surreptitiously funded them for future attacks and provided for their cover. Through the High Commission, the Saudi government kept these terrorists in business.

And then another file of fifteen Saudi nationals along with their mugshots. Of the fifteen, two Saudis were from the United Arab Emirates, one from Egypt, and another from Lebanon. The fifteen Arabs had formed a cell in Hamburg. For some reason, they had left Hamburg, traveled through Kandahar, and wound up at a Florida flight school. The file didn't contain any more information than that.

Now the question became what to do with this overload of new information. After all, she still worked as an asset. She needed to inform Langley immediately and not the Tel Aviv Station Chief whom she circumvented. She went above his head. She used the telephone in her husband's study to place the call to Langley. Naturally, she had to wait an hour to get into direct contact with the Deputy. The wait and the many transfers from one person of authority to another irritated her to no end. With every minute on hold, her pulse raced, and her head swam in a pool of urgency and dread, as she was unable to make the connection between her husband's planned coup, his collusion with the Russians, his treachery in Bosnia, and the faces of the Saudis who had relocated to Florida for flight training.

"Officer, Aspen," answered the Deputy on the other end, finally. "What a surprise. How's married life been treating you, sweetheart?"

"Not well, sir. We have a serious problem."

"There shouldn't be any problems. Aren't you on long-term assignment?"

"Sir, it's my husband."

"Oh, yes, you must give him my regards. I hope you two are doing well."

"Sir, he has planned a coup here in Saudi Arabia," she said excitedly. "He plans to arm the *ulema* against his own family with Russian help, and since the Russians are now working with the Iraqis, the Iranians, the Taliban, and Osama Bin Laden, it only follows that something terrible is going to happen soon and happen in a huge way. The Saudi High Commission where he works in Bosnia is actively hiding and funding terrorist. One puts fifteen Saudi nationals in the United States, but I have no reason why. I haven't figured it out."

"Hang on a second, Officer. Now just calm down, okay? Where did you get this information?"

"I'm in my husband's office right now, sir. I have access to all of his confidential files. He is in Russia as we speak. All of it is outlined here, except for the link to the

Saudi nationals stateside."

"So, you are at home right now?"

"Yes, sir."

"Okay, Officer. Your earlier suspicions from the reports you have already filed have been proven valid. And you say your husband is now in Russia?"

"He is Moscow now dealing with them. He wouldn't divulge the reasons for his visit, so I had to find out for myself. Now we know."

"Good work, Officer. A promotion is in the works for you. For now, though, just sit tight. Let me make people aware of it on this end. It will take until tomorrow for this information to circulate to our Station Chiefs. In the meantime, stay put. Don't leave the house. Call me tomorrow night at which time I'll give you further instructions. Is that clear, Officer?"

"Yes, sir, but how long do you want me to stay here? Don't you want to fly me to Florida? We can bust the cell of Saudis and pull them in for questioning. We have no idea what they're up to."

"Let me take care of that. You just sit tight and call me tomorrow night for further instructions. At any rate, you did the right thing by calling me. Excellent work, Officer."

"Thank you, sir."

After the phone call and for a few hours following it, Sherry could hardly sit still. She passed the time wringing her hands and pacing about the house nervously. A dark night had settled in over the holy city. She was unable to sleep, although she tried. She got up again and returned to her husband's study where she copied and uploaded all of the classified files in question to Langley. Once she did, she realized that she had to get out of the city right away. Doubtlessly, though, she would be stopped if she tried to leave from the main airport in Jeddah. As a Saudi public figure, immigration control would have never let her travel without her husband with her. And then came another idea, a result of her burning mind that turned with the ferocity of a lion looking for its prey. The only way she could possibly leave the city was to dress in her husband's clothing and go in disguise.

She ran to the bedroom and ransacked through his closet. She donned his white garb and a white Arab *taqiyah* with a black headband to hold the cloth in place. Carefully, she crept downstairs and entered the kitchen, making sure not to wake the servants who slept soundly in adjacent rooms. She opened the cabinet where her husband stored old bottles of French and Italian wines. She quickly opened one of the bottles. With the bottle's cork in hand, she burned one end of it with a lighter that she found in another drawer. In the bathroom upstairs, she smeared the black soot from the burnt cork all over her blonde face. She made sure to darken her entire face and most of her neck, so that none of her white skin showed. She looked herself over in the mirror. Her disguise looked like it would fool anyone. But then, she had no idea how she'd take off from Jeddah without a passport and a picture that looked like the new person in disguise. She looked like a totally different person, yes, a dark male Arab to be precise, but without a photo identification. She was stuck inside Saudi Arabia and would have to hide out in Mecca.

She had stayed awake all night when dawn stretched over the city. She called the Deputy for further instructions, but for some reason, she couldn't get a hold of him even in spite of what she told him the night before. At least she had found a pair of her husband's aviator sunglasses to complete her disguise, her lovely blue eyes hidden by them. She was about to call a cab from her husband's study until she saw from the window, to her genuine horror, two black cars with black tinted windows pull up next to the house. Four armed Saudi men in black suits got out and approached the home, their automatic weapons poised and ready to fire. The only one who could have ordered them to her home had to be the Deputy Director of Intelligence. They were Saudi GID henchmen sent by the Deputy to silence her in the worst possible way.

She had little time left. She needed to get out of the house and get out immediately. She heard the four thugs enter the household as stealthily as they had arrived, probably thinking she was asleep in the upstairs bedroom. Shit. Shit. Shit. Still in her Arab disguise, she ran into the bathroom and locked the door. She turned off the lights, stepped into the shower, and pulled the curtain shut. She then waited in the darkness.

The creaking of the stairs and the heavy footfalls upon them told her that one of the men approached the bedroom. When the man got to the bathroom door, he jostled the doorknob but couldn't open it, since Sherry had locked it. She almost yelped when he broke down the door. He turned on the light. Sherry held her breath in the shower, her heart racing out of control and a bead of nervous sweat trickling down the side of her face. She clenched her fists tightly as she heard the GID Officer walking through the bathroom in search of her. He passed the shower. She made sure not to move, not to breathe. Just when she had thought he had turned around to leave, the brown Saudi operative yanked the shower curtain open and found her standing there in her Arab disguise.

Before he fired his gun, she delivered a hard blow to his nose that blurred his vision. His gun fell to the tile floor. She then kicked him hard squarely in the balls. Within moments, the Saudi GID operative dropped to the floor, clutching his crotch and wincing in pain. She leapt out of the shower and retrieved the gun that had slid over to the toilet. She picked up the heavy piece of metal and fired three shots into his chest as he lay on the floor and clutched his balls. One down and three to go. After hearing the shots, the other GID men raced upstairs to the bedroom. Sherry then lay herself prone on the tile floor of the bathroom, her loaded gun aimed at the door.

She heard footsteps beyond the door, and when one of the men opened it, she fired the gun in rapid succession from the floor, sparks from the flurry of bullets ricocheting off the walls lighting up the interior darkness like a fireworks display. She yelled into the darkness while pulling the trigger wildly, not knowing where those bullets landed. She fired madly at the shadows at the door so many times that she had emptied her gun of all of its ammo. She couldn't let go of the trigger, as though her finger had been petrified there and rigor mortis had set into her firing hand. After all of the bullets had been fired, the three remaining Saudis lay dead just beyond the threshold of the bathroom door. She had survived the ordeal without being shot.

She picked herself up and stepped on the pile of dead bodies on her way out. She ran downstairs at top speed, passed the small gathering of worried servants who had been scared shitless by the turn of events. She flew out of the household with her white garb and *taqiyah* waving from her body and dove into the driver's seat of the first black Dodge Charger she found in the driveway. The keys still in it, she fired up the engine, slammed the gear into drive, and peeled out of sight beyond the gates of her husband's property and into the city of Mecca. By the time she found the road to the Jeddah-Mecca Highway and passed underneath the illustrious Mecca Gate, she sped along the long flat road at 120 miles per hour. No one stopped her along the highway, considering she drove a government car with license plates to match. She headed towards the city of Jeddah in her Arab disguise.

She didn't know how she'd escape from Saudi Arabia, now that she had freed herself from the holy city. She understood, though, that now both her own Company and the Saudi GID were in hot pursuit. The faster she drove down the barren desert highway, the better.

As she headed out of town, she felt her chest expanding and her heart beating beneath it, just like when she climbed Mount Sinai and swore that she felt the presence of God within her. Her beating heart came with a relief of mind that put her at ease, as though her beating heart along with its new connection to her riddled mind granted her new life. Even though she ran from her own people too, she did not fear them anymore. She didn't fear anyone.

Because when the heart and the mind connect, that awkward oddness at the center of the chest that takes its own sweet time to open, may produce a beautiful woman who shows up at the front door. Or, if she is already there, perhaps her man notices her all over again and finds her as stunning as when he had first laid eyes upon her. Maybe this woman is not so unlike Sherry who keeps running to stay alive, keeps falling in and out of the arms of men that give her temporary comfort, until she moves on once more, running through her own life and searching for her own freedom. Perhaps that's what Sherry found on the long highway to Jeddah that early morning. Either way, she kept running and running, never at rest, her life and her new freedom never-ending, no matter how horrific the tragedy that soon hit her beautiful country back home.

THE END.

Selected Bibliography

Ahmed, Ali, and Lester Grau. *Afghan Guerilla Warfare - in the Words of the Mujahideen Fighters*. St. Paul, MN, MRI Publishing Company, 2001.

Byman, Daniel L. "Comparing al Qaeda and ISIS: Different Goals, Different Targets." *Brookings*, Brookings, 29 Apr. 2015, www.brookings.edu/testimonies/comparing-al-qaeda-and-isis-different-goals-different-targets/.

Borovik, Artem. *The Hidden War: A Russian Journalist's Account of the Soviet War in Afghanistan*. New York, Ny, Grove Press, 2001.

Coll, Steve. *Ghost Wars: The Secret History of the CIA, Afghanistan, and Bin Laden from the Soviet Invasion to September 10, 2001 by Steve Coll*. Penguin Press, 2004.

Esposito, John L. *Unholy War: Terror in the Name of Islam*. Riyadh, Internat. Islamic Publ. House, 2010.

Gambetta, Diego. *Making Sense of Suicide Missions*. Oxford Oxford University Press, 2012.

Grimmett, Richard. "U.S. Arms Sales to Pakistan." Congressional Research Service, 24 Aug. 2009.

Hoffman, Bruce. *Inside Terrorism*. 3rd ed., New York, Columbia University Press, 2017.

Iqbal, Anwar. "US Hands over Used Combat Aircraft, Other Weapons." *DAWN.COM*, 7 May 2015, www.dawn.com/news/1180506#:~:text=WASHINGTON%3A%20The%20United%20States%20has%20handed%20over%2014. Accessed 30 May 2022.

ITV Documentary. (2016). *Saudi Arabia Uncovered*. United Kingdom.

Jones, Ishmael, and Inc Ebrary. *The Human Factor: Inside the CIA's Dysfunctional Intelligence Culture*. New York, Encounter Books, 2010.

Kessler, Ronald. *The CIA at War: Inside the Secret Campaign against Terror*. New York, St. Martin's Griffin, 2004.

Karsh, Efraim. *The Iran-Iraq War, 1980-1988*. Oxford, Osprey Publishing, 2010.

Marsden, Peter. *The Taliban: War and Religion in Afghanistan*. London ; New York, Zed Books, 2002.

Moran, Lindsay. *Blowing My Cover: My Life as a CIA Spy*. New York, G.P. Putnam's Sons, 2005.

Omrani, Bijan. *Afghanistan: A Companion and Guide*. Hong Kong, Odyssey Books & Guides, 2011.

Robert Anthony Pape. *Dying to Win: The Strategic Logic of*

Suicide Terrorism. New York, Random House Trade Paperbacks, 2006.

Reich, Walter. *Origins of Terrorism: Psychologies, Ideologies, Theologies, States of Mind*. Washington, Dc, Woodrow Wilson Center Press ; Baltimore ; London, 1998.

Sageman, Marc. *Understanding Terror Networks*. Philadelphia, Pa, University Of Pennsylvania Press, 2004.

Saiyid Quṭb, and Albert Bergesen. *The Sayyid Qutb Reader : Selected Writings on Politics, Religion, and Society*. New York, Routledge, 2008.

Joseph John Trento. *The Secret History of the CIA*. New York, Mjf Books/Fine Communications, 2007.

"Washington Eviction Process (2022): Grounds, Steps & Timeline." *IPropertyManagement.com*, ipropertymanagement.com/laws/washington-eviction-process#flowchart. Accessed 30 May 2022.

Weiner, Tim. *Legacy of Ashes : The History of the Central Intelligence Agency*. New York, Doubleday, 2007.

Also, facts and images have been researched from numerous Wikipedia articles and Google Searches online.

HARVEY HAVEL
Author

Harvey Havel has been a short-story writer and novelist for over thirty years. His first novel, *Noble McCloud, A Novel*, about a young, struggling musician was published in November of 1999. He now has nineteen books which include novels, short stories, and two collections of essays on current affairs and political matters. His latest book is a serialized novel, *The Queen of Intelligence: A 9/11 Novel*, has just been released through Kindle Vella on Amazon.com in 2021.

Havel is formerly a Lecturer in English at Bergen Community College in Paramus, New Jersey. He also taught writing and literature at SUNY Albany and the College of Saint Rose, also in Albany, New York.

He currently lives there with his pet cat, Marty, and has many more books in store for his many fans in future.

Copies of his books and short stories, both new and used, may be purchased at Amazon.com, Barnes & Noble.com, Smashwords.com, or at your favorite local bookstore.

An excellent interview with Harvey Havel by Robert Nagle of Personville Press in Katy, Texas, can be found at Imaginary Planet.net.

His readers are encouraged to leave their honest comments about his work anywhere his fine books are sold.